THERE IS NO HONOUR AMONGST THIEVES...

...OR IS THERE?

BLACK MAIL

MICHAEL STOKES

Matador
9 Priory Business Park,
Wistow Road, Kibworth Beauchamp,
Leicestershire. LE8 0RX
Tel: 0116 279 2299
Email: books@troubador.co.uk
Web: www.troubador.co.uk/matador
Twitter: @matadorbooks

ISBN 978 1785899 645

British Library Cataloguing in Publication Data.
A catalogue record for this book is available from the British Library.

Printed and bound by CPI Group (UK) Ltd, Croydon, CR0 4YY
Typeset in 11pt Aldine401 BT by Troubador Publishing Ltd, Leicester, UK

Matador is an imprint of Troubador Publishing Ltd

For

H. C.

"Never Forgotten"

&

in memory of

Police Dog Troy

"I have been informed by a person named Abel Magwitch, that he is the benefactor so long unknown to me."

"That is the man", said Mr Jaggers, "in New South Wales."

"And only he?" said I.

"And only he," said Mr Jaggers.

"I am not so unreasonable, sir, as to think you at all responsible for my mistakes and wrong conclusions; but I always supposed it was Miss Havisham."

"As you say Pip," returned Mr Jaggers, turning his eyes upon me coolly, and taking a bite at his forefinger, "I am not at all responsible for that."

"And yet it looked so like it, sir," I pleaded with a downcast heart.

"Not a particle of evidence, Pip," said Mr Jaggers, shaking his head and gathering up his skirts. "*Take nothing on its looks; take everything on evidence. There's no better rule.*"

– Charles Dickens *Great Expectations*

"Say first, of God above or man below
What can we reason but from what we know?"

– Alexander Pope *Essay on Man*

PROLOGUE

It was not yet light and bitterly cold when the man lifted his coat and squeezed the mobile phone into the front pocket of his leather overtrousers. He walked slowly towards the large wooden gates and opened them as wide as they would go. Flurries of snow were picked out in the beam from the torch he held in his other hand. Moments later, a light-coloured van pulled in quickly and drew to a halt, the tyres crunching on the frosted gravel. The driver signalled to him, smiled and drove the van into the old foundry building, disappearing from sight. The man looked at his watch. It was just 5.03 a.m. Everything must have gone to plan. He closed and bolted the gates, then pulling his scarf more tightly about his neck, followed the van inside. Taking one final look into the still darkened sky, he shut the doors behind him. Only the smoke belching from the chimney gave a clue that anyone was there.

★★★★

CHAPTER ONE

Thursday, 17 December 1998

'How much?'

'Nearly 2 million.'

Detective Chief Inspector Henry Hood shook his head in disbelief.

'What's the exact figure?' he asked. 'Do we have the exact figure?'

'Well, according to the manager, 1.9 million pounds. He's just confirmed it a few minutes ago.'

Detective Constable Wendy Knight winced as she spoke. 'By the way, sir, the ACC has been asking after you. It sounds pretty urgent.'

'I know,' replied Hood despondently. 'She's left two messages on my mobile already. I'll go and see her immediately after the briefing. Hopefully, I'll have something positive to tell her, though I doubt it.'

'There's not much to tell at the moment,' said Knight.

She had only recently been transferred to Hood's team but already admired him both as a man and a detective. It was well known that he had endured a deal of jealous backbiting when promoted to chief inspector, some of it mildly racist in origin. He was the son of a West Indian bus driver and an English mother who hailed from a small village in north Nottinghamshire. Mrs Hood had established herself as a sought-after teacher of English literature after much study and a first-class honours degree from the Open University. Their son took a more orthodox educational path, thanks to their unstinting support. After obtaining excellent A levels from his comprehensive school in Mansfield, he graduated with upper second-class honours in English and philosophy from Leeds University and, to the initial consternation of his parents, went straight into the West Yorkshire Police Force on the graduate entry scheme. He had found it difficult to begin with but his natural talent marked him out as a likely high-flyer. His resolute work ethic merely served to underline the impression he had created with his superiors and promotion was rapid but well deserved. Of course, there were some who disgruntledly put his advancement down to political correctness and the seeming desperation of the higher echelons to identify and advance a police officer of ethnic or mixed racial origins.

For his own part, Hood relied on his well-established abilities. He refused, despite real pressure, to join the black police officers' association and made no bones about his views of such organisations. Divisive he called them. More likely, he thought, to put up barriers than to remove them. Indeed, he had little time for political correctness of any kind. He regarded it as a device that caused people to express views they did not really hold and to reserve their genuine opinions for those they imagined held similar prejudices. Worst of all, it tainted what he still believed was the innate decency of the majority of his fellow citizens. Much better, he thought, if people said what they actually thought whatever the consequences, providing, of course, they acted within the law. It also made his job easier if everything was out in the open. It particularly annoyed him that one assistant chief constable under whom he had previously served thought his views on political correctness were in fact a deliberately contrived tactic to advance his career as a police officer – a sort of double bluff in which he happily relied on the already established requirement of the police service to genuflect before such totems while at the same time eschewing such views himself. And what a totem that would become when the *Macpherson Report* was published. No one expected it to do anything other than damn the Metropolitan Police which would have a knock-on effect on every other constabulary in the country. Not that Hood was one to seek advantage of such circumstances – but he had seen the leaks published in the newspapers and was a good enough politician to realise that Macpherson was unlikely to damage *his* professional standing.

But there were still the occasional digs that the accident of his birth assisted his rise and would go on doing so, and he never forgot the way his father had been treated and the vulgar abuse and worse to which he had been subjected on a few occasions at school. While he strongly approved of anti-discrimination legislation he was fervently against the imposition of quotas or the substitution of diversity for competence which he had dryly observed was fast becoming an unassailable dogma. Still, the world had changed since his father's time and he was in many ways a contented man, happy in his work and enjoying, when he could, his wife and family. Although he had been with Mid-Shires for only four years, he was up for further promotion, providing nothing went wrong before the board assembled in the new year. The only drawback was that it would involve a transfer to the West Midlands as the vacancy was with the Birmingham Metropolitan Constabulary. He knew his wife would not want to move from their present home so it would mean a deal of commuting on his part. Still, he had done very well for someone who had yet to celebrate his thirty-second birthday. Only his superiors were aware of his application and were loath to lose him, but as they spent a disproportionate amount of their own time seeking further advancement, they could hardly stand in his way.

He had arrived at the police station only half an hour before. He was supposed to be on extended leave over the Christmas period but events had dictated otherwise. As the most experienced and successful detective with Mid-Shires, it had fallen to him to begin the investigation into what was to become "Operation Christmas Carol". Hood always followed a strict alphabetical chronology in naming his major investigations rather in the fashion of Mr Bumble, the beadle in *Oliver Twist,* who chose the names of the foundlings who entered parish servitude in like fashion. As an ardent reader of Charles Dickens, he liked to use either a novel or a Dickensian character to identify a high-profile case. As they were up to the letter C, having been through the alphabet once since he joined Mid-Shires, "Christmas Carol" it would be unless, of course, someone came up with a better idea. One of Hood's most endearing characteristics was that he never assumed that his view of anything was necessarily the right one. Such a philosophy might well adversely affect his prospects of reaching the top of his chosen profession but there was nothing he could do about it. That was simply the way it was. He continued to read the crime report.

'How's the security guard?' he asked.

'Not good. It's his heart. The shotgun cartridge was loaded with rock salt, so the actual injuries caused by the blast are not that serious. But it seems the shock brought on a heart attack. It's touch and go at the moment.'

Wendy Knight ran her hand through her auburn hair as she spoke. She was almost twenty-five years of age but was about to complete her fourth year in the force, as she still preferred to call it. She had originally trained as a nurse but abandoned that caring profession and joined the old Leicestershire Constabulary before the merger with the other East Midland police areas. She was regarded by Hood as effective, intelligent and quick thinking and by her immediate colleagues as rather attractive with it. Several had attempted to date her but without success. Her current boyfriend, Greg Oldham, was a university lecturer in statistics. They had met at a mutual friend's wedding and hit it off straight away but that had been nearly eighteen months ago and she was beginning to resent some of Greg's disparaging remarks about her job. Deep down she knew, that for the moment, her career would come first and she was slightly worried that Greg was beginning to realise that too. Hood never inquired about his junior officers' private lives but he hoped and believed Wendy Knight had the good sense to keep her professional duties separate and apart from the rest of her life. He was certainly impressed with the way she repeatedly brushed aside all attempts from other officers to take her out. She had made it a cardinal rule only to socialise with them in a group or when at the gym although she had joined Hood on several occasions on his early morning runs until he and his family moved out to the suburbs. Hood regarded her as a very real prospect for promotion and had supported her recent application to become a sergeant even if it meant he would lose her from his team.

'I see they set the security vehicle on fire as well?'

'Yes sir. They must have planned to do that from the outset. One of them jumped on the roof as the security van was passing through the gate. The windscreen was put in with what appears to have been a small pickaxe then petrol was poured all over the place. Some of it went on the driver and the senior guard. Threats were then made to set them on fire. No wonder they got out as quickly as they did! Of course, the fire was only started after they'd forced the guards to open the rear doors and retrieved the security bags. Very clever when you think about it. If the guards had remained inside the van, there's no way the robbers could have got at the money in time.'

'And I thought cash in transit robberies had gone out of fashion. There's bound to be a problem in laundering that amount of money.'

Knight nodded as Hood loosened his tie and undid his top button.

'Any information as to who did this?'

'Negative. We've had the feelers out but we have nothing to go on as yet. The CCTV is being checked but that's going to take time. It's a professional job all right. It doesn't look like any of the local villains would have been up to this.'

'You may well be right. Could have been some big boys from outside but there will have been a local contact. This has not been planned long distance. They'd have to have someone on the ground. Incidentally, where's DS Hooper?'

'He's still on leave. He won't be back until the new year. Skiing in Val-d'Isère I believe.'

'Marvellous! Who do we have available?'

'Apart from ourselves, there's DS Lunn and DS Burgess, but Debbie's due to go on maternity leave at the end of February. As you know, DS Lunn is working on a major fraud – "Operation Beadle" – appropriately named given the progress he's made.'

Hood laughed. 'I remember suggesting that "Beadle" was, perhaps, unsuitable for a fraud inquiry – sounds as if I may have been right.'

Knight smiled and continued. 'We're very stretched at present, what with Christmas coming up – and this flu that's going about. We could move a couple of DCs from "Beadle" but Ian Lunn won't like it. As you know, DI Palmer is still on long-term sick, so Ian's been virtually running "Beadle" on his own.'

Hood sighed. 'This means we'll have to use uniformed officers to do the leg work. But Ian will have to take a break from "Beadle". This inquiry will have to have priority.' He paused. 'Who's dealing with the CCTV?'

'No one in particular as yet but we'll have to assign an officer pretty quickly. Uniform are still collecting it. With any luck, we should be able to ID the vehicle from the street cameras or the CCTV from the compound. We've already got the tapes from there and the service road but we shall need the pictures from cameras over a wider area. What we have so far is being set up in the incident room as we speak.'

'Right, I'll have a look at those before I go and see the ACC. Then we'll visit the bank that dispatched the money – we'll take in the Charnwood Centre on the way. If you ask me, this has the smell of an inside job. It can't be a coincidence that they struck when so much money was available for the taking. Someone has provided them with the information.'

He handed the crime report to Knight. 'I want you to concentrate on the money. There must be a record of what was stolen. We have to get the serial numbers publicised as soon as possible. We'll look very foolish if any of it starts turning up and isn't noticed.'

Hood and Knight walked out of the chief inspector's office and made their way to the incident room where a large whiteboard had been erected. Civilian employees were setting up several computers. A detective constable was busy pinning photographs taken that morning on to the board, the middle of which was covered with a large-scale plan of the area around the shopping centre.

'Gather round,' said Hood to the six officers who stood up as he entered the room. Three of them were in uniform. Detective Sergeant Ian Lunn appeared at the door as the others took their seats. Hood invited him to join them. The detective sergeant chose to stand at the rear. He was obviously not happy. Hood cleared his voice.

'As you probably know, early this morning a security van delivering a substantial amount of cash to the Charnwood Shopping Centre near the airport was attacked as it entered the secure compound.'

'Wasn't very secure then,' quipped one of the uniformed officers.

The chief inspector glared at him. 'No comedians *please.*' He continued, 'The information we have so far is that 1.9 million pounds was stolen.'

'Phew, nearly 2 million! The manager wouldn't disclose the precise amount when I spoke with him earlier this morning. I can see why. Shouldn't we have been informed so much cash was on the move?'

It was DS Debbie Burgess who had spoken.

'A good point, Debbie,' said Hood. 'That's one of the matters we shall be inquiring into. Now, this was obviously a professional job and was carefully planned. One of the guards is in intensive care in the Queen's Medical Centre in Nottingham. Latest reports suggest he's in a bad way so this may well turn into a murder inquiry. We have the CCTV from the compound and I suggest we start there. Those who are attached to the squad dealing with this case will then be given their individual actions to carry out. Munt, close the blinds.'

The probationary constable did as he was asked, smiling to himself that Harry the Hood, as the chief inspector was known behind his back, actually knew his name. The video recorder was switched on. It became immediately apparent that the system used at the shopping centre was multiplex and a snapshot was taken only every second or so of the action inside the compound and on the service road. This gave the individuals on the screen a stilted look, rather like a film from the early days of cinema.

'That was a bit extreme wasn't it, sir? Smashing the windscreen like that and setting the security van on fire – someone could have died.'

Munt's probationary period was about to finish and he was keen to stay with the case. Although he was older than most probationers – he had gone to college for two years and acquired two "A" levels – he was still in appearance a somewhat gangly youth, his thin frame and above-average height giving the impression that he was not entirely in control of his movements.

'They'd been watching too many American films,' said one of the others. 'But it won't half have put the wind up the security guards.'

'Very risky, though,' said Hood. 'It set the fire alarms off and drew a lot of attention. They must have been very confident of a quick getaway. Fortunately, the security lights inside the compound were not affected by the fire. I suppose we should be grateful for that.'

'And very confident that no security guards from the Charnwood Centre would get in their way,' said Debbie Burgess. 'It's difficult to believe, sir, but they have none on duty after the place closes for the night.'

'Is that right?' asked Hood.

'Yes, sir. I've already run a check. There are three visits during the night by mobile patrols, but none permanently on site.'

A look of complete disbelief passed over Hood's face. 'Play it again,' he instructed, 'and stop it when I say.'

At the first pause he was able to identify the van used by the robbers as a light-coloured transit. The registration number was reasonably clear.

'Make a note of that and get it checked, though it's bound to be bogus.'

'Already done it, sir,' said Munt who had viewed the tape himself after collecting it from the shopping centre. 'According to Swansea, it's registered to a police vehicle in Nottingham.'

'Cocky bastards,' commented one of the uniforms.

Hood could hardly conceal a smile. It would seem that he was dealing with professionals. A nice touch that, using a police-registered number on their getaway vehicle.

'Do we all agree there were three of them?' he asked as the tape was completed a second time. No one dissented.

'Plus the driver, of course,' said Wendy Knight. Hood nodded in agreement.

'All of them seem to be wearing balaclavas or ski masks and dark overalls. One man is obviously taller than the others. Just our luck that the bit where the guard had a go at one of them hasn't been recorded too clearly. Why they don't go the whole hog and provide continuous CCTV in such a sensitive area I really don't know. But the blast from the gun is pretty clear. And it's the taller man who fired it. Anyone make out anything about the driver?'

'Difficult to tell. He's wearing a balaclava too. I suppose they'd all be dressed the same.' said Knight.

'What I don't understand, sir, is how they managed to *reverse* their van into the compound, straight after the security vehicle. The guards must have seen it before they opened the gates.' It was Munt, again, who made this contribution. 'Looks very sloppy on the part of the security team, if you ask me. They don't seem to have been very alert and they did nothing to prevent one of the robbers jumping on to their vehicle.'

'That's what the petrol was for.'

Detective Constable Robbie Sleath, whose Scottish monotone so irritated his colleagues, hardly looked up as he uttered these words. He was usually loath to say anything at such gatherings unless it was to correct a colleague or demonstrate his superior powers of analysis. He was one of those occasionally effective officers, repeatedly passed over for promotion, who thought he had been badly treated by the system and was counting the days until he received his pension. He'd put in again for promotion to sergeant but was not over optimistic. It was over nine months since he'd passed the revamped examinations and he had a long way to go before he could hand in his papers and collect the generous retirement benefits paid to police officers. He thought that five years in uniform and eight years as a DC was more than enough to prove he deserved a step up the ladder, but a vacancy had to arise first. He knew he had the brains for it and if he made sergeant it would get him out of some of the routine work that drove him to distraction and made him unpopular with some of his colleagues. His cynicism, however, knew no bounds and he did not suffer fools gladly. He was fast reaching the conclusion that young Munt fitted into that category. Who did this probationer think he was? When Sleath had been a probationer the golden rule was to keep your mouth shut at all times but here was Malcolm Munt making comments as if he were a seasoned detective. He needed to be put in his place. Sleath was just the man to do it.

'That's why they used the accelerant after putting in the windscreen. Would you hang around in a vehicle that's just had a couple of gallons of petrol poured over it? I wouldn't. Once the guards were out of the van, all it took was a sawn-off shotgun pointed at their heads to ensure their complete co-operation. The surprising thing is that one of them had a go. I bet that isn't in the training manual.'

His tone was condescending and almost brutal, as if he were merely stating the obvious.

'But there was no need to shoot him, was there?' insisted Munt. 'The guard who had a go had been pushed well back before the gunman shot him. It was completely over the top.'

'Away and raffle yourself,' replied Sleath, who undoubtedly had, as fellow Scots might have said, a good conceit of himself. 'He wasn't going to shoot him while he was still wrestling with his mate, was he? Otherwise he'd have probably shot him as well and we'd have had more DNA than we'd know what to do with.'

Munt looked towards Sleath but bit his tongue. Hood frowned.

'Play it again', he ordered, 'then let's see what the technical boys can do about enhancing it.'

There was no chance of identifying any of them from what could be seen on the CCTV. After several viewings of the tape, Hood gave his instructions.

'We are short of bodies at the moment, so the final make-up of the squad will have to wait. For the time being, DC Sleath here will act as co-ordinator.'

Hood glanced at Sleath who smiled and nodded. That sort of task was usually reserved for a detective sergeant. Did this mean his promotion was on the cards? Not that it improved his temper. Co-ordinating an inquiry like this one would be hard work. And with Christmas round the corner, he could see it might well interfere with his domestic arrangements.

'All actions are to be returned to him. The other guards are to be interviewed as significant witnesses. I want them taped, and if possible, videoed. There's a chance one or more of them may be involved. Their body language may give them away. And I don't exclude the one who was shot. It's perfectly possible he was in on it and the shooting staged to make him look a hero.'

'But he can't have thought he was going to have a coronary, can he?' said Sleath continuing his obdurate attitude. 'If he was in on it, it's going to be very difficult to prove, always assuming he survives. And another thing, if forensics are able to detect any blood from the villain who was punched, and provide us with his DNA – in my book that would exclude the guard from being involved. He'd have to be a real idiot to provide potential evidence against one of his own.'

'We assume nothing,' replied Hood firmly. 'We assemble the evidence and see where it leads us. The guard might simply have overdone his part. He must have known he would be captured on CCTV and that we would see it, so he'd want to make it look realistic – if he were in on it. But I agree it's a bit of a long shot.'

Sleath shook his head but said nothing further. Hood turned and spoke to Debbie Burgess.

'Now, Debbie, what can you tell us about this shopping centre?'

Hood pointed to the plan fixed to the whiteboard and the several photographs. 'Any of you ever been there?

A number of heads shook.

'What, nobody?'

'It's miles from where we live,' said Sleath, 'and it wasn't even built when I was in uniform.'

'I've never been there but I've done a bit of preliminary research,' said Burgess. 'As you can see from the plan, it's a huge place. Covers over 124 acres if you include the car parks – which are enormous. It opened early last year to a huge amount of controversy. It was built on an essentially greenfield site, swamping the hamlet that used to be there, and incorporating the old quarry, which has been turned into a lake. There was a lot of opposition at the time. The government eventually let it through because of its position between the airport and the motorway. It also provided a large number of jobs. But the protests went on for months. If you remember, it took a huge amount of policing at the time.'

Ian Lunn, who had played no part in the discussion so far, nodded. He knew all about the protests. He'd been brought in to co-ordinate the prosecutions of the few who were identified.

Detective Sergeant Burgess continued, 'But if you study the plan you will see that the service road which passes the secure compound circles most of the complex – and this is interesting – there are only a limited number of barriers to prevent access to most of it during the night.'

Burgess traced the route with her hand and pointed to where the barriers were positioned.

'Why?' inquired Sleath.

'Why what, Robbie?' asked Burgess somewhat testily.

'Why so few barriers and no security at night?'

'Two reasons,' said Burgess, trying hard to keep her temper in the face of what she considered to be deliberate provocation. 'First, because the big stores have deliveries during the night into the early hours of the morning. So there's a lot of activity when there is no security on the site at all – apart from what individual stores provide for themselves. Secondly, they're still constructing a new multi-storey car park on the eastern side of the main building, so the service road is being used for the time being by customers to access the main car parks.'

'Well that is decidedly odd,' said Sleath giving no quarter. 'No security at night at a place like this?'

'That's a question for the management company and the security firms – but I suspect it comes down to cost – like everything else.'

Hood intervened. Sleath was beginning to try his patience too.

'Nevertheless, it's something we need to look into. I'm sure this team of robbers was aware there was no security there when they carried out this job.'

He addressed Burgess. 'I want you and Ian to lead on the interviews of the other guards. I'll sit in if I can. Oh, and see if you can get DS Hooper back from France. We are going to need him.'

Lunn indicated his agreement but it was clear he was none too keen. Hood then directed his attention to the others.

'Debbie, here, will give you your orders. Now let's get on with it.' He paused. 'Unless anyone has anything else they want to say?'

'There is one thing, sir,' said Munt with a degree of hesitation. He looked at Sleath but the detective constable turned away. 'As I understand it, the security firm that handled the delivery we are interested in is one of the security firms employed at the complex.'

'That's right, sir,' said Burgess. 'Langdale Security. They have an office in Loughborough but their HQ is in Hinckley. They're one of two firms who handle the day to day security at the shopping centre.'

Sleath almost laughed. 'That's a bit of a coincidence isn't it?'

'Coincidences do happen, you know, Robbie,' responded Hood sharply. He looked at Knight. There might well have been something in what Sleath had said although the manner of his saying it hardly helped.

'A visit to Langdale Security would seem in order. Can you fix something up, Wendy? Robbie may be right.' He glanced at Munt. 'On the other hand he may be wrong. But everything has to be checked out. Later this afternoon will be convenient.'

Knight nodded. Hood looked round at his colleagues. 'Anything else?'

'Any sign of the getaway vehicle?' asked Lunn, showing a modicum of interest in the proceedings.

'Not so far,' replied Hood. 'We'll find it burnt out somewhere, I suspect.'

He looked at his watch as the meeting broke up.

'Have we christened the operation yet?' asked Burgess running the palm of her hand over her extended abdomen. Hood paused and turned towards her, his mood lightening.

'I've given it some thought,' he said, smiling. 'As we're up to "C" and given the time of year, I thought "Operation Christmas Carol" would be suitable. Anyone got any other suggestions?'

No one spoke. Sleath shot a look at Munt who wisely said nothing.

'OK. "Operation Christmas Carol" it is.' He made a sideways glance at Sleath. 'Perhaps Robbie here can play the part of Scrooge!'

The others laughed and even Sleath took it in good heart. Hood walked quickly from the room and headed to the car park. The early morning sleet had turned to rain and he pulled the collar of his coat closer as he made his way to his car. He then drove the few miles to Police Headquarters, an extravagantly extended building in the middle of nowhere. He often questioned the logic of having the centre of operations for several counties so far removed from the major cities the combined constabulary was supposed to serve. He showed his warrant card as he passed through security and made his way to the third floor. As he came out of the lift, he saw ACC Margaret Knowles standing at her open door. She ushered him inside her office and invited him to sit down.

'This is a bad one, Harry,' she said. 'I've already had the chief on from his holiday apartment in Florida. Apparently, it's been on *Sky News*, so he picked it up on his TV. He probably knew about it before I did.'

All right for some, thought Hood, but he simply agreed with his superior. 'Yes, ma'am, and it looks like a real professional job. It's not going to be easy.'

'As I understand it, we are rather thin on the ground at the moment? Do we have enough officers available for such a major investigation?'

'Not really, ma'am. I may have to take a few off the major fraud that DS Lunn has been investigating for the last nine months. He's getting nowhere fast so it may be the only option.'

'Well, I may be able to help there. I've been given permission to increase our establishment of detective officers. I have my eye on a couple of our own who have shown a bit of initiative and there are two or three others who've applied from outside. I've been authorised to transfer them in if they pass the board. That should help.'

Hood nodded. He was not very happy being landed with inexperienced detectives but things were pretty desperate. He wasn't going to complain.

'In the continuing absence of Superintendent Latham I shall be heading this inquiry personally,' she added. 'Frank Simpson is already overwhelmed with the investigation into the children's home scandal, so I can't spare him and Tony Craven has taken over the specialist major crimes unit. He's based in Nottingham for the moment – so he's out of the picture too. You'll remain in day-to-day control but you will be reporting to me. I shall require an update on a regular basis.'

'Of course, ma'am. Do we know when Philip Latham will be back?' he asked.

'No idea. His inquiry into the alleged corruption in the Met seems never ending. Until he returns, you will have my full authority. Just keep me informed.'

'I'll do my best ma'am.'

'I'm sure you will.'

She smiled and picked up a copy of the crime report from her desk. 'Now, what thoughts have you had so far? If that guard dies we'll be under intense media scrutiny, you know. He's an Asian man from a large family. We can't afford another cock-up after that acquittal in the Khalid murder case. No wonder Ronnie Palmer went off sick. He's lucky he wasn't disciplined. I expect he'll be putting in for early retirement. Between you and me, that will be for the best. I shall certainly not be encouraging him to stay.'

'If we're being frank, ma'am, I noticed some time ago he was cutting too many corners. His team was far from happy with his leadership. He won't be missed. And I certainly wouldn't want him involved in this inquiry.'

'Good. I'm glad we agree on that. Don't forget that Macpherson will be reporting shortly and we'll have to steel ourselves for some pretty sharp criticism. From what I hear – and I've seen the leaks in *The Guardian* – the Met is going to be accused of institutionalised racism – whatever that means. So I don't want us to be tarred with the same brush.'

Hood smiled to himself. No risk of that with him, but the ACC was going to have to watch her language in the post-MacPherson era. She obviously didn't know the origin of the expression she had just used. But Hood realised she didn't mean anything by it. But others might not. Knowles turned to the subject in hand.

'Anything you'd like to share with me about this case? They were pretty ruthless setting the van on fire before they made their escape.'

'I think that was done simply to intimidate the guards and make sure they got them out of the security van. I've seen the CCTV and they were very careful to make sure they had all the security bags away before they torched it. Ruthless yes, but well planned. I'm not excluding any of the security guards as possibly being involved, including Mr Patel. The cartridge was loaded with salt so it could be a blind.'

'Go carefully with that, Harry. I don't want any comebacks. If he were involved, he'd hardly have attacked a robber with sufficient force to cause him to bleed. That may well provide crucial DNA evidence.'

'I appreciate that, ma'am. As you know, I can be quite discreet when I have to be.'

Knowles smiled. 'Will you run the investigation from Loughborough or from Central in Leicester?'

'Leicester, I think. An incident room has already been set up and most of the team is based there.'

'Any leads at all?'

'It's early days, ma'am. But it has the look of an inside job – to some extent at least. It can't be a coincidence that these villains struck at a time when there was double the usual amount of money being delivered. It's also more than a little curious that we were not informed. We're usually told if such a large amount of cash is to be moved.'

Knowles shook her head. 'That certainly used to be the position. But it's not as common as it once was. I was informed at a meeting a few weeks ago that some of the banks prefer not to tell us in case the information leaks. We are not trusted as we used to be. And, just a thought, but isn't it possible that the cash was as much as it was because it's Christmas next week?'

Hood did not disagree. 'As I said, it's early days and we have little enough to go on. But rest assured. There will be no cock-ups this time. I shall be visiting the compound this morning then I'm off to see the manager at the bank.'

'What about the security firm?'

'The other two guards are being treated as significant witnesses and will be interviewed today. I shall be seeing the operations manager at the security firm this afternoon.'

'Well, keep me informed, won't you?'

'Yes, of course.'

'By the way,' added Knowles, 'I hope your promotion doesn't come through until after this is sorted. We simply can't manage without you at the moment.'

Hood smiled, sheepishly.

'There's no guarantee I will get it,' he replied. 'It's a big jump from DCI to superintendent.'

'You've no worries on that score,' she said with a wry smile. 'I only wish we had a vacancy here. We probably will have in a year or so when Superintendent Millington retires. If you were to hang on until then, you'd walk straight into his job – I could virtually guarantee it. No one would bet against you.'

'That's very kind of you, ma'am, but I don't really want an administrative post. The job in Birmingham is overseeing serious crime. I do like to get my hands dirty sometimes.'

'I understand. There'll be plenty of time for bureaucracy when you join the ranks of assistant chief constables, eh?'

'I never think that far ahead.'

CHAPTER TWO

Irish Bernard and his brother Colin had enjoyed an uneventful journey from Holyhead to Dun Laoghaire. They had stashed their share from the robbery in the spare wheel compartment in their hired car and driven it off the ferry in to Dublin without attracting any undue attention. Within a matter of a couple of days, they'd turned most of it into Irish punts. Although the euro was being introduced into Ireland at the beginning of 1999, it would be quite some time before the new euro notes came into circulation. They had taken a bit of a hit from the third party who had managed the exchange but no suspicions had been aroused. And the Donnelly brothers liked that; they were always keen to ensure their activities remained hidden and went unnoticed by the authorities. They anticipated having a very pleasant Christmas!

Bernard and Colin Donnelly had not been involved in the planning of this particular criminal enterprise. They'd been brought in to provide the muscle and been paid an agreed fee for their trouble. And Bernard certainly had the muscle. He stood well over six-foot tall and weighed seventeen stone. Although he was now entering middle age, he kept himself fit and made regular use of the equipment in one of the several gyms he owned in the Dublin area. Colin was physically smaller, but what he lacked in inches he made up for in determination, especially in a crisis. His natural nervousness seemed to disappear in the excitement of the action and his older brother regarded him as both indispensable and completely reliable.

The two brothers only committed serious criminal offences now in England – in Ireland they were establishing themselves as legitimate businessmen. They had carried out several offences in various locations in the UK and had never even been arrested. They knew Michael Doyle, initially through the building trade, and had set themselves up in Dublin as property developers using money obtained in a VAT carousel fraud masterminded by Doyle, not that anyone else involved had an inkling that he was the brains behind it.

Then there was the family connection. Doyle's younger sister had been in a brief relationship with Bernard's youngest brother, Sean – the respectable member of the family. But that had finished two years before – and it was personal – this was business. The breakdown of a relationship would never be allowed to interfere with the prospect of making large profits from crime. Doyle's mother had been born in Cork and she had moved back to Ireland years before when her marriage broke up, taking her younger daughter with her. Doyle, however, had remained in England. An older sister had emigrated to New Zealand but the Donnelly brothers no longer had any contact with Doyle's Irish-based relatives. They felt it was safer that way.

Originally from County Waterford, the two brothers had moved to the Dublin area as comparatively young men. Bernard Donnelly was always particularly careful about any criminal enterprise he joined. His assessment of risk was given absolute priority over everything else. He and his brother were pleased to get the bonus Doyle had given them when the take from the robbery had proved more than expected, but as far as Bernard was concerned, that was it. Any subsequent problems that might arise were not his concern. True, he had been very impressed with the way Doyle had organised the whole thing, especially as robbery was a new venture for him – but not for Bernard. He was an old hand and well practised in inducing terror in his victims. Nothing had been left to chance. Every eventuality had been considered. The detailed planning was nothing less than breathtaking in its simplicity and attention to detail. Bernard was particularly impressed by Doyle's insistence that no one should be told anything more than he needed to know to carry out the particular task assigned to him. It reduced the risk, if anyone was caught, of implicating the others. What they didn't know, they couldn't reveal.

The police would never find the van used to commit the robbery, not because it had been destroyed but because it was back in its original livery as a post office parcels van. Doyle had "borrowed" it, sprayed it a dull white with a specially prepared solution and fitted false plates. It was quickly restored afterwards by removing the white colouring with a high-pressure hose. The interior was cleaned thoroughly and it was returned with its original plates to the side street by the overcrowded parking area of the depot from which it had been temporarily removed. No one would be the wiser, except the dishonest post office driver who had assisted Doyle in previous criminal activity when it had been necessary to interfere with the postal service. He was paid a couple of thousand for leaving the keys in the ignition and parking the vehicle in the street away from the security cameras. But he was given no information as to the use the vehicle was to be put – not that he would have been interested anyway.

Neither did the Irish connection know anything about the vehicle used to commit the robbery – not until they saw Jules, Doyle's long-standing girlfriend, handling the high-pressure hose with such aplomb back at the foundry. Bernard had laughed when he saw the original paintwork re-emerge and commented on the intelligent and shrewd idea to use a post office van. He naturally attributed the idea to Doyle. It never crossed his mind that Doyle's girlfriend might have been the originator of that aspect of the plan.

'Using this van guarantees the police will get nowhere even if they discovered it was the getaway vehicle. Once it's back in use by the Royal Mail there'll be DNA from dozens of postal workers all over it.'

Jules had laughed as she'd explained the reasoning behind it. Bernard nodded and filed the information away in his prodigious memory. Might very well come in handy one day. The satchels, the overalls and face-coverings along with the sawn-off and the mobile phones were burnt in the old foundry furnace. Nothing survived. Bernard had initially protested when the new banknotes started to be thrown in as well – three hundred thousand pounds going up in smoke? There had to be another way, didn't there? No! It was Jules who had been so insistent. 'It's not worth the risk,' she had warned. 'None of the other notes can be traced – these can. Think about it. It's a fraction of the take and the only part that could lead the police to us. I'd say it's a price worth paying to avoid detection and the prison sentence that will follow if any of us are caught.'

'Jules is right,' Doyle had said. 'It's simply not worth the risk.'

After a short discussion, everyone had agreed. Bernard had even joined in the fun chucking the bundles of notes into the flames. After all, given the amount they had to share between themselves, they literally had money to burn.

Charlie Benson, however, had not joined in the merrymaking. When he'd returned to the foundry he was nursing his nose and his mouth. The bleeding had proved very difficult to stop and Jules had eventually pushed cotton wool up his nostrils until the blood clotted and told him to hold a towel to his cut lip. Bernard had been unsympathetic. 'Some people are natural bleeders,' he had commented, acidly. He had also insisted that Benson was sent on his way before the clean-up began. A sixth sense had told him that Benson was not to be entirely trusted, especially after he got himself involved physically with one of the guards. 'He's better off out of the way,' he had told Doyle before Doyle too vanished from the foundry. He had disappeared within a very short time of their arriving back from the robbery – but it was none of Bernard's business. He'd heard the motorcycle starting up outside but Jules had placed her finger over her mouth and looked at him sweetly, so he'd said nothing. He hadn't seen Doyle again and he had no desire to do so. Jules had managed all that needed to be managed with effortless efficiency. Colin, however, continued to worry, even when they were back in Ireland.

'But what about Benson?' he had said to Bernard, more than once. 'I never really trusted him; he struck me as being a bit lightweight and he had to go and bleed all over that security guard. That could cause us trouble if he's picked up by the police.'

'Don't worry about him,' said his older brother. 'He knows nothing about us, absolutely nothing. The *eejit* thinks we're from Scotland. That's what I told him. He asked if he could visit us in Dundee. I said he was very welcome.'

Bernard laughed, then suddenly appeared more serious. But he was not panicking. He was savouring the wisdom of his insisting that no one with a criminal record should go on the job. That was why Doyle remained behind at the old foundry. His fingerprints were probably still on record from his arrest in '93. Robbery was not really Doyle's scene but he had become quite excited at the prospect and had planned to drive the getaway van. But Bernard wasn't having that. He and his brother had never been caught and they aimed to keep it that way. Benson, on the other hand, was clean – Bernard knew that for sure. Because he had not been too happy about him, he had checked him out personally through a bent copper he knew in the Met. He'd been assured he had no previous and so Benson was allowed to go on the job. But not Doyle – even though it was his venture. That's why Jules had to do the driving; Bernard simply would not hear of Michael Doyle going along. He'd have called the whole thing off rather than take the risk. But there was no time to find a substitute driver. The job could not be put off and although Doyle had agreed to his ultimatum, Jules had had to replace him. She'd made a pretty good fist of it too. She hadn't batted an eyelid when Bernard shot the guard. 'You had no choice,' she had assured him afterwards. But as for Benson? Like Colin, he had not been impressed with him at all and he was beginning to regret he'd allowed him to join them. Now the risk of a DNA match rankled. Although the police had nothing on record about Benson, if he were to be caught for some reason, a DNA match would be a certainty. So, it was sensible to ensure the police did not get hold of him. Providing that didn't happen the DNA wouldn't help them one little bit. They'd have nothing to compare it with.

'We'll be all right,' said Bernard. 'There's no need to panic. Just make sure that Doyle gets him out of the country. Jules assured me it would be done – just as a precaution.'

He pulled on his coat and opened the door. 'I'm going down the pub. Are you coming?'

Colin shook his head. 'No. I'll give it a miss. I'll give Jules a bell, just to make sure she did as she said she would. See you later.'

CHAPTER THREE

Hood spent very little time at the Charnwood Centre. Having surveyed the compound where the robbery occurred he left the scenes of crime officers to continue their detailed investigations and drove with Wendy Knight to the National Commercial Bank of Great Britain in Loughborough. Having passed through the elaborate security procedures, the two detectives made their way to the office of the general manager. A secretary, smartly dressed in a black skirt and cream blouse, looked up and smiled as they entered. She was very attractive and knew it.

'Detective Chief Inspector Hood?'

Hood nodded.

'Mr King is expecting you. Please come this way.'

Moments later Hood and Knight were ushered into the presence of the manager. Hood looked around the room. It was much larger than he had expected and expensively furnished, quite a contrast with the nondescript, modern brick-built building in which it was housed. He had been quite surprised when he'd arrived at the sprawling industrial estate in the suburbs of Loughborough. To the outsider, Bridgeford House, as the complex was known, looked like a large warehouse operation set apart from most of the other buildings on the estate. It was surrounded by a high-security fence and Hood had noticed that there were security guards in larger numbers than he had anticipated throughout the building and an unusually extensive CCTV system. The manager greeted them but not warmly.

'Welcome to Bridgeford House. Would you like a cup of tea or coffee?' he asked, indicating for them to sit.

They both declined and showed him their warrant cards before sitting on the hard-backed chairs in front of his large teak desk. Knight took out her notebook. Hood looked at him quizzically. Reginald King was a middle-aged man, slightly overweight and balding. He was dressed in a cheap looking three-piece suit that had undoubtedly seen better days. The top button of his off-white shirt was undone and his colourful tie askew. His security pass dangled from a blue lanyard around his neck. Hood noticed that the photograph was rather flattering – obviously several years old. King played with his biro as he spoke, passing it between his nicotine stained fingers, nervously.

'This is a bad business, Chief Inspector. It will do my career no good at all. It is essential you catch these people and recover our money.'

Hood continued to look at him before he spoke. 'It was a lot of cash to move without telling us, wasn't it?'

King shook his head and smiled. 'What's to tell? We move very large sums regularly. This sort of thing has never happened before and all the banks involved decided when this shopping centre opened that secrecy was of the essence. Only those who needed to know were aware of the details. That did not include the police.'

He was not pulling his punches. His initial nervousness was diminishing rapidly.

'I presume you'll be able to tell me which of your employees knew of this consignment?'

'Yes, of course. But I assure you no one here will have had anything to do with the robbery. We are very careful in choosing our senior staff.'

Wendy Knight interjected. 'Did you say, all the banks, sir? What do you mean by all the banks?'

King sighed. 'It's perfectly simple. There are dozens of ATMs in the Charnwood Centre and in lots of other similar establishments. If all the banks which supply the cash for such facilities had to replenish them on an individual basis, it would become too well known and money would be arriving there far too frequently. It would be too easy for would-be thieves to work out how to take advantage of such a system. So we have combined and rotate the task. One week, we provide the cash for all the machines, another week one of the other banks does the same. That way we reduce the risks of anything going wrong by limiting the number of deliveries. The only downside is that very large amounts of cash are involved but the security firm is supposed to manage that. Obviously, on this occasion they failed to do so.'

'One of their guards was shot. You do know that, sir.' Hood's intervention prompted a slight change of tone in the manager.

'So I saw on the TV news. That is very unfortunate but the failure of security is down to them.'

Hood glanced at Wendy Knight then turned his attention back to the manager.

'You will have a record of the notes that formed this consignment?'

The manager adjusted his position on his large leather chair and looked distinctly uncomfortable. He cleared his throat before he replied. 'Some.'

'What do you mean, some? Surely a consignment of this size would be fully recorded – a consignment of new notes?'

'Well, that's the point, Chief Inspector. Most of the notes forming this consignment were not new. They were very high quality – they would have looked new to the average person – but most were in fact used notes. Only three hundred thousand pounds' worth was new. Of course, I can provide you with the serial numbers of those.'

He opened his desk drawer and took out several sheets of paper which he handed to Hood. The chief inspector examined them, before passing them on to Wendy Knight.

'The new notes were all twenties and tens?'

King nodded his head in agreement. 'In fact, all the notes making up this consignment were twenties and tens – no fives. Inflation you know.' He forced a smile.

'And we have the serial numbers for only three hundred thousand? You've made our job much more difficult, you know.'

'Well that can't be helped. We have neither the staff nor the technology to make a record of used notes. No bank has. They come in here from all over the place: shops, post offices, supermarkets – all sorts of businesses. We simply can't record the serial numbers of every note we deal with, any more than you could. Do you know the serial numbers of the cash in your wallet?'

Hood shook his head trying to think whether he had any cash in his wallet at all.

'I thought not,' said King, looking very satisfied with himself.

Hood pressed on. He was anxious to retain the advantage as the interview progressed.

'So what do you do here? This is not a typical bank, is it?' He looked directly at King but the manager remained poised and cool. He sighed, like a schoolmaster with a particularly difficult pupil. His description of the procedures at Bridgeford House was obviously well rehearsed. He clasped his hands together as he spoke.

'It's not really a bank at all. This is a service centre or, if you like, a counting house. Amongst our many functions is the processing of cash we receive daily from our branches and, of course, the Bank of England.'

'A counting house?' queried Hood.

'Yes. We have several scattered over the country – as do the other banks. This is the largest in the Midlands. We are gradually closing the smaller units and concentrating our operations in larger centres.'

'And they all fulfil the same purpose?'

'Yes,' replied King, hardly bothering to conceal his irritation. 'Strange as it may seem, our main function is simply to count money.'

The manager stood up and moved to the glass wall behind his desk and beckoned Hood to join him. He pointed to the large warehouse-like room below. Hood looked down and saw a series of tables and machines with individuals feeding what appeared to be banknotes into them.

'This is one of our machine rooms. We put all used notes through our counting machines which spot forgeries or foreign currency and select those notes that are suitable for further use. Others that are past their useful life are returned to the Bank of England for destruction. Most of the notes that made up this consignment were sourced in this way. As you will have gathered, we also provide new notes for our branches and when necessary for the ATMs. These people were very lucky. On another occasion all the notes might have been new and we'd have had a full record.'

'I don't believe anyone can be so lucky,' said Hood returning to his seat. King pressed a switch and an automatic blind started to cover the glass.

'They don't like to think I'm spying on them,' he said with another seemingly forced smile.

'Isn't it very tempting for your staff,' queried Knight, 'you know, to help themselves to cash – especially the banknotes that are due to be destroyed?'

'One can never remove temptation, I suppose,' answered King, 'but security is very tight. Everyone is searched on the way out – as you will discover for yourselves – and visitors are searched on the way in, as an additional precaution. There are no exceptions. Anyone who is caught is subject to instant dismissal; and we haven't had to dismiss anyone for, what… nearly eighteen months?'

'What happened eighteen months ago?'

'A temporary employee; I believe he was a university student. We'd taken him on when we were very short-staffed that summer. He was caught with three hundred pounds down his underpants. The machine room manager sacked him on the spot. I was on leave at the time. We've had no trouble since.'

Hood leant forward in his seat. 'You didn't prosecute then?'

'Oh, no,' replied King, slightly taken aback. 'We didn't want to risk any unfortunate publicity.'

'You must be a very tempting target for robbery though,' said Knight.

The manager shook his head. 'In so far as anywhere is robbery proof, I think we are. Always assuming anyone could get in, we have a foolproof overriding system that would ensure any thieves would never get out. Our own security people here have no control over it. You may have noticed on the way in that this information is prominently displayed once you pass through the security barrier.'

Hood had not taken in any such warning when he passed through security but he nodded anyway. 'So any would-be thieves would have to attack the security vehicles after they had left the premises?'

'Exactly – and the CCTV cameras cover the whole of the staff car park and the exit route as far as the main road. I have preserved the tapes for you for the last fourteen days. We keep them for twenty-eight days before they're taped over. So if you want the rest, just say so.'

'Thank you,' said Hood. 'If you could let DC Knight have them – all of them – they may prove useful.'

Hood continued his questioning. 'The security vehicle that was attacked was carrying a very large amount of cash, wasn't it?'

Knight sat with her pen poised, waiting for King to answer.

'I hope you're not suggesting we altered our usual practice for this consignment? It was only as large as it was because of Christmas week. The demand is much higher. This year was no different to last.'

'And there was I thinking everyone used plastic nowadays,' said Knight.

King smiled. 'Oh, you would be surprised how many transactions are still carried out in cash, you know. Far more than you would think. That's why we encourage the use of credit and debit cards. Handling large quantities of cash is very expensive for us, never mind the cost of security. Anyway, there are much larger amounts sent to the Bank of England for destruction. We've had as much as 15 million sent in a single consignment. Mind you, they wouldn't be much use to thieves. The notes are put through machines that mark them with a dye; those that are too badly damaged to go through the machines are cut in two.'

'Who decides whether a note should be destroyed?' asked Hood.

'In the first place, it's down to the machines. If they are rejected, the operator has a discretion whether to put them aside for return to our branches or if they're very worn or damaged to place them in the hoppers for destruction. But I fail to see the relevance of these questions. None of the stolen money fell into either of these categories.'

Hood tried to conceal his irritation. He had already decided there was something about Reginald King that he did not like. 'I simply want to understand how the system works,' he said with some emphasis. 'We shall need to see the relevant members of your staff. Can you let us have a list?'

The manager nodded. Hood was beginning to realise the enormity of the task before him. 'By the way,' he added, 'have you had any difficulties recently with any other members of your staff? I mean someone in a more senior position. Has anyone left under a cloud, so to speak?'

King looked bemused. 'I don't think so. Our senior staff members have been here for years. But I'll ask my secretary to examine our employment records for you.'

'How many members of staff would have known precisely when this consignment was due to leave here?'

'Me, obviously,' replied King. 'Steven Lloyd – he's the machine room manager – and his assistant, David Taylor, although I think David was due to go on leave before the delivery was made. In fact, I signed it off. I was here until gone 4 a.m. – then got called back almost as soon as I got home – so I am anxious to get away again. I've had very little sleep.'

King looked at his watch as he stifled a yawn. Hood had no intention of allowing tiredness to delay his investigation. 'You have two managers to monitor the machine rooms?'

'Yes. Because we have two rooms now – since the expansion – so David and Steven move between both of them – it keeps the operators on their toes. I suppose I should include my secretary, Mrs Jarvis, amongst those in the know. But I trust her absolutely. She's been with me for over six years.'

'Wouldn't the people who work in the machine room have a good idea too?'

'Why should they? They may handle the cash and record the inflow and outflow but they are not privy to the arrangements the security firms make for the transportation of the security bags. That is kept very much under wraps. It's the security firms that decide when to collect. We have employees working here 24/7 – so they can choose exactly when they wish to move a consignment. They inform Steven Lloyd or David and they arrange for the appropriate number of satchels to be made available. As you would expect, the security firms stagger the times they collect. It would be very difficult for an outsider to work out when a particular consignment was going to be moved.'

'But not impossible?' commented Hood.

'I suppose anything's possible,' said the manager, yawning again, 'but if you ask me, if there's been a leak, it probably came from the security firm not from here.'

'How many work in the machine rooms?' asked Knight.

'We have three shifts, since we expanded last summer, so in total, about forty-six, I guess. As I said, I can let you have a full list. The numbers are very much reduced at night, though. Not many are keen to work that shift.'

He yawned once more as if to make a point.

'And, it would be difficult if not impossible for any of them to work out *when* a particular consignment was due to leave here?'

'That's the general idea,' said King. 'They may be able to predict that a consignment is due to leave within a day or two, but the security people only give Steven Lloyd or David Taylor a few hours' notice of when they propose to collect. They do tend to deal with most of the larger consignments in the early hours of the morning, so I suppose anyone studying when they arrive here might get lucky. But most of the consignments that are destined for ATMs are nothing like as large as this one. As they use exactly the same vehicles for everything, even a keen observer would not be able to tell when a consignment of this size was going to be dispatched. The weak link has to be the security firm.'

'But who decides on the number of satchels that are to be dispatched? The security firm doesn't decide how much money is to be transported, does it? That must be decided here.'

'Yes, I suppose it is. But we have a fairly consistent itinerary. We inform the operations manager at Langdale Security by telephone immediately before collection. I assume that the guards must know the number of satchels that are due to be picked up and transported by the time they arrive. You'll have to ask them how they handle their side of things.'

'We shall. You need not concern yourself about that.'

Hood spoke as if he meant business. Knight then asked a question.

'What's the procedure before the cash leaves here?'

The manager took a deep breath before he replied.

'It's prepared after counting and placed in cages which are sealed and locked and then brought to our strongrooms. The cash that is destined for the ATMs or delivery to our branches is placed in satchels, which are also sealed, locked and placed in the strongroom. There is usually two hundred thousand in twenties in a satchel or one hundred thousand in tens. That means that as far as this consignment is concerned there were…' He paused and glanced at a note on his desk. 'Fourteen satchels – five containing twenties and nine containing tens.'

'Each with ten thousand notes in it,' said Knight.

'That's right,' replied the manager, obviously impressed with her mental arithmetic.

'And the new notes?' asked Hood.

'As the sheets I have given you will make clear, two hundred thousand in twenties and one hundred thousand in tens. So, only two of the satchels contained new notes.'

'Were the satchels containing the new notes different in appearance to the others?'

'No,' replied the manager. 'Exactly the same.'

'Well, that's something I suppose. If we do recover any of the cash, there'll be some chance of at least a few of the new notes being in there.'

'I wouldn't know,' said King, assuming an air of indifference.

'And when the security van reaches the compound? What is the procedure at that point?'

It was Knight who took up the questioning.

'The practice changed about twelve months ago. When the centre opened in '97, the satchels were taken in to the strongroom by the security guards and received by staff working inside. But we were advised that this created too many risks so procedures changed. A chute was built into the wall of the strongroom and the security guards simply place the satchels onto the chute, which carries them down to the strongroom floor. No internal employees are present. When they arrive later they check the bags and arrange for the distribution of the cash. You'll have to ask them how they go about that.'

'Hardly relevant,' said Hood. 'The cash never got that far on this occasion.'

Touché, thought Knight to herself, but she said nothing. The manager frowned. Hood could not resist smiling.

'Why is there no one present inside the strongroom when the cash arrives?' he asked.

'Health and safety, I suppose. We realised that there was no need for them to be there providing the strongroom was secure – which it is – and it removed the risk of staff being taken hostage should a robbery take place. It also meant that deliveries could be made during the night. And another thing, once the cash is deposited, our responsibility ceases. The risk passes to the centre's management. Most of the machines in the centre are operated by them or individual stores, not the banks.'

'But on this occasion, none of the money was deposited – so the risk and the losses remain with you.'

'Exactly, which is why you have to do everything possible to get it back. Unless we can establish negligence on the part of the security firm, this bank will have to stand the loss. Ultimately, I shall be held responsible. As it is we are going to have to make a further delivery tomorrow of another £1.9 million.'

'Are you insured?'

'No. The premiums were too high and we never anticipated anything like this could happen – not on this scale.'

'Well, I suggest you have a police escort on the next occasion. It'll cost you of course.'

Hood shot a knowing glance at Knight.

'That has already been arranged,' said King, looking at his watch again. He was plainly keen to bring the interview to a conclusion. Hood was not.

'How much does one of these satchels weigh when full of cash?' asked Knight.

'I'm not sure exactly. There's no difficulty manhandling them. But I can find out for you.'

King picked up the phone and dialled a number. 'Steven, Reg here. I need your help. Tell me, how much does two hundred thousand pounds in twenty-pound notes weigh?'

There was a short pause. 'I see. Thanks very much.'

He replaced the receiver and looked at Hood. 'A twenty-pound note weighs approximately one gram. Ten thousand notes would therefore weigh...'

'Ten kilograms,' interrupted Knight.

'Precisely!' The manager smiled in acknowledgement of Knight's further demonstration of her mental agility.

'Very impressive,' said Hood, looking at Knight.

Knight almost blushed. 'It's perfectly simple,' she replied. 'That's the beauty of the metric system. All you have to do is move the decimal point!'

Hood turned his attention back to the manager. Maths had never been his strong point.

'And the bags containing the ten-pound notes would weigh about the same would they?'

'More or less,' replied the manager. 'Same number of notes so approximately the same weight.' He paused then added, 'Perhaps slightly less – the dimensions of a ten-pound note are smaller.'

A self-satisfied grin reappeared on his face. Hood pressed on.

'And the bags themselves?'

'A few pounds at the most. That can easily be checked. In fact, I shall ask them to weigh each bag before tomorrow's delivery is made. You will have the precise weights then, if it will assist your inquiries.'

'It may. I like to consider every detail.'

'Do you know, yet, when the security firm will collect the cash tomorrow?' asked Knight.

'On this occasion, yes,' came the reply.

'Why is that?'

King leant forward before he answered. He spoke with feeling. 'Because we had to give your lot advanced notice otherwise you wouldn't have been able to provide the additional security. That's why.'

Hood was almost taken aback by the vehemence of King's reply. He looked slightly uncomfortable as he realised why the police had not been informed of earlier consignments. It would clearly have opened up another area of risk.

'Were there any other security measures taken?'

King quickly regained his composure. 'None.' He paused and continued playing with his pen. 'Believe it or not, we were planning to change the whole system immediately after Christmas. We shall not be using these security bags in future. The plan is to place the cash in specially prepared cartridges that spray indelible ink on the notes if they are interfered with.' He looked up and smiled. 'A German invention, you know. Any interference would render the notes valueless. A real deterrent, don't you think? It's a pity we hadn't got that in place before this happened.'

'Closing the stable door after the horse has bolted,' commented Hood. 'Is there any reason why the move to these cartridges did not take place earlier?'

King took a packet of cigarettes from his jacket pocket, removed a cigarette and placed it between his lips before quickly removing it. 'Smoking is not permitted inside the building,' he said. 'Sometimes, I forget.' He replaced the cigarette in the packet which he casually deposited on his desk. 'It's not just a question of the cartridges. The machines have to be adapted too. That's due to take place over the holiday period. It's a major job. And we have another large delivery to make on Sunday. A bit ironic that. If they'd waited until then, they would have got away with another quarter of a million.'

'Why is the Sunday delivery so much larger?'

'Christmas. The centre is open all day on Sunday and there won't be any further deliveries until the new year – not by us anyway.'

Knight persisted with her questions. 'Why are you making two large deliveries in such a short space of time. I thought you said you and the other banks took it in turns?'

'We do.' King sounded quite exasperated. 'Do you have any idea how much cash is removed from these machines during busy periods? They have to be replenished on an almost daily basis at this time of the year. We are not the only bank delivering during the Christmas period, you know.'

'But why are you making another large delivery so soon? Why not send one very large consignment?'

King looked increasingly annoyed. 'It's partly a question of security but the main reason is simply one of availability of cash. We can't deliver what we haven't got. Used notes are coming in here all the time. We have to check them and decide which ones are up to the required standard. If we had sent a single delivery of 4 million pounds we would have had to use far too many new notes. Once you understand how we operate, it will all become perfectly clear.'

Hood nodded.

'And as things have turned out we'd have lost over 4 million rather than just under two. I suppose we should be grateful for that.'

Knight took up the questioning again. 'How is it decided how many new notes should be included in a consignment?'

King paused before he answered. He was trying not to sound too impatient. 'It decides itself, really. The policy of the Bank of England is to restrict the provision of new notes – on cost grounds. They're not cheap to print, you know.' He dropped his voice as if he were disclosing some confidential information. 'So we use as many used notes as we can. But the amount we receive varies enormously from day to day so we are sometimes obliged to use more new notes than we would like.'

'And this was one of those occasions, was it?' asked Hood.

'Not really. As I've already said, most of the notes in this delivery were used. They have to be of a certain standard to ensure the machines don't get clogged up. Had we had more suitable used notes, we wouldn't have had to include the new ones at all.'

'So there's no consistency in either the number or condition of used notes that you take in?'

'Precisely. There have been a few occasions when we have been obliged to send out a consignment made up entirely of new notes – when we've been short of suitable used ones. But that is fairly rare. But as I say, if we'd sent the Sunday consignment with this one, there would probably have been a majority of new notes. And that would never do. The Bank of England wouldn't like that at all.' He looked at Hood. 'Anything else I can help you with? But I would like to get home and go to bed. It's been a very long night.'

Hood shook his head. 'No, you've been very helpful, Mr King.'

Knight handed him her card. The two of them left the office. King watched them from his door as they walked down the corridor.

'What do you reckon to that?' said Hood as they approached the security barrier. 'We have the serial numbers for only a fraction of this consignment and it all takes place just before the system is made virtually foolproof. There has to be an inside connection. No one can be that lucky.'

Knight did not reply. After passing through security, they got into Hood's car. As they drove slowly through the car park, Hood noticed two security vans emblazoned with "Langdale Security" markings parked in an adjacent compound, separated from the bank's premises by a high mesh fence. He applied his brakes and stopped. He pointed to his right.

'Look at that, Wendy. That must be Langdale Security's Loughborough premises. How very convenient.'

'Yes, sir. I didn't realise they were so close. And there's a yard or something belonging to the bank immediately adjacent.'

'That's very interesting. It would be the easiest thing in the world for someone at the bank to pass information to someone on the other side of that fence, wouldn't it?'

Knight nodded and grinned. 'If he's a smoker. That must be the area set aside for smoking.'

'There's still a few around,' said Hood, 'including Mr King. Did you notice his fingers?'

'Yes,' replied Knight. 'He must have been smoking for most of his life.'

'Not that I have ever indulged. Well, not for years anyway – not since I was in the Boy Scouts.' Hood smiled.

'Me neither,' replied Knight. 'I think it is a disgusting habit. I've been trying to get Greg to give up for over a year. He's nearly there but he still has a crafty drag when he thinks I'm not looking.'

'Keep this to yourself for the moment, eh, Wendy? I'll slip it into the conversation when we see Langdale's operations manager. It will be interesting to hear what he has to say about it.'

CHAPTER FOUR

Chief Inspector Hood and DC Knight were shown into the boardroom at Langdale Security's headquarters. The firm was housed in the offices of a former knitting factory that had long ago ceased trading and the furnishings paid handsome tribute to the prosperous business that had once been conducted there. But like many similar establishments, foreign competition had more than decimated the industry and the premises had been picked up for a song by the founding fathers of Langdale Security Associates Limited. The boardroom had been listed by the local council, Grade II, and remained in its original state, panelled in what Hood took to be dark-coloured oak. It gave the room a rather sombre appearance on a dull December day. A chandelier graced the centre of the ceiling but did little to dispel the gloom, and a large oil painting of a distinguished looking Edwardian gentleman, suitably framed and lit, hung on the wall directly behind an elaborately carved chair placed at the end of the long directors' table. There was nothing on the highly polished surface apart from a blotting pad encased in a leather cover and a white telephone placed within easy reach of any occupier of the carved chair. Several chairs of simpler design were placed along each side. Hood was about to pull one of them out and sit himself down when a smartly dressed man walked briskly into the room.

'Chief Inspector Hood?'

'Yes,' said Hood, proffering his hand.

'I'm Langdale, Simon Langdale, managing director of Langdale Security. I'm afraid our operations manager has gone off sick.'

Simon Langdale shook hands and Hood introduced his colleague. Langdale then intimated that Hood and Knight should take a seat before he positioned himself at the head of the table, in the elaborately carved chair. He placed a fairly thick brown-coloured file immediately in front of him.

Knight took out her notebook. Langdale was a good-looking, slim man of about forty. Knight noticed he did not have a local accent and he gave every appearance of being someone who kept himself reasonably fit. His dark blue suit was particularly well cut and had plainly not been purchased off the peg. His tie, properly knotted, bore a crest of some kind and his nails were obviously manicured. Knight found him curiously attractive.

'I take it you're here about the robbery? Our operations manager has gone down with something – so I thought I would make myself available. I'm very hands-on, so I can probably deal with anything you want to know.'

'That's very good of you, sir. We shall still have to speak to him, but that can wait. What's the latest on Mr Patel?'

Hood was genuinely concerned for the man and, of course, he wanted to interview him.

'Still in a bad way, I'm afraid. The latest bulletin described him as "critical" but there are signs he might pull through. That's what I keep telling myself, anyway. The alternative does not bear thinking about.'

'Were you aware he had a heart condition?'

'No – and, so far as I know, neither was he. He's fifty-one years of age and one of our most experienced operatives. Never had a day's illness – not even when he was attacked a few years ago.'

Langdale opened the file and took out a sheet of paper. 'His record shows that he had a full medical last May. He was pronounced A1 by his own GP.'

'Married with children, I believe?'

'Yes. Four children I think. The eldest is about twenty-two – I'm not sure about the others but Ashock talks about them all the time. He's a very proud father. The eldest boy worked for us on a temporary basis for six months before he went to university. A nice lad as I recall. Very keen to learn. I don't know what he's doing now, although he has helped us out on a couple of other occasions when we've been short-staffed.'

Knight looked up from her notebook. 'You said "not even when he was attacked" … could you give us more details?'

'Certainly, though I would have thought you would have known all about it. It was nearly three years ago. He was set upon whilst delivering cash to a post office, somewhere in Nottingham, but he fought off his attacker and held on to him until the police arrived. Got a commendation for his bravery.'

'Was he hurt?' asked Hood.

'A bit shaken I think, but nothing that required any treatment. I told him to take a couple of days off but he declined. Back at work the next day. He said he couldn't afford any time off – not that that would have been an issue, you understand. I'd have seen to that.'

'How is he paid?' asked Knight.

'He *was* on an hourly rate but after his heroics in '96 he was put on a salary with a discretionary bonus. He was also promoted to senior guard.'

He examined the file again. 'His present salary is… £16,500 and he was paid a bonus of… £385 last year. He's one of our higher paid guards.'

Langdale grinned, then continued. 'Most of them are on an hourly rate. As you might expect we have quite a turnover of staff – it's not the most interesting of work – but Ashock has been with us now for over six years.'

'What did he do before he joined you?'

'You'll have to ask him that yourself. We don't seem to have that information in his file any longer. I'm fairly sure, though, that he had not worked in security before. It was most unfortunate this happened when it did. He wasn't even supposed to be working last night.'

Hood glanced at Knight then concentrated his attention on Langdale. 'What do you mean?'

Langdale studied his file again. 'It was his day off. He agreed to come in because one of the others – Jim Henderson – fell off a ladder while decorating his sitting room at home. Apparently, he's broken his ankle. He'll be off for at least six weeks.'

'When did that happen?'

'The details are not yet clear but his wife phoned in late on the fifteenth. Ashock agreed to stand in for him. Rotten luck when you think about it.'

'Yes,' agreed Hood, his voice failing to conceal one of his pet theories biting the dust.

'Who asked him to come in?'

'The operations manager. Ashock was always eager to earn extra money – and he'd have been paid double time for working on his day off. He'd undoubtedly have contacted him first.'

'So he can't have known in advance he'd have been on this particular job?'

'Not unless he's psychic, no. And he could easily have been assigned to one of the other deliveries.'

'But as the senior guard, would he not have been detailed to do the Charnwood run?'

'I suppose that's right. But it would have been a matter for Bill Mostyn to decide. He may well have put him in charge of the Charnwood run because the vehicle they used had to be picked up in Loughborough. As the senior man, Bill would have trusted him with the keys.'

Langdale closed his file. Hood paused. He would not yet bury his theory that Patel might be involved but he recognised it was definitely a hypothesis that was on its last legs. He sighed then turned to a different topic.

'Tell me a bit more about the firm. I understand it was started by a couple of retired police officers?'

'That's right. My late father was – like you – a detective chief inspector. When he retired after thirty years in the force, he started the business with his former sergeant, Mike Piddock. Dad put most of the capital up so they named it after him. Piddock, as a trading name, didn't quite give the right impression anyway.'

Langdale smiled. Hood did not. 'Your father's dead?'

Langdale became serious. 'Yes. He died two years ago – lung cancer. He never could give up on the cigarettes. One of the habits he picked up in the police.'

'And Michael Piddock?'

'He retired last year, but he still owns 35 per cent of the shares and he remains a non-executive director – not that he shows much interest these days – as long as he gets his pension and his dividends.'

Knight pointed to the portrait on the wall behind Langdale. 'Who's the guy in the painting, then?'

'That', said Langdale, rising to his feet and walking towards the portrait, 'is Mr Amos Watkins, founder of Watkins and Sons, the knitting manufacturer that used to occupy these premises. A former lord mayor of Leicester and later high sheriff of the county he was. Dad always liked it and I've never had the heart to remove it. Gives the place a certain ambiance, don't you think?'

Hood nodded but did not comment. He wanted to get on. 'How long have you had the contract with National Commercial?'

Langdale resumed his seat. 'Since Bridgeford House was opened. I must admit, I was a bit surprised when they came to us rather than one of the big national companies, but it's apparently their policy to use local businesses when they can. This is the first time we've had even a hint of trouble.'

'Do you deal with all their secure deliveries?'

'As far as I'm aware, yes. They're one of our most important clients and we've expanded the business mainly on the work they provide. Our Loughborough office would not exist but for this contract.'

Hood ignored the reference to the Loughborough office – for the moment. 'What about the Charnwood Centre itself? I understand you have the contract there as well?'

'That's partly true. We initially did only the mobile visits – you know – during the night when the centre is closed. Group Eleven has the contract during the day. We got a piece of that six months ago when they couldn't provide enough cover – the building works going on there required extra staff – but we only have a limited role when the centre is open. They still do the bulk of it.'

'Did you make your mobile visits as planned?'

Langdale re-opened the file and looked at his papers. 'According to the records, yes. The mobile patrols – we send two of them because of the size of the place – were there at midnight and 3 a.m. When they returned just after 6 a.m., the robbery had already taken place. Your boys were there in force.'

Hood glanced towards Knight, then continued. 'What precisely are the arrangements for delivering to the Charnwood Centre?'

'Highly confidential,' replied Langdale, looking about him, as if to emphasise the point.

The chief inspector pressed him. 'As you will appreciate, sir. We have already visited Bridgeford House and spoken with the manager. We need to look at the operation from your point of view if we are to catch these people and recover the money. That's why we will need to speak to your operations manager. Presumably he will have been aware of the details of this consignment well before the delivery took place?'

'Obviously he would have some advance notice. I hope you don't regard him as being involved in any way. He's always been regarded as completely trustworthy. I'm sure he wouldn't do anything to compromise the business.'

'Has he been with you long?'

Langdale looked in his file again and produced a separate piece of paper. 'Bill Mostyn has been with us for seven years. He's an ex-copper too. Hails from the West Midlands. My father had known him for ages. They worked together on a big robbery case. Post Offices had been targeted all over the place. Blagging, I believe they called it in those days. It was a joint investigation with several forces.'

'When did he go off ill?'

'Only this morning. He reported sick after he was told of the robbery – but I don't think the two events are connected. He'd been going down with a cold for a day or two. I expect him back next week. It's nothing serious. At least I hope not. His wife confirmed earlier this afternoon that he wouldn't be in for a few days. It looks like flu. She's confined him to his bed. There's a lot of it about.'

'He was here last night?'

'Let me see.'

Langdale consulted his file again. 'Yes. He went off duty at 2 a.m. – all the early deliveries had been assigned by then. I expected him back again at three this afternoon but his wife rang in at about eleven to say he wouldn't be in. His deputy had rung his home when we heard about the robbery and she gave no indication then that he was any worse.'

'Who's his deputy?'

'Well, deputy is probably a bit of an exaggeration. She's really his secretary and assistant, Melanie Newman. She's been with us for at least three years. She also helps with the accounts. She will be arriving for the night shift any moment now.'

'So Mostyn didn't return immediately after he was told about the robbery?'

'No.'

'Does that not strike you as odd, you know, not rushing back here after such an incident?'

'Not really. There wasn't much he could have done – and security is only one aspect of his role here. I have prime responsibility in that area. I came straight here. It's what our customers expect.'

'Will you be able to assist us with everything in the meantime? We need to know exactly how this delivery was organised from your end.'

'Yes, I understand that, but I will need to speak to Mr King before I reveal any details, even to the police.'

'Would you do that now? I'm sure he will give you the OK. He was pretty open with us.'

Hood looked at Knight as he spoke. She did her best to conceal a smile. Langdale stretched for the phone. 'Lisa. See if you can get Mr King at Bridgeford House, will you. Thanks.'

He replaced the receiver. 'I hope you don't think I'm being difficult, Chief Inspector, but it has not escaped my notice that National Commercial may try and land us with responsibility for this robbery so I'm not minded to give them any basis for further complaint. We are due to make another delivery to the Charnwood early on Sunday morning. I'm having to organise that in the absence of Mr Mostyn.'

'Could I ask something while we're waiting?' asked Knight.

'Of course.'

'How healthy is your business at the moment?'

Langdale initially looked slightly surprised at the question but then smiled. 'Before this little incident, we were doing very well indeed. In fact, I have two offers on the table from national companies wishing to merge with us – that's how they put it but they really mean to take us over. If I were to accept either offer, I'd be set up for life.'

'You haven't accepted?'

'No, I have not.'

Langdale emphasised his reply and moved forward in his chair. 'I turned them both down but they're continuing to press me. Security is big business these days, you know. This company was my father's pride and joy and if we were taken over, I haven't the slightest doubt I'd be out of a job very quickly. These big firms are pretty ruthless when it comes to redundant managers.'

'But, as you said, you'd be set up for life. You could retire.'

Langdale looked at Knight and smiled. 'I'm thirty-nine years old. Why on earth should I retire? I enjoy doing what I do. I'd be bored stiff sitting on a beach all day drinking cocktails. How did Shakespeare put it? *If all the year were playing holidays; To sport would be as tedious as to work.*'

He glanced at Hood who gave no indication of recognising the quotation. '*Henry IV*, I think – and there's something else. My wife wouldn't like it. I'd be under her feet all day and that simply wouldn't do, would it?'

Knight smiled broadly and even Hood appreciated the comment. His own wife had sometimes expressed similar sentiments when he'd been on extended leave.

'Now to get back to the business in hand, I'm sure we could survive and prosper without being absorbed by one of the major players. There will always be a market for smaller operations like ours. Security should, in theory at least, be tighter in a firm like this.'

'Does Mr Piddock share your view?' asked Hood.

Langdale's expression changed at once. 'No, he certainly does not.' He shook his head. 'He wants to sell, but as the minority shareholder, he can't force my hand. Not without spending a lot of money on lawyers anyway.'

'What are his shares worth?'

'Nominally, not very much. But when you consider the business assets and the goodwill, I'd say at least a quarter of a million pounds, probably more.'

Hood took a sharp intake of breath.

'You could buy him out.'

'Can't afford to. I've considered it, but the bank wouldn't play ball. They think I should sell out too. We had to borrow quite a bit to set up the Loughborough office and purchase additional vehicles.'

'Who do you bank with?'

Langdale smiled. 'Not National Commercial. We were tempted to transfer our account to them when we got the Bridgeford House contract. But on reflection, it didn't seem appropriate somehow.'

'And if they were to cancel your contract?'

'Well, Piddock's shares would be worth a hell of a lot less. But he'd not go hungry.'

Hood then raised the question of the Loughborough office. He had noted that Langdale had been completely open about its existence. 'What exactly happens there?'

'Loughborough? Well it's really there to give us immediate access to Bridgeford House. Bill Mostyn spends quite a bit of his time there and we store some of our vehicles in the adjacent compound.'

'Was Bill Mostyn there last night?'

'I don't think so. You'd have to ask him but I'd be surprised if he were. If he goes there it's usually during the day. But one of the vehicles from the compound at Loughborough was used to make the delivery to the Charnwood. One of our newer ones.'

Langdale opened his file again, took out a document and showed it to Hood. 'It's a complete write-off now of course. We shall have to replace it. Thank God it was fully insured.'

He sighed. Hood continued his questioning.

'How did the guards get to Loughborough? Assuming they started their shift here.'

Langdale closed his file again. 'They'd have clocked on here at Hinckley in the usual way and travelled in one of the other vans that left from here.

It's not uncommon. You see, it's not easy keeping track of our vehicles from one shift to another. It only takes a breakdown or traffic problems and we can end up with a vehicle in the wrong place.'

'So who was on duty at Loughborough over night?'

Langdale looked bemused and shook his head. 'No one. It's only manned for part of the day. We do all the administration from here. As I mentioned earlier, as the senior guard, Ashock would have had the keys for the compound. It was just a question of collecting the van and locking up again. The office would have closed at 3 p.m. He'd only have to go in there to get the keys for the security vehicle.'

'Very interesting,' said Hood. 'When would he have been told that the van he was to use was at Loughborough?'

'I assume Bill would have told him when he clocked on. I don't think anything turns on that though. As I said, it's a real nightmare keeping track of our security vans. Ashock is completely trustworthy and we needed an extra van at short notice. The Sheffield delivery was only booked that afternoon. We tend to get a lot of extra work at this time of the year – we sometimes can't deal with all the requests we receive. The Sheffield crew had two other deliveries to make afterwards – from different service centres. It can be demanding working out the logistics. That's, principally, Bill Mostyn's brief. And very good at it he is.'

Hood paused and adjusted his tie before continuing. 'So Mostyn knows where every vehicle is or should be at any given time?'

'I suppose he does, yes.'

Hood continued. 'We were at Bridgeford House earlier today, as you know. I noticed that the bank's smoking area is immediately next to your vehicle compound.'

Langdale was still looking bemused. 'Is that of some significance? I can't think why it should be. We don't allow smoking inside any of our premises either. It's becoming fairly common everywhere these days.' He smiled. 'Health and safety, you know. Tell me, is it still allowed in police stations?'

'Not in my room,' replied Hood. 'But it's still permitted elsewhere, much as I deplore it. What concerned me about the set-up in Loughborough was that it might afford an opportunity for someone at the bank – say on a smoking break – to indicate something to one of your operatives, that's all.'

Langdale's expression hardly changed. 'What sort of thing?'

'Oh, I don't know. Passing on information, perhaps as to which delivery might be worth targeting.'

Langdale laughed. 'I think that's highly unlikely, Chief Inspector, don't you? A robbery like this would need a bit more planning than that, wouldn't it? And remember, these deliveries are made at very short notice. That's part and parcel of the security we impose. The team who delivered to the Charnwood can't have known they were going there much before 11 p.m. last night.'

Hood nodded. 'You're probably right, sir. It was only a passing thought.'

The telephone rang. Langdale picked up the receiver. 'Good afternoon, Reg. How are you? Sorry about that. I didn't know you had gone home. It's a bad business all round. I have Chief Inspector Hood with me. I believe you have spoken with him already. I just wanted your agreement before I reveal any details to the police. Yes. I see. Really? Well. I'll bear that fully in mind. We'll talk later. Goodbye.'

Langdale replaced the receiver and looked at Hood. 'Oh dear. Reg King had left for the day. They put me through to his home. Apparently, he's been up most of the night. He wasn't very happy about it.'

Hood said nothing. Langdale then picked the phone up again. 'Lisa. I am not to be disturbed, understand.' He then unplugged the telephone from the socket in the wall, resumed his seat and turned towards Hood. 'Now, Chief Inspector, how may I assist you?'

★★★★

'Well,' said Hood as he and Knight walked towards his car. 'There goes my theory about Patel. He wasn't even supposed to be on duty when the robbery occurred.'

'Doesn't follow that he isn't involved though, does it sir? Or it could have been one of the others.'

'Perhaps. But it knocks out any suggestion that his attacking the robber was all a charade. If that had been part of the plan they'd have had to be certain he was going to be one of the security team. It's asking a lot to assume that this other guard – what was his name, Henderson? – broke his ankle deliberately to ensure Patel was working that night. Doesn't stand up to scrutiny at all.'

'We should still look into it, sir.'

'Of course we should, but I hate to admit it, DC Sleath is probably right when he says Patel can't have been involved. With Henderson unfit, it doesn't follow that Patel was bound to be the one asked to help out.'

'But once he was asked to help out, from what Langdale said, it would be a virtual certainty he'd be put on the Charnwood run, especially as they would obviously trust him, as the senior guard, with the keys to the Loughborough compound.'

Hood nodded in agreement.

'But we still have the problem of him working on that shift at all, don't we? He couldn't have engineered the other fellow breaking his ankle could he?'

'I suppose not, sir. But I shall check it out nevertheless.'

'You do that.'

CHAPTER FIVE

'Is the champagne cold enough?'

'Should be by now,' replied Matthew. 'It's been covered in ice since this morning.'

'Well don't get it too cold; you know Mr Beresford doesn't like it *too* cold.'

'Yes, Mr Allingham, 'I'll be taking it out of the bins one hour before we start, just like you told me.'

'Good lad.'

Geoff Allingham walked back to the clerks' room and sat down. He had been the senior clerk in chambers for almost five years. Following service in the Royal Navy, in which he reached the rank of commander, he had obtained his present position thinking his administrative and leadership skills could be put to good use in the somewhat ramshackle world of barristers' chambers. But while he found the work – and the salary – rewarding he had been known to contrast his former vocation and his current role unfavourably. Managing chambers, he had once confided to his wife, was rather like running a kindergarten when compared with commanding a frigate. Herding cats would have been easier than trying to organise the professional lives of over forty-six prima donnas (of both sexes) each of whom thought his or her practice should be his only concern. But he really had little to complain about and would be able fully to relax when the Christmas period was behind him.

The week before Christmas was always hectic. As in previous years, the chambers' Christmas party was proving too much of a distraction. If he'd had his way there would be no Christmas festivities in chambers. It was just an excuse for the members and their guests to drink far too much champagne. Geoff had also noticed a reduction in concentration by his junior clerks. They got caught up in the general merriment well in advance of the actual event and standards started to slip. After all, the courts were still sitting until the twenty-third and there was plenty of work to be getting on with.

'Miss Lassiter's on the phone,' said the young woman sitting to his immediate right.

'Is she? Can't you deal with her, Edwina?'

The young woman shook her head. 'She specifically asked to speak to you.'

'What does she want this time?' he asked in a resigned tone. 'If she thinks I'm sending one of you off to pick up her dry-cleaning, she's going to be disappointed. We're far too busy.'

He lifted the phone and smiled before he spoke. It was obviously a contrived, well-practised and disingenuous grin. 'Yes, Miss Lassiter, what can I do for you?'

Harriet Lassiter was an important member of chambers whose influence was growing. She had taken silk three years before, somewhat to Geoff's surprise, but had already established herself as a major player both in London and on the Midland and Oxford circuit. Her services were in demand both defending and prosecuting and Geoff had been forced to acknowledge that he had underestimated her abilities when he'd advised her back then that her application to become a QC was, perhaps, a tad premature.

'I may be late tonight, Geoff. The judge has decided to start his summing up – on a Friday afternoon – and I'm almost bound to miss the 4.25. Peter is in London anyway – so I shall meet him at chambers. If I'm as late as I anticipate, make sure you keep him well away from Julian Beresford, won't you? We don't want another scene.'

'OK, will do,' replied the senior clerk.

'Oh and Geoff, get Matthew or someone to pick up my dry-cleaning will you? They'll be closed by the time I get back. The ticket is on my desk. Bye.'

The line went dead. Geoff replaced the receiver and inwardly cursed. 'Matthew,' he shouted. 'Get in here will you?'

The junior clerk appeared at the door.

'Matthew, be a good lad and go to Miss Lassiter's room and look on her desk. There should be a dry-cleaning ticket there. Find it and cut along to Sketchley's on Theobolds Road and pick up her dress. She'll need it for the party. Take some money from the petty cash and make sure you leave the receipt in there.'

'But what about the champagne?'

'Never mind the champagne. It can look after itself. Now off you go.'

'Mr Beresford's on line three, Geoff,' said Edwina, 'and the listing officer from Derby has been chasing you. They need a recorder for three days next week. They're desperate. She wants to know if we have anyone available.'

'Ask Mr Rymer. His trial cracked today and he needs to get some sitting time in. And don't take any nonsense from him about not wanting to go to Derby. There's a decent enough train service.'

'Will you speak to Mr Beresford?'

'Yes. Put him on,' sighed Geoff. 'Yes, Mr Beresford, what can I do for you?'

★★★★

The party was in full swing by the time Harriet Lassiter arrived. She was greeted at the front door by her husband, Peter Callaghan. He had declined to join the noisy throng in the large atrium in which the merriment was centred. He had hung around the front door, glass in hand, exchanging a few words with a solicitor he had met at a similar social evening in the summer.

'At last,' he said, kissing his wife on the cheek, 'I thought you were never going to arrive. You know I regard these events as something close to purgatory.'

'I'm sorry, darling. The train was delayed at Bedford – signalling problems north of Luton – and there was a huge queue for taxis at St Pancras. I thought I'd never get here. Let's go up to my room so I can change. I promise you we won't stay too long. A token appearance is all that's required.'

Harriet glanced at Julian Beresford, her head of chambers, as he held court in the middle of the heaving mass of bodies. He raised his glass in mock acknowledgement and inclined his head as she and Peter climbed the stairs before turning his attention back to the High Court judge with whom he had been trying to speak. The clamour of voices made conversation almost impossible so Beresford ushered the judge out of the main room into the corridor and into a smaller room where fewer were assembled. Young Matthew and his girlfriend, entranced with each other in the corner, were the recipients of a steely glare, but they took the hint and plunged back into the main arena, hand in hand. Charles Cavan-Henry and his actress wife remained as did a few others. Beresford carefully directed the judge towards them.

'You know Cavan-Henry, Judge?' he said in his most oleaginous voice.

'Yes, of course,' replied His Lordship, trying desperately to place him. He certainly remembered Mrs Cavan-Henry, or Belinda Raynor, as she was more generally known. He'd seen her playing Gwendolen in a revival of *The Importance of Being Earnest* at the Theatre Royal in Nottingham when he was on circuit and the two of them were soon in animated conversation, leaving the two barristers to their own devices.

There was no love lost between Cavan-Henry and his head of chambers. Charles Cavan-Henry had failed in his application for silk and long suspected he had not had the support that was due to him from Beresford. He considered himself the better advocate of the two and resented the fact that Beresford had been in silk for almost ten years while he remained a mere senior junior. But while Cavan-Henry's practice was expanding, Beresford's was in decline as even he must have appreciated and his tenure as head of chambers was about to expire. He had resisted the attempts of his fellows to introduce a fixed term of three years for the headship but had been forced to concede the point following a particularly rowdy chambers' meeting at which he was ingloriously defeated. It particularly riled him that the lovely Harriet Lassiter was the obvious choice as his successor, although there were three other silks her senior. Two of them practised entirely in the commercial court and had no interest in chambers' politics and the third, Brenda Hardy, was desperately trying to maintain a leader's practice in the family courts in the face of anticipated cuts in legal aid and a broken marriage. She had refused even to consider Beresford's suggestion that she stand.

'I'm worried about Harriet taking over,' Beresford confided to Cavan-Henry. 'Hers is mainly a circuit practice. She doesn't really spend enough time in London to keep an eye on chambers.'

'I don't know about that,' responded Cavan-Henry. 'She strikes me as being highly efficient and very committed. I think she'll do just fine. I shall definitely be supporting her.'

'Well that is certainly your prerogative, Charles – but having headed these chambers for over eight years, I am naturally concerned that we should have a smooth and successful transition. Harriet spends very little time in chambers. Why, she's only just arrived here tonight. It really wouldn't be good enough for the head of chambers to be absent when our distinguished guests start to arrive, now would it?'

'Perhaps we shouldn't invite our *distinguished guests* or anyone from outside chambers. That's certainly the view of the younger members… and there's the cost to consider as well. Are we really giving the right impression of the Bar in these increasingly straightened times, dishing out expensive champagne to a bunch of judges and hangers-on? It doesn't seem to do us any good.'

'Really, Charles, we must uphold the finest traditions of the profession… you especially should realise that if you want to get silk.'

'Yes, but we do that by doing the job properly in court, don't we?'

There was an embarrassing silence, neither man wishing to continue the conversation. Eventually, Cavan-Henry spoke.

'You must excuse me. I need to speak to Harriet. She's leading me in a murder after Christmas and we need to liaise about a conference.'

After checking that his wife was still occupied with Mr Justice Welford, he went in search of Harriet, leaving Beresford open-mouthed and shaking his head. But the head of chambers quickly recovered, removed a bottle of champagne from a passing junior clerk and obsequiously topped up the glasses of the judge and Belinda Raynor.

Charles Cavan-Henry found Harriet with her husband outside the main reception area talking to Brenda Hardy and her significant other. Brenda had recently divorced and had to juggle her career with caring for her three school-age children, their father having run off with a much younger woman who worked with him at a well-known investment bank in the City. Brenda was plotting how to impoverish him in due course, employing her considerable expertise in the divorce courts to her own and her children's advantage.

'He's a brave man,' said Peter Callaghan. 'He must surely have realised you'll take him to the cleaners?'

'He's a reptile,' said Brenda between gulps of champagne. 'A dishonest, selfish and adulterous reptile – not that I would say that in front of his children. Do you know he's only seen them a couple of times in over eight months? Poor Hamish – he's my eldest – says he won't see his father again whatever any judge may say, and I don't blame him.'

'Now, Brenda. You mustn't let yourself get worked up,' said her escort whom she had introduced as Martin Hughes, a bloodstock agent from Newmarket she'd met on holiday in Dubai. He had spent nearly ten minutes trying – unsuccessfully – to persuade Peter and Harriet to buy a couple of racehorses before Cavan-Henry joined them.

'What about you, Charles? Ever considered buying a racehorse?' asked Peter, a multi-millionaire building contractor who intended to stay that way and had no intention of entering the risqué world of horse racing.

'Never again,' replied Cavan-Henry. 'When I was in chambers in Manchester about six of us bought a yearling. We were told it was bound to win but after we'd spent an absolute fortune in training fees the bloody thing went and broke its leg on the gallops. That was enough for me. Never even got to the races.'

'You *were* unlucky,' said Brenda. 'Martin had a half share in a two-year-old that won the *Lowther* at York this year.'

'That's right,' said Martin enthusiastically. 'We sold it at Tattersalls a fortnight ago for over seventy-seven thousand guineas. Not bad when you think we only gave twelve thousand for it at the Doncaster sales last year.

'Guineas?' queried Peter.

'Yes,' replied Martin. 'It's not only the Bar that likes to keep up its traditions. Of course it's translated in to pounds immediately. Tradition is one thing but money is money. And it's all tax free.'

'That's what we were told,' said Cavan-Henry mournfully. 'A racehorse is considered to be a wasting asset, so no tax is payable if you make a profit, providing it's not a business venture. Ours certainly came into that category. A completely wasted asset!'

Harriet laughed. 'But you can afford it. And you're bound to get silk next year.'

'Like our horse was bound to run and win? I'm not counting my chickens, I can tell you,' said Charles, mixing his metaphors.

He assumed a particularly glum posture.

'Oh, come on Charles. No one gets it on their first application, and at least you'll be at the races this time. You're only forty. Plenty of time to make it to the front row.'

'How old were you, Harry, when you took silk?' asked Charles. Like all the best cross-examiners, he already knew the answer to the question.

'Thirty-eight,' replied Harriet, 'but I'm a woman, as I hope you have noticed – and in these increasingly politically correct times, we have a distinct advantage over you white middle-class males!'

'Who's middle-class?' queried Charles. 'My father was a vicar in an inner-city parish in Salford. Contrary to appearances, I was not born with a silver spoon in my mouth.'

'Yes, but you captured Belinda, didn't you? Wasn't her father an earl or something?'

'An impoverished Irish earl,' moaned Charles. 'He didn't even have a seat in the House of Lords. And she never uses her courtesy title.'

'Well, I wouldn't hold that against her,' interrupted Peter. 'She's a real charmer and almost as good-looking as Harry here!'

'And ten years younger,' added Harriet with a rueful smile.

'Eight, actually,' corrected Charles looking around for a champagne-carrying clerk.

Martin and Brenda had drifted away to talk to a solicitor who sent Brenda most of her work. Charles took the opportunity to mention the upcoming murder trial.

'You and I have that murder case in Leicester in January. That's really what I came to talk about – you don't mind if we talk shop for a minute, do you, Peter?'

'Not at all,' sighed Peter, who had long ago realised that was all lawyers could talk about to each other. Their fascination with each other's cases was something he had never been able to understand and when they were engaged in the *same* case, objection was utterly pointless.

'The CPS rang today. They want a conference next week. The psychiatrist you advised should examine the defendant has come up with something and they want our views. Trouble is, Belinda and I are off to Cyprus on Sunday and we won't be back until the eighth. And the trial starts a couple of days later.

'I'll deal with it,' said Harriet. 'Peter and I are staying in the UK this Christmas and my jury is going out sometime on Monday so I should be able to fit them in.'

'I assume Tom Campion will be the trial judge,' said Charles. 'There won't be a High Court judge there in January.' He looked across the room to see if he could spot Campion, a former member of chambers, whom he knew had been invited to the party. 'It's been released from the High Court list so it should be a reasonably pleasant couple of weeks.' He was unusually quietly spoken – just in case he was overheard by the man in question whom he noticed was now speaking to Belinda in the atrium.

'I did hear', whispered Harriet, who had noticed Campion too, 'that Susan Stillwell has been approved to try murders – so it might well be her.' The QC was obviously being provocative.

'What?' replied an astonished Charles. 'They've given Serious Sue a murder ticket! What is the world coming to?' Several people looked in his direction. His voice was now back to its usual volume.

'You mean Her Honour Judge Susan Stillwell, QC,' hissed Harriet. 'Oh, she's all right – once you get used to her. In fact, she's quite a good judge really – and she's obviously angling for promotion. But I wouldn't worry too much. I doubt if the resident judge would let her loose on our case. Too many potential traps for the unwary.'

'Let's hope you're right – look, I'd better go and get Belinda and say hello to the judge. It won't do any harm to keep on the right side of him and he doesn't know me as well as he does you. Happy Christmas if I don't see you before.'

Cavan-Henry took his leave, threading his way through the increasingly crowded reception area.

'Cyprus, eh?' said Brenda who had drifted back leaving Martin to his sales pitch with her solicitor. 'He must be doing very well.'

'Better than Martin,' observed Peter looking across the room as the solicitor made his excuses and hailed one of the junior members of chambers. Martin rejoined them, not in the least downcast.

'And where are you and the children spending Christmas?' asked Harriet.

'Newmarket. Martin has invited all of us to his house for three days so Imogen will have her fill of horses and I shall be waited on hand and foot. Martin, amongst his many other talents, is an excellent cook.'

She gave him a sideways glance. Martin almost blushed.

'Can we slip away now?' asked Peter. 'I think you've done your duty.'

'We must go too,' said Brenda. 'Babysitter, you know. She gets very difficult if we are late back. See you next term.'

'I'll just have a quick word with Tom Campion while you get the coats,' said Harriet. 'I've heard a rumour that he might be transferring from the Midlands to London to sit at the Bailey. I really must find out if there's anything in it. He'll be a tremendous loss if it's true. I promise, I won't be a moment.'

She was true to her word. By the time Peter returned with her coat she was extracting herself diplomatically from the company of both Campion and Welford, smiling as she did so. Charles and Belinda took the opportunity to detach themselves too.

'You must come to dinner soon,' whispered Belinda. 'I've been teaching Charles how to cook and we need someone we know *really* well to experiment on!'

'Sounds positively dangerous,' replied Harriet. 'But we'd love to come. I like to live recklessly occasionally. We'll speak in the new year.'

Charles smiled but said nothing.

'Enjoy Cyprus.'

The Callaghans said their goodbyes as Peter helped Harriet on with her coat. Beresford spotted them as they headed for the front door. The party was still in full swing. If anything, the noise had increased in direct proportion to the amount of champagne consumed and the younger element, at least, were becoming extravagant and loud in their behaviour.

'That's exactly what I mean,' said Beresford to no one in particular. 'She simply doesn't have time for chambers. She and her wealthy husband will always have something more important to do.'

Whether anyone heard him he neither knew nor cared.

CHAPTER SIX

Tuesday, 22 December 1998

Five days had passed since the robbery and the investigation had produced little in the way of evidence. Hood was pinning his hopes on a DNA match from blood found by scenes of crime on the uniform of the guard who had punched, then briefly wrestled with, one of the robbers and a few spots that had been identified on the adjacent wall. It would be several days before any results were known and with Christmas round the corner, it could be the new year before anything useful was revealed. Hood wasn't even sure if the blood on the uniform came from the robber. Although the cartridge was loaded with rock salt, the impact and range was such that salt had penetrated the guard's uniform and damaged his chest, so there was a chance that the blood was his. All he knew from the witness statements of the other guards was that the robber who was punched by their seemingly plucky colleague had sustained a severe nosebleed. His face covering would have absorbed most of the blood, but the fact that he bled so freely gave Hood some hope that a DNA match might be possible. He was almost convinced that the guards were innocent of involvement, despite the apparent ease with which the transit reversed through the compound gates before they could be closed. The imminent threat of being barbecued seemed a sufficient explanation for their almost complete compliance. They could hardly be blamed for getting out of the van pretty sharpish. It was also obvious that the robbers were waiting for the security van to arrive. Neither of the guards who had been interviewed recalled anyone following them at any stage of the journey – further proof if it was needed that essential information had been passed to the robbers from somewhere.

To add to his troubles, Hood had received a phone call from DS Hooper, in whom he had always placed a great deal of confidence. Hooper was unable to fly back to the UK before the new year. An air traffic controllers' strike in France had grounded most European flights. He would not be back until the 2 January at the earliest. But there was good news on one front. The injured guard was making steady progress. He was still too ill to be interviewed but he was conscious and had been moved from intensive care to high dependency. Hood was not expecting he would be able to give any useful information but had decided he would interview him personally when the doctors gave the OK.

He had called a conference of the officers assigned to his, as yet, limited team. ACC Knowles could not attend. She, like many others, had gone down with flu, so Hood was left in total charge, which quite suited him. Her last act had been to confirm the increase in the detective strength in his division. Applications had already been received from candidates in outside forces and from existing Mid-Shires officers. Interviewing boards were to be held in January. Most of the applicants came highly recommended so at least three new detective officers would be on board by mid February. "Of course," she had added, "you'll have resolved matters by then." *Some hope*, Hood had thought. This was going to be a long, drawn-out investigation.

Wendy Knight and Debbie Burgess arrived at his office together. Hood noticed that Debbie was really showing the fact that she was almost five months pregnant. She wasn't going to be around for very much longer to assist in the inquiry. DC Alan Eccles arrived a few minutes later with the newly commissioned PC Malcolm Munt – no longer a probationer. Given the shortage of officers, Hood had decided to try him out for a week or two in the hope his youthful enthusiasm might be put to good use. The other uniformed officers who had been doing the leg work were not invited. DS Lunn had been ordered to defer his fraud inquiry for a few weeks and had taken over from DC Sleath as co-ordinator. Sleath, unfortunately, had gone down with the flu and called in sick. Lunn was still far from happy that "Beadle" had been deferred and he lurked at the back of Hood's office, declining as on the previous occasion, an invitation to take a seat.

'To be brief,' said Hood, 'we are getting nowhere fast. I think we can proceed, for the moment at least, on the basis that the security guards were not involved. I've seen the videos of their significant witness interviews and they strike me as truthful and they were undoubtedly traumatised by what happened to them. Anyone disagree?'

No one dissented.

'We have not yet interviewed Mr Patel, but the chances of him being involved must be pretty remote. His actions in thumping one of the robbers may well give us our only clue. He also established his credentials as a bit of a hero three years ago. I've checked the information Wendy and I got from his employer and it's all kosher. In July 1996, he was delivering cash to a post office in Nottingham when he fought off an attempt to rob him. Not only that, he hung on to the villain until assistance arrived, so he played a major role in our getting a conviction. The judge was certainly impressed. He handed Patel a commendation and a reward from public funds, so it doesn't look as if he's our mole. But as he was the senior guard, I don't propose to jump to any conclusions until he's been interviewed.'

Again, he looked about the room to see if there was any contrary opinion.

'And there's the fact that he wasn't even supposed to be working that shift,' added Wendy Knight. 'We've checked out the guard who supposedly fell off a ladder while decorating. Although his ankle turned out to be sprained rather than broken, it's pretty clear he was painting his sitting room that week and he *was t*aken to A & E. He's also been off work since the fifteenth.'

Hood continued. 'Wendy and I will be interviewing the operations manager from the security firm tomorrow – assuming he's fit. He's been off with flu. He was a DS with the West Mercia before he took the job at Langdales. From what we were told by his employer, he would have had all the details of the consignment we are concerned with, so he has to be regarded as a possible candidate for the leaking of information to the gang. He spent a lot of his time at the Loughborough office too, which is immediately next door to Bridgeford House. He could easily have set up some form of communication with one of the bank's employees.'

'But he was one of us, sir,' said Eccles with only a slight hint of sarcasm.

'One of us or not, until he's excluded as a suspect, we keep an open mind on the subject.' Hood stood up. 'If we are going to solve this one, it's going to be through basic, systematic police work and hard graft. It's not the sort of case where anything is going to fall into our laps. We've had no luck at all so far; we haven't even found the getaway vehicle, probably because it's been destroyed. I value your views – so don't be shy.'

He looked at each of his officers in turn. No one said anything.

'We are still waiting for the results of the DNA analysis of the blood on Mr Patel's uniform and the swabs SOCO took from the area around the burnt-out security van. The ACC has authorised fast tracking but I doubt if we'll get anything before the new year. We can't even be sure that the blood came from the robber.'

'What about Langdales, sir?' asked Eccles. 'Can we give the owner a clean bill of health?'

'Wendy and I have seen the managing director. He seemed genuine enough. Contrary to what Reg King told us, he was aware of these new-fangled cartridges that the bank is about to introduce – not because of anything National Commercial had told him – but because they already have a couple of building society customers who use them. So it must have been in his contemplation that National Commercial would be using them in the future.'

'Doesn't that put him in the frame, sir?'

'Not necessarily. He has a number of very good reasons for not wanting this robbery to have occurred which must remain confidential for the moment. He has a co-director; some of you may remember him as Sergeant Mike Piddock – used to be with the old Notts. constabulary. He's retired from active involvement in the business but I don't think that he and the MD see eye to eye about the future of the firm.'

'You think he might have put them up to it, sir?'

'I don't think we can assume that. As I've said before, we can't assume anything. We must see where the evidence takes us.'

He smiled and looked at each of the more experienced members of the team in turn before his gaze settled on young Munt.

'Remember Malcolm, what Mr Jaggers said to Pip in *Great Expectations* after he discovered his benefactor was Magwitch and not, as he thought, Miss Havisham?'

Knight understood what he meant. She had heard the question asked before as had the others. The young constable looked rather vacant. Hood continued to look at him waiting for some flicker of recognition of one of Charles Dickens' most famous stories. But he was wasting his time. Munt, alas, was one of the many victims of the modern English system of education. Although he had spent the statutory number of years at a comprehensive school, he had hardly received a comprehensive education. He was not a great reader and while his natural aptitude for maths and science had ensured he obtained no fewer than 8 GCSEs and two A levels (taken after he had left school and attended the local further education college), his only encounter with the works of Dickens had been when he'd watched the film version of the musical *Oliver!* on television the previous Christmas. He'd never heard of Mr Jaggers, although he did have some distant memory (in black and white) of Pip and Magwitch and their encounter in the churchyard on the Kent marshes. He'd seen something of the sort on television years before but was unable to place it in context. Hood shook his head and explained.

'Pip complained to the lawyer – Jaggers – who coincidentally acted for both Miss Havisham and Magwitch, that he had been misled by circumstances. Jaggers corrected him in words which should, in my humble opinion, be carved in stone over every police station and courthouse. *Take nothing on its looks. Take everything on evidence. There's no better rule.*'

Munt nodded, half pretending he'd got the point. Hood continued. 'And that's what must drive us on in this investigation – evidence. So far we have none.'

He turned and picked up some papers from his desk then looked at Munt once again.

'But there's nothing wrong in our establishing the most likely way in which this robbery was planned and executed. Indeed, it's an essential part of a detective's function that we do. So while we can never discount the fact that coincidences do occur, we must nevertheless try and establish a few basic facts which *have* to have been present for this job to have been pulled. So the first question we have to ask is surely this; what did the robbers have to know in order to make the risks they were taking worthwhile?'

Munt, anxious to re-establish his credentials with his superior officer, was first to speak.

'They would have to have known when these new cartridges were going to be introduced and pull the job before then otherwise the whole thing would have been pointless.'

Hood smiled. 'That is undoubtedly of importance, but there is something of greater significance than even that.'

Wendy Knight answered. 'They had to know that the bulk of the consignment would be made up of used notes – notes that couldn't be traced.'

Hood's face lit up. He was pleased that at least one of his team had the wit to spot the essential point in the case and, if the truth were told, it gave him an additional fillip that it was Wendy Knight who had analysed the situation so well.

'Exactly. Whatever the risks of these new cartridges being introduced, there would have been little point to the enterprise if all the notes had been new. The serial numbers would have been known and laundering the stuff would have been that much more difficult and the profits correspondingly reduced. So they would have been taking tremendous risks for possibly very little reward.'

Hood paused. 'And what does that tell us?' He didn't wait for an answer. 'It tells us that someone at the bank must have leaked the necessary information to the robbers. Only someone at the bank would have known for sure how this consignment was going to be made up. And, don't forget, he – or she – would have to have been able to communicate that information in sufficient time for the robbers to go about their business.'

He noted several heads nodding. 'Wendy, you've been co-ordinating the taking of statements from the bank staff – anything you've picked up that might lead us to the mole?'

'Not much to report yet, sir. The manager has confirmed in his statement that three security vans picked up cash after midnight on the seventeenth. One went to Sheffield and one to Nottingham. The one we are concerned with, the third van, was carrying by far the most cash. The other two only had three hundred thousand on board and they arrived without incident. The vans were identical – all from Langdale Security, with one slight exception. The one we're interested in was brand spanking new. It had enhanced security features and would have been much more difficult to break into. The CCTV from the bank confirms that two of the three vans left one after the other, including the one we are interested in. Both of them followed the Ashby Road towards the M1. Our van didn't go on the M1 – it stayed on the A6 – then took the country route. The other continued to junction 23 and on to the M1 to Nottingham. The Sheffield-bound van had left thirty-five minutes earlier.'

'That's why they waited at the Charnwood,' said Eccles. 'They couldn't possibly have known which van held the most cash when they set off. And another thing. I don't think we should run away with the idea that this job was as well planned as we are giving them credit for. It might be sheer coincidence that the take was as much as it was. Sometimes they just hit the jackpot.' Eccles paused. 'And it stands to reason that there would probably be the most money in the van heading to the Charnwood because of the number of ATMs in the place.'

'I agree,' said Hood. 'But as I said before, however much money was present, their prime target must have been used notes.'

He looked again at Knight. 'Have we got anywhere in identifying the local connection? It's unlikely that the informant at the bank, assuming he is at the bank, and the link with the gang who did this is the same person. It would have to be someone with enough experience to set this in motion and he'd have to have the contacts. Robberies on this scale are not carried out by amateurs.'

'That would depend,' said Knight. 'It could be a local villain with connections or an outside gang with a direct link to someone inside the bank. It's too early to form a settled view about that. Debbie's been looking at a few possible candidates, haven't you, Debs?'

'Yes. There is no intelligence about this job at all. It seems to have come from out of the blue, which supports the theory that the perpetrators are not local. As we are assuming there must be a local connection, there are three possible names in the frame – Alex Stringer, Jimmy Fallon and Michael Doyle.'

'Jaguar Jimmy! He's not up to this, surely?' said Eccles. 'He's a good class burglar and con man, not a robber.'

Lunn, who had decided, at last, to take some part in the proceedings, agreed. 'You can forget Fallon,' he said. 'He's inside. He's not due out until May. We interviewed him last September in "Beadle". This isn't his scene. He's also in prison in Lincolnshire – North Sea Camp – so he's hardly local.'

'What about the other two?' asked Hood. Debbie Burgess looked at her notes.

'Doyle's a fly one all right, but he's never gone in for violence. He's a fraudster and a money launderer – not that he's been convicted of anything for years. Apart from a motoring matter, you have to go back to 1986 for his last conviction – nothing has been made to stick since then. He's been in more tight corners than Mika Häkkinen but he's always walked away. Stringer sounds more likely. Since he came out from that twelve-year stretch – and that was for a series of robberies – intelligence suggests that he's been looking to get into something big. He's well worth a pull.'

'We are not necessarily looking for a thug,' cautioned Hood. 'Someone like Doyle might well have fed information to some hard men from elsewhere for a share of the proceeds. The local connection could be a card-carrying pacifist for all we know and simply set up whatever the outsiders needed locally in order to pull the job. I think we should have a word with both of them.' He turned to Lunn. 'Ian, in the absence of Andrew, I'll leave it to you to make contact with them. But take it easy, at least to begin with. We have nothing to justify arresting anyone at the moment.'

Lunn nodded, then suggested an alternative candidate. 'What about Gus Grayling? He's been very quiet of late. I would have thought this sort of caper would be right up his street. He used to run a team of really hard villains. They'd think nothing of pulling a shotgun out *and* firing it.'

'The Fish?' queried Burgess. 'I thought he'd retired. He's moved down south, hasn't he? Somewhere near Hastings. Started growing orchids I'd heard.'

'Orchids or not, this is exactly the sort of job he'd be more than capable of planning – even if he got someone else to carry it out.'

Lunn had once had a run-in with Grayling and had come off second best. Nothing had been proved and the Fish had not been prosecuted. Lunn, however, had not forgotten. To say he harboured a degree of resentment was an understatement. Burgess viewed matters more objectively.

'He'd need a local connection though. Intelligence reckons he's hardly left the south coast in recent years. Apparently he's not at all well. And he's getting on a bit. He must be well over sixty now.'

'That won't stop him,' snapped Lunn. 'He'll never change. It's ingrained in the man. And don't forget, Alex Stringer was definitely working for him. Pity we could never prove it.'

'That's the problem, isn't it?' said Burgess. 'We never could prove anything against Grayling. He's lived a charmed life.'

Lunn turned away and shook his head.

'Is there any intelligence that Doyle and he have been in touch?' asked Eccles. 'If Doyle is involved he'd have to go somewhere to hire the muscle for a job like this. And Grayling was definitely regarded as number one for mindless violence on this patch a few years back.'

Lunn looked up and disclosed something of Grayling's past. 'It was rumoured some years ago that Grayling had lent Doyle a sizeable amount when he needed to re-finance after a mortgage fraud had gone wrong – but it was never properly investigated. I haven't the slightest doubt they were both in cahoots with each other but we had too much on and the chief superintendent halted the inquiry after Doyle's trial fell apart.'

'Not our greatest moment, that,' added Burgess, glancing at Hood. 'I think the then chief constable wanted to draw a veil over the whole investigation.'

Hood looked vaguely curious. 'Obviously before my time?'

'We lost a couple of promising officers too. Someone always has to carry the can.'

'We mustn't let that divert us,' said the chief inspector, making a mental note to dig out the papers on the aborted trial. 'Do we have anything that suggests this fellow Grayling might have been involved in the robbery?'

Wendy Knight was quick to answer. 'Nothing, sir. Nothing at all.'

'I agree,' said Burgess, hastily. 'He's been off the radar for years. I'll run a check on him but I suspect it'll be a waste of time. Anyone fancy a trip to the south coast?'

'I don't think the direct approach with Grayling is necessarily a good idea,' instructed Hood. 'If he has provided the gunman he'll have ensured the trail doesn't lead back to him. We don't want to waste time and resources on speculation. If we get some evidence he may have been involved, I shall reconsider – but for now let's resist wild goose chases, shall we? But I shall want to see the file on that inquiry – assuming we still have it?'

There was a sense of relief around the room with the exception of Lunn. Nothing would have pleased him more than to put Grayling in the frame for the robbery and anything else that came to hand. But it was not to be.

'Well, unless anyone has any further contribution, we'll call it a day.' Hood stood up which prompted the meeting to start to break up. He turned as he reached the door. 'After I've seen Mostyn tomorrow, I shall not be here until the twenty-seventh. I'm *supposed* to be on leave. If anything does turn up, give me a ring at home. But try not to ring on Christmas Day. Sarah will only take it out on me if you do.'

CHAPTER SEVEN

Wednesday, 23 December 1998

It was still drizzling when DS Lunn approached the Salvation Army hostel in Ratcliffe Street. He turned his raincoat collar up against the cold wind as he crossed the road, narrowly missing a passing motorcyclist who raised a contemptuous finger in his direction. Although it was not yet five o'clock, it was already dark and the street lighting made little impression in this run-down area of the city. He had located Alex Stringer after speaking to the probation service. Stringer had been paroled to a probation hostel in Kirkby-in-Ashfield after his release from prison. He'd been permitted to leave providing he lived where directed and for the last two weeks or so he had lodged at the "Sally Ann" pending a flat becoming available in Beeston. According to his somewhat naive probation officer, who had not yet succumbed to cynicism about her charges, Alex had been behaving himself since his release and had only missed one appointment owing to a mix-up over the date. That apart, things were looking up for him or so she had assured Lunn. Ian Lunn, whose knowledge of serious criminals was more extensive and more soundly based, was not so certain. He had heard all this before. He walked through the main entrance and spoke to the duty manager. The manager took him into a small office and checked the records. It seemed that Stringer had been logged in as present when the doors closed at 11 p.m. on 16 December and was shown as being there for breakfast at seven thirty the next morning.

Lunn was directed to the first floor where Stringer's room was located. The hostel had originally served as a lace factory and had been converted some years before. It now provided basic accommodation for up to forty men. Many of them were ex-prisoners, drug addicts or recovering alcoholics. Several had continuing mental health problems. Most of them would otherwise have been living on the streets. Lunn was no stranger here. He had visited on other occasions and had arrested more than a couple of the residents in the past. Every time he came he wondered at the commitment of the Salvationists. There was no side to them, they did not judge or comment but offered shelter and sustenance to those whom society preferred to pretend did not exist. Whatever it was that informed their actions, Lunn had always thought there should have been more of it about.

'Hello Alex. Long time no see.'

Alex Stringer, unshaven and dressed in a grey hooded sweater and jogging bottoms with a pair of heavily scuffed trainers on his feet, smiled in acknowledgement. He had certainly changed since Lunn had last seen him. His hair was thinner and streaked with grey. He looked twenty years older and had developed quite a paunch. No longer the slim, athletic twenty-seven-year-old of yesteryear.

'Well, if it isn't Detective Constable Lunn,' he said sarcastically. 'Brought me a Christmas present, have you?'

'Detective sergeant actually,' responded Lunn. 'Unlike you to be behind with the news, Alex.'

'Well, I've been away for rather a long time, as you know, Mr Lunn; eight years to be precise. Only got paroled in September. I was knocked back the first time. How did you know I was here? I only left the probation hostel a couple of weeks ago.'

'Well, Alex, as you're on parole licence we're supposed to know where you are.'

Lunn looked along the passageway as an elderly man shuffled past, talking to himself. His eyes followed the man until he opened a door with a key and disappeared from sight.

'Bit of a comedown, this, isn't it Alex? The probation hostel must have been better than this.'

'Nowhere else to go, Mr Lunn; they wanted me out of the hostel and I'd no wish to stay there. Full of crooks, you know.' Alex half smiled as he turned the key in the door behind him. 'And Linda didn't wait for me this time. She's in Australia now, with her fancy man. A quantity surveyor from Melton Mowbray by all accounts. Divorced me three years ago and married him. Perth – that's where they are now. Very nice climate, I believe. Taken the kids with her as well.'

'I'm sorry to hear that, Alex. I always thought she would stick by you. Had plenty of practice, hadn't she?'

Stringer ignored the remark. 'I'm sure you haven't come here to talk about that.' He pushed the door open. 'I suppose I should invite you in.'

Lunn followed him inside. The bed-sitting room was small but tidy. Apart from the single bed, there was a wooden wardrobe and a table in front of the window with an old television perched on it. A couple of framed photographs stood on a rickety looking bedside unit and a few paperbacks were piled on the floor. A large haversack had been pushed into the corner. The walls were quite bare save for a Nottingham Forest football poster and a copy of the fire regulations securely fixed behind a Perspex cover.

'I can't offer you a drink; it's not allowed here. Get caught twice and you're out. Very strict they are.' He sat down on the bed and pointed to the only chair by the table.

'Have a seat,' he said, 'and tell me what brings you here. I'll tell you straight away, whatever it is, I didn't do it. I've had enough of prison. I'm not going back there.'

Lunn pulled the chair from under the table, turned it round until it faced Stringer and sat down. He leant forward as he spoke. 'I'm not here to accuse you of anything, Alex. Just thought we'd look you up, that's all.'

'Come on, Mr Lunn. Don't give me that. You've not come here to wish me the compliments of the season. What you working on at the moment? Anything interesting?'

'Right up your street, actually, Alex. The robbery at the Charnwood last week. You must have read about it.'

'I've heard about it, obviously. Got away with 2 million, they reckon.' He looked at Lunn and laughed. 'You don't think I had anything to do with that, do you Mr Lunn. I'm flattered, I really am but I doubt if I'd be here in this shithole if I'd got away with 2 million quid!'

'No, Alex. I don't suppose you would.'

Lunn looked around the room. 'This is a long way from your penthouse flat overlooking the river isn't it, Alex? You'll not want to be hanging about here for too long?'

'That depends Mr Lunn. I'm still looking for a job. It's not easy with my record, you know. A twelve-year stretch doesn't half put them off taking you on. And I did a few courses when I was inside. I've got certificates.'

Lunn smiled. 'What happened to your flat?' he asked. 'That must have been worth quite a bit.'

'Wife got that in the divorce. Sold it for two hundred thousand. I didn't see a penny. I suppose I should never have put it in her name, but that's what we all did in those days.'

'So how are you managing?'

'Benefits, Mr Lunn. Can you believe it? Alex Stringer on the social – what a comedown!' He took a cigarette from his pocket and searched his jogging bottoms for his lighter.

'Must be very tempting to go back to the old ways, eh, Alex?'

'No way, Mr Lunn.' He spoke with determination, the unlit cigarette bobbing between his lips. 'Them days is over. I'm not going back inside. I couldn't face it. This place is little better than a doss house, but I can go out when I like, within reason, and I can do my own thing. I couldn't do another long stretch. I'd kill myself first. Anyway, I should be getting a flat in a week or two, if I keep my nose clean.'

Lunn took out his own cigarette lighter and offered it.

'Thanks,' said Stringer, lighting the cigarette. He drew deeply on it. 'I'd offer you one, Mr Lunn, but I've only a couple left.'

'No problem,' said Lunn. 'I'm trying to give them up anyway.'

The detective sergeant stood up and retrieved his lighter then walked to the window and looked out over the back streets and alleyways. The constant drizzle obscured his view and the darkness had closed in but he could see that it would not have been impossible for someone to climb out of the window and slide down the drainpipe into the rear yard. There was a fairly high wall to surmount in order to get into the street, but it would have been well within the capacity of the Alex Stringer he had arrested nearly nine years before. He turned and faced him. But this was not the Alex Stringer of nine years ago.

'About this robbery, Alex. Heard anything on the street have you? We assume it's a team from out of town. No one here could have organised a job like that.'

Stringer drew on his cigarette again. 'I'm not a grass, Mr Lunn. If I did know anything, I wouldn't tell you. But the truth is, I've no idea who could have done it. Very professional, but you don't need me to tell you that, but a bit over the top wasn't it, shooting the guard? What was the point of that? Only gets people's blood up that does which means you boys have to pull out all the stops.'

'You've handled a sawn-off in your time, though, haven't you, Alex?'

Stringer smiled. 'What if I have? They were never loaded. I never shot anyone. I was always very careful in that regard. Not that the judge saw it that way. Bastard gave me twelve when my brief said I'd only get eight if I pleaded.'

It was Lunn's turn to smile. 'The evidence was pretty overwhelming, as I remember.'

Stringer shrugged his shoulders.

'Had any contact with Gus Grayling since you came out?'

Alex Stringer hesitated then shook his head. 'And why would Gus Grayling be interested in me, Mr Lunn?'

'Come on, Alex. We know you were working for him when you pulled those robberies.'

'Was I, Mr Lunn? That was never proved now, was it?'

Lunn did not want to argue the point. 'I just thought he might have shown a bit of gratitude, that's all. You really carried the can for the whole team, didn't you?'

'Well, look around Mr Lunn. Does it appear to you that anyone's lending me a helping hand? Anyway, as I said, I'm no grass. When I was inside, the word was that Gus had retired. Living down south somewhere isn't he?'

Lunn frowned. Alex Stringer was obviously not going to drop anyone in it – least of all his old boss.

'What about Michael Doyle? Think he might be involved?'

Stringer smiled. 'Mickey Doyle? No chance. He'd run a mile at the sight of a gun. He's into fraud and that clever stuff that you lot can never understand which is why he's where he is and I'm where I am. Not his bag at all.'

'He and Grayling have done business together in the past, haven't they?'

'Have they, Mr Lunn? I wouldn't know. I've never been involved in planning anything – I just do as I'm told.'

'Well, if you'll accept my advice, Alex, I'd keep well away from both of them. Unless you want to go back inside of course.'

Stringer smiled. 'I'll do as you say, Mr Lunn, not that Doyle would have anything to do with me. He would never use anyone with a record like mine – whether the job was legit or not.'

'You may be right about that. Where is he, exactly?'

'Who, Doyle? I dunno. I haven't seen him since I came out.'

He looked up. 'And as I've told you, I'm quite sure he wouldn't want to see me. I did think about touching him for a loan – you know, for old time's sake, but I thought better of it. Last thing I heard he was living with some posh bird in Leicester – name of Jules. That's all I know.'

'We knew that, Alex but we can't seem to find him. His neighbour hasn't seen him since around the time of the robbery – which is interesting of course. If you do hear anything, there's a drink in it for you if you let us know. You and he go back a long way, don't you?'

'We was at school together – but that's as far as it ever went. He was always the clever one was Mickey. Top of the class he was. Could have gone to university if he'd wanted to. Not like me. I was rubbish at everything – except P.E and football. I could always beat him at that.' He paused. 'But look at me now. I'd have a job running for the bus.'

He looked down at his paunch and his stained jogging bottoms. 'Anyway, I told you, Mr Lunn, I'm no grass. If I was Mickey and I had what he has, I'd be spending Christmas in the sun – not here.'

'But you did hang about together didn't you, a few years back?'

'I wouldn't put it that way. I worked for him for about twelve months in the eighties, when he was running his building company – before he went into financing timeshares and holiday homes abroad alongside his property business here. I wasn't much use to him in that line – so we parted company.'

'Word was that you took that breathalyzer for him, you know, when he crashed his Porsche on the bypass.'

'That's what you lot would like to think. The truth is that I *was* driving. He was too pissed and he asked me to get him home. All he got done for was allowing me to drive without insurance. I'd had a few myself and I got banned for eighteen months but Mickey paid the fine. The car was written off and we drifted apart after that. He accused me of sniffing round after his younger sister. She was only fifteen at the time but a real looker. Then I met Linda and the rest is history.'

'So you and he don't keep in touch?'

'Look, Mr Lunn. I was inside for over eight years. I never heard a thing from him – not once. As you can see, we move in different circles. What would he want with me?' He paused and his voice softened. 'What would anyone want with me? I'm nobody.'

He looked away, his eyes filling with tears. Lunn realised that there was nothing to be gained by continuing the conversation. This was a man who'd hit rock bottom or so it seemed. The intelligence that he was looking to involve himself in serious crime seemed unreliable. He decided to leave.

'Just for the record, Alex, can you remember where you were on the night of 16/17 December?'

'What day was that?'

'Wednesday night into Thursday morning.'

'I'd have been here, of course. Like every other night… in my bed. Doors are locked at 11 p.m. If I wasn't in by then, the night manager would have recorded it. It's easily checked.'

Lunn nodded. 'Just a formality really, Alex. My governor likes to do things by the book.'

'I'm glad to hear it.'

'Well, I won't keep you. Nice to talk to you. In case you change your mind, I'll leave you my card. You can get me on that number any time.'

Lunn handed his card over, together with a packet of Benson & Hedges and a twenty-pound note.

'What's this for?' said Stringer, regaining his self-control. 'I ain't told you nothing.'

'Christmas present', said Lunn, 'for old time's sake.'

Alex Stringer looked at the crisp note in his hand. He was tempted to return it but times were hard. 'Thanks, Mr Lunn. As long as you understand – I'm no grass.'

★★★★

'How did it go?' asked Hood when Ian Lunn returned to the police station. It was getting late and the chief inspector was anxious to get home.

'I don't think he knows anything. Do y'know, I hardly recognised him. If that's what eight years inside does for you, I'm glad I'm doing what I do. I really doubt if Stringer would be up to it – and his alibi seems pretty solid. And he says he's heard nothing from Grayling. What about Mostyn? Did he shed any light on things?'

'Haven't seen him,' said Hood. 'He was taken to hospital this morning in the early hours. He's not at all well, apparently. This case gets more difficult by the minute. Both men who know most about this delivery are now in hospital. Even I'm beginning to wonder whether this can just be a coincidence.'

'Makes you think, doesn't it, sir? Do they know what's wrong with him?'

'Won't say. I spoke with his wife – she seems nice enough – she says his flu got worse; he had difficulty breathing, then he collapsed during the night. She called an ambulance and he was taken to Leicester Royal Infirmary. That's all I know. It certainly doesn't look good.'

CHAPTER EIGHT

Friday, 25 December 1998

Christmas morning in the Hood household began early as the chief inspector's two young children leapt on his bed and demanded that he get up. His wife was already downstairs preparing the festive lunch.

'Come on, Dad,' said his son, Philip. 'Mummy says we can't open any presents until you come down.'

Hood opened his eyes and smiled. He picked up the alarm clock from the bedside table, looked at the time and groaned. He pulled the duvet back over his head.

'Oh, Daddy,' shouted young Amy. 'Don't go back to sleep.'

She jumped on top of him, followed by Philip. With a mighty roar, Hood lifted both up and carried them from the bed. The two of them were screaming in mock terror trying to wrestle themselves free.

'All right, all right,' cried their father. 'You win. I'll be right down.' He released them and grabbed his dressing gown.

'Go and tell Mum you can start opening the presents while I get dressed.'

'No,' said his daughter. 'Mummy says you have to come down *now*.' She folded her arms and looked at Hood with a determined frown. He knew when he was beaten. She was only eight but she was her mother's daughter.

'OK,' he sighed, 'you lead the way Amy.'

The children marched ahead, triumphantly, then, when they reached the bottom of the stairs, rushed through the hallway into the sitting room whilst Hood followed slowly, checking his dressing gown pocket. He had already decided he would not bother with his morning run and he was pleased that they had attended Midnight Mass the night before, although in accordance with the modern practice, the service had commenced at

9 p.m. thus enabling families to attend without risking involvement with those whose first port of call had been a public house. His religious duties having been observed, only the ordeal of Christmas lunch with the usual relatives remained. His wife was standing by the Christmas tree, smiling, as he entered the room.

'Good,' she said. 'You can supervise them. I have a lot to do in the kitchen. They'll be arriving sooner than you think.'

"They" was a reference to Hood's parents, his wife's mother and Uncle Winston, a confirmed bachelor of seventy-two. Every Christmas had been the same – at least since the children were born. Hood got on with his mother-in-law pretty well and she with him but she had never let her daughter forget that the family would have preferred her to have married Jonathan, Sarah's boyfriend from university. He was now a successful barrister in London, earning far more than a detective chief inspector and she had cajoled Sarah for several months to stick with him as their relationship began to deteriorate. Jonathan was very career-minded and Sarah was made to feel that she came a distant second to his establishing himself at the Bar. Her father had died suddenly just after her graduation and while Jonathan had been particularly helpful and understanding immediately after the funeral, he had then moved permanently to London. As Sarah's continuing education was in Sheffield, they saw far less of each other and when she moved to Nottingham to take up a position in the main hospital, contact became even less frequent. Her mother encouraged her to visit Jonathan as often as possible but it was not to be. Sarah had met Hood during her final year at Leeds university. They had been friends for some time, whilst she was still involved with Jonathan. He had never pushed their relationship but their friendship developed steadily as her interest in Jonathan waned. They did not become lovers until she and Jonathan had gone their separate ways and by the time her mother found out about them, the die was cast.

Mrs Ravenscroft was initially shocked that her extremely clever and attractive daughter had taken up with a man of mixed race. But she was no racist. Her husband had been a consultant with the Race Relations Council and she, like him, had publicly supported multiculturalism, never, of course, thinking that her own daughter would bring the issue so close up and personal. But she had just taken a little longer than Hood would have liked to come to terms with their relationship. Hood was very good-looking in those days and reminded Mrs Ravenscroft of Sidney Poitier, although he was much lighter skinned. Hood's own parents were quite the opposite. They thoroughly approved of their son's choice of wife. They thought Sarah was quite wonderful. After the wedding, a simple and private affair, they had kept a reasonable distance but when the grandchildren arrived, there was no holding them. Like any grandparents, they spoilt and idolised their grandchildren. Nothing was too much for them They even moved to within a couple of miles of the Hoods' home so they were always available for babysitting duties. It was the arrival of the grandchildren that eventually brought about a civilised if slightly cool accommodation with Mrs Ravenscroft. She was always polite, perhaps too polite, but she had little in common with Hood's parents and family gatherings were always a little tense and strained as a result, but the ice had thawed gradually as the children grew older.

Hood's relationship with his mother-in-law reached its zenith after she read in the social pages that Jonathan's marriage to the daughter of a wealthy baronet had broken up after only a couple of years. Perhaps her daughter had made the right choice after all? Sarah, now an established consultant psychologist, had an explanation for everything and anything but she was somewhat reticent about expressing any opinion on her own mother's views. She worked only part-time now, as she had succumbed very early to an overwhelming desire to spend as much time as possible with her children. No doubt she had an explanation for that too.

Hood could not resist grinning as he entered the room. He produced a small present from his dressing gown pocket. 'For you,' he said, kissing his wife on the lips. The kitchen was forgotten about for a moment as Sarah tore away the decorated paper, revealing a dark blue velvet-covered box which she opened slowly, gazing delightedly at the contents. She looked at her husband and then back to the box.

'They're beautiful. You shouldn't have.'

She took the string of pearls from the box and placed them against her throat, then looked at herself in the mirror over the fireplace.

'Well, I can always return them,' said Hood, a twinkle in his eye.

She turned away from the mirror and took him in her arms, her eyes bursting with gratitude.

'You'll do no such thing.'

She kissed him and he held her tightly in his arms. This was the bit of Christmas that he looked forward to. The gathering of the relatives later for lunch he could have done without but that's what Christmas was all about, he supposed. He'd get through it, as he had in previous years.

'Sarah,' he said, as he looked towards his daughter, 'should Amy be doing that?'

Sarah turned and faced her daughter who was busily applying lipstick to her younger brother's face. She smiled.

'Leave her, after all it is Christmas and Pip can look after himself.'

CHAPTER NINE

Monday, 4 January 1999

Chief Inspector Hood was sitting behind his desk reading witness statements and thinking. He was a great believer in standing back (or in his case, sitting back) and thinking about an investigation. Progress had been slow, but that was to be expected. He appreciated that while he was under a degree of pressure to move the matter on he had to be patient while the numerous enquiries he had put in hand were given the chance of bearing fruit. He recalled a lecture at Hendon years before. Previous major inquiries had been put under the microscope and the essential leads identified. He remembered the bungled Yorkshire Ripper inquiry and almost shuddered as he recollected how it was that two uniformed officers on patrol just doing their job and applying a bit of common sense had led to Peter Sutcliffe's arrest and the later retrieval of two of his weapons, a ball-pein hammer and a knife. All the complex inquiries and cross-referencing that had gone on for months before had achieved nothing, apart from a failure to detain Sutcliffe on earlier occasions. He had then gone on to kill again.

Then there was the Great Train Robbery. Although the robbers were eventually apprehended and convicted, it was never established who had tipped them off. Hood simply could not accept that they had struck lucky and managed to stop a train which was carrying over 2 million pounds in untraceable notes. Someone in the know had to have given them the essential information. Just like the robbery at the Charnwood, this was not a lucky strike. Someone, somewhere knew this consignment would include a substantial number of untraceable banknotes. Hood was determined to identify that individual as well as convict those who'd carried it out.

He had still not spoken to Bill Mostyn. He was, in the words of his wife, "still seriously ill". At least Hood could rest assured that his condition was genuine. It had crossed his mind that Mostyn might have been trying it on and feigning sickness to avoid being interviewed.

His telephone rang and he sat up with a jolt. He looked at his watch before he picked up the phone. It was almost 6 p.m. He should have been home hours ago.

'There's an Inspector Crawford from Humberside on the line for you, sir,' said the officer on the switchboard.

'Put him on.'

Hood settled back in his chair. He knew and liked Crawford. They had attended a conference on knife crime a few months before; part of the continuing training that was an essential feature of the modern police service along with the never-ending round of pointless meetings.

'Hello Jack. How are you? I thought you'd be in Spain. Don't you always spend New Year in that villa of yours?'

'We did, but you know what it's like, we had to get back early this time. How are you getting on with that robbery investigation?'

'It's early days yet. But to be frank, we've not made much progress so far.'

'Well I think your luck is about to change. I might well have something for you.'

Hood sat up straight in his chair. 'Go on…'

'We have one of your target criminals here – unconscious in the infirmary. Smashed his car up. It seems he was after catching the ferry to Rotterdam on Saturday night. But what may be of interest to you is this – he had a suitcase with what looks like about half a million quid in it – all in twenties and tens.'

'Who is he?'

'His passport says he is Michael James Doyle; ring any bells?'

Hoods faced broke out into a wide smile.

'It certainly does! What have you done with the money?'

'Well that's a bit embarrassing, actually. The bobbies who attended the accident missed it. But the car recovery people phoned in and told us about it first thing this morning. We have it safe and sound. It occurred to me it might have something to do with that big robbery in your division before Christmas. We can't link it to anything in this area.'

'You could well be right. I'll get someone over tomorrow. Don't let anyone touch the notes and for God's sake don't count them. We'll want to test them for prints and DNA first.'

'I've already given instructions, but I think the car recovery people may well have contaminated the notes. A lot of them had burst out of the suitcase in the collision – or so they say – and they thought they were doing the right thing putting them back.'

'Can't be helped, I suppose. But this could be our first decent lead. How's Doyle?'

'He'll live – but he won't be going anywhere for a while. He seems to be in some sort of a coma but I gather the damage is not that bad – unfortunately!'

'Have you put him under observation?'

'Of course. There's an officer at the hospital as we speak on bed watch. As soon as he comes round, I'll be informed. And you'll know as soon as I know. Oh, and I hope you think this is sensible – we've kept his identification secret – at least for the time being. Only the medics know who he is.'

'Good man, Jack. I think I'll come over myself but it won't be before Wednesday. I'll ring you later tomorrow, sometime after six – if that's OK with you.'

'No problem – I shall be back on duty at four tomorrow. Speak to you later.'

Hood hesitated. 'By the way, Jack, has anyone been asking after him? If this cash is from the robbery, he'll have been taking it abroad to launder it. Someone's bound to have missed him by now.'

'No one's been in to the hospital and as far as I know no one's been asking after him. We've released no information about the accident yet, so the chances are no one will know where he is at the moment.'

Hood smiled. 'Shall we keep it that way? At least until I get over there.'

'Will do.'

'Thanks, Jack. Hope to see you on Wednesday. Cheers.'

CHAPTER TEN

Julia Hamilton was lying in bed half-asleep when her mobile phone rang. She hesitated before picking it up and checking the caller's number. She glanced at her alarm clock. It was 6.45 a.m. Only Michael would ring her at that time. She'd expected him to be in touch with her the day before but she had heard nothing. They were seldom apart for more than a few days and while she appreciated that he had a phobia about his telephone calls being traced, he should have called her when he'd arrived in Holland. She looked at the alarm clock again and then at her phone. She recognised the number and smiled. 'Hi darling, I was expecting to hear from you yesterday at the latest.'

But it wasn't Michael who answered.

'Jules, it's me, Max. I'm ringing about Mikey.' Max always called her lover Mikey, much to her annoyance.

'Is he not with you?'

'No. He didn't arrive on the ferry. I arranged to meet him at the usual place but he didn't show. Have you heard from him?'

'I haven't, no.' Jules was concerned. She was now sitting up and pulling her fingers through her blonde hair; the tiredness had vanished. 'I don't understand it. We took the usual precautions. He left his mobile here and he was going to ring me using your phone when he met up with you.'

It was an invariable rule on his trips abroad that Doyle never took his mobile. On the rare occasions he did, he always used a phone that could not be traced back to him. He and Jules changed their mobiles every few months. Doyle knew that a mobile phone was essentially a radio receiver and transmitter and he had developed what amounted to an obsession that the police would be able to trace his movements by plotting the position of his phone at any given point. He much preferred to use public telephones for any important communication or – at a push – someone else's mobile. Assurances from Jules that the police could not prove where he had been through such analysis did not provide him with any comfort. "If they can't do it yet," he used to say, "it's only a question of time before they can."

'Well, he's not been in touch. I've checked with the ferry company,' said Max. 'He had a booking but he never embarked. That's what they told me. I waited for the next boat in case he was delayed by the bad weather but he wasn't on that either. Unless he shows soon, we'll lose the chance of converting the money. My contact won't wait.'

'Where are you at the moment, Max?'

'I'm still at Europort, but I'm about to go in to Rotterdam. I can't hang around here any longer. Customs will start to get suspicious. There isn't another ferry anyway until tomorrow.'

Jules was now very worried. 'Something must have happened. God, I hope he hasn't had an accident. The weather was terrible here as well over the weekend.' She paused and tried to think. 'Look, Max, leave it with me. I'll get back to you when I find out anything. Love to Marieke. Bye.'

Jules placed the phone on the bedside table. She had put on her dressing gown and was carefully inserting her contact lenses when she heard the bell ringing followed by several loud bangs on the front door of the flat. She'd heard that sort of commotion before when she'd been with Michael in his penthouse apartment on the top floor. It could only mean one thing – a visit from the local constabulary. Her reaction was immediate. First, she switched the phone off and placed it in a specially constructed niche in the bed-head, and closed the small wooden panel over it. Then she quickly brushed her hair and checked her appearance in the mirror. Voices were calling for the door to be opened. She walked through the hallway and casually opened the front door. Two uniformed police officers and another she took to be a detective, were standing there. She yawned as she looked them over.

'He's not here,' she said. Jules recognised the heavily suntanned detective. She'd crossed swords with him before. 'He has his own apartment upstairs – the penthouse.'

'We know that, we have a warrant to search those premises. As he's not there, we thought you might have a key. It would save us breaking the door down.'

It was the detective who spoke as he waved a piece of paper in front of her.

'May I see that,' replied Jules, letting her dressing gown slip just enough to attract the concentrated gaze of the other two. One of them smirked and elbowed his colleague. She took the search warrant and glanced at it. The detective was impatient to get on with the search.

'It's all in order; now are you going to assist us or not. I'm more than happy to get one of these strong boys to kick the door in.'

The two constables looked vacantly at each other.

'Of course,' said Jules bowing in mock deference, and exposing even more of her breasts to the appreciative audience. 'But, you'll find nothing to interest you, I can assure you.'

'I'll be the judge of that,' replied the detective, retrieving the warrant.

'Well you'd better come in while I get dressed. I'm not going upstairs in my negligee.'

Hooper and the two constables followed her into the flat. She rented it from Alpha House Holdings Limited, a company still controlled by Doyle. Although she spent most of her time in the penthouse, she was careful to maintain her own residence, if only for the sake of appearances, not that the detective sergeant was deceived in the slightest as to the true position.

'Nice place you have here,' said Hooper. 'I bet this costs you a pretty penny.'

'Actually, the rent is quite reasonable.'

'Could that have anything to do with the fact that Doyle owns the entire building?'

Hooper had done his homework and was quite familiar with most of Doyle's known assets.

'I rent it from Alpha Holdings – and I pay a commercial rent.'

'But Doyle *is* Alpha Holdings, isn't he?'

'Is that a fact? You know more about Michael's interests than I do.'

'I very much doubt it,' said Hooper cynically.

Jules ignored him.

'Do you mind if I get dressed, now? I don't have much time to spare. I'm due in court in Nottingham at ten o'clock. And I have a taxi arriving to take me to the station in forty minutes.'

Hooper looked at his watch. It was not yet 7.00 a.m.

'You've plenty of time to get there.'

Again, she ignored him and walked out of the lounge into her bedroom. Minutes later she returned, immaculately dressed in a dark blue skirt and jacket and a white linen blouse. The two constables gawped at her, open mouthed. Hooper coughed.

'Still working for those Derby solicitors?'

'Not that it's any of your business, but no I am not. I'm freelance now. I work for a number of solicitors, including the Derby firm. I'm assisting in a case at Nottingham Crown Court at the moment, for Evans and Partners; perhaps you've heard of them?'

'Can't say I have,' said Hooper. 'Can we get on? I wouldn't want to make you late for court. That would never do.'

He indicated to the two constables and the party of four left the flat and, after Jules had carefully locked her door, made their way to the lift. Within a minute and a half, they were standing outside Doyle's penthouse apartment. Jules opened her handbag and took out a key which she handed to Hooper.

'It's all yours, do try not to make a mess.'

'You can stay while we carry out the search, if you like,' said Hooper.

'No thank you. It's nothing to do with me. And I don't want you trying to use my presence to justify what you're up to. I'm sure Mr Doyle will be consulting his solicitors about the legal basis for that warrant.'

With that, she turned and walked haughtily away from them. The eyes of the two constables followed her all the way to the doors of the lift.

'Legal basis for the warrant,' muttered Hooper. 'Who does she think she is?'

He put the key into the lock and turned it and the three officers went into the flat, closing the door quietly behind them.

Jules waited for the lift to arrive, turning to look at Doyle's apartment as the doors opened. She descended to the first floor and went back into her own flat. She picked up her briefcase, retrieved her mobile phone and left the apartment, locking the door behind her. She headed for the stairs but as she passed the lift, she hesitated. She thought again about Michael. Then, quite suddenly, she pressed the call button which caused the lift doors to re-open. She took the lift back up to the top floor and approached Doyle's apartment. She knocked on the door and after a few seconds Hooper appeared. He looked as if he had been half expecting her to return.

'I've changed my mind,' she said. 'You lot simply can't be trusted. I shall stay here until the search is completed.'

Hooper opened the door wider and stepped back to let her in.

'Good,' he said, 'you'll be able to let us know where things are.'

'I wouldn't count on that,' she responded. Jules took the few steps into the open-plan living area and sat down on the leather chesterfield couch, placing her briefcase at her feet.

'Don't mind me,' she said. 'Carry on.'

Hooper pointed to her briefcase.

'What have you got in there,' he asked.

'None of your concern. They're only papers in respect of the case I'm covering and are subject to legal privilege. If you search this bag, the judge will be informed and you will be for the high jump.'

Jules paused for effect.

'On second thoughts, do take a look. When the judge is told what you've done he'll probably have to stop the trial, which will be very much in my client's interests because it's not going very well for him at the moment.'

She put on her best artificial smile, showing her almost perfect teeth to their best advantage.

It was Hooper's turn to hesitate. He was not over fond of judges and remembered how one of his colleague's over enthusiasm had contributed to the CPS decision to drop the charges against Doyle in the mortgage fraud some years before. He wasn't going to be caught out doing something similar.

'I was only asking,' he said. 'I have no desire to search either you or your briefcase.'

Hooper directed the two officers into the second of the two bedrooms, nothing of interest having been found in the first, whilst he continued his search of an antique walnut desk in the corner of the main reception room. He had already taken possession of a few pieces of paper and a mobile telephone he'd found on the coffee table. This was the phone that Jules had deliberately left in that precise position so that it would be discovered by the police should they ever chance on searching the flat. There was, of course, nothing in its memory apart from a few innocuous messages that she had placed there from time to time using her mother's phone and another mobile obtained especially for that purpose. Jules smiled inwardly as she observed Hooper trying to check if there were any messages.

'Whose is this?' asked Hooper, holding the phone so she could see it clearly.

'I think it must be Michael's,' she replied, looking slightly puzzled. 'I wonder why he didn't take it with him?'

'Perhaps he has another one,' said the sergeant.

'He may well have,' replied Jules, 'but he's always losing them. He still prefers to use a land line, you know, he's not keen on mobiles at all. He thinks they can give you cancer.'

'Really,' replied Hooper, failing to access the message facility. 'Do you happen to know the code to get in to this thing?'

'Try four zeros.'

He did and gained access but discovered nothing of relevance.

'Can I help you with anything else, officer?' asked Jules.

'We'll be taking the phone and these papers; Williams here will write out a receipt.' One of the others who had returned to the living area, took out a pad, and started to log each of the pieces of paper the sergeant handed him. Jules was turning over in her mind whether she should ask about Michael. This wasn't the first time the police had turned up looking for him with a warrant to search the flat but she had noticed on the magistrate's order that he was under suspicion of committing robbery. She decided to take the risk. Indeed, her principal reason for coming back to the apartment was to find out what had happened to Michael. Part of her didn't want to know, because she feared the worst, but she realised the question had to be asked.

'What's this all about?'

She stood up and looked directly at Hooper.

'I was wondering when you might ask. I take it you know where Doyle is?'

'As far as I know, he's in Holland, on business.' She paused and allowed a look of concern to cross her brow. 'Why? Has something happened to him?' Jules was now *really* worried, much more than before. She had already worked out that the arrival of the police at the flat probably meant that Michael had been arrested or worse.

'He's not in Holland. He's in Hull Royal Infirmary. He's been involved in a road accident, by all accounts.'

Hooper was quite unable to conceal a certain delight in making the announcement. Jules, on the other hand, was shocked. She went quite pale and had to sit down.

'Is he…?'

Hooper interrupted. He realised this was news to her. Either that or she was a bloody good actress.

'Don't worry,' he said. 'He'll live.'

'May I see him?' asked Jules, the relief only too evident.

'You may not,' replied the sergeant. 'No one will be allowed to see him until he's answered a few questions, especially not you. Don't think you fool us, love. We know you're up to your eyeballs in his crooked activities. You can see him after he's been charged and not before.'

'Charged? Charged with what? He hasn't done anything. I can vouch for that.'

'Can you? Well, we'll just have to see, won't we?'

Jules asked to see the warrant again. She examined it in greater detail and mumbled some of the words in an increasingly incredulous tone.

'Suspicion of robbery on 17 December? What does this mean?'

'Don't you come that with me. You know exactly what that means; you were probably in on it with him.'

'Well, you'd better arrest me then,' said Jules defiantly. She stood up and faced Hooper. He was not impressed. He looked her directly in the eye and spoke with deliberation.

'I will, if we get the evidence.'

'He wasn't even here on 17 December,' countered Jules. 'We were planning to go to Dorset for Christmas. If you look at some of the papers you've seized, you can see that for yourselves.'

'Of course you were,' replied Hooper. 'No doubt you were preparing his alibi for him.'

'That's a ridiculous suggestion. Michael went down there on the morning of the sixteenth. I couldn't go because the case I was covering ran over. You can check with the court if you like. A juror was ill and we couldn't sit for two days the week before. The verdict didn't come in until the eighteenth. I went down on the train on the nineteenth and Michael met me at the station. So if this robbery of yours took place around here, Michael simply couldn't have been involved.'

'What makes you think the robbery took place around here?'

Jules almost sniggered as she replied. 'If it didn't – you wouldn't be the investigating officer, now would you?'

Hooper did not reply. He had to give her that one. He walked out of the sitting room and quickly rechecked the main bedroom, glaring as he passed the second officer who was exiting the second bedroom, his expression indicating that nothing had been found in there either. Hooper opened the fitted wardrobe and ruffled through the hanging garments. He then went to the set of drawers, opening them one after the other and sifting through the contents. Jules watched him from the doorway.

'I don't think he trusts you two,' she said, glancing towards the constables.

They looked at each other but said nothing. Hooper closed the top drawer and made his way towards the door. 'Right. We'd best be on our way.'

Williams handed Jules the receipts. Hooper pushed past her, handing her the key as he did so.

'Good morning, Miss Hamilton. We'll see ourselves out.' As he approached the front door he paused. 'There is one thing you can help me with.' He turned and faced her. 'Where exactly were you and Doyle over Christmas?'

Jules answered straight away.

'We spent the whole of Christmas in Dorset,' she replied. 'Right up to the day before New Year's Eve. You can check with the hotel if you like – if you think the receipt you've taken is a fake. I'm sure the receptionist will remember us. Michael is a generous tipper.'

'I bet he is,' said Hooper. 'What's the name of the hotel?'

'It's quite clear on the receipt if you can be bothered to look – High Trees House Hotel. It's between Dorchester and the coast. I can recommend it. The *Coquilles St Jacques* is to die for.'

Hooper hated shellfish. It didn't agree with him – but he made a mental note and opened the door. The constables followed. Jules remained at the front door, smiling, until all three of them got into the lift. She then closed and locked the door and returned to her own flat. Once in her bedroom, which overlooked the front of the building, she glanced discreetly through the Venetian blinds. The police officers got into the same unmarked car and drove away. After a few moments, she took her mobile phone from her handbag and switched it on. She had several calls to make.

CHAPTER ELEVEN

'Along the corridor, turn left then right and you'll find it on the left-hand side about three-quarters of the way down. Room 401 D.'

'Thanks.'

PC Raymond Craddock raised his hand to acknowledge the hospital security officer and trudged off in the direction given with a marked lack of enthusiasm. He was not a happy man and that was not simply because he was soaking wet having walked to the infirmary in the pouring rain. He had been looking forward to an easy time on the night shift back at the station. It closed to the public at 10 p.m., which meant only light duties for the rest of his shift. A bit of filing, answering the telephone when the switchboard girl was on her break and, inevitably, making tea for the sergeant manning the desk – that's what he'd had in mind. Plenty of time to read the crime thriller he'd been given for his birthday. He'd been told when he joined the Humberside Constabulary nearly four years before that you could never predict what might happen in the police service as it was now known. Not a police force any longer as it had been in his father's day. Unpredictability! That's what made the job so interesting and occasionally exciting. Well, young Raymond begged to differ. His experience of police work was largely one of unremitting boredom and mind-boggling bureaucracy accompanied by a regular diet of abuse and worse from drink-sodden youths on the Ermine estate or in the city centre. The only thrills he got were from the detective novels he devoured by the dozen. But the money was quite good and he had plenty of time off; only another twenty-six years to go before he could retire on a decent pension and do something useful with the rest of his life.

He often thought he should have gone to university. He had three good A levels and one not so good – a D in physics – but he was certainly brighter than the average recruit. His late father had reached the rank of superintendent and many of the older officers still remembered him – some with affection. It had always been his ambition to follow in his father's footsteps but nearly four years on he was beginning to have his doubts. He'd taken and passed his sergeant's exams but had been told there were no actual prospects of promotion at present. Of course, there had been the four months or so when he had been temporarily promoted to acting detective constable in the only murder case with which he'd had any real involvement. While there had been other homicides, his sole contribution in those cases had been standing outside the property where the dastardly deed had been done to prevent unauthorised access or spending most of his shift on his hands and knees searching for possible evidence, all to no avail. He had certainly enjoyed his brief tenure as a detective although his sole task had been to view numerous hours of CCTV captured from city centre cameras and compile a video recording of the relevant images in strict chronological order. His logical mind and careful editing had made a singular contribution to the conviction at trial, or so he had been told, and he received a commendation from the trial judge and the chief constable. His mother was very proud and hung the somewhat over-elaborate and framed certificate in her front room. Raymond was very pleased to have been chosen for this task, until his friend Eddie informed him he'd been the only volunteer. "Who wants to spend all day watching CCTV?" Eddie had asked in disbelief when Raymond had told him he would be out of uniform for a few weeks. "I'd rather patrol the Ermine than that!" Still, his success had triggered his application to become a full-time detective. But, despite his efforts to impress and success in his examination he'd been told that there were no vacancies, at least not in Humberside. So he had put in for a transfer to Mid-Shires Constabulary. That was over a month ago but he was still waiting even for an acknowledgement of his application. And he hadn't told his mother either. She wouldn't like it and there was no point upsetting her if nothing came of it. On the other hand, if he did get a transfer it might improve his love life. He'd heard the girls in Nottingham and Leicester were good-looking and living at home had always proved a handicap when he started to get anywhere with a woman. Yes, a move to the East Midlands would be just the job. He paused as he turned into the second corridor by no means sure he was going the right way.

Why should I have to do this? he thought to himself. *Spending all night guarding an unconscious crook who's incapable of escaping*. He had taken the precaution of bringing his novel with him in the confident assumption there would be nothing required of him, save his presence.

'Why me, Sarge?' he'd moaned as he'd brought in the sergeant's tea. 'There's nothing worse than bed watch. It's so boring.'

'Because there's no one else, lad, that's why. Eddie Farnsworth has been there since two o'clock and someone has to take over. Inspector's orders; there has to be an officer with him all the time, in case he comes round. Anyway, it'll give you a chance to chat up them nurses. It's about time you found yourself a steady girlfriend.'

Sergeant Perry smiled. Raymond ignored the reference to his non-existent love life, which, for reasons he'd never understood had become the talk of the station. He suspected Eddie Farnsworth had something to do with that as well.

'What do y' mean chat up the nurses? I'll be too busy for that. He might try and escape.'

'I doubt that very much. He's going nowhere. He's got a broken leg and a few cracked ribs. He's been out cold since they brought him in. He might even have brain damage. So you've no worries on that score. But he might try and contact someone or give something away if he comes round. So we need a bright lad like you there to keep an eye on him. Inspector Crawford's relying on you.'

Raymond was not impressed with the mention of the inspector. He'd been told that a dozen times before as an incentive to get him to do something no one else wanted to do but no good had ever come of it. Not for him anyway.

'What's he supposed to have done anyway?'

'I've heard nothing officially,' said the sergeant in the tone he always adopted when about to reveal some inside knowledge, 'but they reckon he's wanted for that armed robbery before Christmas, the one near Nottingham, you know, the one where they got away with nearly 2 million quid.'

Raymond perked up a little. That was a serious case.

'I read about that. Didn't they shoot a security guard?'

The sergeant nodded as he opened his tin of chocolate digestive biscuits.

'But what's that got to do with us? Mid-Shires police should be dealing with that.'

'They are lad, but this character crashed his car on the way to the ferry. Apparently, he was on his way to Rotterdam. But he never got there. He came to grief on Clive Sullivan Way to be exact – you know, not far from the infirmary. He had a stash of stolen money in the boot. That's why they reckon he was in on that robbery. If you want to know more of the details you can find them on the crime report on the computer – I wouldn't bother though if I were you. As soon as he's fit, Mid-Shires will take him back to the East Midlands. Two of their lads will be over here in a day or two to check him out.'

Raymond knew from past experience that "What Sergeant Perry hadn't heard officially'" was usually not very far from the truth but he decided he was interested enough to check the crime report for himself before he left the police station. His application to Mid-Shires was still on his mind. *You never know*, he thought to himself, *a few basic facts about the case might come in handy*.

'So what am I supposed to do with him?' he asked as he searched the computer for the relevant briefing.

'Absolutely nothing – that's the beauty of it. Just keep an eye on him until you're relieved. If he comes round, radio in and let me know. I'm on until six. Inspector Crawford will do the rest.'

'Doesn't mention him on the briefing notes,' said Raymond.

'They're keeping mum about him at the moment. Mid-Shires don't want his name released. Crawford knows who he is, but he's not letting on. I can understand why. There must have been a few others involved and if they find out this one's been nicked the chances of finding them will be less than zero.'

Raymond could see the point of that but was far from happy that he'd seemingly drawn the short straw yet again.

'Is there anyone who can give me a lift?' He glanced through the window as he logged off.

The sergeant looked up from his crossword and took a swig of his tea.

'It's only down the road. You can walk. Do you good.'

'But it's pouring down outside.'

'Well. You'll get wet then, won't you? Now get on with it!'

★★★★

'Hello, Eddie,' said Raymond. 'Anything to report?'

'Nothing,' came the uninterested reply. The recumbent police officer stretched out his arms and yawned. 'He's sleeping like a baby. I've had nothing to do for the whole bloody shift. If you ask me, it's a complete waste of time having anyone here. The medics could tell us when he comes round.'

Eddie Farnsworth got up from the chair and looked at his watch. 'Another ten minutes and he's all yours.' He stretched his arms again. 'They must think he's pretty important to go to all this bother. Have you found out who he is? No one here seems to have a clue.'

Raymond looked around to check if anyone could overhear before he answered.

'Well, according to Sergeant Perry, Mid-Shires think he's one of the villains who did that robbery just before Christmas. You know – the one at that huge shopping centre near East Midlands Airport – where the guard got himself shot.'

Raymond conveyed these details to his colleague in the manner of one who had been given highly confidential information.

'Oh, I know *that*,' replied Eddie. 'I read the newspapers you know. I just thought you might have used that brain of yours to find out *who* he is. There's nothing written on his notes to identify him and every nurse who comes in here asks me the same question; who is he? All this secrecy makes them think he must be some kind of celebrity.'

'Well I checked the updated crime report before I came,' said Raymond. 'There are no names given. It looks as if they hadn't a clue who pulled off this robbery; not 'til now, anyway.'

'You would do that, wouldn't you?' replied Eddie grudgingly, failing to conceal just a hint of admiration. 'Still after being a detective then?'

Raymond nodded. 'Anything's better than this. This isn't what I joined the police for.'

Eddie laughed. 'You're too keen, that's the problem with you, Raymond my boy. Too keen. And they'll just keep taking advantage of you. You need to relax a bit. There's a lot more to life than police work, you know.'

Raymond sighed. 'What's wrong with him, anyway?' he asked. 'Is he at death's door or what?'

'Now that I can help you with,' replied Eddie. 'He was in the high dependency unit until this morning but they've transferred him here because we don't want him on a general ward and they needed the bed in HDU for someone else. Fortunately, this room was available and they moved in all the necessary equipment. Trouble is the nurses are in and out like yo-yos. Until a couple of hours ago they've been checking him every thirty minutes or so – but he's more settled now.'

With that, he opened the internal door, crept from the anteroom into the patient area and picked up the clipboard from the end of the bed. He took a quick look at the sleeping man and tiptoed back. 'Here you are. You're the would-be detective. Take a look at this.'

Raymond took the clipboard from him and glanced at the medical notes. 'This doesn't tell me much,' he said handing the clipboard back.

'No, but the nurses can,' replied Eddie, looking very pleased with himself.

Raymond was not in the least surprised. Eddie had a way with him when it came to getting things out of nurses or any woman. Raymond had often wished he'd had Eddie's easy manner with the opposite sex.

'He's got a broken leg – nothing too serious, several fractured ribs and a nasty knock to his head.' Eddie grinned as he added, 'That's what comes of driving too fast along Clive Sullivan Way in heavy rain – although I don't suppose the burst tyre will have helped.' He continued with his diagnosis. 'They're expecting him to come round sometime soon. His concussion isn't the most serious but neither is it trivial. And he's had a CT scan – apparently there's no need to open him up. The swelling on his brain is responding to conservative treatment.'

Eddie adopted a mock professional tone as he repeated the medical opinion confided to him by one of the nurses. 'By the way, we're not supposed to know any of this – it's confidential.'

Eddie walked back to the patient area and replaced the clipboard. He took another quick look at the man in the bed before he returned.

'Well, I don't recognise him. He's certainly not from round here. Want to take a butcher's?'

'Later,' replied Raymond. 'I've got all night for that.'

'You sure have,' said Eddie. 'Another thing – we're not supposed to go in there where he is – apparently it's unhygienic. But you can see all you need to see through that window.'

Eddie pointed to a pane of glass set in the partition that separated them from the patient immediately adjacent to the door that led to the other room. 'You can slide it back like this – Eddie demonstrated – so you can hear the monitors when the nurses forget to turn them down. But it drives you daft after a while. Oh, and no one can get into his room unless they come in here first. So if someone comes to knock him off, you'll be able to stop them.'

'Why should anyone want to knock him off? Sergeant Perry never said anything about anyone knocking him off.' Raymond didn't like the sound of that. He checked his belt to see if he had his CS spray with him.

'Well you never know, do you?' replied Eddie. 'The rest of the gang might think he'll talk and give them away. Don't forget, they got away with nearly 2 million quid – so they must be professionals. And look what they did to that guard. I read he was still in intensive care at the QMC in Nottingham; at least he was last week.'

'You're having me on,' said Raymond. 'They wouldn't leave you and me on our own if there was any chance of that.'

'Correction,' said Eddie. 'You – you're on your own. I'm off. I've got some leave due and me and Alison are going up to Durham to see her mum and dad. No pressure, of course, but I think I'm being given the final once-over.'

'Well, so long as no one turns up here to give me the once-over.' Raymond suspected Eddie was winding him up. Eddie enjoyed winding him up.

'I wouldn't worry too much,' said Eddie. 'They'd never find their way up here through this labyrinth of a place. They'd have to get a map.'

He *was* winding him up. Why did he always fall for it? Raymond changed the subject. 'So you're finally making an honest woman of Alison, are you?'

'Certainly looks that way. Time you found someone, Raymond. Time's getting on!'

Raymond sighed. 'What are the nurses like?' he asked as he lifted up part of the blind and looked outside. Eddie smiled in that knowing way that Raymond had seen all too often in the past. Another wind-up seemed to be on the cards.

'There's been two in so far. You know, to check on him and replace his fluid bags etc. I suppose the doctors have knocked off for the night. One of them is just your type, Raymond.'

'Oh, yes,' said Raymond, releasing the blind.

'Only one of them, mind you. Other's a bloke!' Eddie laughed and looked at his watch. 'Three days' leave starting about now!'

He made for the door. He paused and pointed at a discarded plastic sandwich wrapper and an empty Pepsi bottle by the comfortable chair.

'I suppose I should get rid of that,' he said, 'unless you deal with it?'

Raymond sighed. 'Leave it to me. Anything else I need to know?'

'Nope. Just remember to call in when he comes round. The DI wants to talk to him before the lawyers get the chance to interfere.' Eddie opened the door. 'I suppose it's still hammering down outside?'

Raymond nodded. With that, Eddie was gone, leaving Raymond standing in the middle of the room listening to the heavy breathing from the bed and the occasional ping of the monitor that could still be heard even with the glass screen closed. He removed his utility belt, sat down in the comfortable chair, stretched out his legs and took out his novel. He was not looking forward to his stint at the hospital. Eddie's cocky attitude reminded him that his search for a decent girlfriend had been about as unproductive as his application to become a detective. Girls didn't seem as keen to go out with coppers as in his father's day – with the exception of Eddie, of course. Eddie never had any trouble in that department. Raymond had lost count of how many women he'd seen him with. If only he could find someone like Alison. She was a cracker. He'd only seen her once or twice because Eddie hadn't flaunted her like he had the others, so even he must have regarded her as a bit special. Eddie had introduced her to him as his fiancée at the Divisional Christmas party – and she was everything Raymond thought he wanted in a woman. Tall and slim, she had legs to die for and a figure to match. She was also intelligent; apparently she taught French at a comprehensive school in Hessle, or so he'd heard. *Completely out of my league*, he'd thought as he lusted after her across the room. But what he'd really noticed were her lovely hands. Raymond's mother had told him that a woman's hands revealed a great deal about her character and when he danced with Alison at the party on that single occasion, holding her hand in his for only a few moments, he regarded this as proof positive of the truth of his mother's advice. He shifted on the chair and turned the page. It was going to be a very long night.

CHAPTER TWELVE

Raymond must have started to nod off because he didn't hear the door from the corridor open and he certainly wasn't expecting what appeared in front of him. He quickly got to his feet feeling very awkward and more than a little embarrassed. Had Eddie been winding him up about the nurses? The two who'd been in earlier when Raymond had been wide awake were nothing special. Raymond couldn't have described them further if his life had depended on it. They were just nurses. This one, however, was something else.

'Hello there, how are you?' said the vision of loveliness.

Raymond noticed the lilt of an Irish accent. *Nothing surprising about that*, he thought. *Lots of nurses come from Ireland*. But he couldn't take his eyes off her. He had long thought that no one could surpass Alison in looks. But here, standing right in front of him, perfectly proportioned and with the most beautiful face he had ever seen, was Alison's undoubted comparator. She smiled as she spoke revealing almost dazzling white teeth. Her red hair, cut short, which Raymond didn't usually like, framed her exquisite features. Her uniform seemed a little too big but it merely emphasised the perfection of the body that moved within it. And her hands! Raymond was transfixed by her hands. Long fingers with perfectly manicured nails. And what was more – no ring.

'Are you all right?' she asked oblivious to the effect she was having on him.

'Yes, you startled me, that's all. I think I was starting to nod off.' Raymond thought confessing the truth was the only option, at least until he started thinking straight. He tried to read her name on the identity badge secured to her belt but it was lopsided and he couldn't make it out.

'Well, I can't stand here all night talking – I've got a patient to see to.'

She opened the door into the patient area and busied herself, checking the monitor and reading from the papers on the clipboard. She leaned over the patient as if checking his breathing and Raymond could see the black strap of her bra as her uniform was pulled to the side when she stretched over the bed. He looked at his watch. It was 2.35 a.m. He must have nodded off. He watched through the glass panel as she moved to the other side of the bed, smiling at him as she did so. She then opened the door into the en suite and disappeared from his view. He heard a tap running. Raymond was beside himself. Was this what Sergeant Perry had meant? The chance of chatting up a really good-looking nurse? What should he do? Should he ask her name? She seemed friendly enough. Then the doubts set in. She was bound to have a boyfriend if not a husband – someone with her looks simply couldn't be available, could she? But there was no ring. Perhaps nurses take them off when working? But perhaps they didn't? Someone as good looking as her… His mind was racing. She reappeared, looked once more at the still sleeping patient, before coming back into the anteroom.

'Would you know, officer, what happened to the patient's clothes?' she asked.

Raymond was taken by surprise by her question. What did she want with his clothes? He had no idea. He assumed they would have been seized along with his wallet, if he had one, and everything else.

'I'm not really sure,' he replied. 'I expect they've been taken by the forensic boys. You know, to try and work out who he is.'

'You mean you don't know? Surely the car he was in would have given you a clue? And he must have had some documentation with him.'

Raymond was beginning to feel more than a little foolish. Of course, she was right. The reason there was no name over his bed or on the clipboard was because it had been decided by someone on high that he was to remain anonymous. And he knew that. Sergeant Perry had as good as told him. He ventured this as an explanation that would re-establish his standing in her eyes. And they were beautiful eyes. A delectable shade of green and sparkling like emeralds. He tried to assert himself, adopting a quiet but knowledgeable tone.

'We believe him to be a dangerous criminal and… and, eh… we don't think it appropriate that his identity should be made known, not at this stage of our enquiries.'

'Is that a fact, officer? Do you think we'll be safe with this *dangerous criminal* amongst us?'

Was she laughing at him? Raymond wasn't quite sure. But he had to keep the conversation going. He'd rehearsed several times what he would say if such an opportunity arose, but his mind had gone a complete blank. He had to say something.

'There's no need to panic.' Raymond's voice now acquired that reassuring timbre that he had learnt from experience in giving unwelcome news to members of the public. 'I'm afraid I don't know your name? I can't read it on your identity badge.'

'I'm Moira.'

'Oh, and I'm Ray.' Raymond thought his full name might not create the right impression. Most people called him Ray, except Eddie, Sergeant Perry and his mother. With them it was always Raymond.

'Well, we'll be safe I suppose while you're around to protect us.' She smiled. But this time Raymond detected no sarcasm at all. He grinned and drew his stomach in, anxious that she shouldn't leave. What was he to say next?

'You're not from round here I take it. That's an Irish accent, isn't it?'

'There's no fooling you, to be sure. I'm from Carrigaline. But I've been over here for quite some time.'

Raymond wished he'd paid more attention in geography lessons at school.

'Carriga…'

'Ay, a lovely place it is – just outside Cork.'

Now Raymond had heard of Cork. His grandfather on his mother's side was from County Cork.

'Is that a fact?' she replied when he disclosed this titbit of family history. 'Have you ever been there?'

Raymond replied in the negative. 'I've never been to Ireland… always wanted to go though.'

She tossed her head back in mock surprise. 'So you've never kissed the Blarney Stone?'

The tongue-tied Raymond wished he had. She stepped back a pace and looked him over.

'We might even be related. You never know. Nearly everyone in Ireland's related. We're all descended from kings, you know.' She smiled at him again.

He was sure they weren't but he loved the way she said "related". 'Do you live locally, then?' he asked. 'You can hardly commute from Cork.'

'Commute from Cork? Indeed, I do not – the very idea! It's bad enough getting here from Brigg.' She smiled that smile again. 'But I don't give out personal information to just anyone, you know. We are advised about such things. It wouldn't be safe what with all these *dangerous criminals* about the place.'

She stepped closer to him. He could smell her skin and he felt her warm breath on him.

'What's that you're reading?' she asked.

'A detective novel,' he replied. 'It's the original Inspector Frost novel, you know, by R. D. Wingfield. I've read some of the others but never been able to get hold of his first one.' His eyes turned down for a moment and he smiled, sheepishly. 'A birthday present from my mother.'

He handed her the book. She took it from him and glanced at the cover as she walked around the anteroom then placed it back on the table.

'I like detective stories too,' she said, looking directly at him.

She almost giggled. Raymond was growing in confidence. They had something in common – apart from their Irish ancestry. She turned and looked for a second towards the patient.

'I shouldn't really ask,' she said, 'but we've all been wondering what this fellow's supposed to have done. He must be a really *desperate criminal* if he has to be guarded by a big, strong policeman like you.'

Raymond found himself unable to resist telling her everything he knew spiced up with a few things he didn't.

'I shouldn't really be telling you this.' He lowered his voice and beckoned her away from the open internal door. She stood next to him again, still smiling. 'We reckon he's a major criminal from the Midlands whose involved with that big robbery that took place near Nottingham just before Christmas; you know, the one where the guard was shot. You must have read about it?'

'I never read the papers. It's *so* depressing. What makes you think he was involved?'

Raymond leaned forward so that his face was only inches from hers. He was now whispering. 'Because he had a suitcase full of cash in the back of his car. It burst open in the crash. CID reckons it came from the robbery. Apparently, Mid-Shires Police have been after him for years, but they've never been able to get anything on him. But it looks as if he's for it this time.'

'Is that so? Where's the money now?' She was whispering too.

'Oh, it'll be with forensics. They'll be looking for fingerprints and DNA. They'll be checking the serial numbers too. There should be a record somewhere of what was stolen.'

'Is that a fact?' She looked impressed. 'And you're working on the case are you?' Her green eyes seemed to be growing larger as she stared straight into Raymond's face.

'Oh, yes,' he said. 'That's why I'm here. In case he comes round and says something that may give him away or at least give us a lead.'

'How fascinating! You have a really interesting job, don't you?'

Do I? thought Raymond. He was almost in a trance but the spell was broken by a second and louder alarm coming from the stack of monitors by the patient's bed.

'What's that?' he asked.

'It's nothing. The stats probe will have come off. He's probably starting to come out of his coma. Hang on a minute.'

She rushed into the patient's room and adjusted the probe on his finger. She then reset one of the monitors. The patient seemed to have moved his position slightly but continued in what Raymond supposed was a coma.

Please, God, he said to himself. *Don't let him come round, not yet*.

She picked up the clipboard and appeared to write something on the notes, then returned to Raymond.

'Is he coming round?' he asked. That would be just his luck when he fancied he was getting somewhere with Moira.

'I don't think so. He'll not be fully awake for a while yet. Now, where were we? I find this *really i*nteresting.'

Thank you, God, thought Raymond. *Keep him under for a bit longer*.

She sat down on the hard-backed chair and indicated to Raymond to sit. He didn't need a second invitation. 'So, have you caught any of the others? Was it a big gang? Did they have guns? How much did they get away with?' The questions were coming thick and fast. She seemed to be looking at Raymond with increasing intensity. Anxious though he was that the conversation should continue, he really didn't know anything else. Well, not anything he should reveal. He played for time.

'Well, it's very early days and we won't know much more until he talks or forensics come up with something positive.'

He had learnt a long time ago with police work that mentioning "forensics" to members of the public was an excellent way of covering up for a complete absence of evidence. There was always a chance with the scientists that something might turn up. She giggled with excitement, raising her feet on to the chair and placing her hands around her legs. Raymond's attention strayed from her face to those legs, encased as they were in black nylons. He wondered whether she wore tights or stockings and suspenders.

'But supposing he doesn't talk?'

Raymond put on what he thought was his *macho* look.

'He'll talk – they always do in the end.' He knew this wasn't true. He'd had limited experience of the hard men of Hull but he knew that real villains usually never say anything to the police, not on the record anyway. Interviewing them was usually a complete waste of time. Then he added something he shouldn't have mentioned that he'd seen on the updated crime report.

'One of the guards – the one who got shot – had a go at one of the robbers and punched him in the face. It must have been a pretty powerful blow 'cos it made the robber's nose bleed. I reckon we'll be able to get a DNA match from the crime scene. If it matches him in there he'll go down like a stone. I reckon he'll get at least fifteen years, maybe more if the guard doesn't pull through.'

'Really?' She was no longer smiling. 'As much as that?'

'Well,' said Raymond, warming to his task, 'if the guard dies it'll be charged as murder and then it'll be life!'

'But there's not much chance of that, is there?'

'Too early to say, but I did hear he's out of intensive care now.'

'Well, that's good,' she said. 'The poor man was only doing his job.' She paused and looked away then turned to Raymond. 'But what if it doesn't match? What if he wasn't even there?'

'I'm no lawyer, but whether he was there or not, if he's involved in any way, he'll be for it.'

Raymond noticed something of a change in her. She was no longer smiling. She looked away from him again. Had he frightened her or what? He sometimes forgot that people could be a bit squeamish about serious crime. Reading about it in the newspapers was one thing, hearing about it directly quite another. Then she spied the sandwich packet and the empty Pepsi bottle, still on the floor where Eddie had left them. Her manner towards him changed abruptly.

'Are *you* responsible for that?' She took her arms from her legs and her feet from the chair and stood up pointing to the offending items.

'Not me – it was the officer who was here before me.' Raymond got to his feet, the embarrassment and awkwardness returning. How he wished Eddie had taken his rubbish with him.

'I don't care who left it there.' The almost hectoring tone was noticeably different. 'It's unhygienic. This is a hospital, you know, not the police canteen. Come on now. Get rid of them. There's a bin down the corridor.'

'But I can't leave the room. It's more than my job's worth.' Raymond realised how pathetic he must have sounded.

'Stuff and nonsense! Your man in there is going nowhere and I'll wait here until you get back – as long as you're quick about it.'

She took Raymond by the shoulders after he'd bent down to pick up the litter and guided him towards the external door. 'Down the corridor, you say?'

'That's right. To the left and down near the lifts.' Raymond was about to open the door but he paused, took a couple of steps back and picked up his utility belt and put it round his waist. 'I can't leave this lying about.'

She was smiling again and opened the door for him. 'Now don't be too long, I've lots of other patients to see to.' Her voice had softened and she was looking him directly in the face again. He thought for a moment she was going to kiss him. He lingered for a moment on the off chance that she might. But she didn't.

'I shan't be a minute.'

She closed the door behind him. Raymond hurried down the corridor. *She definitely said to the left*, he thought to himself but when he got to the end of the corridor there was no sign of the lifts. The lighting was dimmed and there was no one about to ask. He looked above him at the mass of information hanging from the ceiling. Eventually he noticed a blue arrow with the word "Lifts" next to it. He went in the direction indicated, along the corridor and round the next corner. He picked up speed and arrived in a better lit area with several routes marked in different colour codes. The sign for the lifts seemed to have disappeared. Neither could he see any waste bins. Just then, a nursing auxiliary appeared. She was short, fat and unattractive.

'Are you lost, love?' she asked in the way women of a certain age address men they regard as hopelessly impractical. It reminded him of how his mother spoke to his late father.

'I suppose I am – a bit. I'm looking for a waste bin.'

The auxiliary noticed the rubbish in his hands. 'Give it to me,' she said, in a weary tone, 'I'll get rid of it for you.'

'Thanks very much.' Raymond handed the debris over and turned to retrace his steps, desperately trying to remember the route back. This place really was a labyrinth. All the corridors looked the same. He didn't notice the auxiliary shaking her head as she walked off in the opposite direction. But he wouldn't have cared. He wanted to get back to the pretty nurse. He was making progress with her and she was obviously impressed with him – or so he thought. There was a rare bounce in his step as he rushed back towards room 401D. 'Bugger,' he said to himself as he reached another junction of corridors. 'I don't remember this.' He turned round and rushed back in the direction he had come. He tried again, and this time his luck was in. He found the right corridor and then the room and opened the door. But anticipation immediately turned to despair. She was gone. He checked the patient's room. The heavy breathing, the ping of the monitor – everything was the same as before. But Moira was gone. 'Bugger,' he repeated. 'You've done it again, Raymond. You've cocked it up. She's got fed up of waiting.' He flopped down in the chair and sighed. He looked at his watch. Just over three minutes had passed. Perhaps she wasn't that keen on him after all? Still, he'd soon find out who she was. He knew she lived in Brigg and Brigg wasn't that big a place. *Should be a piece of cake to find her* he thought to himself. He'd found several missing persons in his time and this investigation would be a real pleasure. *And you never know she might come back before my shift is over*. He settled down in the chair, picked up his novel and started to read. 'Yes,' he said to himself almost audibly, 'I shan't let this one get away.'

★★★★

It was almost half past three when the door opened again. This time Raymond was awake and alert. He was on his feet in an instant hoping that Moira would appear. It was not to be. A male nurse walked in.

'Fancy a cuppa?' he asked.' I brought an extra one just in case.' He placed a plastic tray on the table with two paper cups containing some undefined tepid liquid.

'Is Moira still about?' asked Raymond, casually, as he took one of the drinks from the tray. He hoped he didn't sound as if he was trying too hard to seem disinterested.

'Moira? Moira who?' replied the male nurse. 'I don't know any nurses called Moira. What's the rest of her name?'

It suddenly dawned on Raymond that he didn't know her surname. He looked the nurse over. He reckoned they were about the same age and, so far as he could judge, he thought him heterosexual.

'I don't know, but you'd remember this one,' said Raymond. 'She's an absolute cracker.'

'It's not ringing any bells at the moment. Mind you, it's a big hospital, and I can't say I know all the nurses but if she's as gorgeous as you say, it would have got round. There's not many here who fall into that category.'

He smiled then took a sip from his cup. 'Of course, she might be one of the irregulars.'

'One of the irregulars?' queried Raymond. 'What's that mean?'

'An agency nurse; you know, a part-timer who's called in when we're short-staffed. And are we short-staffed at the moment – what with all this flu about!'

'But there'll be a record of her somewhere, won't there?'

'I suppose there will be, eventually, but there's a lot of staff off in administration at the moment. The flu, you know. And some of the agency nurses only come here once or twice. They work all over the place.' He paused. 'Why do you want to trace her? She's not in trouble or anything?'

'Nothing like that,' said Raymond. 'I just want to contact her, that's all.'

The male nurse nodded. He looked at Raymond knowingly and spoke slowly.

'Of course, a lot of these part-timers are married, you know, or single mums. That's why they don't work full-time.'

'Really?' said Raymond. A picture of Moira, child in arms, popped into his head. He took a sip of the unidentifiable liquid and screwed up his face. It tasted terrible.

'Why all the interest in John Doe?' asked the nurse, changing the subject and nodding towards the still sleeping patient. 'We don't usually have police officers guarding our road accident victims? And another thing, what's with all the secrecy? Why's his name not been disclosed?'

Raymond decided to be mysterious. After all, this wasn't Moira. 'I'm not at liberty to say,' His tone suggested that further enquiry would be a waste of time. The nurse took the hint.

'Well, I'd better go and check on him, I suppose.' He put his cardboard cup back on the tray and went about his duties. Raymond remained seated. He wasn't interested in what was happening next door; he was still thinking about Moira. How was he going to find her? If she didn't usually work here and he didn't know her surname she might be more difficult to trace than he first thought. Then the alarm went off again and the nurse called out. 'I think he's coming round – I do believe he is.' Raymond heard a snorting sound then the nurse spoke. 'It's all right mate. You're in hospital; you're going to be OK.'

Raymond looked through the glass panel, unclipped his personal radio and walked into the corridor. It was time to call in. 'He's coming round. You'd better tell the DI. I know he's off duty but he wanted to know as soon as… well that's up to you. I'm staying here until I'm relieved.'

Raymond was perfectly happy to stay at the hospital for as long as it took. He was fast losing interest in the unnamed villain next door. His enquiries would concentrate on finding Moira. That would be his priority as soon as he went off duty.

★★★★

Raymond went straight home when his shift finished. His mother had prepared him a cooked breakfast but he picked at it; he was still thinking of Moira.

'That's not like you, Raymond,' said his mother. 'Aren't you hungry love?'

'No,' he replied. 'I just don't fancy it this morning. I think I'll pop upstairs and get some sleep. I'm back on duty at four thirty.'

'That reminds me,' said his mother. 'A letter came for you this morning. Looks very official.'

She handed Raymond the envelope. He noticed the words "Mid-Shires Constabulary" next to the postmark.

'Oh, it's nothing,' he said, 'I'll read it later.'

Raymond ran up the stairs into his room and threw himself on the bed. He tore the envelope open and unfolded the letter inside. 'Yes!' he said to himself. 'At last!' The letter informed him that if he were still interested in a move to Mid-Shires as a detective constable, he was to attend a board on 11 January in Leicester. A telephone number was given for him to ring to confirm his attendance.

His mother called from downstairs.

'I'm just popping next door, love, to see if Mrs Middleton wants anything from the supermarket. Won't be long.'

This was Raymond's chance. He waited until he heard the door slam and rushed down the stairs to the hall telephone. A few minutes later he had confirmed his attendance for the eleventh at 2.00 p.m. He was too excited to sleep but he resolved he would not tell his mother anything until he knew for sure that he was on the move. And he wasn't going to tell Eddie either. If he said anything to Eddie it would be all round the station in no time. Then his mother would find out. No point worrying her, yet. It might still come to nothing. An hour later, as he tried to get some sleep, he suddenly realised he hadn't thought of Moira once since he opened the envelope.

CHAPTER THIRTEEN

Hood and Wendy Knight travelled towards Hull through some pretty atrocious weather. The rain was hammering down and Hood was eventually forced to stop at a roadside cafe, a few miles short of their destination. He had delayed his visit to the east coast by several days in order to give Doyle more time to recover. He had despatched DC Eccles and a uniformed officer to collect the cash seized from Doyle's car shortly after the call from Crawford. A blood sample was also collected and taken immediately to the forensic science laboratory where it was undergoing DNA profiling. Hood was banking on a match that would rapidly resolve the issue of Doyle's participation in the robbery. Coffee was ordered and he and Knight sat at a table next to the window. The break gave them time to review progress and plan their strategy when they spoke to Doyle.

'Of course, the fact that he had the money in his possession doesn't necessarily mean he took part in the robbery, does it?' said Knight. 'He could simply have been laundering part of the proceeds.'

'True,' replied Hood. 'But we don't need to place him at the scene. I shall be suggesting a charge of conspiracy – always assuming we can prove the money came from the robbery.'

'There's bound to be at least some of the new notes in there, isn't there? According to King, it would have been virtually impossible to distinguish the old notes from the new. And no one's going to get rid of three hundred thousand pounds just because the notes might be traceable.'

Hood was not so sure. 'Possibly... but the serial numbers would have been in consecutive order on the new notes and Doyle's a clever one. It wouldn't surprise me at all if he'd noticed the difference and saddled someone else with those notes. Let's hope that his natural greed does for him. We'll just have to wait and see.' Hood took a sip of his coffee and grimaced. 'I don't think much of this,' he said. 'But at least it's hot.'

Wendy Knight smiled. 'Any further news on the DNA?' she asked.

'That's the really good bit,' replied Hood. 'They've got a full profile and the blood is definitely not from the guard – initial grouping tests showed that. It's just a matter of obtaining a match. Doyle is not on the database but Crawford got a sample of his blood while he was still unconscious – one of the nurses was highly co-operative. If our luck holds and the scientists come up with a match it'll be game over for Michael Doyle.'

'When will we know?'

'His sample only arrived a few days ago – so it will be a while yet – unless it's fast tracked as the ACC promised. As I said, he's not on the DNA database but thanks to the nurse there should be no problem checking his profile.'

'Always providing it's his blood.'

'Obviously. Let's hope our luck holds.'

'What about the alibi his girlfriend's told us about? The checks we've done at the hotel support what she says. Doyle arrived there during the early afternoon of the sixteenth. The head waiter remembers him very well – he ordered a very expensive bottle of wine at dinner – Chateau Margaux '77. They only had two bottles of it in stock and he reserved the other one for Christmas day. It has the ring of truth about it.'

'Forgive my cynicism, but does it not also suggest that he wanted the waiter to remember he was in the dining room that night? His girlfriend didn't get down there until the nineteenth. Why didn't he wait for her before splashing out nearly two hundred pounds on a bottle of chateaux bottled claret? My wife would have my guts for garters if I'd done that in her absence.'

Knight pictured in her own mind a confrontation between her boss and his wife over such a trifle. Somehow, she just couldn't quite see it. Mind you, she'd have been pretty annoyed if Greg had done such a thing – in her absence. She continued to adumbrate the problems, as she saw them, with Hood's theory.

'But he had breakfast in his room the next morning. The waitress remembers it well. He gave her a big enough tip.'

'Exactly. That's my point. He gave her a ridiculously large tip to make sure she remembered him.'

'But sir, it's over 200 miles from the Charnwood to this hotel. If he were simply wanting to produce a false alibi, why not book into a hotel in

Leicestershire? He would create the same problems for us, but at much less inconvenience to himself.'

'He was thinking well ahead and covering all his bases –which is exactly what you would expect with Doyle. There's nothing more impressive to a jury than a seemingly cast-iron alibi. The further away he puts himself, the more impressive it looks. And we mustn't lose sight of the fact that if he organised this job, it wouldn't be necessary for him to have been there anyway. After all, that's his usual modus operandi, isn't it? He keeps himself well away from the action. And another thing, Doyle is a planner, not an innovator. If we can shake him up a bit, he might just say something that gives him away.'

'I suppose so. But it would be so much more damning if we could put him in that compound. As things stand, we haven't really got anything to show he was involved with the planning.'

Hood sighed. 'I suppose you're right. But, if the DNA comes up trumps it won't matter if he has a hundred alibis. He'll be dead in the water.'

Hood took another sip of his coffee. 'The real question is whether we wait for the results before we interview him or we get on with it, always assuming he's willing to speak to us.'

Wendy Knight frowned as she stirred her espresso. 'I did have a thought about that, sir. Might it not be better to get one of the Hull officers to interview him about the accident first, without letting on we know about the money. He's more likely to give something away if he is lulled into a false sense of security. I know if I were him, I'd be thinking about the money more than the accident – once I realised I was OK. If that's what's on his mind he might well let something slip.'

Hood remained silent for a few moments and took another sip of his coffee. The taste was less offensive than before as he considered Knight's suggestion. 'Do you know, Wendy, I think you might be on to something there. I'll certainly give that some thought; softly, softly, catchy monkey, eh?'

'Exactly, sir. Andrew Hooper reckons he'll say nothing anyway but if we don't let on we know about the money and he's only interviewed about the accident, we might get something out of him, especially if we use a traffic officer to ask the questions.'

Hood winced at that suggestion. 'That might be a bit risky. The traffic boys are not the sharpest knives in the box. It could go badly wrong. If we did get something out of him, we might not be able to use it. You know how hot the CPS is on breaches of procedure these days.'

'There must be at least one bright copper in Hull, sir.'

He laughed. 'I hope so, I really do.'

Hood finished his coffee and stood up. He noticed that the rain was easing off and pointed through the window to his car.

'Let's get on,' he said. 'You drive and I'll ring Jack Crawford. If we go with your suggestion, he should be able to recommend a suitable uniformed officer to question Doyle about the accident. We can always put a traffic officer in with him to add a bit of authenticity.'

CHAPTER FOURTEEN

Michael Doyle sat in his chair, his left leg outstretched and resting on a stool. He was wearing a hospital-issue dressing gown. The below knee fracture was fixed with plaster but with a modicum of effort and the aid of a walking frame he was able to get about with minimal assistance. His ribs were still sore but his headaches had subsided. His memory of events, however, remained very hazy. He was also desperate for a cigarette but would have to manoeuvre himself outside if he wanted a smoke and thus far the effort required had proved too much. He put down his copy of the *Daily Mail* and looked around him. He had now been conscious for several days and was beginning to wonder why he had not been transferred to an ordinary ward. "Bed blockage," he'd been told by a doctor. "You're lucky you're not on a trolley in a corridor. I'd be very grateful if I were you." He had noted the glass panel in the wall of his room and the anteroom beyond. He'd also observed on a couple of occasions the presence of a uniformed police officer. He'd asked one of the nurses why they were there but she had dismissed his concerns.

'They'll want to talk to you about the accident, that's all. You could have been killed from what I've heard. I hope you're well insured and have got a good solicitor.'

He had already asked about his clothes which had been in a separate bag in the rear of the car next to the suitcase containing the cash. But what was really on his mind was the money. He could remember that all right but many other details were still not in place. The knock on his head had certainly affected his recollection. Had the police seized the case containing the money? He simply didn't know. If they were treating this as a road accident caused by the bad weather, the suitcase should still be securely locked in the back of his hired Mercedes and it would simply be a question of getting hold of it before they did. On the other hand, if the police had opened his suitcase and discovered the cash they'd be looking to question him about it. They were bound to link it with the robbery. He needed to see Jules. He needed to know what they knew. He also needed to get in touch with Trevor Parker, his solicitor of long standing.

'Has anyone heard from my girlfriend yet?' he'd asked the nurse. 'Surely she must know about the smash by now?'

'You can phone her yourself,' he was told, 'now that you're out of danger. I can get the phone trolley to you if you like.'

He did like but he was still waiting. Then the waiting was over. He'd just finished what passed in the hospital for a cheese omelette and salad when two uniformed police officers walked into his room. One of them was holding a clipboard.

'Hello, there Mr Doyle. I'm PC Raymond Craddock and this is PC Rogers.'

The officer with the clipboard nodded.

'We'd like to ask you a few questions about the accident, if you're feeling up to it. We realise you were knocked about a bit, so if you'd rather, we could come back later.'

Raymond deliberately adopted a casual attitude, as if he were just going through the motions. He didn't want to put Doyle on his guard. But Doyle didn't answer. Did this mean the police had not discovered the money? Was the nurse right when she said they only wanted to talk to him about the accident? These two were ordinary PCs – not detectives. If they'd found the money they'd have had a senior officer to question him. He decided to play for time.

'I can't really remember much about it, to tell you the truth,' he said, putting his hand to his head. 'I was knocked out and the doc reckons I'm suffering from amnesia. The last thing I can remember is driving in to Hull in that appalling weather – then everything else is a blank.'

'Well, I can understand that,' said Raymond. 'Do you think you could tell us about the vehicle? We understand it was a hired car.' Raymond rushed through the words of the caution before continuing.

Doyle paused before answering. He didn't like the fact he'd been cautioned. 'What's the caution for?' he asked. 'I haven't done anything to be cautioned for.'

'Just following the rules, sir,' replied Raymond. 'You know, in case there's a charge arising out of your driving.'

Doyle grunted his reply. 'I see.' He was trying to think. As he'd been cautioned he could choose to say nothing. On the other hand, he wouldn't find out about the money unless he discussed matters with the police. Eventually, he spoke. 'What do you want to know?'

'Well,' said Raymond, 'I suppose we should start with the car. We understand it was hired? The traffic department has already checked the registration details and insurance.'

Why are you asking me then? thought Doyle. But he couldn't see any harm in confirming what the police already knew. 'That's right. I hired it before the new year from a firm in Leicester. I hire lots of cars from them. Everything's above board and the insurance will sort out any damage. All the paperwork should be in the glove compartment. Do you know where the car is now?'

'It's still at the recovery yard, as far as I know,' replied Raymond. 'We've informed the owners. I suppose it's up to them to decide where it should go to be repaired, always assuming it isn't written off.'

'Was it very badly damaged then?' asked Doyle

'I haven't seen it myself,' replied Raymond, 'but John Rogers here attended the scene and got the ambulance to you.'

Rogers gave a description of what he had seen, refreshing his memory from his original note. 'The front nearside and the whole of the nearside passenger door area are pretty badly damaged. It looks as if the car must have spun after the initial impact because there's quite a lot of damage to the rear off-side and the back end.' He looked up from his notes. 'In fact the door at the back – you know, the hatchback – burst open, so I reckon you must have hit something pretty hard. Oh, and two of the tyres are deflated.' He looked again at his notes then faced Doyle. 'It might have been a burst tyre that caused the accident for all we know. I reckon it's probably a write-off, which takes some doing with a Mercedes estate. You also demolished a lamp post and almost went through a metal barrier on the side of the road.' He smiled. 'You must have been going some speed.'

Doyle looked impassively at both officers. 'As I said, I really can't remember. All I do recall is that it was absolutely pissing down when I came into Hull.'

'Not exactly unusual in these parts. Where were you heading?' asked Raymond.

Doyle realised the police must have seen the ferry ticket and his passport. He'd found his wallet in the bedside locker after he'd regained consciousness but it was pretty obvious that someone had gone through it.

His passport was there too but not the keys to the car. So there was no point concealing where he was going.

'I was booked on the overnight ferry to Rotterdam. Obviously, I never made it. If I was driving a bit on the fast side it was because I'd been held up by an accident on the M18. I was stuck there for over an hour. I do remember that.'

He decided to bite the bullet and ask about his luggage. 'Have you recovered my bags from the car? I could really do with some of my things. As you can see, I'm desperately in need of a shave for starters.' Doyle brushed the growth on his face.

'We've got a bag with us. It's outside with one of the nurses. I don't see why you shouldn't have it.'

Raymond walked to the door and stepped briefly out of the room. Doyle's confidence rose. Perhaps they hadn't found the money? But his hopes were dashed as Craddock returned carrying a soft fold-over leather bag and placed it in front of him.

'This is it, I think.'

'That's one of them,' said Doyle. 'There should be a suitcase as well.'

'I haven't seen a suitcase,' said Raymond, quite truthfully. 'Can you describe it?'

Doyle started to show signs of stress. His immediate thought was that the case containing the money had been jettisoned in the collision or, worse, someone had stolen it. Perhaps one of the recovery people. You couldn't trust anyone these days. He tried as best he could to hide his concern.

'As far as I can recall it was a red hard suitcase – not like this one – about two and half feet by two feet with wheels. There was a strap around it; I think a brown leather strap with my initials on it. It was in the back.'

'Anything valuable in it, sir?' asked Raymond, casually.

'Do you know,' replied Doyle, 'I really can't remember. But I would like it back.'

'Have you seen a red suitcase, John?' asked Raymond.

'I didn't check the luggage area,' replied Rogers. 'I was more concerned about getting him to hospital.' He grinned at Doyle. 'You looked in a bad way, sir.'

'Where did you get this from?' asked Doyle, indicating the soft fold-over bag.

'From the recovery people. They removed everything from the car or so we assume. We haven't searched it, not yet anyway. We got the vehicle documents from them too. As I said, we concentrated on getting you to hospital. I don't mind telling you, I thought you were a goner.'

'Well, I'm very grateful but all the same I would like all my property back, if you don't mind.'

Doyle had half convinced himself that the suitcase with the cash must have been stolen by the recovery people – or these two coppers were playing mind games with him. His initial anger subsided when he realised if it had been stolen, there would be nothing to tie him to the robbery. And he knew exactly how to get it back. Even if he could do nothing in his present condition, he knew a man who could.

'Perhaps I'm mistaken then,' he said. 'Perhaps I didn't have another case with me after all. My memory could be playing tricks with me.'

Raymond smiled as Rogers made a note of Doyle's description of the suitcase on the report form. 'If you'd just sign this, sir. I'll see what I can do.' He offered the clipboard to Doyle who declined to take it.

'Is that really necessary,' he asked. 'I don't like signing things without checking what it is I'm signing, and to tell you the truth, I'm feeling pretty groggy again. And I don't want to make a claim for another bag if I'm wrong about it.' He paused and felt his head. 'I think I need to get back to bed. Could you ask the nurse to come in? I can't manage to get into bed without assistance.'

Raymond looked at Rogers. 'That's OK, sir. We'll leave it at that for now. If you're feeling better tomorrow, I'll get someone to pop in and we'll see if we can locate your other bag – if there is one.'

'You do that,' said Doyle, 'and another thing, I need to phone my solicitor. I take it you have no problems with that.'

Raymond could not help noticing that Doyle was showing very real signs of stress. Beads of sweat had appeared on his forehead and he was moving about in obvious discomfort on his chair. He leant forward and rubbed his raised leg. He was clearly concerned about his red suitcase, thought Raymond, or perhaps he really was feeling bad again. Rogers returned to the question of the accident.

'We're still trying to work out what happened when you crashed the car, sir. There's no decision been made yet about any charges in relation to the accident. You never know, it might all come to nothing. But if you want to speak to a solicitor, you go ahead and do so. That is your right.'

Doyle said nothing. He didn't believe what he'd been told. If there were no charges contemplated, why had he been cautioned? He decided to remain silent. There was a lengthy pause. No one said anything. It was clear to Raymond that the conversation was over. He decided to leave. Doyle sat back in his chair. His eyes followed the two police officers as they walked towards the door.

'Just a minute,' he said. 'Has anyone told my partner about the accident?'

Raymond turned and faced him. 'If you give us the details, I'll see to it personally.'

Doyle frowned. His leg was causing him pain and he was beginning to get angry again about the money. It must have been stolen. Those thieving recovery people. They'd nick anything. The reaction of the two police officers admitted of no other conclusion. It took an immense effort on his part to appear unconcerned.

'No, never mind. I'll give her a ring myself – if they ever bring the phone trolley to me.'

'Very good, sir. We'll leave you in peace.'

Raymond walked through the anteroom and along the corridor. Rogers followed him. Another uniformed officer was standing outside an administrator's office in the adjacent corridor. Raymond knocked on the door and he and Rogers walked in. Sitting at a table, eager to hear his report, were Inspector Crawford, Chief Inspector Hood and DC Knight. Hood stood up as they entered.

'Well done,' said Crawford, after Raymond recounted what had occurred. 'He's as good as admitted the suitcase is his. Over to you, I think, Harry.'

'He's also about to telephone his partner,' added Raymond. 'He's just waiting for the phone trolley to arrive.'

'We'd better make sure it doesn't – at least for the time being.' Hood turned and spoke to Crawford. 'Can I leave you to deal with that, Jack?'

'No problem,' replied Crawford. 'They're always in demand by patients. I'll make sure he's well down the list. And he hasn't got a mobile with him, not that he'd be allowed to use it if he had.'

'Good. I don't want him knowing we've already turned over his flat and his office. Not before we've had the chance to speak to him.'

'That means we can't put it off much longer, sir,' said Knight. 'His girlfriend knows we're on to him. It's only a question of time before he finds out from her.'

'I agree. First thing tomorrow – and we'll have to get him a solicitor if he wants one. We don't want any difficulties down the line. I've spoken to

Andrea Fleming at the CPS. We will run admissibility risks if we interview him under caution outside a police station. This will have to be treated as a voluntary interview not under caution and will have to be restricted to any explanation he may wish to give for his possession of the money. Anything else will have to wait. Has anyone spoken with the medics about when he'll be fit to be discharged?'

Crawford answered. 'Not for another three days. That's what I was told. The medics have been very decent with us so far. They have not told him of our interest in him apart from the road accident.'

Hood looked concerned.

'That isn't going to last much longer. He's no fool and the longer we keep Julia Hamilton away from him, the sooner he'll cotton on. It's only a matter of time before she gets here and there's nothing we can do to stop him seeing her – not unless we arrest him – and I'm loath to do that before we hear from the scientists. Hopefully we'll have something by tomorrow morning. And another thing, could I ask you to remove the uniformed officers who have been keeping an eye on him? Now that he's on the mend and has been spoken to by young Craddock here he'll become suspicious if he sees uniformed officers hanging about. A plain-clothes officer would be less obtrusive and he should keep to the corridor rather than the anteroom.'

'That shouldn't be a problem,' said Crawford. 'I'll arrange it straight away.'

'Thanks, Jack. You've been very helpful. I shan't forget it. It won't be for long. We're going to have to move on this pretty quickly, do you agree Wendy?'

'Seems like we have no choice, sir,' said Knight. 'Tomorrow it will have to be.'

★★★★

Hood spent a disturbed night in his Travelodge bed. His room was comfortable enough and the cost well within his allowance but he simply couldn't sleep. He was constantly turning over in his mind how the interview was likely to proceed the following morning. He had considered every possible avenue of approach and Doyle's likely response. His alarm sounded at six forty-five and after a shave and a shower, he met up with Knight at a nearby cafe for breakfast. He treated himself to a full English – something he rarely got at home from his diet-conscious wife. Knight restricted herself to fruit juice, coffee and toast. She was buttering her second slice when her mobile phone rang. It was Hooper. He'd heard from the lab. The news was not good. She passed her phone over to Hood.

'No match with Doyle? Damn. Who? Who's he? Do we know anything about him?'

Hood paused and listened. 'I see. Yes. Well keep them at it. Let me know as soon as anything comes up. Cheers.'

Hood sighed as he handed the phone back.

'The blood is definitely not Doyle's. They pulled everything out to get a quick result and it's not his. Belongs to someone called Charles Anthony Benson, whoever he is. No previous and lives in Birmingham. No connection with Doyle at all, so far as we know.'

He returned to his breakfast briefly then put down his knife and fork and pushed the plate away. Knight was only too aware of his frustration.

'That's not what we wanted to hear, is it sir?'

'It certainly isn't.'

'What about the money?'

'They're still working on that. Nothing so far. They're only testing a small percentage of the notes taken at random. Obviously they can't test them all.'

'But surely we can check them against the serial numbers of the new notes – every one of them?' said Knight.

'Of course,' replied Hood, 'but that's a matter for us – the scientists are just testing for fingerprints and DNA. Examining every note against the serial numbers will be a very long job. I was hoping to short-circuit that by finding a forensic link between some of the notes and the stolen money. I suppose it was always a bit of a long shot but the difficulty is, as things stand, we can't prove that the money in Doyle's suitcase came from the robbery. I don't think we have enough to arrest him.'

Hood sat back in his chair and sighed. Knight tried to humour him. 'I don't know, sir. Isn't it a bit of a coincidence? A robbery takes place in which nearly 2 million is stolen – all in twenties and tens and Doyle just happens to have several hundred thousand – also in twenties and tens, which he is taking out of the country? And he's travelled from the very area where the robbery occurred.'

'I agree. I don't think it's just a coincidence either but I doubt if it would be enough to hold him. As you've already pointed out, if Doyle said he was merely laundering the money and had nothing to do with the robbery we'd be hard pressed to prove him wrong without a definite link to events in the compound. At the moment we can't even prove for sure that the money came from the robbery.'

'Is it wise for us to interview him then?'

'That's exactly what I've been thinking.' Hood paused and stroked his chin. 'Probably not. I think we're going to have to call on those two Hull officers again. We don't want to reveal our interest unless and until we have enough to arrest him.' He picked up his coffee cup and took a sip. 'One of them seemed pretty switched on, didn't he? What was his name? Craddock?'

'Yes, sir. Raymond Craddock. Quite good-looking, too.'

Hood half smiled. 'Jack Crawford tells me young Craddock's put in to transfer to Mid-Shires. Wants to be a detective apparently. He certainly looks promising.'

'I've come across worse.'

Knight stirred her coffee as if deep in thought. 'This DNA match, sir?'

'Yes, what of it?'

'If this man Benson has no record, how can they be so sure of the match? What have they compared it with?'

'He's on the database. Apparently, he volunteered a sample in a big exclusion exercise in the West Midlands some time ago and his profile was never removed. It's quite different from Doyle's. There's no possibility of a mistake.'

'And no way of linking him to Doyle?'

'Not at the moment. Birmingham have been asked to pick him up. We'll have to take it from there, always assuming they can find him. I wouldn't mind betting that he's out of the country. Andrew's alerted ports and airports but I suspect he'll be long gone by now.'

'It would be interesting to see Doyle's reaction if we asked him about Benson.' Knight smiled at her own suggestion.

'Interesting but too risky. We don't want to blunder in without knowing a great deal more about Mr Benson.'

Knight pushed her cup aside. 'Lucky he was on the database, sir?'

'That's certainly true. But we needed a bit of luck. We've not had much so far. And it won't do us much good if we can't trace Benson.'

'But we can't really leave interviewing Doyle any longer, can we sir? I thought we agreed yesterday, his girlfriend's bound to be in touch soon and he'll know we've searched his flat then. So he's bound to realise we're on to him.'

'I know that Wendy, but we're better off doing nothing for the moment. Better to let him speculate about what we might know rather than proving we have insufficient evidence even to arrest him.'

'What do you propose, then?'

'Nothing.'

'We do nothing?'

'Exactly. In fact, I don't think we want to see Doyle at all. I think we'll have to leave it to Humberside for now. Come on, drink up. We need to see Jack Crawford.'

CHAPTER FIFTEEN

Raymond Craddock was feeling very pleased with himself. He'd been praised by Inspector Crawford for his questioning of Doyle and in front of a DCI from Mid-Shires! And, what was more, only a couple of days before his interview to consider his application to transfer to Mid-Shires. What a stroke of luck! And here he was on his way back to the hospital because Inspector Crawford had informed him the DCI wanted him to speak to Doyle again. This time he was to ask him specifically about the red suitcase and the money. It was his opportunity to impress Hood. Sergeant Perry had advised him to take it steady and avoid a confrontational approach. "This is not the time for the third degree," he had told Raymond. "Don't suggest anything to him. Just make it clear you want to know where the money came from, that's all." That seemed reasonable enough to Raymond. Doyle would be expecting such a question once he realised the police had seen the money. He would be suspicious if he wasn't asked about it.

Raymond headed for the same office at the hospital as before. Inspector Craddock wasn't going to be there this time, just the DCI from Mid-Shires and that attractive detective constable. If she was an example of the girls in the East Midlands, he couldn't wait to get there. Crawford had also advised him as to his approach. "Forget about your application for a transfer," he had warned. "You're not there to impress the DCI but to deal with a specific query. Don't get carried away." He waited for the lift to the fourth floor thinking about Wendy Knight. He wouldn't have minded being carried away with her. The lift doors opened and there, standing right in front of him, was Moira. The attractive detective constable went straight out of his head.

'Moira,' he enthused. 'How nice to see you again. What happened to you the other night? You'd gone when I got back.'

Moira smiled but looked distracted.

‘I was called to another patient,’ she said. She was civil but showed no interest in continuing the conversation. Raymond allowed the lift to go. He wasn’t going to let this opportunity escape him. His new-found confidence drove him on.

‘I was wondering,’ he said ‘if we might go out for a drink some time?’ He almost surprised himself with his daring.

Moira looked at him but did not answer.

‘Just a drink, that’s all.’ Raymond must have resembled a young puppy such was the pleading look in his eyes.

‘Aren’t you too busy working on your big case to go out for a drink with the likes of me? You are still on the case, aren’t you?’

‘Yes,’ said Raymond. ‘In fact, I’m on my way to have a word with him now. You know, about the money he had in the car.’ Raymond lent forward and whispered this highly confidential information to her.

Moira seemed more interested. ‘Really? How exciting. Do you think he’ll tell you anything?’ She paused again and smiled but this time it was like the way she’d smiled the other night. ‘I’ll think about it. Do you have a number I can contact you on?’

Raymond fished in his pocket for his card. He took out a pen and wrote his mobile number down on the reverse. ‘Don’t ring me on the station number,’ he said. ‘That’s my mobile on the back.’

She took the card and looked at it. ‘I’m not promising anything,’ she said. ‘I’ve got a lot on at the moment. Look, I really have to go. I’ve been on duty all night.’

With that she rushed off towards the main concourse. Raymond watched her until she was out of sight. ‘Raymond, my boy,’ he said to himself, ‘this really is your lucky day!’

He was still smiling to himself when he found the office. Hood was looking out of the window as he entered. Wendy was sitting at the desk. She looked far from happy. Hood turned and faced him. He looked unhappy too.

‘I’m afraid I’ve got you here under false pretences, Craddock,’ he said. ‘Doyle discharged himself early this morning. There was nothing anyone could do to stop him.’

Craddock was unable to disguise his disappointment. ‘I see, sir. I thought he was going to be here for another couple of days?’

‘That’s what we thought, but he left with his solicitor at 6 a.m. We’ll have to take over now. We assume he’ll have gone back to his apartment in Leicester. But thanks for your help. It won’t be forgotten, if you understand my meaning.’

Craddock hoped that referred to his application to transfer to Mid-Shires. It couldn't refer to anything else, could it? 'Thank you, sir. Will you be wanting me for anything else?'

Hood smiled. 'No. You can go. Take care.' He turned to Wendy Knight as Craddock left the room. 'Well, that solved our dilemma, eh Wendy? There's no prospect of interviewing Doyle now – not unless we find him and arrest him.'

Knight stood up and started packing up her things. 'It can't be helped, sir. We still have his admission that the bag containing the cash was in his possession. And his initials are on the strap. If we can prove it came from the Charnwood, we'd have enough to arrest him then.'

'That's a big "if" and the longer we have to wait for the scientists, the greater the chance of Doyle making himself scarce.'

Hood's phone rang. He answered it and smiled. 'Well that's something at least. When will he arrive in Leicester?' The chief inspector listened intently and nodded towards Wendy Knight. 'We're on our way. And, Ian, I don't want anyone talking to him until I get back, understood?' He glanced at Wendy. His mood had changed for the better. 'Benson's been picked up by customs in Portsmouth.'

'Trying to leave the country?'

'Quite the opposite, actually. He was returning from France with his girlfriend. We need to move. The Hampshire police have placed him in the custody of Andrew and Ian. They're on their way back with him. I want to be there when he arrives.'

⋆⋆⋆⋆

At Harbour Buildings, Jules and Doyle were discussing a phone call they had just received from Tricia Gooding, Benson's girlfriend, who had informed Jules of his arrest.

'What's he doing coming back into the UK?' asked Doyle, his anger mounting. 'He was supposed to keep away.'

'It's Tricia's mother,' replied Jules. 'Apparently she had a stroke just after Christmas. She's in a bad way in hospital in Birmingham. Tricia wanted to see her.'

'But why was he arrested? He's supposed to be clean. They'll match him with the blood on the guard's uniform now. How can they have had his DNA on record?'

'Well it seems they have. There can't be any other reason for arresting him. Perhaps the information Bernard got from his contact in the Met was wrong.'

Doyle grabbed his crutches and staggered to the window.

'I bet the police are out there keeping a watch on this place. If they connect Benson with us, we'll be in real trouble. Thank God we didn't go to his engagement party in Birmingham. Your migraine couldn't have been timed better.'

'But why should they connect him with you, or me for that matter? He'll not say anything to them…'

Doyle looked out of the window, pulling the blind back as he did so. 'Won't he? Can you be sure of that? And if he does, the first thing we'll know about it is when we're pulled in too. They obviously searched this apartment and my office because of the cash I had in the Merc. Thank God we got rid of the notes that could be traced.' He made his way back to the sofa and sat down. He looked at Jules. 'Good decision of yours that. I'd be under lock and key if we hadn't burnt them.'

She smiled. 'That's as may be. But what about Benson?'

'We need to find out what – if anything – he's said, and that won't be easy.'

'And Tricia? Do you think he's told her anything?'

'I doubt it. I'm more worried what he might say to the police.'

Jules sat down on the sofa next to Doyle. She put her arms round him as she spoke.

'If they charge him, he'll appear in court, probably at Loughborough. I could ask Alex Stringer to report back on what occurs. Benson doesn't know him and he did ring and tell me about the visit he had from the police just before Christmas.'

'Stringer? Can he be trusted?'

'I think so. He wouldn't say anything to the police on principle and he's anxious to get in on any future jobs you might pull.'

Doyle smiled. 'But this was the last one. We're retiring abroad, remember? When Trevor's sorted out the problem with the Revenue and disposed of all my interests here, we'll be sunning ourselves a long way from Leicester.'

'Yes, but he doesn't know that, does he? We can play him along for a bit. And I have one or two other ideas to find out what the police are up to.'

'Well, don't tell me. What I don't know, I can't spill – even by accident.'

CHAPTER SIXTEEN

Benson was brought into Interview Room 2 by a uniformed officer. He looked quite at ease with himself. Hood reckoned he was about the right height for the robber on the CCTV whose nose had been injured. He was also the right build. Hood examined his features. He had a certain boyish charm about him. His light brown hair was unfashionably long and highlighted with blonde streaks. He had a gold tooth which became quite obvious when he smiled which he seemed to do nearly all the time as if his arrest did not trouble him at all. Earlier checks had revealed that he was thirty-two years of age and had no previous convictions. No disclosure had taken place. Hood knew he would not be able to spring the DNA evidence on him without informing his legal advisor in advance but he wanted to see his reaction. So he proposed to mention it immediately after caution, then offer Benson a break to consult with his lawyer. That was what he intended but things did not always work out as expected even in the best planned interviews.

The tape player was switched on and the usual formalities observed. Benson was asked to identify himself for the purposes of the tape, but he said nothing. His solicitor, a young man called Richard Goddard, confirmed his presence. Hooper then cautioned him.

'You do not have to say anything. But it may harm your defence if you fail to mention when questioned something which you later rely on in court. Anything you do say may be given in evidence. Do you understand the words of the caution, Mr Benson?'

He nodded.

'Could you say yes for the tape, please? It can't record a nod.'

Benson remained silent. The solicitor spoke.

'Mr Benson understands the caution. I discussed it with him when we conferred earlier. I am instructed to tell you that he will not be answering any questions at the moment. He relies on his right to silence.'

Hood intervened. 'Very well.'

'Could I remind you, Chief Inspector,' continued the solicitor, 'there has been no disclosure thus far. My client is entitled to know on what grounds he has been arrested and detained and his car seized.'

'Of course he is, Mr Goddard,' agreed Hood. 'Mr Benson has been arrested on a warrant issued by a magistrate in Loughborough. He is suspected of robbery during the early hours of 17 December last at the Charnwood Centre. Nearly 2 million pounds in cash was stolen and a security guard shot at close range. We believe that Mr Benson was one of the robbers.'

Benson's expression did not change. He hardly seemed interested in the proceedings.

He sat back in his chair and yawned.

'And your evidence for this allegation?' queried Goddard.

'DNA, Mr Goddard. One of the security guards had a go at one of the robbers. We say, Mr Benson here. He was punched – on the nose.'

Hood lent forward and looked closely at Benson's face. There was no sign of injury, apart from the remnants of a graze to his lower lip. His nose seemed intact and unmarked. He continued. 'It was a decent enough punch in the circumstances because it made the robber's nose bleed quite heavily. They were also in physical contact with each other for a few seconds. We have obtained a DNA profile from a sample of that blood. I am advised that it matches your client's DNA profile – exactly. Unless he has a twin brother, as far as we are concerned that puts him there at the scene participating in the robbery.'

'And the shooting?'

'That was one of the others. But you know the law on joint enterprise as well as I do They must all have known about the gun and the accelerant that was used to threaten the guards.'

Benson remained unmoved. His facial expression did not change. He took out a handkerchief and pointedly blew his nose. But he said nothing.

The solicitor continued. 'My instructions remain the same. My client denies these allegations. He does not accept the accuracy of the DNA analysis. We shall, of course, be seeking our own tests in the event of his being charged.'

Benson looked at Hood and smiled but remained silent. The solicitor continued. 'You may question my client. I cannot prevent you from doing that but, as I have already indicated, he will not be answering any questions at this time.'

'No problem,' replied Hood. 'I would also like to make it clear that if you or he wishes to speak privately following the disclosure I have just made and then continue the interview, I would be perfectly content to accommodate you. This inquiry has a long way to go yet.'

'That won't be necessary,' said the solicitor. 'I have my instructions. I repeat, Mr Benson has nothing to say at this stage.'

'Very well.'

Benson smiled but said nothing.

'By the way,' said Hooper, 'when did you last see Michael Doyle?'

Hood looked at Benson intently as the question was asked. He thought he detected a slight change in his expression – was it a look of concern? His eyes blinked rapidly just for a second or two. Then his face resumed the same vacant look. He said nothing.

'Right, then,' said Hood looking at Hooper. 'Take him back to the custody sergeant, will you, Andrew? I want him remanded overnight and ready to be interviewed further tomorrow morning. The clock has started to run. We don't want to waste any time.'

Benson was removed by a uniformed officer. Hooper followed. The solicitor smiled at Hood after his client had left the room.

'I suppose bail is out of the question, eh, Chief Inspector?'

'You suppose right,' replied Hood.

★★★★

The following morning, solicitor and client conferred together for half an hour. Hood arranged for the medical examiner to be on hand to obtain a swab to confirm the DNA analysis. Hooper had it rushed to the laboratory. The chief inspector wanted immediate confirmation that the profiling was accurate. He realised he was going to look particularly foolish if there had been an error.

The interview began as before. Like before, Benson declined even to acknowledge his name. Goddard had to do it for him. Like before, he declined to answer any questions. This time he was asked specifically about Michael Doyle. This time, Benson gave nothing away. He relied on his right of silence. He was asked about his movements over the last four months, his relationship with his girlfriend and his finances. He said nothing. He wouldn't even say "no comment". After forty minutes of questioning the buzzer sounded, indicating that the tape was coming to an end. Hood decided to call it a day. He appreciated he was unlikely to make any real progress until the DNA was confirmed and that would probably take another two days even with fast tracking. The ACC had approved an extension of time to continue the questioning and had prepared the appropriate application to seek a further extension from a magistrate should that become necessary. Hood had little doubt that it would. In the afternoon, Benson was interviewed further. Again he said nothing.

Overnight he was lodged in a police cell and the following day Hood sent Hooper to the courthouse to find a Justice of the Peace to obtain an additional extension. There was no problem. The DNA profile was good enough for the nervous magistrate. But Hood was fighting against time. It was a weekend and only a skeleton staff was on duty at the laboratory. Once it was confirmed that the blood was Benson's he intended to charge him. He wanted him to realise that the game was up. He told him there would be another interview the following day and left him to stew. Had he had his way, he'd have charged him there and then but the CPS had reviewed the evidence by telephone. Although they approved Hood's proposal to charge conspiracy to rob rather than robbery they insisted the profile had to be confirmed first. As usual, the no-risk policy of the CPS prevailed.

Benson was taken on this occasion to a cell some distance from the interview room. The heavy door closed and the key was turned in the lock. He saw a face through the slot in the door for a moment or two then it, too, was slammed shut. He heard the footsteps echoing as the jailer walked slowly down the passageway, humming to himself. He was now quite alone. The first night he had managed – just. But a second night – that was a different proposition. He looked around at the cream painted brickwork and saw the tiny window deliberately placed so high he could see nothing out of it. Not that he tried. He stood motionless for several minutes. Then he sighed and sat on the ledge that was built into the wall opposite the door and served, he assumed, as a bed. There was neither pillow nor blanket provided. He noticed the stainless steel WC fitted in the far corner but in full view of the hatch in the door. He felt an aching emptiness in the pit of his stomach as a deadening sensation of complete isolation swept over him. His head dropped into his hands. For the first time in his life he understood why suspects confessed. Anything to relieve this feeling of quite terrifying loneliness. He'd been quite cocky with the police at first – at least before he was interviewed. He'd told the sergeant at the desk when he was booked in that they'd made a terrible mistake. They'd be hearing from his solicitors – no question about it. They'd got the wrong man. But the DNA evidence altered all that. The DNA was the knock-out punch. There was no getting away from it. He'd half remembered the sample he'd given three or so years before in Erdington which he had dismissed because he'd been told it would be destroyed at the end of the exclusion exercise. He'd never bothered to check whether the police had made good their promise. He recalled a letter he'd been sent about it but he'd had other things on his mind at the time and had simply binned it. Obviously they hadn't removed his profile from the database or he wouldn't be in this mess.

He'd read about the manhunt in the Birmingham paper at the time. The exercise had been one of the largest ever carried out. Over three thousand men had volunteered to give a sample. He had been one of them. He saw no harm in it at the time; he was not contemplating a life of crime back then. If only he hadn't become addicted to gambling. If only! But it was too late now. He remembered that the Birmingham culprit had been caught and convicted, after a trial, of serial rape. He'd been sent down for life. Now it looked like he was going to suffer the same fate simply because he'd played the good citizen and co-operated. There was no need to wait for the sample he'd just given to come back from the lab. He knew what the result was going to be. Whatever alibi he arranged it would be exploded by the DNA. He was done for and if he said anything to anyone about the others, the rest of his life wouldn't be worth living either. In fact, there wouldn't be a rest of his life. The big man with the sawn-off had made that absolutely clear.

He stretched out on the bed and placed his hands behind his head. He had to hang in there. The urge to talk to someone, anyone, was becoming overwhelming. But he knew the consequences if he did. He realised, of course, why he'd been asked about Doyle. Just so he would know they were on to him – in the hope he would be persuaded to give him up. But he didn't dare. Not that it was Doyle who scared him. It was that mad man with the gun. He remembered how he'd shot the guard at close range without a moment's hesitation. It would have made no difference if the cartridge had been loaded with pellets rather than salt. He'd have done it just the same. He would never forget that look as he pulled the trigger. Cold, indifferent, the whites of his eyes standing out against the black of the balaclava. The man was a psychopath. He knew that when the swab confirmed the DNA profile, his solicitor would advise him to put his hands up, despite his assurance to his lawyer that the scientists had got it wrong. Then there would be hints dropped about getting a shorter sentence. Letters in brown envelopes to the judge to say how much he'd co-operated. He'd been warned by Jules exactly what it would be like. They all had. The tactics the police would employ were second nature to her. She'd seen it a hundred times in her paralegal work. But he remembered, too, what all of them had agreed. If they were picked up they were to say nothing – absolutely nothing. If they said nothing, Doyle had guaranteed it would all work out. It was as simple as that. Say nothing and ways and means would be found to make sure that no sentence would be served. Talk – well, if anyone did that, the consequences would be too terrible to contemplate.

★★★★

Benson slept hardly at all that night. He'd been given a meal of sorts at 7 p.m. and a blanket and a pillow later on, but there was no way he could get to sleep. When he closed his eyes, he saw Tricia, his fiancée, crying as he was taken into custody by the customs officers at Portsmouth. Thank God he hadn't involved her or even told her what he'd been up to. She was curious about his new-found wealth, but he'd told her how he'd won a few thousand on a particularly lucky day at the races. That was partly true. He'd had a good day at Newmarket at the close of the flat season in November but those winnings had all gone by the middle of December. His gambling addiction had got seriously out of hand and he was desperately in need of money. He had fallen into the hands of an illegal off-course bookmaker who was quite prepared to use ruthless methods to achieve payment. Like many punters, while Benson had his good days, the bad days easily outnumbered them. The robbery was his idea, or so he had led Doyle to believe. He and Doyle had kept observations on the secure compound for a couple of weeks but Doyle and Jules had done all the donkey work. Planning a crime of this nature was well beyond him. He'd just gone along for the ride really. They hadn't expected any real resistance, not after Colin had smashed in the windscreen and poured petrol all over the van, some of which had soaked a couple of the guards. They'd jumped out of the van like no one's business. Doyle had got the idea from a film he'd seen earlier in the year. Just like in the film, it worked a treat – until the senior guard had a go and punched Benson hard in the face. It was some punch; Benson was knocked backwards, but held on to the guard's other arm. He had then pushed him away as Bernard fired the gun. There was no resistance after that. The guard went down, clutching his chest and the other two nearly fainted with fear. In fact, one of them begged for mercy and told Bernard about his wife and family. Bernard was unmoved, pushed the sawn-off into the back of his neck and told him to open the rear doors. The guard did as he was told. And so must he; it was not in his interests to reveal anything to the police about any of the others.

He replayed the events after the shooting in his mind as he lay in his cell. Although he had been shocked by Bernard's actions, he had quickly come to and assisted in removing the security satchels and transferring them to the other van that had been manoeuvred into the gateway to ensure that the electronic gates remained open. Once the money was removed, the guards were ordered to join their injured colleague who was already prostrate on the ground and the security van was torched. An additional can of petrol had been placed in the back to ensure it was destroyed. They'd heard the explosion as they made their escape down the service road. Within twenty minutes, they were back at the foundry.

He turned on his side in the almost pitch darkness. Oh, how he regretted that he had become involved! He could hear a drunk singing loudly in an adjacent cell and another inmate threatening him with serious injury if he didn't shut up. It had no effect. The singing continued for another hour until, exhausted, the drunk fell asleep. Benson had no such luck. By the time breakfast was brought in at 6.30 a.m., he reckoned he'd slept for no more than thirty minutes. After breakfast, he was allowed out of the cell and taken to a washroom where he shaved and splashed cold water on his face.

At 9 a.m., he was back in the interview room. Hood was still waiting for information from the lab about his sample. Benson refused to say anything. The interview was terminated. At 10.40 a.m., he was removed from the cell again. The same ground was covered once more, Benson maintaining his silence. Then the message arrived. The results were still not available and wouldn't be for another fifty-six hours. There was no one working over the weekend that was qualified to give an opinion. Budget cuts had removed all overtime, whatever the urgency. So much for fast tracking! The solicitor pointed out that Benson could not be held for that length of time without charge and demanded that he be bailed. Benson's heart leapt. If he got bail, they'd never see him again. Whatever conditions were imposed, he'd be off! Hood was furious and terminated the interview in order to speak with the CPS. Benson was taken back to his cell, his spirits raised by his solicitor's assurance that he would have to be released on bail if he were not charged by the end of the day.

Andrea Fleming was not available – she was not contactable over the weekend. Hood went to the top and insisted on speaking to the chief prosecutor, James Frazer, who fortunately (or, perhaps, unfortunately) was both available and aware of the basic facts of the case but was not prepared for the onslaught he received from Hood. He was initially insistent that Benson should not be charged.

'If he were bailed, he could be re-arrested once the match was available. Conditions could be imposed. His passport could be retained.'

That was not good enough for Hood. If Benson were bailed he would never be seen again, passport or no passport. He insisted that the CPS review its original decision not to charge before the new sample was tested against the crime scene sample. Frazer hesitated then promised to speak to the chief scientist at the laboratory – if he could get hold of him. But it was the weekend – it might not be possible. Two hours later, Frazer telephoned Hood and agreed that as it had been confirmed by the very disgruntled scientist who had been dragged from the golf course that as it was a virtual certainty that the original profiling was accurate, he would take the risk and authorise that Benson be charged. If the test on the sample taken on his arrest were not identical with the sample from the crime scene, however, the case would have to be discontinued. That was as far as he was prepared to go. The chief inspector breathed a sigh of relief. The decision was good enough for him. There really couldn't be much chance of a mistake.

Benson was removed once more from his cell and walked through to the custody desk. The solicitor had somewhat sheepishly and apologetically told him that he was to be charged and placed before the magistrates' court the next day. He was immediately plunged back into the depths of despair. However much he tried to hide it, Hood had no difficulty detecting that Benson was in a state of near hopelessness. If only he could have interviewed him again, he might have got somewhere but time and the law were against him. Once charged, that would be it. No more interviews. Hood maintained his professional attitude, carefully concealing his delight that permission to charge had been given, no matter how reluctantly. Hooper, although he tried very hard, was quite unsuccessful in his attempt to emulate his superior. The grin on his face simply grew as the charge was read out. The custody sergeant cleared his throat before he spoke. An officer of the old school, he put the allegation in very formal language.

'Charles Anthony Benson, you are charged that between 1 December 1998 and 18 December 1998, you conspired with others unknown to rob David Jameson, Roderick Lane and Ashock Patel of a quantity of cash, the property of the National Commercial Bank of Great Britain, against the peace of our Sovereign Lady the Queen, her Crown and Dignity.'

Benson was again cautioned but made no reply. He felt quite faint and the proceedings, for him, began to take on a surreal element as if he had been plunged into what seemed to be a never-ending nightmare. He simply looked at Hood and then at Hooper and grimaced. He did manage to remain upright but there was no arguing about it, he was in a state of shock. The custody sergeant wrote everything down on the record and Hood checked it religiously. He didn't want any mistakes. Benson was told he would be produced before the magistrates' court the next day when he could apply for bail. He was told, of course, it would be opposed.

'On what grounds?' asked the solicitor, desperately trying to regain the high ground and impress his client. 'Might I remind you, Mr Benson has no previous convictions.'

'Interference with the course of justice and risk of failing to surrender,' replied Hood as if he were reciting a formula. 'He's looking at something in the region of fifteen years, minimum, I would have thought, wouldn't you, Mr Goddard, even on a plea? There are not many who would hang about waiting for a sentence like that, not when they have contacts abroad like your client. And we are yet to apprehend any of the others. We don't want Mr Benson doing anything that might prevent us catching them, now do we?'

But Benson heard none of this as he was escorted back to his cell. This was a bad dream from which there would be no awakening.

CHAPTER SEVENTEEN

Monday, 11 January 1999

A heavily suntanned Charles Cavan-Henry walked in to the robing room at Leicester Crown Court. 'Have you seen Harriet Lassiter? She's leading me in "Emmerson".'

James Critchley looked up from his newspaper. He was a middle-ranking barrister with a large family. He was prosecuting a violent disorder in court five. 'Popped out with Bill Savage. He's for Emmerson and he's doing it without a leader – obviously trying to impress someone. Must be in for silk next time. Harriet said something about a psychiatric report…'

'Yes. I was aware it was on the way. Thanks, James, I'd better find her.'

Cavan-Henry threw his bags on the robing-room table and rushed from the room.

'So Charlie's being led by Harry, is he?' said a voice from the far side of the room. It was Randell Richards, criminal hack. He was still a junior after forty-eight years at the Bar but had an intimate knowledge of virtually everyone in the profession. Times were hard for him and his few contemporaries who were still trying to earn a living. Most of his vintage had taken silk, gone on the bench or died. Randell had stubbornly declined to do any of these things, not that he had any prospect now of becoming a judge. His age and his history were against him. Indeed, judicial ambition had died in him long ago when he was put off the road when sitting as an assistant recorder back in the early eighties. He had once had a lucrative practice in the days when legal aid was plentiful and the fees exceedingly generous and, like many others, had been invited by the Lord Chancellor to sit as a part-time judge in the Crown Court. He had started well enough but his inability to remain silent on the bench and his playing to the press gallery eventually took its toll. He never got his full recordership and was effectively prevented from sitting again after the press turned against him when he sentenced a bus conductor to immediate imprisonment for stealing twenty-six pounds from his employers. The defendant's deprivations had probably been much greater but twenty-six pounds was all that could be proved. Randell sentenced him to three months' immediate imprisonment for what he described as "a grave breach of trust." The miscreant's colleagues took a different view – they all went out on strike in sympathy and did not return to work until the Court of Appeal quashed the sentence and substituted a conditional discharge. Randell's photograph had appeared in all the newspapers and on the television news. He was subject to harsh and offensive criticism including a leading article in *The Times* decrying the unnecessary use of imprisonment for minor offences and bemoaning "out of touch" judges. That, in effect, ended his embryonic judicial career.

His practice at the Bar, however, did not suffer noticeably, or at least not immediately, and he remained in demand and continued to make a decent living. But times had changed and he had had to give way to younger advocates – and to greatly reduced fees. His clientele had suffered too, as the managing clerks in the old solicitors' firms on whom he relied for work began to retire or die or the firms gradually amalgamated into larger, impersonal conglomerates, their main preoccupation being the preservation of their profits. He still had a couple of firms who briefed him but even they looked elsewhere for the more serious cases. The major criminals wanted younger, more aggressive barristers, apparently. But his overheads were low and his mortgage paid. He had been a widower for over ten years and both his children were grown up so he was able to survive – just. And there was always a chance that he might get instructed in a long trial, perhaps being led by the likes of Harriet Lassiter? Well, he could dream. Reality was quite different. For the most part, he had to get by on committals for sentence and breaches of probation orders and the odd plea when no one else was available. It was over eighteen months since he had done a jury trial.

'Got something interesting today, Randell?' asked one of the young barristers, looking towards his colleagues and making no effort to disguise his provocative tone.

'Quite a complicated committal for sentence, actually.'

The others laughed. Randell placed his battered wig on his head, picked up his solitary brief and stomped towards the door. He turned before he left the room.

'And just for that I shan't tell you what I picked up over Christmas about the resident judge!' He slammed the door behind him. The younger element looked at each other, grinning, as Bill Savage and Harriet Lassiter came into the room.

'Something amusing you all? I do hope you're going to share it with us.'

'It was nothing,' said James Critchley piously. 'Just taking the piss out of old Randell Richards.'

'You really should be more respectful to Randell,' said Harriet, disapprovingly. 'He must be one of the oldest practising members of the Bar and he's a very sound lawyer. He could certainly have shown you lot a thing or two in his younger days.'

'You wouldn't say that if you'd been here a bit earlier,' said Critchley still grinning. But Harriet was no longer interested in their juvenile behaviour. She turned to Savage.

'Are we agreed then, Bill? Your chap will plead to manslaughter on the ground of diminished responsibility?'

'That will be his plea. I hope the judge won't cause any difficulties. Emmerson has already been transferred to Arnold Lodge and you've seen the latest reports. All the doctors agree.'

'Don't you worry about Tom Campion. He'll be as good as gold. He's a first-class judge and will have plenty of other work to be getting on with.'

She turned to the younger advocates, half smiled and continued, 'I expect you'll miss him when he goes to London.'

Critchley stood up. There was a look of real concern on his face. The room became suddenly silent. 'Tom Campion's leaving us?' His voice was incredulous. 'Where's he off to? He's far too young to retire.'

'Yes,' said one of the others, 'and he's got a two-year-old son. He'll *never* be able to afford to retire.'

Harriet noted their concern. 'Rumour has it that he's going to be made a senior circuit judge and sit at the Old Bailey. He's not due to start there until after Easter, so enjoy him while you can.'

'How do you find out these things, Harry? You're a mine of information,' said Savage who hardly wanted to admit, even to himself, that such a piece of golden gossip had escaped him.

'He was at our chambers' party before Christmas. He was a tenant with us, you know, before he went on the bench and a bloody good barrister.' She smiled in a superior way. 'Someone let it slip. It's still highly confidential of course. So don't gossip about it, will you?' Harriet turned away. She knew that was precisely what they would do. Gossip was the lifeblood of the Bar. Critchley and the others looked far from happy. They appeared regularly at Leicester and regarded Campion with both respect and affection.

'I bet that's what old Randell was on about,' said one of the others. 'I wonder who'll take over from him?'

'Not Serious Sue, I hope,' said a voice from the back of the room. 'She'd be dreadful. She has no sense of humour.'

'Or Izzy Scrope – but she's probably too inexperienced.' Critchley sighed and resumed his seat, casually picking up his newspaper and placing his feet on the table. 'They could even send us another woman. Imagine it? Three women in a court centre this size. If we were sent another one like Sue or Izzy we'd have a veritable convent. I can see it now, "The sisters of little mercy"!'

Several of the others laughed.

'And what if they did?' said Harriet. 'You men have had it all your own way for far too long.'

'I have nothing against women judges,' responded Critchley, pompously, removing his feet from the table and sitting up straight in his chair. 'So long as gender and diversity are not allowed to trump ability. The last thing we need is a politically correct judiciary.'

'I entirely agree,' said Harriet, 'but if we are to judge wholly on merit, Susan Stillwell must be the favourite – and she's just been given a murder ticket. I'm sure that's no coincidence.'

'They might parachute someone in, I suppose,' moaned Critchley. The mood in the robing room was now quite sombre. 'A judge from Birmingham, or even Nottingham, perhaps?'

'Unlikely... and there isn't anyone else locally,' interrupted Savage who had an opinion on everything, particularly himself. 'Unless, of course, they appoint someone straight from the Bar – perhaps Harriet here might be interested?'

He smiled as he awaited Harriet's reaction. She countered the suggestion quickly.

'It's not for me,' she insisted. 'I'm not even a recorder.' She paused before tossing the idea back to him. 'Perhaps you should apply, Bill. I'm sure you would make an excellent circuit judge. And you have a good few years' experience of sitting part-time.' She paused and looked mischievously at the assembled company. After a few seconds, she turned her attention back to

Savage. 'But tell me, Bill, have you finished your anger management course yet? That would be an essential prerequisite in your case, wouldn't it?'

Loud laughter broke out. Savage, however, was not amused. His ambition was to take silk and make a lot of money. He had accepted appointment as a recorder simply to enhance his prospects of becoming a QC.

'I wasn't suggesting myself,' he replied, smugly. 'A judicial career holds no attraction for me. Anyway, I'm far too young.'

He smiled then glared at Harriet.

'Thank God for that,' someone whispered from the corner.

Harriet looked away. She could hardly resist smiling at his obvious discomfort. She knew Savage was only a year younger than her and despite the hours he spent in the gym he was already beginning to lose his youthful good looks – well, that was what she thought. Others obviously took a contrary view if the stories of his conquests were to be believed. She and Charles moved to a corner of the room. Savage pretended he had not heard what had been said but he was anxious to re-establish himself in the eyes of all present.

'Can't imagine anything worse,' he said, ensuring the whole room could hear him maintaining his disinterest in becoming a judge. 'Even the High Court bench doesn't attract me. What a life, dragging round the country staying in those dreadful lodgings. I like to sleep in my own bed – whenever possible.'

'That's not what I've heard.' It was Critchley who spoke, looking up from his newspaper. He was not smiling.

'Stirring again, are we James?' responded Savage indignantly. He paused and tried to look as if the remark had caused him real pain. 'My relationship with your junior tenant was fleeting and entirely platonic. It's hardly my fault if she misunderstood my intentions. I wouldn't mind the rumours if anything had happened, but it didn't. Lunch at Simpsons is hardly a hanging offence, is it?'

Savage had married when very young then quickly divorced. He had a bit of a reputation in his chambers when it came to female members of the Bar or, indeed, females of any kind. He was a decent advocate and a pretty good lawyer but his favourite subject – by a country mile – was himself. Outside the facts of the particular case he was dealing with, it was difficult to get him to talk about anything else. It was as if his life were continuously reflected in a mirror that followed him around and the only reflection he could see was his own.

'And dinner at the Savoy?' continued Critchley, determined to add to Savage's discomfort.

'And didn't I hear of a long weekend in Cumbria?' said one of the others. 'And there was that weekend in Brighton with that gorgeous looking solicitor's clerk?'

The entire room was now looking in his direction. Savage was not a popular man. His numerous indiscretions were too well known and there were still a few gentlemen practising at the Bar who heartily disapproved of his attitude towards young women. Critchley, who had trained to be a Jesuit for three years before turning to the law, was one of them. Savage glared angrily at him and adopted a superior tone.

'I don't quite understand what you are implying?'

The atmosphere was turning quite unpleasant. Harriet was even a trifle concerned that her initial comments had caused things to get rather out of hand.

'Shall we go in to court?' she said opening the door and calling an end to the cross-questioning. 'The judge will be coming in soon and I need to speak to Charles. He's having a word with the officer in the case about the proposed plea.'

CHAPTER EIGHTEEN

'How did she take it?' asked Eddie Farnsworth.

Raymond had phoned him immediately after giving his news to his mother that he had passed the board and was on his way to join Mid-Shires Constabulary as a trainee detective constable. As he had guessed, Eddie already knew about his transfer. A woman officer in administration had let it slip. Women officers were always letting things slip where Eddie was concerned.

'That's what I can't understand,' replied Raymond. 'She was pleased for me. Said it would do me good to get away from Hull. She was positively enthusiastic about it.'

'Well, there you go, Raymond my boy. Nothing to worry about was there? She's probably glad to get you out from under her feet!'

'I don't know about that. She made me promise I'd come back to see her at least once a month.'

'Perhaps we should go out and celebrate your success,' said Eddie. 'I've got nothing on tonight. Alison's got a parents' evening and I'm on rest day tomorrow. So you and me can go out on the town. How about it?'

'No can do, Eddie. Not tonight. I've got a date.'

'You're kidding? Who is she? Anyone I know?'

'No. She's a nurse I met at the hospital when I was on bed watch. And I'll tell you now, she's a real cracker!'

'Where are you taking her? I wouldn't mind a butchers at her myself. I could always give you a few tips.'

'I bet you could – but it's not going to happen. You've got Alison, remember. I'm not letting you anywhere near her. And your tips I can do without.'

'Oh, go on, Raymond. I won't say anything, I promise. Just tell me where you're taking her and I'll just nosey along and give her the once over. I'll keep my distance. You won't even know I'm there.'

'That's true, 'cos you won't be. You won't get within a mile of her!'

'Please yourself. I suppose I can always go and play snooker with the lads. See you, lover boy. Be careful – if you know what I mean!'

★★★★

Raymond arrived at the Mermaid a full twenty minutes before Moira was due. He found a fairly private table in one of the smaller rooms and took occasional sips at the low calorie tonic water that he had purchased at the bar. He had brought his car with him in the hope he might get a chance to drive Moira home and was determined not to exceed the drink-drive limit. If he stuck to non-alcoholic drinks until she arrived, he calculated he could risk a gin and tonic when she made her appearance. Unlike Eddie, he had never been a beer drinker. In fact, he disliked the taste which only added to his reputation amongst his colleagues as a bit of a mummy's boy. "Orange juice for you, is it?" was the usual comment when he joined other officers for a drink at the end of a shift. Not that they complained when he was able to drive them home at the end of a session. "Sober as a judge is our Raymond," they used to say. At least his move to Mid-Shires would bring that to an end. They'd have to make their own way home in future.

He glanced at his watch again. So far so good. Ten minutes to eight. He took another sip of his tonic water and looked at the menu on the blackboard behind the bar. He didn't really fancy anything to eat; he could still taste his mother's chicken casserole that he'd gulped down before spending an inordinate length of time in the shower preparing himself for his encounter with Moira. Still, she might be hungry so he'd have to join her if she fancied something. He looked at his watch again then at the now crowded lounge. He'd overlooked the fact that it was quiz night. The quiz contestants were ordering pints and taking them through to the larger room on the right of the bar. Many of them were ordering food too. 'That's the end of the plaice,' he heard the barmaid shout. 'Plenty of haddock and cod though.' The bar area began to empty. Raymond looked at his watch again. It was nearly eight o'clock. He could feel butterflies in his stomach, vying with the half-digested chicken casserole. Then she appeared. Her head peeped around the corner and she gave Raymond a dazzling smile, her perfect white teeth contrasting with her very red lips.

'Found you,' she said. 'I went in through the other entrance and couldn't see you in the main bar – still, here we are.'

Raymond, who had remained sitting down as she made her appearance, jumped to his feet.

'You look wonderful,' he said. 'What can I get you to drink?'

'A glass of dry white wine would be lovely,' she answered, sitting herself down in the chair opposite and opening her cerise coloured coat which revealed a similarly coloured close-fitted dress that emphasised her slim waist and proportionate bust. A gold chain with a crucifix hung around her neck.

Raymond could hardly take his eyes off her as he stumbled over a vacant chair to get to the bar. She was wearing more make-up than when he had first seen her at the hospital which made her look slightly older than he remembered. Her red hair was more carefully styled than before. Raymond had never really fancied redheads before. The ideal woman of his dreams had always been blonde, rather like Eddie Farnsworth's Alison. She would have looked fantastic in Moira's dress. Mind you, Moira would have looked outstanding in anything or nothing, if it came to it. If he had been prejudiced against redheads before, Moira had blown away such sentiments entirely.

'Careful, now,' she cautioned as he arrived at the bar after righting the chair he had knocked over.

He smiled, not without embarrassment, and ordered two glasses of dry white wine.

The barmaid took the money and eyed Moira before grinning at Raymond. He did not respond. He guessed what she was thinking as he carried the two glasses of wine to the table and placed one of them in front of Moira.

'There you are, cheers!'

He took a sip from his glass.

'That's perfect,' she said. 'Are you going to sit down?'

Raymond negotiated the extra chair on his side of the table without incident and sat down.

'Well, here we are. This is very nice.'

She smiled again and looked around the room, fingering the crucifix nervously. There was a couple sitting at the next table, deep in conversation, holding hands and oblivious to everyone. There was no one else sitting at the other tables and Raymond would have preferred it if they had moved on, but, much as he would have liked to follow their example, he decided not to risk such intimacy with Moira – not yet anyway. He felt his confidence wilting as he gazed at her. He simply couldn't take his eyes off her. Could she really be interested in him? He had rehearsed imaginary conversations with her as he took his shower and again as he drove to the pub, but now she was actually in his company, his mind had virtually gone a complete blank – just like at the hospital.

'How's your mother?' he asked, desperately thinking of something to say.

'My mother?'

'Yes, you said on the phone you were going back to Ireland because your mother was unwell.'

Moira hesitated before replying. 'I did indeed. It's nothing to worry about. She has this long-standing condition and has periods when she can be quite ill. She's going into hospital at the end of the week – just routine you know – but she wants me to be there. I'm all she has – since my father left.'

'I see. I hope everything goes well. Will you be returning when she's recovered?'

'We'll have to see about that. She's getting on a bit now and she'd like me to stay at home but I have to work and jobs are not easy to get in Cork at the moment – and the money's not as good as it is over here. But I'm looking elsewhere; something will turn up.'

'Well, I hope you do come back.'

She looked down and fluttered her eyelashes. 'So do I.' Her voice was soft and tender. Raymond was smitten. She then looked up and smiled again, turning her eyes away. Raymond regarded this as a good sign. Almost a bit of a come-on, at least that's what he hoped. She looked up towards him and leant forward. He could smell her perfume.

'What about you? What are you up to at the moment? What happened to that dangerous criminal you were guarding at the hospital? Has he confessed everything?'

'Oh, him.' Raymond spoke almost contemptuously. He turned and looked at the couple on the other table before leaning towards Moira and whispering his reply. 'I shouldn't really be telling you this but it turned out there was no evidence that the money he had in the back of his car came from the robbery so he was never arrested. He discharged himself from the hospital early. I don't suppose you saw him again either.'

'No. I was working in another department last time I was there. I get around you know.'

'You don't work there all the time then?'

'Oh, no. I'm an agency nurse. I go wherever I'm required. There are no full-time jobs there at the moment.'

'That must be a bit of a pain; never knowing where you're going to be?'

'I don't mind. I get a lot of variety but it would be nice, I suppose, to work in one place for a while. I might get to know a few people then. I hardly know anyone, you know, not over here anyway. I flit about from here to there.'

She half giggled. Raymond was quite pleased to hear that. It might explain why there appeared to be no one special in her life. He noticed there were still no rings on her fingers.

'I would have thought they'd be queuing up to get to know you.'

Moira almost blushed at his attempt at gallantry.

'I've had my moments. Most men seem to think I must be in a relationship with someone, but there's no one special – not at present. I had a boyfriend back home but we've sort of lost touch since I came over here.'

Her eyes, those lovely emerald-green eyes looked away from him again. Raymond could hardly believe it. He prayed the boyfriend back home really had lost interest, though if he had he must be blind – or mad.

'Do you have a girlfriend?' she asked.

Raymond answered quickly. 'No one special. Not at the moment, anyway.'

He could feel himself beginning to blush. For a few seconds neither of them said anything. She averted her eyes again. Raymond was searching desperately for something to say.

'I have got a bit of news, though.' He sounded confident. She looked up. 'I've got a transfer to the East Midlands. I'm joining the Mid-Shires Constabulary. I might even get in on the investigation of that robbery. I'm becoming a detective constable – although I'll be a trainee for a few months. I'm really excited about it. I start at the beginning of next month.' He tried his best to sound modest but could not conceal the pride he felt in his promotion. He looked at her intently but did not receive quite the reaction he had hoped for. She hesitated and a look of concern crossed her face.

'Really? Well, isn't that fine? But that'll mean you won't be here if I come back from Ireland, doesn't it?'

Raymond thought that her mood had changed quite markedly. Perhaps she really did fancy him and was upset he was moving from Hull? He almost placed his hand on hers before he replied but withdrew at the last moment. She looked down and seemed reluctant to speak. The tension was broken by loud cheering coming from the adjacent quiz room. Raymond moved closer.

'It's not that far away. I'll be back here quite a bit, you know, to see my mother and keep in touch with my… friends.'

Moira was silent for quite some time, then she looked up and smiled.

'Well, congratulations – I hope you enjoy your promotion. Do you think you'll be put on that robbery case – they haven't given up on the fellow who was in the hospital, have they?'

'I don't think so. I suspect they're keeping an eye on him.'

Raymond drew closer still and whispered. 'But I did hear they had arrested one of the others. Banged to rights by all accounts. They have his DNA from the crime scene – so he's done for.'

Moira looked surprised. 'Is that a fact? I thought these robbers were supposed to be so professional. Why take someone on the job who has his DNA on record? Sounds a bit amateurish to me – not that I would know anything about such things.'

She hesitated as if she'd said a little too much then laughed. 'Weren't you hoping that the DNA would match the one from the hospital?'

'That's what we hoped but there was no match, more's the pity. Mid-Shires was pretty pissed off at the time. I heard that they'd been after him for years and it looks like he's given them the slip again.'

It was Raymond's turn to hesitate. Because of his involvement in questioning Doyle, his inspector had kept him up to speed on the progress of the investigation, on a strictly confidential basis. But there couldn't be any harm in telling Moira, could there? Maintaining the aura of confidentiality, he whispered to her.

'Look, this is really hush-hush and mustn't go any further but we only got the other one because he'd given a sample a few years ago in Birmingham – it was a big exclusion exercise, a serial rapist was on the prowl. I think they got him in the end but this bloke's DNA was never removed from the database. Lucky when you think about it. Without it we'd have nothing on him.'

Moira looked impressed. 'Yes. Very lucky. Seems strange somehow that luck should play such a big part in convicting someone of a serious crime.

But I suppose he'll be able to tell you about the others, if he has no other way out.'

Raymond assumed a cynical look. 'I doubt it. Real life isn't like detective novels, you know. From what I've heard he's not said a word. If we're going to get the others, we'll have to prove it in some other way. Try and establish some connection between him and them.'

'But surely you can get him to talk, can't you? Can't you offer him a deal or something?'

Raymond laughed. 'We're not allowed to do deals. The most we can offer is to put a letter before the judge to try and get him a lower sentence if he co-operates but we can't even guarantee that. It's up to the judge at the end of the day.'

'So those detective novels are not really true to life?' Moira did not try and hide her disappointment.

'Not really, no. But we might be able to connect him to the bloke from the hospital – that would be a start anyway. That's what they're working on at the moment – but I don't know if they've got anywhere. I'm out of the loop at present – since that fellow Doyle was discharged from the hospital.'

'Was that his name?' said Moira. 'You know we were never told who he was. That's what made us so curious. We thought he must be someone who'd done something really serious.'

Raymond realised that he had said something he should have kept to himself. He instinctively looked around the room to see if anyone else had heard him. The couple on the next table were still entranced one with the other and the barmaid was busy washing glasses.

'I shouldn't have mentioned his name,' he confessed. 'You will keep that to yourself, won't you?'

'Of course,' she replied, 'the name means nothing to me. Sounds as if he might be from my part of the world, though. There are a lot of people called Doyle in County Cork.'

She smiled and placed her hand on his. 'Don't worry. I shan't say anything to anyone – I promise.' She squeezed his hand gently. 'But you're still after him, aren't you?'

Raymond sighed with relief and anticipation. He took hold of her fingers then answered.

'Oh, yes. And the detective in charge is not one to give up, I can tell you. Once Harry the Hood gets his teeth into something he hangs on in there.'

'Harry the what?'

'Detective Chief Inspector Hood. That's what they call him – behind his back, of course.'

Moira giggled. 'Well don't let him catch you calling him that or he'll have you off the case and we don't want that do we?'

Raymond pursed his lips and released her hand from his. He suddenly looked a little forlorn. 'I'm not sure that I'll be on the case when I start there. They may put me on some big fraud that's been going on for months. It's getting nowhere fast so, knowing my luck, I'll probably get lumbered with that.'

'When will you know?'

'Not 'till I get there. I can only hope that the work I've done so far will stand me in good stead with the chief inspector.'

'I'm sure it will.'

Raymond looked at her again. He noticed that she had almost finished her drink.

'Fancy another one?' He drained his glass as he spoke.

'Why not? I've got nothing on tomorrow and I'm off to Ireland the day after. Do you think I could have a Baileys this time?'

'Anything you like,' he replied. 'I think I'll have a gin and tonic myself.'

He picked up both glasses and headed for the bar. Perhaps this was going to be his lucky night after all?

★★★★

Raymond's head was still spinning when he crawled from under the duvet following his night at the Mermaid. This, he assumed, was what a hangover felt like. It was new experience for him. He had never been drunk in his life before and, privately, did not concede that his condition the previous evening was quite so bad as to be so described. *I was only tipsy*, he assured himself as he examined his alarm clock and tried to focus on the time. Memories started to flood back. That first gin and tonic had been followed by several more. If only he'd stayed on the tonic water. But Moira had seemed quite determined to ply him with alcohol and his resistance had folded very quickly. He had noticed, though, that her consumption of Baileys and Amaretto had no discernible effect on her, while the drinks he was putting away were gradually rendering him both indiscreet and ever so slightly out of control. They had stayed at the Mermaid until after half past ten and it was Moira who had suggested they should leave. He recalled with real embarrassment his clumsy attempt to kiss her passionately as they fell into the back seat of the taxi that she had called. Her resistance had been partial but effective, and although their lips had touched briefly, she had gently removed his hands from around her waist and placed him in the corner of the seat before kissing him again, gently and quite chastely, on his forehead.

'Raymond,' she had said, sounding just like his last girlfriend. 'Not here.' She extracted his address from him and ordered the taxi driver to proceed.

'Is he all right, luv?' the driver asked. 'I don't want him throwing up in my cab.'

'He's fine,' she said sweetly. 'Just had one too many, I think. We have been celebrating.'

'Well as long as there's no celebrating in my cab,' pronounced the driver wearily.

She had then allowed Raymond to cuddle her as they journeyed to his home. Raymond's insistence that they should go on somewhere else was met with an implacable refusal. "I have a lot to do in the morning," she had said. "And I have a plane to catch the next day, remember?" Raymond accepted defeat. His original idea had been to drive her home in the hope he might be invited in for a coffee. There had been no question of that. Moira had been very firm about it. 'Think of your career,' she had reminded him. So his car was left in the car park. The alcohol was gradually having a quite soporific effect upon him and by the time they reached their destination, he was almost asleep. Moira paid the fare, waited until he staggered to his front door, then blowing him a kiss through the open taxi window went on her way. "I'll be in touch," she shouted. Raymond watched as the taxi disappeared down the road, vowing he would never drink alcohol again. This had been his big chance and it looked like he had blown it. *I bet she was just saying that*, he thought to himself.

'Want any breakfast, luv?' his mother shouted up the stairs as he dressed himself.

Thank God it was a rest day. He'd have to retrieve his car from the Mermaid, but that could wait. But breakfast? He knew he had to show willing or his mother would think he was ill. 'I'll just have a poached egg. Only one slice of toast though.' That was all he thought he could manage. He located the Alka-Seltzer in the bathroom cupboard then dropped two tablets into a glass of water and downed the bubbling liquid in one. It tasted disgusting but Eddie had told him it always did the trick and no one had greater experience of such things than Eddie. He'd had quite a few hangovers in his time. Raymond then looked around his bedroom and spied the half-packed suitcase in the corner. He would be off to Leicester in a couple of weeks and had quite a lot of preparation still to do. He had found some digs in one of the more pleasant areas of the city, a couple of miles from the police station where he was to report for duty. He could hardly wait.

'You were back late last night,' said his mother as she poured out the tea.

'We were celebrating my promotion,' said Raymond. 'I think I had a couple too many.'

Mother looked a tad disapproving. 'I bet it was that Eddie encouraging you, wasn't it?'

Raymond shook his head. 'Eddie wasn't there.'

His mother looked at him a little more closely. 'Are you all right, luv?'

'I'm fine – just a little tired. I've got a lot to do before I leave for Leicester.' He looked at the egg, squatting precariously on a rather thick piece of well-done toast.

'Do you know, Mum? I'm not really that hungry.' He pushed the plate away and picked up his tea.

'I hope you're not sickening for something.' She sounded quite concerned. Raymond shook his head again. Of course he was sickening for something, but he wasn't going to tell his mother, or indeed, anyone else about Moira. Not yet anyway.

CHAPTER NINETEEN

Thursday, 21 January 1999

Chief Inspector Hood made himself as comfortable as he could in the chair which he assumed ACC Margaret Knowles had placed immediately in front of her desk. This suggested a more formal meeting than the previous updates he had been giving her when they had both been seated on the more comfortable, soft, easy chairs next to the window. He noticed, too, that there was no offer of coffee or any refreshment despite the 8 a.m. conference call that had caused him to come into the station earlier than usual. Knowles' secretary had told him that the ACC had been slightly delayed but her apology did not include the usual offer of a hot beverage. He had been shown into the ACC's room and asked to wait. That was when he had spied the solitary chair. He looked around him at the plain but functional room and wondered what accommodation he would be given should his application to join Birmingham Metropolitan be successful. He had been more than a little annoyed to discover that his board had been postponed for two months. He correctly suspected interference from Mid-Shires. They really couldn't manage without him at present he had been told, so the quicker he resolved his present inquiry, the sooner he would learn his fate in Birmingham. He looked at his watch. It was almost ten past eight. He stood up and walked towards the window, and looked out over the half-empty car park. The trees in the distance appeared stark against the rising ground behind them. The rain had come on as well, hammering on the car roofs and striking the office window forcefully. This was the time of year he disliked most. That empty lull before the spring when nature appeared to have fallen asleep, seemingly never to awake. His phone rang. It was Wendy Knight.

'What? When? Well that's just what we didn't need. Thanks for letting me know.'

He switched his phone off and placed it in his breast pocket.

'A penny for them, Harry?'

ACC Knowles had arrived. Hood turned and faced her.

'I was really thinking about a cup of coffee,' he ventured, optimistically.

'No time for that,' replied Knowles. 'The chief wants to see us – both of us – now!'

'Have there been developments? Something I don't know about?'

'Nothing like that. He just wants a first-hand account of the investigation so far. I think someone's been on to him but he won't say who. Probably that MP; you know the one who used to be on the police committee when he was a councillor? He's been making a lot of fuss about the guard who was shot. Come on. The lift isn't working – again. We'll have to walk up to the top floor.'

'After you, ma'am. And by the way, there's been one unfortunate development. I'll tell you when we get upstairs.'

Harry followed his superior up the stairs. He noticed she was quite out of breath when they got to the top, another indication that promotion had its downside. Sitting behind a desk all day was undoubtedly a health hazard. He skipped up the stairs without catching a breath.

'Steady on, Harry,' said Knowles. 'We don't want to appear too eager.'

They passed through the outer office, Knowles acknowledging the two secretaries who seemed to be doing nothing in particular.

'You're to go straight in,' one of them said. 'The chief is expecting you.'

Knowles tapped briskly on the door and opened it. Hood followed her in.

'Come in, come in,' said the chief, 'no need to stand on ceremony.'

Hood noticed that he did not stand up. He simply pointed at a number of chairs forming a half circle in front of his huge mahogany desk. This was equality in action he presumed. No standing for women officers any more.

'Would you like a coffee or something?' he asked.

Before Hood could say anything, Knowles had declined for both of them. Hood noticed that the chief had a coffee in front of him and a copy of *The Guardian*, half-opened to his left, now *de rigueur* for ambitious police officers. A half-eaten croissant peeped from under a lever-arch file to his right.

'Breakfast,' he said, indicating the plate. 'I've been in since seven.'

Kevin Langley had been chief constable of the combined police service for nearly eighteen months. He had been appointed from an outside area in order to avoid any suggestion of unfairness or bias. Two of the former chiefs had applied unsuccessfully for the job. Onewas now in Northern Ireland and the other had effectively undermined his chances by publicly opposing the amalgamation. He was now a deputy in charge of administration and discipline, not a role that would ever have appealed to Hood.

Langley had long since mastered the modern management-speak that was becoming endemic in the higher ranks. Political correctness leached out of him, but he still liked to think of himself as one of the lads. Fortunately, he had little notion of what "the lads" thought of him. The chief did not usually invite his subordinates to his office. He much preferred to make his presence felt by appearing suddenly and without notice on the floors below or in distant police stations, a practice which was not appreciated by the lower ranks. As he had once been an assistant chief constable in Cheshire before joining the Met as deputy commissioner, he was known, behind his back of course, as "the Cheshire Cat" – given his habit of appearing and then disappearing. Hood had only been in his office once before – when Langley was first appointed. He observed, on this his second visit, that the room had been expensively refurbished. When the forces merged, large sums of money had suddenly become available, courtesy of the Blair Government. The flow of cash was such that desperation had set in as to how to spend it. So chief officers had persuaded themselves and the police authority that they could only carry out their increasingly complex and difficult role if they were accommodated in the lap of luxury with a support staff that would have been appropriate for a medieval prince but looked a little excessive for a chief police officer.

The furniture, whilst modern, was obviously from the top of the range. Several paintings adorned the walls and a personal bathroom and a dressing room had been constructed from the storeroom that had abutted the office on Hood's previous visit. He would not have been surprised if a bedroom had been tacked on somewhere as well. The chief took a sip of coffee and then proceeded to business.

'No doubt you are wondering, Hood, why I have asked to see you and the assistant chief in charge of crime?'

The chief inspector noticed the formal approach.

'Yes, sir. I was, of course, aware of your interest in my present investigation. ACC Knowles has kept me informed.'

'And you, she?' he continued.

'Yes sir.'

'You are aware, I believe, that Macpherson will be reporting shortly?'

'Yes sir.'

'We are anticipating that the report will be highly critical of the Met.'

'So I believe, sir.'

'But it won't only be the Met who the media will be having a go at. We shall all be in the firing line too.'

'I suppose we will,' agreed Hood.

'I have been privy to some of the likely recommendations – unofficially, you understand. We expect the main recommendation to relate to a redefinition of a racist incident. It will encompass anything which is perceived to be racist by the victim or, indeed, by anyone else. That means that this robbery you are investigating, together with the attempted murder of the security guard will be categorised as a racist incident.'

Hood looked surprised. 'Really, sir? I can't think why.'

Langley grimaced.

'Isn't the security guard who was shot Asian?'

'Yes, sir – but I don't know what that has to do with anything. He wasn't shot because he was Asian. He was shot because he had a go at one of the robbers.'

'You may think that,' replied Langley. 'But that is not how it will work in the future. An Asian citizen has been shot and nearly killed during a robbery. As far as I am concerned that makes it a racist incident – with all the consequences that will follow.'

Langley folded his arms and sat back in his chair. Hood was not impressed.

'What consequences?' he asked. He forgot to add the customary "sir".

'Resources will have to be increased and efforts redoubled. The individual who fired the gun must be apprehended and convicted. It is clear to me that our performance in future will be judged largely on our success in combating racist crimes.'

Hood sighed inwardly. This was precisely the sort of reaction he could do without.

'I have no objection to increased resources, sir. But I have real difficulty in understanding how this can possibly be regarded as a racist incident. The motive for these offences was greed – pure and simple. The security guards were in uniform and wearing helmets. It was also dark. I very much doubt that any of these villains knew or cared about their racial origins.'

Knowles started to look apprehensive. She nursed ambitions to reach the top of the tree and was more than happy to fit in with the latest mores – whatever they might be.

'I'm sure Harry is as keen as any of us to track down all of the offenders, sir.'

She looked at Hood and nodded.

'Of course I am,' replied Hood. 'But I fail to see how categorising this robbery as a racist incident is going to help – resources apart.'

'Well,' said the chief. 'I'm surprised you don't see it as I do, very surprised.' He shook his head. 'I would have thought you of all people would have understood.'

Hood began to get irritated. 'So, we are talking about my racial make-up now, are we?' He'd forgotten the "sir" again.

Hood stood up and walked away from the desk before turning and standing before the chief. Langley was not impressed.

'May I remind you, Chief Inspector, who you are talking to?' said Langley, a trifle pompously, pointing to Hood's chair.

Hood sighed and sat down.

'I'm sorry sir, but I don't see how this is going to assist us catching the others. I have spoken to Mr Patel, very briefly, at the hospital. His doctors only gave me two minutes. He wasn't fit enough to make a statement but I'm sure he doesn't regard what happened to him as racist – and it never occurred to me either. And I ought to add that I am not yet wholly convinced that Patel or one of the other guards were not involved.'

The chief constable raised his voice, glancing at Knowles then looking directly at Hood. 'I hope you realise what you're saying. As far as I can see this man's a bloody hero. There's no evidence that he was involved. No evidence at all! And I've read your interim report. It seems that he'd behaved in a similar heroic manner on a previous occasion.'

'I agree, sir. In fact, *all* the evidence is to the contrary. All I'm saying is that it's too soon to reach any firm view, one way or the other. This robbery was not a chance encounter. It was carefully planned. Someone leaked information to the robbers. It could well have been one of the guards.'

'I doubt if you'll get anywhere going down that route,' said Langley dismissively. 'The man wasn't even supposed to be on duty that night. Did you see the TV interview with his wife? She's been devastated by what happened to her husband. She's so upset she wants to go back to India. And you think he might be involved in some way? The idea is preposterous!'

'No sir, I didn't see the interview but I can well understand how she feels. Nevertheless, treating this as a racist incident isn't going to help. If Patel doesn't regard it as such, why should anyone else?'

The chief leant forward, smiling as he did so. It was obviously time to change tack. 'Look Harry. That is precisely why we *must* regard it as a racist incident. We have to be ahead of the game. Patel may not think that at the moment but I predict the passage of time will bring about a change of view on his part. Just you wait and see.'

It will if this nonsense is put to him, thought Hood, but he said nothing. He had noticed the ACC's pleading look and decided discretion was necessary, at least until he left the chief's office.

Langley looked at Knowles, then continued. 'And I'm bound to say, Harry, progress seems to be painfully slow. What is the problem? I'm only here to help, you know.' Langley was now well in to avuncular mode. Hood settled in his chair again and replied calmly.

'Well, sir. We have one of them, as you know. The evidence against him is pretty overwhelming. We have his DNA at the crime scene. He isn't going anywhere soon.'

The chief did not appear impressed.

'But there were at least three others, probably more. No progress at all seems to have been made in even identifying them. The getaway vehicle has not been found, neither has most of the money. I don't regard one arrest out of four or more as anything like good enough.'

'Neither do I, sir. But I do expect to make progress.'

Knowles interrupted. 'We have good reason to believe that Michael Doyle is involved. It would be premature to make a move on him yet. He's under constant observation. I agree with the chief inspector's approach. We could arrest him, but there plainly isn't enough to hold him. Not at the moment anyway.'

'I'm sure there's a connection between him and Benson,' said Hood. 'It's only a question of time before we can prove it. Pulling him in now would only alert him to our interest in him. Far better to leave him where he is. He can't go far with his broken leg.'

The chief took another sip of his coffee before pushing the cup away.

'So what is being done to prove a connection?'

Hood looked at Knowles who indicated that he should continue.

'We are working on the assumption that there has to have been an inside connection at Bridgeford House. We haven't excluded the possibility of one of the other guards being in on it, but someone at the bank must be favourite. What I can't buy is that it was purely coincidental that the robbers swooped when a larger than usual amount of cash was being delivered in used notes. This theory is strengthened when we bear in mind that the whole system was going to change after Christmas. Once those German cartridges start to be used, the proceeds of such a robbery would be of no value – because of the dye that would stain the notes if the cartridges were broken open. The security guards did not know about the proposed change – not in relation to National Commercial – neither did the security firm. The bank had not yet informed them. The mole is much more likely to have been inside Bridgeford House. Only the bank would have known how the money was to be made up.

The chief stroked his chin. 'That seems logical. But if there was a tip-off, it could equally have come from someone in management at the security firm couldn't it?'

'The security firm could not have known that the bulk of the 1.9 million was to be made up of used notes – not unless someone at the bank told them. That seems to me to be the most important factor in the case. New notes could be traced and would be less valuable to the robbers as a result. This robbery took place when it did because most of the notes were untraceable. That is key to understanding the case.' Hood paused. 'As I said, sir, we haven't excluded anyone. But I've spoken with Simon Langdale who runs the security firm. He seems perfectly genuine – and Langdale had a very good reason not to be involved in anything like this at the moment.'

'Oh, what was that?'

'He has offers on the table from two of the national security companies. This little problem will make his business less attractive in the short term and reduce its value, which, in turn, will reduce what he would get for his interest in the company. So I think we can safely exclude him.'

'What about the operations manager? You don't seem to have got anything out of him.'

'That's right, sir. And I'm afraid we won't. He's dead!'

Langley and Knowles looked stunned. Hood glanced at Knowles. 'That's the development I mentioned downstairs, ma'am.'

'What? How did that happen?'

'As you know, I had arranged to see him before Christmas but he went down with the flu. His condition deteriorated and he was taken to hospital.

He seemed to be making progress but pneumonia set in and he died last night. I was informed a few minutes ago.'

'Well, that is a blow.' Langley appeared quite shaken.

'Yes, sir. We have not been exactly lucky with this investigation.'

'He can still be checked out of course.'

'In good time, sir. But I don't think it appropriate to start asking his family questions just yet.'

'No. You must use your discretion, Harry. I understand that.'

'Thank you, sir.'

Langley paused for a few moments then turned again to the question of the leak.

'If the leak was from the bank, any ideas yet who the source might be?'

'We have not excluded anyone at the moment. We are investigating all of them – from the manager down.'

'And…?'

The chief looked directly at Hood.

'Nothing so far. We are examining the employees' records – including some temporary short-term workers.'

Knowles interrupted. 'There can't be many of those, surely?'

'More than you would have thought, actually. Last summer they were very short-staffed when the operation expanded. They took on several workers through an employment agency. The last one left in early November. We've traced all of them bar one. My sergeant has given them all a clean bill of health. The exception is a woman called Lorraine Townley. We have not been able to find her. The address she gave in Loughborough turned out to be a student bedsit. The owner has very dodgy records, although her name does appear on a rent book he's produced. He says he has no idea what she looks like. Apparently it was his wife who arranged everything – and she doesn't speak English, or so he says.'

'What about the other tenants?'

'The trouble is the turnover is considerable. Hardly surprising when you see the place. It's a real dive. No one living there at the moment can remember her.'

'You've checked her National Insurance number, I presume?' said Langley.

'Of course. There is a number that matches but the address the Revenue has for her is on Tyneside. The only contributions made in the last two years are for the period she worked at Bridgeford House. The tax position is the same. If she is a student – which is what she told the agency – that might explain things.'

'Still sounds a bit suspicious. Is she registered anywhere as a student?'

'Not that we know of. She was in Newcastle – but that was months ago. But she did produce something to the agency that suggested she was studying somewhere or was applying to do so. Unfortunately, they didn't keep a copy of it.'

'What about Bridgeford House? They should have a copy of everything, including her photograph. Even the most basic security would require that.'

'You would have thought so – but all her records have mysteriously disappeared – which suggests to me that if she has anything to do with it, she was not working alone.'

'Well someone must remember what she looks like?'

'They most certainly do, sir. She's a good-looking woman who kept herself to herself by all accounts. We have a sketch of her – looks like a film star. Auburn hair and hazel eyes. All the men remember that.'

'What was her job at Bridgeford?' asked Knowles.

'She was a machine operator for the most part – but she did some secretarial work as well.'

Langley looked unimpressed.

'Doesn't sound as if she would have access to the necessary information – unless she got herself involved with one of the managers?'

Hood smiled. 'That's exactly what we are investigating at the moment. The general manager and his wife are heading for a divorce from what we can tell, but the word is he's involved with his secretary. He's probably a bit old for this one, anyway. She's only twenty-seven and he must be pushing fifty.'

'There's no fool like an old fool,' said Langley disinterestedly.

Hood thought it diplomatic to ignore that comment. He knew Langley was fifty-five next birthday.

'There is something else, sir. According to the manager – and this is what makes me really suspicious – not only have her employment records gone but her identification pass has disappeared too. Apparently, she never handed it in when she left but the copy, which is supposed to be retained for twelve months, can't be found either. The agency she was registered with doesn't have a photo – so we're reduced to a photofit of her. It certainly makes you think.'

Langley started to get interested.

'Does she have a passport? There will be a photo of her on record with them.'

'Apparently not. Swansea has no record of her either.'

'She doesn't hold a driving licence?'

'No sir.'

'Quite the mystery woman, isn't she?' said Knowles.

'Yes, ma'am. But this may all be a blind alley. Tyneside has been asked to check her out – but they've had no joy so far.'

'What about Doyle? He had four hundred grand in his possession in notes of the right denomination?' Langley had obviously studied Hood's reports fully.

'Not a single note corresponds with the three hundred thousand that we have the serial numbers for. There are no prints or DNA. In fact, there are only about two or three notes with consecutive serial numbers. That must just be coincidence. The CPS tell us that the fact he was travelling from this area with notes of the same denomination isn't good enough. The case would be kicked out of court unless we can prove a link between him and the crime scene – which for all practical purposes means a link with Benson. I should add that his alibi checks out, too. He arrived at the hotel in Dorset well before the robbery occurred. And he's made sure that the staff at the hotel remember him. He was dishing out tips like there was no tomorrow.'

'Perhaps he didn't take part. Perhaps he just set it up and ensured he had a rock solid alibi?'

'Perfectly possible,' replied Hood. 'As I said, we haven't excluded anything or anyone – yet. And there's something else. I discovered this morning that Hull has dropped the careless driving charge. The metal signs before the roadworks he crashed into had blown over in the bad weather and the flashing warning was not working that night. The CPS has decided there is insufficient evidence to prosecute.'

'This man sounds untouchable,' said Langley. 'Is anything going our way?'

'Not at the moment, sir. We've checked out Alex Stringer again, after he turned up at the magistrates' court, but there's nothing to connect him. He said he only came to get a look at Benson – just to see if he knew him. He didn't, or so he says. Sergeant Lunn knows him of old. He's pretty sure he's clean – at least for the moment.'

'Stringer is an armed robber, isn't he?'

'Yes sir. At least he was. He's just come out from a twelve-year stretch but I don't believe he had any involvement. His alibi, too, is rock solid.'

'But what's his connection with Benson? Why did he turn up at court if he doesn't know him?'

'He told Ian Lunn that he'd seen it in the local paper – that Benson had been arrested. Ian had spoken to him about the robbery before Christmas. He was just being nosey. After all, sir, it used to be his trade – armed robbery.'

Langley cleared his throat. 'So, what do we have? Is this man Benson likely to give us any assistance?'

Knowles took up the narrative. 'Benson has not said anything. He's probably too scared. He was only inches away when the shot was fired. He has no previous so he does seem a bit out of his league. Someone must have recruited him.' She turned to Hood. 'His background is being thoroughly checked, isn't it Harry?'

'Yes, ma'am. As you know, we are investigating him from the Birmingham end but we have drawn a complete blank so far. No one has a bad word for him and there's no intelligence to suggest he was ever involved in anything criminal or even dodgy. All we have is that he lost his job in September. He worked as a sales rep for a paint company. Made redundant because he failed to meet his targets. Seems he's a bit of a gambler too. But doesn't seem to owe anything. He had a big win in the autumn. The clerk at his usual betting office remembers him because of that. He won over two grand. He told the regulars all about it.'

'Well his luck has run out now,' commented Langley, gruffly.

'Yes, sir. It certainly has. His girlfriend seems genuine enough, but we reckon he knows Doyle and that she could prove it – but her mother died recently. She had a stroke over Christmas, so we have to take it gently with her at the moment.'

'Not too gently, I hope?' said the chief.

'We'll be seeing her again, no doubt about that. She has a sister who's a lawyer of some kind – so we have to tread carefully.'

'What about CCTV from the shopping centre?' asked Langley.

'There's masses of it. I have two officers going through it. We have CCTV from several cameras on the service road but nothing that can assist in identifying anyone. So we have uplifted CCTV from several locations, including pubs and restaurants as well as some of the major stores. We are working on the theory that observations must have been carried out before the robbers struck. We have some CCTV up to the day of the robbery. It's of varying quality and doesn't go back too far in time, but you never know, something might turn up. If we are to be given more resources, I could put more officers on to this.'

'Well, I've promised you two of the new trainee DCs who start next month,' said Knowles. 'You'll have to monitor them, of course, but they're pretty bright. You know one of them. He helped you out in Hull.'

'Yes,' replied Hood. 'Young Craddock. He has some experience of analysing CCTV. Got a judge's commendation for it, I believe.'

'A thankless task for a new recruit, isn't it?' said Langley.

'Well someone has to do it and he's got the experience.'

Langley frowned.

'Well that's up to you. As you know, I never interfere in operational decisions.'

It was Hood's turn to frown but he resisted the temptation.

'We still have the money, I take it,' added the chief. 'We haven't given it back to him?'

'No sir,' said Hood with emphasis. 'Doyle's brief is threatening proceedings but we are holding it until he proves where he got it from. So far, he's provided no evidence and unless and until he does, it stays with us.'

Langley nodded then drew the proceedings to a halt.

'All right, I have another appointment, so we'll bring this meeting to a close. But I want to be kept fully up to speed on this investigation – understood?'

'Yes, sir,' said Knowles. Hood nodded as he stood up.

'And Harry, don't forget to categorise this as a racist crime, will you?'

Hood looked at Knowles, then at the chief but said nothing.

'I'll ensure that's done, sir,' she said.

Hood hoped the chief did not notice the scowl on his face as he and the ACC left.

CHAPTER TWENTY

Andrew Hooper's trip to Newcastle upon Tyne produced only one piece of useful information. David Taylor had omitted to tell them something of potential relevance. The second in command in the machine rooms at Bridgeford House had been involved with the lovely Lorraine Townley. Theirs had been but a brief fling, according to Miss Townley, a young woman with a history of depression and bipolar affective disorder. She was detained in hospital because she could no longer cope with the breakdown of what she had believed was going to be a permanent relationship. Poor woman – she had started a number of "lasting relationships" in her young life, none of which had proved anything of the kind. Taylor was no exception. It had continued only a few weeks before he remembered his obligations to his wife and family. And, thinking of his wife and children – such had been his excuse – had called it all off. It was an old story. He'd swept her off her feet and promised to leave his wife. Their weekends away had been extravagant and sensual. She had particularly enjoyed the three-day trip to Glasgow, he having told his wife he had been sent on a course by his employer to Bournemouth. Marriage had been mentioned and preliminary vows exchanged but when the practicalities started to make an impact and passion had begun to subside, the cold light of reality had won the day. As her short-term contract came to an end, her lover's interest waned and floundered. She waited for him at her miserable bedsit in Loughborough, pending her hoped for return to a prospective place at New College in Leicester, but he simply failed to show. His mobile number was not answered and her attempts to contact him at Bridgeford House proved unsuccessful. He had carefully avoided giving her any accurate information about his domestic circumstances, although she knew he was married with children, so she was unable to locate his home telephone number. Like all of the managers at Bridgeford House, he was ex-directory. Then the letter arrived. She still had it and allowed Hooper to take it away with him. She could not bear to have it read to her.

So, as had happened before in her brief existence, she had taken an overdose of paracetamol and, after a brief confinement in a local hospital was sectioned under the Mental Health Act and transferred back home to Newcastle. Her detention was later varied which meant she could be detained for up to six months in hospital for her own protection, although the doctors had said she should be well enough to be released before then. But as the day of her release drew near, her anxiety had increased and her stay in hospital extended. She was in a fairly pleasant unit without any obvious or oppressive security and seemed to prefer to stay where she was. She had told her story to Hooper in a matter-of-fact way, entirely without emotion. Hooper wondered how such an attractive young woman could have ended up in such a predicament. Obviously, looks were not everything. He had left her lying on her bed, clutching a soft toy in her hand and staring at the ceiling. The nurse had assured him she was on the mend and that the medication she had been prescribed was having its effect. She would soon be discharged, whether she wished to be or not, but where she would go had yet to be decided. Hopefully, she would be able to make a written statement in the near future confirming what she had told him.

'Ask him to come in, will you, Andrew?' Hood had said after reading his sergeant's notes. 'From what she told you, our Mr Taylor may have been in need of extra funds. It can't be easy or inexpensive running a home and keeping a mistress on the side.'

'I wouldn't know, sir,' Hooper had responded. A bachelor still, at twenty-nine, the detective sergeant had escaped marrying his long-term partner for over three years, despite the many hints she regularly dropped, sometimes in the presence of senior officers.

'Do you think he was responsible for her records disappearing?' Hooper had asked.

'Undoubtedly,' Hood had replied. 'The question is why? To cover up his affair, or to cover up something far more serious? And, Andrew, make it clear to him, this is not an invitation he will be allowed to decline.'

★★★★

Hood had never met Taylor before. His witness statement had been taken by Wendy Knight. Hood read it again before the assistant manager arrived at the police station. There was no mention of Lorraine Townley. He decided to conduct a formal interview of the machine room deputy manager and to tape the proceedings. He would not be arrested – yet – but the more formal surroundings of the suspects' interview room were fully justified. Hood thought he deserved nothing less.

Taylor arrived looking very apprehensive. His earlier witness statement had been taken at Bridgeford House. The request for him to attend at the police station for a further interview had unnerved him, as Hood intended it should. Taylor had asked others at the counting house if they had been invited for further interviews. He was the only one. Hood was fully aware of the likely psychological impact on him. He intended to take full advantage. He deliberately kept him waiting and then sent a uniformed officer to conduct him to one of the interview rooms in the basement. No point having a consultant psychologist as a wife and not taking advantage of her knowledge of human behaviour under stress! Hood and Hooper walked into the room and sat down opposite Taylor. Hood said nothing for a minute as he took in every facet of the individual sitting nervously across the table. He certainly didn't have the look of a Lothario. He was not particularly tall and his brown hair was turning grey at the sides. He looked rather haggard and the bags round his eyes suggested he had not been sleeping well.

'Thank you for coming in, Mr Taylor,' said Hood after brief introductions. 'Do you mind if we record our conversation?' Hood indicated the tape machine with his hand. 'It saves Sergeant Hooper here having to write everything down.'

Hood smiled but not in a friendly way. His prey half laughed then nodded his head.

'Whatever you think is best,' he replied. 'But I don't think I can add anything to what I've already told you. I really know nothing about this robbery. I was halfway across the Channel when it took place.'

'Yes,' said Hood. 'We know. You were on your way to France, weren't you? Euro Disney wasn't it? With the family?'

Taylor tried to laugh it off.

'That's right. With my wife and family. I produced all the documentation to that nice lady detective last time.'

'Don't worry about that, Mr Taylor. We don't think you're one of the robbers.' Hood paused for effect. He then leant forward. 'If we did, you'd already be under arrest.'

Hood sat back in his chair and looked intently at the man opposite. Taylor swallowed hard and opened his mouth as if to say something but nothing emerged.

'Is there something you want to tell us, Mr Taylor, perhaps something you omitted from your earlier statement?'

'I don't think so, no. I repeat, I know nothing about this robbery. Nothing at all.'

Hooper smiled as Hood inserted his hand into his inside pocket and removed two sheets of paper, which he slowly placed on the table in front of him, smoothing out the pages as he did so. Taylor's head dropped as he recognised the letter he had written to Lorraine Townley.

'We have asked you here today Mr Taylor, to discuss your relationship with a former employee of the bank, a Miss Lorraine Townley. I'm obliged to point out to you that you are not under arrest. You can leave at any time, but I would be grateful if you would remain and help us with our inquiries. Do you understand?'

Taylor lifted his head, looked at Hood and then at Hooper and nodded.

'Does my wife have to find out about this?' he asked.

'It depends, Mr Taylor. Have you said anything to raise her suspicions?'

'No, of course not,' Taylor replied with a little more spirit.

'Well, Mr Taylor. I always say that when a man has repeatedly lied to his wife about his conduct and forgotten his marriage vows, it should be left to him to decide whether to confess all to her, unless of course, there is a criminal aspect to that behaviour.'

Taylor said nothing.

'I take it you did lie to her. I don't suppose your trip to Glasgow is something she knows anything about, is it?'

'So you know about that, do you?' sighed Taylor.

'We certainly do. And a few other things besides. Do you know where Lorraine is now?'

Taylor suddenly became quite animated. 'She's not here is she?'

'No, she's not here. She's in Newcastle, or to be accurate, a few miles north of Newcastle. In hospital. Seems she's had a bit of a breakdown. Sergeant Hooper's been up to see her. That's how we got hold of your letter.'

Taylor lowered his head again.

'Do I need a solicitor?' he asked.

'That's up to you. Do you feel you need a solicitor?'

Taylor raised his head. He was plainly embarrassed.

'Look Chief Inspector. I admit I had an affair with Lorraine. But that had nothing to do with this robbery. Half the men at Bridgeford House were after her. She's a good-looking woman.'

'And she chose you, did she?'

'Well, she was helping me out with a backlog of paperwork – one thing led to another, you know how it is – and things just developed from there.'

'No. I don't know how it is, Mr Taylor. Perhaps you would enlighten me? Did she know you were married?'

'Of course. If I hadn't told her, someone else would have done. Anyway, there's a photograph of my wife and kids on my desk.'

'Did you know she was mentally vulnerable?'

Taylor sighed. 'Not at first. It was only after we got back from Glasgow when she seemed to become very dependent on me – and very clinging. She wanted me to be with her all the time. It became quite stifling after a while. Then she threatened to tell my wife. There was a staff social event on the horizon – at the end of November. It happens every year and although she was due to leave before then, the manager had said all the temps would be invited. My wife would have been there so I had to tell her it was all over.' He paused. 'She didn't take it very well. If she hadn't been due to leave, I'm sure there'd have been a scene at work.'

'And you told her by writing her this letter, not face to face?'

'Yes. I know it looks like a coward's way out but I could never have done it otherwise.'

'Were you responsible for all her paperwork disappearing?'

Taylor looked quite surprised at the suggestion. 'No – I didn't know it had.'

'You would have access to the personnel records would you not? We understand that temporary employees come directly under your jurisdiction?'

'Yes, but why would I want to get rid of her records? Everyone knew she had worked for us for nearly four months. What would be the point?'

Hood changed the subject.

'How much do you earn, Mr Taylor?'

'What's that got to do with anything?'

'Will you answer my question, please? How much do you earn?'

Taylor eventually answered. 'Thirty-one thousand pounds per annum plus a discretionary bonus. Last year it was just under four thousand. I don't suppose there will be one this year, though, what with the robbery and everything.'

'And you are married with three children. Is that correct?'

'Correct, yes.'

'Does your wife work?'

'Yes, part-time. She's a veterinary assistant.'

'How much does she earn?'

'I'm not sure to the exact pound, but it's in the region of eleven thousand.'

'Tell me, Mr Taylor. How did you manage financially? You know, entertaining Miss Townley, taking her to hotels for the weekend and then there's the Glasgow trip. How was all this paid for from your earnings? I would have thought things must have been pretty tight anyway with a wife and three children to support?'

Taylor shook his head and sighed.

'So that's what all this is about, is it?'

'What do you mean?'

'You think I'm the mole; the one who gave the robbers the tip-off. That's what you think, isn't it?'

'What makes you think there was a mole? We haven't suggested that, have we?'

Taylor almost smiled. 'It's the talk of the bank,' he replied. 'It's never been specifically raised but it's perfectly obvious that's what your people have been trying to find out. Someone must have tipped off the robbers.'

'It's something we feel we have to consider, Mr Taylor. After all, if you were in our shoes, wouldn't you be asking the same question?'

'Well, it isn't true. I had nothing to do with it. How many times do I have to say this?'

Hood glanced at Hooper, who took up the questioning.

'You haven't answered the chief inspector's question Mr Taylor. Where did you get the money to wine and dine Lorraine? She told me you and she were having a whale of a time.'

Taylor closed his eyes and leant forward. For a moment Hood thought he was going to faint but he opened his eyes, put his hand in his jacket pocket and produced a credit card bill.

'You'd better look at this,' he replied as he handed the document to Hood. The chief inspector opened it up and examined it. He whistled through his teeth, then passed it to Hooper.

Taylor started to give his explanation.

'It's a new credit card account I opened nine months ago. I get twelve months' interest free credit then I have to pay it back – at 26 per cent. As you can probably guess, that's going to be a bit of a problem, especially if my wife finds out.'

'Six and half thousand pounds,' said Hooper, unable to resist grinning. 'I hope you think she was worth it.'

Taylor ignored the remark.

'As you can see, Chief Inspector. The hotel bills as well as the flights to and from Glasgow were all obtained on credit. I'm trying to pay it back a little at a time. If I lose my job over all this, I'll never manage it.'

'Why should you lose your job, Mr Taylor? Your secret is safe with us, providing you're telling us the truth. Then there's the question of the disappearing paperwork, of course.'

'I can assure you, that's not down to me. There were one or two members of staff who were more than a little suspicious about Lorraine and me, so as I said before, what would be the point?'

'Are you suggesting someone else might have removed her file?'

'I'm not suggesting anything. I simply don't know. Temporary workers' files are never thought of as being particularly important. Once they've left, no one ever looks at them. They're destroyed after twelve months anyway.'

'But only Lorraine's is missing. All the others were still in the filing cabinet in Mrs Jarvis's office. I don't like coincidences Mr Taylor. Someone removed that file and I want to know why.'

'I'm sorry, I can't help you. It wasn't me.'

Hood paused. He was dealing with a man who was obviously an accomplished liar. He'd lied convincingly to his wife and to Lorraine Townley but he had to concede in his own mind that the motive for such effective deception may have had no bearing on his investigation.

'All right, Mr Taylor. That's all for now. You can go. But I'd like you to agree to both your office and your home being searched. Sergeant Hooper will be as discreet as he can.'

A look of panic crossed Taylor's face.

'I don't mind the office being searched,' he said, 'but do you have to search my home? If I had taken the file, I'd hardly stash it at home, now, would I?'

'Perhaps not. But we still have to check. You'd be surprised what we have found when searching homes in the past. People do the strangest things.'

Hooper looked towards Hood.

'We could always search his home when his wife is at work, I suppose, sir.'

'Is she at work now?' asked Hood, checking his watch.

'Until 7 p.m. She works late on Thursdays.'

'All right, Andrew, the house first, then the office. No doubt Mr Taylor will go with you. Thank you for your co-operation. I may need to speak to you again. So don't go anywhere without informing us, will you?'

Taylor stood up and walked to the door. He was obviously relieved but paused and turned and faced Hood. 'I'm sorry about Lorraine,' he said. 'I really did fall for her. It was the children that brought me to my senses. I couldn't have left them. I simply couldn't. I didn't realise that until it came to it. Funny, isn't it?'

'Never tempted to take her abroad, then, Mr Taylor? Or was that impossible because she didn't have a passport?'

Taylor appeared puzzled.

'What do you mean? She did have a passport. I remember seeing it. I commented on her photograph. She wanted me to leave my wife and run off with her to Italy. We even planned a trip to Venice. She speaks Italian, you know. I think she lived there for a while when she was younger.'

'Mr Taylor, we checked with the passport office. No passport has ever been issued to Lorraine Townley – not to anyone of her age anyway.'

'But her passport wasn't in that name. It was in her maiden name. She was briefly married a few years ago to a man called Townley, but he was an unpleasant bully by all accounts, so she left him after only a few months.'

Hood sat up and leaned forward. 'But she continued to use a passport in her maiden name?'

'I suppose so, yes.'

'What was her maiden name?'

'Benson. She was Lorraine Benson.'

CHAPTER TWENTY-ONE

When Hood gave Knight the news about Lorraine Townley, or Lorraine Benson, as he now referred to her, she was quite taken aback. They were sitting in Hood's office discussing the progress of the investigation. Hood was taking advantage of the temporary absence of his two detective sergeants, both of whom he had despatched to Birmingham earlier to make further enquiries of Benson's family following David Taylor's disclosure of Lorraine's antecedents. He valued Wendy's cool, logical mind and her ability to remain detached when assessing the legitimate parameters of potential evidence.

'That's a turn up, sir. But it's a fairly common name. It doesn't necessarily mean there's a connection.'

'I know,' replied Hood. 'There are over forty of them in the local phone book.'

'We'd better get someone over to Birmingham with Lorraine's photofit. See if she's part of the same family. She's certainly not Charlie's sister. We checked out his immediate family after he was arrested.'

'Already in hand. Ian Lunn is over there with Andrew as we speak and I've asked Tyneside to check her out as well. An officer has gone to the local register office to see what she can discover about her background. She has her date of birth, so it shouldn't be too much of a problem to come up with a basic family tree.'

Knight shook her head. 'It never occurred to Andrew to ask her for her maiden name?'

'We live and learn, Wendy, we live and learn. I suppose you would have done. It's the sort of thing that would have occurred to a woman.'

Hood smiled as he spoke. Knight knew he wasn't being sexist. He was a great supporter of women in the force.

'I don't know about that, sir. Seems obvious with the benefit of hindsight but whether I would have thought to ask, I really can't say. I don't think it occurred to any of us that she might have been married.'

Hood was still smiling. 'I suspect you would have asked though. I must confess, it never occurred to me either. It goes to show you one should never assume anything.'

'But let's suppose she is related. Let's suppose she's been in contact with Charlie. Perhaps she was at his engagement party? Question is, would she have known enough to tip him off?'

'It's not a question of supposing,' replied Hood. 'We need some clear evidence. Even if she is related to Benson, that in itself doesn't prove a thing.'

'I agree, sir. But if she is, we'd just *have* to see Taylor again, wouldn't we? He could have mentioned something to her, you know, inadvertently. What do they call it? Pillow talk? And she could have passed it on to Benson. If she was desperate for Taylor to leave his wife and go off with her, it would probably have led to his giving up his job and the two of them would need money from somewhere. They'd need more than love to keep them warm in the long winter nights – even in Italy.'

'Possibly. Or perhaps it was Taylor himself. Although he decided against it in the end, he was completely obsessed with her to begin with and he could have been making similar plans. I doubt if he wanted to embrace poverty as well as Lorraine! But you're right, we need to see him again – if there's the slightest hint of a link.'

Knight immediately started to have second thoughts. 'But would Taylor have told us her maiden name if he were involved? Somehow, I doubt it. It sounds as if he didn't appreciate the possible relevance of what he told you. And another thing. We haven't got any evidence to suggest he knows Charlie Benson or that he knows of any connection between Benson and Lorraine.'

'Well, there's no point speculating until we have established some basic facts. We should be hearing from Ian or Andrew shortly. And we mustn't forget, none of this is going to help us in proving a link with Doyle. That's our prime objective and we have a long way to go, a very long way. If Doyle is the main man behind this job, I'd much rather have some evidence of a link between Lorraine and him.'

Knight remained in a pensive mood. 'It could still be perfectly innocent, though, couldn't it, sir? You know what it's like at a party when the booze is flowing. A few drinks too many. An unguarded comment about his job. A reference to the proposed change to these cartridges. Benson's ears a-flapping? Not enough to arrest Taylor, really.'

'That's what I like about you, Wendy. You are capable of retaining an objective viewpoint and don't let your imagination run too far ahead of the evidence. Unlike one or two of your colleagues. Another feminine virtue, I suppose?' Hood was silent for a few moments. 'But Taylor was a very worried man when Andrew and I had a chat with him. If we invite him in again, I'm sure he'll co-operate. If he doesn't we shall have to think again about our Mr Taylor.'

Hood's mobile rang. He looked at the screen.

'It's Andrew.'

Silence ensued for a couple of minutes. Then Hood spoke. There was more than a touch of excitement in his voice.

'Very interesting, Andrew. Is she willing to make a statement? Good. I'll see you in my office in the morning.' He switched his phone off. 'Curiouser and curiouser.'

'What do you mean, sir?'

'You're not going to believe this. Benson's sister recognised the photofit. Better than that, she produced a photograph of Lorraine. It was taken at Benson's engagement party in October. I think you must be psychic, Wendy.'

The detective constable laughed.

'I wouldn't go as far as that, sir. Just a lucky guess.'

'But it gets better. Lorraine had a man in tow. An older man. And the description fits Taylor to a tee. Pity they didn't have a photo of Taylor with them to show her. But we can soon remedy that.' Hood's face was a picture and he had become very animated. 'And it doesn't stop there. Lorraine and Charlie are first cousins. How's that for a bit of luck?'

Wendy Knight remained calm.

'But what about Doyle? Did she recognise him?'

Hood's face fell.

'No joy on that front. She hesitated when she was shown his mug shot, but didn't recognise him. But we can't have everything I suppose.' But Hood was already planning his next move. 'When Andrew gets back, I think we definitely need to see the assistant manager of the machine room again, and quickly. And we need further words with Lorraine. I think you ought to go up with Andrew this time. She might be more responsive with you.'

'Whatever you say, sir.

★★★★

When Hooper returned from Birmingham, Hood called both him and Knight into his office. A decision had to be made as to whether Doyle should be arrested. The pressure from the top was becoming intolerable. The chief constable wanted some action. Hood put forward his carefully considered theory that Doyle had travelled from Dorset in order to take part in the robbery then returned to the hotel to consolidate his alibi.

'But the car park, sir. There's a barrier. It opens automatically for incoming vehicles until midnight, then it's locked. If he came back in the early hours of the morning, he'd have had to contact the night porter to get the barrier raised. And there's no way he could have got that Mercedes *under* the barrier. The hotel had it specially designed to protect vehicles left in the car park over-night; and the CCTV showed that the Merc did remain in the car park on the night of the sixteenth/seventeenth. It didn't leave until Saturday lunchtime when Doyle went to pick up Hamilton at Bournemouth Station. He had to go to reception to get the code in order to lift the barrier.'

'Exactly,' replied Hood, taking on board Hooper's scepticism. 'A perfect alibi – assuming the only transport he had was the Mercedes.' Hood paused and looked at the two junior officers in turn. 'What if he had some other means of transport stashed well away from the hotel? The Merc couldn't get out of the car park – but he could certainly leave the lodge area without anyone being the wiser. Question two: Why are we assuming he had no other means of transport? Isn't that exactly what he wants us to believe?'

Neither Hooper nor Knight responded.

'I also did a bit more checking on Doyle. He had two speeding convictions when he was in his early twenties. He was disqualified from driving the second time which suggests he was going extremely fast.'

'That doesn't prove anything, does it?'

Knight looked puzzled but Hood continued.

'No, it doesn't – and it took some digging to get the details, I can tell you. Most of the case papers have been destroyed. But some bright spark did put a bit of interesting information onto microfiche. On both occasions, Doyle was riding a high-powered motorcycle.'

'You mean he had such a machine stashed near the hotel, left on the bike, pulled the job and got back to the lodge before breakfast?'

Hooper sounded more than a little sceptical. Hood pretended not to notice.

'Exactly. He had a "Do not disturb" sign on the *outside* door of the lodge and had ordered a full English for 9 a.m. When his breakfast arrived he was in his bed. Quite an alibi, when you think about it. And he made sure he was noticed in the restaurant the night before by ordering that very expensive bottle of wine.'

'Chateau Margaux '77. Not one of the better years but still out of my price range,' said Knight.

'Is that so?' said Hood. 'One hundred and ninety pounds for a bottle of wine does seem a bit excessive. You mean he could have paid more?'

"78 and '79 are reputed to be better years – but the hotel did not have them in stock.'

Hood was again surprised at Knight's knowledge. But she simply smiled.

'It's Greg's main interest – outside statistics. He looked it up for me in his wine encyclopaedia. He reckoned it was quite a good price given that it was served in such a well-known and expensive restaurant. They usually double the price you'd pay from a wine merchant.'

Hooper sighed. 'So it was quite cheap really?' he said, smiling. 'So that won't help us break his alibi then.'

Hooper's sarcasm did not escape Hood. Knight also added a note of dissent.

'But why go to all this trouble? As I pointed out before, sir, he could have organised something like this in a much handier location – somewhere nearer the Charnwood.'

'Let me finish before you shoot me down,' said Hood. 'I also did a bit more checking – or Debbie did. Why do you think he hired such a large estate?'

'Because he's a rich show-off?' said Hooper dismissively.

'Perhaps. But you can get quite a big motorcycle in the back of one of those Mercs. Debbie visited Premier Cars yesterday; it seems they were not very happy with Mr Doyle. They found some oil on the rear carpet of the vehicle when it was returned. Now what do you think could have caused that?'

'A motorcycle carried in the back? But will it be possible to get it tested?' asked Knight, warming to Hood's theory.

'Unfortunately not. They put in a new section of carpet and got rid of the offending piece, but the fact of the oil stain is noted in their records.'

'Do their records show whether Doyle gave an explanation for the oil?' asked Hooper.

'No. He's one of their best customers.' Hood almost scowled. 'So no one liked to raise it with him. Remember, he hired the same vehicle from them early in January. The one which he smashed up in Hull. It was written off and has since been broken up for spares. So there's no way we can carry out any tests. It's a pity Humberside didn't hang on to it – but I suppose it was impossible once they dropped the careless driving charge. All we have are some photographs taken after the accident.'

'It would be very handy if we could find a motor cycle that belonged to him,' mused Knight.

Hood laughed. 'And the chances of finding that are...?'

All three answered together.

'Zero!'

'Well?' said Hood. 'Do we pull him in or leave him until we get something a bit more definite?'

'We leave him,' replied Knight. 'With respect sir, unless we can explode his alibi, this will be dismissed as a mere theory. Now, if we could link him directly with Benson, we would have a chance. Questioning him now would simply give him more time to come up with a convincing explanation.'

'That must be right, sir,' added Hooper. 'Chances are he wouldn't say anything anyway. We have to leave him until we can link him with Benson. There's no other way.'

'And there was nothing to link him with Benson's car? The one that was seized in Portsmouth?' asked Knight.

'Absolutely nothing,' replied Hood. 'The forensic boys went over it with a fine toothcomb. Every test was negative.'

'Well, we can't touch him, sir. Wendy's right. If we move too quickly, we will merely demonstrate how weak our case is.'

'I think that must be right,' said Hood thoughtfully. 'We'll see what we get out of Taylor and Lorraine and push on with examining the CCTV. If we can establish a link, the CPS reckons his possession of the cash will add a bit more weight to our case – even though we can't prove for definite that it came from the robbery.'

'I think the CPS is being typically weak on that sir – as per usual,' said Hooper. 'Unless Doyle comes up with an innocent explanation for having so much cash – in the right denominations – in the back of his motor as he was leaving the country, the only conclusion is that he was laundering money from the robbery. You'd have thought that forensics would have come up with something to link it with the cash from the Charnwood.'

'But they haven't.'

'I suppose we could arrest him on suspicion of money laundering,' added Knight. 'He'd have to come up with something then, wouldn't he?'

'Not necessarily,' said Hood. 'We'd still have to prove the money was the proceeds of crime. Anyway, I don't want him going down for that. He'd be out in twelve months. I want him for the robbery and attempted murder. He'd be out of circulation until I retire if we can pin that on him!'

'So we leave him, do we, sir?'

'For the moment – yes. It's my wedding anniversary soon. I thought I might take Sarah down to this hotel in Dorset for the weekend. I can make a few further enquiries while I'm there.'

'Don't forget, sir', said Knight with a smile, 'the '78 and '79 are superior years.'

'I don't think we'll be drinking Chateau Margaux – not at those prices – thankyou very much.'

CHAPTER TWENTY-TWO

Wednesday, 3 February 1999

David Stuart Taylor sat nervously in front of the table in Interview Room 3 at Police Headquarters. Hood had decided to ratchet up the psychological pressure on him by bringing him to the centre of operations of Mid-Shires rather than by interviewing him again at the station where "Operation Christmas Carol" was based. Interview Room 3 also had the advantage of a transparent or one-way mirror, so ACC Knowles could observe events. She was under considerable pressure from the chief constable and wanted to see for herself what progress was being made with the inquiry.

Nothing of interest had emerged from the search of Taylor's office or his home. His wife had left her work early with a headache on the afternoon the search had been carried out and arrived at the house as Hooper and two uniformed officers were about to leave. Taylor had had to lie to his wife again to explain their presence but while Hood assumed he was now quite practised in deceiving her he hoped her undoubted displeasure at having her home turned over by the police had made a further impact on his conscience. He certainly looked pretty upset as he waited for Hood and Hooper, and the single, silent, uniformed officer standing motionless by the door hopefully added to his discomfort.

Hood and Hooper walked somewhat casually into the room. Taylor started to fidget. He took a handkerchief from his pocket and wiped his brow.

'Thanks for coming in again, Mr Taylor. Hopefully we won't keep you too long.'

This assurance had no discernible effect on Taylor. If anything it added to his apparent distress. He swallowed hard and placed his hands together on the table, trying to present as calm an impression as possible. In that he was singularly unsuccessful. Hood sat down opposite him and placed a file of papers somewhat ostentatiously on the table. He then leaned over and started the tape player. As it rumbled into action, Taylor spoke.

'I would like a solicitor if I'm to be questioned further. I have told you everything I know. I had nothing to do with this robbery.'

'Of course you can have a solicitor, if you wish, Mr Taylor,' said Hood. 'But you are not under arrest and I have no present intention of arresting you – you can leave any time you like – I just have a few more questions arising out of what you told us the other day. As before it would be convenient if we recorded your answers.'

Taylor looked slightly relieved but still unhappy.

'I see. If that's the case, why was I brought here? You could have questioned me at Bridgeford House or even at home – now that my wife knows about this.'

'Sorry about that, sir,' interrupted Hooper. 'But we had no idea she would come home early that afternoon. As I understand it, neither did you.'

Hooper looked towards Hood who already knew the position.

'Left work early with a headache, sir. Caught us as we were just finishing off.'

'So, does she know about Lorraine now?' asked Hood mischievously.

'No – she does not!' responded Taylor, his spirits rising. 'And I'd be obliged if she wasn't told. I have enough problems at home without her finding out about Lorraine.'

'We'll do our best, sir,' assured Hood, 'but we can't help the gossip at Bridgeford House, now can we? It might be better if you confessed all to Mrs Taylor. You never know, she might be more forgiving than Lorraine.'

The assistant manager looked startled.

'What do you mean? What has Lorraine said?'

'Well, as you might expect, we are speaking with her again and with other members of her family.'

Taylor's head dropped. Hood pressed on.

'You may have read in the newspapers that we have a man in custody charged with conspiracy to rob – a man called Charles Benson. Turns out he is Lorraine's cousin.'

Taylor looked up. His face told it all. 'I didn't know that. I really didn't – not when I first saw his name in the paper – then I put two and two together after you interviewed me. I didn't know for sure, but I thought it was too much of a coincidence, you know, the names being the same.'

'It's not exactly an uncommon name, is it? When did you first discover her maiden name was Benson?'

Taylor could hardly control himself. He unburdened himself in one long, rambling and confused confession.

'We were planning a trip to Venice – I believe I mentioned it when you saw me last time. I was trying to book a flight over the Internet – I'd never tried to do that before. It's not as straightforward as they say, you know, or perhaps you don't. I don't know about you but I usually use a travel agent… I thought using the Internet would be more confidential. I had to have her passport number, though. You have to enter it on the application form. I suppose I should have realised that. She showed me her passport and I noticed the name. I had no idea she had been married before then. She'd never mentioned it previously. I didn't know, honestly, you have to believe me.'

Hood said nothing for a moment. He knew when he had someone on the rack and he aimed to keep Taylor there for a little longer.

'But you didn't go to Venice, did you?'

The disclosures continued at a pace. Taylor hardly drew breath.

'No. I couldn't find a flight back on a suitable date. That's why we went to Glasgow. My wife was going away for a long weekend to see her mother. She was taking the children with her. Half term it was. I told her I had to go to a conference in Bournemouth – which was half true. There was a conference that weekend that I could have gone to, so it was all coming together – but I had to be back by the Tuesday and there were no flights available until Thursday, so Venice was off the agenda.'

'Glasgow doesn't seem much of a substitute.'

Taylor dropped his head and said nothing for several seconds. He breathed hard then looked up, his self control returning.

'Chief Inspector, we are both grown men. Let's be realistic, shall we? We spent most of our time in the hotel bedroom. The location was of secondary importance. We simply wanted somewhere well away from here. I didn't want to run the risk of bumping into someone we knew.'

Hooper interrupted. 'Did you go anywhere else with Lorraine – apart from the double bedroom in Glasgow?'

Taylor squirmed with embarrassment. 'You've seen my credit card bill. Most of the places we stayed are on there.'

'No mention of Birmingham – on the credit card bill?'

Hooper had examined it with care. Taylor dropped his head again and sighed.

'Yes, we went to a party in Birmingham. I didn't think I would be able to get away that weekend. It was a last-minute decision. We stayed in one of those Travel Inn places. Paid cash on that occasion.'

Hood looked at Hooper.

'Did you meet any of Lorraine's family, her extended family, I mean?'

'I remember being introduced to her cousin, a woman about the same age – I can't remember her name, Liz or something, I believe. Her aunt was there as well. A tall, thin woman with really bad halitosis. Apart from that we kept ourselves pretty much to ourselves.'

'Charlie Benson – the man we have in custody – he was at that party. In fact, it was his engagement party. Surely you and Lorraine must have been introduced to the happy couple?'

Taylor hesitated.

'There were a lot of people there. Well over 120 I would say and I didn't know any of them. It was also very noisy. But I saw him at a distance. There was some kind of presentation made – you know – an engagement gift was handed over on a sort of small stage towards the end of the evening. He made a few remarks – well I assume it was him – and then the dancing started again. Lorraine and I left shortly afterwards. As far as I can recall, I didn't speak to him.'

'What about Lorraine?'

'She could well have done. She disappeared for ten minutes at one time. I was left entirely on my own. I didn't speak to anyone. I thought she'd gone to the loo. You know what women are like on these occasions – and there are never enough loos.'

He smiled. Hood did not.

'Tell me about these cartridges. The ones that were being introduced last month to replenish ATMs. Did Lorraine know about them?'

'I expect so. It's not a secret. We had a big consignment of them delivered in December – just as I was about to go on leave. I guess almost everyone at Bridgeford House knew we were going to start using them.'

'That was in December. Lorraine left in early November. Who knew about them in, say, September? Who knew they would be coming into use in January 1999 at the time you attended the party in Birmingham?'

'Senior management knew. We discussed it at a management meeting in September. Mrs Jarvis would have known – she took the minutes. I suppose anyone who looked at the minutes would have known but they have a very restricted circulation.'

'Would Lorraine have known?'

Taylor began to look nervous again. He did not reply.

'Well, Mr Taylor. Did Lorraine know about the changeover before you went to the party in Birmingham?'

'I don't know. She might have done. She did some secretarial work for me. She might have seen the minutes. Anyway, everyone knew they were being used by other institutions. There'd even been a TV programme about them.'

'Did you tell her they were about to be used by the bank? You know, trying to impress her, perhaps. Letting it slip out, unintentionally?'

Taylor looked down before he answered.

'How would that impress her?'

He paused again, then added, 'I might have done. I can't remember.'

Hood looked at his quarry, then at Hooper.

'You see how it looks from our point of view, Mr Taylor? You are having an affair with Lorraine. She at least thinks this is the real thing. She hopes you are going to leave your wife and go off with her. You don't need me to tell you the likely effect of that on your finances. You would need money. One way of getting it would be for someone, you or her – perhaps both of you – to leak to these robbers the date of the changeover. Or are we to presume it was pure chance they struck two weeks before the changeover was due to be made?'

Taylor looked up. He spoke slowly and firmly as if his life depended on it.

'I don't know about Lorraine. All I know is I never leaked anything to anyone – not knowingly anyway. I just wouldn't do that. I just wouldn't.'

Hood picked up his papers and selected a photograph – a photograph of Doyle. He handed it to Taylor.

'I want you to look at this photograph. Study it carefully. Tell me, do you recognise him?'

Taylor did as he was asked. He started to shake his head.

'No, I don't know him. Who is he?'

'That doesn't matter.'

Hood retrieved the photograph, then produced another one. This time it was of Charlie Benson. Taylor looked at it. Almost at once his head nodded.

'This is him. The chap at the party. The one who was getting engaged.'

'Thank you,' said Hood, placing the photograph back in his folder.

'Finally, take a look at this one, would you?'

Hood took out a smaller photograph – of Julia Hamilton. It was not a particularly good likeness as it had been taken without her knowledge as she left Harbour Buildings. Taylor looked at it for some time.

'Good-looking woman,' he volunteered. 'She looks a bit like Lorraine, apart from the hair. But I don't think I've ever seen her. Was she at the party too?'

'I don't know,' replied Hood. 'I wasn't there. You were.'

'As I've said, there were a lot of people there. I'm sure I'd have noticed someone like her had she been there.'

He handed the photograph back to Hood.

'I really can't say – one way or the other.'

Hood replaced the photograph in his file.

'Tell me about the cash, please, Mr Taylor. How many people working at Bridgeford House would know how a particular consignment intended for ATMs would be made up?'

'What do you mean?' Taylor genuinely appeared not to understand.

'The consignment that was stolen was made up of both used notes and new notes – yes?'

'Agreed,' replied Taylor.

'Who determines whether new notes or used notes – or a combination of the two – is used to make up the consignment?'

'I've already dealt with this in my witness statement. It depends on how many suitable used notes are available. The policy is to limit the use of new notes. They are only used to make up the numbers.'

'I appreciate that, Mr Taylor. What I am asking is *who* decides when new notes should be used?'

'Mr King has the final say but either Steven Lloyd or I usually make the decision – if you call it a decision. It really makes itself. If there aren't enough used notes of suitable quality, the balance is simply taken from the new notes stored in the other strongroom.'

'On this occasion, three hundred thousand pounds were in new notes. The serial numbers of those notes were therefore known – agreed?'

'Yes.'

'We were told by Mr King that sometimes a whole consignment can be made up of new notes. On this occasion most of the notes were used and there was, therefore, no record of their serial numbers.'

'Yes.'

'When did you become aware that only three hundred thousand were going to be in new notes?'

'Oh, I see,' said Taylor, nodding his head. 'You're suggesting that I tipped off the robbers to let them know that the bulk of this consignment would be in used notes. That's what your suggesting, is it?'

'I'm not suggesting anything. Merely trying to get to the truth.'

'Well, you're way off target so far as I'm concerned. I was given the numbers only a few hours before Langdale Security collected. The information came directly from Reg King or his secretary not three hours before they arrived. I checked the secure program on the computer and realised we would have to use some new notes to make up the numbers. I arranged for three hundred thousand to be removed from the smaller strongroom. It's all logged. In fact, because I was going on leave, I think you'll find that it was Reg King who signed off the delivery – not me.'

'I'm aware of that, Mr Taylor. We have checked the paperwork. It's in apple-pie order – as you would expect. Mr King remained on the premises all through the night in question. He didn't get home until the early morning. You left – the record shows – over two hours before Langdale Security arrived.'

'I see,' said Taylor. He was now much more animated and speaking with renewed energy. 'You're suggesting that I passed on the details. In effect, telling these criminals this was the consignment to go for. Well, I'm sorry to disappoint you, Chief Inspector, but it didn't happen. I told no one anything. I went straight home and two hours later my wife and family were heading for Dover. We caught the early morning ferry. If there was a leak – it had nothing to do with me.'

Hood smiled.

'What about the Sunday consignment?'

Taylor looked surprised.

'The Sunday consignment?'

'Yes. We understand from Mr King that an even larger delivery was to be made to the Charnwood early on the Sunday morning?'

'What has that to do with me?' Taylor seemed genuinely unconcerned. 'I wasn't going to be there to deal with that. Anyway, I have since heard that it all went smoothly – with a police escort.'

'Who organised that?'

'I don't know. I assume it would have been Mr Lloyd or Mr King. I was on leave.'

'So you were.'

Hood glanced at Hooper before he continued.

'I also understand that the entire Sunday delivery was made up of used notes?'

'Was it? I don't know. You'll have to ask one of the others.'

'We shall, Mr Taylor, we shall.'

Taylor looked about him, nervously. Hood continued to press him.

'Can you explain why three hundred thousand in new notes was included in the delivery that was stolen if there were sufficient used notes to form an even larger consignment a few days later?'

'I've no idea,' replied Taylor confidently. 'Perhaps some were held back for the Sunday delivery – I don't know.'

Hood suddenly stood up. 'Thank you, Mr Taylor. That will be all – for now. Can I offer you a lift back to Loughborough?'

Taylor, no longer nervous, looked away and declined.

'I can make my own way back, thank you,' he said. 'If you wish to question me further, I shall require my solicitor to be present.'

Hood smiled.

'Of course, Mr Taylor, but I doubt if we shall need to trouble you again.'

Hooper and Hood followed Taylor out of the interview room.

'Shows you the wisdom of the old adage, doesn't it?' whispered Hood when Taylor was out of earshot. 'Do not adultery commit. Advantage seldom comes of it!' I wouldn't want to be in David Taylor's shoes when he gets home.'

CHAPTER TWENTY-THREE

Monday, 8 February 1999

Wendy Knight's trip to Newcastle hardly advanced the inquiry. As she'd been in hospital well before the robbery occurred, Lorraine was never considered to be a suspect, but she did corroborate Taylor's account in most respects. She had spoken to her cousin and his fiancée at the engagement party but didn't think Taylor had. "He's very shy with people he doesn't know," she had said in her bland, unemotional way. She also agreed she had told her aunt and Liz where David worked and what he did, but this she said was just general chit-chat. She didn't think anything of it and neither did anyone else. But she was able to give some assistance on one point that had long troubled Hood. Although the changeover to the cartridges was supposed to be known only to senior management, she remembered she had actually typed a letter to the German manufacturers in September whilst helping out in the office and she reckoned most of the employees would have known the system was due to be changed at some time in the future. She didn't know when, but she did know that the ATMs would have to be adapted before the new system could become operational. As Hood had foretold at the outset of the investigation, gossip was as prevalent at Bridgeford House as it was anywhere else, so when Knight revealed this piece of information to him on her return, he rechecked the witness statements of the other employees and wondered aloud why not a single one had mentioned it. All, save senior management, had stated they had no knowledge of any likely alteration to their working practices. Perhaps someone at the counting house had something to hide after all? Or perhaps they were too scared to state openly what they knew?

The senior guard, Ashock Patel, was now fit to be interviewed. Hood decided to take Knight with him when he travelled to the small and rather exclusive estate in Oadby, just outside Leicester, where the

Patel family resided. He was initially surprised that a security guard could afford to live in such surroundings until he was told that the bungalow was rented from a relative of Mrs Patel. They had lived there for nearly seven years and were well liked in that small community of mainly white retired residents. Two of their four children were at home when the two detectives called but were rushed outside by their mother as Hood and Knight were shown into the sitting room. Although the property was indistinguishable outside from other homes in the avenue, the living room had a distinct Indian ambience. The wallpaper was heavily embossed and mainly gold in colour and a large effigy of an Indian god gazed benignly from an alcove. Knight, who had recently completed a diversity course at Hendon, recognised it at once as *Shri Ganesha,* the remover of obstacles and lord of beginnings. *Perhaps it's an omen*, she thought to herself as she accepted an offer of tea from Mrs Patel. Hood declined. Ashock Patel remained seated in an armchair. Hood shook his hand and asked how he was, observing he looked much better than when he had last seen him in hospital. He was being rather economical with the truth when he said that; Patel looked anything but well.

'I'm still a little weak, but much better than I was,' he replied. He had hardly any accent, unlike his wife, but he had an open and seemingly honest face. 'I hope to return to work – eventually,' added the security guard.

Hood sat on the settee close to Patel's chair. A return to work appeared out of the question, at least for the foreseeable future.

'There is no question of that,' said Mrs Patel as she brought a tray with four cups and saucers into the room and placed them on the coffee table in front of her husband. 'This country is not safe for the likes of us,' she added. 'If I had my way we would return to India.'

Patel smiled indulgently. 'And what would we do there, Nirmala? How would we live? I am used to this country. We have a good life here – and the children are doing very well.' He turned to Hood. 'My eldest son, Amrit. He is at university in Sheffield. He graduated with 2:1 honours. He is to become a teacher when he finishes his postgraduate course in May. That is what I hope.'

'He doesn't want to be a teacher,' contradicted Mrs Patel. 'And if he did he could be a teacher in India. India is the future – not this country. I do not like it here. We would be safe in India. Amrit will go there when he finishes his studies.'

Patel looked at his wife and shook his head.

'He is only going there on a trip – not to stay there. You know that, Nirmala.'

Patel turned towards the chief inspector. 'Amrit is going on an adventure holiday when he finishes his exams in May, Mr Hood. He and a few friends are travelling overland to where my family comes from. That is all.'

'Sounds like fun,' said Hood. 'My wife did something similar when she graduated – but in the opposite direction. It was all the rage in those days.'

'Amrit should stay there and not come back. We should go there and not come back.'

Mrs Patel was quite adamant.

'Forgive my wife, Inspector. She is worried for me. She wants me to change jobs – but what else can I do? I have no qualifications. None at all.'

'You would appear to have a great deal of courage though, sir. That's something of a qualification, isn't it?' said Hood.

'And that will get him killed,' said Mrs Patel, pouring the tea. 'That is all that will do. Get him killed. Then what would become of me and the children.'

She offered Knight a cup of tea. Hood again declined, but politely.

'Could I ask you, sir, why *did* you punch that robber? You must have seen one of them had a gun and they'd already poured petrol over you and the driver. What on earth made you do it? Your two colleagues were terrified. They didn't lift a finger to help you.'

'I don't know. I just did it. I thought they might kill us anyway. It was just a reaction. That is all. I didn't do it to be a hero.'

Patel took a cup from his wife and started to heap spoonfuls of sugar into his tea. Hood counted three before the tea was stirred and the spoon placed in the saucer. He continued with his questions.

'When did you first notice the other van – you know, the van that must have contained the robbers?'

'I saw it as we were about to turn into the compound. I operated the remote control and waited for the gates to open. I saw this white van parked further down the access road. Engine started up as the gates were opening. It had no lights on. I remember that.'

'How long did it take the gates to open?'

'Too long. I complained about this before. The gates slide back but the security van cannot get in till the gates are fully open.'

'Where was the other van when the gates opened?'

'Behind us. I thought it was going past but it turned then reversed in after us. A man jumped from nowhere on to our van – then tried to smash our windscreen before we had a chance to pull down the protective mesh.'

'Why was the mesh not already down? Isn't that the usual practice?'

'Yes. But it had been trying to snow and my driver had difficulty seeing. The petrol would have got through the mesh anyway.'

'This man who jumped on your roof. Where did he come from?'

'I don't know where he came from. He had a weapon. He smashed the windscreen then he poured petrol on us. It was very frightening.'

'I bet it was,' murmured Hood.

'Why did you open the doors?'

'He had a big lighter. He said he would set us on fire if we did not get out.'

Patel used his hands to illustrate what he meant.

'You didn't sound the alarm?'

'Yes I did!' Patel was quite insistent. 'I pressed the alarm before I got out. It is silent but informs Langdale we are under attack.'

Knight looked up from her notebook and underlined what Patel had just said.

'Your colleague in the back didn't sound his alarm. Do you know why?'

'I cannot help you. He is quite new. He was probably too scared. The whole thing was very frightening.'

Patel took a sip of his tea then smiled towards his wife. She scowled and raised her hands in disapproval. Hood changed the subject.

'Were you aware you had a heart condition?'

Patel smiled. 'No. I do not understand it. I had a medical in 1997. Nothing was wrong, nothing at all. I was passed A1.'

He shook his head vigorously. 'I must have a full assessment before I return to work. Mr Langdale insists. I do not know what will happen.'

Mrs Patel coughed and cleared her throat before she spoke.

'He will not need an assessment from anyone. We will go back to India. That is what will happen.'

Patel looked at Hood and smiled. 'Mr Langdale has been very good to me. He says I will receive full pay for as long as it takes. He is a very nice man.'

Mrs Patel simply glared at her husband, but said nothing. Hood continued his questioning, firmly but gently.

'I want to ask you, sir, about the arrangements that morning for picking up the cash from Bridgeford House. I'm not able to ask Mr Mostyn. I think you are aware he died in hospital recently.'

'Yes. That was very sad. And he was only slightly older than me. He was always very good to me too.'

Mrs Patel grunted.

'My husband always say these people are good to him. But truth is he is good to them. They take advantage.'

Hood nodded. He silently wished that Mrs Patel would find some domestic chore to get on with so he and her husband could speak without interruption.

'How long before you set off for Bridgeford House that morning did you find out how many satchels you were to deliver to the Charnwood Centre?'

'I received written instructions about an hour after I arrived for my shift. They came directly from Mr Mostyn. Until then, me and my crew would not know the size of the delivery. That was how the system worked.'

'You had no idea you would be going to Bridgeford House?'

'Not definitely, no. But we usually do ATM deliveries if we are on early shift and we do more ATM runs from Bridgeford than other banks. In fact, we had to collect the van from the depot in Loughborough. I had to get the keys from the office. It's right next to the bank.'

'And you arrived at work, when?'

'I was helping out on the 11 p.m. to 6 a.m. shift because Jim had injured himself painting and they needed another guard. I was checking one of the other vans when they brought out the schedule – just like they always did. Mr Mostyn then said that my team would be using one of the vans in the compound at Loughborough. So we had to travel there in one of the other vans.'

'Was there a shortage of vans at Hinckley that night?'

'I don't think so. Mr Mostyn said we were to use the new van that had ended up in Loughborough for some reason – he didn't explain why. I think he wanted us to use it because it is more secure than some of the others. Not that it turned out to be. And I shouldn't really have been there. Isn't that what you in England call an unfortunate coincidence?'

'Of course. You should not have been working that night, should you?'

Patel opened his mouth to answer, but his wife was too quick for him.

'That's right, and look what happens. He nearly gets killed!'

Mrs Patel then burst into tears. Knight attempted to comfort her. Patel smiled meekly.

'I was just helping them out. That's all.'

'So you knew you would be collecting nineteen bags at about midnight?'

'Around that time, yes. Perhaps a little later. It is all written on the schedule we are given.'

'And Mostyn had not told you before then?'

'No. Why should he? It doesn't make much difference to us how many bags there are.'

'Did you know how much was in the security satchels?'

'No. We are only told the number of bags we are to pick up and deliver. But we get used to the weight. They are usually about the same.'

'Do you have a mobile phone, Mr Patel?'

'No – apart from the one provided in the van. Each van has a mobile phone – but I do not have one myself. Amrit says he will get me one for my birthday, but I don't have much use for a phone. We have a phone here, of course. Land line.'

Mrs Patel interrupted. Her tears had gone.

'My husband knows nothing about technology. My son, on the other hand, knows everything. He has degree in computer science and is doing a Masters in business studies. He will not waste his talents being a teacher!'

Patel shook his head.

'Now, Nirmala. Don't say that. It is a good thing to be a teacher. Amrit will do the right thing.'

His wife shook her head, too, but more vigorously, then turned and spoke to Hood as if her husband were not present.

'He only talks about teaching because his father wants it. He has more sense than him, just wait and see.'

She started to clear away the tea things. Patel glanced at Hood but said nothing further. Hood waited until Mrs Patel left the room before continuing with his questions. He was mightily relieved that she had gone.

'When you punched the robber, did you have any idea of the effect it had on him?'

'It was a lucky punch, I think. I was wearing leather gloves – like I always do – but I did feel it hurt him. He went backwards then grabbed me and pushed me away. I could see his eyes. They looked scared.'

'He was wearing some sort of face covering, wasn't he?'

'Oh, yes. But I could see his eyes and I knew I had hurt him because I saw blood spurting from his mouth which was not covered. I may have dislodged one of his teeth.'

'His mouth?' Hood looked at Wendy.

'Yes. I'm sure I hit him in the mouth. That's what it felt like. I have hit a man in the mouth before and you can feel the impact on the teeth.'

'Not his nose?'

'Oh, no. His nose was covered by his mask, but his mouth I could see. And I remember the blood spurting out. Then I was shot and remember nothing until the hospital.'

Mrs Patel returned from the kitchen. Her mood had not changed.

'Yes. They shot him. He had a heart attack.'

She started to weep again. Knight comforted her as before. Patel looked on; his concern was readily apparent. Knight hesitated but then mentioned something that Benson's girlfriend had said to her.

'I seem to remember that Benson's girlfriend did mention that he had some dental treatment while they were in France.' Knight retrieved this information from the back of her mind. She also remembered it had not been included in Tricia Gooding's statement. 'But I don't think it was because of damage caused by trauma. She said he had lost a filling.'

'That wasn't in her witness statement,' said Hood, recalling the graze he had observed on Benson's lower lip when he had interviewed him.

'No sir. No one thought it relevant. The other guards reckoned the robber had a nosebleed.'

'Perhaps you damaged both his teeth and his nose?' said Hood looking at Patel,

He asked Patel to make a fist. When he did so, Hood noticed he had very large hands. A decent punch could well have caused damage over a wide area.

'Could be,' said Patel, nodding in agreement. 'But all I remember is blood coming out of his mouth. Then nothing.'

Mrs Patel interrupted again. She had dried her eyes on her apron.

'I remember my husband lying in hospital, hardly breathing. That is what I remember. My son came from university – all the way from Sheffield – and sat with him three days and nights. Three days and nights. He would not leave his dad.'

She dabbed her eyes with her apron again.

'He is very good son,' agreed Patel. 'He was the first person I recognised when I came round.'

There was then a long pause before Knight suggested that she start to take a statement in writing from the injured guard. It was a long and slow process and Hood eventually had to insist that Mrs Patel left the room. He suggested she show him the garden (he couldn't think of another excuse to get her out of the room) and left Knight to take Patel's witness statement. The garden was small and was mainly laid to lawn, but a few daffodils were poking through the borders. Hood was no gardener himself; that was Sarah's department and it proved impossible to sustain any conversation between him and Mrs Patel on the niceties of spring bulbs and mulching, but Hood noticed an old Land Rover parked on a hard surface, partially covered with tarpaulin, at the side of the bungalow. It looked as if it were undergoing restoration. Mrs Patel explained it was the vehicle her son was going to drive to India in May with his friends when he had completed his examinations. He was working on it on his occasional weekend visit to his parents, with the assistance of her second eldest son who was an apprentice mechanic. Mrs Patel plainly regarded her eldest son with a degree of awe as well as normal parental pride and affection. Hood got the firm impression she was keen for him to stay in India and work there. Amrit's permanent presence in the subcontinent would then support her argument that the family should move back there. Hood had the feeling that she would eventually have her way. Whatever Mr Patel's views on the subject, mother and son had already resolved the issue. Hood could not see Mr Patel holding out for long.

Eventually, they both returned to the sitting room. Mrs Patel was much calmer now and did not interrupt as her husband read through then signed his statement. The two detectives said their goodbyes and left. They were both relieved to do so. As they walked slowly towards Hood's car, Knight was the first to speak.

'Sorry about that, sir, I should have told you before.'

She was referring to Benson's dental work that Tricia Gooding had told her about when she had taken a statement from her. 'It didn't seem relevant.'

'You're not the only one, Wendy. I recall, now, that Benson had a graze on his lower lip when we arrested him. I hope to God that's on his custody record. I'd entirely forgotten about it. Mind you, it probably won't matter. The DNA will do for him.'

'Did you notice, sir, Mr Patel claims to have pressed the alarm but we found no evidence at Langdale Security that the alarm had been triggered until several minutes after the robbery had taken place?'

'I did. We need to go over the timeline again. It may well be of significance. My recollection is the same as yours. The first call to the police did not come from Langdale. It came from one of the security officers from the store almost next door. I suppose it's possible there was a fault somewhere in the system…'

'Or Patel is lying,' interrupted Knight.

'Unlikely. He seemed remarkably honest and open to me. There's probably a simple explanation. As I say, we need to check it out again. Neither of the other guards suggests that the alarm was triggered.'

'There's another thing, sir. While you were talking to Mrs Patel in the garden, I noticed a couple of Air India brochures under the coffee table. You don't think the Patels really are planning a trip do you?'

'It wouldn't surprise me, Wendy. If Mrs Patel has her way – and I certainly wouldn't bet against it – they'll be gone before the end of the summer. She's pretty determined and I don't think Ashock will be able to stand in her way. He may be a brave man, but it's she who makes the decisions in that household, mark my words. And if they are going to go back to India, good luck to them. He's not had much luck here, has he?'

CHAPTER TWENTY-FOUR

Monday, 15 February 1999

Craddock had spent his first day as a Mid-Shires detective at headquarters. He had initially attended the central police station in accordance with his written instructions but had then been driven to the new HQ building outside the city. There, he was introduced to ACC Knowles and put under the tutelage of Detective Constable Wendy Knight. Knowles had apologised for the absence of the chief constable. "He always likes to welcome new officers," she had told Raymond, "but he is attending an ACPO meeting in London. I'm sure you'll bump into him sometime soon."

'You can bet your life on that,' Wendy Knight disclosed to him later as they drove back to the police station. 'He has a habit of turning up when you least expect it, so be on your guard.'

'I don't suppose he'll be interested in me,' said Raymond. 'I'm more concerned about Mr Hood. What's he really like?'

'Well, you've had dealings with him already, of course. But there's a few things you should know about him. He's very bright and very well liked. But there are a few officers who don't get on with him. They're jealous I suppose and think he's risen too fast. But he's very well thought of by the top brass and he's always been fine with me. As long as you pull your weight, you'll be OK. One thing, though, don't call him "guv". He hates it! We had a DC from the Met working with us last year and he called him guv all the time. Hood got really angry with him. By the way, he's a great fan of Dickens. I think he's read everything that's been written on the subject.'

'What do you call him?'

'Sir. You won't get into bother if you stick to that!'

'Will I be definitely working on his team?'

'Of course. The chief inspector thought you could make a contribution because of your earlier assistance in Hull. Anyway, you have to work with me for the next three months as I am acting as your mentor – so the decision was quite easy, really.'

Raymond was delighted and said so. He really liked DC Knight. Working with her for three months was more than he could have wished for and there was no one he would have preferred as his mentor. He almost forgot about Moira when he looked at Knight but he quickly discovered from others that she was unavailable when it came to socialising. "You'll get nowhere with her," young Munt had told him. "Many have tried and all have failed. She's virtually engaged to a bloke from the university. None of us has any chance with her."

The following day Chief Inspector Hood saw him in his room and brought him up to date on the progress of the investigation, such as it was. It only took a minute or two before the subject of CCTV was mentioned and the chief inspector referred to Raymond's commendation from his earlier case in Hull. Hood explained that most of it had been viewed already but it was necessary for a full review to take place. Raymond was not in the least put out. He regarded this as an opportunity for him to make an immediate impact. Wendy Knight took him to the incident room to view the photographs of the individuals he would be looking for. He carefully scrutinised the large photograph of Doyle. He looked younger than he remembered him from the hospital but he would be able to spot him if he appeared on the CCTV. Benson was also quite distinctive. It was the third photograph he was shown that took him by surprise – and it showed.

'Do you recognise her?' asked Knight, her curiosity aroused by Raymond's reaction.

Raymond did not reply immediately.

'Who is she?' he asked.

'Julia Hamilton, Doyle's girlfriend. He calls her Jules. Are you sure you don't recognise her?'

Although her hair was blonde and her eyes blue, Raymond thought he saw a distinct resemblance to Moira. He swallowed hard.

'No, not really,' he replied. 'She just, eh, has a look of someone I used to know – but it isn't the same woman. I'm sure of that.'

But Raymond was not really sure of that at all. He hoped he was wrong but he was starting to feel he might have been taken advantage of by an attractive but clever operator. Her features resembled Moira to an uncanny degree. The hair colouring was different and the make-up over the top, but the similarities seemed too great to be coincidental.

'Looks like one of your girlfriends, does she?' asked Knight, smiling in a way that reminded him of Eddie.

'No, just someone I met on a couple of occasions.'

There was no way Raymond was going to say anything more. 'What do we know about her?' he asked, trying to sound objective and professional.

Knight picked up the photograph and revealed the little that police intelligence had discovered about Julia Hamilton.

'She's twenty-eight years of age; born in St Albans. Left school at seventeen before taking her A levels – some talk of an improper relationship with a teacher, I believe, but nothing was ever proved. She trained as a nurse for two years before giving it up and going to secretarial college. She was then employed by a large solicitors' firm in Derby and gradually moved up and became a paralegal, working in the criminal field. That's when she met Doyle. The firm acted for him in a mortgage fraud – got him off too! It didn't even go to the jury. The CPS dropped the charges. The firm broke up a year later – it split into two. A solicitor called Trevor Parker went off and formed his own outfit with a man called Peter Hobson – they act for Doyle now. The bulk of the old firm concentrates on other areas – they've given up crime altogether. She got involved with Doyle during the mortgage fraud case. She was still very young then but after eighteen months or so she gave in her notice and set herself up as a freelancer – what used to be known as an outdoor clerk. You know the sort of thing I mean – she sits behind barristers in court, visits witnesses to take statements, goes to prisons to take instructions. She's very popular by all accounts but I suppose the fact she's so good-looking must help. You know what these lawyers are like! She and Doyle have been an item for a good few years. He keeps her out of his dodgy dealings, or so we assume.'

'So she trained as a nurse did she?'

'What if she did?' asked Knight, smiling. She was now sitting on the desk, her long, shapely legs stretched out in front of her, her eyes fixed on Raymond. 'If you must know, so did I. But I only lasted eighteen months, though. Is it important?'

'No, not really. I wondered why she packed it in so close to qualifying? It's a three-year course isn't it?'

'That certainly used to be the position. It was hands-on training in my day. You learnt the job on the wards rather than in a classroom. But like everything else, it's probably all changed now. Anyway, I did hear that she had a bit of a fling with one of our police officers before she got involved with Doyle. He was like you – you know – a bit of a high-flyer. Made sergeant in no time at all.'

Raymond smiled.

'I'm hardly that. I've been in the force for over four years and I've only just made acting detective constable.'

'Don't let that worry you. The DCI thinks you're someone to keep an eye on.'

Raymond almost blushed. 'Still, I wonder why she gave it up – nursing, I mean?'

'Well I can't speak for her, but I didn't like the hours nor did I like many of the doctors. They were an arrogant bunch, particularly the surgeons. Treated us little better than slaves.'

Raymond was still feeling more than a little foolish but continued to put on a professional air.

'Can I keep a copy of these photos?'

'Of course, if you like. There ought to be copies in the CCTV room. Malcolm Munt and DC Sleath have been viewing the footage in there for the last two weeks. They haven't found anything of evidential value, so don't build your hopes up, will you?'

'Well, I'll make a start if I may,' said Raymond.

'OK. It's just next door along the corridor. I'll call in later to see how you are doing. Malcolm will show you the ropes.'

When Raymond entered the CCTV room, Munt was already viewing a tape. The quality was pretty poor and it was only in black and white.

'This is the camera opposite the main car park entrance,' he said. 'I don't suppose there's anything of interest.'

'What date is it?' asked Raymond.

Munt produced a handwritten chart.

'We're up to 13 December at the moment. We've been trying to keep in some sort of order but more tapes are arriving all the time, so it is a bit confusing.'

Raymond sat down in front of the screen. Munt moved out of the way.

'It's hardly exciting stuff,' he moaned. 'Robbie Sleath and me have spent hours on this. We didn't get on to begin with, but he seems better on closer acquaintance. He's not as bad as I thought he was – for a Scot. Mind you, rumour has it he's about to be promoted to sergeant so he's in quite a good mood at the moment.'

'Where is he?' asked Raymond.

'He's on leave this week. We all expect his promotion to be announced when he gets back. So it's just you and me for the moment. But the good news is he'll probably be put back in uniform for a bit – so he'll be off this inquiry.'

Raymond said nothing and started examining the schedule. He noticed it was not in strict chronological order, a failure he felt obliged to comment on.

'I've got it all on the computer,' insisted Munt. 'Don't worry. It will be in order – eventually.'

Raymond looked at the equipment. There were three screens, two video recorders and several photographs on the table in front of him.

'Trouble is,' added Munt, 'a lot of it is quite useless. Either the quality is terrible or the individuals are too far away. When we enlarge it with the computer program, the images become even more difficult to make out. The DCI won't send anything else for professional enhancement unless he considers it relevant. It cost a bomb to enhance the tapes from the compound and it didn't really do any good. I think we are wasting our time on the street CCTV. We should be concentrating on the stuff from the pubs and shops. It's much better quality.'

Munt then pointed to a plastic tray containing several video tapes.

'I was about to start on these. You can have a go if you like. I'll get us a coffee while you get the hang of things.'

'I have done this sort of thing before,' said Raymond hoping he didn't sound too arrogant. 'Forget the coffee. I'd rather press on.'

Munt gave him a disdainful look.

'Please yourself, I'll take my break now so you can settle in. See you in twenty minutes.'

With that, Munt left the room leaving Raymond in sole control. If the truth were told, he preferred it like that. He required peace and quiet when carrying out such duties otherwise the chances of missing something important increased. He checked the video recorders then selected a tape, carefully noting the information written on it. He didn't expect to find anything of use, but he was determined to examine everything in minute detail. In the murder case in Hull where he had assumed a similar role, it was on a piece of tape that had been missed on initial inspection that he observed the man who was eventually proved to be the killer leaving a public lavatory immediately adjacent to the nightclub where the stabbing had occurred. It helped to blow away his alibi. If only he could do the same again!

The first tape he examined was from the entrance to a large department store. It was a fixed camera and recorded customers entering and leaving. The quality was pretty good but after viewing it for twenty minutes, he started to get distracted. Munt returned and sat down next to him. They did not speak but gazed intently at the same screen. The tape lasted for sixty-five minutes before it gave out.

'See what I mean,' said Munt. 'Nothing, and there are hundreds of hours of the stuff. We could be here for ever.'

'Well, it has to be done,' said Raymond. 'Perhaps we should split them and look at them separately. That should halve the time.'

'The DCI thinks there's a better chance of spotting something if two of us view the tape at the same time.' Munt sounded fairly insistent.

Raymond was not so sure.

'Last time I did this – in a murder inquiry in Hull – I viewed them myself. In the event of my finding nothing, they would have been viewed again by two of us, as a check. That seems to me to be more logical. As it happened I did spot something that had been missed, and it proved very useful.'

'OK, I'm happy to do it that way – providing *you* tell the DCI!'

'Well, let's give it a go. I'll mention it to Wendy when she comes in. She can decide whether we tell the DCI.'

Munt moved to the other side of the desk and pulled round one of the screens. He selected a tape from the tray, made a note on his schedule and started to play it. The two of them sat in silence until lunchtime. Nothing of any relevance had been spotted by either of them. Knight popped her head round the door.

'Come on, you two,' she said. 'You've done enough for one morning. Let's show young Craddock here the delights of Leicester at lunchtime. Anyone fancy a curry. I'm starving.'

Munt needed no second invitation. Raymond was not so fast off the mark.

'Come on, Ray,' said Munt. 'You need a break doing this sort of work otherwise you might miss something. And you won't find anywhere better than round here for Indian food.'

'It's not my favourite,' replied Raymond, 'but I'll give it a go.'

When he returned fifty minutes later, Raymond wished he hadn't given it a go. He felt quite bloated. At least he wouldn't need any supper, or so he thought. He settled down again and started viewing a tape from a public house fairly close to the compound. In fact, the rear door of the Lady Jane pub led directly to the taxi rank, some 200 metres or so from the entrance to the security gates in question. Munt had dashed off to the gents, cursing the chicken vindaloo he'd gorged on in the restaurant. Raymond watched the tape for twenty-five minutes before it ran out. There was nothing of interest on it, although the quality was good. He stretched his arms and yawned. The screen was blank as the unused tape continued to run through the machine. Raymond noted the details on his schedule and was about to rewind the tape when further images suddenly appeared. They were much the same as before. A constant toing and froing from bar to tables and the occasional close-up of individuals sitting enjoying themselves. He felt the chicken balti moving inside him. He would be following Munt to the loo in a few moments. Then he saw it. The camera hovered for a few seconds over a table and he saw, clear as anything, a closeup of Benson, the remains of a pint in front of him on the table. He checked the time on the tape. It was 21.19 but there was no date showing. He wound the tape back and viewed it again. It was definitely Benson. He let the tape run on. There then followed a sharp intake of breath. A second person appeared at Benson's table and sat down, opposite him. Raymond could only see the back of this individual at first, but he then half turned and Raymond gasped. It was Michael Doyle. He couldn't quite believe it. He rewound the tape and watched it again. Yes. He was sure. There couldn't be any doubt about it. Doyle and Benson together, sitting at the same table in a public house, only a few metres from the secure compound. And obviously in conversation. He forgot all about his stomach, jumped from his chair and headed down the corridor.

'What's up?' asked Munt as Raymond almost collided with him in his excitement.

'Where's the DCI?'

'I don't know. I suppose if he's in, he'll be in his room. Why? Have you found something?'

'Come with me,' said Raymond. 'See for yourself.'

'I don't believe it,' said Munt as they viewed the tape together. 'Robbie Sleath and me have been stuck here for a fortnight and found nothing. You've been here five minutes and you've cracked it. Guess who'll be the DCI's blue-eyed boy?'

'I don't have blue eyes,' said Raymond, pointedly.

Munt ignored him and picked up the phone and dialled a number. Hood answered almost immediately.

'Sorry to bother you, sir, but we've found something you ought to see. Yes, sir. In the viewing room. Thank you, sir.'

Raymond looked at Munt. 'We?'

'Well, you know what I mean. Don't worry. I'll tell him you found it. The glory's all yours.'

Munt bowed in mock deference.

'To tell you the truth, Malcolm, I found it by accident. I thought the tape had finished but I let it run on while I made a few notes and these further pictures just appeared. I reckon they must have reused the tape and then changed it before they recorded over the bit we're interested in.'

'Trouble is there's no date on it. Must be an old system,' said Munt.

'Yes,' said Raymond. 'But look at the bar. Look at the decorations. There's no date on the tape, but they're Christmas decorations, aren't they? Look at that Santa Claus on the end of the counter. This must be the period we're interested in. It just has to be.'

'We'd best get round there and take a statement from the manager. Someone might remember one of them. It looks very busy but there's every chance the barman or someone will remember something.'

Hood rushed into the room.

'Right, what have you got?'

'Look at this, sir,' said Raymond. 'I think you'll find it interesting!'

Raymond played the tape and noticed the smile on the chief inspector's face grow by degrees.

'Well done,' said Hood. 'Very well done.'

He then shot a look at Munt.

'Pity this wasn't spotted before.'

Munt cast his eyes down and Raymond felt it appropriate to confess his good fortune. He told Hood how he had come across the section of tape.

'Well, there's nothing wrong with a bit of luck,' said Hood. 'We could certainly do with it in this investigation. Now make sure this is preserved and copied. I want it enhanced and stills taken and I want you two to get down to this pub with Wendy and interview the staff who were on duty in the days leading up to the robbery. Wait for the stills and show the photos of these two to anyone who happens to be there. OK?'

'Yes, sir. What about Doyle?' asked Munt.

'Don't you concern yourselves with him. Sergeant Hooper and I will deal with him.'

Hood played the section of tape again.

'Pity there's no date on it, but the decorations around the bar area should be enough to place it in the Christmas period. And we know Benson was out of the country shortly after the robbery so we can safely exclude any chance of this being picked up on CCTV *after* the offence had been committed.'

'Yes sir. And even Doyle can't be in two places at once. The staff at the hotel in Dorset are on record that he was there by early afternoon on the sixteenth and he didn't leave until the twenty-ninth. It must follow that this bit of video was recorded before the robbery took place.'

'Absolutely, Malcolm. Few of us are given the gift of bi-location. This is the break we've been waiting for. But we mustn't get too carried away. This only places the two of them together near the scene of the robbery, as you say, before it occurred. It doesn't necessarily prove that Doyle was in on it.'

'But won't the money Doyle had with him have some relevance now, sir? We can't prove for definite that it came from the robbery but when you put it all together, it's mighty suspicious.'

'But Doyle is no fool. It won't take much thought on his part to explain everything away. We must keep on digging.'

The two constables looked at each other and smiled.

'Well, what are you waiting for?' said Hood. 'Let's get on with it.'

The chief inspector left the room with a broad grin on his face. Back in his office he first telephoned ACC Knowles and told her the good news, then he went in search of Andrew Hooper. He had decided to let his sergeant make the arrest, always assuming Doyle was where he was supposed to be. Harbour Buildings was under constant observation and he had received no report suggesting Doyle had left the premises. Then Hooper had phoned him. Doyle had gone! There was no response from either his penthouse flat or Julia Hamilton's apartment. Hood was furious. Someone's head would roll for this and he wasn't over interested in whose it might be.

CHAPTER TWENTY-FIVE

Michael Doyle sat in front of the custody sergeant at Loughborough Police Station on a particularly uncomfortable wooden bench. He had been arrested at East Midland's Airport bound for a flight to Nice. Julia Hamilton had been with him and had been arrested too. It was Ian Lunn who had arrested them. A sixth sense had sent him directly to the airport when he'd heard that Doyle was missing. Doyle was seething and determined to take full advantage of his semi-disabled condition. His crutches had been removed from him at the airport and he was not inclined to try and even stand up without assistance, let alone walk, although both actions were well within his capabilities. But he had been literally carried from the police vehicle that had been used to transport him to the station and placed upon the unpadded bench positioned directly in front of the raised desk. The custody sergeant was not minded to rush the booking-in procedures. He was an old hand who preferred the more leisurely paper-based approach and lacked the necessary keyboard skills that were now essential in the computer age. DS Lunn, as the arresting officer, was obliged to explain the reasons for Doyle's arrest as the custody officer had a discretion to refuse his detention if not satisfied that the arrest was justified. He had already "refused charged" Julia Hamilton. He only had two more years to go before he collected his pension and was not going to be rushed into making any decision that might rebound on him. She had been walked through to the public area of the station and waited there, impatiently, for news of Doyle.

If she and Doyle had been intent on leaving the country permanently, they had been quite intelligent in concealing their real objective. The flight tickets, now in the possession of Ian Lunn, showed an apparent intention to return in a fortnight's time. Neither were they cheap. Both were business class and the return fare was more than Lunn earned in three months.

The custody sergeant had resisted Lunn's attempt to keep her in custody by pointing out that she could not be accused of assisting a fugitive or attempting to pervert the course of justice because Doyle was not the subject of an arrest warrant nor had there been any previous attempt to arrest him. And, for good measure, there were no proceedings in being that anyone could be said to have perverted – not in relation to Doyle at any rate. Sergeant Bullock was particularly pleased that his view of the law had been confirmed by the telephone call he had made to the duty CPS lawyer. He'd had fewer qualms when it came to Doyle. Ian Lunn had explained that Doyle could be linked with Benson through the recently discovered CCTV which raised the evidential value of the cash seized from him in Hull. The mere mention of the conclusive DNA link between Benson and the crime scene was more than sufficient even for an astute and careful custody officer like Sergeant Bullock. The duty doctor had been and examined Doyle and authorised him fit to be detained, despite Doyle's assertion that the problems caused by the broken bone in his leg were far from resolved.

Sergeant Bullock continued typing the details into the computer using only two fingers. Doyle was becoming visibly more irritated as the custody officer pressed each key methodically but slowly, pausing between strokes. Lunn had searched Doyle as best he could at the airport and had carried out a more thorough examination in the glass-fronted cell that abutted the custody area. He had found nothing further of evidential value but retained possession of Doyle's passport, wallet, watch and cheque book, which he now placed next to the flight tickets on the desk in front of him. There was over ten thousand French francs and a couple of thousand in travellers' cheques inside the wallet. Doyle's tie and belt were also removed from him.

'We don't want any accidents, do we?' said Bullock as he continued to make his entries on the custody record. The sergeant eventually looked up from the keyboard and asked the questions which had become second nature to him.

'You have the right to have someone informed of your arrest and the right to free legal representation. If you do not have a solicitor, a solicitor will be made available free of charge...'

'Cut the crap,' interrupted Doyle. 'Get me Trevor Parker. He's my solicitor. I don't want anyone else, especially not some legal-aid bumpkin. And I shall be holding you responsible for any financial loss on them tickets. Cost me an arm an' a leg they did.'

He winced in apparent pain as he spoke.

'Do you have Mr Parker's telephone number available?' asked the sergeant. 'I can look him up if you haven't.'

'You'll find his card in my wallet,' replied Doyle sarcastically. 'I never go anywhere without it! Jules is out there somewhere as well. I wouldn't mind betting she's already got hold of him.'

Bullock looked inside the wallet and took out an American Express charge card and several twenty-pound notes. He found the solicitor's card and passed it to a constable working at a table behind him and instructed him to make a telephone call to Parker. He looked up at Doyle.

'We'll follow procedure if you don't mind, Mr Doyle. Miss Hamilton must take her own course.'

'You'd better ring his mobile,' grumbled Doyle. 'He won't be in the office at this time.' He automatically raised his arm and looked where his watch had been before realising it had been removed from him by Sergeant Lunn.

'What time is it anyway?' he asked indignantly. Sergeant Bullock did not answer but pointed to the clock on the wall behind him.

'Don't forget,' added Doyle, 'the clock is ticking. I shall be out of here before long, then it will be your turn to worry. Trevor Parker will see to that.' Doyle knew enough to appreciate that he could not be held for more than a day unless a superintendent authorised it.

But Sergeant Bullock had heard such threats a thousand times before. It hardly troubled him. No one had ever sued for false arrest, not where he had been involved anyway. He looked up and smiled. Once twenty-four hours had passed it would be up to the superintendent or a magistrate. Nothing to do with him.

'Well, Mr Doyle,' he replied. 'You must take such action as you may be advised but I have decided to authorise your detention for questioning on suspicion of robbery and attempted murder. You do not have to say anything but it may harm your defence if you fail to mention when questioned something which you later rely on in court. Anything you do say may be used in evidence. Do you understand?'

'No comment,' said Doyle.

The custody sergeant then placed Doyle's property into a clear polythene bag and sealed it with a blue plastic tie.

'If you could sign for your things, please Mr Doyle?'

Bullock pressed a button and a printer rattled into action. Several pages of the custody record were printed off and passed to Doyle. He looked only at the property section, carefully checking each and every item. He then scribbled his initials on the document where directed and passed it and the biro back to Lunn who placed it on the desk in front of Sergeant Bullock.

'And I know exactly how much cash there is in there,' said Doyle. 'It had better all be there when I get out of here. I know what you lot are like.'

Bullock ignored him, checked the signatures on the custody record then turned and spoke to the young constable.

'All right, you can take Mr Doyle through now. The bridal suite, I think. We don't want him complaining about our facilities now, do we?' He handed the constable a copy of the codes of practice.

'Something for you to read, Mr Doyle.'

The constable passed the booklet to Doyle then returned to his position behind the desk. Doyle glanced at it then threw it on to the floor.

'I don't need this. And I want my crutches back!'

'All in good time, Mr Doyle,' said the custody sergeant calmly. 'All in good time. We don't want you hurting yourself with them, do we?'

'This is ridiculous,' replied Doyle, now quite furious. 'What do you think I'm going to do with them? Beat myself senseless? I need them to get about.'

'Rules are rules, Mr Doyle and you won't be going anywhere for some time, I suspect. The constable will assist you to your cell. Mr Parker is on his way,' whispered Sergeant Bullock, without a hint of sarcasm as Doyle was assisted towards his unwanted overnight accommodation by the reluctant constable. 'Sleep tight! Breakfast is at seven.'

'Rather you than me, Ian,' said Bullock, as Doyle disappeared. 'He's going to be a handful is that one. You mark my words.'

'He won't be my problem,' replied Lunn. 'The boss will want to interview him. I doubt if I shall get a look in.'

'Well, I would be thankful for small mercies if I were you, I really would.'

CHAPTER TWENTY-SIX

Chief Inspector Hood made arrangements for Michael Doyle to be transferred from Loughborough to the main police station in Leicester. The facilities at Loughborough were limited and he wanted to be in close proximity to the incident room when he interviewed him. He had decided that Detective Sergeant Hooper should accompany him, despite the latter's firm view that Doyle would say nothing. He had already spoken with ACC Knowles to ensure the appropriate permission would be given to extend Doyle's presence at the police station once twenty-four hours had elapsed. Wendy Knight was alerted to make an application to a magistrate should the additional time that could be granted by Knowles prove insufficient.

Doyle had been arrested at 5.15 p.m. This meant an early start and Hood planned the first interview for 8 a.m. He was well acquainted with such evidence the team had assembled and, as was his custom, he placed the case papers to one side and found time to read (or re-read) a Dickens' novel. He found it cleared his mind and put him in a better mood for the labours of the following day. He lay in bed, his wife by his side, gently chuckling to himself as he turned the pages of *Little Dorrit*, one of his favourites.

'What are you laughing about?' his wife asked him as she looked up from a paper on "Psychological Insights" she was preparing for a lecture she was due to give in a few days' time.

'Nothing, really. I was just thinking how the circumlocution office – one of Dickens' better creations – bears a remarkable similarity to the modern police service. Never give a straight answer to anything. Obfuscation, that's the thing now – and it'll get worse after Macpherson reports. You mark my words. Everything will be carefully processed through the filter of political correctness.'

'It won't be as bad as that, surely?'

Sarah continued to edit her notes.

'Ask me again in ten years,' said her husband blandly.

After a few minutes, Hood chuckled again. His wife looked up from her papers and adjusted her reading glasses.

'Honestly Harry, how many times have you read that novel? Don't you think you should move on? How about trying someone a bit more up to date?'

Hood placed his book on the bed and smiled at his wife.

'But that's the beauty of Dickens, my love. He is *so* up to date. It just goes to show that people never really change – superficially yes – but deep down, I don't think so. What motivates us, how we regard others, the stupid things we do; I don't think human beings have changed that much since his day.'

'Now you're trespassing in my field!'

'Part of my job. But I'm always open to advice. I've got an important interview tomorrow – and the interviewee is likely to say nothing other than "no comment". Any tips you might have to get him to talk would be very welcome.'

Sarah put her papers down and removed her spectacles.

'This is the one you have in the frame for the armed robbery, is it? The one you prepared the interim report on for the ACC?'

'Yes. We reckon he's the brains behind it. And it's serious stuff. The security guard was shot, remember?'

Sarah nodded.

'But I thought you'd got one of them for that?'

'Not the one with the gun. We haven't identified him yet. But we have the one the guard had a go at – Charles Anthony Benson by name. He's not talking – too scared, I suspect. He'll not walk, though. We can place him at the crime scene through DNA but this fellow, Doyle, all we have on him is the cash he had with him when he crashed his car in Hull and a bit of CCTV showing him with this other chap at the Charnwood a few days before the robbery. Not much when you think about it.'

'So an admission would be welcome?'

'It sure would. But it's highly unlikely. And there's a risk he might get bail if we don't get something out of him. If that happens we'll never see him again. He was on his way out of the country when he was arrested. I expect him to be remanded if we charge him but if we persuade a magistrate to keep him in, he could apply for bail to the Crown Court so anything extra would really assist.'

'Why are you waiting until tomorrow to interview him? Why not get on with it? You've interviewed suspects in the middle of the night before now.'

'I thought you, my darling, would be the first to appreciate that. He's a fly one is Doyle and he probably won't say anything but a night in the cells might soften him up a bit. He'd have expected us to get on with it. The fact that we haven't might frustrate him to the extent that he'll let something slip. He has quite a temper on him, according to Andrew Hooper. He's dealt with him before.'

Sarah frowned.

'Do you think you'll be able to charge him?'

'Again, I'm not sure. That'll be up to the CPS after we've questioned him – but you know my views about their reluctance to make a swift decision.'

Sarah smiled.

'I thought you said the CPS lawyer in this case was OK?'

'She is – but I doubt if they'll let her make the decision. The chap in charge is a real worrier – he's no *Tulkinghorn* – that's for sure.'

'Now that's a name that rings a bell. Didn't *Tulkinghorn* come to a sticky end?'

'He certainly did. Shot in his own chambers as I recall, though I haven't read *Bleak House* for a few years.'

Sarah, too, had read the novel, but many years before.

'Yes, I've never forgotten Dickens' description of that particular lawyer,' she said. 'Remember? I read English as a subsidiary subject in my first year at uni. I must have read at least seven of his novels, including that one. Particularly hard going as I recall.'

'Not at all,' replied her husband. 'It's one of his best.'

Sarah gave him one of her looks then hesitated and closed her eyes as if trying to recall a distant memory.

'*Smoke-dried and faded… dwelling among mankind but not consorting with them.*'

Hood smiled. 'Very good, and pretty accurate too. Though I doubt if anyone would take a pot shot at Frazer, mores the pity! But he's certainly living on another planet, if you ask me; dwelling with mankind but not consorting with them.'

Sarah laughed but it was her husband who claimed to have won the argument.

'You see; Dickens is still relevant today. You've proved my point!'

'What if I have? That's no reason why you shouldn't broaden your range. Try a bit of Trollope for a start. I quite enjoyed him, too, when I was at university. You never know, after that we might get you into the twentieth century.'

But Hood's head was buried in the trials of *Little Dorrit.* A few moments later he raised his eyes and looked at his wife. His mind was once again turning to the following day's agenda. Unusually, his concentration was waning. He put the novel down again.

'And Doyle's bound to get some expensive brief working on his case – assuming we can charge him. Frazer is more of a politician than a lawyer. He's more concerned whether the CPS will get sued than he is in putting away villains.'

'Be fair, darling. We do live under the rule of law, don't we?'

'Yes, but in practice it seems like the rule of lawyers – not quite the same thing.'

Sarah frowned and, thinking her husband wanted to continue to discuss what was evidently dominating his thoughts, obliged him as she had done many times in the past.

'So, you can put him at the Charnwood *before* the robbery occurred?'

'Yes.'

'But not at the *time* the robbery occurred?'

'No – not directly, no.'

'And he was found in possession of cash from the robbery some time later?'

'Well, not exactly. We *believe* the cash came from the robbery – but we haven't been able to prove it yet – not scientifically. Neither can we prove that the serial numbers on the recovered notes match any of the notes known to have been stolen. Most of the cash was made up of used notes – so there's no record of them. And that's another thing. They must have known most of the cash would be untraceable. So the whole thing has been very carefully planned.'

'Well, that *is* a problem. Where does he say he got the cash from he had with him?'

'He hasn't given any real details. Intended for some kind of business deal abroad. That's all he's disclosed. Obviously, he was taking it abroad to be laundered.'

'But you can't prove that?'

'No. And the lawyers say that the inference that he was about to launder it can only be drawn if we can first prove the money was stolen. And as things stand – we can't.'

'So, you're back to first base?'

'Virtually, yes.'

'Is he the sort of person who would involve himself in such a violent crime?'

'He has no form for violence – but neither has Benson. Benson has no previous convictions at all, but we know he was there because his DNA was found on the security officer – the one who was shot.'

'And Doyle?'

Hood sighed. 'He's only been arrested once in the last ten years. Andrew Hooper's convinced he was the organiser of a huge mortgage fraud in the late eighties but if he was, he got away with it.'

'Tell me about him.'

'Doyle?'

'Yes.'

'Well he's no fool, that's for sure. He runs several businesses – all legit – at least they seem to be. He's very wealthy but appears to own very little. Everything is in a company name or hidden away in a complex web of nominees and trusts. His girlfriend is some sort of lawyer – not qualified – but as sharp as they come.'

'What sort of businesses?'

'Well he owns the block of flats where he lives – or his company does – and that must be worth a couple of million. But he pays a commercial rent on his penthouse apparently – as does his girlfriend. She lives in the same block. They pretend not to live together. He's also involved in property purchases abroad – mainly in Europe. That's where he was supposed to be going when he smashed the car up in Hull.'

'So he's not short of a bob or two?'

'Quite the reverse – though it may not last. The Revenue is after him. They've been very helpful over the last few days and given us quite a lot of information about our Mr Doyle. They reckon he owes them a small fortune. At the moment, I think I pay more tax than he does.'

Sarah smiled, sympathetically.

'So why would he involve himself in this sort of thing?'

'Because he's a greedy bastard. We are working on the theory that he came by the information about the used notes and just couldn't resist having a go. I reckon this was his last big job. Intelligence suggests he's planning to leave the country. Probably in an attempt to avoid the tax man.'

'What's the basis for that?'

'Apart from the fact we lifted him at the airport? Well. His property empire is up for sale and he's already found a buyer for Harbour Buildings. He owns a few other commercial properties too, including one only a few miles from the bank where the money was sorted. The Revenue's keeping tags on everything. They've served a big tax demand on him so a few hundred thousand in cash would be just what the doctor ordered. It would be enough to set him up abroad and there's bound to be a bit left over in the UK even if the tax man takes him to the cleaners.'

'Sounds like he's very careful.'

'Exactly.'

'Not the sort to take unnecessary risks?'

'Unnecessary, no. Carefully calculated, perhaps?'

Sarah mused on the information she'd been given. 'But he didn't die? You know, the one who was shot?'

'No, but he came pretty close. He had a heart attack. The cartridge was loaded with salt.'

'Well, there's a clue for you.'

'What do you mean?'

'Well if these were psychopaths, they wouldn't have bothered with salt – they'd have used the real thing. Someone has taken care to ensure that if the gun were discharged, no one would get hurt, not too badly anyway.'

'And no –one could have predicted the guard would have a coronary, I suppose.'

'Of course not. Anyone who thought that far ahead wouldn't have got involved. But someone has certainly considered the obvious risks and taken steps to reduce them. So you are not dealing with a bunch of would-be killers. You're dealing with someone who has given a lot of thought to the enterprise. This fellow Doyle may well fit the bill.'

'You mean the psychological profile?'

Sarah smiled.

'Now you know what I think of such descriptions?'

'Yes, I know, darling. I'm none too keen myself!'

Sarah placed her papers on the bedside table in order to concentrate on her husband's problem.

'Of course, if you really wanted a full *psychological profile* on this man, I'd have to know a great deal more about him. Do you know anything about his childhood?'

'Not a great deal. He was pretty bright at school, apparently. Could have gone to university. He went into the building trade and started his own business. He was in some minor trouble in his late teens and has a couple of convictions for speeding, that's all.'

'Doesn't sound like his upbringing caused him to go off the rails. He seems to have taken to serious crime later in life – and he seems to be quite good at it. More of a career choice I'd say.'

'So he's not a psychopath?'

'Correct.'

'What about a personality disorder?'

'Too early to say, but I doubt if he'd fit the ICD-10 criteria. Not all criminals do, you know.'

'I'm glad to hear it. It's somehow comforting that there are still some villains out there who are responsible for their own actions.'

'Well, that's not quite the same thing. As you know, I've been working on...'

Hood interrupted her. 'I don't know and I don't want to know. Leave me something to believe in, please.'

Sarah noticed the pleading look in her husband's eyes.

'Oh, all right. Have it your own way!'

She sounded only slightly irritated as she spoke but her interest had been aroused. She liked a good crime thriller as much as the next person.

'Tell me about the guard who was shot.'

'What do you mean?'

'Well, you've mentioned before that you hadn't excluded him, right?'

'Right.'

'If he were involved, he would presumably know about the cartridges not being full of shot. So his dramatic intervention – his playing the hero – may well be part of the plan. Always assuming he didn't anticipate having a coronary!'

'I think it's safe to assume that.'

'So he might well have been in on it?'

'It's a bit of a long shot. And, as a theory, it has found very little support, particularly with the chief constable. The argument is that he wouldn't have had a go at Benson had he been part of it. The other two guards nearly died of fright. Why should this one have had a go at all? He could hardly be criticised for doing exactly as he was told in the circumstances.'

'Oh, come on Harry. If the guard were part of the gang, what better way of making him look innocent than getting himself shot?'

Hood paused. This was a thought that had passed through his own mind at the outset of the inquiry. But he had as good as dismissed it when he discovered that Patel was not due to work the shift in question.

'I don't know about that. I've seen him a couple of times now and I found him to be quite impressive. And he really played the hero about three years ago when he stopped a robbery as he was delivering cash to a post office. And there's one more thing. He wasn't due to be working that night. He was called in at the last minute when one of the other guards failed to show. Apparently the other guard fell off a ladder while decorating his front room.'

Sarah paused and nodded.

'Well that blows a bit of a hole in my theory. I suppose you checked out the employee who didn't turn up?'

'Of course. And it all seems pretty genuine. I don't think we could prove he fell off the ladder deliberately if that's what you mean.'

Hood laughed. Sarah pursed her lips and continued to think aloud.

'But just suppose the information that the used notes were part of this consignment only became known at the last minute.'

'Yes,' said Hood. 'That's a possibility – but they'd have to have had the job pretty well sorted by then. And the information would have to come from the bank in the first place.'

'Exactly. So if Patel were in on it, he couldn't guarantee to be working the shift in which the robbery was to take place. Like in any job, he'd have to have rest periods?'

'Yes…'

'So if the information came through the night before…'

'Let me stop you there. The evidence suggests very strongly that the decision to supply so many used notes was only taken a few hours before the delivery was made – not the day before!'

'I see.'

Sarah paused. She then smiled broadly.

'I think you might have missed something there.' She turned and looked directly at her husband.

'Suppose the decision was confirmed on the night of the delivery but someone at the bank realised the day before that it was inevitable that most of the consignment would have to be in used notes? It must be possible in this sort of organisation to predict pretty accurately what the make-up of a consignment would be. After all, they're doing this sort of thing on a daily basis, aren't they?'

'I suppose that's right. But there's no pattern to it…'

'Well there you are then. It must have been known well before the seventeenth that the bulk of this consignment would be made up of used notes. There is no pattern because this single consignment was always intended to be the one that the robbers targeted. It would be perfectly simple for someone with sufficient authority to ensure that there was a build up of used notes to limit the number of new notes that would be assigned to this delivery.'

She clapped her hands in apparent triumph, then kissed her husband.

'Hold on a minute, Sherlock,' he replied. 'There were two other deliveries that left at about the same time. How do you suggest the used notes were kept back for this consignment without raising suspicions?'

'Well, were they?'

Hood cast his mind back. The delivery to Sheffield had been made up entirely of new notes and the Nottingham consignment had been split two thirds/one third in favour of new notes. He gave Sarah this information then pondered why he hadn't given this combination of banknotes more thought previously. It meant that only one hundred thousand in used notes had been used for both of the other deliveries.

'There you go then,' she said. 'Someone must have decided to reserve most of the used notes for the Charnwood delivery. All you have to do is find out who.'

She looked very pleased with herself.

'I don't know about that,' said Hood. 'There was only three hundred thousand in the other two deliveries that night – six hundred thousand in total. There was 1.6 million in used notes went to the Charnwood.' He smiled. 'I don't think your little theory actually stands up to examination when you think about it.'

'Nonsense, Harry. Look at the arithmetic. Half a million in new notes went to the other destinations and only three hundred thousand to the Charnwood. Three hundred thousand out of 1.9 million! Someone had to decide where the used notes went. Why not send six hundred thousand in used notes to Sheffield and Nottingham?'

Hood remained far from convinced. 'Let's suppose you are right – just for the sake of argument you understand. How does this prove that

Patel was in on it? Even if it were known the night before, how did he get the other fellow to fall off a ladder so he could take his place? There was no need for him to be there at all if the leak was at the bank. Why involve one of the guards if the information the gang needed came from someone at the bank? It reduces the amount available for the rest of the gang.'

Sarah's enthusiasm was slightly dimmed.

'I see that but given how this robbery was put into effect, it would still have been very useful to have had someone on the inside. The other two guards panicked, didn't they? If Patel was in on it, he could ensure that things didn't get too out of hand. I mean, suppose the guards hadn't abandoned the security van? It could all have gone horribly wrong.'

'Yes, but it's all very speculative…'

Neither of them spoke for a minute or two. Then Sarah sought to strengthen her theory.

'And remember, the fact that he's played the hero before gives him the perfect cover for doing it again – but this time he would have *known* he couldn't be seriously hurt because he knew the cartridges were loaded with salt!'

Hood shook his head. 'That, my love, is where your theory breaks down completely. Think about it. If – and we know this to have been the case – Patel was only there because this other fellow had injured himself the day before there can't have been a pre-arranged plan to shoot him as part of a charade. Patel must be the genuine article. A real hero.'

'Oh, please yourself,' said Sarah, irritably. 'I was only trying to help.'

She adjusted the duvet around her then turned and puffed up her pillow. She was beginning to lose interest, rapidly. She looked at her husband quizzically.

'So nothing I've said actually helps you?'

He grinned and kissed her on the forehead. 'I wouldn't go as far as that. It always helps to talk things through with an intelligent bystander.'

Sarah poked him in the ribs. 'Bystander, eh? Tell me, where does this fellow Doyle say he was at the time of the robbery?'

'He hasn't said anything yet. But his girlfriend says he was nearly 200 miles away – at a hotel in Dorset. She joined him there a couple of days later.'

'That doesn't ring true.'

'What do you mean?'

'If he is your main man, he doesn't sound to me like he's someone who would be 200 miles away when the plan – his plan – was put into operation. He's a details man. He can't trust anyone 100 per cent. He simply wouldn't be able to help himself. He'd have to be somewhere near.'

She turned, sat up and looked directly at her husband. 'Look. He's planned everything to perfection. Somehow, he's found out that most of the cash is practically untraceable. He's taken careful steps to limit the damage the gunman could do. He might even have set up the shooting of the guard. He might not have taken part in the actual robbery but I think he'd be pretty close to the action – not sitting in some hotel in Dorset.'

She punched her pillow then placed her head down and faced her husband. Hood revealed more.

'Well his alibi is pretty solid. Everything checks out at the hotel, but there are a couple of things that might suggest it's all bogus.'

'Such as?'

'Well, if it is all a set-up to give him a false alibi, he certainly didn't come back up here in the car he drove down to Dorset. There's no doubt it was parked up in the hotel car park all night. It could be part of an elaborate lie.'

'So? He had access to another vehicle?'

'That's what we have to establish. Unfortunately, the car he used was written off in an accident in Hull – you know – when we suspect he was taking some of the cash from the robbery abroad. It's been scrapped – but we do know there was a patch of oil in the back of the estate car – and Doyle certainly knows how to ride a motorbike. He's got convictions for speeding on one when he was younger.'

'So he might have had a motorbike in the back? Have you located a bike?'

'No. And I don't suppose we will – not now.'

Sarah stretched out her arms and stifled a yawn.

'So you can't break his alibi?'

'Not at the moment. But I shall be having a good look around the place next week – so I haven't given up hope.'

'Next week? I thought we were going away to celebrate our wedding anniversary next week. Remember, your parents are having the children for three whole days!'

'We are.'

Sarah looked at him suspiciously. She sat up, suddenly alert.

'You don't mean you're taking me down to this hotel in Dorset?'

Hood laughed.

'Well it *was* going to be a surprise. I wasn't going to tell you.'

She poked him in the ribs again, this time less playfully.

'So my wedding anniversary is going to be spent with a man whose primary concern is to try and break a suspect's alibi, is it?'

Hood tried not to look too embarrassed.

'It won't be like that, I promise. *You* will be the centre of things, you really will. And there are advantages. We get the room on expenses and the travel, too. But as you're coming, I have to stand the cost of the meals. And it's a pretty classy hotel, I can tell you.'

Sarah smiled

'I should hope it is. I suppose my coming with you provides a bit of cover does it?'

'Not really, but it does kill two birds with one stone. The ACC crime has approved the expenses. And another thing – Macpherson is reporting next week, so I'd rather not be around. That's going to cause a real fire storm, I can tell you.'

'Well that's all right then,' said Sarah sarcastically. 'I wouldn't want to spend my anniversary weekend anywhere without the approval of the assistant chief constable! And I suppose Macpherson will be all over the newspapers anyway?'

She frowned again then realising there might well be advantages to be gained from the arrangement, smiled sweetly at her husband.

'So it's a classy place is it?'

'It has a *Michelin*-starred restaurant!'

The smile grew broader as she flopped back on to the pillow.

'How many stars?'

'I don't know. But the food is supposed to be fantastic and the wine list is formidable and pretty expensive, by the way.'

'Good. Sounds just the ticket. I shall pack my sexiest negligee. I might even give your case a bit of thought. No charge of course!'

She hesitated, then smiled, coyly, raising her head from the pillow and leaning on her elbow. 'I've been thinking, darling.'

'Oh yes.'

Hood, who had picked his novel up and started reading again, turned the page with deliberation.

'If you get your promotion to superintendent, we could afford another child, couldn't we?'

She snuggled up against him. He closed his book and placed it on the duvet but continued to look straight ahead.

'Well, the room I've booked at the hotel has a four-poster bed and I've ordered a bottle of champagne for when we arrive.'

He turned and looked her full in the face. 'But we don't have to wait until then, do we?' She giggled and turned off her bedside light. Hood forgot all about Michael Doyle and *Little Dorrit* as he turned to his side and switched off his light too.

CHAPTER TWENTY-SEVEN

Wednesday, 17 February 1999

Chief Inspector Hood arrived early at his office the following morning. He hummed to himself as he walked down the corridor, passing several bemused junior officers.

'He's in a good mood,' whispered Munt to Raymond Craddock as he passed them by.

'Perhaps he's come up with something?' replied Raymond, naively.

'I think there's a more down-to-earth explanation,' commented Andrew Hooper as he made his way towards Hood's office. He grinned at the two would-be detectives. 'You'll understand when you're older.'

'What does he mean?' queried Munt, blankly.

'I dunno,' replied Raymond.

The two of them made their way down the corridor to continue their inspection of CCTV tapes, Munt shaking his head.

Hooper knocked on Hood's door and entered. Hood was sitting behind his desk, strumming his fingers on his blotting pad and humming a tune that Hooper was quite unable to identify.

'You're very cheerful, aren't you, sir?'

'Am I?' responded Hood. 'I can't think why. I'm not expecting a particularly easy day, interviewing Doyle.'

The strumming ceased as did the humming.

'No sir. I'll be surprised if we get anywhere with him. His solicitor's been with him for over forty minutes, so I don't think we'll be catching him unawares.'

'We can but try, Andrew. We can but try. Have you given his solicitor the disclosure I indicated?'

'Yes, sir. I handed it over at seven twenty. It's been noted on the custody record, just to be on the safe side.

'Good. We don't want any complaints do we?'

'No, sir.'

The prospect of a morning with Michael Doyle did not appeal to Hooper who remained wholly convinced that nothing would come of it.

'How are we going to play, it sir? He's a stubborn so-and-so – and I reckon his brief is going to present us with a prepared statement. He's been writing away in the interview room since I handed over the disclosure.'

'So he'll probably say nothing?'

'Doyle and I go back a long way. Three days I spent with him on that mortgage fraud. He never said a word. And it did the trick for him, didn't it? The case against him collapsed. Never went to the jury.'

'But that was because of a cock-up in the investigation – not because he went no comment. I've studied the papers. There was a case to answer all right. It was the non-disclosure that killed it, not Doyle's refusal to answer.'

'But we don't really have that much on him, do we sir? We can't break his alibi and the fact that he was in the same pub as Benson doesn't really prove anything does it?'

'It's not compelling, I agree. But when we put everything together, including the money, we at least have something to take forward. And that additional statement from the hire company is interesting. Anyway, I'm seeing Andrea Fleming this afternoon with the barrister she's instructed. A chap called Markham-Moore. Have you heard of him?'

'Yes, sir. Edward Markham-Moore. He prosecuted those travellers in that big conspiracy case. They were all convicted. He knows what he's doing.'

'Good. He might have some ideas of his own. Let's hope he's a bit more flexible than Frazer.'

'No comment, sir.'

They both laughed. Hood looked at his watch and handed the file from his desk to Hooper.

'Let's get on with it.'

★★★★

Hooper was proved right. Doyle refused to answer any questions and his solicitor produced a short prepared statement in which all the evidence Hood had assembled was ostensibly explained but without much detail. After thirty-five minutes Hood gave up and authorised his further detention, at least until the conference with counsel had taken place.

'I have an appointment with the CPS later this afternoon,' he explained, 'so there will be no further interviews until after 1800 hours. Mr Doyle will be returned to his cell until then. Good morning to you.'

Hood picked up his file and followed Hooper out of the room. Craddock was waiting in the corridor.

'We've found another bit of tape, sir, which shows Doyle and Benson standing in the taxi queue three days before the robbery took place. It's pretty good quality and it's timed and dated.'

'The taxi queue at the Charnwood?'

'Yes sir, almost opposite the compound.'

Hood broke into a wide grin.

'Well done, Raymond. Let me see it. I've got enough time before my meeting with the CPS and counsel.'

After viewing the tape, Hood's confidence rose. It was just what was wanted. Even Hooper was optimistic.

'Surely, sir, this additional CCTV can't be explained away so easily – not when you place it with everything else.'

'Well, we'll know soon enough. Frazer has insisted on attending the conference this afternoon and it's not too difficult to guess what his take on the evidence is likely to be. You'd better get a copy of the taped interview and the CCTV over to him so he can consider them before we meet with counsel. I don't expect it will change his mind, but he ought to see everything we have. You never know, this latest tape might persuade him to let us charge Doyle but I'm not building my hopes up.'

'Markham-Moore is bloody good, sir. He'll see there's a case. You mark my words.'

★★★★

Hood's meeting with James Frazer and Andrea Fleming was arranged for 4.30 p.m. at counsel's chambers in Nottingham. Although Edward Markham-Moore practised from London, he was a door tenant at Lace Market Chambers and he had agreed that a conference could be held there to save Hood the inconvenience of travelling to the Temple. Time was of the essence if Doyle was to be charged. Hood and Wendy Knight arrived in good time to find James Frazer anxiously smoking a cigarette outside the main entrance.

'Is Andrea here?' asked Hood. He felt very much in need of her support and knew she, at least, was keen to proceed against Doyle.

'She's inside with Mr Markham-Moore,' said Frazer. 'I'll be in shortly. They don't allow smoking in there.' He took a drag on his cigarette then flicked the ash on to the pavement. Hood nodded and opened the heavy outside door. Perhaps he'd have a chance of speaking with counsel before Frazer started to undermine the case against Doyle? Knight followed him through into the reception area. They were greeted by a young male clerk who introduced himself as Peter Blakemore and led them directly to a conference room on the first floor. Both declined the offer of coffee as they shook hands with Andrea Fleming's choice of counsel. Andrea smiled and nodded towards the officers as they sat down, but said nothing.

Neither Hood nor Knight had met Edward Markham-Moore before. He was a tall, slim individual dressed in traditional black jacket and striped trousers. A heavy gold chain stretched across his waistcoat and Knight noticed his cuff links looked particularly expensive. *Were they really diamonds in the centre of each stud*? she wondered. He wore a stiff white collar and his tie, bearing the crest of one of the Inns of Court, was carefully knotted. Knight thought he was about thirty-five years of age. A few fine streaks of grey stood out in his otherwise dark brown hair and a signet ring with what appeared to be a particularly large ruby sparkled on the little finger of his left hand. He had the confident air of someone who knew exactly what he was doing.

'Shall we get on,' he asked, 'or should we wait for James Frazer? He's outside having a cigarette. Filthy habit. We don't allow smoking inside chambers.'

That's a good start, thought Hood. *Perhaps Frazer's opinions will not count for much with this fellow*.' Any such hopes were quickly dashed.

'I'm bound to say, Chief Inspector, James Frazer thinks the case against Doyle is a bit thin. Have you got anywhere linking the cash he had with the proceeds of the robbery?'

'Not yet, no – apart from the inference that it could have come from the robbery.'

'Could have won't be good enough, you know. Has he said anything? You've been interviewing him this morning, haven't you?'

'Nothing that comes close to an admission. Mr Frazer has a copy of the tape. But there has been another breakthrough with the CCTV. We've got a second bit of film with him at the Charnwood a few days before the robbery and he's in the company of Benson again.'

'Is that so? Could be useful that. So we have two instances of him at the Charnwood before the robbery and on both occasions he's with Benson who we know for sure was involved.'

'Yes, sir.'

'But we can't place Doyle at the compound when the robbery took place?'

'No.'

'And there's the question of his alibi, which seems pretty solid.'

Markham-Moore was adopting his usual approach of mentioning the downside before he turned to the more positive aspects of the case. Hood felt impelled to challenge him.

'But he wouldn't have to have been in the compound to be involved, would he? Andrea and I were thinking of a charge of conspiracy.'

Hood half turned in his chair as Andrea acknowledged what he had said.

'He could have organised and run the whole thing from the hotel in Dorset.'

'There's that phrase again,' said the barrister, shaking his head. 'Could have. We have to be able to make the jury sure. Could have won't do. I don't suppose there's any chance of Benson co-operating and fingering Doyle?'

'Not a chance,' replied Hood. 'He's never said a word. Too scared, I reckon.'

The barrister sighed. Knight intervened.

'Isn't the fact that he had four hundred thousand in twenties and tens – the precise denominations of the stolen money – of some significance? He was heading out of the country within a fortnight of the robbery from the very area where the offence took place and refuses to give any details of where it came from, apart from mere generalities.'

'It's not unhelpful,' confided counsel, 'but I gather from the papers you've sent me that his legitimate businesses deal in a lot of cash?'

'That's certainly true,' said Hood. 'That's why the Inland Revenue and Customs and Excise are after him.'

'But before a jury can draw an adverse inference based upon his undoubted possession of the cash, they have to exclude any and every reasonable alternative explanation. It's ironic, but the fact that he's the subject of an Inland Revenue investigation – for not paying tax on cash receipts – is likely to help him.'

'That's what James Frazer thinks,' ventured Andrea Fleming, glumly.

At that moment, there was a tap on the door and Frazer walked in, the stale aroma of tobacco wafting in with him. Markham-Moore grimaced.

'Ah, James,' he said, forcing a smile. 'Do take a seat. You know Mr Hood and Miss Knight I take it?'

Frazer nodded and sat in the one remaining chair furthest away from Markham-Moore's desk. The barrister had obviously placed it there deliberately. Frazer made an initial attempt to move it closer but it was heavy and cumbersome and got caught up in the Persian rug. He quickly abandoned the idea. Hood was pleased that the Chief Crown prosecutor was, geographically at least, outside the immediate circle of discussion.

'I've been going through the main features of the evidence with the officers,' Markham-Moore informed him.

Frazer interrupted.

'Is there anything new? It seems to me we simply do not have enough to charge him. I've listened to the tape of his interview this morning. He hasn't admitted anything and as for that new bit of CCTV, what does that prove?'

Frazer was clearly not impressed with the latest development. Hood intervened.

'This was before the meeting in the pub. So any suggestion that this is all a coincidence doesn't stand up. And this clip is taken from a camera not fifty metres from the compound.'

Frazer did not alter his opinion. He shook his head but said nothing further.

'There's something else you won't know,' added Hood. 'There was a delivery of cash to the compound at 3.55 that very afternoon. DC Knight has checked the schedules of all the security firms who deliver to the Charnwood. Langdale Security made the delivery.'

'From Bridgeford House?' asked Frazer.

'So we understand. There was a bit of urgency about it. Several of the cash machines had run out. There wasn't another delivery due until the one we are concerned with so National Commercial helped out. It was only a small consignment, a hundred thousand.'

'Are you suggesting Doyle knew there was to be a delivery that afternoon?'

'I don't know. If there was a leak from the bank, it's perfectly possible.'

'And perfectly possible he was just doing a bit of shopping.'

Frazer was obviously prepared to pour cold water on anything suggestive of Doyle's guilt.

'Unlikely, Mr Frazer,' said Knight. 'He didn't have anything with him. That much is clear from the CCTV.'

'Perhaps nothing took his fancy?'

Frazer sat back in his chair and folded his arms. Markham-Moore was impatient to get on. He had an appointment in London later in the evening and he was anxious to get there in time.

'I think I shall have to see this CCTV. When will a copy be available?'

'It can be viewed now at Central,' replied Hood. 'Or I can get a copy to you by this time tomorrow. But could I point out that a decision about Doyle will have to be made before then. Time is running out.'

'You could always bail him to return to the police station at a later date,' suggested Frazer.

'If we do that,' replied Hood, 'we'll never see him again.'

'We could retain his passport.'

'That won't stop him. If we don't charge him by this time tomorrow, he'll be off. He's obviously disposing of all his assets with a view to moving abroad. He was arrested at the airport, remember.'

'Yes, but with a return ticket,' countered Frazer.

'That was a blind,' replied Hood, firmly. 'Believe me, this man is no fool. He knows we are on to him and once he's out of custody he'll disappear.'

Markham-Moore, who had observed the verbal fencing between Hood and Frazer without interruption, decided to bring the meeting to order.

'You have instructed me to give my opinion, at this stage I emphasise, as to whether there is sufficient evidence to *charge* Doyle. I gather that you, James, remain concerned about that.'

Frazer nodded. 'I most certainly do.'

Markham-Moore continued. 'The case against Doyle depends in the first place on the case against Benson. The DNA shows without doubt that Benson was the man who was attacked by the guard. Agreed?'

Everyone nodded.

'So to implicate Doyle, we have to establish a connection between them. Not simply that they may know each other but a connection which establishes they were party to the same criminal enterprise. On the available evidence we can't place Doyle either at the compound or even in Leicestershire at the relevant time. Indeed, there is, superficially at least, some pretty good evidence he was in Dorset, some 200 miles away. On the other hand, he was undoubtedly in possession of a considerable amount of cash that *could* have been part of the proceeds of the robbery. At the moment, there is no scientific evidence to prove for definite that this cash came from Bridgeford House. If there were any such evidence, in my view that would go a long way to proving conspiracy against Doyle. If it could be proved that those notes had passed through Bridgeford House a jury would be entitled to infer they were part of the proceeds of this robbery – always providing the link with Benson can be established.'

'Forgive me,' interrupted Knight. 'Most unidentified cash passes through such places at one time or another. That's clear from the statements of the manager and the staff. Doyle could argue that the money he had came from various sources after it had passed through a counting house. And there are dozens of similar establishments all over the country. We can't even prove that any of it had been touched by Benson. And if we'd found a print from Doyle – which we haven't – he could easily explain that away as he maintains this is his money.'

'Exactly,' said the barrister. 'That is my point. It's no good looking at this cash as a lot of individual notes. Neither would a fingerprint from Doyle prove anything. It has to be viewed as a tranche of four hundred thousand pounds.'

'I don't follow,' said Frazer. Neither did Hood, but he had the good sense to keep quiet.

Markham-Moore looked at Knight. He had already identified her as the most likely in the room to grasp the importance of what he was saying. The barrister continued.

'Without the link with Benson, Doyle could simply say what he said this morning in his prepared statement or he could even try and get out of the robbery by saying he was laundering the money and had no idea where it came from. So linking him with Benson and proving Benson was one of the robbers is absolutely essential.'

He glanced at Hood. 'But I think you already appreciate that, Chief Inspector?'

Hood nodded. The barrister then turned to Knight.

'How many of these notes were consecutively numbered?'

'Only two or three, I think,' she replied.

'So Doyle hasn't collected it from his bank. Had he done so there would have been numerous consecutively numbered notes and a record of the transactions.'

'But he dealt with that in this morning's interview,' said Frazer impatiently. 'He doesn't claim to have drawn it from his bank. He said in his prepared statement he'd collected it from various sources over a period of months. How do we disprove that? Bridgeford House has no record of the used notes that made up this consignment.'

Markham-Moore looked sceptical.

'That doesn't sound very convincing even if he runs part of his business on a cash basis. Whatever he may have said this morning, the analysis by the revenue investigators shows that well over 80 per cent of his income goes through his bank at one time or another.'

'That still leaves a hell of a lot of cash transactions,' said Frazer. 'That's why the Revenue's after him – there's no evidence that he has ever declared his cash in hand transactions so he could well claim that the four hundred thousand came from that.'

'It's possible,' replied Markham-Moore, feigning agreement with Frazer.

'Of course he will,' said Frazer. 'He might lose the money but it would keep him out of prison. It's a no-brainer, if you ask me.'

Markham-Moore shook his head. 'Well I, for one, don't buy that…'

Frazer cut him short.

'In the absence of any evidence to the contrary, all he has to say is that he was taking it out of the country because he hadn't paid any tax on it. The fact that the Revenue is already investigating him for that very reason will lend support to any such story.'

'Precisely,' said Markham-Moore. 'That's why we must look at this tranche of cash as a whole.'

'And supposing we do? What then?' The Chief Crown prosecutor plainly didn't understand the barrister's point. But neither did anyone else. Even Wendy Knight looked puzzled.

'I shall need to see these banknotes. I don't have any photographs and before I say anything else I need to see their condition. Where are they now?'

'They're in the property store at Central,' said Hood. 'By the way, when they were counted we were about 200 short of four hundred thousand.'

'I'm not worried about that,' said Markham-Moore.

'I am,' said Frazer. 'Doyle is threatening to sue for return of his cash – all of it.'

'But he hasn't, has he? Don't you think that is significant? He'd have to give chapter and verse as to where he got it from and he won't do that. Not while he is facing a charge of conspiracy.'

Hood sat up in his chair. 'You mean there's sufficient evidence to charge him?'

Markham-Moore paused. 'To charge him, yes. He has been given the opportunity, more than once, to explain where he got the cash from and he has failed to do so. Unless he comes up with a credible explanation, I think there is *just* enough to proceed against him. That second bit of CCTV, if it shows what you say, strengthens the link with Benson.'

'And what if he does give sufficient details as to the origin of this cash?'

Frazer's tone betrayed his unhappiness with the opinion ventured. It was not what he had expected and he was paying for it out of his already stretched budget.

'But there's something else. Once he's charged, we shall be on much stronger ground in obtaining a production order against his bank. At the moment we are relying on information provided by the Revenue and they've only let us have it on the basis that we don't use it in evidence. Strictly speaking, they shouldn't be disclosing a taxpayer's details when they haven't charged him. I bet Doyle has carried out numerous transactions in Europe. That's a major part of his business. It will be interesting to see how many of them involved cash. I'd be surprised if many of them did.'

Frazer was not impressed. 'So all he has to say is that he was evading tax! And we all know that even if he were to admit it, he's unlikely to be charged. The Revenue will agree some compromise with him. All they want is the money. If he can pay the penalty, that will satisfy them.'

He unfolded his arms, stood up and walked over to the window in a forlorn attempt to hide his exasperation. Markham-Moore continued in his business-like manner as Frazer returned to his seat and sat down. The barrister looked directly at the two police officers.

'My advice is, however, subject to investigations continuing, particularly into the source of this cash. And I mean very rigorous investigations. A judge will probably kick the case out at half-time if Doyle comes up with anything approaching an explanation.'

He nodded in the direction of Frazer.

'I've had a couple of thoughts myself but I want to discuss the matter with a statistician friend of mine before I say anything more. Do you know Greg Oldham?'

He smiled and gazed intently at Knight. She almost blushed.

'Intimately,' she replied, quickly recovering herself.

'We were at university together you know. Has he never mentioned me?'

Markham-Moore's smile broadened.

'Not that I can recall, no. But I take it he's mentioned me?' said Knight, smiling sweetly.

'I believe he did. The last time we spoke over the telephone. But we haven't seen each other for a while. Time we were in touch again.' He grinned boyishly. 'And you haven't discussed the case with him?'

'Certainly not,' Knight replied with emphasis. 'I never discuss work with him. It's something we agreed on shortly after we met.'

'Really? Well, this may have to be an exception.'

Markham-Moore spoke with the easy confidence of someone who was not used to having his views contradicted. Knight, however, was not intimidated.

'Well, you'll have to wait a few days. He's in America at the moment at a conference in Boston. He won't be back until the end of next week.'

'No rush,' said Markham-Moore, seemingly unconcerned. 'Once Doyle's charged it'll be a couple of weeks or longer before he gets to the Crown Court for a preliminary hearing. Plenty of time, assuming what I have in mind works out.'

'It would be of great assistance if you could go into a bit more detail now,' said Frazer, dejectedly. He obviously remained concerned at the advice given.

'I'd rather not, if you don't mind. Not until I've seen the exhibits. I'm in the Court of Appeal next week in a case that's likely to last two or three days so I won't be able to get over to Central until about this time next week. But tell me one thing. What condition are these banknotes in?'

'Pretty good,' said Hood, his curiosity aroused. 'They could pass for new, but we know none of them is, not the ones we have recovered.'

'Good. Excellent. Just what I wanted to hear. One other thing. Did you recover any other cash from him, you know, from his business premises or his home?'

'Yes, we did,' replied Hood. 'There was about twenty-six thousand in his office safe.'

'And has that been examined?'

'Well, it's been counted, but there's nothing to suggest it has anything to do with the robbery. It's probably what he's collected in from rents and the like. He's probably telling the truth about that.'

'But you still have it. You haven't given it back?'

'No. We still have it, but Mr Frazer thinks we should hand it back. Don't you, sir?'

Frazer nodded. 'If it's nothing to do with the robbery we can't lawfully hold it. If the Revenue reckons he hasn't paid tax on it, it's up to them to seize it.'

'I disagree,' said Markham-Moore, decisively. 'That cash is or may be valuable evidence. It's essential it remains with the police – at least for the foreseeable future.'

'I don't understand,' said Frazer. There was more than a touch of irritation in his voice.

'You will,' responded the barrister. 'I'll explain it all later. But please don't hand it back. Not yet anyway. And don't let the Revenue or Customs and Excise get their hands on it either.'

Frazer remained concerned. 'I would feel a lot better if you explained why.'

'All in good time. I don't want to say anything more until I have checked my theory out; trust me, please. If I'm right – and I have every reason to believe I am – the case against Doyle will get a lot stronger.'

He looked at Hood and smiled.

'I will certainly get over next week.'

'And until then?' said Frazer sulkily.

'Give him one more opportunity to explain where he got this cash from. I suggest he is asked directly whether he was simply laundering the stuff. He won't say, of course, but at least the option of his admitting as much will have been put to him – then charge him, put him before the magistrates and make sure he's kept in custody. I agree with the chief inspector. If he gets bail, he'll be on his toes.'

'What about the attempted murder? He hasn't been interviewed about that and if we charge him, no further interview will be possible.' Frazer was unrelenting in his determination to find fault with the advice he had been given. Counsel glanced at Hood before he replied.

'I gather he's indicated he won't answer any further questions?'

Hood nodded.

'Well, put the allegation to him. If he refuses to answer, charge him with that as well. If, as we think, he's the organiser, he must have been aware of the gun.'

'But it was loaded with salt. How do we prove an intention to kill?' Frazer could not conceal his displeasure. The barrister dismissed his concerns with a wave of his arm.

'We can drop it later, if necessary. If you want to keep him inside, a charge of attempted murder should do the trick. We have to work in the public interest even if it means stretching the rules a bit. I haven't the slightest doubt if this man gets bail, whatever conditions are imposed, we'll never see him again.'

Hood couldn't believe what he was hearing. A veritable Daniel come to judgement! But he lapped it up.

'More easily said than done, given the state of the evidence,' moaned Frazer. He fixed his narrow, mean eyes on Hood as he spoke. Hood did not respond. He was quite happy to leave everything to Markham-Moore.

'Oh, I don't know. I doubt if the magistrates will give him bail given the seriousness of the case and I can get someone from chambers to oppose bail if he applies to the Crown Court… or Andrea here could do it. She knows the case inside out from the quality of her instructions to me.'

Andrea Fleming smiled, nervously.

'I'd rather you did it,' she said.

'Well, we'll see how things pan out.'

Frazer interjected. His tone had not changed in the slightest.

'You'll put your advice in writing, will you, Edward? I would like it in writing in the circumstances.'

'Of course. I'll let you have it by tomorrow. It will be short but to the point. In the meantime, you can serve the statements I have seen and get some photographs taken of the cash.'

'That's already been done,' said Hood. 'We're just waiting for the prints to come through.'

'Excellent. If you could let me have copies in due course.' The barrister rubbed his hands together. 'Well, if that is all, I have a train to catch. Thank you all very much.'

Markham-Moore started to bundle up his papers.

'Thank *you*,' said Hood. 'Let me know when you can get to the police station. I'll have everything lined up for you.'

CHAPTER TWENTY-EIGHT

The estate agent was very impressed with The Old Bakehouse. He was being shown round by Mrs Celia Campion who was very much in two minds as to whether her husband's forthcoming transfer to the Old Bailey was such a good idea. The work would be more demanding and stimulating, no doubt, and the extra money would be welcome, but she had grown used to living in the Leicestershire countryside and was not exactly looking forward to resuming suburban living in London. Her husband had suggested staying where they were leaving him to commute on a daily basis. After all, the train from Market Harborough only took an hour and although it was a good stretch of the legs from St Pancras to the Central Criminal Court, it would keep him fit if nothing else. And he could always spend the odd night at his club. They had decided to sleep on it but when everything was taken into account, they both realised a move to London would be more practical in the long run. A bad winter could play havoc with a commuting judge.

Their two older children were both at university, one of them at the LSE, and young Christopher had yet to celebrate his third birthday, so his education could easily be organised at a suitable school in London. The Campions had not planned to have a third child; it had just happened, but their initial shock when Celia discovered she was pregnant at the age of forty-one had quickly turned to delight after the child was born. They had once again assumed the role of doting parents and young Christopher had quickly become the centre of their lives. Mrs Campion had noticed that her husband was getting home much earlier than had previously been his practice. Quite simply, he was enchanted with his son. He couldn't do enough for him. It was the judge's desire to spend as much of his spare time with young Christopher that had really determined their forthcoming move to London.

The estate agent walked through the French windows into the magnificent garden that Celia Campion had both designed and planted when they had first moved into the eighteenth-century property, just outside the village of Foxton. Even in early spring, its proportions and style were self-evident. The agent was already composing in his mind the description of the exterior he would prepare for the particulars – always assuming he was given the opportunity. 'Is that yours too?' he asked pointing to the two-acre paddock adjoining the stable block.

'Yes. It's rented to the local farmer. He grazes his sheep on it in the spring and summer. It helps to keep the grass under control. There's nothing much happening with it at the moment, though.'

'Well that will up the price. Very attractive that is. We can fairly describe this as an equestrian property. How long have you been here, may I ask?'

'Just over six years, I think. Yes, we came up from London in '93. Quite a bargain it was at the time. And we got a very good price for our Edwardian semi-detached in Richmond.'

She hesitated.

'We've never had horses here, you know, but there are three stables. We haven't altered them at all.'

But the agent was hardly listening. He had already calculated the commission he would be receiving on the completed sale.

'The market was still pretty bad then – outside London,' he said, trying to pick up on the conversation again. 'Much better now, of course. I think you'll be pleasantly surprised.'

He gazed appreciatively towards the horizon. There was no sound, save for two thrushes squabbling over a few scraps of bread on the lawn and a motorcycle droning in the distance.

'Nice and quiet, too,' he added. 'That's always a selling point.'

Mrs Campion nodded in agreement.

'But I sometimes think it's too quiet. We are quite some distance out of the village. Our nearest neighbour is several hundred yards away.'

'That won't affect the price,' said the agent. 'A house like this gains value from having no immediate neighbours. People with this sort of money prefer to be well away from prying eyes!'

Mrs Campion didn't quite follow his meaning. She steered the conversation towards the question of the London property market.

'Prices will have gone up in London, too, I expect. I wonder what our house in Richmond will be worth now.' She was not expecting the nine hundred thousand Mr Denyer wrote down as a suitable guideline price for The Old Bakehouse to purchase very much in London, even on the outskirts. She had visions of a mansion flat in Victoria or a terraced house in East Sheen. After all, if they were going to live in London, there was no point in living so far out that her husband would be spending all his time commuting.

'Oh, yes. There's no doubt about that. You'd need a couple of million to get anything like this in the metropolis. And you can forget about a two-acre paddock – even at that price. London is like another country when it comes to property prices.'

Mr Denyer nodded his head as he spoke. Mrs Campion looked anything but surprised.

'That's what I expected. And a couple of million we most certainly do not have!'

'I can get one of our London offices to keep an eye out for you, if you like,' said Mr Denyer, helpfully. 'And we'll have this on the market by tomorrow – we should get an immediate response. Properties like this don't hang about for long.'

'That would be very good of you. Would you like a cup of tea? I think I heard my son waking up from his afternoon nap. Shall we go inside?'

CHAPTER TWENTY-NINE

Wednesday, 24 February 1999

His Honour Judge Thomas Seymour Edmund Campion TD, QC Honorary Recorder of the City of Leicester, arrived home slightly later than he had anticipated. As usual, his two-and-a-half-year-old son was standing at the French windows waiting for him as he drove his Land Rover Discovery through the automatic gates in to the open carport at the rear of The Old Bakehouse.

He locked his vehicle and walked purposefully towards the back door. As he entered the house he could hear young Christopher calling him, "Daddy, daddy". Christopher toddled into the kitchen where Mrs Campion was already pouring out a glass of white wine in anticipation of her husband's arrival. The judge kissed her on her forehead, took a sip from the glass she handed him and picked up his son.

'Daddy, daddy,' repeated Christopher, placing his arms round his father's neck. His father nuzzled him.

'Bad day?' asked his wife. 'You look like you needed that drink.'

'Nothing out of the ordinary,' replied the judge.

He put his son down but kept hold of his hand.

'But enough of that. What about your day. Any progress on the house sale?'

His wife smiled.

'It's been like Piccadilly Circus here today, hasn't it Christopher? We've had three viewings and a couple of them looked very interested. Denyer was quite right when he said there'd be lots of interest.'

'That makes seven in the last week, doesn't it? But still no offers?'

'Not yet, but he says it's only a matter of time.'

'Who came today?'

'Well, there was a second viewing by the wife of that QC you know from London. She sounds very keen. Then there was a first viewing by the wife or significant other – that's how she described herself – of some American professor who is coming over here for a couple of years. He'll be on some sort of exchange visit at the university. She was really interested and asked all sorts of questions, but I suppose that's what Americans do.'

'But would they want to buy somewhere? It'll be a temporary exchange visit, I suspect. And the third?'

'A Mr and Mrs Jackson, I think they said. I got the impression, though, that they thought we were a bit remote from the village. He was quite mature – a lot older then her. And, I can't say for sure, but she looked pregnant to me. She was very interested in Christopher's nursery.'

The judge placed his wine glass on the table.

'By the way, they couldn't provide anyone to show the American woman round. I had to do it myself – just after lunch too – most inconvenient. The other two came this morning. If she puts an offer in, perhaps we should ask for a reduction in the commission we'll have to pay?'

Campion smiled. 'Let's get an offer first – then we can argue about the commission.'

'But we should get an offer soon. It's a really lovely house when you take everything into account. I was having second thoughts about selling this morning.'

'None of that now – we've discussed this at length, remember? And we can't really do anything about London until we get a definite offer. That house in Fulham will not be on the market for very long. It'll be snapped up for sure.'

He looked down at his son, who was trying to pull him in the direction of the drawing room. Mrs Campion smiled. 'He's got his Thomas the Tank set laid out in there. Mind you don't fall over it. It took me over half an hour to lay it out.'

The judge removed his overcoat and looked down at his son. Mrs Campion shrugged her shoulders and held out her hands. 'Give it to me,' she said, taking the coat from him. 'You take charge of him.'

'Come on, then. Let's play trains, Christopher. Then it's off to bed for you.'

'Supper in twenty minutes, and don't keep him up, will you? He should really have been in bed half an hour ago.'

'Not tired,' said the boy, peevishly.

Campion smiled, picked his son up, then taking the glass of wine with him, walked towards the drawing room. Neither he nor his wife had noticed the solitary individual lurking across from their home in the descending darkness, mobile phone in hand. The hooded figure put the phone to his ear and spoke for about a minute before climbing on to a bicycle and pedalling in the direction of the village.

CHAPTER THIRTY

Charles Cavan-Henry walked into the clerks' room at his chambers in Bedford Row.

'Where's Geoff?' he asked Edwina.

'He's on leave this week; he's gone to the Norfolk coast with his wife and sister-in-law. Anything I can help you with, sir?'

'Rather him than me in this weather,' said Cavan-Henry. 'It'll be perishing cold up there.' He shivered in mock sympathy.

'This brief from Evans and Partners. It's drawn up as a trial. They can't be serious? The DNA will do for this defendant. It's open and shut.'

'Well, they want a conference before the Crown Court hearing. It will mean a trip to Lincoln. He's being held there. His application for bail was refused by the stipendiary.'

'That's hardly surprising given the evidence. I see they want me to make a further application to the judge at Leicester. That's a waste of time and money. I take it he's on legal aid?'

'Afraid so, but I'm sure you'll think of something. You usually do. Incidentally, the solicitors think the case merits a junior. What do you think? It could be your first case in silk if everything goes to plan on Maundy Thursday.'

Cavan-Henry smiled.

'I wouldn't put any money on that if I were you. Maundy Thursday is a long way off and I'm trying not to think about it.'

'It's not that far away, sir. April the first.'

'How appropriate. All Fools' Day! Have you fixed a conference yet?'

'No. But it will have to be arranged in the very near future. There was to be a hearing in the Crown Court soon but it's been delayed because they've charged someone else as well and the CPS want them to appear together. Miss Lassiter is being instructed for the other one – privately paid too.'

'Just my luck! Better make it on Friday then – if it suits the solicitors. I suppose we should show willing. I'll have a word with the new pupil. I set her to work to see if there's any legal manoeuvring available in respect of the DNA evidence. If we can't exclude it, Benson is dead in the water.'

Cavan-Henry left the clerks' room and climbed the stairs to the top floor. He walked into the room reserved for pupil barristers and smiled as Laura Mitchell looked up from her desk. She removed her spectacles and sat back in her chair. She pulled a few strands of her straw blonde hair from her face before she spoke.

'I think I may have come up with something, Charles.'

'Really?' said Cavan-Henry feigning surprise. He had chosen Laura Mitchell to do the research for him because he judged her the ablest of the three pupils who had started in chambers the previous October. If anyone could find a way round the DNA evidence, she could. Her double first from St Hilda's, Oxford had impressed the pupillage committee and her personality and sense of vocation had resulted in her receiving the largest of the three chambers' pupillage awards.

'There may be some chance of keeping out the DNA evidence.'

'Go on.'

'Well, I may be taking a bad point, but it seems to me that without the DNA evidence the prosecution would have no case.'

'Correct. It's all they have – certainly at the moment – but it's all they need, assuming it's admissible. The chance of its being someone else's DNA is put at less than one in a billion. So we can abandon that possibility right away.'

Laura Mitchell sensed that Cavan-Henry was not at all confident that a defence worthy of the name could be put forward. This was her opportunity to demonstrate both her worth as a future member of chambers and her powers of legal analysis. She was not going to let this chance slip her by.

'From my reading of the papers it seems tolerably clear that Benson would never have been identified but for the fact he had volunteered a sample in 1995 in an exclusion exercise. It was that profile, when matched with the sample from the crime scene that led to his arrest.'

Cavan-Henry pulled up a chair and sat down. His interest had been aroused. The young barrister continued.

'But if you look at the relevant legislation, that profile should never have been kept on the database. Had the police complied with their legal obligations, the profile would not have been there for them to match the sample from the crime scene. It should have been removed.'

Cavan-Henry's brow furrowed. He put forward the counter argument he anticipated the prosecution would seek to rely on.

'But the Crown is not relying on that profile. They're relying on the sample they took from him *after* his arrest. That sample was taken perfectly lawfully, so far as I can see. They've just disclosed the earlier stuff as unused material.'

Young Laura was not in the least put out. She stuck to her guns.

'I appreciate that, but surely it must be arguable that their initial failure to comply with the law renders the subsequent DNA analysis inadmissible? The law required them to destroy the sample from 1995. Had they done so they would never have been able to identify him. In fact, instead of carrying out their legal duty they did the exact opposite. They kept it on their database. So their entire case is dependant on a deliberate and unlawful act on their part. Look at the words of the section.'

Laura handed over the volume of *Archbold Criminal Pleading and Practice* she had been consulting and pointed to the provisions of the legislation. Cavan-Henry read it out slowly but audibly.

'Where samples are required to be destroyed... and subsection 3 (A) does not apply, information derived from the sample of any person entitled to its destruction. shall not be used in evidence against that person or for the purposes of any investigation of an offence...'

He sat back in his chair.

'See what I mean,' said Laura. 'The word is "shall" not "may". It's mandatory.'

'That can't be right, can it?' said Cavan-Henry, somewhat bemused. 'It would drive a coach and horses through criminal investigation procedures if a judge were to rule that is the correct interpretation. It would mean that if the police had a sample, say in a murder case, derived from some earlier incident and matched it with the crime scene, they wouldn't be able to rely on it if that is what led them to identify the suspect. That would be madness. What's the exception referred to?'

But Laura had her answer ready.

'That doesn't seem to assist the Crown here. The only exception is where the defendant has been convicted of a recordable offence. It's OK to keep the sample then – so in most cases the problem will not arise as most defendants have previous. The DNA sample will be preserved, and not destroyed in those circumstances. The police would be perfectly entitled to keep it on their database. But Benson has never been convicted of anything. His sample came from a *voluntary* exclusion exercise and he was promised that it would be destroyed once the investigation was concluded. Here's the letter from the police admitting they made a mistake.'

She handed Cavan-Henry a document from the papers spread over her desk.

'Some mistake,' drawled Cavan-Henry as he finished reading the letter.

'My thoughts exactly,' said Laura. 'Although to be fair to them, this exclusion exercise did take place just after the change in the law. And all the volunteers' samples were put on the database. They couldn't have carried out the exercise without doing that. They simply failed to remove this one.'

Cavan-Henry handed the letter back but said nothing for a few moments then, recalling something he had read in his brief when it first arrived, pointed out another interesting feature.

'It's also the case, isn't it, that he was charged with the offences before the prosecution obtained the match from the sample he gave in interview?'

Laura nodded.

'Spot on. He was arrested and charged solely on the basis of the profile on the database being matched with the sample from the crime scene. The match from the sample he gave when in police custody was not obtained until a week or so later. On a proper construction of the legislation, it looks as if they have no case. There's no other evidence and he made no admissions in interview.'

Cavan-Henry read the section again. He couldn't quite believe it but there it was in black and white.

'You may well be right, Laura. But we don't want to go overboard with this. They haven't served all of their case so there may be something we don't yet know about. On the other hand…'

Cavan-Henry read the section a third time then, closing the book firmly, congratulated the pupil barrister.

'Well done Laura. At least we have something to go on now. I was beginning to think I'd have to advise him to plead – and that would never do.'

Laura, now flushed with enthusiasm, smiled broadly. She had expected this senior member of chambers to shoot her down in flames but here he was apparently agreeing with her.

'But keep this to yourself for the moment,' cautioned Cavan-Henry. 'We shall need to look at the European Convention as well. A deliberate breach of the law like this may give us an additional argument.'

'I'll continue researching the matter. There are a couple of authorities against us, but they relate to the state of the law before the amendments introduced by the 1994 Act.'

'Well get them all out. I shall study them before I see Benson in conference. Incidentally, would you like to come? It'll probably be on Friday. You found the point – so if you want to follow it through, you're more than welcome. It will mean a trip to Lincoln but I can give you a lift up there if you like?'

'That would be wonderful,' said Laura, smiling. 'I shall have to ask my pupil master first, but there shouldn't be a problem.'

'If there is, let me know. I'll have a word with Giles if he kicks up. Is he doing anything interesting on Friday?'

'Just a few pleas at St Albans.'

'Well, I'm sure this will be more educational. Have a word with the clerks when you've spoken with Giles. It will probably mean an early start. I'll pick you up from your flat at 6.30 a.m. on the dot.'

'I'll be ready.'

CHAPTER THIRTY-ONE

The rain had changed to drizzle as Harriet Lassiter rushed from the taxicab towards the communal entrance of her London apartment building. Her husband had purchased the then dilapidated first-floor suite of rooms twenty-five years ago, before they met and married. Cadogan Gardens in SW3 had been pretty exclusive even in those days but the gradual refurbishment of the entire period structure and the rapid rise in house prices in London meant that their financial future, at least, was secure. It was now worth over eight times what Peter had paid for it. Not that she had any real worries on that score. Her husband's property business had gone from strength to strength and they could both have retired on the proceeds of that alone, but neither was so inclined. Peter Callaghan had always been very sensible with money and his business had survived the property crash of the late eighties because he had never engaged in reckless borrowing. If he were ever inclined to consider retirement they would have been very comfortably off even if they never made the *Sunday Times* rich list. But as they had not been able to have children and had never got round to considering adoption, their respective professional lives were very important to them. As she pushed open the door to the apartment, Harriet reflected whether Michael Doyle's future, financial and personal, was as secure as her own. She had been instructed by Trevor Parker to represent him and had been pleasantly surprised when she saw the fee marked on the brief. It was by far the largest she had ever commanded and had caused consternation and more than a little jealousy in chambers. "He must be very guilty," commented her head of chambers as he looked askance at the words "legal aid" marked on the papers he had picked up from the clerks' room at the same time.

Harriet knew that her husband had already arrived at the flat and she called out as she dropped her briefcase by the sofa in the sitting room. 'I'm in the kitchen,' replied Peter. 'I thought we'd have a mushroom risotto tonight. Is that all right with you?'

Harriet, who regarded any meal she did not have to prepare herself as more than all right, readily agreed. 'I'll just have a quick shower,' she said, 'then I have to read some papers after supper.'

'Not again,' responded Peter, dejectedly. 'Can't we have a night when we just relax?'

Harriet popped her head into the kitchen and kissed him on the cheek.

'It's a big case,' she said, 'and it's worth a lot of money.'

'But we don't need the money,' said Peter, resplendent in his chef's apron.

'That's not the point – and you know it.'

'How much?' he enquired, trying his best to pretend he was not really interested.

'Twenty thousand on the brief and eight hundred a day,' replied Harriet, looking very pleased with herself. Peter seemed slightly stunned.

'He must be guilty then,' he said, putting on his best impression of what he thought a hanging judge would look like.

'That's what Julian Beresford said.'

'So we agree about something – at last!'

Harriet pulled a face at him.

Peter smiled. 'Go and have your shower; it's almost ready. I've opened a bottle of the Jean Thévenet. Take a glass with you.'

'That's a bit extravagant isn't it – with mushroom risotto?'

'Not if you're being paid that much to defend some villain.'

'Don't say that darling. You never know, he might be innocent!'

'That'll make a change. Now hurry up. I don't want it spoiled.'

Thirty minutes later, Harriet was curled up on the larger sofa in the splendid sitting room of their apartment. Although the building was early nineteenth century, Peter had modelled the refurbishment on largely contemporary lines. He had retained the high ceilings, which gave a marvellous impression of space, but some of the period features had been removed. Harriet had persuaded him, after many months of pleading, to restore the marble fireplace, now fitted with a modern coal-effect gas fire, which added a warming glow, much appreciated, even by Peter, on a cold February night. The furniture was a mixture of both modern and antique, some of the pieces being inherited by Harriet when her father had died. A large figurative painting by a recently deceased artist of Peter's acquaintance took up a substantial part of the wall opposite the main window. Harriet would not have chosen it for herself, but she was gradually beginning to appreciate its attributes following a recent valuation by Sotheby's. *There's no accounting for taste*, she thought to herself when a sum which would have purchased a medium-sized chateau in France was given as its present-day value.

"A dead artist always commands a higher price," intoned the specialist from the auction house as he examined it. "And this fellow was taken up by the Islington set a few years before he died. A very canny investment, if you don't mind my saying so." Peter did not mind, and neither did Harriet, but they had not yet decided whether to put the expert's opinion to the test by offering it for sale.

Harriet was now engrossed, reading her instructions in the case of *The Queen against Michael James Doyle.* Her third glass of wine was to hand and she was feeling more than content if a little tired. Her husband was sitting at what had been her father's William and Mary walnut desk by the window, studying a spreadsheet. The seduction duet between Don Giovanni and Zerlina from Mozart's opera was playing softly in the background. Harriet had always found she worked more effectively when listening to music. She had always loved opera and since she and Peter married he had become similarly enchanted. She looked up from her papers.

'That was very nice, darling. Your culinary skills are coming on no end!'

'I get plenty of practice.'

'Well, you knew what it would be like when you married me. Being a barrister is not a nine-to-five job.'

Peter merely grunted. He looked up.

'What's he supposed to have done anyway?'

'Who?'

'The villain you're representing.'

'So you are interested?'

'Whatever it is, I suspect it's more interesting than my quarterly accounts.'

He stood up and stretched his arms then casually walked towards his wife singing to himself.

'Veini, mio bel diletto.'

Harriet responded – almost in tune with the music.

'Mi fa pieta Masetto.'

Peter laughed and sat down on the edge of the sofa before snatching a glance at the papers spread out around Harriet. She pulled them away from his prying eyes.

'These are confidential,' she said, putting on her spectacles and assuming her best barristerial persona.

'Don't be like that, darling. You know I won't tell anyone. Let me play devil's advocate. It will focus your mind. You never know, it might even help.'

Harriet looked bemused. She picked up the remote control and switched off the tape player. 'Oh, all right. Basically, he's accused of being the prime mover behind a major robbery that occurred before Christmas in the Midlands – just north of Leicester. One of the security guards was shot at close range. Happily, he survived – just.'

'He'll be going away for a long time then?'

'If he's guilty, yes.'

'Well is he?'

Harriet removed her spectacles. 'I don't know, do I? It doesn't matter to me whether he's guilty or not.'

Peter frowned. 'No. It's just your job to get him off!'

'If the evidence isn't there, yes. And what's wrong with that? I wouldn't want to live anywhere where the rules were different. Would you?'

Peter nodded, sagely. 'I suppose not.'

There was a pause before he spoke again.

'What have they got on him then?'

'I don't have all the papers yet. They haven't been served. They want me to go up to Leicester next week to make a bail application.'

'I thought QCs didn't do bail applications?'

'We do if we're paid enough.'

Harriet smiled knowingly. Peter grinned.

'The labourer is worthy of her hire, eh?'

She hissed in derision.

'Actually, they don't seem to have much of a case against him – not on what I've seen so far.'

'So he might really be innocent?'

Peter did not succeed in disguising a touch of incredulity as he spoke. Harriet smiled.

'Well, everything seems to turn on his connection with his co-accused. Charles is defending him – on legal aid!'

'Poor Charles.'

Peter dropped his head in mock sympathy.

'Yes. He seems banged to rights, unless Charles can think of some way to keep out the DNA evidence.'

'You mean he left his DNA at the crime scene?'

'So it appears. All over the guard who was shot.'

'Well he is an incompetent thief. He deserves all he gets. What about your chap?'

'Nothing to connect him to the crime scene at all. He also has what looks like a cast-iron alibi.'

'So what is there?'

'They have him on CCTV on a couple of occasions before the robbery in company with this other man – Charles Benson – at the shopping centre where the security van was hi-jacked. And then there's the money.'

'The money?'

'Yes. He was effectively caught with four hundred thousand pounds in tens and twenties trying to leave the country. The notes are all in the same denominations as the stolen money.'

'Well, that's him down the tubes, too, isn't it?'

'Now, darling, you're reacting just like an over-confident policeman. They have no evidence that the cash in his possession had anything to do with the robbery.'

'What? You mean they have no record of the serial numbers?'

'No. They were all used notes.'

Peter was not to be put off by that. His interest was aroused.

'How much was stolen?'

Harriet glanced down at her papers.

'1.9 million.'

Peter whistled through his teeth. 'All in used notes?'

'No. Three hundred thousand was in new notes. They have the serial numbers for those.'

'And…?'

'None of the notes in the possession of my client matched any of the serial numbers of the stolen new notes.' Harriet smiled, more broadly this time. 'Neither do they have any DNA or other scientific evidence to link any of the recovered money with the stolen cash.'

A look of triumph graced her features.

'Apparently, the cash was destined for ATMs and because of pressure from the Bank of England, the practice is to replenish the machines with used notes as much as possible – so there's no way of identifying where a particular banknote has come from.'

Peter was silent for a few moments.

'Apart from the new notes?'

'Yes – and he didn't have any of those.'

'So you said. What was he doing with four hundred thousand in used banknotes?'

'He hasn't given any detailed instructions about that – yet.'

'Still thinking up an explanation is he? Or exercising his right of silence?'

'Oh, Peter, really! You're so cynical. One thing we do know; the Revenue is after him for unpaid tax. Perhaps he was exporting money he'd avoided paying tax on.'

Peter corrected her. 'Not avoiding – that's legitimate. You mean he was evading tax. Not the same thing at all.'

Harriet smiled. 'Touché.' Then added. 'Whatever he was doing it doesn't prove he was involved in the robbery.'

'Mmm... Sounds a bit fishy to me. What does he do for a living, this innocent client of yours? Apart from armed robbery of course.'

Harriet poked her husband playfully in the ribs.

'Very amusing. He's a property developer. In the same line as you I suppose? But in recent years he's been purchasing a lot of property abroad.'

'Not in the same line as me at all, darling. I need hardly remind you that I'm an upstanding citizen who pays all his taxes on time. No comparison. My last tax bill alone must have been enough to run an entire hospital for a year.'

Peter took the back sheet out of Harriet's hands and looked at it.

'Michael James Doyle? Never heard of him.'

'He runs several companies...' Harriet listed some of them. 'Alpha House Holdings, Riverside Developments, Wreake Construction...'

'Still doesn't ring any bells. I ask again, if he's legit, what was he doing with all that cash?'

Harriet adjusted her position on the sofa. 'All he's said is that he was acting for a client he declines to name in a property transaction in Holland.'

'And you believe him?' Peter snorted with laughter. 'Has he heard of inter-bank transactions? There's no need to use cash in a property purchase, not even in Holland.'

'But they haven't brought in the euro yet, have they?'

'What if they haven't? Ever heard of a banker's draft? You can get them in any currency you know. Or he could have paid the cash into his bank over here and it could have been converted into whatever they use in Holland – guilders I think – and wired to the lawyer carrying out the transaction. No need for cash at all.'

Harriet pretended to ignore him and continued to read her brief. Eventually, she looked up and repeated her earlier comment.

'Even if he were up to no good, it still doesn't prove he was participating in this robbery. He has several witnesses, including I might add, a suffragan bishop, to prove he was 200 miles away at the time.'

'A suffragan bishop, eh? How on earth did he arrange that?'

Harriet poked her husband again, this time less playfully.

'Apparently he was dining in the same hotel in Dorset. It was just a coincidence. He bought the bishop a glass of vintage port. That's how the Right Reverend gentleman remembers him. You really are being unduly critical Peter.'

'He's no slouch, your chap. I'll give him that. Fancy getting a bishop as an alibi witness. Even if he is only a suffragan. You couldn't make it up!'

Peter's face was a picture of mirth as he continued in his efforts to undermine the defence case. 'You must call him, darling. I might even come and watch. A bishop alibiing a suspected armed robber. It's bound to make the *Church Times* at least!' Peter was now laughing out loud. Harriet was not amused. She was beginning to get cross with her husband who was having difficulty controlling himself. She snatched the back sheet from him and started to pick up the papers strewn about the sofa and coffee table. Peter immediately became serious.

'I'm sorry darling. I'm only trying to help. Pointing out the pitfalls.'

Harriet did not reply. Peter tried again.

'I suppose that is a defence, is it?'

'What?' She was no longer in the mood to humour him.

'You know, that he's a money launderer rather than a robber.'

He was starting to enjoy being provocative again.

'Oh, Peter, really! He's thirty-seven and he's never been convicted of anything – not for years anyway. And he's not charged with money laundering.'

The property developer continued to try and find flaws in the barrister's defence of her client. 'You said that 1.9 million was stolen?'

'Yes.'

'And 1.6 million was in untraceable used notes?'

'That's right.'

'How many robbers?'

Harriet looked at her brief again. 'Three – plus the driver.'

'So, four in total.'

'Yes…'

'So if we assume – for the sake of argument – that they were the only individuals involved, if they got rid of the new notes, that would still leave them four hundred thousand each, wouldn't it?'

'Yes.'

'Which just happens to be the precise amount your chap had with him. Case proved, members of the jury!'

He stood up, bowed and awaited acknowledgement of his prowess. Harriet was unmoved.

'That's pretty speculative though, isn't it, Mr Prosecutor? There may have been more than four involved. Indeed, if Doyle was not one of the four who actually carried out the robbery that would make a minimum of five. And you are overlooking the fact that at least a few of the traceable notes would have been discovered in a haul that size. No one's going to destroy three hundred thousand pounds on the off chance they might be traced.'

Peter shook his head. 'Why not? They'd still have 1.6 million. Not bad for a night's work. Perhaps this man Doyle is a bit cleverer than your run-of-the-mill criminal. He's certainly drawn a much cleverer barrister than usual to represent him.'

Harriet was not impressed with the attempt at a backhanded compliment.

'You won't get back into my good books quite so easily.'

But she couldn't help smiling as she spoke. Peter turned away and walked across the room to the bookcase where he selected a volume. He was flicking through the pages when he suddenly turned towards his wife. Something significant had occurred to him.

'What have you thought of now?' asked Harriet, suspiciously.

'Where had the stolen cash come from?' said Peter. He now sounded deadly serious.

'One of the major banks, why?'

Harriet noticed the change of tone in his voice. She sat up and looked at him with a degree of concern.

'A bank or a counting house?'

'What do you mean, a counting house?'

She knew what she meant by that expression. She hesitated as she asked the question and wondered what her husband understood it to mean? Peter walked back to her and put his book down on the coffee table.

'The big banks have a number of service centres or counting houses. All the money they take in at their branches is sent to one or other of these centres for processing. It's then counted, checked and redistributed or, if the notes are badly worn, sent back to the Bank of England for destruction. Only the really good quality notes would be reserved for ATMs.'

Harriet smiled and started to relax but only a little.

'You are remarkably well informed. That's more or less what my instructions say but they're silent as to the exact procedures. The prosecution hasn't served all the statements from the bank yet. I don't suppose they would be very keen on such information getting into the public arena.'

Peter was now on a roll. 'Remember, darling, my casual employees are still paid in cash. My accounts' clerk has to do weekly trips to the bank to obtain the money.'

'So?'

'Well, I have noticed that some of the notes we get are in pretty poor condition. Certainly not good enough to be used in cash machines. I even complained on one occasion.'

'And your point is?'

Peter sat down on the sofa next to Harriet.

'The cash that's drawn from ATMs is usually in tip-top condition, either new or as good as new, agreed?'

'Yes, otherwise the machines might get clogged up.'

'Exactly. Now what sort of condition was this four hundred grand in?'

Harriet started to sound apprehensive again.

'I don't know for sure; I haven't seen it yet.'

'Could I suggest that you examine it?'

'When I do, what should I be looking for?' She looked at her husband disdainfully. 'Banknotes are banknotes aren't they?'

Peter shook his head.

'Oh come on, Harry. Get those little grey cells working.'

Harriet stifled a yawn. 'It's getting too late for that and I've had a very long day.'

'Nonsense. Think about it. All this cash has been prepared in one of these counting houses. None of it is in sequence, none of the recovered cash was new, right?'

'Yes.'

'And all of the recovered cash is in the same denominations as the stolen money?'

'Yes, but what does that prove? Lots of people use cash. You've already said you pay your casual staff in cash.'

'Yes. But mine comes from a high street bank – and its condition is variable. If this four hundred grand is suitable for use in ATMs it stands to reason it must have been prepared in one of these service centres for that specific purpose.'

'What if it was prepared there? You've just said all the cash the branches take in is sent to these places.'

'Yes, my darling, but not all of it is sent out again to fill up these cash machines. Only the notes that are of good enough quality.'

Harriet was beginning to see the point. She thrashed around for an answer.

'But lots of people deal in cash, don't they?'

'Not these days.'

He looked her full in the face. 'Come on, darling. Who deals in cash nowadays? Bookies and… criminals. When I sell a property I even have to check the passports of the purchasers just to prove who I'm dealing with. We never *deal* in cash.'

'But how does this prove that the cash my chap had in his possession came from *this* particular counting house?'

'It doesn't. But I reckon I could prove beyond any doubt that it was prepared for use in ATMs, which means it must have come from *a* counting house.'

'How?'

'Simple. Take the four hundred thousand to one of these service centres and put it through their counting machines. If it has been collected over a period of time from a variety of sources – which is doubtless what your chap will tell you – the machine will reject a significant proportion of it as not being up to the required standard.'

'And if it isn't rejected?'

'Well, that will prove that this four hundred grand had been prepared to be placed in cash machines. The chances of anyone having that amount of cash made up only of notes of that quality must be what?' He paused. Then he smiled, knowingly. 'Four hundred thousand to one!'

Harriet looked at him quizzically. She said nothing for well over a minute then casually dropped the papers onto the coffee table.

'I give up. You're probably right.' She sat up straight. 'If Doyle's cash really is all of that quality, I suppose that's the only inference that can be drawn. My solicitor says there are some photographs. He's going to let me have them when I see him next week.'

Peter adopted a more sympathetic tone. 'They might help, but really you need to see the money.'

'But I can't ask the prosecution to put it through those machines. It'll give the game away. They obviously haven't realised. And it's not my job to help them convict my client.'

Peter opened his mouth as if to say something but thought better of it. His wife placed a finger on his lips, then hugged him.

'Darling, you're a genius. I can honestly say I would never have spotted that, not in a month of Sundays.'

Peter smiled, preening himself. 'Not bad for a brickie, eh?'

'You're hardly that now, darling, even if you started out as one.'

'Isn't that what your head of chambers still calls me?'

'He's a snob – and probably thought he was being funny. Besides, he's undoubtedly jealous. You earn far more than the whole of chambers put together – as I feel it necessary to remind him from time to time. And don't forget. He won't be head of chambers for very much longer.'

She kissed her husband. He stopped smiling.

'You're still planning to take over as head?'

'Yes. I know what you think, but there really isn't anyone else, and we can't let Julian carry on. People would leave.'

Peter looked disconsolate.

'Is it so important that you become head of chambers? We might as well sell the house in Surrey then. You'll never have time to go there.'

'There's no need for you to worry your head about that. The first thing I shall do as head of chambers is to appoint a chambers' director. Geoff can then stick to clerking. We have to make the administration more efficient and professional. Do you know that some of the younger members are owed thousands in fees that have never been collected?'

Peter sighed. 'Have it your own way. I suppose I'll get used to it. It's those infernal social occasions I can't stand.'

He smiled, rather pathetically. But Harriet became serious as her attention returned to Michael Doyle and the four hundred thousand pounds.

'Mind you, it won't exactly help my client if the penny drops with the prosecution.'

Her husband brushed his hand through her hair.

'Forty million pennies to be exact. Of course, I could be wrong. Some of this cash may not be in tip-top condition.'

Harriet shook her head. 'I don't know. Trevor Parker says in the instructions it could all be taken for new but I shall have to check that for myself.' She half laughed. 'He thinks that helps us. You know, the fact that none of the recovered notes matches the serial numbers of the new notes means that this lot can't be part of the proceeds. He reckons that at least a few of the new notes would have been there – if it were part of the stolen money. He obviously hadn't spotted your point either. Let's hope no one else has!'

Peter nibbled her ear then kissed her. 'If this chap Doyle has anything approaching a brain, he'd have had no problem appreciating which of the notes were brand new. They'd have had consecutive serial numbers.'

She looked at him admiringly.

'I know. I shall have to take specific instructions from him about the money. In writing! You've put me in a very difficult position. Ever considered a career at the Bar?'

And she wasn't necessarily joking.

'No chance. I'd look stupid in one of those wigs!'

CHAPTER THIRTY-TWO

Chief Inspector Hood was sitting in his office still musing on the weekend he had spent with his wife in the hotel in Dorset. Macpherson had also reported and the consequent tumult, particularly amongst the higher ranks, had to be seen to be believed. Hood thought he detected a degree of panic in the summary rushed out in the chief constable's name by the ACC (administration). Those at the coalface took a more philosophical stance and carried on much as before. The chief constable had called what he described as a "Macpherson Seminar" to which all ranks above and including chief inspector were required to attend.

Hood had read a summary of the report and agreed entirely that both the attitude of the Metropolitan police and its investigation into the racist murder which had prompted the enquiry were lamentable. The ineptitude of the police officers involved was marked. Hood would have been personally ashamed had he conducted such an error-strewn investigation. But he, like many others, was unable fully to comprehend the notion of institutionalised racism, the phrase that had fast become the lodestar of the enquiry's report. And he immediately spotted the circular reasoning that defined a racist incident as any incident perceived to be racist. For his part, he did not recognise the vast majority of his colleagues as real or even unwitting racists and he wondered aloud whether the outcome of the enquiry and the terms in which it chose to represent its conclusions might simply further undermine the morale of officers who, on the whole, were doing their best in frequently difficult circumstances. Worst of all, he dreaded a politically correct police service, fastening on to every fashionable and passing fad instead of getting on with its principal function of preserving the Queen's peace. *God save us*, he said to himself, *from the day when senior police officers are regarded by the public in the same venal terms as most politicians.*

He put considerations of Macpherson to one side and smiled as he contemplated the delightful time he and his wife had enjoyed at High Trees House hotel on the Dorset coast. The weather had been unexpectedly kind and he and Sarah had revelled in the long walks along the beach when the sun had broken from behind the scudding clouds. On one occasion the rain had suddenly returned and they had then appreciated the huge log fire that had greeted them in the hotel lounge when they'd arrived back, dripping wet. He had almost forgotten about the secondary purposes of the trip – to investigate first-hand Doyle's alibi. He had, of course, measured the distance from his home to the hotel and noted the time their journey had taken. Even he was beginning to have doubts about his theory until he started chatting with the night porter as he ordered a newspaper for the following morning. No one had taken a statement from Ronald Earnshaw, a former sergeant in the Queen's Regiment. He'd been spoken to but the local police had deemed him unimportant as far as the inquiry was concerned. He had been on duty on 16 December and had fallen into conversation with Doyle. Later, noticing that Doyle, like Hood, had not ordered a newspaper for the following morning, he had telephoned the lodge were Doyle was staying.

"It was at about 9.45 p.m.," he'd told the chief inspector. "He'd finished dinner a good hour before. Funny thing was, there was no reply. I didn't think much of it at the time. I thought he might have been in the shower or gone to bed early, but I recall it vividly. Easy to remember Mr Doyle. Very flash with his money he was. Gave me the biggest tip I've had in a long time." Hood had remedied the omission and taken a short but detailed statement from Mr Earnshaw, though he had not sought to match the tip Michael Doyle had proffered.

Sarah, of course, had been much more interested in the culinary delights offered by the hotel's restaurant. They had enjoyed an excellent dinner and consumed a whole bottle of wine between them. True, the wine had not been of the standard enjoyed by Doyle and Julia Hamilton, but the lesser growth Margaux had nonetheless been fully appreciated. Their lovemaking afterwards had been unusually passionate. Hood had winced then smiled the next morning when his wife warned him that he had better get his promotion as she was anticipating another mouth would need feeding nine months hence.

Hood smiled then turned his mind once more to the enigmatic observations of Edward Markham-Moore. The barrister had declined to add anything to his analysis of the cash seized from Doyle's Mercedes in Hull, at least, not until he had seen the banknotes for himself. Hood had examined the photographs of the cash that the forensic scientists had taken but he had yet to view the actual exhibits. He had instructed Munt to bring all the cash seized from Doyle up to his room from the property store. "Get Craddock to assist you," he had said, "and make sure you don't mix them up." He recalled that Markham-Moore had insisted that the cash removed from Doyle's safe must also be retained. Hood remained puzzled about that. He couldn't see how it was relevant to the case. The Revenue's interest he could understand but, try as he might, he couldn't see how it affected his inquiry. No one suggested that the money from the safe had anything to do with the robbery. Apart from anything else, when it was examined and counted, there was a large number of five-pound notes – and no five-pound notes had been despatched to the Charnwood from the counting house. But the fact that the barrister was so insistent that it be retained continued to bug him and he could not get it out of his mind. He'd even discussed it with his wife but she could not shed any light on the conundrum either.

He stood up and walked to the window, his hands in his pockets. The break in the weather he had relished in Dorset had passed. Leicester was cold, wet and miserable, typical conditions for the end of February. The rain lashed against the window and he smiled as he noticed Wendy Knight and Andrew Hooper rushing from the car park trying to keep themselves dry by sharing Wendy's wholly inadequate umbrella. They were returning from a further visit to Langdale Security following Hood's careful examination of the series of calls to the police immediately after the robbery. Langdale was the fourth out of the seven calls received by the control room. If Mr Patel had pressed the silent alarm, as he insisted he had, Hood wanted to know why fully four minutes had passed before the police were alerted by the security company. Surely, they should have been the first to call the police? Those four minutes might have been crucial in enabling the robbers to escape from the Charnwood. Three other calls from various stores in the vicinity of the compound had been received before the alert from Langdale, the first fully two and a half minutes after the security van had been torched. Something didn't seem quite right. Hood was determined to get to the bottom of it. Amongst her many other accomplishments, Wendy Knight was a dab hand with computers and he was hoping that her examination of the computer system at Langdale Security might provide the answer.

The knock on his door was followed by the entry of two bedraggled specimens in the form of Detective Sergeant Andrew Hooper and

Detective Constable Wendy Knight. Hood could not resist grinning as they approached his desk.

'Sit down,' he said. 'You look as if you could do with a cup of tea.' He pressed the intercom and ordered three cups then sat down himself.

'Anything to report?'

Knight looked at Hooper, who nodded and she then related what they had discovered.

'It's very interesting, sir. The emergency warning system at Langdale is fully computerised, as we thought. It's also subject to a full test on a regular basis. Bill Mostyn was responsible for ensuring it remained in working order.'

'How is the testing carried out?' asked Hood.

'Very straightforward, sir. He chooses – or should I say chose – the time and an operator in each van pressed the alarm. He then checked the responses on the computer. That, according to his assistant, is how it was done. In the event of a genuine emergency, the computer triggers an audible alarm in the operations room at Hinckley. There is no direct communication with our control room. A call has to be put in by the person on duty – who at the time we are interested in was Mostyn's assistant.'

'We know a call was put in, but not immediately,' said Hood.

'Yes, sir. Melanie Newman called control as soon as the alarm sounded.'

She looked at Hooper again and indicated that he should continue with the report.

'The thing is, sir – someone had tampered with the computer program. A four-minute delay had been inserted. So the alarm only sounded four minutes after Patel pressed the silent alarm in the security van.'

'Are we sure about that?' asked Hood.

'As sure as I can be,' replied Knight. 'We'll probably have to get a real expert to examine the system, but it seemed pretty clear to me.'

'And Mostyn's computer controls the system does it?'

'Yes, sir.'

'So the late Mr Mostyn was in on it, was he?'

'Looks that way, sir,' said Hooper.

'And he had left before the robbery occurred?'

'Yes, sir. Melanie Newman was on duty at the time.'

'I suppose if he hadn't been taken ill, he could have reprogramed the system afterwards and no one would have been the wiser?'

'Yes, sir.'

Hood was silent for a few seconds.

'When was the last test carried out?'

Knight looked at her notes.

'The twenty-third of October.'

'That's very odd, isn't it?' said Hood. 'You'd have thought they would have tested the system more frequently than that. On a weekly basis, at least?'

'Seems they didn't,' said Hooper. 'It looks as if Mostyn was a bit slack when it came to testing it. Of course, they hadn't had an incident for over three years.'

'Did anyone else have access to Mostyn's computer?'

'Not officially, no sir.'

'What do you mean, "not officially"?'

The two officers looked at each other, then smiled. Hooper hesitated before replying.

'There are four docking stations in the operations room. Each member of staff has a password. Our Mr Mostyn's, though, was known to most of the them.'

'What?' exclaimed Hood. 'Why was that?' Knight took up the story.

'You know, sir, if you try and gain access to a computer and you have to insert a password?'

'Yes,' said Hood slowly. He had been meaning for some time to upgrade his computer skills.

'If you type in the wrong password, a message comes up telling you that the password is incorrect?'

'Yes.'

'Well, Mostyn was a bit of a joker it seems. That was his password. "Incorrect". Melanie Newman certainly knew it; that's how we gained access to his computer.'

Hood considered what had been said.

'So… if his password was generally known, someone else could have altered the program?'

'It's a possibility, sir. But he has to be the prime candidate.'

Hood sat back in his chair as his secretary appeared with a tray containing three steaming mugs of tea and placed it gingerly on the desk. They each helped themselves. As his secretary left the room, Hood almost chuckled as he spoke.

'Do you know what I find so interesting about this investigation? Every time we think we have established something with certainty, there's always a little twist. Always a slight possibility that there's another explanation for what seems pretty clear.'

He shook his head. His frustration was obvious.

'A full examination of the computer system will be able to demonstrate exactly when the program was changed. Right down to the minute,' said Knight. 'We can then check from the employee time sheets exactly who was on the premises at the time it was altered.'

'That will narrow it down, I suppose,' said Hood. 'And it hasn't been changed since the robbery?'

'No sir, we organised that at the outset. Simon Langdale agreed not to alter anything as a condition of our allowing the firm to continue to use the system. Fortunately, there hasn't been another robbery.'

'So there's always a possibility that Mostyn wasn't there when the alteration was made,' continued Knight.

'I hope not,' responded Hood forcefully. 'I really do. If he's excluded, we'll be right back to square one!'

'Well, sir, it does help clear up one matter. Patel was obviously telling the truth when he says he pressed the alarm in the van. We can surely exclude him now?'

Hood nodded.

'That's progress, I suppose. Robbie Sleath was right about him. At least the chief will be pleased. He was quite determined that Mr Patel should remain a hero. It looks like he'll get his way after all.'

Hood took a sip of his tea.

'But it doesn't help us. If someone else did interfere with the computer program, all he has to say is that it was down to Mostyn. We'll never be able to prove that wasn't the case.'

'That's true enough, sir,' replied Knight. 'Unless he was on leave at the time the interference took place, we won't be able to prove he wasn't there. He was regarded as management. He didn't have to fill in any time sheets.'

Hood shook his head and finished off his tea. But he said nothing.

'How did you get on at the hotel, sir?' asked Knight, sensing a change of subject might be helpful.

'Sarah enjoyed it,' said Hood, 'and I did get a better impression of the place than I'd gained from the witness statements taken by the local bobbies.'

'What about the wine, sir?' asked Knight, cheekily. 'I don't suppose you stretched to a Margaux?'

Hood smiled.

'Not a first growth,' replied the chief inspector. 'But it was our wedding anniversary so we had a bottle of the '87 Prieuré-Lichine, which, as Greg will tell you is a Margaux. Very acceptable it was too! But only a fourth grow, I believe.'

Knight was impressed.

'I'll ask him about it,' she said.

'Yes. Quite a nose it had and very well structured. A bit heavy on the Merlot, I thought, but otherwise very acceptable.'

Hood laughed at his own parody of a wine expert. Knight joined in. Hood then became serious. 'As for the investigation,' he continued, 'I did establish that Doyle was not answering his phone after 9.45 p.m. The night porter rang him. There was no reply.'

'That's interesting,' said Knight.

'But hardly conclusive,' responded Hood. 'I also took a look at his room – or should I say suite? The entrance to the lodge can't be seen from the hotel and there's a convenient balcony that gives access to some woodland behind. There's a well-worn path that leads to a main road – not three hundred metres away.'

'Also interesting,' rejoined Knight.

'But, again, not conclusive. No one saw him with a motorcycle either.'

'But it remains at least a possibility that he came back to Leicestershire that night?'

'A possibility, yes. But proving it is another matter altogether. Remember what Markham-Moore said? What we require is proof.'

'Yes, sir,' said Knight. 'I've been trying to get my head round what he said about the money too. I didn't mention it to Greg – like we agreed – but I still can't see the relevance of the cash from his safe. That can't have anything to do with the robbery, can it?'

'That's my view too. It's probably cash he hasn't paid tax on. There's no way it can form part of the proceeds of the robbery. There are hundreds of fivers in it and no five-pound notes were included in the consignment.'

'The barrister will be up here in a day or two won't he, sir?' interrupted Hooper. 'All will be revealed then, I suppose.'

'Yes, I suppose it will,' said Hood. 'But it would be nice if we could solve the riddle without his assistance all the same. We're supposed to be the detectives – not him!'

Hood leant forward. 'To that end, I'm having the cash brought up from the property store. All of it. The money from the Mercedes and the cash from Doyle's safe. I think we should take a good look at it.'

'Will that help, sir?' queried Hooper.

'Well,' explained Hood, 'Markham-Moore wants to see it before he says anything further. So I thought we should have a good look at it first.'

Neither Hooper nor Knight looked particularly convinced. Hood sat back in his chair and looked at the two of them in turn, then smiled.

'Did I ever tell you about my old DCI in Leeds?'

'No sir.'

'Well he was quite a character and a very clever detective. He's dead now, God rest his soul. Had a stroke within a year of retiring. Very sad. Keen on poetry. He never had much of an education himself, but he was a voracious reader. Quite an authority on Dickens too, though that isn't the only reason I liked him.'

He chuckled to himself. Then he leant forward again. 'He also had a very practical piece of advice for young detectives. "Always look at the exhibits Hood," he used to say. "Always look at the exhibits." Sound advice that, don't you think?'

'But we have the photographs, sir. We've had a good look at those.'

'It's not the same, though, is it? You don't get the feel of things from just looking at photographs. And if Markham-Moore wants to see the cash, there must be a reason.'

Hood pressed his intercom and waited for his secretary to respond.

'Yes, sir?'

'Any sign of those exhibits I asked for, Shirley?'

'Not yet, sir.'

'Chase 'em up, will you?'

He sat back in his chair, scratched his left ear and addressed his two colleagues. 'I suppose we'll be losing Robbie Sleath, now that he's made sergeant?' The other two noticed the twinkle in his eye.

'Yes, sir,' said Hooper. 'He's going back into uniform – at least for the next twelve months. That reminds me sir, we haven't collected your contribution towards the party.'

'Party? What party?'

'We're giving him a bit of a send-off next week. He's transferring to the Nottingham division– traffic management.'

All three smiled, knowingly. Sleath was not the most popular of colleagues.

'Well, he was the one who wanted promotion. But I suppose we'll miss him. He was right about Patel though, wasn't he?'

There was no reply, as Hood searched his inside pocket for his wallet.

'What's the going rate?' he asked.

'Inspectors and above, a tenner,' replied Knight.

'Ten pounds?' queried Hood. 'Where's this celebration taking place? The Ritz?'

Knight laughed. 'No sir. At the Seven Stars Inn – the pub in the village near where he lives. They're putting on a buffet too.'

'I should think they are,' replied Hood, taking a crisp ten-pound note from his wallet. 'I only took this out of the cash dispenser this morning.'

Knight searched in her shoulder bag and produced a motley bunch of notes tied up with an elastic band.

'Wendy's acting as treasurer,' pointed out Hooper. 'She's the only one we could trust with the money.'

She removed the elastic band, smoothed out the notes then added Hood's tenner. She was about to place the elastic band around the notes again when Hood intervened.

'Just a moment, let me see that cash – all of it.'

Knight looked at Hooper. What did Hood mean? There was a look of astonishment on his face – as if he'd had a sudden revelation.

'There's not that much sir. I think with your tenner we should have about ninety pounds. We haven't collected from everybody yet. You know what coppers are like when it comes to parting with money.'

She placed all the cash on the desk. Hood spread it out so that each note was fully visible. He looked at the two detectives in turn. His excitement was obvious.

'What do you see?' he asked. Hooper did not understand what was happening. Hood seemed suddenly exhilarated. As if he'd just discovered he'd won the lottery jackpot.

Hooper sighed. 'Three tens, two twenties and… one, two, three… four fivers. That's ninety pounds, like Wendy said.'

'Not the amount,' said Hood impatiently. 'Look at the condition of the notes!'

Hooper and Knight stared at the cash now strewn over the desk then looked at each other.

'Describe what you see,' insisted Hood.

'The fivers look pretty well used, sir. Your tenner looks like a new note and the others look pretty much of a muchness.'

'Which means?'

Hooper looked blank. Wendy Knight started in similar vein then hit her forehead with the palm of her hand.

'That's it. That's what Markham-Moore meant! He said we had to look at Doyle's money as a *tranche* – not at the individual notes.'

Hooper continued to look bemused as Hood pushed the banknotes about, turning them over and stroking them. What was he doing that for? This wasn't Doyle's money. It was what had been collected for Sleath's party.

'And…?' said Hood, looking directly at Knight. She sounded almost as excited as Hood when she answered.

'This cash, looked at as a whole, cannot have come from a cash dispenser and it follows it cannot have been prepared for replenishing a cash machine!'

'Exactly! Well done Wendy. You've got it. How can we have been so stupid?'

Hooper continued to look vacant. 'But I thought you said, sir, that you'd got that tenner from a cash dispenser this morning?'

The penny had clearly not dropped with him.

'It's been staring us in the face all these weeks,' said Hood ignoring Hooper for the moment. 'That's why Markham-Moore wants us to retain the cash from the safe. By way of comparison.'

Hood looked at the still uncomprehending face of Hooper. Knight noticed the chief inspector was almost ecstatic. He got out of his chair and walked round and round the room, quite unable to remain in any one place for more than a second or two. Eventually, he stopped behind his desk and leant forward, placing his elbows on the desktop, and looking directly at Wendy Knight.

'I'll lay even money that when we examine the cash from Doyle's car, it looks like my tenner. That's what the photographs suggest. But the cash from the safe will have come from all over the place. It'll be just like this lot you've collected for Sleath's party – some of it might be good enough for a cash dispenser – but a lot of it won't.'

He glanced at Hooper, who was still completely unable to understand his chief inspector's manifest excitement.

'Which means…?'

'We haven't any photos of the cash from the safe, have we sir?' said Hooper.

Both Hood and Knight looked at him and smiled. It was Knight who answered Hooper's question.

'That's right. The cash from the safe has not been photographed yet. But it will have to be. If, as we suspect, it looks like the party money it will mean that as a *tranche* of cash, it can't have been prepared with a view to refilling a cash dispenser.'

Hood nodded, a broad smile covering his face.

'Whereas…?'

'The cash from the Mercedes *must* have been prepared for cash dispensers which means it must have passed through a counting house.'

'Absolutely! We've got him, Wendy. We've got him!'

Hood pressed his intercom again. 'Shirley, where are those exhibits I asked to be brought up from the property store?'

'They're on their way, sir.'

'Good. Tell them to get a move on.'

Hood flung himself back in his chair and hit his desk with his hand in delight. Hooper continued to look about him as he stared first at Hood then at Wendy. He had no idea what they were talking about.

'Will someone please explain?' he asked. 'I only want to know what is so significant about the cash we've collected for Sleath's party.'

'Tell him, Wendy,' said Hood. 'Andrew wasn't there when we saw Markham-Moore. Go on, let him in on the biggest clue we've had in the whole investigation – a clue we've all missed! We should be ashamed of ourselves.'

Wendy was about to begin her explanation but was disturbed by a noise from the corridor outside Hood's room. Hood got up, walked to the door and opened it.

'About time,' he said. 'Where have you been?'

Munt and Craddock, in their shirtsleeves, were manhandling a somewhat ancient-looking trolley filled with polythene bags containing cash. Neither of them had ever witnessed Hood in such a buoyant mood.

'Sorry about that, sir,' said Munt meekly, 'the property store couldn't immediately locate the cash from Doyle's safe. His solicitor had asked to see it yesterday and it hadn't been put back in its proper place.'

'Had he indeed? It's all there I take it?'

'Oh yes, sir. The solicitor wasn't allowed to open the exhibit bags. He was told he would have to get the permission of the CPS to do that.'

'Excellent,' said Hood. He knew how long it would take the CPS to make a decision about that. 'Bring the trolley in.'

The trolley was wheeled, squeaking, into Hood's office.

'The bags on the top contain the cash from the Mercedes,' added Craddock. 'The cash from the safe is on the bottom. They're clearly marked.'

He handed over a box of latex gloves to the chief inspector. 'Sergeant Watson said you'll need these. There are some new plastic ties as well – just in case you need to open any of the bags.'

'Thank you – that will be all.'

'Anything else we can do?' asked Craddock, anxious to discover the purpose of bringing the cash to Hood's room.

'No. Not at the moment. You can come back in about forty minutes,' said Hood. 'We'll have finished with it by then. You can take it back to the store – and make sure it's put back where it belongs and properly signed for. I shall hold you and Munt responsible!'

'Yes sir,' nodded Craddock.

He and Munt departed. Hood opened the box of gloves and offered a pair first to Knight and then to Hooper. He put a pair on himself then picking up one of the polythene covered parcels of cash from the top section of the trolley, pulled at the plastic tie securing it. It was immovable.

'Try this, sir,' said Hooper, taking a penknife from his jacket pocket.

Hood cut the tie and opened the polythene bag.

'Get rid of those notes,' he told Knight, pointing to the collection money. Knight picked up the banknotes and replaced them in her shoulder bag. Hood emptied the polythene bag on to his desk, spilling the twenty-pound notes over the surface.

'As I predicted,' he said, relishing the moment. 'These notes are as good as new. There's nothing to choose between them.'

Hooper and Knight joined in the examination of the banknotes. Neither of them could find a single one that was other than in excellent condition. Hood started to pack the notes back into the bag. He resealed them with a new tie and signed the exhibit label, dating and timing to the precise moment he had cut the original. He then picked up a second bag and repeated the exercise. Again, all the banknotes were in very good condition. A bag of ten-pound notes received similar treatment. Then, the penny dropped with Hooper.

'I've got it sir,' he said. 'Sorry to have been so slow.' He grinned in embarrassment.

'All these notes are good enough to be placed in cash dispensers. The chances of having so many notes in such good condition that have *not* been prepared for cash dispensers is so remote as to be fanciful.'

'Well done, Sherlock,' said Hood. 'That's why Markham-Moore wants a statistician to look them over. One of these university geniuses will be able to work out the precise odds, I shouldn't wonder. Of course, it will have to be someone other than Greg. We have to avoid any suggestion of bias.' He glanced at Knight. 'Now let's have a look at the cash from Doyle's safe.'

When those polythene bags were opened – only two in number – the condition of the banknotes was wholly different. Many of them were badly worn, particularly the five-pound notes. Several of the other notes were also in poor condition.

'No chance of this lot having been prepared for placing in a cash dispenser,' said Knight. 'They'd block the machine in no time.'

'Some of them would be good enough,' commented Hooper, 'but I don't suppose that matters.'

'Not at all,' said Hood. 'We have to look at them as a whole. As a single *tranche.* That's the point. Had this lot been put through a counting machine at Bridgeford House, a good proportion of them would have been rejected as of insufficient quality to be sent out to be placed in cash machines. On the other hand, the cash we retrieved from Doyle's car must have been prepared for replenishing ATMs. There is no other credible explanation.'

Hood could hardly contain his excitement.

'There is one thing, though, sir,' said Knight. 'Although this might prove the cash seized from the car was prepared for placing in cash dispensers, it doesn't necessarily prove it came from Bridgeford House, does it?'

But Hood was not to be deflected.

'I agree, Wendy. But how many robberies have taken place where this much cash has been stolen from a counting house? Only this one, so far as I'm aware. Remember? We did a nationwide check several weeks ago. This is the only one.'

'So we've got him, sir.' Hooper was delighted. He was almost as animated as Hood. 'Michael James Doyle is going to go down for twenty years. At last!'

CHAPTER THIRTY-THREE

Tuesday, 2 March 1999

'Do you really think it's a runner?' asked Harriet Lassiter.

She was sitting at her desk in chambers reading the notes prepared by Laura Mitchell for Charles Cavan-Henry, who was lounging in Harriet's well-worn leather armchair opposite, smiling broadly. He'd just had a rather unexpected victory in the Court of Appeal and was feeling very pleased with himself.

'Well, I can't think of a way round it,' he answered. 'Whoever drafted this statute certainly didn't foresee the circumstances we find ourselves in. But they never do, do they?'

Harriet remained sceptical. She always operated on the basis that if something sounded too good to be true then it probably was just that – too good to be true.

'But it doesn't make sense. Why exclude evidence that proves a man's guilt without a shadow of a doubt? There must be a contrary argument, surely?'

'Ours not to reason why,' said Charles. 'It's a gift from the gods, as they say, and when you think about it, it's entirely consistent with article 8 of the European Convention. By doing what they did, the police undoubtedly interfered with my chap's right to a private life. It simply depends how you look at it.'

'Yes,' said Harriet, 'but article 8 doesn't deal with absolutes. What are the words? "Everyone has the right to *respect* for his private and family life…"'

'Well, that must include your DNA, surely?'

Charles was in no mood to be contradicted.

'Especially if you've given a sample voluntarily for a specific purpose and the police promised to destroy it afterwards. They did the exact opposite and kept it on their database. We can't have the police deliberately breaking the law, now, can we?'

Harriet continued to appear somewhat less than convinced.

'I understand the argument. It's superficially attractive and it's succeeded at least once before.'

'Really? Laura couldn't find any reported cases directly on the point.'

'Well, there is one.'

'Don't keep it to yourself, Harry. Where's it reported?'

'It's not in the law reports, but I'm hoping to get a transcript of the ruling.'

'Where did you dig this up from?'

Charles was even more ebullient.

'I didn't. My junior did.'

'I thought you'd been lumbered with that old has-been Randell Richards? Couldn't you insist on someone a bit more, er... how should I put it... contemporary?'

'There's nothing wrong with Randell,' cautioned Harriet. 'Did you know about this rape case in Carlisle? It's not in the law reports but Randell knew about it. An old mate of his was the defence junior. The judge – it was Francis Willoughby, you know, the one who has just been promoted to the Court of Appeal – ruled out a DNA profile in almost identical circumstances.'

'Fantastic! But didn't the Crown appeal it on a reference? Surely, it must have gone to the Court of Appeal?'

'That's where Randell comes in again. Apparently, the CPS messed up and put the appeal in too late. There's a strict time limit. So as far as we know there hasn't been a ruling from the CACD yet.'

'So ours may be the first case to get to the Appeal Court, assuming we can convince the trial judge that it's a good point? We might even get as far as the House of Lords. Now that's something to think about.'

Harriet removed her spectacles.

'Even if the Crown appeals, as the law presently stands, it would only be of academic interest and, of course, a precedent for future cases. Our potentially guilty clients would still walk free. There's no power to reverse the ruling so as to convict a defendant.'

'I had thought I'd have to advise Benson to plead. It looks as if he'll be getting out without the matter even going to a jury.'

'You're going to make an application to dismiss?'

'Certainly. You must too.'

'There's the question of the money in my case. The prosecution hasn't spotted it yet, but if they do, I may still be in trouble.'

'What do you mean? If Benson goes, how can they connect your chap with the robbery?'

'Supposing they can prove that the money they found in his motor car came from the counting house that supplied the cash to the Charnwood Centre?'

'Can they do that? None of the serial numbers has been recorded.'

'I think they could, if they thought about it. It's all in such good condition you see; that quantity of cash can only have been prepared for placing in cash dispensers. The chances of having so much cash in almost new condition with virtually no consecutive serial numbers is so remote as to be nigh on impossible.'

Charles furrowed his forehead.

'I see – or do I? It's hardly conclusive is it?'

'It might be if the prosecution realised it and put the money through the machines at the bank. A low rejection rate would be virtually conclusive.'

'Of course,' said Charles, slowly, as the obvious and irresistible point dawned on him. 'It's as plain as a pikestaff when you think about it. But they'll never cotton on to that, will they?'

Harriet was not so sure.

'Edward Markham-Moore is prosecuting. I bumped into him over at the Law Courts yesterday. He was looking very confident. He certainly knew you and I were in the case. He even asked me if we're going to offer to plead.'

'Edward always looks confident,' said Charles dismissively. 'It doesn't mean a thing. But clever old you, Harry, thinking of that. I must confess it had never occurred to me.'

Harriet almost blushed.

'Actually, I didn't.'

Charles looked surprised.

'Not Randell again?'

'No. It was Peter. He thought of it.'

'Good for him,' said Charles. 'He'll keep it to himself, of course?'

'Of course he will. But I'm going to have to raise it with my client – just in case.'

Charles looked pensive.

'Do you really think so? It's not for me to say, Harry, but I'd leave it for the moment, if I were you. If we both make applications to dismiss and succeed in keeping out the DNA it will deal a mortal blow to the Crown's case. The most they could get your chap for would be money laundering. As for Benson, he'd be free as a bird.'

Charles was quite insistent.

'And Doyle hasn't been charged with money laundering – yet.' Harriet smiled as she spoke.

'Exactly,' said Charles. 'Let's not jump our fences until we get to them!'

'I'd still like to know what his explanation is about the money, though.'

She stood up and walked to the drinks cabinet by the door. Charles jumped out of the wing chair and followed her.

'No you don't. He might say something that will embarrass you – professionally – and you don't want that to happen with that brief fee, do you?'

Harriet frowned.

'Of course not. But I'm not easily embarrassed. Fancy a gin and tonic, Charles?' She looked at her watch. 'It's gone six o'clock.'

'I thought you'd never ask. Not too much gin though. I'm driving.'

'I'm staying in London tonight. Peter has a dinner at the CBI.'

She poured an over-generous measure of gin then tipped some of it into a second glass.

'There's no ice I'm afraid. I really ought to get a fridge in here. I suppose if I become head of chambers, I shall be expected to run a free bar for the rest of you.'

'There's no doubt about that,' grinned Charles, 'although Beresford has only offered me a rather indifferent sherry on the rare occasions I've ventured into his room.'

'That's more than he's ever offered me!'

'You're still standing I take it, Harry? The headship, I mean. No one else is in the running. I haven't heard a dissenting voice – Beresford apart.'

Harriet handed Charles his drink in a heavy cut-glass tumbler.

'I don't suppose he'll vote for me?'

'In my humble opinion, there won't be a vote. No one else will stand – and Julian would be too embarrassed to stand himself following the last chambers meeting. No, I confidently predict you'll be elected *nemine contradicente.*'

'Cheers,' said Harriet, smiling. 'I hope you're right.'

'Good luck – not that you'll need it.'

Harriet took a sip of her drink and returned to her seat.

'What are we going to do about these bail applications? I was hoping they'd be listed before Tom Campion, but Edwina says he's away on a JSB course at Warwick. I've been instructed to get my chap bail at all costs. He's not coping at all well inside. Will Sue Stillwell have to deal with them?'

'It's worse than that, I'm afraid. Edwina heard a whisper that they're going before old Welford at Northampton. The presiders haven't released the case to Campion yet – so they've got to be put before a High Court judge.'

'I thought he was retiring?'

'Not until after Easter. He's off to Worcester from Northampton. That'll be his final sitting.'

'Well that's a bit of a blow. I can't remember Bernard Welford ever giving bail in a major case. It's almost as if the Bail Act didn't exist with him.'

'I know exactly what you mean. We've got no chance. That's why I think we should keep our powder dry. If we raise this DNA point on the bail application, it will put the Crown on notice – and I bet they haven't spotted it. And we want to keep it that way for as long as possible.'

Harriet sighed.

'But I'll have to put up a bit of a show. Doyle won't be there but that girlfriend of his will be lurking outside – assuming she doesn't talk her way in. And she's no slouch when it comes to judging advocacy. You've probably come across her. She's a freelance. Does a lot of work for Midland solicitors?'

'Oh, I know the lovely Miss Hamilton, all right,' replied Charles, taking another drink. 'I've never trusted her but she's very popular with the punters. You might just have to explain our predicament in advance. If we win the dismissal application they'll be out of custody anyway.'

Harriet nodded in agreement.

'But we'll have to raise the DNA point at the dismissal application, of course. Wouldn't we be better waiting until the trial and taking them by surprise?'

'We could, but what about your chap? I doubt if we'll get a trial date much before July and Tom Campion will be off to the Bailey before then. My client's equally eager to get out of prison. He's in Lincoln, don't forget. He's finding it very hard.'

'I see. Who would deal with a dismissal application? If it's released and Campion is on his way to London, it would probably go before Susan Stillwell, wouldn't it? I'd rather have Tom Campion. At least he's intellectually honest.'

'I agree. We've a far better chance with Campion. And I reckon if we put in a dismissal application it will be released to him rather than Stillwell. And if we win the dismissal application, there won't be a trial. He's more likely to take the point in our favour than any of the others who sit at Leicester.'

'I can see that too,' said Harriet. 'I suppose if he deals with the dismissal application, he'll have to keep the trial if we don't succeed on the DNA point?'

'Hopefully, yes. It could follow him to the Bailey. It's certainly serious enough – but I can't see how we can fail on a dismissal application. It just has to be an abuse of process for the police to ride rough shod over the law this way.'

Harriet was not so sure.

'It just doesn't seem right somehow. I can't put my finger on it, but I just have a feeling it isn't going to do the trick.'

'Is this that famous feminine intuition of yours?'

'I don't know what it is.'

She looked puzzled and took another drink.

'Don't get me wrong, Charles. I've no doubt that my solicitor will want to go for a dismissal too. Doyle won't want to wait until July to be tried either.'

She looked up.

'When do you think a dismissal application could be heard?'

'Well, it will have to be before arraignment and that's bound to be before Easter.'

Harriet sighed.

'Doyle won't want to wait even until then.'

'He'll just have to be patient. A few weeks inside is nothing to what he'll get if he's convicted.'

'I suppose you're right. Let's hope it is released to Tom Campion.'

'I think that's a virtual certainty. Unless the presider does it himself?'

Harriet shook her head.

'Unlikely. Rupert Frobisher is lined up for that body in the lake case in Birmingham later this term. Do you know, I was offered the leading brief in that trial, but I had to turn it down.'

'Legally aided, was it?'

Harriet laughed.

'That had nothing to do with it! Geoff had accepted a retainer in Doyle's case – so I have to give it priority. You know me, I always stick to the rules.'

Charles drained his glass.

'A retainer as well, eh? I didn't know about that. They must be keen to have you.'

He got to his feet.

'Look, I shall have to dash. I'm picking Belinda up at the National Theatre. She's rehearsing for some awful Brecht play they're putting on after Easter. Unfortunately, I shall have several free tickets – if you're interested?'

Harriet sent him on his way with a promise she and Peter would attend. Peter was quite keen on Brecht.

'Watching Belinda is always a joy – whatever she's in.'

'Well don't say you haven't been warned.'

Charles paused before he walked through the door.

'We're in agreement about the bail hearing are we? We don't mention the DNA?'

Harriet nodded.

'It's your point, Charles. If you want to play it like that, I shan't interfere.'

'Cheers Harry. See you in Northampton.'

He closed the door behind him.

Harriet settled back in her chair, opened her copy of *Archbold* and started to read. She cast herself in the role of prosecutor and considered Laura Mitchell's argument from that perspective. Try as she might (and she really did try) she could not discover a logical flaw. The police had undoubtedly acted unlawfully by keeping Benson's DNA on the database. It seemed open and shut. It was beginning to look like Michael Doyle was going to walk, despite what Peter had said about the cash from the Mercedes. She wasn't going to be up in Leicester as long as she had expected. Or so it seemed.

CHAPTER THIRTY-FOUR

'So, you worked it out, did you, Chief Inspector?' said Edward Markham-Moore as he, Hood and Detective Sergeant Hooper made their way towards Hood's office after their visit to Bridgeford House.

'It was a long time coming,' he confessed. 'But we got there in the end – and before you proved your point when the cash was put through the machines.'

'Well,' replied the barrister, with unaccustomed humility, 'I would have looked particularly foolish if the demonstration had not worked out as I anticipated.'

'As a theory it seemed quite perfect,' replied Hood. Then he leant towards Markham-Moore and whispered, 'I wonder why Mr King never suggested it?'

The barrister laughed.

'Well you're the detective. Perhaps it's something you should follow up?'

Hood smiled.

'There's always been something about Reg King that didn't quite ring true, and he didn't seem a bit surprised when your demonstration went according to plan. Only 45 per cent of the money from Doyle's safe passed muster but nearly all of the cash from the Mercedes was good enough to be placed in cash dispensers. Did you notice his reaction? It was if he had expected it all along.'

'Will you question him further?'

'I shall certainly think about it. He didn't know about the money from the safe of course, but I do find it surprising that he never suggested putting the cash from the Mercedes through his counting machines. After all, it as good as proves that the four hundred thousand belongs to his bank.'

The barrister suddenly stopped, a few feet from Hood's door.

'But it's the difference between the two that's important,' he insisted. 'We mustn't lose sight of that. That's why I didn't want you to release the money from the safe, despite what James Frazer said. The comparison is damning; don't you think? I can't see Doyle talking his way out of that one!'

'I look forward to his attempt to do so,' replied Hood. 'When we receive Professor Lee's statement, I fancy it will be game, set and match whatever Doyle says. Good of Greg Oldham to recommend him.'

★★★★

As predicted the bail applications did not go well. Harriet travelled up to Northampton on the train from Euston – which was twenty minutes late and very over crowded. There was a queue for taxis at the station and the rain was incessant. But both she and Charles Cavan-Henry did their utmost to persuade a very uninterested judge to grant bail, subject to stringent conditions and sureties. Mr Justice Welford would have none of it. It wasn't even necessary for Edward Markham-Moore to address the court. Bail was refused.

'There is', ruled the judge, 'a significant risk of the defendants fleeing the jurisdiction and committing further offences. No conditions could reduce such risks to acceptable levels. The applications must be refused.'

Julia Hamilton was furious.

'It was one of the best bail applications I've ever witnessed,' Parker assured her. 'The judge just wouldn't have it. No one could have done it better.'

She eventually calmed down when Harriet promised she would visit Doyle in prison in two days' time. Parker had made an appointment several days before the application was heard. In his mind, there never had been any doubt that bail would be refused.

'Not a very good idea for her to have put herself forward as a surety,' said Harriet after Doyle's girlfriend had gone. 'Welford didn't like that when he realised she had been arrested too.'

'That's what I told her Miss Lassiter, but would she listen? Of course not. She thought she knew better. Doyle isn't going to like it either when he finds out he's been refused bail. I suppose he's in for the duration now. The trial won't get on before the summer – not with the state of the lists in Leicester.'

'Well, Mr Parker, there is a point of law in this case which I shall discuss when I see Doyle on Friday. If I'm right about it, Doyle will not be in custody for much longer.'

Parker looked more than curious.

'A point of law? You mean the money?'

'No, it's not the money. Cavan-Henry and I think we can keep out the DNA evidence!'

Parker looked shocked.

'Really? But without Benson's DNA going in they haven't got a case, have they?'

'That's the argument; I much prefer relying on a point of law rather than the lay client's evidence. Much more reliable. You have no idea of the number of defendants who convict themselves by going into the witness box.'

Harriet smiled. Parker, of course, did not need telling. He was a great believer in a guilty client staying securely in the dock and not venturing into the witness box. Dangerous territory the witness box. But would they listen to him? Of course not, and Doyle would be no exception.

'I shall explain it all on Friday when we see Doyle at the prison. If we are right, we can get the matter listed before the trial judge on a dismissal application. But don't say anything to Doyle yet.'

'Whatever you say, Miss Lassiter. A point of law, eh? Whatever it is, it's passed me by. Oh, I nearly forgot. I managed to book one of the interview rooms at the prison so we should be able to speak quite freely. It'll be better than having to see him in the same room as the domestic visits.'

'Good. I'll see you on Friday then Mr Parker. One thirty I believe.'

'That's right. One thirty. We've got a full hour with him.'

'I don't think I shall need that long.'

CHAPTER THIRTY-FIVE

Michael Doyle paced the floor in the consultation room at Leicester prison. His leg was no longer giving him trouble, save for the occasional wince of pain when he remained immobile for too long. The support had been removed six days after he had been remanded in custody. He had been hoping that would mean a trip to the local hospital but the prison medical service had managed the task without calling on more expert assistance.

The consultation room at the prison had been originally designed and constructed as the boardroom. There was still a pair of heavy velvet curtains at the large window, the lighter patches offering some evidence that the sun shone into the room at least occasionally, but bars had been placed outside making any hope of escape a forlorn one. The walls were panelled in a light coloured wood and while the door gave the impression from the inside of simple oak solidity, its outer skin had been reinforced with a heavy steel jacket. Doyle had taken all this in when he had seen Jules on her single legal visit the day after his incarceration. His second visit to the room merely served to confirm that there was no realistic chance of escape. He had no choice but to place his future in the hands of his lawyers.

Trevor Parker had been the first to arrive. He had spent more years than he cared to remember waiting – for juries, for clients and for counsel – and had developed an ability simply to sit, calmly and silently, until events dictated he should do otherwise. Doyle continued to pace the room like the caged animal he was.

'How long do we have to wait for her, Trevor?' he asked impatiently. 'We've only got an hour and there's a lot to get through.'

Parker looked up from the newspaper he was reading.

'She'll be here directly. She's probably got held up in security. You know what it's like here.'

'Actually, I don't Trevor. You see I'm stuck in here. I don't come in and out of the place like you and Jules. Not since you failed to get me bail!'

Parker moved in his chair. He had not been allowed to forget that bail had been refused and even he was getting more than a little tired by Doyle's constant harping on the subject.

'It was always going to be a big ask, Michael. Judges don't usually give bail in cases as serious as this.'

'Well it's time they did. I'm innocent and I'm locked up in this dump with a load of drug taking criminals. What about my human rights?'

'If Miss Lassiter is right – and she's seldom wrong – you won't be here much longer.'

Doyle stopped. He pulled out a chair from the table and sat down.

'Say that again Trevor.'

Parker immediately regretted his remark, but he had to say something. He folded his newspaper and laid it on the table.

'Miss Lassiter reckons she has a legal argument that will mean the trial won't go ahead. Don't ask me what it is – I don't know – but when she's here she'll explain it. All I know is it's something to do with Benson's DNA.'

'But what's that to do with my case? They haven't got my DNA anywhere. Don't forget, Trevor, I was 200 miles away when this robbery took place. There must be ten or more witnesses who can vouch for that.'

Parker sighed. 'As I've tried to explain, Michael, the case against you is largely dependent on the case against Benson.'

'Whoever he is,' interjected Doyle, looking away.

Parker tried but failed to conceal his irritation.

'If the prosecution fails against him, the case against you will be weakened to the point of collapse.'

Doyle stood up again and searched his pockets for his cigarettes. As he did so, there was a knock on the door and Harriet Lassiter was introduced into the room by a uniformed prison officer. He closed the door behind her. A key was heard to turn in the lock.

'I'm sorry to have kept you,' said Harriet. 'I've had one hell of a job getting through security. They even confiscated my Polo mints!'

Doyle grinned. He remained standing and Parker joined him.

'It's because they think I might escape through the hole in the middle,' he quipped.

Harriet smiled.

'Very witty, Mr Doyle. Let's hope you are as quick in cross-examination – if we get that far.'

Doyle's face fell.

'What do you mean, if we get that far? I'm not paying you what I am in order to cop a plea.' His voice betrayed a note of concern.

'No one's suggesting you should do that, Mr Doyle,' said Harriet. Parker then formally introduced Doyle to her. She shook his hand then sat down in the chair previously occupied by Parker and removed her gloves. She did not remove her coat. She was not intending to remain for long.

'What should I call you?' Doyle asked as he sat down opposite her placing his packet of cigarettes in front of him after he had removed one and put it between his lips.

'I hope you aren't going to light that,' said the barrister. 'It's very stuffy in here and I abhor smoking.'

Doyle glanced at Parker and sighed. 'All right,' he said. 'I suppose I can wait.'

Harriet continued. 'I'd prefer it if you called me Miss Lassiter. It's more professional. I don't approve of this practice that seems to be creeping in of addressing everyone by their first names as if we were all friends or relatives. Ours is a purely professional relationship and it's better if we keep it that way.'

Doyle looked at Parker again. His expression was not a happy one but he was not minded to argue with the barrister who was costing him a tidy sum.

'Anything you say, *Miss Lassiter.*'

Harriet noticed the emphasis he put on her name.

'Good,' she replied. 'Now that the ground rules have been established we can get on.'

She opened her case and took out a lever-arch file of papers and a notebook. The file remained closed but she opened the notebook, put on her dark-rimmed spectacles and perused the jottings she had made in preparation for the meeting. This was a preliminary consultation and she had no intention of going through the evidence with her lay client, but she required the notes of her conversation with Charles Cavan-Henry to ensure she did not depart from the agreed approach to the DNA evidence. She had decided, after a deal of anxious consideration, that her colleague's advice not to engage in specific questioning of her client was sound. At this stage of the proceedings, at least, she didn't want to know anything from

Doyle. Not even his instructions as to where the money in his car came from. Doyle looked her in the face as she removed her glasses. Before she could say anything Doyle raised the issue of bail.

'What happened at the bail application?' he asked. 'I thought there would be no problem in getting bail – given the state of the evidence.'

'That was unfortunate,' confessed Harriet, 'but hardly surprising. The charges are very serious. Judges rarely give bail on a charge of attempted murder.'

Her answer did not satisfy him. 'But I wasn't even there,' he insisted. 'I was over 200 miles away. How can they do me for attempted murder?'

'I agree it's not the strongest of cases on that count,' observed Harriet, 'but as I understand it, the prosecution will be putting the case on the basis that you were the prime mover in this whole enterprise. Whether you were present or not is neither here nor there.'

'Joint enterprise,' said Doyle, knowingly.

'Exactly,' replied Harriet. 'I see you've heard of the concept.'

Doyle nodded. 'Yeh. It's just a way of convicting the innocent, if you ask me.'

Parker smiled to himself but said nothing.

'What's this point of law then?' Doyle continued. 'Trevor here hasn't been able to explain it. He said you would.'

Harriet glanced at Parker and smiled.

'It's very simple,' she said, sitting back in her chair and looking directly at Doyle.

'The prosecution case depends on two essential propositions. First, your connection with your co-accused, Benson. Secondly, the money you had in the car that crashed in Hull.'

Doyle interrupted.

'*Alleged* connection.'

'Alleged connection,' she repeated, 'but hear me out Mr Doyle.'

'But the money is nothing to do with the robbery,' he interjected. 'It was mine.'

Harriet raised her hand.

'Please, Mr Doyle. Let me finish. I don't want to know where you got the money from – not yet at least. I am not curious. Don't tell me anything about it. It is not relevant at this point.'

Doyle sighed, nodded and leaned back in his chair. 'All right. I'm listening,' he said. 'But make it good. I'm paying you enough, after all.'

Harriet frowned then turned again to her explanation. 'Without your *alleged* connection with Benson the case against you is likely to collapse. The prosecution cannot prove the money you had in the car came from the robbery other than through inference which depends on your *alleged* connection with Benson too.'

'Yeh, I understand that,' said Doyle. 'I'm not stupid, you know.'

'Quite. But the case against Benson is wholly dependant on the DNA profile from the blood he *allegedly* shed at the crime scene.'

She paused.

'Well that's obvious too,' said Doyle. 'I don't need an expensive QC to tell me that!'

'But what would you say, Mr Doyle, if that evidence was to be ruled inadmissible by the judge?'

Doyle looked at Parker, then at Harriet and almost laughed.

'Well, he ain't going to do that is he?'

It was Harriet's turn to smile. 'Oh, but he may have to.'

'Why?' asked Doyle, a look of astonishment on his face.

'Because he was identified from his profile on the DNA database that had been left there unlawfully by the police. That's why!'

Doyle was silent for a few moments. 'Run that past me again.'

Harriet sighed. 'A few years ago Benson volunteered a DNA sample in a big exclusion exercise carried out by the police in Birmingham in an attempt to trace a serial rapist. Over 3,000 men gave samples. They were promised that those samples would be destroyed after the culprit had been caught. Well, it seems he was caught and sent to prison for life. But the police broke their promise. Some of those profiles of entirely innocent men were placed on the national DNA database and not removed. One of those profiles belonged to Benson. It was because of that profile being on the database that he was identified as one of the robbers.'

'So?'

'Well, Mr Doyle. In this country, no one is above the law. Not even the police. They acted unlawfully in keeping his profile, so they cannot now use it as evidence against him.'

'Why not? If it proves he's guilty…'

'Because that would involve the court countenancing an illegal act by the police. And we can't have that can we?'

'And that's the law, is it?' Doyle could not quite believe it.

'It is. As laid down by Parliament. There's already been a similar case in the north where the judge ruled out DNA evidence for this very reason.'

Doyle was still unable to understand what he was being told.

'But that's bloody daft. Why should evidence be ruled out if it proves someone is guilty?'

'That's the law,' said Harriet firmly. 'At least that is what we shall argue the law is.'

Doyle got up from his chair and started to pace the room again.

'If that's the law – and I'm bound to say it sounds stupid to me – why am I still in here? If that's the law, I should be out on bail.'

'It's a question of tactics, Mr Doyle. It's quite obvious that the prosecution has not spotted this point. We want to give them as little notice of it as possible. If we had raised it at the bail hearing it would have given them too much time to try and find a way round it. Our best option is to leave it until the trial and then object to its admissibility…'

'But when will that be? I can't stay in this place waiting for months for a trial. It's already driving me mad. There's some very nasty people in here you know, Miss Lassiter.'

'I understand that. That's why Benson's counsel and I are considering an application to dismiss the case. We would have to alert the prosecution in order to do so but not yet. We can wait until all the papers are served.'

'What's an application to dismiss when it's at home?'

Doyle pulled his chair out and sat down again. He remained sceptical but if this proved to be a way out of prison he wasn't going to let it slip him by.

'It's something we can insist on as soon as the papers have been served and before you are arraigned. Probably in about a month. We should be able to get a hearing in about a month.'

Parker interrupted. 'The Plea and Directions hearing is the week before Easter – in about four weeks. It took some doing I can tell you to bring it forward. The prosecution wasn't at all keen.'

'Four weeks? I can't be doing with that! I've been here over two weeks already. That'll be six weeks I'll have been in here! I can't have that. I want bail – now!' Doyle slammed his fist on the table and looked away.

'That's out of the question Mr Doyle. A month is nothing compared with the sentence you'd pick up if you were to be convicted.'

He was now beginning to try Harriet's patience. Doyle looked directly at his counsel. He narrowed his eyes as he spoke. She noticed his expression had changed his features dramatically. He looked very menacing indeed.

'But that's not going to happen, is it?' he said, his tone matching the unpleasantness of his appearance. 'I'm innocent. And don't let anyone forget that.'

He then broke into a smile and appeared to relax. He sat back in his chair and stretched out his arms.

'It still sounds too good to be true, though. I hope you people know what you're doing.'

Parker spoke.

'Miss Lassiter knows exactly what she's about, Mr Doyle. I can assure you of that.'

The solicitor turned and spoke directly to Harriet.

'I do have one question, if I may? The prosecution is not relying on the profile from the database but the sample Benson gave when he was arrested. Will that make a difference?'

'Not in the least,' replied Harriet, confidently. 'The real question is what led to the identification of Benson as one of the robbers. No matter how you look at it, you are driven back to the fact that everything begins with the illegal actions of the police. They only knew who to arrest because of their unlawful retention of his profile. I really can't see a way round it. Their actions were wholly unlawful.'

Doyle shook his head. 'What if the judge rules in my favour and the prosecution then appeals can they do that?'

'They can,' replied Harriet in a matter-of-fact way.

'Well, that means I'll still be stuck in here, doesn't it? It could take years before any appeal is heard.' Doyle began to get angry again.

'No,' replied Harriet firmly. 'It does not mean that at all. Although the prosecution can appeal it has no binding effect on you. It is purely academic. You will be released if the judge rules in our favour. If Benson goes, so do you. There would be insufficient evidence for the case to continue against you.'

'What?' said Doyle. 'You mean even if they won the appeal it wouldn't effect me?' He shook his head in disbelief. 'Who makes up these laws?'

Harriet smiled. 'MPs in Parliament,' she replied. 'Oh, I have no doubt the Parliamentary draftsmen are already working on a change in the law – but none of that will affect you. There's no doubt about that, I assure you.'

Doyle started playing with his cigarettes, pushing the unsmoked roll-up along the surface of the table to the edge, then blocking its fall with the packet. He repeated the manoeuvre several times before looking up.

'It still sounds a bit iffy to me.'

'It may, as you say, sound a "bit iffy", but the words of the statute are quite plain.'

He shook his head again. 'I don't get it. There must be a catch.'

'There's no catch,' assured Harriet.

'And any appeal can't affect my case? That's definite is it?'

The QC started to pack away her papers. She closed her case and stood up.

'Mr Doyle. If the judge dismisses the charges, so far as you are concerned, that's the end of it. There's no trial, no jury. It's over. Finished. You might find your name in the law reports but I suspect that will be of little interest to you.'

Doyle was silent, his head bowed. He then looked up.

'But how can you be so sure this judge will chuck out the charges? He might think of a way round it, just to keep me in here.'

'He might,' admitted Harriet. 'The prosecution is not going to give in and walk away or you wouldn't need me. But believe me, when they see our application they'll be worried – very worried.'

She looked at her watch. 'I really must go. I have a train to catch back to London and it'll probably take me twenty minutes to get out of here. My junior and I will come and see you immediately before the application is heard. Just to ensure we haven't missed anything of relevance.'

She proffered her hand to Doyle who shook it vigorously.

'Thank you, Miss Lassiter. I hope you're right about all this, I really do.'

Harriet nodded. 'Leave it to me. We have an excellent chance of getting you out of here by Easter.'

'Pity it can't be before then,' grumbled Doyle.

Harriet did not respond. She simply smiled and looked at the solicitor.

'Goodbye, Mr Parker. I shall be in touch.'

Picking up her case from the table, she knocked on the door. After a few seconds, the sound of a key turning in the lock was followed by the door swinging open. A bored looking prison officer poked his head inside.

'Ready are we?' he asked.

'I am,' said Harriet briskly. 'I believe Mr Parker will be staying for a few more minutes.'

'Is that right, sir?' asked the turnkey. 'That's not very convenient, you know. It'll mean two separate trips through security.'

The officer looked mournfully at Parker, hoping to attract his sympathy. He failed.

'That can't be helped,' replied Parker. 'We have at least another twenty minutes.'

'If you insist,' moaned the officer. 'You'd better come with me, miss.'

Harriet looked at Parker and rolled her eyes.

'Goodbye… again,' she whispered.

She followed the officer through the door, closing it behind her. The key turned again in the lock and Doyle reached for his cigarette, lighting it quickly and drawing deeply.

'I hope she knows what she's doing,' he said. His tone was now much more aggressive. He didn't feel it necessary to keep up even the pretence of civility when he was alone with his solicitor.

'I tell you what, Trevor, this had better work or there'll be hell to pay. I can't cope in here for much longer. I'm sure Jules has told you the same.'

Parker stood up and moved to the chair vacated by Lassiter and sat down directly opposite to Doyle.

'Calm down, Michael,' he said. 'There's nothing to be gained by getting yourself worked up. You heard what Miss Lassiter said. You should be out of here by Easter.'

'Calm?' replied Doyle. 'Why should I keep calm? I shouldn't even be in here. I should be on bail. Can't we appeal or something?'

'No. Not unless there's a change of circumstances. If there's a change of circumstances, we can make another application.'

'When can we do that?'

Parker looked bemused. 'If there's a change of circumstances.'

'What does that mean?'

'If something fundamental changes, we can apply again for bail.'

'What, to the same judge? And what's the point of that? He'll only say no again, won't he?'

'Not necessarily to the same judge. The judge who refused bail is retiring soon and we have a good idea of who the trial judge is going to be. Any further application would probably be before him.'

'Who's this judge, then – if he's not the bastard who refused me bail?'

'Judge Tom Campion, QC – he's the Recorder of Leicester – the senior permanent judge at Leicester Crown Court. He's tough but fair.'

'Is he?'

Doyle drew on his cigarette again. 'Jules has mentioned him. She says he goes in to bat for the prosecution when the CPS cocks things up. He's not going to be very sympathetic is he?'

'I wouldn't say that. I've always found him to be very fair, although I agree he's no slouch when it comes to sentencing.'

'Oh, that's all we need, isn't it?'

Doyle slammed his packet of cigarettes onto the table and took a final drag from the one he was smoking.

'Well, if Miss Lassiter is right, it won't come to that, will it?'

Doyle stubbed out the remains of his cigarette in the small, round tin provided.

'Well, she'd better be right. I don't really understand what she's on about. It sounds very iffy indeed to me. But if it gets me out of here – bring it on!'

Parker smiled. 'I don't think there'll be much of a problem. If the DNA evidence is excluded, you should both walk.'

'So there'll be no trial as such?'

'That's about it. Miss Lassiter will argue the matter purely as a point of law. If she succeeds, the judge will dismiss the case.'

'And that's it?'

'That's it.'

Doyle was deep in thought for a few moments. 'So the whole thing turns on what this judge decides?'

'Yes.'

'No one else?'

'No one else.'

'No jury?'

'No jury,' confirmed Parker.

'What about the prosecution?'

'They'll get to have their say, of course. But at the end of the day, it's up to the judge.'

'And if they appeal?'

'As Miss Lassiter said, it's academic. If the Appeal Court disagrees, it doesn't affect the case against you. It serves as a precedent for other cases in the future, but it doesn't affect you.'

Doyle sighed, and took another roll-up from the packet on the table.

'So it's all down to this one judge?' he repeated, lighting his cigarette.

Parker nodded and moved uncomfortably in his chair. He didn't like the direction in which the conversation seemed to be moving.

'How much do these judges earn?'

'I'm not sure of the exact amount,' replied Parker, 'but what's it to you?'

'Well,' replied Doyle, coyly. 'They say everyone has his price.'

Parker reacted with alarm. 'Don't even think of it,' he insisted. 'This is England. English judges don't take bribes. They'd have you in the funny farm if you tried that on.'

'How do you know?' demanded Doyle. 'If he's open to a bit of commerce, he's not going to advertise it in the *Yellow Pages* is he? It would have to be done on the q.t.'

'Well, it's not going to be done by me,' replied Parker, emphatically. 'Do you know what you'd get for even attempting such a stunt? They'd make an example of you and throw the key away!'

Doyle paused and then chuckled, blowing smoke towards Parker who waved his hand in a hopeless attempt to avoid it.

'I was only having you on, Trevor. You do fall for it, don't you? Every time.'

Parker frowned. 'Just leave it to Miss Lassiter, Michael. She knows what she's doing.'

'Well, I hope for your sake she does.'

Parker couldn't help noticing a hint of menace in Doyle's voice. 'What do you mean?'

'If I go down for this, I'll be taking a few others with me. That's all I'm saying.'

'I think you should explain that remark,' said a concerned Parker, looking about him.

Doyle stood up. 'Oh, come of it Trevor. You know what I'm on about. Remember? That big hole in your client account about two or three years ago. The one you filled with *my* money!'

Doyle leant forward over the table until his face almost touched Parker's. Trevor Parker looked down and beads of sweat started to appear on his forehead. After a few seconds he raised his head.

'You promised you wouldn't mention that again. And you said you'd destroyed the copy ledgers that I let you have.'

Doyle's expression did not change.

'I lied. Jules has still got the originals. They're safely stashed away – just in case we needed them.'

Parker stood up. The two men were face to face with only the table between them. Parker was the first to weaken.

'You wouldn't?'

'Wouldn't I, Trevor? Just you try me. You get me out of here or they go to the Law Society. Jules has got it all worked out. She reckons you'd get three years if it went to court.'

A look of panic crossed Parker's face. 'Court? Why should it go to court? Nobody lost anything. All the clients got their money back. No one even knew anything untoward had occurred.'

'Not quite, Trevor. I didn't get my money back, did I? Not until last year. And I'm a client, aren't I?'

'But you said…' Parker slumped down in the chair. He looked thoroughly dejected. '…it was a loan.'

'Never mind what I said. You get me out of here – whatever it takes, understand? If I go down for this, you'll be coming with me – just to keep me company!'

He glared at Parker and smiled but not in a friendly manner and then turned his back on him.

'But you said that was a loan… and I paid you back – with interest,' whimpered the solicitor, repeating himself. Doyle turned round and smiled.

'Look Trevor…'

His tone had changed. He stubbed out his cigarette and sat down. He sounded almost reasonable again. 'Jules is pregnant with my child – yes, she told me the other day. I'm not spending ten years inside and missing it growing up. I want out of here. And I don't care how I do it. Do I make myself clear?'

Parker hesitated. He took out his handkerchief and mopped his brow. His voice was now little more than a whisper.

'Let's leave it to Miss Lassiter, shall we? I have every confidence in her.'

Doyle's aggression returned. 'Well, you'd better be right about her. She's costing me a bloody fortune and I don't suppose I shall see my four hundred grand again, will I? Whatever she says.'

Parker swallowed hard. 'It depends…'

'It depends! Well that's not good enough. I want out of here. No ifs and buts – definite – understand? I'm not bothered about the four hundred grand; there's plenty more where that came from. You get me out of here, Trevor, and I guarantee, you'll never see me again.'

That was a prospect Parker welcomed. Heavy footsteps were heard in the corridor, then a knock on the door followed by a key turning in the lock. Parker was about to speak.

Doyle raised his hand and cut his solicitor short.

'Hear that, Trevor,' he whispered threateningly. 'That's what it's like in these places. Locks and turning keys. All the time. You never really get used to it.'

Parker almost wilted. The same uninterested officer popped his head round the door. 'Time to go,' he said, stifling a yawn.

A second officer appeared and called on Doyle to accompany him back to the remand wing. A pair of handcuffs dangled from his left hand.

'There's no need for those,' said Doyle. 'I shan't be any trouble. And as my solicitor will tell you, I always keep my promises. He looked sideways towards Parker. 'Don't I, Trevor?'

Parker did not reply.

CHAPTER THIRTY-SIX

Trevor Parker pulled into the car park at Harbour Buildings and stretched across to open the passenger door. He had arranged to drive Julia Hamilton the few miles to Glen Parva Young Offenders' Institute where his particularly loathsome nineteen-year-old client, Cameron Ferguson, was being held on remand. Parker had a legal visit arranged to see Michael Doyle at Welford Road Prison later in the morning so it wasn't much of an inconvenience to drop Jules off at the former borstal. The solicitor had instructed Bill Savage as counsel, someone with whom Jules had enjoyed a brief fling a few years ago before she became involved with Doyle. It was not for her, of course, to decide which barrister Trevor Parker should employ but, if truth were told, she wished he'd chosen someone else. In the years that had passed since the affair ended they had exhibited a tolerable degree of cold politeness on the few occasions their paths had crossed, but Jules had never quite dispelled the feeling that Savage had used her for his own ends, just as he had taken advantage, so it was rumoured, of many women since. Parker, who knew nothing of the affair, could nevertheless tell from the expression on her face as she slipped into the passenger seat that she was not looking forward to renewing her contact with this forceful advocate, but that was hardly relevant. Savage was instructed because he was persuasive and effective; exactly what was required in the case of Cameron Ferguson.

Jules had been tempted to withdraw from practising as a paralegal until Doyle's case was resolved but Parker had advised that she continue her work at least for the time being. He would not permit her to have any direct dealings with her lover's case but saw no reason why she should not assist him and other solicitors with unconnected criminal litigation. It might also help keep her mind off Doyle's predicament. The only condition he imposed was that she should not attend the prison where Doyle was housed other than in a private capacity. To this she had reluctantly agreed. So, while Welford Road was out of bounds professionally speaking, Glen Parva YOI was not and Parker, who was as appreciative of Jules' obvious physical attributes as the next man, recognised that repeat offenders did not demand his firm's services simply because of his reputation as a criminal defender. A conference with counsel that included the beguiling presence of Julia Hamilton was a great selling point. Although he no longer commanded her services on an exclusive basis, the link between Jules and his firm was well established in the minds of many of the incarcerated and testosterone fuelled youths who might otherwise have looked elsewhere for representation. Neither was Jules blind to the opportunities that might arise for her to assist Doyle "on the quiet" if she remained in contact with the legal scene. The robing room was always a hotbed of gossip and her position as a well-established paralegal gave her unobtrusive and easy admittance.

'Thanks for the lift,' said Jules as she smoothed her skirt and made herself comfortable. 'It's very good of you.'

'My pleasure,' replied Parker, 'but I can't pretend my motives are entirely altruistic. I thought it would be a good opportunity to have a word about a couple of matters – you know – out of the office.'

Jules said nothing but adjusted the seat belt, which had previously been used to anchor the more ample proportions of Mrs Parker.

'Have you come across young Cameron before?' asked the solicitor, as he started up the engine.

'No, I don't think so. But I assume from his record that he's a bit of a regular.'

'You can say that again. He's a complete idiot is our Cameron. He left his DNA all over the point of entry and the police found the stolen laptop and some of the other proceeds in his mother's garden shed. He'll have to plead.'

'But he'll be put away this time, won't he?' responded Jules, trying to show some interest in the case. 'This is the third time he's done a dwelling house burglary. There's a mandatory sentence isn't there?'

'Correct, and his wretched background and drug dependency will not save him this time I'm afraid. That's why he wants to fight it. He doesn't fancy a three stretch at his tender age.' He glanced at Jules as he spoke. 'That's why I instructed Bill Savage. If he can't get him to plead, no one can.'

'I think I'd have gone for someone else – but that's not my decision, is it?' Jules pursed her lips as she spoke.

'No – but I understand where you're coming from. He's a bit of a one when it comes to the ladies isn't he?'

Jules did not reply. Parker laughed then became more serious.

'I wanted to ask you about a matter that has been bothering me. It's a bit personal.'

Jules looked at him, her curiosity aroused.

'Did Michael ever mention a loan he made to the firm about three years ago?'

Jules' expression did not change. She had long suspected as much but Doyle had never discussed it with her.

'No – he didn't. Is it important?'

Parker hesitated.

'Not really. The firm has repaid him in full, of course. It's just that he had a copy of our client's account ledger as security – just a print-off of a few pages you understand.'

Jules smiled. She realised what was coming next.

'That sounds like Michael. Did he let you have it back when you repaid him?'

Parker paused. He could not fail to notice the wry smiled that played on her face.

'Well, not exactly. He told me he had destroyed it. I was just wondering whether he kept a copy, that's all.'

Parker brought the Volvo to a halt at a zebra crossing and waived an elderly couple across. Jules was no longer smiling.

'Have you asked him?'

'Yes.' Parker seemed unwilling to go on.

'And… what did he say?'

'Well, he was a bit vague but I got the impression that he might have filed a copy away somewhere?' He pressed the accelerator and drew away. 'To tell you the truth, I'm not at all sure that he meant what he said. You know what he's like.'

It was Jules' turn to pause. She looked ahead for a few seconds before she answered.

'Oh, I know what he's like all right. I've copied a number of documents for him over the years but I don't recall copying a ledger – certainly not one that concerned your firm. But he never throws anything away – not if it's related to money.'

Parker concentrated on the road.

'You would tell me if you still had a copy, wouldn't you?'

Jules smiled sweetly. 'Of course I would Trevor. I suspect Michael is just having you on.'

She knew this was not true. She had seen the copy ledger more than once but had never studied it or asked Michael why it had been filed away. She would have to look at it again. It might come in useful if Parker proved unco-operative in the future. The solicitor turned and looked at her. He appeared to relax, but only slightly.

'You're probably right. He's under a lot of pressure in that prison. That was the other thing I wanted to talk to you about. I'm very worried about him. When I saw him three days ago, he was not himself at all.'

Jules almost scoffed. 'Of course he isn't. Can you blame him? That's why you should have got him bail. I warned you about this at the outset. He simply can't cope in prison.'

Her voice was now raised. Parker swallowed hard. He was beginning to regret mentioning Doyle's case. But there was no going back.

'There's no point going over old ground. He'll have to stay where he is until things sort themselves out.'

He drove on in silence debating in his mind whether he should mention the new evidence that had recently been served. He decided to risk it.

'We received some additional evidence yesterday…'

'Additional evidence?' she replied coldly. 'As far as I was aware they have no evidence apart from Benson's DNA which hardly concerns Michael.'

Parker got the distinct impression that Jules did not really believe what she had just said.

'Well, eh, a stack of further evidence arrived yesterday afternoon. I'm seeing Michael about it later this morning. I haven't studied it all yet but it's to do with the money – from the Mercedes. They reckon they can prove it came from the service centre that supplied the cash for the Charnwood.'

Jules smiled. 'I thought I was supposed to have nothing to do with his case?'

Parker sighed and tried not to appear irritated. 'Michael has specifically asked me to keep you up to date. I am merely complying with his instructions.'

'And how precisely do they think they can prove Michael's money has anything to do with this robbery?'

Parker explained the essentials to her so far as best he could. She did not give the appearance of being convinced.

'That's all speculation,' she said dismissively. 'There's no record of any of the notes. They're clutching at straws.'

'I'm not so sure,' replied Trevor. 'They've got some professor from Leicester university, Gordon Lee, to validate the statistics. I don't pretend to understand it myself but I shall be going through it with Michael when I see him.'

'What does Harriet Lassiter make of it?'

'I don't know. She'll only have received her copy this morning. No doubt we'll hear from her soon enough.'

'Well, they'll need more than that to prove Michael was involved.'

Trevor decided to change the subject. He was now regretting that he had raised the matter at all.

'Any more news on the pregnancy?' he asked. 'I think that's the one thing that's keeping Michael going, you know.'

Jules replied in a matter-of-fact way. 'All's well at the moment. But I shall have to give all this up in another two months. That's what the hospital said. Too much stress is bad for baby. And we can't have that, can we?'

'I suppose not – do you know what it is yet?'

Jules nodded. 'Yes. But I don't want Michael to know. I had a scan yesterday. It – as you put it – is a boy.'

A broad smile appeared on Parker's face.

'Why, that's wonderful news – but why don't you want Michael to know? He'll be delighted.'

Jules frowned. 'You've just told me he's not coping well in custody – which I already knew – and I know what you men are like when it comes to producing little replicas of yourselves. I agree with you. Michael will be over the moon – for about ten minutes – then he'll feel even worse than he does at the moment. His being where he is will bear down on him more than ever, and I don't want that. All he needs to know is that we are both OK.'

Parker did not dissent.

'And I mean it, Trevor. I don't want you telling Michael. I know what you can be like. I don't want it slipping out. Understand?'

Parker nodded his head vigorously and raised his right hand. But he did not pretend to understand her objection – not that he had ever really understood anything about her.

'You can trust me. Scout's honour!'

He said nothing further on the subject and concentrated on the road. When he next spoke it was about Doyle's case.

'I've also received Harriet Lassiter's skeleton argument on the dismissal application. It's very impressive.'

'I should think it is given what she's being paid.'

'Yes. I just hope this new evidence about the cash Michael had doesn't undermine it.'

'Am I allowed to see a copy?'

Jules tried to sound casual as if she didn't really care either way.

'I don't see why not. I've run you a copy off. It's in that folder on the back seat.'

Trevor braked and brought the Volvo to a halt at a red traffic light. Jules glanced behind her, stretched out her right hand and picked up the blue folder. She opened it and started to read.

'Rather you than me,' Trevor murmured as he noticed the sign for the young offenders' institution. 'I've never liked Glen Parva. Terrible place – especially for youngsters like Cameron Ferguson. I don't see how putting them in an institution like that does any good.'

But Jules wasn't listening. She was engrossed in Lassiter's argument objecting to the admissibility of the DNA evidence that would place Benson at the crime scene.

'It doesn't seem to put them off committing offences though, does it?' he mumbled to himself. 'I've lost count how many of them I've seen in there.'

Jules read on, turning the pages swiftly.

'Well, it's all good for business, I suppose.'

The lights changed to green and Trevor looked to his left then pressed the accelerator and the automatic gearbox engaged and took them forward. The journey continued without another word for a couple of miles while Jules studied Lassiter's argument. Eventually, Trevor broke the silence.

'How are you going to get back, by the way? I'm seeing Michael at eleven o'clock at Welford Road so I won't be able to pick you up.'

Jules looked up. 'I'll get a taxi.'

She continued to read.

'Or you could ask Bill Savage to give you a lift into Leicester. I think he'll be in his car. He's got another conference at Lincoln this afternoon so I doubt if he'll be relying on the train.'

Jules half smiled.

'What? Let him give me a lift? I think I'd rather walk. I'd be asking for trouble getting into his car. You know what he's like. Anyway, I'm supposed to be seeing Michael at one thirty at the prison and I don't want Bill Savage of all people knowing anything about it. Really, Trevor, I don't know why you keep instructing him.'

'Because he's bloody good, that's why.'

'But not as good as Harriet Lassiter?'

'No. Not for a case like Michael's.'

'Well, I hope you're right. This reads pretty well though. When will we get the prosecution response?'

'They have fourteen days. That was the direction given by the judge. He's given his directions in writing. Sign of the times I suppose.'

'And it's definitely Campion, is it? He's the trial judge?'

Parker nodded and turned the Volvo from the main road into the side road that led to their destination. The massive red brick walls loomed up before them. Jules shook her head.

'How well do you know him? Have you ever sat through a trial when he's been the judge?'

Parker paused. 'No. I don't think I have. I haven't the time – and it isn't cost effective – not on legal aid anyway. But I'll be there for Michael's trial of course, if there is one.'

Jules sighed. 'So you're banking on the dismissal application succeeding, eh, Trevor?'

'I don't see why it shouldn't. Miss Lassiter has every confidence…'

'And if it doesn't?'

'Well, they'll still have to prove the case against Michael before a jury. And you know yourself the evidence isn't that strong.'

'And if Benson pleads?'

'If we lose the dismissal application he will have to…'

'But that won't help Michael, will it? If Benson pleads they'll rely on his conviction to prove the link between them. They won't need the DNA.'

'They'll try, I suppose,' replied Parker.

Jules did not respond. She was thinking about the new evidence, about the money. She didn't like the sound of it. She and Doyle had convinced themselves that the provenance of the unused notes would be incapable of definite proof. Parker looked at her sympathetically.

'Snap out of it Julia. I don't know why you're sounding so pessimistic about keeping the DNA out. When the CPS sees this skeleton argument they'll be wetting themselves. I can't see an answer to it myself. I really can't.'

Jules remained silent as if weighing her reply.

'But you're not Judge Campion, are you Trevor? You may not have seen him in action but I have. I've studied him over quite some time. I've seen him in a few trials in fact – and I agree with you. He's very good – very good at getting convictions! Do you know, I don't think a single client of yours has been acquitted when he's been the trial judge.'

Parker almost laughed. 'Well, we can't win them all.'

Jules did not share his obviously contrived levity.

'But seriously, Julia, he is fair, isn't he? That's certainly his reputation.'

The Volvo came to a halt in the car park. Jules looked at her watch. She had plenty of time before her conference with Savage and the wayward Ferguson. This was her opportunity to get a few things clear with Trevor Parker. She had not, perhaps, fully understood all the nuances of leading counsel's argument but she was as experienced as anyone with Judge Tom Campion's trial technique. She turned and looked Trevor full in the face.

'That's exactly what I mean. He seems perfectly fair but once he's decided where the truth lies he's not one to let legal technicalities get in his way. Don't you remember that case eighteen months ago? I forget the client's name but he was charged with a really nasty aggravated burglary in Loughborough. Some old woman was badly injured and dragged out of her bed.'

Parker leant forward deep in thought.

'I remember the case, yes. Elliott – that was his name – Jeffrey Elliott. Right little toerag. In fact, I think it was Bill Savage who defended him. He's doing ten years as I recall.'

'Precisely! Savage was able to demonstrate at least three breaches of the Code of Practice by the police – but Campion still admitted the evidence. He finessed his way round Savage's arguments with ease. At the end of the day he decided they were merely technical breaches that didn't affect the fairness of the proceedings. Not that Elliott saw it that way – not when the jury convicted him.'

'But he was obviously guilty wasn't he? There was a lot of other evidence against him. He certainly didn't get anywhere on appeal.'

'But that's my point. Campion dressed it up perfectly. So perfectly the appeal was dismissed. Deliberate failures by the police to comply with the law and he still let the evidence in. And it might have gone over the heads of some, but it was obvious to me *why* he let the evidence in. Because he thought Elliott was guilty and he wasn't going to let him escape on a technicality. Once he let in the conversation in the police car Elliott was bound to be convicted. And when he summed up he had the jury eating out of his hand. They always do what he wants them to do.'

Parker sat back in his seat and paused before he replied.

'Well, we're stuck with him now, but Michael's case is quite different when you think about it. This isn't just a breach of the code – it's a deliberate failure to comply with the mandatory requirements of an Act of Parliament. And it's worked before. Randell Richards found a case in Carlisle where a High Court judge gave a similar ruling and the case was dropped. That's a precedent. We are on much stronger ground. Miss Lassiter deals with it all in her skeleton argument.'

'Are we? I'm not so sure.'

Jules started to undo her seat belt and took hold of her briefcase from the footwell. She placed the blue file inside it and made to open the door. Trevor Parker grasped her arm.

'Look Julia, let's leave it to counsel shall we? She knows what she's doing. And remember, there's really no other evidence against Michael that puts him at the scene whatever this new stuff about the money might show – and that's bound to weigh with the jury if it gets that far.'

She started to get out of the car.

'That's what worries me,' she said. 'Campion will know that if he excludes the DNA evidence Benson will walk. And we all know he's guilty. There's no innocent explanation for the DNA. And if Benson walks it increases the chances of Michael getting off. This judge is no fool, you know. He'll see that straight away.'

'Read Miss Lassiter's submissions again,' counselled the solicitor. 'That will reassure you. Believe me. And if Benson walks I guarantee so will Michael.'

Trevor Parker smiled to himself as he started up the engine and waved Julia goodbye but he was concerned, very concerned. He had long ago worked out where the brains lay in the Doyle/Hamilton partnership even if no one else had and he had no doubt that Doyle was not the party with the superior claim. The last thing he wanted was Julia Hamilton taking matters into her own highly capable hands. But he relaxed somewhat when he thought again about Lassiter's skeleton argument. Worth its weight in gold that was. And if it didn't succeed Doyle still had a good run in front of the jury. He had one of the best alibis Parker had ever encountered. He simply couldn't see the prosecution breaking it.

He looked at her standing by the entrance greeting Bill Savage as he climbed out of his series 6 BMW. Then, as he turned out of the car park and on to the road, she was out of his sight.

★★★★

As Savage opened the door for her and she walked into the reception area of the YOI, Jules thought she felt her child move inside her. Was that an omen? Could she contemplate a future without Michael? If he were convicted she would be on her own for a considerable period of time. Parker reckoned the sentence for the conspiracy alone would be at least sixteen years after a trial and she had no reason to doubt his assessment. Alone and with a child to bring up? Alone for the best years of her life? The time had surely come when she had to think of herself and her future. Although she had fallen big time for Doyle, she had always held just a little of herself in reserve. She knew all about his criminal activities and she'd always realised there was a risk he might be exposed one day. She was beginning to regret that she had acted as a substitute driver on the raid at the Charnwood. Benson could easily give her up for that, if he had a mind to. It was time she looked to her own protection. She resolved there and then that she would put her own interests first. Nothing and no one would stand in her way – even if it meant abandoning Doyle.

The conference with young Cameron took hardly any time at all – once he was brought to the conference room – which took more than twenty minutes. Although she had once regarded Bill Savage as a self-serving, self-centred and arrogant scumbag (those being her precise words when she'd described him to her mother after the disastrous weekend in Brighton), she had to admire his technique in conference. She couldn't help noticing, too, that he seemed better looking than she remembered him. She'd had no professional dealings with him for over twelve months. While others might not share her view, she thought he was possibly one of those men who, like the best wine, seemed to improve with age. Neither was there any shilly shallying or honeyed words with Savage. He told Cameron Ferguson straight that he had no option but to plead guilty and get whatever discount on sentence might still be available to him. After an initial grunt and a half-hearted, "I thought you were supposed to be on my side," the youthful burglar surrendered unconditionally. Savage assured him he'd pick up less than three years – he would see to that. 'OK boss,' he whispered. He then looked up at Jules and smiled then turned his head slightly and muttered to Savage, 'I bet you wouldn't mind giving her one, eh boss?'

The uncouth youth smirked and showed what remained of his yellowing teeth. Julia looked away, suppressing a giggle, while Savage, who would have loved to do exactly what Ferguson had suggested, adopted as severe a look of shocked disapproval as he could muster.

'Don't be impertinent,' he said, standing up and placing his papers in his bag. 'I'll see you in court at the end of next week.'

'Sorry about that,' he fawned after they had passed through the laborious security procedures and headed for his car, 'but you can understand where he's coming from.'

He smiled, revealing his unnaturally brilliantly white teeth. Then he added, almost in a whisper, 'I haven't forgotten our weekend in Brighton, you know.'

'Neither have I – although I have tried very hard to do so!'

Jules spoke coldly and without emotion. It certainly put Savage in his place. His recollection of their time together was obviously clouded by his over consumption of champagne. Plainly, hers was not.

'May I offer you a lift?' he said. He was no longer smiling but going through the motions of professional politeness. He was not expecting a favourable response. But Jules didn't fancy ringing for a taxi. It had started to rain and something inside her told her she should keep on the right side of Savage. He seemed different from how she remembered him, almost vulnerable in a strange sort of way. And he might prove useful to her, so she accepted the offer, but seemingly reluctantly.

'If you could drop me off at Welford Road, I'd be very grateful.'

Savage brightened up immediately and opened the passenger door for her. The short journey to the prison passed initially in silence. Jules had no intention of revealing the real reason for her visit. "Just another client to proof," she told the over-attentive barrister when he queried why she was going there. Savage looked at himself in the rear-view mirror and adjusted his bow tie with his left hand. He seemed to have entirely expunged her put-down from his memory. She smiled wearily but tried to remain at least outwardly pleasant while showing a distinct lack of enthusiasm for anything he might propose. She was really in two minds about him. After all, he didn't have to have offered her a lift – and she didn't have to have accepted.

Jules decided to take advantage of the circumstances and do a little probing about Tom Campion. She knew Savage had done quite a lot of work in front of him.

'What do you reckon to Tom Campion – as a judge?' she asked, casually.

'Campion?'

Savage paused as if in thought.

'He's bloody good – unless you happen to be guilty. He knows how to run them in all right. His summing up reads perfectly on paper, but he always manages to convey what he thinks the verdict should be – it's a joy to listen to – unless you happen to be in the dock.'

He laughed.

'But if the prosecution case is weak, he'll give you a decent run. I'd rather have him than many of the others – providing I've got a reasonable defence.'

He paused again then cursed a motorist driving a Range Rover who had presumed to change lanes directly in front of him.

'He won't be round here much longer though. He's off to the Bailey sometime after Easter.'

Jules already knew about that. It was the talk of the robing room.

'I've heard he's a decent lawyer too?'

'First class.'

He leaned across and whispered in Jules' ear.

'Did you know he's been asked to sit in the CACD? Quite a feather in his cap! Not many circuit judges get the opportunity to sit in the Court of Appeal.'

Jules did her best not to sound impressed.

'I hadn't heard that, no.'

'Well, keep it to yourself for a while will you? It's supposed to be confidential. He's ex-army, too, you know. I think he did three years in the parachute regiment and he was in the Territorials after that. He certainly did at least one tour of Belfast. Got wounded too – nothing serious, you understand.'

That last piece of information was news to Jules. Savage had his uses after all – although she would have felt happier if his leering countenance had been further away from her. Why had she accepted a lift? What was she doing? She thought he was about to touch her on the knee when her mobile phone rang. It had a salutary effect and Savage concentrated on the road. Jules looked at the screen. It was Trevor Parker. What did he want?

She assumed he must have finished his conference with Doyle because mobile phones were not allowed to be taken into prisons – not even by respectable lawyers.

'I'm phoning to let you know that Michael is very upset. I've been through this new evidence with him and it's a bit more damaging than I first thought.'

'Define "a bit more damaging",' replied Jules slowly. She had already realised the potential effect of the evidence as soon as Parker had revealed it. She noticed that Savage was paying her attention again. She turned away from him, placing her hand over her ear as Parker revealed his concerns.

'What they've done – and it's very clever when you think about it – is they've put the four hundred thousand Michael had through the counting machines at the service centre and virtually all of it turned out to be of good enough quality to be used in ATMs.'

'Well, what does that prove?'

Jules appreciated exactly what it might prove but she wasn't about to say as much to Parker.

'It's not just that – they put the cash they seized from Michael's safe through the same machine and a larger percentage of that would not have passed muster. It would not have been suitable for ATMs.'

'So?'

'Don't you see, Julia? What they'll be saying is that the four hundred thousand must have passed through this service centre and been put aside for filling ATMs. The chances of having so much cash – obtained randomly – nearly all of which is suitable for replenishing ATMs, is virtually zero – and they're using the money from the safe to prove it. They're comparing one with the other. It took some time to explain it to Michael but it really rocked him when he realised the possible repercussions.' He paused. 'By the way, he's still not given me any clear instructions where he got it from.'

Jules ignored that last remark but her brain was in a whirl. 'It's all a bit speculative, isn't it? And it proves absolutely nothing. We already know that most cash from the banks ends up in these service centres.'

But Parker was not to be diverted. 'That's why they've gone to this professor from the university. He says the prosecution's conclusion is a virtual statistical certainty.'

'You'll have to find another professor then won't you – one who thinks that it isn't a virtual statistical certainty? Honestly Trevor, I don't see what you're getting so worked up about.'

Silence.

'I suppose I will.'

Jules switched off the phone.

'That sounded very interesting,' commented Savage, his curiosity aroused. 'I take it that was about the robbery case? I know Trevor's representing Michael Doyle. I was hoping to get a brief myself. I couldn't believe it when Trevor gave the junior brief to Randell Richards. I'd have given an arm and a leg to be in that trial.' He paused then added, 'Friend of yours, isn't he – Doyle I mean?'

Jules did not reply immediately. Her brain was once more in overdrive. She had to think quickly. 'He used to be,' she heard herself saying, 'but after he got me arrested, I terminated our relationship.'

'Really?' queried Savage. 'He got you arrested? I didn't know that!'

'Yes – we were supposed to be going on holiday together so I was with him when he was arrested at the airport. They took me in as well. I was released pretty quickly of course. Taught me a valuable lesson that did. Not to mix business and pleasure.'

She gave Savage one of her looks but he was not put off in the slightest.

'Does that mean you're not, err… involved with anyone at the moment?'

Jules noted the sudden injection of enthusiasm in his voice.

'No,' she answered. 'I suppose I'm not. And I'm not looking to start a new relationship either – before you ask.'

But she smiled, coyly, as she spoke.

'Pity,' said Savage. 'I've always wanted to make it up to you. You know, that disastrous time we spent together in Brighton all those years ago.'

Jules smiled. 'It's all forgotten. Ignore what I said earlier.' Her smile broadened and she spoke more warmly than before. After all, Savage might well prove a convenient diversion while Michael was in custody.

'Where would you like me to drop you?' he asked. 'We're nearly there.'

'I'm a bit early for my appointment,' she replied. 'Just drop me off outside the Tigers' ground. I can get a cup of coffee in the cafe nearby. I don't want to go in to the prison before I have to. Place gives me the creeps.'

Savage nodded in agreement.

'I could join you if you like,' he said, beaming as only he could, 'if only I could find somewhere to park.'

He slowed down and looked for a gap in the limited on-street parking.

'There's nowhere round here,' responded Jules neutrally, 'and you have to get off to Lincoln, don't you? I did hear there had been an accident on the A46 this morning. There was a huge tailback mentioned on the local news earlier today.'

This was a deliberate lie but she made it sound completely credible. Jules was, in fact, a very accomplished liar. Far better than most of her clients. But this was a come-on. She wanted to judge Savage's reaction.

'Really? I must have missed that.' A slight look of alarm spread over his face. 'Well, I can't be late. It's a rather important case – another murder, you know – I'd better get off, if it's all the same with you.'

Jules smiled. She fully appreciated she was in complete control. As she now proposed to demonstrate. 'There again, it's bound to have cleared by now. The announcement I heard was at half past six.'

She looked at him and smiled again. Savage relaxed just as a parking space appeared. He drew the BMW to a halt.

'Well, providing I get off in half an hour. I should love to buy you a coffee.'

Jules thanked him. She hadn't yet decided how Savage might be of use but she would certainly keep her options open. And she didn't see why she shouldn't at least tolerate his company for thirty minutes or so.

CHAPTER THIRTY-SEVEN

Bill Savage stayed for only quarter of an hour. Jules' lie about the accident on the A46 played on his mind but before he departed he had invited her to the local Law Society dinner. He was to be the guest speaker and he said he would deem it an immense honour if she would be his escort for the evening. Jules surprised herself by gracefully accepting his invitation. She could hardly fathom why, but accept she had. That would set a few tongues wagging – which was precisely what she wanted. If she decided to finish with Doyle, her appearing at such an event with Savage would certainly convey a definite change of circumstances. She smiled to herself. Who better to publicise such a notion than William Savage, Esq.? It would be all round the circuit within forty-eight hours that he had resumed his liaison with the wonderful Julia Hamilton! Knowing as she did that Savage and champagne did not mix, she determined to ensure that he should consume a sufficient quantity of the bubbly liquid – after he had completed his speech – so that she could control any groping he might be minded to attempt. Amongst her many talents Jules was able to drink champagne cocktails one after the other seemingly with little or no adverse effect. The same could not be said for those who attempted to match her consumption. More than one ambitious male had been left prostrate by his unsuccessful attempt to drink her under the table. But she remembered she was pregnant. She'd have to cut down on the alcohol!

Her thoughts turned to Michael. She pictured him sitting forlornly in his prison cell. And what if he were convicted? She couldn't face nine, ten or more years on her own. Not with a child to bring up. She really had to make a decision. She couldn't put it off much longer. But how was she to decide? If Parker was right and Michael was bound to get off, their lives could proceed as before. But something at the back of her mind told her this was not going to be. And if Michael was going to have to spend years in prison, she was going to have to look to her own position, regardless of her feelings.

After Savage had left, she opened her briefcase and took out Lassiter's skeleton argument. After she had digested it a second time she was forced to agree it was an impressive piece of work, but something still rankled. She just couldn't accept that a judge of the calibre of Campion would fall for it. Not if he were driven by legal considerations alone. And Lassiter's argument did not take account of the new evidence. Jules was particularly annoyed about that. She could not believe she had missed what she now realised was such an obvious point about the cash found in the car. In the weeks during which Michael had been incarcerated, she had allowed her mind to contemplate a variety of ways of getting him out of prison – all of which she had rejected as unworkable. She had taken some preliminary steps in furtherance of a particularly daring endeavour which she had then had second thoughts about but she had, she thought, obtained some very useful information should such an audacious undertaking be resurrected in the future. Wiser counsel had prevailed, however, when difficulties in recruiting the necessary muscle proved, temporarily, at least, insuperable. So she had then more or less decided that Parker's strategy of using the law to free him was the best available. Now she was not so sure. She looked at Lassiter's document again. Sceptical though she was, she now realised that Campion would have to be persuaded that Benson's DNA should not be admitted in evidence if Doyle were to be certain of an acquittal. If it went in, chances were he'd be convicted. But if it were excluded – well, that would be another story altogether. Without the DNA which linked Benson to the crime scene there would be nothing to connect Michael to the robbery. He might go down for money laundering if she couldn't think of a way round this new evidence, but the sentence for money laundering would be much more manageable – for both her and Doyle.

Then there was the Revenue to consider. The tax man was bound to relieve Doyle of a considerable portion of his assets – the ones they knew of at least. And then there was the Fish. He'd been pretty quiet since Michael had been arrested but he wouldn't stay like that forever. So sticking with her lover might mean their anticipated life of luxury abroad would become a thing of the past. What was she to do? Her choices were limited but clear. Either she stuck with Doyle and hoped for the best, risking a lengthy period alone in a style to which she had no desire to become accustomed or she started to make tracks and begin a new life for herself – well away from Leicester – possibly outside the UK.

But what about the child? An abortion remained a possibility but Michael would kill her if she did such a thing. And he was bound to get out of prison at some time. But the odds now clearly favoured a new start away from Doyle. It was looking more and more likely that he would be convicted – whatever Lassiter and Parker might think. She stared out of the window, weighing her options carefully.

She shivered with anticipation. Jules had always been decisive. Doyle always regarded that as her greatest attribute. She could not tolerate people who couldn't make decisions. She finished her coffee, put the blue file back in her briefcase and walked slowly out of the cafe. Her mind was now made up, her course of action determined. She knew exactly what she was going to do. Her first port of call had to be the prison. She was not looking forward to it, but do it she would. If Michael was as upset as Parker said, this was the ideal moment to put phase one of her plan into operation.

CHAPTER THIRTY-EIGHT

Andrew Hooper rushed into Hood's room at Central. He was so excited he forgot to knock.

'What on earth's the matter?' asked the chief inspector.

'It's about Doyle,' said Hooper, unable to contain himself.

'He's offering to plead guilty is he?' asked Hood, without a hint of sarcasm.

'No sir – not yet anyway – but he's in the hospital wing at Welford Road. He's in a right state.'

Hood seemed unimpressed.

'Calm down, Andrew, and sit down. Now, take it slowly. What's Doyle been up to?'

'It's not him as such, sir. It's that girlfriend of his – or should I say, ex-girlfriend?'

Hood closed the file he had been reading. This was something he had to hear.

'What do you mean?'

'Well, sir, I've just finished speaking to the liaison officer at the prison. As you know I keep in touch with him on a regular basis. It seems Doyle received a visit from Julia Hamilton the day before yesterday. It all started out OK but then turned into a slanging match. Doyle had to be restrained and she was taken out of the visiting area. She's also asked to be taken off his list of contacts and told him she won't be visiting him again.'

Hood looked puzzled. He did not reply immediately.

'That sounds decidedly odd. Have they fallen out over something? I'd always thought she was going to be called as a defence witness?'

'And there's something else, sir. She's pregnant it seems and Doyle is *not* the father – that's what she's told him. He went completely bananas and attacked one of the prisoners who intervened to protect her. The welfare officer is really worried about him. They think he might try and top himself.'

Hood did not speak for a full minute.

'I don't think so. That is definitely not Doyle's style. This is genuine, is it? It's not another ruse?'

'I don't see what's to be gained if it isn't true, sir.'

'I don't know,' replied Hood, stroking his chin. 'When was the additional evidence served – you know – the evidence about the cash found in his car? If he thinks that will convict him, they might be trying to manufacture some psychiatric defence. There's nothing else left to him now.'

Hooper paused.

'What? Not guilty by reason of insanity? Sounds a bit far-fetched, sir. He's perfectly sane by all accounts. Just terribly upset.'

'Well, I'm not going to rush to any conclusions. She's visited him two or three times before and by all accounts they were all lovey-dovey with each other.'

'That's what the liaison officer reported back. But why should it all suddenly change?'

Hood did not answer for a few seconds. Then he stood up.

'I'm not falling for that. Not until we have it checked out. First things first. Let's find out if Julia Hamilton really is pregnant. She doesn't strike me as the mother and apple pie type.'

'How do we do that, sir? Medical matters are confidential.'

Hood frowned.

'We could always just ask her, couldn't we? It would give us the opportunity of delving into the matter a bit more deeply too. She's still living in that apartment at Harbour Buildings, isn't she?'

'Yes, sir.'

Hood checked his watch. 'It's gone six – she should be home by now. Well, what are we waiting for? Let's go.'

The two detectives rushed down to the car park and set off for Julia Hamilton's address in Hood's car. They were only a few hundred yards away from her flat when Hood pulled into a convenient lay-by and switched off the engine.

'Is there a problem?' asked Hooper.

'I was just wondering whether we are going about this the right way,' replied Hood. 'If this is a scam by Doyle we're doing exactly what he would expect us to do. It might be more sensible to react in a way he might not expect; don't you think?'

'I suppose so, sir? But if we don't speak to the Hamilton woman, who can we speak to?'

'Why don't we just leave it? Why do the intricacies of his domestic life concern us? If all this is true it will simply make Doyle more vulnerable, won't it? Make him easier to cross-examine. If he has gone to pieces because Hamilton has abandoned him – all the better.'

Hooper did not reply for a moment.

'But has she abandoned him? If she has, why? As you said before, sir, they've always been very close.' Hooper paused again. 'But to tell you the truth, I've always regarded her as a bit of a gold-digger myself. Doyle isn't the first man with money she's had her claws into. She was involved with a DS a few years back. And he must have come into money. He bought a hotel when he jacked the job in.'

'Well, if that's the case, perhaps she's heading for pastures new? Perhaps she thinks Doyle is not going to be able to provide for her in the future?'

'It makes you think, sir.'

'Exactly, Andrew. We've done too much rushing about in this case and not enough thinking. Perhaps we should speak to Markham-Moore before we go running off after the lovely Julia?'

Hooper nodded.

'Perhaps you're right, sir.'

Hood turned the car around and drove back to the police station.

'Let's just leave it for a day or two, shall we?'

CHAPTER THIRTY-NINE

Three days later, Hood returned to his office after a period of leave. He was now convinced his wife was pregnant again and the test she had carried out was affirmative. She had made an appointment to see the GP the next day. He really was going to need his promotion now. The successful prosecution of Doyle would be a real feather in his cap when he went before the postponed promotion board.

There was a message from the ACC waiting for him. She wanted to see him immediately at HQ. No reason was given. When he arrived he was surprised to see both Frazer and Markham-Moore sitting in Margaret Knowles' outer office.

'Is there a problem?' he asked.

'You can say that again,' scowled Frazer. 'I want it on the record that I was opposed to prosecuting Doyle from the outset.'

He turned away. Hood looked at Markham-Moore who appeared downcast. Hood turned towards one and then the other. 'Will someone please inform me what is going on?' he said.

Markham-Moore raised his head.

'I take it you haven't seen the application to dismiss.'

'The what?' enquired Hood.

Markham-Moore stood up. He started to pace the floor.

'The defence has put in an application to dismiss the charges of attempted murder and conspiracy to rob in respect of both Benson and Doyle.'

'I don't understand,' replied Hood. 'Where is the ACC?'

Markham-Moore remained stoney-faced.

'She's on her way here. All will be revealed when she arrives.'

Hood looked concerned. 'I thought the evidence we've assembled – proving the cash in Doyle's car came from the counting house – was just what we needed to convict him? You know, the final nail in his coffin.'

Markham-Moore sighed.

'If you remember, Mr Hood, I advised that the cash was sufficient to convict him *providing* we could establish the link with Benson.'

'But the CCTV does that. You said as much.'

'I agree – but everything is dependent on proving that Benson took part in the robbery. A chain is only as strong as its weakest link and it seems that we are going to have a real problem proving Benson was at the compound when the robbery occurred.'

Hood shot a look at Frazer then moved closer to the barrister. He half smiled. Surely, this was a joke – a joke in very poor taste?

'But the DNA does that. There's never been any question about it. The DNA puts Benson in the compound grappling with the guard who was shot.'

'Not any more it doesn't,' said Frazer, glaring at Markham-Moore. 'It isn't admissible – because *you* charged him before the result came through from the lab on the sample he gave after his arrest!'

Hood looked puzzled.

'I don't follow. You authorised the charge. And anyway, the DNA sample he gave on arrest matched the sample from the crime scene.'

Markham-Moore intervened.

'Please gentlemen,' he said raising his hands. 'It won't do any good if we fall out with each other.'

He glanced at the chief prosecutor who looked desperately in need of a cigarette.

'Anyone mind if I smoke?' asked Frazer.

Margaret Knowles' secretary interrupted.

'I'd rather you didn't. Mrs Knowles doesn't allow smoking up here. You'll have to go outside.'

Frazer shrugged his shoulders and put his cigarettes back in his pocket. Hood noticed he was facing away from Markham-Moore as if he didn't wish to be associated with him.

'How long is she going to be? I have got other business to attend to, you know,' the Chief Crown prosecutor said truculently.

Hood looked increasingly alarmed.

'Are you saying we've cocked up somehow in respect of the DNA? Is there some sort of problem with it?'

'You can say that again,' said Frazer, cynically, turning to face them. 'Mr Markham-Moore will explain it all in due course, no doubt.'

Markham-Moore shook his head. Hood could not help detecting the ill feeling flowing in the direction of the barrister.

'It's not as simple as that, James. It doesn't make any difference that Benson was charged before the result from his arrest sample came through. It's much more complicated.'

Further discussion was halted by the arrival of ACC Knowles. She appeared extremely perturbed.

'Come in, will you?' she said, quietly, opening her door and leading the trio into her room. She closed the door firmly behind them. When they were all seated she handed Hood a copy of the dismissal application.

'This arrived on my desk this morning. The chief has seen it and he's not very happy with it.'

She looked at Markham-Moore. 'Is there any way round it? It seems a question for the lawyers, if you ask me?'

The barrister cleared his throat before he spoke. 'On the face of it, no.'

Frazer raised his eyes towards the ceiling.

'Well, we're well and truly stuffed then, aren't we? They'll both walk.'

Hood was occupied reading the document. He glanced towards the ACC.

'This can't be right, surely? It's ridiculous. How were we supposed to know that Birmingham Metropolitan had retained Benson's DNA illegally? It just doesn't make sense.'

He continued reading. Frazer resumed his surly expression. He was determined to pass the buck – in any direction – providing it was away from himself.

'What doesn't make sense is that counsel instructed on our behalf didn't spot this!'

He looked at Markham-Moore who smiled wearily.

'Counsel is only as good as his instructions, James. Where in my instructions did you state that Benson's DNA had been held on to by Birmingham when it should have been destroyed?'

'That's not the point. This statute has been in force for some time. I expect experienced counsel to know the law. That's why we instruct you.'

He folded his arms.

'As always, James, I take your point but I think you're being a bit unreasonable in all the circumstances. I was specifically instructed, if you remember, to advise about the money. That I did and I stand by my advice.'

'Gentleman, please,' interrupted the ACC. 'Looking to apportion blame for this will get us nowhere. Is there anything practical we can do – or do we have to drop the case? The chief will have a fit if we do.'

No one spoke for some time. Then Markham-Moore gave his views, trenchantly but without rancour.

'These applications arrived with the CPS four days ago. We have another ten days or so to respond. If there is an answer, it's obviously not staring us in the face. But it seems to me that if Benson's DNA is excluded by the judge we will be in difficulties with both of them. There's no other evidence against Benson and without the link to Doyle, we shall have problems keeping him in too. The evidence about the money, while it might still prove he was in possession of cash from the robbery, probably won't be enough to establish he was part of the robbery team. The most we could get him for would be money laundering – and that would not be a foregone conclusion either.'

'And what would he get for that?' queried Frazer. 'Eighteen months tops!'

The others looked at him. His attitude was anything but helpful.

'So, what do you advise?' asked the ACC, looking at Markham-Moore and trying but failing to conceal her irritation with Frazer.

'I've spoken to my head of chambers about this, informally of course.'

'Of course,' repeated Frazer. His tone had not changed.

'My suggestion is that he is instructed to give an opinion…'

'What!' said Frazer, raising his voice and standing up. 'Harold Cronshaw QC – we can't afford him! He spends all his time in the Court of Appeal and the House of Lords. We're already over budget this year. The DPP would have my guts for garters.'

Markham-Moore sighed.

'It's precisely because he spends nearly all his time in the appellate courts that I suggest we use him – not for the trial – just to deal with this application. If he's restricted to this question his fee will be perfectly reasonable. He's already said as much. As a favour to me.' He smiled. 'I was his pupil you know.'

'Oh, yes. And what about that rapacious clerk of yours?'

'He'll do as he's told.'

Frazer started to calm down. Hood finished his reading.

'Is this really the law? It's ridiculous if it is.' He shook his head.

'If anyone can find a way round it, Harold Cronshaw's the man,' said the barrister. 'I think it's worth a shot. But you needn't take my word for it.

Hal has looked at it already and is working on an answer. If he'd thought it was a waste of time, he'd have said so.'

'We've got to give it a go,' said Hood. 'We can't just give up.'

'But a judge has already ruled on the point in similar circumstances. That case in Carlisle. It's exactly the same point. It's all in the skeleton argument.'

Frazer sounded anything but optimistic.

'I agree with the chief inspector,' said Knowles. 'We've invested too much time and effort to give up now, especially as it seems absurd that evidence which proves beyond doubt that Benson was there in the compound should not go before a jury.'

Frazer paused and reached for his cigarettes, then spying Knowles' expression put them back in his pocket.

'All right,' he said, appreciating he was in a minority of one. 'We'll instruct Cronshaw to give his opinion in conference. I suppose his reputation will have some effect on the judge – but, mind you, he's being instructed on this point only – not for the trial. If the judge dismisses this application you're on your own for the trial.'

'Agreed,' replied Markham-Moore. 'I'll set it up, hopefully for next week.'

'Will it be in order for Chief Inspector Hood to attend?' asked Knowles.

'Of course. I think the chief inspector and Harold Cronshaw have worked together before?'

'That's right,' smiled Hood. 'It's a few years ago now – when I was in West Yorkshire – but he was very impressive. Got a result too as I remember.'

'Good,' said Knowles bringing the proceedings to an end. 'No doubt the chief and I will be informed of the outcome.'

The three men nodded in unison.

'Anything else?'

'There is one thing,' said Hood. 'Doyle's girlfriend has apparently given him the push. He's taken it very badly. It probably means she thinks he's going to be convicted and she's looking to her own future – always assuming it's not some sort of ploy.'

'They hardly need a ploy given this little difficulty,' said Frazer, sarcastically.

'Perhaps she doesn't know about it,' suggested Knowles.

'Highly unlikely, ma'am,' said Hood. 'I have no doubt that Doyle will have kept her in the loop – at least until a few days ago. My sergeant thinks this bust-up is genuine. He's always reckoned she was nothing more than a gold-digger and that she's simply pulling out because she knows Doyle is going down for a long time.'

'Cutting her losses, eh?' said Markham-Moore.

'Possibly. But whatever the truth may be, it seems to have hit Doyle pretty hard. He was moved to the hospital wing for a couple of days.'

'Good,' replied Markham-Moore. 'But I suspect someone like Doyle will soon get over it. On the other hand, any advantage in cross-examination is always welcome.'

'If we get that far!' added Frazer, excusing himself and putting a cigarette in his mouth.

He noticed Knowles glare in his direction. 'Don't worry, I'll wait until I get outside before I light it.'

The two lawyers left the room. Hood remained.

'This is a bit of a blow, isn't it?' said the ACC after the door had closed.

'It's ridiculous,' said Hood. 'Are they seriously suggesting that evidence that proves Benson's guilt should not be put before a jury? I just can't believe it.'

Knowles smiled.

'What was it Mr Bumble said, Harry? "The law is an ass"?'

Hood corrected her.

'Not quite, ma'am. The words Dickens put into his mouth were slightly but importantly different. What Bumble actually said was *"if* the law supposes that then the law is an ass, a idiot." The "if" is significant – at least I hope it is in our case!'

'Let's hope Harold Cronshaw can demonstrate the law is not as daft as Mr Frazer seems to think it is, eh?'

'Well, ma'am, if he can't we really are in trouble.'

The ACC changed the subject.

'What do you reckon the truth is about Doyle's girlfriend? Is it some kind of scam they're working on?'

'It's possible – but if they have this legal loophole going in their favour, there wouldn't seem much point to it. Perhaps she really has given him the elbow? Perhaps she's unaware of this legal complication?'

'I'm not so sure. She's pregnant, isn't she?'

'So she says. We've not had any confirmation either way.'

'Well if she is, and he's the father, I would take some convincing before I'd believe they're no longer an item. Although I suppose if she were to have an abortion, that would confirm the relationship had ended.'

'I wouldn't wish that on anyone and it would depend anyway on whether he really is the father. But she's told him he isn't. That's what we've heard from the intelligence officer in the prison.'

'They could still be up to something, Harry.'

'If they are, I can't think what it is. I thought at first they might be trying to lay the foundation for a psychiatric defence, but Doyle's apparently recovered his composure and been moved back to a cell.'

'Just take things carefully. That's all I'm saying. Let's not jump to any conclusions.'

CHAPTER FORTY

Tuesday, 16 March 1999

'What's she up to?' asked Doyle. 'Come on Trevor, you must have spoken to her.'

Trevor Parker was in two minds about what to say. Doyle was not like a normal client. As a solicitor, he realised he had become far too close to him and his affairs and it was going to be difficult if not impossible to retreat into a typical lawyer/client relationship. He was in too deep. And he hadn't forgotten that Doyle probably had a copy of his client account ledger that could cause him professional problems should it come to the notice of the Law Society. His conversation with Julia Hamilton had, after due reflection, made him even more nervous that Doyle would take full advantage of any hold he thought he had over him. While he was not certain that a copy of the ledger had been retained, he couldn't take the risk of putting his doubts to the test. But he had determined in his own mind that a line had to be drawn somewhere. There were certain things he was simply not prepared to do.

He'd managed to book the private interview room again so he and Doyle could speak freely without the risk of being overheard. While Doyle was happy to have been released from the hospital wing and serve only three days in the segregation unit, he showed not even a spark of gratitude for his solicitor's efforts on his behalf.

'Well Trevor,' Doyle repeated, 'what's going on? I know she's definitely pregnant. I've seen a copy of the scan. Why is she saying I'm not the father?'

He looked at his solicitor who seemed reluctant to speak. He asked the question again.

'Who's the father if it's not me?'

'I don't know,' insisted Parker. 'I'd always assumed it was you. That's what she told me at the outset. Now she's saying you're not. I asked her who it was and she told me in no uncertain terms to mind my own business.'

'She told me the same,' replied Doyle. 'I'll tell you this for nothing. If she's been having it away with someone else behind my back...'

'Please, Michael,' interrupted Parker. 'It'll do no good talking like that. We need to concentrate on your case and get you out of here – then you can sort out Julia for yourself.'

'And when exactly am I going to get out of here? I'm paying you and that stuck-up QC a bloody fortune – but I haven't seen much return on my investment so far.'

Trevor Parker sighed.

'It's still early days, Michael.'

Doyle reacted angrily.

'Not for me it isn't – not that I've got much to look forward to if I do get out of here. Jules gone – and then I've got the Revenue to deal with. And then there's this so-called evidence about the four hundred grand...'

The solicitor shook his head.

'Don't get down-hearted. I know this evidence about the cash in your car doesn't help but Miss Lassiter doesn't think that it's enough to convict you – not on the present charges anyway. Unless they can put Benson in the compound when the robbery was taking place, the most they can do you for is money laundering. And they might not even get you for that if you gave me some clear instructions where the money came from.'

'All in good time, Trevor. All in good time. If the QC doesn't want to know what I was doing with all that cash, why should you? All you need to know is it was for a business deal.'

Parker looked forlorn.

'It would make me feel a great deal more comfortable if you told me where the actual cash came from – that's all.'

Doyle took out a cigarette and placed it between his lips. His solicitor produced a lighter and lit it for him.

'And what if I don't get out of here? What if Harriet Lassiter is wrong about Benson's DNA? What do I do then? How will I ever find out if this child is definitely mine?'

'We can deal with that – if it comes to it. We can get a court order to have his DNA checked. If he's your child, the DNA analysis will prove it. You needn't worry about that.'

Doyle looked up.

'You said "he", Trevor.'

Parker hesitated and removed his spectacles. Doyle glared at him.

'It's a boy, isn't it? She's told you it's a boy. She never said anything to me about it being a boy, and you couldn't tell from the scan I saw.'

Parker took out a handkerchief and started to polish his glasses, vigorously.

'Did I? I don't know,' he responded unconvincingly. 'I just said "he". Could be a girl for all I know.'

'Don't lie to me, Trevor. I can tell from your face your telling porkies. She's told you it's a boy and she's told you not to tell me, hasn't she? If you and her are up to something…'

Doyle leant forward, his temper rising. Parker squirmed in his seat but responded forcefully.

'I'm not up to anything. I'm doing my best for you in very difficult circumstances. If you're not satisfied you can always get someone else to represent you.'

He replaced his spectacles and looked at Doyle. Doyle seemed taken aback for a moment. He sighed and shook his head.

'All right. I withdraw what I said. But it's hit me pretty hard, you know.' He paused and looked away and became emotional. 'I thought she loved me, I really did. And just when I need her the most she does this to me.'

Doyle extinguished his cigarette and placed his head in his hands. For a brief moment Parker thought he was going to break down. He almost felt sorry for him.

'Look Michael…' His voice softened. 'I don't know what she's up to. I really don't but if you ask me it doesn't add up. When I saw her a few days ago she was really concerned for you. I showed her Lassiter's skeleton argument and she gave me the impression she was genuinely worried that it might not do the trick. She was visibly upset.'

Doyle leant back in his chair, and looked intently at Parker.

'What do you mean?'

Parker did not reply. His client became more insistent.

'Are you keeping something from me, Trevor?'

'No.' The solicitor shook his head. 'I'm keeping nothing from you. It's just a feeling I have.' Parker sighed deeply. 'Look, I'm not holding back on anything, Michael. She was in touch again a day or two ago – by phone – about one of the cases she's handling for me and I saw her in the office yesterday. I told her on the phone I was coming to see you today. She asked how you were getting on and I told her you'd got into trouble with another prisoner and you'd been put in the segregation unit.'

Doyle was now calm. He was obviously thinking fast. He said nothing for some minutes.

'How did she react when you told her that?'

'She didn't say anything.'

'What? No message? There you go then. She's only being polite to you. She's not interested in me.'

'I don't know. By the way, it was the Law Society dinner the other night and she was there.'

'Was she? She's hasn't been to that for years. Why did she go?'

'I don't know, Michael. She came as my guest four years ago, but I don't think she's been since.'

'Who invited her?'

'Not me. She was there with a barrister, Bill Savage. He was the guest speaker.'

'Was she?'

Doyle slammed his hand down on the table. Then placed his head in his hands again. When he looked up he was calm. He changed the subject.

'What about the Revenue? I suppose I'll be penniless as well by the time I get out of here?'

Parker was glad to move the discussion away from Doyle's relationship with Julia Hamilton. As always, he felt much more at ease dealing with practical matters.

'I've managed to put that on hold. I think they're waiting to see the outcome of these proceedings. You needn't worry about that for the moment – the accountants have got everything in hand. They've been in touch with you directly, I presume?'

Doyle nodded.

'We need to concentrate on this case, Michael. The tax man can wait.'

But try as he might, Doyle couldn't get Jules out of his head.

'Why is she interested in this Savage character? What's he to her?'

'I don't know, Michael. Perhaps she simply wanted to go to the dinner. It's a very popular event.' Then he added something, anxious to return to practical matters. 'Incidentally, she was asking me about some of your properties.'

'She was what?' Doyle's temper began to rise again. 'What properties?'

'She was very interested in that land in the Vale of Belvoir. You know, the ninety acres you sold to that property company last year?'

'Subject to planning permission,' interjected Doyle. 'We've only received a percentage of the selling price. We won't get the rest until it's approved. And we have to repay most of it if the permission doesn't come through.'

Parker smiled. No matter how down Doyle might feel, he was still on the ball when it came to questions of money.

'And you haven't given possession either, remember? But that shouldn't be too much of a problem. They were very keen to get their hands on it and there's unlikely to be a problem with the planners. Not anymore. They're as confident as we are. We're just waiting for the planning committee to rubber-stamp it. We should have that sorted before Easter.'

'It's taking a long time.'

'Well it's not straightforward, I agree. But the planning committee now favours the development, so I wouldn't worry about that. All the other interested parties are heavily in favour. Even the county council has come round to our point of view.'

Doyle seemed to relax a little.

'But why would she be interested in Orley Farm? There's only that tumbledown house and those big barns that haven't been used for years. And it's in the middle of nowhere.'

'It's not just that property. She wanted to see the particulars of sale on the units at Riverside and she asked me how the sale of Harbour Buildings was progressing. She also asked about the farm in Ireland. I didn't even know she knew about that.'

Doyle slammed his hand down on the table again.

'She knows about everything – we were planning to move abroad, remember? She was helping me to sort it all out with the accountants. And that farm in County Limerick is in her sole name. The accountants recommended that. My sister and my mother were supposed to be moving in there to look after it. I never intended she should get her hands on it.'

He paused.

'You don't think she's going to make a claim against me – you know, try and get a share of my assets? What with the Revenue after me as well…'

He stood up and walked towards the barred window. 'That would be very handy, that would, wouldn't it? I go down for a long stretch and she goes off into the sunset with her fancy man and a few hundred thousand of mine.'

'Somehow I don't think so,' said Parker, anxious to contain his client's worries. 'You're not going to go down – not according to Harriet Lassiter – and as for Julia, she seems to be acting wholly out of character. And, remember, you're not married so she'd find it very difficult to pursue a claim against you. Of that I am sure. I have a lot of experience in that area of the law. She simply wouldn't get anywhere – and she has sense enough to realise it.'

'Does she? I just don't know any more. She could do me a lot of harm if she wanted to.'

He took out another cigarette and lit it. Parker, with some hesitation, continued his explanation of the law.

'Mind you, the child is another matter. If it's yours – she would be entitled to look to you for support.'

'But she's saying it's not mine.'

He looked away. When he spoke his tone was bitter. 'She's always been interested in money has Jules. She knows she's a looker and she thinks that means she should never go without – and she's not getting any younger.'

He paused and took a long drag on his cigarette.

'That's why she tagged along with me in the first place. I'm not that naïve, you know, Trevor. She didn't put her lot in with me just for my good looks.'

He half smiled and brushed his hand through his hair. 'Not that I ever went short in that department.'

Parker ignored Doyle's attempt at humour.

'Yes, but you've been together for over five years now. I just can't believe she would suddenly go off you like this. There must be some other explanation.'

'Well, if there is, she hasn't let me in on it.'

Parker stood up and put his hands in his pockets. He looked at the floor then at Doyle. He was deep in thought.

'I'll be completely straight with you Michael – I'll tell you what I really think.'

Doyle scrutinised him carefully.

'You'd better.'

The solicitor resumed his seat and cupped his hands together on the table. Doyle walked over and sat down opposite him. Parker was not at all sure about what he was about to say, but it might have a beneficial effect on his client. Doyle looked at him closely.

'Go on then. And it better be good.'

Parker hesitated. 'This is only my opinion, you understand. I've nothing solid to go on. But I think she's up to something – not to harm you, but – in her own way – to help you.'

'You what?' Doyle's face was a picture of incredulity. 'But that doesn't make sense. If she was trying to help me, why not let me in on it?'

The solicitor paused. Should he go on? Would it make matters worse? He was already regretting saying anything.

'Look Michael, I've never mentioned this before but Julia is a clever young woman. She doesn't have much in the way of qualifications but she's very bright. I've always thought so. If I can be blunt, she's a lot cleverer than you – or me for that matter.'

Doyle half closed his eyes but he didn't interrupt. A smile played on his lips. He'd always rated Jules too. Not that he liked the suggestion that she was brighter than he.

'I reckon she's kept you out of whatever it is she's got in mind in order to ensure you're not implicated. If she was visiting you or telephoning you while you're stuck in here it could rebound on you – especially if it all went wrong. As things stand, you can't be held responsible for anything she might do.'

Doyle took a drag on his cigarette.

'Go on, Trevor. Don't stop now.'

'She obviously knew how you'd react. The fact that you went off the deep end – and got yourself locked up in solitary – is exactly what she'd expect. After all, she knows you better than anyone. She calculated that telling you that you're not the father of her child would have exactly the result that it did.'

Doyle screwed up his face.

'You think she lied about it? Lied to *me?*'

'Yes, I do. She was plainly telling me the truth in the office when she first said she was pregnant and she made no bones about it then.'

Doyle shook his head slowly and stubbed out his cigarette.

'I don't get it. She could have told me what she was up to and I could still have got myself locked up in the segregation unit. It's easily done you know. I think you're barking up the wrong tree here, Trevor.'

Parker shook his head.

'Maybe I am. But that's my point. She knew you were finding it hard inside so she used that knowledge to make sure you reacted as you did.

That's what's so clever about it. She didn't want to rely on your acting ability – which, if you'll permit me to say so – is pretty lousy.'

Doyle remained thoughtful, then his anger returned. He stood up.

'No. I don't buy that, Trevor. She's up to something with that barrister, that's what all this is about. She's obviously wanting to get me completely out of her life. Anyway, what can she do that isn't being done already by you and the QC?'

'I don't know. It's just a feeling I have. I have no idea what she's planning – I'm just convinced she's up to something.'

Parker wished he'd never raised the subject. Doyle glared at him then smiled.

'Perhaps she's going to seduce the judge?'

Parker almost laughed. 'Now that would be a stupid thing to do. And Julia is not stupid.'

'I don't know about that. They're a randy lot some of theses judges. I read the papers, you know.'

But Doyle was only trying to hide the sick feeling in the pit of his stomach. He'd lost her and that was all there was to it. It was fanciful to think there was any other explanation. He was not one to clutch at straws but he pressed his solicitor further.

'You're not just saying this are you, Trevor? She's not told you to say this? You know, just to keep me quiet?'

'I give you my word, Michael. She's said nothing at all to me. Only what I've told you – and she didn't even want me to disclose what I have. But there must be some reason for her sudden change of attitude. When I saw her yesterday she was completely different. It was as if she didn't care about you at all. She has to be up to something.' He looked down. 'That's what worries me. Whatever she's got in mind, it's probably not legal.' He raised his head and looked earnestly at Doyle. 'And I can't have any part in anything dodgy. I want to make that very clear. I've been a solicitor for thirty-four years and I want to retire in good standing.'

Doyle scowled at Parker. He started pacing the room.

'I wouldn't worry your head about it, Trevor. It's over. That's all there is to it. I've just got to learn to accept it. Anyway, what else did she say to you yesterday? You'd better tell me everything, and I mean everything.'

'Well, I thought she was particularly cruel when she mentioned your French holiday…'

Doyle perked up at the mention of France. 'What about it?'

'Are you into films, Michael?'

'Films?'

'Yes, she said something very odd before she left the office yesterday. She asked me to give you a message. She said to tell you "we'll always have Paris". I'd almost forgotten about it.'

Doyle suddenly felt elated. But he wasn't going to show it – not to Trevor Parker. He feigned surprise. 'She said what?'

'She said, "Tell him we'll always have Paris". You know – what Humphrey Bogart said to Ingrid Bergman at the end of *Casablanca.* Remember? It was his way of getting her to go off with her husband, the war hero – what was his name? Victor Laszlo? She left Bogart standing at the airport with Claude Rains. Very emotional. Always gets to my wife that bit does.' Parker paused. 'Pretty unpleasant thing for her to say in the circumstances, I thought. But she can be unpleasant when she wants to be. Very unpleasant. I was in two minds whether to tell you.'

But Doyle was not listening. He turned away from his solicitor and walked towards the barred window, gazed at the courtyard below and smiled. And what a smile! Everything that he'd just said about Jules vanished from his mind. He took it all back. That was the message he'd been waiting for – the message he thought would never come. "We'll always have Paris." That was what she had told him when she saw him for the first time in prison. "Whatever happens, however bad things seem, wait for that message. Then you'll know everything is prepared." He shook his head. He'd been a fool. How could he have mistrusted her? How could he have doubted her? His spirits soared. She was still his. The child, too, was undoubtedly his. Just as she'd first told him. Whatever she was up to with Savage, he knew she still belonged to him. Whatever she was about was plainly a diversion of some kind. He could have jumped for joy – but he knew he mustn't. Neither must he let on to Parker that his initial suspicions about Jules' behaviour were correct. She had obviously not trusted him; neither must he. The smile vanished as he returned to the table in an apparent state of depression. He might not be much of an actor in Parker's opinion, but he could carry this off all right. He looked at his solicitor – a picture of misery. He was even able to produce a tear. 'The bitch,' he said, shaking his head.

'My sentiments, exactly,' replied the solicitor. 'I couldn't have put it better.'

CHAPTER FORTY-ONE

Hood travelled to London with Detective Constable Wendy Knight. He had left Hooper to make discreet enquiries at Leicester prison to try and ascertain the truth about Doyle. Hood had given strict instructions that Julia Hamilton was not to be approached. He judged that there should be no contact with her until he had a more definite idea of what, if anything, was happening between her and Doyle. As for Jules, she was giving every indication that her relationship with Doyle was well and truly over. She had attended the local Law Society annual dinner in the company of Bill Savage, which had caused a deal of gossip. "They make an attractive couple," Charles Cavan-Henry had commented to his wife, and he wasn't being wholly sarcastic. What Charles could not know – and neither could anyone else – was that Julia Hamilton would adamantly refuse to spend the rest of the night with her escort, a fact which Savage could be relied on to keep a closely guarded secret. To do otherwise might have exposed his unsuccessful attempt at seduction and damage his reputation in the eyes of those he imagined admired his technique with the ladies.

The train arrived at St Pancras on time and the two detectives took a taxi to the Temple where the consultation with Harold Cronshaw, QC was to take place. Markham-Moore was waiting for them in the reception area at 14 King's Bench Walk. Frazer had prayed an urgent appointment at CPS headquarters and had despatched Andrea Fleming in his stead to take a careful note of the proceedings.

The contrast between the centre of operations in chambers and Cronshaw's room on the first floor of the seventeenth-century building could not have been more marked. Banks of computers were arranged along the centre of the clerks' room with every known technological gadget prominently on display. Hood thought it resembled the action centre of an investment bank or the bridge of the starship *Enterprise* rather than the staid environment he had imagined would be *de rigueur* in a London barristers' chambers. Cronshaw's room was much more to his liking and met his expectations to the letter. There was no sign of any technology. Even the telephone resembled one he remembered from his childhood. When he and Knight were ushered into the room, the eminent barrister was sitting behind a huge mahogany desk, the faded green leather top partially covered with papers and several legal textbooks. A large oil painting of a truly beautiful woman encased in a carved golden frame was positioned on the wall behind him. The other walls were lined with what Hood took to be leather-bound law reports interspersed with cartoons of judges and distinguished barristers, each volume in its correct chronological position. An intricately carved fireplace with what appeared to be a real coal fire burning in the grate added the final touch.

Cronshaw rose as they entered, Andrea Fleming taking up the rear with Markham-Moore.

'Chief Inspector Hood, I believe,' smiled Cronshaw, proffering his hand. 'It has been a long time.'

'Yes, sir,' said Hood. 'It was 1993 if I remember – the case of Richard Cummings in Leeds.'

'Was it that long ago? Nasty business that. Well, do sit down.'

Hood introduced Knight and Andrea Fleming before taking a seat. He noticed that Cronshaw looked older and thinner than when they had last met and there was, he thought, a certain sadness in his countenance which vanished only when he smiled. Then his face was quite transformed.

'Mr Markham-Moore needs no introduction,' added Hood.

'None at all,' said the great man. 'He was my pupil, you know.'

He smiled sheepishly as he glanced at his colleague. 'Mr Frazer not with you?'

'No,' said Fleming. 'He had an urgent appointment with the deputy DPP.'

Cronshaw nodded and chuckled to himself.

'James certainly knows where his priorities lie.'

Harold Cronshaw was a barrister of the old school. Called in 1968, he had taken silk in 1985 and rapidly developed a leader's practice which was the envy of his fellows. He had been the scourge of the prosecuting authorities as a junior, exposing weak cases and suspect evidence with apparent ease. He did not win every case – that was simply impossible – but even when his clients were convicted they appreciated the efforts made on their behalf. No one, of course, really knew the hours of dogged preparation and research that had gone into his cases but all were mesmerised by his advocacy. In silk, the CPS tried, without success, to monopolise him, simply to prevent him appearing on the other side. Judges quaked when they saw his name on the list and rushed to their law books in a forlorn attempt to give the appearance, at least, that they could match him for learning. Then, when he was at the height of his powers as an advocate, tragedy struck. His wife of only seven years was killed by a drug-ravaged drunken driver on the North Circular. He was devastated. After taking six months off and declining a judicial appointment he returned to the fray. He took a flat in Gray's Inn, the smallest but most tranquil of the Inns of Court, where he lived alone during the week and returned every Friday evening to the Elizabethan manor house in Oxfordshire which he and his wife had been renovating at the time of her death. It was to be her memorial. He never socialised, other than at his Inn during the working week. All social invitations at weekends were refused to the extent that few were now received. His limited spare time was devoted to his daughter who, even before she reached the age of nine, had shown a remarkable resemblance to his late wife. It was his dear wife who appeared in the painting behind his desk, a portrait he had commissioned after she had died from a photograph he had taken while they were on holiday in Provence.

Nowadays the bulk of his practice was in London. He rarely travelled on circuit. There was more than enough for him to do in the Court of Appeal and the House of Lords. Very much in demand, he could pick and choose his cases. His *métier* was legal argument. He seldom appeared in trials but before the appellate courts he had no equal.

But he deplored what he saw happening around him and was concerned for the future of his profession. For him, the Bar was a vocation akin to the priesthood. Its bedrock was a high level of competence and learning, personal integrity and genuine independence. He had no time for the management apparatchiks who seemed to be taking over its governance or talk of partnerships or teams or direct access to clients. He declined, year on year, to contribute to the various publications that purported to rank barristers one against the other, or the modern practice of extolling on websites their alleged attributes and the listing of their successes. "Mere advertising" he would say, dismissively. "A barrister is as good as his last case." Despite his refusal to accommodate these modern practices he was chosen on one occasion to be "Barrister of the Year" by some publication he had never heard of. He declined both the nomination and the cheap looking trophy that went with it. "I am not a celebrity," he intoned to his disappointed senior clerk who had been looking forward to the ceremony and the dinner at a City livery company.

Although his chambers operated a website – the younger members insisted – he refused to be photographed for it or to have any of his cases listed. All that appeared under his name was his field of practice and his qualifications. In this he was almost unique – but it did not affect in the slightest the demand for his services. He would appear for either prosecution or defence with but one exception. He would never act for either side in a case concerning death by dangerous driving – not even to argue a point of law.

Harold Cronshaw possessed neither a computer nor a mobile phone. Such technological advances were entirely foreign to him and, if they featured in a case, he had to rely on his junior to explain their workings. He stubbornly continued to write his opinions in longhand using the fountain pen his late wife had given him on his thirty-ninth birthday. But his reputation and importance to chambers was such that "upstairs Margaret" as the chambers' sole typist was known, had been kept on when the rest of the typing pool had been declared redundant as barristers began to type their own opinions and pleadings with the introduction of computers. She operated from a tiny room on the top floor and could read and understand every nuance of his opinions, correcting, without prompting, the occasional solecism or error in spelling, which was indeed a rarity.

He opened the papers, which lay on the desk, carefully untying the white tape and placing it to his right-hand side. He spoke slowly, choosing his words with precision.

'Edward and I have discussed this case in detail already.'

He placed his large hands together and smiled.

'I will come to the point at once – no doubt you have a train to catch?'

Hood protested that he was under no pressure of time.

Cronshaw smiled again, sat back in his chair and eyed the individuals before him one after the other.

'Whilst nothing about any criminal litigation can be certain,' he opined, 'I am satisfied that there is a logical argument that can be put forward to circumvent the literal meaning of this *very* badly drafted piece of legislation.'

He paused as if to underline his view of the Parliamentary draftsman – which was not a high one.

'The greatest difficulty I foresee – and I don't regard it as insuperable by any means – is the decision of Lord Justice Willoughby, as he now is, in the *Carlisle* case – but from what Markham-Moore tells me, the point was not well argued on that occasion. Indeed, it appears to have been missed altogether.' He smiled broadly. 'That is not an error that will be repeated!'

Hood sighed in relief.

'Willoughby is a good man,' continued Cronshaw adopting an almost confidential tone, 'but he really ought to stick to charter parties and collisions in the English Channel. I'm afraid that serious crime is well outside his professional experience. Hopefully, his recent elevation will ensure that any further contributions he may make to criminal jurisprudence will be limited and qualified by the presence of two other judges.'

He looked tentatively towards Markham-Moore but although junior counsel smiled he said nothing. He knew when not to interrupt. Cronshaw returned to the matter in hand.

'I am confident that we would carry the day in the Appeal Court – providing, of course, we drew the right constitution – but that should not be too difficult to arrange.'

He chuckled to himself as if he had the influence to choose the judges who would sit on any appeal. Hood, for his part, never doubted it.

'But that will be no good,' interrupted the chief inspector. 'Mr Markham-Moore has made it clear. We have to win in the Crown Court or they walk.'

'Agreed,' said Cronshaw. 'That's another piece of legislation that needs amending. It almost makes you think these politicians are on the side of serious criminals.'

He chuckled to himself again. Cronshaw seemed to do a great deal of chuckling – for such a serious person. But every now and again a look of extreme sadness would suddenly cloud his features as if something had awakened a long forgotten and painful memory.

'The question is whether the trial judge will be brave enough to go against Willoughby's ruling – such as it is. I'm sure the other side will point to his recent promotion as some support for their submissions – a sort of crutch, if you understand my meaning.'

Hood noticed a distinct note of derision as those words were uttered. Markham-Moore then had his say.

'I think that Tom Campion might well be persuaded that the *Carlisle* decision is wrong. He's a good judge and does not like guilty men escaping on technicalities. Providing we put forward a cogent enough argument, he'll go for it. Of that I'm sure.'

'Confident as ever, I see,' observed Cronshaw.

The great man then turned again to the papers before him and set out the basis of his argument. As he unfolded his thoughts, Hood immediately appreciated that his thesis was a combination of legal learning and adroit tactics.

'First,' said Cronshaw, now adopting a very serious air indeed, 'we must underline the fact – at the outset – that both of these… criminals… (he paused and emphasised the word) will escape justice if the judge does not accept our submissions. That should put him under the right degree of psychological pressure. I see no point in relying on secondary considerations or alternative offences. If we are to succeed, the judge must be made to realise that we shall not proceed further with the case if our argument on the admissibility of the DNA is rejected.'

Hood was minded to interrupt and mention all the work that had been done to establish that Doyle's cash must have originated from the counting house, but the barrister waved his objections aside.

'Secondly, we must also concede that Benson's DNA profile was unlawfully held by the police following the discovery of the actual perpetrator of the offences they were then investigating in Birmingham. It should, indeed, have been destroyed and not kept on the DNA database.'

'But if we concede that…' said Hood. The barrister raised his hand again and refused to give way.

'Permit me to continue, Mr Hood. In conceding these matters we are merely accepting that there is no contrary argument on these preliminary questions that has any prospect of succeeding. We are not conceding the main issue. Neither are we seeking to draw any meaningful distinction between the profile on the database and the sample you took from him on his arrest. We nail our colours to a straightforward and common sense principle. The police in this case, by which, of course, I mean your good selves, acted in the utmost good faith. You were not responsible for the actions of the other constabulary retaining the profile on the database. It would be irresponsible and contrary to the intention of Parliament to prohibit a DNA sample – providing it was either lawfully acquired or voluntarily given – from being used to establish participation in an unrelated and subsequent criminal offence. As a former Lord Chief Justice has said, the investigation and prosecution of serious crime is not a game.'

Hood nodded in agreement.

'There is, in my considered opinion, no overriding requirement to give an over literal interpretation to this legislation. The failure to comply with the seemingly mandatory requirement to destroy the sample is but the starting point; it does not answer the real question. The real issue is whether the failure to comply with that requirement necessarily has the *inevitable* consequence that such cogent evidence should *always* be rendered inadmissible.'

He paused to let his audience catch up. Hood was certainly well behind.

'We shall argue it does not. The court must have a discretion whether to admit such evidence bearing in mind there is already a statutory code which is available for determining such questions. I refer, of course, to section 78 of the Police and Criminal Evidence Act. In short, we shall argue that Parliament purposefully did not enact a blanket ban on such material being admitted because the court already has sufficient powers under section 78 to determine, in a particular case, whether the admission of such evidence might adversely affect the fairness of the proceedings. It is significant, in my opinion, that section 78 includes a requirement on the court to take into account the circumstances in which the evidence was obtained. There is no such requirement in relation to this statutory provision. Parliament, in its wisdom, plainly thought that section 78 was more than adequate.' He paused again then added with more than a hint of sarcasm, 'Always assuming they gave it any thought at all!'

Hood did not pretend he followed such labyrinthine arguments. He was only interested in the conclusion.

'In other words,' said Cronshaw, clearing his throat, 'it is entirely consistent with statute, general principles and the common law that this question should be determined on the particular facts of each case. And given the cogency of the evidence in our case, it simply cannot be realistically argued that there would be any unfairness in admitting evidence which proves conclusively that Benson participated in this robbery. Indeed, it is not suggested in the dismissal application that the DNA evidence is unreliable merely that it should not be admitted.'

He paused and looked directly at Hood who seemed far from convinced. Cronshaw decided to put his advice in simple form.

'If I might use the vernacular, Mr Hood; once we nail Benson – everything else follows.'

He unclasped his hands and adjusted his cufflinks. 'I have always held fast to the principle, Chief Inspector, that common sense is more important in such matters than the arbitrary workings of the parliamentary process. Any other conclusion would have, frankly, quite absurd consequences. Mind you,' he added, with a twinkle in his eye, 'I shall get on to my friend the Attorney-General and suggest that this statute is amended post-haste. Hopefully, when the question is next considered in the House, the honourable members will be awake and alert to the problems such sloppy drafting can produce.'

Cronshaw gazed at his audience. No one spoke for a few moments.

'What about the human rights point?' asked Wendy Knight. 'The defence seems to be making a great deal of that?'

'Oh, I wouldn't concern yourself over much with that,' responded Cronshaw confidently. 'Article 8 is not quite as all consuming as some commentators suggest. If we are correct, any interference with Benson's rights which might be established by the use of this sample would inevitably be regarded as legitimate and proportionate. Questions about the admissibility of evidence are matters for the national courts – that is already clearly established. These rights are not absolute you know, although I suspect they are going to cause a deal of trouble to majority opinion in the future.'

'Will you be drafting a response to the defence application?' asked Andrea.

'Already done, my dear Andrea,' replied Cronshaw. 'You can pick up a signed copy from the clerks' room as you leave. I've checked it for typos and initialled it. And I think I can say, without contradiction, that Edward here agrees wholeheartedly with my conclusions.'

Markham-Moore nodded. 'Absolutely,' he replied. His relief that his former pupil master had come to his rescue was evident to all.

'And you will appear to conduct the argument?' continued Andrea Fleming. 'Mr Frazer is very keen that you should...'

'If you think it necessary, although I expect Edward could manage it, now that the basic argument has been ironed out!'

Cronshaw smiled impishly.

'I don't think so,' responded Markham-Moore. 'The judge will take a great deal more notice of you than he will of me.'

'I suppose he might,' conceded Cronshaw. 'Very well. Let my clerk know the details and I shall arrange to be there. I suppose it will mean a trip up to Leicester, will it?'

Fleming nodded.

'I haven't been there since 1992. I suppose it's changed quite a lot since then?'

'Indeed it has,' replied Hood.

'I expect it will be over with within the day. The judge will probably read the skeleton arguments in advance, so there won't be that much to add. If he's as bright as you say, Edward, he should have the point firmly fixed in his mind before he comes into court.'

He stood up as if to indicate the audience was at an end.

'Well, goodbye Chief Inspector. I look forward to seeing you in court. I take it you will be there?'

'Of course, sir. I wouldn't miss it. Let's hope it goes as well as in the Cummings case.'

Cronshaw smiled.

'I see no reason why it shouldn't.'

CHAPTER FORTY-TWO

Bill Savage was more excited than he could remember. He was lounging in his flat in Twickenham when his clerk telephoned him to reveal that he had heard on the "grapevine" that he was certain to get silk on Maundy Thursday. His source had been a middle-ranking clerk in the Attorney-General's chambers (one of Savage's clerk's drinking companions) who claimed he had seen the list which would not be published until Thursday.

'Are you sure, Clive?' Savage asked with unbecoming modesty. 'Or is this just a wind-up?'

'Oh, no sir,' replied Clive. 'It's genuine enough. The Attorney always gets advance notice. I remember when Mr Goldstraw took silk three years ago, I had the same indication, so it's likely to be correct.'

'Did you tell Mr Goldstraw?'

'No sir, I couldn't. He was skiing somewhere in Austria and I couldn't get hold of him.'

'But what about that fellow in Piers Court, you know, the one who ordered all that champagne and then discovered he hadn't got it after all. That turned out to be anything but accurate, didn't it?'

'Nothing to do with me, sir. I don't know where that came from. And he did get it the following year. But my source is pure gold. I'd put my pension on it.'

'Well you'd better be right, Clive. I don't react well to disappointment as you know.'

His clerk sounded a little apprehensive as he replied.

'But you'll keep it to yourself, won't you, sir? Just until they publish the list in *The Times* on Thursday. If it gets out before then there'll be hell to pay.'

'I see. This is one of those secrets of yours is it, Clive?'

'Yes, sir. I can keep a secret – no problem. It's just the people I tell who let me down!'

They both laughed.

'All right. I'll keep it to myself until Thursday. Not that there's anyone I'd want to tell anyway.'

That was not strictly true and Savage had no intention of keeping to his word. Within ten minutes of putting the phone down on his clerk, he was ringing Julia Hamilton's mobile. There was no reply. *Damn*, he said to himself. *I'll have to try later*. But he could not settle. He decided to go into chambers and test the lie of the land. When he'd eventually threaded his way through the central London traffic, Clive had left and the two junior clerks were finishing off the day's business.

'You're in late, Mr Savage,' said Lulu, the junior criminal clerk. 'Worried about Thursday I suppose, sir?'

'What do you mean?' replied Savage. 'Have you heard something?'

'No, sir. We won't know anything until Thursday morning – not unless one of us gets the first edition of *The Times* on Wednesday night.'

Savage looked hard in her direction. He repeated his question.

'What do you mean?'

'You can usually get a copy of *The Times* just before midnight. I got one last year to see if Mrs Robinson was on the list. Didn't do her any good though. She didn't get it.'

'I didn't know Sheila Robinson had applied for silk?'

'No sir. She didn't want anyone to know. She's gone on the bench since, so I suppose she's out of it now.'

This information caused Savage to pause. It seemed that Clive's contact was not as infallible as he represented.

'I suppose Clive has gone home has he?'

'Yes, sir. It's his snooker night. He's got his mobile with him if you need to speak to him.'

Savage said nothing. He left the clerks' room and walked upstairs, bumping into Fiona Mason on the landing. Fiona had been one of Savage's early conquests and the two hardly acknowledged each other these days. But on this occasion, Fiona smiled.

'Only three more days, Bill?'

'To what?' he responded indifferently.

'You know. Maundy Thursday. The silks' list. Everyone thinks you're bound to get it.'

'Do they?'

'Of course they do!'

She leant towards him and whispered. 'I did hear that Clive's already ordered the champagne.'

Savage was neither fully convinced nor amused. He still had a lurking doubt whether Clive had got it right.

'Has he? Well, I hope he's going to pay for it if the Lord Chancellor doesn't agree with the rest of you.'

'Don't worry,' she replied. 'You'll get it. I must be off. My fiancé will be waiting for me. Bye.'

Fiancé? thought Savage. *I really must get in to chambers more often.*

Once in his room he telephoned Clive. The senior clerk was still on the train, heading for his stately pile in Essex.

'Yes, sir. What can I do for you?'

'It's about our little secret. Did you know that Sheila Robinson applied for silk last year?'

'Of course I did. But she'd also put in for the circuit bench – and she didn't want anyone to know.'

'Well, what did the Attorney's clerk say about her?'

'Nothing.'

'Nothing?'

'Yes, sir. She'd withdrawn her application. She had to make a decision pretty smartly. She couldn't be in for both so she plumped for the bench. Wise decision. She had no chance of silk in my opinion. She's the family judge at Luton now – God help her.'

'Yes, I know that – but how come I knew nothing about her applying for silk?'

'Confidential, sir. Not for me to discuss applications by other members of chambers.'

'I see. So your source knew she had withdrawn?'

'Oh, I very much doubt it, sir. He only gets to see the list of the successful candidates – not the no-hopers who've withdrawn.'

'Well, why was Lulu despatched to get the first edition of *The Times*?'

'She's told you that has she? I'll have to have a word with her. Look, sir, she wasn't despatched anywhere. She did that off her own bat. Judge Robinson was in the West Country with her family. I knew she'd withdrawn but no one else did. You know what it's like with the silk round – everyone gets exited. Lulu went for the early edition to see whether Judge Robinson had got it. She didn't know she had withdrawn. Only me and the head of chambers knew that.'

'But everyone knows I'm in for silk.'

'Yes, sir. But that's because you've told everyone!'

Savage paused then let out a sigh of relief.

'So you're still sure I'll be on the list?'

'Absolute certainty sir – providing you keep it to yourself. I've heard rumours of names being removed before now.'

'Really?'

'Yes, sir.' He paused for effect. 'But only because of administrative cock-ups. Oh and there was that chap from Manchester who got breathalysed the week before the list came out. That did for him for a couple of years.'

Savage sighed again.

'You will have your little joke, won't you Clive?'

'Sorry, sir.'

'Do you know any other names?'

'No sir. That would never do. I'm only told about my own members. And you're the only applicant this year, as far as I know. Your letter should be in chambers on Wednesday morning.'

'But I'll be on my way to Brussels that evening – and I want to be in Leicester on Wednesday morning to hear Cronshaw's submissions in that robbery case.'

'That's not a problem – if you give me permission to open it.'

'Oh, all right, Clive. But you are to ring me as soon as it arrives. And that's an order. And no messing about. I want a simple yes or no. None of your wind-ups. Do I make myself clear?'

'Yes, sir. I'll come in early to catch the post.'

'Good.'

'How long will you be in Brussels, sir? You'll have to get back for the ceremony. It's on the first day of next term. Then there's the fitting for the silk's outfit.'

'Can't you sort that, Clive? Ede and Ravenscroft have my measurements. I've bought enough suits from them. I really have to deal with my aunt's estate – and I won't have another chance if I'm going to be as busy as you say.'

'All right, sir. I'll have a word with Wilfred at Ede and Ravenscroft. You should only have to come in for the final fitting. Have a nice break in Belgium.'

Savage replaced the receiver, sat back in his chair and stretched out his arms. He was now fully relaxed. 'William Savage, one of Her Majesty's Counsel learned in the law,' he said to himself. He put his feet up on the desk, took his mobile phone from his breast pocket and rang Julia Hamilton. This time she answered. 'Julia,' he said, 'I've got the most wonderful news.'

CHAPTER FORTY-THREE

Wednesday, 31 March 1999

'All rise.'

Malcolm Hemming – the only male usher employed at the Crown Court in Leicester – raised his voice at precisely eleven fifteen to announce the entry of Judge Campion. The usher's eyes darted about the packed courtroom seeking out any malcontent who dared to disobey his order. He then relaxed as the judge passed him and took his seat in Court 2, the largest of the six courts in the modern red-brick building. It was a beautiful day outside, the temperature soaring to almost 20 degrees centigrade – a quite wonderful if unexpected spring morning. But inside the hushed courtroom, from which all natural light had been excluded by architectural design, there was a sombre atmosphere. Counsels' benches were filled to overflowing; several barristers with no immediate need to be elsewhere sat attentively, anxious to see and hear the arguments, which had already been weighed, discussed and, depending on one's original preconceived opinion, rejected or accepted in robing rooms all over the circuit. If there were a majority view, it was slightly in favour of the defendants – although wiser heads recognised that the presence of Harold Cronshaw, QC on the side of the angels, might well have an important bearing on the outcome.

Amongst those sitting at the back of the court – unrobed – was Bill Savage. He sat quietly, preening himself and occasionally nodding as whispered congratulations were passed to him. Clive had been right. The letter had arrived in the first post and confirmed his elevation to the rank of Queen's Counsel. Savage, of course, had seen no need to keep the news to himself.

The female clerk stood up and cleared her throat.

'Will the defendants please stand.'

Doyle and Benson rose to their feet, the burly dock officers rising with them.

'Are you Charles Anthony Benson?'

'Yes,' came the nervous reply.

'And are you Michael James Doyle?'

'Yes, ma'am,' replied Doyle confidently, looking around the room to see if Jules had attended. He could not see her anywhere in the large public area. But he was not alarmed – no doubt she was busy elsewhere, doing whatever had to be done.

As for the unfortunate Benson, he had been repeatedly drilled on the way to court by Doyle on the importance of silence at all times. The likely consequences of any breach of this ordinance were graphically explained. This was an unlooked for opportunity seized upon by Doyle, and provided courtesy of Group Eleven, the security firm charged with transporting Benson from Lincoln prison to the Crown Court at Leicester. As had occasionally happened before, the security co-ordinator had diverted the van to Welford Road to pick up prisoners from that institution, thereby destroying the carefully managed arrangements of the police to keep the two men separate and apart. This was later explained to an enraged Chief Inspector Hood as a "bit of a cock-up" caused by a shortage of security vehicles and, of course, the need to enhance the company's profits. The disinterested security men even placed the two defendants in adjacent compartments within the van, another unfortunate coincidence that Doyle regarded as an omen, anticipating, as he now did, a successful conclusion to the application before the court.

'Sit down,' said the clerk before returning to her seat and busying herself at her desk.

Lassiter and Cavan-Henry had agreed that he should begin. Although Doyle was regarded as the prime mover in the offences set out on the indictment, the Crown Prosecution Service, in its wisdom, had followed its usual unthinking practice of indicting them in alphabetical order. Markham-Moore indicated to both Harriet and Charles that he would be seeking an amendment in due course to place Doyle at the head of the charges. "They haven't been arraigned yet," he said, "and can't be until this application has been resolved. It will be put right for the trial."

"Assuming there is a trial," Harriet had commented, with a wry smile.

In any event, it was Laura Mitchell who had spotted the point while doing research for Charles, and so professional courtesy required that he should go first, and, of course, the DNA he was seeking to exclude related to his client. The pupil, resplendent in her new wig and gown, sat immediately behind him. By happy chance, the second six months of her pupillage commenced this very day. Her pupil master had given her permission to accompany Cavan-Henry rather that attend a somewhat boring fraud case he was prosecuting at Inner London.

'If it please your Honour…' began Charles, after which he introduced the other counsel in the case. Harriet thought she spotted a slight incline of the judicial head when Cronshaw's name was mentioned. Yet again, his reputation had preceded him. But Charles was in a confident mood. His letter from the Lord Chancellor's office had been opened in chambers by Geoff Allingham, on his instructions, that very morning. As the senior clerk thrust the letter opener into the envelope, he reassured the barrister over the telephone "it's a thick one, sir – not like last year." Indeed, it was as the clerk had foretold, Charles Cavan-Henry, too, was to be advanced to the rank of Queen's Counsel. The letter warned him that these tidings were to remain confidential until the list was published on Maundy Thursday – but no one ever took any notice of that. Charles had already been congratulated by everyone in the robing room, including the great man himself. Even Savage had managed to be pleasant about it, before revealing his own good news.

'Well done,' said Cronshaw, warmly. 'I am sure you will prosper – but, hopefully, only after the present case has concluded.'

Campion, too, was aware of Cavan-Henry's promotion – the rumour mill extending well inside the judicial corridor – but he thought it prudent not to make any observation in open court, and had determined to invite the new silk into his chambers to offer his congratulations at the end of the court day.

Charles went through his submissions strictly in accordance with the skeleton argument he had prepared weeks before. He emphasised the plain meaning of the words set out in the statute and the importance for the rule of law of the police being required by the court to obey, to the letter, the Act of Parliament. Campion only interrupted him once – simply to raise a possible distinction between an error by the police in failing to remove a profile from the database and a deliberate decision to act contrary to the law. Charles dealt with it – he thought – more than adequately. In the absence of any explanation as to why the DNA profile of a *volunteer* had been retained on the database, one could only draw the inference, he argued, that the police had behaved deliberately improperly. In any event, having sent out a letter stating they would not preserve such profiles, they had more than demonstrated bad faith on their part by failing to remove Benson's. The judge looked slightly sceptical but said nothing more.

Charles sat down after forty minutes, satisfied that he had put his case as well as it could be put. Then it was Harriet's turn. She began by adopting Charles' submissions in their entirety then attempted to anticipate the arguments she expected would come from Cronshaw. Unlike Charles, who had spoken in deadly earnest throughout, she tried to lighten the proceedings with just a hint of sarcasm and a touch of humour. She quoted from *Alice in Wonderland* as she insisted that the words of the statute could bear only the meaning that an objective construction gave them.

'The Crown,' she observed, 'in the style of Lewis Carroll, is seeking to argue that a word or phrase means whatever they want it to mean, so as to produce a predetermined conclusion, predetermined in the Crown's favour.' She cast a friendly eye towards Cronshaw. Then, quoting directly from Carroll's masterpiece, '*When I use a word, Humpty Dumpty said in a rather scornful tone, it means what I choose it to mean – neither more nor less*!'

A ripple of laughter ran through the court. Even Cronshaw smiled. He hoped he was not being compared to the character in question.

Harriet pressed on. 'I need hardly remind your Honour what happened to Humpty Dumpty – he suffered a great fall and all the King's horses and all the King's men couldn't put Humpty together again. (Another ripple of polite laughter.) Rather like the Crown's case – when we examine it carefully, the pieces begin to fall apart. No matter how distinguished the advocate (she nodded again towards Cronshaw), once separated out, like Humpty, the Crown's case cannot be put together again – not in a sensible fashion at any rate. It can succeed only by doing great violence to both the English language and the plain intention of Parliament.'

She then adopted a serious air and referred the judge to the *Carlisle* decision. She had acquired a transcript and annexed it to her skeleton argument. The issue, she submitted, was exactly the same.

'Mr Justice Willoughby's decision, whilst not strictly binding on your Honour, is of immense persuasive authority. He has, as you know, since been appointed to the Court of Appeal which adds further weight to his ruling. As you can see from the transcript, he excluded the DNA evidence in that case for exactly the same reason we submit your Honour should exclude the DNA evidence in this case. To admit it would negate the plain meaning of the statute and undermine the rule of law.'

Campion nodded, indicating he understood the point – but said nothing.

Harriet then emphasised the mandatory language of the provision in question. She quoted the words of the statute – '*Where samples are required to be destroyed... information derived from the sample...* ***shall*** *not be used (a) in evidence or (b) for the purposes of the investigation of an offence.*'

'The police in Birmingham', she continued, 'acted in complete defiance of that statutory requirement.'

She paused and looked at the judge. Campion's expression did not change. Neither did he comment, but made a note in his book and underlined it. She went on to submit that the obligation on the court was to ensure that a sample which fell within the statute should not be used either as an investigatory tool by the police or admitted in evidence by the court, no matter how cogent it might otherwise be, evidentially. When legal principles clashed – as here – the words of the statute, carefully selected as they must have been by Parliament, must be given their natural and literal meaning.

She continued. 'Parliament was here seeking to strike a balance between the use of DNA samples to investigate and prosecute serious crime on the one hand and the need to protect the rights and interests of members of the public on the other. It was plainly the intention of Parliament that in unusual circumstances such as we have here, the rights and interests of the citizen should prevail.'

It was approaching one o'clock when Harriet sat down. A murmur of approval passed around the room. The judge had not interrupted her at all. He looked at the clock.

'I'll hear you at five past two,' he said to Cronshaw and glanced at the usher.

Malcolm Hemming was quickly on his feet.

'The court will rise,' he announced, in a stentorian tone, almost daring anyone to contradict him. As one, counsel and the entire public gallery stood in silence. Malcolm briefly surveyed the room, then bowed to the judge.

Campion reciprocated, nodded to counsel and quickly disappeared.

'Well done,' said Cronshaw to both Harriet and Charles. 'I think I am going to have to revise some of my response. No time for lunch I'm afraid. Come Edward – we have work to do.'

★★★★

At exactly seven minutes past two, the judge resumed his seat in the still packed courtroom. The temperature had risen by several degrees since the morning session owing to the air conditioning system developing a fault. The court manager had telephoned the relevant contractor – in Brighton – who told her an engineer would be despatched the following week. Until then, nothing could be done. Cronshaw, however, was not inconvenienced in the slightest. Whilst the audience, which had gathered to hear him, fidgeted and perspired in the uncomfortable atmosphere of the courtroom, he rose silently, removed his pocket watch from his waistcoat and placed it somewhat ostentatiously onto his lectern, then standing, ramrod straight, began his submissions. He had no irritating idiosyncrasies. He did not put his hands in his pockets or play with his cufflinks; neither did he place one leg on the seat beside him or advance his arguments by extravagant movements of his arms or by pulling the lobe of his ear as Cavan-Henry was sometimes noted to do. He simply fixed the judge in his sights and deployed the advocates' most telling weapon, a perfectly controlled and mellifluous speaking voice.

'In the early hours of 17 December last,' he began, 'three ordinary, hard-working security men, delivering nearly two million pounds in cash to the Charnwood Centre, thirteen miles north of this court building, were set upon and robbed by a group of criminals, at least one of whom was armed with a shortened shotgun. One of those security men, showing immense courage and presence of mind, sought to prevent the theft by attacking one of the robbers. For his pains, he was shot – at close range – and injured. Although the cartridge was loaded with rock salt rather than the traditional pellets, he was wounded and suffered a heart attack. He very nearly died. The robber he punched was Charles Benson – of this there is not even a scintilla of doubt. That punch, so carefully and effectively delivered, caused Benson to bleed. Some of that blood was deposited on the uniform of the guard, Mr Patel. A full DNA profile was obtained from that blood. It is not disputed – nor could it be – that the blood in question came from Benson. It necessarily follows that Benson was one of the robbers.'

He paused and turned towards the dock. Benson, at least, had the grace to bow his head. Doyle merely smiled. He had been very impressed with Lassiter's performance and could not conceive that any contrary argument could be seen to have any merit.

'We are met here today,' Cronshaw continued, 'to counter the wholly absurd proposition that Parliament in legislating the amendments to the Police and Criminal Evidence Act 1984 introduced by the Criminal Justice and Public Order Act 1994, intended that such cogent and irrefutable evidence should not be put before a jury. Why? Because, it is submitted by my learned friends, that would amount to an interference with the human rights of Mr Benson. He, who by his criminal actions puts at nothing the very lives of others, asserts it would be unfair and contrary to law for such evidence, whatever its cogency, to be used to convict him of an offence of which he is manifestly guilty. I believe that is the crux of the argument advanced by my learned friends.'

Cronshaw smiled benignly in the direction of Harriet Lassiter and Charles Cavan-Henry.

'No one', he went on, 'surpasses me in the respect owed to the workings of Parliament, although my researches do show that the House of Commons was barely quorate when this piece of proposed legislation was discussed in so far it was discussed at all. Neither did any of the honourable members present foresee the use to which, once enacted, it might be put.'

Again he paused. The judge almost smiled. It was well understood in judicial circles that MPs were less than diligent when considering complex legislative proposals concerning "black letter" law.

'It is the simple and straightforward submission of the Crown that Parliament intended no such thing. We concede that the police in Birmingham should not have kept Benson's DNA profile on the database. When their inquiry came to an end it should have been removed and destroyed. That is what the statute plainly demands.'

'That much is accepted by the Crown is it, Mr Cronshaw?' asked the judge.

'Indeed it is. We also concede that had it not been for that error – so clearly identified by your Honour during argument this morning as precisely that – and nothing more than that – the identification of Mr Benson, as one of the robbers, would in all probability never have been achieved. Without his identification, the link to Doyle would also not have been possible.'

Both Benson and Doyle nodded vigorously from the dock. Trevor Parker turned and smiled towards his client.

'But none of that had anything to do with the police officers investigating this robbery and attempted murder. There is not and cannot be any complaint as to the manner in which the senior investigating officer and his colleagues went about their task investigating this case.'

Knight gently nudged Hood and smiled.

'And in any event, that is not to the point. In the absence of bad faith – which cannot here be demonstrated, either on the part of the investigating police officers or indeed, the other constabulary – the history of the securing of this material does not *necessarily* lead to the court ruling out its reception in evidence. Please note I use the word *necessarily* advisedly. We concede there will be some case where such evidence might well be excluded.'

He paused for effect.

'This case is not one of them!'

Cronshaw then directed the judge to the fine detail of his skeleton argument; he rehearsed for several minutes the alleged distinction between mandatory and directory requirements; he pointed to a decision of the House of Lords, which rendered such distinctions – in certain circumstances – both archaic and valueless. It was, he submitted, a pointless exercise trying to fit a particular requirement into one category or the other. It was more important to focus on the consequences of non-compliance. He argued, forcefully, that a distinction had to be drawn between the actions of the police in Birmingham which enabled the DNA profile to remain in existence and the present duty of the court to deal with the position notwithstanding those breaches of the law. He also warned of the probable consequences for the investigation of serious crime if the defence submissions found favour. Campion listened without interruption until Cronshaw referred to the *Carlisle* decision, as it had generally become known. Campion then interrupted.

'Surely, Mr Cronshaw, the point has already been decided by Lord Justice Willoughby. I must, must I not, pay great heed to his ruling on the matter? The principle enshrined in that ruling has never been questioned in the Court of Appeal.'

A low murmur went round the courtroom. That seemed to represent the view of the majority present. Cronshaw was not deterred. He had already decided not to mention in open court that the reason why it had not been questioned was because the CPS had failed to put in the notice of appeal in time. He went straight to the heart of the argument.

'Your Honour should ignore that decision entirely,' he submitted with an air of supreme confidence. 'First, because it is not binding on you and secondly, and much more importantly, because it is manifestly wrong!'

The murmuring in the courtroom grew louder. The usher felt compelled to call for silence.

Cronshaw then explained why it was wrong. 'Not only had the point not been properly argued, the consequences of that decision clearly demonstrated that the resulting exclusion of the evidence could never have been what Parliament intended. The victim of that terrible rape was left in the wholly unacceptable position of knowing that the identity of the man who had ravished her had been established – beyond scientific argument – but, she must also have been informed, that there was no prospect of his being punished by the court because the evidence that proved his guilt was not admissible.'

He paused. 'Did Parliament intend that *her* human rights should be so lightly cast to one side? What of *her* right to have *her* private life respected? Surely, the right not to be raped in her own home stood somewhat higher in the hierarchy of entitlements than the assumed rights of her attacker's interest in his own DNA profile?'

'Not according to Lord Justice Willoughby,' countered the judge, showing only a slight degree of irritability.

Cronshaw smiled and lowered the level of his rhetoric.

'A simple failure', he continued in almost a whisper, 'of the advocates in that case to refer His Lordship to the relevant test of admissibility.'

'Go on,' responded the judge, taking up his pencil with renewed interest.

'Your Honour will have noted that the amended legislation does not deal specifically with the legal consequences of non-compliance?'

'No,' replied Campion shortly, 'it simply forbids, in arguably clear terms, that such evidence should be used at all.'

Both Lassiter and Cavan-Henry nodded in unison. Doyle glanced at Benson and gave a thumbs-up sign. But Cronshaw was not in the least put out. He was experienced enough to know that the abler judges frequently raised such propositions so they were better able to appreciate the contrary argument. Campion plainly fell into that category. The judge continued.

'Given the exclusion of the DNA evidence by the judge in Carlisle because of the breach of the statute by the police, there would be no legal proof that the defendant was the attacker. Are you not assuming that which you would have to prove by using evidence that is admissible in law? Material that is not admissible in law is not evidence.'

Again, Lassiter and Cavan-Henry nodded. Cronshaw shook his head.

'But that, with respect, your Honour, is beside the point. It is not the function of the court to monitor the working practices of the police but to rule on the admissibility of evidence. The statute does not state that a breach of what is argued by the defence to be the mandatory duty to destroy the sample in the circumstances of this case *necessarily* leads to the evidence being automatically excluded. It is no coincidence that these requirements, introduced by the 1994 statute, were incorporated into the Police and Criminal Evidence Act, which already prescribes the universal test of admissibility in criminal cases.'

'You mean section 78?'

'Precisely! Neither should it be overlooked that section 78 itself sets out, we submit by special design, a test of admissibility which includes the manner in which the evidence was obtained, so that the trial judge has an absolute discretion whether such evidence should be admitted. In which case, there is no need to interpret these requirements in the absurd way suggested by the defence. In some cases, the manner in which a DNA profile is obtained or preserved by the police may cause the judge to exclude it. In another case – and we argue – in this case – because there is neither bad faith nor any questions as to the reliability of the evidence – that discretion should lead to the evidence being admitted.'

'I see,' said Campion, nodding his head and sucking on the end of his pencil. 'So you say that section 78 can be used to decide this issue in all cases?'

Cronshaw smiled approvingly.

'Your Honour has the point. It is no coincidence that the legislature incorporated these requirements into that very Act of Parliament.'

'So what was the purpose of the requirements introduced by the amendments to the statute?'

'Exactly,' whispered Cavan-Henry to Lassiter. Cronshaw simply smiled.

'If one reads section 64(3)(B) together with section 78, the provisions are perfectly workable. The police know how they should proceed in such circumstances. If they fail to do so – in other words they do not comply with the requirements of the statute – the court has an absolute discretion to decide whether such evidence as they may have obtained should be admitted. Each case must turn on its own facts.'

The judge mused on the submission but made a careful and extensive note.

'This has the advantage', Cronshaw added when the judicial pencil was still, 'of avoiding the wholly absurd consequences of the construction contended for by the defence, and places the responsibility for deciding the issue in the individual case in the hands of a trained, professional and independent judge.'

He paused and took a sip of water from the glass to his side. He then looked at the judge with a knowing smile.

'After all, your Honour, a criminal trial is not a game. The object of a criminal trial is to acquit the innocent and to convict the guilty. If the submissions of my learned friends become the common currency of construction of this statute, we may as well remove our wigs and gowns and put them aside for there will be no justice for the ordinary, honest citizen – who unlike Charles Anthony Benson – does not plot and scheme to rob and injure but puts his faith in the rationality and fairness of the law. For let me make it completely clear, if this evidence is not admitted, the prosecution will not continue with the case against either of these defendants.'

Cronshaw sat down to absolute silence. You could have heard a pin hit the floor.

'Thank you, Mr Cronshaw,' said the judge, eventually. 'You have given me a great deal to think about.'

He looked towards defence counsel.

'Do either of you wish to respond to Mr Cronshaw?'

Cavan-Henry declined and Lassiter, briefly, sought to counter the Crown's submissions by emphasising again the precise wording of the statute and the correctness of the *Carlisle* decision.

'We are confident,' she said in conclusion, 'that your Honour will not be influenced by the Crown's attempt to persuade you to accept its construction of the statute by publicly announcing that the case will be abandoned if the DNA evidence is excluded. That the Crown states as much merely serves to underline the absence of any other probative evidence and the plain breach of the statutory requirements by the police.'

She then sat down and the judge slowly flicked through the pages of his notebook, adding to the tension in the room. He then addressed all counsel.

'As I indicated at the Directions Hearing, I do not intend to give my ruling today, anxious as I know, the defendants in particular, will be to receive it. I shall give my ruling on Wednesday morning at eleven o'clock. There is no need for leading counsel to attend if they have other commitments – in which category I understand I must shortly include you, Mr Cavan-Henry?'

The judge had changed his mind. He saw no need as the clock approached half past three to pretend that the news of Cavan-Henry's promotion had not reached his ears.

'So it is rumoured,' replied Charles, bowing to the judge. 'I don't think I am able to comment until tomorrow!'

'I shall not press you then. Next Wednesday it is.'

Savage, who was checking his watch, was mildly put out that he was not included in the judge's compliments – he assumed because he was not robed or because his advancement had not reached the judge's ears. In any event he had to dash – he was due to pick up Julia Hamilton in the next ten minutes and drive to London. He then had to get the two of them to Waterloo Station to catch the Eurostar train to Brussels. He anticipated traffic problems on the M1. Malcolm Hemming was quickly on his feet.

'The court will rise.'

The court did as he demanded and the judge departed.

The noise that broke out immediately the judicial door had closed was considerable. Hood and Knight moved smartly forward and congratulated Cronshaw on his efforts. Andrea Fleming, who had been keeping a careful note, added her praise.

'We're not out of the woods, yet,' said Cronshaw, modestly, 'but I'm fairly confident the judge will see it our way. Mind you, he doesn't give anything away does he?'

'Nothing at all,' agreed Markham-Moore. 'He played a very straight bat. It's impossible to say what he was really thinking.'

Doyle looked towards Lassiter as he was taken from the dock and raised his hand. He seemed reasonably satisfied. Benson simply looked embarrassed. If guilt were decided solely on appearances, he would already have been convicted and sentenced.

'What do you reckon?' asked Cavan-Henry, whose confidence had been somewhat dented by Cronshaw's performance.

'We're still in with a shout,' replied Harriet. 'I really don't think the judge knows what he's going to do – yet.'

'I agree,' said Cronshaw, gathering up his papers and folding his lectern. 'It could go either way – although I'm sure we would win in the Court of Appeal!'

He smiled as did Lassiter.

'My client will be content with a victory here,' said Harriet. 'The opinion of the Court of Appeal would be of no interest to him.'

'And would have no effect on him either,' added Cronshaw. 'If we lose, he and Benson will walk. But on this occasion, there would be no question of the notice of appeal not being filed in time. I have already drafted the bare bones of it. Just in case.'

'So you don't think it's a foregone conclusion?'

'Not at all. It will take a courageous judge to go against Willoughby's ruling – although I have high hopes of Campion. I assume he's going to the Old Bailey because he's prepared to take an independent line? He's no slouch, intellectually.'

Lassiter nodded in agreement.

'Will you be returning next week – to hear the judge's ruling?'

'Most certainly,' replied Cronshaw. 'I wouldn't miss it for the world!'

'We'd better go and see Doyle,' interrupted Trevor Parker who was looking particularly pleased. 'He seems happy enough with our performance. I was keeping an eye on him most of the time.'

'All right. Are you coming Charles?'

'I suppose I must,' said Cavan-Henry, but without much enthusiasm. 'My chap seems anything but happy – but I shall have to go and hold his hand and reassure him.'

Harriet collected Randell Richards, who was enjoying his moment in the limelight, discussing the defence tactics with several members of the Bar who no longer treated him like yesterday's man.

'So you found the Willoughby ruling did you, Randell?' said one of them.

'Yes,' replied Richards. 'An old friend of mine was defence counsel. We old timers still know a thing or two.'

He and Harriet walked towards the entrance to the cell block. Cronshaw and his junior made their way to the robing room.

'It is pleasing, is it not,' said Cronshaw, 'that we still live in a country where these serious issues can be fully debated by experienced counsel and placed before an independent judge who, we all know, will give his ruling unaffected by anything other than his desire to do justice in accordance with the law.'

'Indeed,' replied his junior. 'Not that we are really appreciated, certainly not by the tabloid press. I suppose if any government wanted to undermine the rights of its citizens, the first thing it would have to do would be to destroy the independent criminal Bar, then slowly but surely, nibble away at the independence of the judiciary.'

'Not in our lifetime, though,' replied Cronshaw.

'I suppose not.'

CHAPTER FORTY-FOUR

The journey to Waterloo had been smoother than Savage had anticipated. He and Julia Hamilton had arrived in good time; soon enough for him to begin celebrating his elevation by ordering champagne cocktails in the first-class lounge. Julia (as Savage always called her) appeared more than happy to encourage him to buy a second round before they made their way to the departure gate. Then it was announced there would be a delay and further drinks were ordered and consumed at a small bar nearby. When the train eventually pulled out of the station, Savage was already intoxicated. Julia seemed unaffected, largely because she skilfully ensured that Savage drank most of the alcohol provided – including the champagne he ordered on the train. Just as she had hoped, he was already showing signs of weariness and light-headedness as they arrived in Brussels. Having located their luggage, the porter carried it to a waiting taxi that took them to the luxury hotel in Avenue Louise at which Savage had made a last-minute reservation.

'You're certainly pushing the boat out,' she commented as they walked into the reception area of the Steingenberger Grandhotel.

'It's not every day one becomes one of Her Majesty's counsel learned in the law,' responded Savage, pompously, placing one hand on his forehead before adding, 'Do you have any paracetamol with you?'

'I'm afraid I don't, no. All you need is a bit of a lie down. You'll be fine in the morning.'

The hotel porter showed them into a quite splendid suite on the seventh floor after struggling with their combined luggage. Savage stuffed a few coins into his hands and declined any further assistance. He then collapsed on one of the two king-sized beds.

'I'll unpack for you,' said Jules, sweetly. 'You have a sleep.'

'You don't mind?' asked Savage. 'I am very tired. Must be the champagne – and it's been a very long term.'

'Not at all. We have five whole days to enjoy ourselves. The flight back isn't until Tuesday afternoon, remember?'

Savage looked at his watch. He was trying hard not to think of the flight back.

'That's right,' he said, recalling his fear of flying. But he had to get back quickly in order to witness Judge Campion's ruling on the seventh, and there was his celebration party to organise and his fitting at Ede and Ravenscroft. It suddenly crossed his mind that his absence from London at this important moment in his career was quite extraordinary. He imagined the letters of congratulation piling up in chambers and the telephone calls he would not be able to answer. What on earth was he doing in Brussels? Then he recalled why he was where he was. He raised himself up, leaning on his arm, and gazed at Julia. She looked simply stunning! London could wait. Then he added, 'But we have to see the lawyer tomorrow. The whole of Brussels will shut down over Easter and I *so* want to show you my aunt's apartment. I haven't been there for a few years but it's quite remarkable.'

He yawned.

'How did your aunt come to be living in Brussels?'

'It's a long story. I'll tell you all about it tomorrow.'

He removed his jacket and loosened his tie.

'You need a good night's sleep,' said Jules sympathetically. 'You get undressed. I'll deal with everything else.'

Savage was in no condition to argue. He yawned again. Jules went into the bathroom. When she returned, he was already dressed in his vivid scarlet pyjamas and seemed fast asleep. She smiled, knowingly, then slowly and methodically unpacked two of their suitcases. A third case remained untouched until she pushed it with some difficulty under her bed, away from prying eyes. She then undressed and climbed into the other bed. She took a final look at the now snoring Savage and switched off the bedside light. All was going to plan.

★★★★

Savage slept later than he had planned. Jules was already at the breakfast table in a private corner of the dining room when he came down.

'Feeling better?' she asked, pouring him a coffee.

'Much better, thank you,' he replied. 'Sorry I wasn't much fun last night. I shall have to watch the alcohol intake from now on.'

'No matter. You're here to enjoy your success. There's no rush. In fact, I thought it really good of you to book a suite with separate beds. We don't want a repeat of that disaster in Brighton, now do we?'

Jules was putting down an early marker. She had no intention of sleeping with Savage, certainly not at present. He, poor man, had absolutely no recollection of the "disaster in Brighton" other than that Jules had refused to speak to him for several weeks afterwards and had declined any further invitations. His consumption of alcohol had been such that he genuinely had no memory of his allegedly brutish behaviour towards her. She smiled sweetly. He was about to say something but thought better of it. If she thought that he was being discreet and magnanimous he saw no need to inform her there were no other suites available at the time he had made the reservation. Indeed, he felt strangely content that Jules appeared to believe he was capable of thinking such unselfish thoughts. Perhaps behaving like a gentleman had its advantages, after all?

'Yes,' he replied eventually, trying his best to sound caring and submissive. 'I really wanted to make it up to you. I didn't want you thinking I was only interested in your body, beautiful though it is.'

He smiled. She looked down. Was she really having such an effect on him? She caught his eye and tried to appear supportive. She gave him that look of hers and could see he was well and truly smitten. She poured herself some more coffee.

'Well. What have we got lined up for today?'

'We're seeing my aunt's lawyer at twelve, then I thought we could visit the apartment. It's quite a few minutes away, so I suggest we get a taxi. He'll probably come with us.'

'What are you going to do with it? I don't suppose you'll live in it yourself? Not now you're a QC.'

She smiled and placed her hand on his.

'Good God no. I propose to sell it. But the market may not be right at present. They're introducing the euro here you know and it's not a particularly good time to sell.'

'Do you know how much it's worth?'

'No idea! The lawyer says it's in the millions, so let's hope he's right.'

'Forgive my asking, but did she leave you anything else?'

Jules was finding Savage increasingly attractive. He seemed far less brash than she remembered him from Brighton and his newly acquired wealth and status added to his appeal.

'Everything in the apartment, I believe – and a couple of hundred thousand pounds – although she lived here she still had an account with Coutts in the Strand. She liked to keep a connection with the UK and she had a rather nice house in Bournemouth – not that she'd lived in it for some time. She was married to a Frenchman, you know. He got some amazingly important job in the EU – hence the apartment here. He died quite a few years ago, so Aunt Kitty was well set up. It's a real gravy train getting one of the top jobs in Europe.'

'How old was she when she died?'

'Eighty-two, I believe. I think she lived fairly high on the hog until a few years ago. Then she became something of a recluse. Hardly went out, but she did come over to the UK when my mother died three years ago. That was the last time I saw her. I was really worried she might have left everything to a donkey sanctuary or something.'

'Did she like animals?'

'Hated them. But she could be a spiteful old so-and-so when she wanted to be.'

'Well she's done you proud, or so it would seem.'

'Yes. There's no denying that.'

He leant forward.

'She collected pictures, you know. Mainly young artists still making their way – but some of them might be worth something.'

Jules was now quite fascinated with the details of his great aunt and her burgeoning estate.

'Are you the sole beneficiary then?'

'Not quite. She's left her house in Bournemouth to my sister. That's worth a pretty penny. Our parents are both dead and there are no other relatives.'

'So you have a sister, have you? What does she do?'

'She qualified as a solicitor, but she doesn't practise – not since she got married. She has three children. Married to a surgeon. What about you? Do you have any family?'

Jules hesitated before she replied. She rarely spoke of her family and when she did, she hardly ever told the whole truth.

'My father's dead and my mother remarried. I don't get on with my stepfather, but I still see my mother from time to time. She spends a lot of time abroad. She has a villa in Portugal. I don't have any brothers or sisters – a couple of uncles on my father's side but I never see them.'

Savage broke a croissant in half and spooned some strawberry jam from the container in front of him. Jules took a sip of her coffee.

'Great coffee, don't you think?'

'I should think it is,' replied Savage. 'At these prices!'

'Oh, don't spoil it,' said Jules disapprovingly. 'Not when you've come into all this additional wealth – and been made a QC at the same time. You'll be set up for life.'

Savage nodded enthusiastically.

'I can't pretend it's not happened at the right time. It can be quite expensive taking silk. It means starting all over again, you know.'

'You'll be fine – what does your clerk think?'

'Who, Clive? He's a born optimist. He says I'll make a fortune – which means so will he. He's on 12 per cent, you know. Time will tell. But the solicitors who send me work as a junior may take some persuading to brief me as a silk. Take your ex's case as an example. Why on earth did Trevor Parker instruct old Randell Richards? He could have had me for the same money. I'd have given anything to get a brief in that case.'

The smile vanished from Jules' face.

'I'd rather not discuss that, if you don't mind.'

That was the reverse of the truth. She was desperate to find out from Savage what had happened in court the day before but she had to do so whilst giving a quite uninterested impression.

'Sorry,' he said. 'I'd forgotten for a moment – you have an interest in the case, don't you?'

'Not any more,' she insisted, 'although I would have quite liked to have heard Cronshaw arguing the point. He's supposed to be quite brilliant, isn't he?'

'Absolutely. If I were ever half as good as he, I'd be well satisfied. I must confess, I thought it was going in favour of the defence – until he got on his hind legs. He really gave Campion something to think about.'

'So you think the judge will rule in favour of the prosecution?'

'Hard to say which way he'll go. But I did hear in the robing room that the smart money is now on the Crown. Most people reckon that the judge will let in the DNA evidence – which is quite a turnaround, I can tell you.'

'What was Harriet Lassiter like?'

'Bloody good. I doubt if it could have been argued better – but the thing is – and most people tend to forget this – the merits are obviously on the side of the Crown. And that means something with Campion. He doesn't like guilty people getting off!'

Jules' thoughts exactly. Had she not said the same thing to Trevor Parker?

'Well,' she replied, 'as I said, it's all in the past now. Whatever Campion rules, it's no longer of any consequence as far as I'm concerned. Michael Doyle is history.'

She sounded as if she meant it as she placed her cup sharply in the saucer. Savage was delighted. He selected another croissant and called the waiter over for some fresh coffee. Things were looking up!

★★★★

'It was quite wonderful,' said Jules as she and Savage relaxed in the lounge of their hotel enjoying afternoon tea. 'It must be worth a fortune.'

Savage was full of himself. 'You know, I had no idea the old girl had refurbished the place. It's quite fantastic. I might even keep it. It'll make a perfect bolt-hole.'

Jules looked at him quizzically.

'Do you need a bolt-hole? I thought you'd turned over a new leaf?'

'Well, you never know, do you?'

He laughed.

'And what about that painting in the sitting room? Do you think it's genuine?' Jules was now gazing at him intently. He pretended he hadn't noticed.

'If it is – it'll be worth more than the apartment,' replied Savage, his eyes flashing. 'Have you heard of Pieter de Hooch? I haven't, but I've never been into art – until now.'

'Me neither, but it could be worth quite a bit. Had you never noticed it before?'

Jules could feel herself warming even more towards Savage. There might well be a number of advantages being in a relationship with a wealthy man, especially if his riches were totally legitimate.

'Never seen it before. I'll have to get it cleaned and checked out by an expert. If it is the genuine article, there'll be increased death duties to pay no doubt. But there should still be a considerable amount left over.'

Savage could not conceal his excitement. Jules frowned.

'I didn't particularly like it – not as a picture. I don't think I'd give it house room. And the lawyer did say it could be by a follower or a copy even – not by de Hooch himself.'

'That's the likeliest explanation, I suppose. I think it would look quite good in my London flat – but I'd sell it if it's worth anything. I might be able to pay my mortgage off entirely and have enough left over to buy a villa in Italy. Now that really would be something!'

Jules paused. A villa in Italy would have been quite delightful.

'Won't your sister want a cut? If you'd never seen it before, perhaps your aunt had kept it previously in her house in England at some time?'

Savage shook his head and spoke with real determination.

'Don't introduce complications! The will is explicit. We each get her respective residences with the contents *at the time of death*. And the rest of her estate is split equally between us. You can't be clearer that that.'

Jules smiled; here was a man like herself who put his own interests before anything or anyone else. If only she were not pregnant. Then, suddenly, she felt the child move inside her. She thought again of Doyle languishing in his prison cell. And although she was an essentially amoral person, she knew she could never have a termination. Somehow, it just didn't seem right. She put her hand to her abdomen, realising she must be beginning to show her condition, despite the loose fitting dress she was wearing. Not that Savage would have noticed. He was completely absorbed in the detail of his newly acquired riches.

'You'll have to excuse me,' she said. 'I'm feeling a little bloated. I think I over indulged at lunchtime. Do you mind if I have a lie down? Just for an hour or so?'

She stood up. Savage, ever the gentleman, at least superficially, did likewise.

'Not at all. I need to speak to the lawyer again, anyway. He said he'd come here at five, so it's quite convenient as it turns out. You go and have a rest. I can deal with business here.'

Jules kissed him on the cheek. 'Thank you. I'll make it up to you. I promise.'

He waited until she had walked a few yards from the table before resuming his seat and busying himself with the papers from the briefcase at his side. He took a calculator from his inside pocket and was quickly absorbed in revising the extent of his inheritance. He didn't notice Jules smile as she approached a middle-aged man sitting reading a newspaper near the hotel reception desk. He folded the newspaper and followed her towards the lift.

'Hello Max,' she whispered. 'Fancy seeing you here. I have something for you. It's in my room on the seventh floor.'

CHAPTER FORTY-FIVE

'Why are we going this way, Trevor?'

'I have to take a quick look at a property along here for a client; it won't take long. I should have checked it two days ago. But you were insistent we got to your brother's in Norfolk as soon as possible.'

'I should think I was. We were a day late anyway and you know the trouble his wife goes to. She wasn't very pleased we didn't get there until Saturday – and why did we have to come back today? Couldn't we have waited until tomorrow?'

'You know I couldn't. I've got this important hearing on Wednesday – and I've got some work to do before then – assuming you want me to retire by July?'

'You know I do. You should have retired two years ago. When you were sixty.'

Parker slowed down as he approached the long drive that led to Orley Farm. The darkness had closed in, making it difficult to see the turn, hidden as it was by several huge poplar trees and an overgrown hawthorn hedge. He was about to indicate when a black Range Rover pulled out of the drive in front of him, causing him to brake hard. Its windows were tinted and it picked up speed rapidly as it emerged onto the main road and accelerated out of sight in the direction of Nottingham. Parker was unable to note its registration or make out the number of people inside as its tail lights disappeared into the distance.

'I wonder who that could be?' he said. 'At this time of night as well.'

'It's only nine o'clock,' his wife replied. 'We should be home in under an hour – if you get on with it!'

Parker turned slowly into the drive putting his headlights on full beam. He was feeling slightly apprehensive as he inched cautiously along the rutted surface towards the main house.

'Could have been thieves, I suppose. Not that there's anything worth stealing here, apart from the lead on the roof – and most of that's already gone.'

As he reached the yard by the side of the house, he drew his car to a halt. There was no sign of life. The place seemed to be deserted. A solitary owl hooted in the near distance.

'Pass me the torch from the glove compartment, will you love?'

Mrs Parker did as she was asked.

'You're not going to wander around here in the dark are you, Trevor? There's no knowing who might be out there.'

'Just a quick look. I want to check that nothing's amiss, that's all.'

Parker shone his torch on to the side of the house as he got out of his car, closing the door as silently as he could. He walked to the front of the dilapidated building and tried the front door. It was locked. He shone his torch at each of the windows, all of which seemed secure behind the wooden boarding he had arranged to be fitted months before. He then walked quickly to the outbuilding which adjoined one side of the main house. All seemed well. Nothing appeared out of place. He stood at the top of the cellar steps, pointing his torch towards the cellar door. Something caught his eye. It was a large brass padlock.

That wasn't there last time I was here, he said to himself. *Not that I've been here for some months.*

He started to descend the steps one by one until he disappeared from his wife's view. She raised herself in her seat, staring anxiously after him. 'Be careful, Trevor,' she called but he did not hear her.

He reached the cellar door and pushed against it. It did not move. 'Strange,' he whispered. It was not like this on his previous inspection. He shone the torch towards the window next to the door. The large window had been blacked out. It looked like paint had been applied directly to the glass and wooden battens placed across the outside of the window making it impossible for him to see inside. He took hold of the brass padlock and examined it. It appeared to be brand new. He then noticed that a clasp had been drilled into the solid oak door and a brass fitting applied to the architrave to which the padlock had been secured. He pushed hard against the door again, this time using his full strength. There was still no movement. Shining his torch on to the concrete slab immediately below him he spied traces of sawdust – with flecks of black paint – debris, he assumed, from the fixing of the clasp. He scratched his head. He had not authorised any work to be done. Then he remembered that Doyle had gone over his head and instructed his accountants to issue a notice to quit to Julia Hamilton. He must have instructed them to get the place made more secure too, such was his fear that Julia Hamilton might move in. Still, it was very odd that a Range Rover should have been exiting the drive at this time of night. Very odd indeed.

He made his way up a few steps then shone his torch through the small transom window above the door. Although paint had been applied to this window too, there was a tiny section that had escaped the obviously rushed brushwork. By leaning over and placing his free hand against the wall until he almost overbalanced, he was just able to see to the far side of the dank cellar. He noticed that a mattress had been slung on the floor against the back wall and a neatly folded blanket had been placed on top of it. There was a grey coloured bucket nearby. These items had definitely not been there on his last visit. The cellar had been cleared completely prior to the farm being placed on the market the previous year. Someone had obviously been in there. Julia Hamilton? Surely not. If she intended to take possession, she would hardly have set herself up in the cellar; she'd have moved into the house. Anyway, she was in Belgium. She could not have been in the black Range Rover. Parker climbed the steps and walked slowly towards the two large barns on the other side of the yard. The Dutch barn was completely empty, apart from a piece of rusting farm equipment, which he remembered from a previous visit. The smaller barn was closed but the double doors opened easily as he pushed against them. He shone his torch on to the rafters then along the dirt floor. A pair of pigeons flapped as the light from the torch illuminated them. Nothing was out of the ordinary. Parker closed the barn doors and headed back to his car.

'Everything OK?' asked his wife, anxiously, as he made himself comfortable in the driver's seat.

'Nothing to worry about,' he replied. 'Everything seems secure. In fact, it's more secure than I thought. The cellar seems to have been fortified. There's a padlock on the door and someone's put a mattress and a blanket in there. I can't think why? Anyway, we can get off home now.'

Mrs Parker seemed unimpressed.

'I don't know why we had to come here in the first place,' she said pulling her coat more tightly about her and displaying a degree of irritability.

'Acting on instructions,' replied Parker, defensively. 'Michael Doyle was anxious about security. Though why he should be, I simply don't know. The planning permission has come through so it's no longer his problem.'

He turned the ignition key and started the engine before reversing the car.

'The sooner you part company with that man the better. He's nothing but trouble. What is this place anyway? Looks pretty much abandoned to me.'

'It's an old farm he's sold to developers. Nothing to concern yourself about.'

Parker steered his vehicle on to the drive.

'What's it called?'

'What do you mean?'

'Well, I assume it had a name – when it was a farm?'

'I see what you mean, yes. Orley Farm. It was known as Orley Farm. I think they're going to keep the name for the new development.'

'Oh, like the novel?'

'The novel? What novel?'

'Anthony Trollope's *Orley Farm*. Mr Brandon – you know, the tutor at my evening classes – he says it was his best novel; Trollope thought it was anyway.'

'Did he? Well, we live and learn. But I suspect this farm was named after the village down the road.'

Parker sounded quite uninterested in his wife's literary pretensions. He turned out of the drive on to the road and accelerated. Mrs Parker settled down in her seat and closed her eyes.

'Wake me up if I nod off, won't you?'

'Yes, dear.'

CHAPTER FORTY-SIX

Judge Thomas Campion had been the victim of crime on only one occasion. When he was still practising as a barrister, his car was stolen from a car park in Lincoln whilst he was in the middle of a fraud trial. It had proved extremely inconvenient. He had, of course, reported the theft to an uninterested police officer at the nearest police station but he never saw his vehicle again.

'BMW was it?' yawned the officer. 'We'll probably find it burned out somewhere. Taken by joy riders I shouldn't wonder. You'll probably hear about it before we do.'

Campion had completed the requisite form and been given a crime number so he could make a claim on his insurance company. But he never heard from the police again. A single telephone call he made several weeks later resulted in his being told that no one at the police station knew anything about the incident. He didn't bother ringing again. He appreciated, of course, that the police had more important matters to deal with but their apparent lack of interest in his minor problem had remained with him. He was always alert to what he regarded as police laziness and insufficient care or concern for victims of crime. When he became a judge he quickly developed what he considered to be appropriate empathy with those who suffered at the hands of criminals. He had, he thought, sufficient imagination to appreciate how it must feel to wake in the middle of the night and discover a burglar in your bedroom or to understand the trauma caused by being assaulted in the street, although he had never experienced such circumstances himself and hoped and believed he never would. His sentencing policy as a judge was to put the interests of the victim before those of the criminal and he resented the fact that few if any defendants served the full sentences that he imposed. Politicians were quick to criticise if a sentence seemed to be unduly lenient but slow to recognise how the statutory provisions, enacted by them, enabled even serious criminals to be released well before their sentences had been fully served. Saving public money always came before everything else, and running prisons was expensive.

It was this philosophy that caused him to examine carefully the arguments put forward by Harold Cronshaw, QC on behalf of the Crown. He realised, of course, that Charles Benson was undoubtedly part of the team of robbers. It had never been suggested on his behalf that the DNA evidence was unreliable and he never liked guilty men getting away with their crimes. But could he really depart from the judgement of Lord Justice Willoughby in the *Carlisle* case? Could he admit evidence that seemed to have been obtained in plain breach of the rules laid down by Parliament? True, the decision did not bind him but if he were to distinguish it, his reasoning would have to be demonstrably transparent, logical and, above all, right. And he had to find a way round what appeared to be the clear words of the section. Cronshaw's arguments seemed soundly based but he still had a problem with the wording of the statute. But he was satisfied that the police in Birmingham had not acted in a calculated manner, deliberately ignoring the statute. They had simply made a mistake; there were two Bensons who had given a sample in the exclusion exercise. They had removed the one and left the other; exactly the sort of administrative error anyone could make.

He had spent more time than he should considering the matter and drafting and then re-drafting parts of his ruling, much to the annoyance of his wife, who had quite different plans for the holiday weekend.

'It's supposed to be a bank holiday,' she had chided. He acknowledged the essential truth of what she was saying, switched off his computer and drove her and his son to his sister-in-law's home in deepest Northamptonshire. While the two sisters chatted and Christopher played with his five-year-old cousin, he continued to turn the matter over in his mind while half listening to his brother-in-law's analysis of the latest performance by Northampton Saints rugby team. When they eventually returned home at nine o'clock in the evening, he went straight back to his computer and continued his analysis of the issues raised in the case. By the time he was too tired to continue, he had virtually drafted two versions of his ruling, coming to opposite conclusions, in the respective judgments. It was past midnight when he turned on the burglar alarm, locked the front door and climbed the stairs to go to bed.

'What time is it?'

Celia Campion turned on her side as her husband slid into bed next to her.

'It's just gone midnight,' he whispered. 'Sorry to have disturbed you.'

He noticed his wife had not drawn the curtains, but it was a dark night and the morning light would ensure he awakened early. He was able to manage with the minimum of sleep.

'That's all right. But what are you doing coming to bed at this time?'

'I'm sorry, darling. I've been working on the ruling I have to give on Wednesday.'

'Is that all? I thought you said it was pretty straightforward?'

'Well, it turns out it isn't. Not when everything is considered. If I'm not going to follow the previous decision of Francis Willoughby, I shall have to explain why – and in detail. It's bound to go to the Court of Appeal, whatever I decide.'

'I see. So you're thinking of letting it in, are you? The DNA evidence?'

'I'm veering in that direction, although I haven't finally made my mind up.'

'I should think so too. They're obviously guilty.'

Celia fell silent, turned on her side and went back to sleep. The judge switched off his bedside light, kissed his wife on the cheek and settled down under the duvet. He glanced at the digital alarm clock on his bedside table. It was 12.23 a.m. precisely. That was a time that he would never forget.

It was only well after the dreadful events of that morning that he realised it had been about 4.45 a.m. when he and his wife had been disturbed in the most dramatic of circumstances. The first thing he recollected was young Christopher crying out and his wife nudging him in the darkness.

'Your turn,' she had said sleepily. 'Go and see what he wants.'

Then it happened. The main bedroom light was suddenly switched on. Campion sat upright in bed and saw two men, both masked, one holding a sawn-off shotgun which was pointed directly at him. Celia Campion screamed. The judge grasped her hand then put his arm around her.

'Silence,' commanded a slightly muffled voice from behind the shotgun. Campion thought he recognised an Irish accent. He had worked in intelligence for part of his service in Northern Ireland and had become familiar with the slight nuances and variations in tone of voices in the province. This voice, while it resembled the harsh guttural rasp he was used to seemed to have a softer underlying aspect. Was this someone trying to put on an Ulster accent?

'What do you want?' demanded the judge. Although shocked, he tried to give an impression of coolness, his army training kicking in quickly. Celia Campion remained distressed and almost hysterical. He maintained his arm around her.

'Where is my son?' she wailed. 'What have you done with him?'

As she spoke, a third person entered the bedroom, carrying Christopher. 'Mummy, mummy,' the child cried as he was bundled into his mother's arms. For some reason he couldn't quite explain, Campion had the distinct impression this third person was a woman despite her clothing being identical to the others.

'I asked what it is you want?' repeated the judge. 'If you're here to rob us, you'd better get on with it. There's nothing of value up here apart from my wife's jewellery.'

The person holding the shotgun moved closer and pointed the gun in the direction of Mrs Campion and Christopher.

'This isn't a robbery,' said the voice. 'Just do as we say and no one will get hurt.'

He indicated to Campion that he should get out of bed. As he was doing so, the second person unplugged the telephone. Campion put on his dressing gown then told his wife to stay where she was.

'Your wife and son are going for a little ride,' said the voice.

'They're not going anywhere,' replied Campion, firmly.

'They won't be away long – providing you do as we say.'

'What do you mean?'

'Later,' replied the voice. 'Let's deal with Celia and the boy first, shall we?'

So, this was planned? The gunman knew the name of Campion's wife. It was also obvious they were familiar with the layout of the house.

'And if I refuse to let you take them?'

The man laughed. 'And how do you think you're going to stop us? You're not in court now, your Honour. You'll do as I say or live with the consequences.'

The judge moved towards the gunman who responded by pushing the shortened barrels into his chest.

'Do you really want to find out what those consequences will be?'

Campion turned to his wife and then faced the gunman again.

'I cannot permit you to take them. You need to think of the consequences for yourselves – when you're caught, it will be life imprisonment all round!'

The gunman laughed again.

'Will it, indeed? But we're not going to be caught because you're going to be sensible and do as we say.'

Campion made a further move towards the gun.

At that, the gunman struck him across the forehead with the stock of the gun, knocking him back on to the bed. Celia Campion screamed. The child was now crying for his father.

'Now that wasn't very sensible, was it?'

He looked at Celia Campion.

'You have three minutes to get yourself and the child dressed. You can bring one bag with you – that's all.'

He indicated to the third person who pulled Celia Campion from the bed and pushed her gently towards the dressing room. Campion lay on the bed dazed. He called after his wife.

'Celia, stay where you are.'

The gunman struck him again, this time in the abdomen.

'I won't tell you again. Stay down on the bed or it will be the worse for them.'

Celia Campion was now in control of herself. Her maternal instincts were taking over. Her only object was to protect her son. If that meant doing as these criminals demanded, then that was what she would do. She eyed the gunman with a steely determination.

'It's all right, Tom,' she said. 'Just do as they say. Christopher and I will be fine.'

Campion lay back on the bed, still dazed, blood trickling from his forehead. He saw the second person go through the small bag his wife had prepared before thrusting it into her hand. She and Christopher were then marched out of the bedroom, the boy gripping his teddy bear in both hands. He heard them descending the stairs. The gunman pulled up a chair from beneath the window and sat down. The gun was now pointed directly at Campion. The man spoke quietly and slowly.

'I want to impress upon you the importance of doing exactly what we say. If anything goes wrong, whether it's your fault or not, we shall not hesitate to kill your wife and your boy. If we receive the slightest hint that you have involved the police or anyone else, you will leave us no option. You'll be signing their death warrants.'

Campion sat up. He couldn't believe what he was hearing.

'If this isn't a robbery, what do you want of me? If you're looking for a ransom, I have to tell you we have very little money. All we have is tied up in this house.'

The gunman shook his head slowly.

'We don't want your money. We're here to help you reach the right decision in the case tomorrow – that's all. Just find for the defence and your wife and the boy will be freed.'

Campion stared at the man in disbelief.

'Are you mad? Do you really think this will achieve anything? If I were to rule as you say, it would have no legal effect. A ruling induced by threats is invalid. It will be set aside.' He was thinking fast and added. 'I was going to find in favour of the defence anyway, so all this is completely unnecessary.'

The gunman nodded.

'Sure you were. You would say that wouldn't you. Well, that will be just fine. No one needs to know anything about your little adventure with us.'

'I will know,' responded Campion. 'The ruling will not stand. I shall have to recuse myself.'

The gunman sighed and shook his head.

'What do you mean, recuse yourself?'

'It's quite simple. I shall have to remove myself from the case. It will have to be dealt with by another judge.'

'Now, you're not being very sensible, your Honour, and there was I thinking you were an intelligent man. You will not resign from the case; d' you understand? (The way he spoke showed he was unfamiliar with the concept.) You'll give the ruling. We're not interested in its effect in the long term. When Doyle and Benson are free, you can overrule it. You can rip it up – you can stuff it up your arse for all we care. Do what you want with it. We're not interested. You'll rule as we require and the boys will be released. That's what the prosecutor said, isn't it? The case will be dropped. That's all we want. They won't be around for the inquest. And neither will we.'

Campion heard a vehicle starting up outside. He stood up and glanced out of the window. The man stood in his way but not before he observed a dark-coloured Range Rover leaving the yard.

'Where are you taking them?'

'A long way from here. But there's no need to concern yourself. They'll be perfectly safe – providing you do what's required. Twenty-four hours after you give your ruling, they'll be released – unharmed. That's a promise.'

Campion fell silent. He decided to play along with them. He needed time to think.

'I'm not due to give the ruling until tomorrow morning. That's more than twenty-four hours from now.'

He looked at his watch. The gunman was not concerned.

'I know that. You'll carry on as normal until then. We have people on the ground – more than you can possibly imagine. Any little thing that tells us you've blabbed – well, I need hardly remind you what the consequences will be.'

The second man, who had remained silent throughout, nodded. The gunman looked at him.

'Mr Jones here has disengaged your burglar alarm but he hasn't cut your phone wires – much as he'd like to – but we don't want to draw attention to ourselves. If it rings, you'll answer it as normal and give the impression that all is well. We'll be listening on the extension. And now, if you would be so good as to hand over your mobile phone…'

'It's on the bedside table,' said Campion, dejectedly. 'I was going to go to court later today – to finish off preparing my ruling.'

'Well, there'll be a change of plan. You can finish it off here. You have a computer in the study. And I'll be wanting to see it when it's done. You'll drive to court as usual tomorrow. You'll be under observation all the way.'

The gunman picked up the mobile phone and placed it in his pocket.

'Do you have any others?'

'My wife has one but no doubt your associates will have seen to that.'

'To be sure they will. Now, I suggest you get some sleep and I'd see to that cut on your forehead. We don't want you drawing attention to yourself when you arrive at court tomorrow. Mr Jones will be sitting outside your door – so don't try anything foolish.'

The gunman tossed the shortened shotgun to his associate and stood up. 'I think I'll get a bit of shut-eye myself. That couch in your study looks pretty comfortable. Oh, by the way, we have the keys to your Discovery. If anyone calls later today, you'll get rid of them, without raising any suspicions, do you understand?'

Campion nodded. 'Yes, I understand. Not that we are expecting anyone – apart from the milkman.'

'I'll ensure the empties are put out,' replied the man, leaving the room.

His associate broke the shotgun, revealing that it was loaded with two cartridges. He then closed it again before walking towards the door. But he said nothing. Campion observed that both were dressed in what appeared to be dark blue boiler suits. Both were wearing latex gloves and their faces were completely obscured by black balaclavas. There was no prospect of identifying either man. He also noticed that the shotgun was a Purdey; who would saw off the barrels of such a valuable firearm?

He heard talking downstairs and calculated there must have been at least three of them left in the house. He lay back on the bed. There was no prospect of his sleeping but he had to think. The next few hours would require him to make a number of decisions that were truly life changing. He felt sick to the pit of his stomach – and it wasn't through being jabbed with the shotgun. He thought of his wife and little Christopher. Abducted, terrified, not knowing where they were being taken – or why? He comforted himself in the knowledge that Celia was an intelligent woman who would not go to pieces. She was strong and resilient. She would protect their son. But in the final analysis, it was down to him. If he did as these animals required, they would be safe – there was no advantage in harming them. If he did not? He knew he couldn't live with himself if anything happened to them.

He had lied to the gunman when he said he had intended to rule in favour of Benson and Doyle. But no one would blame him if he did when the very lives of his wife and family were under threat. He realised, of course, that both defendants would have disappeared without trace once twenty-four hours had passed from his ruling. One or both of them must be behind this. Only they could derive any advantage from this unprecedented kidnapping of a judge's wife and child. Campion stood up. He suddenly felt a little faint. He put his hand to his forehead and realised he was bleeding. He went into the adjacent bathroom and looked at himself in the mirror. It was not a serious cut, but he bathed it in tepid water. He could see the beginnings of a bruise developing. He was going to have to make up something to explain the mark when he got to court the next day.

He started to wonder whether the gunman was telling him the truth. Did they really have as many men on the ground as he asserted? Campion very much doubted it. But could he risk it? The leader was certainly a thug who knew what he was about. He could well have been one of the robbers; perhaps the one who had shot the security guard? One thing was certain. Whatever he said, he couldn't have anyone on the inside at the court. Campion trusted the staff implicitly and there had been no newcomers in over twelve months. His one opportunity of foiling their scheme would arise when he got to court the next morning. He decided he would go in as early as possible. Nothing out of the ordinary in that. He was usually at court by eight fifteen at the latest and as he assumed these people had been watching him, they would know that. But what of his wife and Christopher? If he said anything to anyone he might be putting their lives at risk. This gunman obviously had no conscience. He was obviously a psychopath. But would he really kill the wife and child of a serving judge? Campion was minded to dismiss this as a remote prospect. Then he remembered that judges had been attacked and at least two killed in Northern Ireland and the leader of this gang could well be from the province. He may well have killed before. He lay on the bed thinking everything through.

Having reached no definite decision, he showered and then dressed himself in casual clothing and knocked on the bedroom door. Mr Jones opened it but said nothing. He indicated with the gun that the judge should go downstairs. He followed him at a discreet distance. Campion noticed that it was now 5.55 a.m. Time seemed to have passed rapidly. He walked into the kitchen and filled the kettle. The original gunman called to him from the study.

'I think we'll all have a coffee, your Honour. I take mine black but the other three will have milk. No sugar though.'

Campion obliged. So there were four of them in and about his home were there? There was always a chance they might leave their DNA somewhere, perhaps on the coffee mugs but he supposed they might well take precautions against that. He was right. They did. After drinking their coffee in the kitchen while Campion was held at gunpoint in the drawing room so he could not see their faces, the leader insisted on the mugs being placed in the dishwasher.

'We are forensically aware, you know,' he boasted. 'The dishwasher will be put in motion before we leave. There'll be nothing to show we were ever here.'

Not quite, thought Campion. He had noticed that the lower panel of the kitchen door had been completely removed – without breaking the glass. He wondered how they had disabled the alarm system.

After a period of time when nothing was said by anyone, Campion asked if he could go to his study to finish preparing his ruling.

'Of course – but there's no rush. You have the whole day before you. If I were you, I'd make yourself some breakfast. Mr Jones here used to be a chef. He's already raided the fridge. We'll be having bacon and eggs ourselves, if you've no objection?'

'Help yourselves,' replied Campion, 'but I have no appetite. I can't think why.'

He spotted a man outside the study window which overlooked the rear of the property. A black Range Rover had been parked under the eaves of the outbuilding, well out of sight of any casual visitor. Was this the same vehicle that had been used to remove his wife and son or did they have two similar Range Rovers? His own Discovery had been moved from its usual position under the carport to the side of the house, making it visible from the road. The gang leader saw him looking through the window.

'It's no good looking to escape. We've moved your Discovery, just to show that you're at home.'

Campion noted that he was the only member of the gang who had uttered a word in his presence throughout his ordeal.

By 1 p.m. he had finished the final draft of his ruling. He had contemplated sending a message by email, but he was prevented from using the Internet. These people were leaving nothing to chance.

'Word processing only,' he was told in no uncertain terms, as his Internet cable was pulled from the computer. He printed off a copy of his ruling and handed it to the gang leader who read it carefully in his still gloved hand.

'That's fine,' he said. 'No one could possibly complain about that. It reads very well. You have a nice turn of phrase, your Honour.'

'You have some legal training, have you?' enquired Campion, sarcastically.

'I have not. But I'm not a fool. It wouldn't take much for this to be changed and for you to rule the other way – not that you'll be thinking of doing that of course.'

He handed the draft back to Campion.

'See that you read it out – word for word. There'll be someone in the courtroom checking that you do.'

Will there? thought Campion, but he realised there was no chance of spotting who that might be.

At 6 p.m., the gang leader switched on the TV in the sitting room and helped himself to some of Campion's single malt whisky. The glass he used was later placed in the dishwasher. After the national news, the local news came on. There was nothing reported about the kidnapping of Celia and Christopher.

'So far, so good,' said the gunman.

At 9 p.m., Campion was told to go to his bedroom. He initially refused.

'Now, your Honour,' said the gunman. 'Be a good boy. Everything's going fine – we don't want to spoil it now, do we? And you need a good night's sleep to prepare for tomorrow.'

'I want to speak to my wife. I need to know she is safe.'

'Haven't I told you she'll be fine – and the boy – providing you do as we say? No talking to her, I'm afraid. We don't want any calls being traced now, do we?'

Campion reluctantly climbed the stairs. There had been no callers to his home all day. No opportunity had presented itself for him to do anything but obey their demands. Although his land line had not been disconnected, no one had telephoned. Then he remembered that his sister-in-law had said she would call Celia around lunchtime to arrange a trip to the theatre in London. She had obviously forgotten, or perhaps she'd been ringing Celia on her mobile? As he entered his bedroom and closed the door, he could hear one of the men taking up his position immediately outside. A chair was placed clumsily against the door. Inside his room, he was silently seething. He could not remember a time when he had been angrier. All his life he had respected the rule of law. It had been the canon which had guided his entire professional life. Now, he could quite happily have taken the shotgun from the gang leader and blown his evil head off. He threw himself down on the bed in frustration. He simply couldn't see a way out of this dilemma.

Although he was determined that no harm should come to his wife and son, he desperately wanted these criminals caught and punished together with whoever directed them to his home. He considered his options as he gazed through his bedroom window. Nothing was happening in the yard or the garden. His Discovery was still parked at the side of the house, but he noticed that the black Range Rover was no longer there. Did that mean that one or more of the gang had left? He sat down on the bed again and placed his head in his hands. He had to think. First, he must not put his wife and son at risk. That much at least was clear. Everything else was secondary to that. But he had taken an oath to deal justly with all manner of people without fear or favour. He was loath to give a ruling which did not represent his real and genuine judgement. Surely, there must be a way of protecting Celia and Christopher and at the same time ensuring the kidnappers were apprehended and the course of public justice preserved? He had all night to think about it. He knew he would not be able to sleep.

He recalled a kidnapping case he had prosecuted years before; the failure of the victim's parents to inform the police until after they had handed over the ransom demand had led to tragic consequences. The girl had died from exposure long before her distraught parents had gone in desperation to the police and then only after the kidnappers had cut off contact with them having failed to return their daughter as they had promised. But kidnappers rarely keep to a bargain especially after they have obtained what they wanted. Always a mistake that. To try and deal with kidnappers personally without involving the police. That was the stuff of novels and TV dramas. Not a mistake that Campion was minded to make. The police might not inspire much confidence when it came to recovering a stolen motor car but making a demand with menaces was something else entirely. They had the experience, training and expertise to resolve such matters, usually without undue harm to the victim. In the case he prosecuted the three gang members who were captured after a long and extensive police investigation were convicted of manslaughter and false imprisonment and sentenced to twenty-five years in jail. He would never forget the anguish of the girl's parents as the trial proceeded. If only they had gone to the police earlier.

But he knew the abduction of his wife and child was no ordinary kidnapping. Celia and Christopher would not be released until Benson and Doyle were freed. Freed because of his ruling. The chances of finding his family before 11 a.m. the next morning were decidedly remote, especially as no one yet knew they had been taken. And if he were able to get a message to the police, they would have insufficient time to find them. Any questioning of Benson or Doyle would immediately give the game away. But he was damned if he was going to let them get away with it. He had to do something. But what?

CHAPTER FORTY-SEVEN

Wednesday, 7 April 1999

It was nearly seven o'clock when Campion awakened. To his slight surprise, he had fallen asleep for a few hours. He felt rested and more confident as a result. After shaving and showering, he dressed himself; white shirt and stiff collar, his Parachute Regiment tie and his grey charcoal suit. He opened the bedroom door. No one was there. The chair that he had heard placed against the door the evening before was still on the landing but was no longer occupied. He started to go downstairs, slowly and quietly. Had the men gone? He walked into the kitchen. It was 7.19 a.m. exactly. No one was about. His spirits started to rise but his hopes were dashed when he heard the voice of the gang leader.

'You're up early, your Honour.'

He turned and saw his tormentor, gun in hand, standing at the dining room door.

'Sit yourself down, Judge. We have a number of matters we need to discuss before you go to court.'

'I shall make myself a cup of tea, if you don't mind,' insisted Campion, checking the kettle before switching it on.

The gunman indicated he could do so. Two of the others then walked into the kitchen. Like before, they remained silent. Campion pulled out a chair and sat at the kitchen table. The gunman did likewise.

'What time do you usually arrive at court?' he asked.

'If you've planned this as well as you obviously have, you will already know the answer.'

The gunman noticed a degree of belligerency which disturbed him. It had not been present the night before. He also noticed the tie that Campion was wearing. He'd obviously seen that before. He sighed in exasperation.

'But I'd like to hear it from you. We have to decide how much we can trust you. The next few hours are going to be very important for you and your family.'

Campion nodded.

'All right. I usually leave home at about half past seven. I like to avoid the rush-hour traffic if I can. I get to court around eight to quarter past most days. I was planning to leave a little earlier today.'

'And when you get there, what do you do?'

Campion paused. Why were they asking him these questions? Were they as well prepared as he had thought? As he had surmised, they had little idea what went on behind the scenes at court. He decided to take full advantage of their ignorance.

'I'm usually the first judge to arrive. I go to my chambers and start to prepare for the court day. And there will probably be some administrative matters I shall have to deal with. I haven't been at court since last Wednesday, remember?'

'So who will you be talking to?'

'The court manager will probably come and see me at about nine o'clock. She lives in Derbyshire, so she doesn't usually get in much before then. The only person I'm likely to speak to when I arrive will be my usher, Malcolm Hemming. He's an early bird too.'

'So there'd be no contact between you and the police?'

'Not in relation to Doyle's case, no. But I expect there will be some chambers' applications to deal with first. Some of those may involve contact with police officers.'

'Explain what you mean.'

'The court has not sat since last week. That means there may be a couple of bail applications to deal with. Nothing out of the ordinary.'

'And these applications – they're done in court are they?'

'No. In chambers. No one else is present. Just a court clerk.'

'So you'd have the opportunity of informing the police about us, would you?'

Campion sighed.

'I'd have the opportunity. But I'm hardly likely to put my family's lives at risk, am I? What could the police do before I'm due to give my ruling at 11 a.m.? No one knows that my wife and son have even been abducted.' Campion spat the words out then looked at the gunman who hesitated before he replied.

'Exactly. I'm glad to see you're being sensible about this. It would be very foolish for you to start getting ideas at this stage. And, by the way, please don't think I didn't notice the tone of your last reply. You will do exactly as we require and you will do it without causing any suspicion!'

Campion looked down.

'I don't seem to have any other choice, do I?'

He got up from the table and poured boiling water from the kettle on to a tea bag he had placed in Celia's favourite mug. He refrained from asking if anyone else wanted a drink. He opened the fridge, took out a bottle of milk and placed it on the table. He then took his mug and sat down again. He eyed the gunman.

'There will be several police officers at court when I give the ruling. You ought to know that. This was arranged last week. I always ensure the police have a number of additional officers at court when I am due to give a controversial judgement. It ensures that nothing untoward occurs. Emotions can get out of control otherwise.'

The gunman appeared unsettled, exactly as Campion had hoped.

'You could cancel those instructions, couldn't you? As you're going to find for the defence, there shouldn't be any trouble.'

'I could, but it would look very suspicious if I did, especially as arrangements will already have been put in hand. The team of officers usually arrives well before the court sits. They're probably on their way now.'

The gunman paused and looked at the other two men.

'Well, your Honour, we don't want anyone thinking something is amiss. Just see to it that you don't make any changes to your ruling – not that affects the result anyway.'

Campion nodded. He then added, 'You should bear in mind that in a case of this nature, there will be some degree of control by the police when it comes to members of the public being admitted into the courtroom. That's also something I authorised last week.'

Campion looked the gunman full in the face as he spoke. He was beginning to enjoy what he fancied was a degree of concern on his part. He also noticed the other two men becoming restless but neither of them said anything.

'What do you mean?' snapped the gunman.

'Well, it's not for me to say, but they may ask for identification on the way in. It's happened before in serious cases. I don't want anything to occur that puts my wife and son at risk. That's why I'm telling you this. You said yesterday you would have someone in the courtroom. I'm not interested who that may be; just make sure he's got some form of ID, that's all.'

The gunman looked at Campion. He visibly relaxed.

'Thanks for the tip, Judge. But you needn't worry about that. Now you'd better be making tracks. You have your ruling with you?'

Campion took a sip from the mug.

'It's in my bag.'

'Good. Off you go – and remember, someone will be watching you, so no clever tricks. The future of your family is in your hands.'

Campion stood up.

'I'm not likely to forget that, am I?'

He moved from the kitchen into his study and picked up his briefcase. He checked that a copy of his ruling was inside it, then walked through the kitchen towards the back door. He noticed that the dishwasher was now in motion and that the glass panel had been refitted to the door. His mug remained sitting on the kitchen table. There was no sign of the black Range Rover.

'On your way, Judge,' said the gunman. 'We shall not meet again.'

He handed Campion the keys to the Discovery. The judge glared at him.

'What about my wife and son? I'd be better able to carry this off if I could speak to my wife.'

'You'll be fine. Don't worry about them. They're perfectly OK. You'll be seeing them by noon tomorrow – providing nothing goes wrong.'

★★★★

As he drove towards the city centre, Campion kept an eye out for the black Range Rover. He had not been able to make a note of the registration number, but he knew from the shape it was a recent model. He presumed it was running on false plates anyway. As he travelled along the A6 through Oadby, the build-up of traffic caused him to slow almost to a halt. He observed the driver of a dark blue BMW looking at him. Was this one of the gang?

When he reached the London Road, the traffic became heavier. He inched his way along. He was unable to make out if he was being followed. He looked at the clock on the dashboard. It was 7.52 a.m. As he negotiated the racecourse roundabout he noticed the BMW close behind him. He decided to pull ito the service station on his left, without indicating. The blue BMW continued on its way. He drove to the pump nearest the exit, switched off the engine and got out of the Discovery. He didn't really need to purchase any diesel – his tank was just over half full – but the pause in the journey gave him additional time to think. He looked about him as he filled his tank. There were four other vehicles on the forecourt, all the drivers busily engaged in replenishing their fuel tanks or paying for their purchases inside the service station shop. No one seemed interested in him. As he replaced the nozzle and made his way to the kiosk, a woman smiled at him and wished him "good morning". He nodded and returned the greeting, but she was not someone he recognised. As he paid with his credit card he noticed her climbing into a red Mercedes sports car and driving off quickly in the direction of the city. He walked back to the Discovery, started up the engine and continued his journey.

He drove past the railway station after what seemed an eternity, and turned to his left then immediately to his right, and swept down towards the Crown Court car park. A security officer waved to him as the metal shutters were raised. He waited briefly, exchanging pleasantries with the guard, then passed through and parked his vehicle as near to the judges' entrance as he could manage. There were only six other cars in the car park. He pressed the five-digit code into the keypad and entered the building. He suddenly felt relieved and comparatively safe. He knew exactly what he was going to do. He took the lift to the first floor and walked along the corridor until he reached his room. No one was about. He threw his briefcase on to a chair and sat at his desk. He looked at the clock. It was now 8.11am. Picking up the telephone, he dialled what he hoped was still the mobile phone number of Detective Chief Inspector Hood. Before he'd been appointed to the bench, some three years before, Campion had prosecuted a murder trial in which Hood, then a detective inspector, had been the senior investigating officer. He had been impressed with Hood and had contacted him directly on several occasions while preparing the case rather then delaying matters by going through the CPS. For some reason that combination of numbers had remained with him. He prayed that Hood had not upgraded his phone. He was in luck. Hood answered.

'Mr Hood. This is Judge Campion. I need to see you immediately. Something of a particularly grave nature has occurred. I am at the Crown

Court. I shall arrange for you to be brought to my chambers through the car park entrance.'

'Of course, Judge,' replied Hood. 'I'm still at home, but I will leave at once. Can you give me some indication of the problem?'

'Not until you get here. I can only say that what has happened is unprecedented. Lives are at risk. It is of crucial importance that you do not give the impression that anything is wrong. Security will let you into the car park. I shall have someone I trust waiting at the judges' entrance for you.'

'I'm on my way.'

Campion replaced the receiver. As he did so Malcolm Hemming knocked on the door.

'Good morning, your Honour. You're in bright and early. But it's a big day today, isn't it?'

'Bigger than you think, Malcolm. Shut the door will you?'

Hemming did as he was bid. He turned and faced the judge and noticed the bruise and small cut on his forehead, but he said nothing. It was not his place to comment on the judge's appearance.

'Sit down, will you Malcolm? I have something important to tell you. It must not go any further.'

Hemming took a seat. This must be really serious. In all his years at the Crown Court he had never been asked by a judge to sit down in his chambers.

'Early yesterday morning, a number of men broke into my home. My wife and young son have been abducted. I have no idea where they are being held. They will only be released if I rule in favour of the defence submissions later this morning and dismiss the charges faced by Benson and Doyle.'

The usher could hardly believe what he had just been told.

'What? How dare they!'

'Well, they dared. I have been told quite clearly that if I were to disclose what has happened to a living soul, their lives will be forfeit.'

He looked down, his voice failing him. The usher leaned forward and spoke quietly but sympathetically.

'I can't tell you how sorry I am, sir. But would they do that? They'd be hunted down and jailed for the rest of their lives. Kidnapping a judge's wife and son. They must have taken leave of their senses.'

Campion looked up, his eyes moist with tears.

'We'll worry about what should be done with them if and when they are caught. My immediate concern is for my wife and son.'

'Of course, your Honour. Will you have to do as they say?'

'I have drafted a ruling which dismisses the charges. It does not represent my real view. But if nothing effective can be done before I'm due to give the ruling, I'll have no alternative but to deliver it.'

'I can see that.'

'I'm telling you, Malcolm, because I trust you implicitly. But it is essential that you say nothing about this to anyone else, and I mean anyone. For all I know these people could have someone on side in the court office. I have asked a senior police officer to see me as a matter of urgency. He's on his way here. There are two matters I need you to attend to. First, make six copies of my ruling, but do not allow anyone else to see them. Secondly, when Detective Chief Inspector Hood gets here, bring him in through the judges' entrance from the car park and up to my chambers. Can you manage that?'

'Of course, your Honour. Leave it to me.'

Campion removed the draft ruling from his briefcase and handed it to the usher.

'Bring the copies to me as soon as they're ready.'

'Yes, sir.'

Malcolm Hemming left and Campion sat back in his chair, contemplating whether he had done the right thing. He was working on the basis that whatever might happen, these men would not dare carry out their threat. He had thought of nothing else since his home had been entered and he had calculated that those holding his wife would have been as forensically aware as the men who had held him prisoner. His wife and son would not be able to identify their captors so there would be nothing to be gained – and a huge amount to lose – if they added murder to their crimes. That was his assessment of the position. He could only pray that he was right.

Fifteen minutes later, Malcolm Hemming returned with six copies of Campion's draft ruling and Detective Chief Inspector Hood. Campion and Hood shook hands. The judge then placed the copies in a drawer and locked it.

'Malcolm, could you ensure that the chief inspector and I are not disturbed. I shall not be joining the other judges for coffee this morning. Just tell them I'm too busy.'

'Yes, your Honour.'

Hemming closed the door behind him. Hood was first to speak.

'It occurred to me on the way here, Judge, that if what has arisen involves the case of Doyle and Benson, as the SIO I may not be the appropriate person to assist. Perhaps some other officer – an independent officer – should deal with the problem, whatever it may be.'

'On the ball, as always, Mr Hood; but it matters not. I've come to you because I believe I can trust you. And as a consequence of what has happened, I shall no longer be able to deal with this case, not legally. You see, I now have a particular interest in the outcome.'

'You do?'

'Yes.'

Campion ushered Hood to a seat.

'Yesterday morning, while my wife and I were still in bed, a gang of at least four men, probably more, broke into my home near Foxton. My wife and two-year-old son have been abducted.'

Campion became emotional but he quickly regained his composure and displayed a degree of anger.

'These bastards have demanded I rule in favour of the application to dismiss – so that Doyle and Benson will be released. The consequences if I don't do as they say hardly bear thinking about.' He paused. 'They said they would kill them.'

Hood said nothing for a few moments. He could see that Campion was under severe emotional pressure.

'I don't know whether this will help, sir. But I doubt very much if these people will carry out their threat. It wouldn't be in their interests to do so. They intended to terrorise you and your wife and they no doubt succeeded, but if it were to come to actually doing what they threatened, well that's a quite different proposition. They will know they'd be hunted down – however long it took and once caught and convicted, they'd spend the rest of their lives in prison. I know it's hard and I'm not guaranteeing anything but if it's any comfort to you, that's my professional opinion. They won't lay a finger on your family.'

Campion sighed then nodded his agreement.

'That's what I calculated. That's why I telephoned you. But it's still a hell of a risk I'm taking It only takes one of them to lose it and there's no knowing what might happen.'

'As I said, there are no guarantees in a situation like this.'

'What are the chances of finding them before I have to give my ruling?'

'I'll be truthful with you – pretty remote. We have nothing to go on.'

'Who would benefit from all this?' asked the judge. '*Cui bono?*'

Hood frowned.

'That's easy. Doyle.'

'No one else?'

'I doubt it.'

'So what do you advise?'

'You must rule in their favour. We'll have to track them down again after your wife and son have been released. Presumably any ruling made in such circumstances will have no legal effect?'

'Correct. The matter would have to be reheard before a different judge. I would have to recuse myself.'

'Well, that's the answer then. Once your family is safe, we can pull out all the stops. We'd find them eventually, I'm sure. Doyle has considerable assets in this country which he won't want to abandon.'

'That will take some doing. They won't release Celia and my son for a further twenty-four hours. Any attempt to keep track of Benson and Doyle will certainly put their lives at risk. And twenty-four hours would give these creatures every opportunity to make good their escape.'

'I can see that. But the safety of your family must come first. Doyle must be behind this. Benson is lightweight. He has neither the money nor the contacts to arrange anything like this.'

'And I suppose if you were to interrogate them, again it would give the game away. They would know I had informed you – which would again put my family at serious risk.'

Hood was thinking fast.

'I agree. That's out of the question. But if this is Doyle's doing he must have organised it from prison – which means he must have had a conduit.' He then added, 'You won't know this Judge, but we had reason to believe that Doyle and his girlfriend, Julia Hamilton, had a big falling out. My sergeant thinks it's genuine. He reckons she's a gold-digger and has abandoned Doyle and got her claws into someone else. I'm not so sure. But our intelligence is that there has been no contact between them for several weeks. The only person who has had any contact with Doyle is his solicitor. We've been monitoring all his phone calls and all his visitors. He hasn't made a call to anyone other than his lawyers in over four weeks and he's had no visitors apart from his solicitor and counsel.'

'What are you suggesting? That his solicitor set this up?'

'I'm not suggesting anything – but it's a possibility. Doyle is a wealthy man. He'd certainly have the wherewithal to arrange something like this.'

'Remind me, who is his solicitor?'

'Trevor Parker.'

'Parker? I can't see him getting involved in something like this, not willingly anyway. He's always seemed pretty straight to me.'

'Perhaps he's been put under pressure too? He's married with a few children, all grown up, I believe.'

Campion stood up and walked to the window.

'That's something I hadn't considered. Perhaps Parker's wife has been kidnapped as well? These people wouldn't hesitate to pile the pressure on a solicitor if they're prepared to kidnap a judge's wife.'

He turned and faced Hood.

'On the other hand, I suppose it's just possible that Doyle is not the mastermind behind this robbery and that someone else has organised this. Someone who wants Doyle and Benson out in case they reveal something they shouldn't?'

'Possible, but unlikely. My gut feeling is that Doyle organised the whole show. I doubt if there's anyone directing his actions, although I have my suspicions about the Hamilton woman. She's very clever.'

'Do you know her whereabouts?'

'As far as I know she's been abroad over Easter. She's on the list at ports and airports. We're informed if she leaves the country. She went to Brussels last Wednesday. She should have returned yesterday. I'll check whether she did.'

He pulled out his mobile phone and pressed a digit.

'Andrew? Any news about Julia Hamilton? I see. Find out where she is now, will you? And Andrew, discreetly. I don't want her knowing we have any interest in her.'

Hood switched his phone off.

'Her flight was delayed. She only got back to Heathrow at nine fifty-five last night.'

'So it can't have been her. I had the distinct impression that one of the gang was a woman. The one who was involved with my wife. I don't know why, I just got that feeling.'

'Is there anything else that might help us trace them?'

'They had a black Range Rover, a recent model, possibly two. I'm pretty sure they took Celia and my son off in one but there was one parked in the yard at the back of the house in the morning. It could have been the same vehicle; I simply can't be sure. I never saw the registration number. One of the gang – the one in charge – had an Irish accent, and a sawn-off shotgun – sounded as if he was from Ulster rather than the south, but he could have been putting it on. He was a big man, distinctly taller than the others. About six-foot four, I would guess. They were all wearing navy blue boiler suits and black balaclavas. They also had surgical-type gloves, light blue in colour. They were certainly professionals. I expect they'll be gone from the house by now and will not have left any trace of themselves behind. They were very careful about that. It won't help you to find them, but only the leader spoke. None of the others uttered a single word in my presence.'

'And you've no idea where they may have taken your wife and son?'

'No. They said it was a long way from Foxton but they could have been lying. By the way, they seemed very familiar with the inside of our home. It's on the market at the moment. We've had quite a few viewings. I suppose it's possible that one of the would-be purchasers was acting on behalf of these gangsters?'

'More than likely, sir. We'll look into that. Who are the agents?'

'Gargans. The chap my wife was dealing with is called Denyer.'

'Did you see any of the people who viewed the house?'

'No. Celia dealt with all that.'

'Right. We'll have a specialist team to your house this morning. Don't worry. They won't draw attention to themselves. As you say, these people are probably long gone anyway. Do you have a key you could let us have? Just in case they've managed to lock the doors.'

Campion took his keys from his pocket and examined them. Much to his surprise his house keys had not been removed. He detached the rear door key. Hood thanked him.

'We know that Doyle has a number of properties in the locality. We could make a discreet search of those?'

The judge shook his head.

'Would that be wise? As you have said, you have nothing to go on – and he'd be a fool to use one of his own properties – and I suspect that's one thing he isn't.'

'Perhaps you're right.'

Hood looked at his watch. 'It's almost eight forty-five. Given the time available, we seem to have no option but to go along with their demands. Anything else you can recall?'

'The sawn-off. I'm pretty sure it was a Purdey. My father owned a pair of them, you know. Who would saw off the barrels of a Purdey?'

'Who indeed?'

Hood made to leave.

'And you will have to keep all this confidential, please, Mr Hood. I don't want this leaking out. They said they'd have someone at court to make sure I keep to their terms.'

'Did they? We'll keep a look out for him.'

'I warned them there would be a heavy police presence. I told them I had put it in hand last week. I hadn't of course. Whoever it is might be expecting to be asked to produce some sort of identification in order to gain admittance to the courtroom. I told them it was extremely likely because of the sensitivity of the case.'

'No problem. I can soon arrange that, without letting on why. At least we'll have a record of everyone who comes in.'

Hood walked towards the door. He turned.

'I shall have to alert HQ though. We have a specialist squad which deals with abductions of this gravity. They are very experienced, and can be very discreet when they have to be.'

'I appreciate that, but nothing must be done that puts my wife and child at risk, anymore than I have done already.'

'I understand, but believe me, you've done the right thing in informing us. By the way, is there any chance of delaying your ruling, without drawing undue attention? Any additional time will be welcome?'

'I doubt it. We sometimes lose court time because defendants in custody arrive at court late. I'm always complaining about it. Too much to hope that it'll happen today.'

Hood nodded

'I'm sure that something can be arranged. I think there might be a lockdown at Welford Road this morning. Leave it to me.'

With that, Chief Inspector Hood opened the door. Malcolm Hemming was waiting in the corridor.

'Malcolm, will you see Mr Hood out? You can ring me on this number if anything occurs. I take it you saved it after we spoke earlier?'

'I did.'

Hood nodded as he spoke.

'I'll be in touch.'

The door closed and Campion collapsed in his seat and placed his head in his hands. All he could do now was pray.

★★★★

Hood was shown by Malcolm Hemming into the court office and then out into the public area. He went immediately to the police room. A solitary uniformed officer was sitting there, checking his notebook. Hood instructed him to go for a cup of tea. As the officer left, somewhat reluctantly, Hood took out his mobile. He rang the liaison officer at Welford Road Prison. The custody vans had arrived but only the van heading for Nottingham had departed. Hood arranged for the remainder to be delayed. He then rang Andrew Hooper. Hooper had established that Julia Hamilton had spent Tuesday night at the Heathrow Hilton with Bill Savage.

'Did she? Is she still there? Get on to reception. And Andrew, I want you at the Crown Court asap. Get Wendy to ring me too. I have a little job for her. I'll explain everything when you get here.'

Hood then telephoned the ACC. She was already in her office at police HQ.

'Good God,' she exclaimed when Hood told her what had happened. 'I'll get on to the specialist unit at once. Do you need any assistance at the court?'

'We have to keep the lid on this ma'am, but I would like a team of uniformed officers here. There's no need for them to know anything other than we have a security alert – code black. They can be told we're concerned that an attempt may be made to free a defendant. I'll be ready to speak to the chief superintendent from the specialist crime unit as soon as he wishes. In the meantime, I propose to deal with matters on a need-to-know basis only.'

'I agree. What is the judge proposing to do?'

'If we don't come up with something before he has to give his ruling, he'll rule in favour of the defence. That will mean that Doyle and Benson will walk. It'll be another twenty-four hours before the judge's family is released, so our chances of re-arresting these two will not be good. Doyle will have arranged to disappear but I don't see we have any other choice. We have to put the safety of the judge's family first.'

'Quite. Do you have any leads at all?'

'I'm working on the theory that Doyle has organised this from inside Welford Road. He must have had help on the outside which means he must have been in contact with someone. As far as we know, his only contact in the last few weeks has been with his solicitor. Julia Hamilton has not been in touch for quite some time. It may be that the solicitor's been put under pressure to do Doyle's bidding. On the other hand, he may have been bribed. He's retiring in July and we know Doyle is asset rich.'

'Or it could be that this is the work of someone else? A dishonest prison officer for instance. He could have been the go-between?'

'That's a possibility but only Doyle and Benson will be the beneficiaries as far as we know. I simply can't accept that Doyle doesn't know about this.'

'Use your discretion Harry, but be careful. We don't want this blowing up in our faces.'

'Yes, ma'am.'

As Hood terminated his call to the ACC his mobile rang again. It was Wendy Knight.

'Wendy, I have a little job for you. I want you to visit the home of Trevor Parker, Doyle's solicitor. Parker won't be there. He'll be here at the Crown Court for the ruling in Doyle's case. I want you to check if his wife is at home and that all is well. The utmost discretion will be required. So no blue lights and sirens. Use your own car and park it well away from the house. They live just outside Derby. You'll get the address from the voters' register. It can't be very far from where you live. Are you still at home?'

'Yes, sir. I was just about to leave. I won't need the register. I know where they live. It's in the next village.'

'Good. Get to it.'

'What's this all about, sir?'

'I can't go into details now but it's of the utmost importance. If she's in and everything seems all right, ask her a few questions about what she and her husband have been up to over the last few weeks. Anything, however seemingly trivial, may assist – understand?'

'It would help if I had an inkling what it is you really want to know. I don't want to put my foot in it.'

'All I can say for the moment, Wendy, is we are checking out whether Doyle's solicitor is being used as some sort of conduit to get information from Doyle to third parties. We can't risk approaching Parker directly, not at this stage – but if you can squeeze anything out of his wife, it just might help focus us in the right direction.'

'Very good, sir. I'll do my best. I'll ring you as soon as I can. I'll have to think of something to justify my questions, though.'

'You do that. I'm relying on you Wendy.'

Hood looked at his watch. It was eight fifty-five. Time was getting short.

Ten minutes later, Hooper arrived at the court. As instructed, he casually joined the queue and passed through the usual security checks before making his way to the police room. Hood related what had happened.

'So the bastard will get away with it? If he's released from here this morning, we'll never see him again.'

'I know, Andrew, I know. But we have to put the safety of the judge's family first.'

'I appreciate that sir, but can't we delay before releasing Doyle and Benson?'

'No. The judge's family will not be released until twenty-four hours after Doyle and Benson are set free. So there'd be no point.'

'And after all the work we've done!'

'Can't be helped, Andrew. Just think of the torment Judge Campion is going through at the moment. He's probably beating himself up for telling us about this. He's taken a tremendous risk. If this goes wrong, he'll never forgive himself – or us.'

'I see that, sir. Let's hope something turns up.'

'That's most unlikely. He's due to give his ruling at eleven. I've done what I can to delay Doyle's arrival here. But we can't put it off forever. That will only draw suspicion on the judge. If these people find out he's told us, there's no telling what they might do – out of sheer bloody mindedness!'

Hood's mobile rang again. As he answered it he directed Hooper to organise the uniformed officers when they arrived.

'There'll be seven of them,' he said. 'I want three of them in Court 2, the rest distributed round the ground floor. Tell them to keep their eyes open. They don't know about the kidnapping and there's no reason why they should. Just tell them to keep alert. Anything suspicious they report it to you. And get Ian Lunn to check out the people who've viewed the judge's house, but discreetly. OK? Gargans are the agents.'

'Yes, sir.'

CHAPTER FORTY-EIGHT

At precisely nine forty-six, an Interflora van pulled up outside The Old Bakehouse. The driver, a young woman, stepped out carrying a large bunch of peach coloured roses. She opened the pedestrian gate and walked up to the front door. After ringing the bell, she waited a full minute before ringing the bell a second time. There was no response. She stepped back and looked up at the first-floor windows; there was no sign of life. After waiting a few more seconds, she returned to the van and started up the engine. She then reversed a few yards and turned into the drive through the already open five-barred gate. The van disappeared behind the house. When it was out of sight of the road, she reversed right up to the back door. The rear doors of the van opened and three armed police officers emerged. The kitchen door was opened and the specialist officers went quickly inside followed by two scenes of crime experts. Minutes later the armed officers returned, having thoroughly searched the house. One of them climbed into the rear of the van, the other two remained in the house, closing the door as the van drove out of the yard and back on to the road. The bouquet of roses was left on the step.

Within seconds, Hood was informed of the result of the search. He telephoned Judge Campion and told him that the house was clear. There was no sign of the kidnappers. 'As we anticipated,' said Campion, glumly. The judge checked the time and called for Malcolm Hemming.

'I shall deal with these three bail applications at ten,' he said. 'In court as chambers.'

'I'm sure Judge Stillwell would deal with them if you asked, sir,' said Hemming sympathetically. 'She thinks her trial will crack.'

'I'm sure she would. But they'll be expecting me to do something between now and eleven o'clock. If I don't, it may make them suspicious.'

'Well, if you feel up to it, your Honour?'

'Yes, I do. Ask the court clerk to pop in at five to, will you?'

'Yes, sir.'

★★★★

In the entrance foyer of the court, Hood spotted Trevor Parker, queuing to pass through security. He watched him as his briefcase was searched. Parker then walked towards the solicitors' room. Hood headed him off.

'Good morning, Mr Parker. Ready for the big day?'

'Hope springs eternal, Chief Inspector. It will be interesting to see which way the judge jumps.'

'What do you reckon?'

'Could go either way. Miss Lassiter has her concerns but if the judge follows the *Carlisle* decision, we should be home and dry.'

'Many a slip between cup and lip!'

'I agree. Your man was very good. He may well have persuaded Judge Campion to go with the merits.'

'You don't think your man has the merits on his side then?'

'Depends what you mean. Benson's as guilty as hell. There's no question about that and you know how this judge hates them getting away on technicalities. Doyle, on the other hand, would still have a bit of a run in front of a jury don't you think? His alibi is as solid as they come.'

'Well, as long as it gets to a jury. That's all I want. Run or no run. Well, I can't stand here chatting. I have other matters to be getting on with.'

Hood looked at his watch. It was nine fifty-four. He walked off towards the police room. As he opened the door, his phone rang again. It was Wendy Knight.

'I think I may have something, sir.'

'Go on Wendy.'

'I saw Mrs Parker. I told her we were doing house-to-house enquiries in connection with a spate of burglaries. It's something she's very worried about. I turned the conversation to the problem of holidays – you know, sir – people being concerned about being burgled when they go away? Well, she invited me in for a cup of tea then started telling me about a trip she and her husband took during the Easter break. She obviously enjoys a good gossip. They had been to her brother's in Norfolk for a few days. On the way back, they called at an old farm in the Vale of Belvoir, Orley Farm.'

'That's one of Doyle's properties, isn't it?'

'Yes, sir. It's on our list. It seems that Trevor Parker was checking that the place was secure – apparently on Doyle's instructions. As they were about to turn into the drive, a black Range Rover with darkened windows pulled out in front of them.'

'A black Range Rover?'

'Yes sir.'

'Did they get the number?'

'No.'

'Pity.'

'But when Parker got back in the car, he said something about a padlock on the cellar door – and this is the interesting bit – a mattress and a blanket that had been put in there too. Sounds as if someone might have been going to hold up in there. It's well out of the way.'

'Or put someone else in there to keep them out of the way? Now why would Doyle want Parker to check out Orley Farm? Isn't that the place he's sold to developers?'

'Yes sir – subject to getting full planning permission.'

'Well done, Wendy. You may well have hit the jackpot.'

'Really sir? Is there some intelligence about Doyle that I don't know about?'

'Yes. Get yourself over here. I'll tell you all about it.'

'Yes sir.'

Hood telephoned the ACC and told her what Knight had discovered.

'You don't think that's where they're being held, Harry? Doyle would be a fool to use one of his own properties.'

'Perhaps he wasn't behind this after all. I think I'm going to have to risk speaking to Parker directly.'

'I don't know about that Harry. You should clear it with Tony Craven first. You know they found nothing at the judge's house.'

'I'm aware of that ma'am. And I shall speak to Tony Craven. But time is of the essence. In the meantime, could we send the helicopter over Orley Farm just to check if there's any sign of anything? It's in the middle of nowhere so the helicopter going over shouldn't raise any concerns.'

'Will do. Speak to you later.'

Hood then had a long conversation with Chief Superintendent Craven. Craven pointed out to Hood that the chances were that Celia Campion and her son would be locked up somewhere without any of the kidnappers being in the vicinity.

'It's a myth that kidnappers keep someone guarding the victims, particularly in a case like this. Once they have what they want they'd simply disclose where the victim was being held, assuming they can be bothered. Sometimes they don't even do that. If they have them securely confined in a remote spot, there'd be no need for them to take the risk of staying there themselves. Why should they? It only increases the risk of being caught. I think it's worth speaking to Parker, but be careful how much info you give him. I'll get my team to check this place out, carefully and with the minimum of fuss.'

Hood immediately headed to the solicitors' room. There was no sign of Parker. He checked, using his phone, whether Doyle had arrived at court. He was still at Welford Road. The governor was playing ball. He had invented an incident that prevented any of the vans leaving the premises. There would be a few judges in the Midlands fuming about the non-arrival of prisoners, but that couldn't be helped. This was far more important. He was then informed by Malcolm Hemming that Trevor Parker was dealing with one of the bail applications in Court 2. Hood waited outside, mingling with a large number of people anxious to hear Campion's ruling in Doyle's case. He glanced at his watch. It was now ten nineteen. One of those waiting patiently outside the court was Harold Cronshaw, QC.

'Good morning, Mr Hood,' he said benignly. 'We should know where we stand pretty shortly, although I hear there's been a lockdown at the prison and Doyle hasn't arrived yet.'

'So I hear,' replied Hood, giving nothing away. 'Does that mean there'll be a bit of a delay?'

'That will depend on the view the defence takes. There's no reason in principle why the judge shouldn't give his ruling in the absence of the defendants.'

'I would have thought they would want to hear it?'

'Perhaps, but I doubt if the technicalities would mean much to them. It's the result they'll be keen to know and counsel can tell them that when they get here.'

'Has Benson been delayed too?' asked Hood.

'Do you know, I haven't heard about his position. He's in a different prison isn't he?'

'Yes. He's at Lincoln. I'll check whether they've arrived.'

At that moment, Trevor Parker came out of the courtroom, looking decidedly out of sorts. His client had been refused bail by Campion.

'Good morning again, Mr Parker,' said Hood.

'I don't see what's good about it,' replied the solicitor. 'I've just been refused bail by Judge Campion when the prosecution wasn't even objecting. Risk of interfering with witnesses. The judge seems to be in a foul mood this morning. Doesn't augur well for our chances later today.'

Cronshaw smiled. Hood did not as he touched Parker on the arm.

'Could I have a quiet word? Nothing to concern yourself about.'

'Certainly. Where shall we go?'

'The police room is just over there. It's pretty private. We shouldn't be disturbed.'

Parker followed Hood into the police room. Hood closed the door and instructed Andrew Hooper that no one was to be allowed in.

'What can I do for you, Chief Inspector?' asked the solicitor. 'You will bear in mind that I am restricted in what I can say to you – if any of this concerns my client?'

Hood indicated a seat. Parker sat down.

'It's a somewhat delicate matter, Mr Parker. I'm mindful of legal professional privilege – and I don't want to put you in an embarrassing position – so if you feel you cannot assist I shall understand.'

'This sounds rather ominous.'

'It's very serious, very serious indeed. Unfortunately, I can't reveal the details but it is no exaggeration to say that lives may be at risk.'

Parker looked alarmed.

'Is this something to do with my client's case?'

'It may be. I'm not in a position to say.'

'This is very mysterious, Mr Hood. Perhaps you should simply tell me what it is you want to know. Whatever it is, can't it wait until after the judge's ruling?'

'No. It's about Orley Farm, you know, one of the properties owned by your client.'

'Orley Farm? What has that to do with anything?'

'We have information that you visited Orley Farm on Monday evening?'

'Yes, what of it? My client was concerned about security. I only went there to shut him up and to double check that he could give vacant possession. He was concerned that his ex-girlfriend might move in there and scupper the sale to the developers. Technically, it's no longer his property.'

'What do you mean?'

'As it's a matter of public record now, there's no harm in my disclosing this. The full planning permission came through last week. I received a letter of notification on Thursday. The outstanding condition being satisfied the transfer can now proceed. Doyle doesn't know that yet. I was going to tell him this morning.' Parker looked slightly perturbed. 'Tell me, how did you know I had been there?'

'That will have to remain confidential for the moment.'

The solicitor continued to look concerned. Hood pressed him further.

'Could I ask if you saw anything suspicious – when you were there on Monday night?'

Parker did not reply immediately. A number of thoughts passed through his mind before he answered. None of them was complimentary of Doyle.

'Well, I suppose I can tell you this as it doesn't seem to me to relate to the prosecution of my client. There were a couple of things that struck me as rather odd. A four-wheel drive vehicle sped out of the drive as I was about to turn off the main road. I thought at the time it was mighty suspicious, especially at that time of night. It was about 9 p.m.'

'Could you identify the vehicle?'

'It was a Range Rover, dark coloured, possibly black. I noticed the windows were shaded but I didn't get the registration number. And before you ask, no, I couldn't tell how many people were in it.'

'Any idea why it was there?'

'None at all. I thought they might have been thieving. We've had things stolen before. Some of the lead went off the roof six months ago. It caused a lot of damage on the inside when it rained.'

'You checked the premises?'

'I did. But only from the outside. I didn't go in. Nothing seemed to have been disturbed. There was something else, though. A padlock had been fitted to the cellar door. It looked pretty new to me. There was still sawdust on the step too, so it can't have been there for long. I assumed Doyle had arranged for it to be fitted; why, I have no idea.'

'But since he fell out with Julia Hamilton, you have been his only contact, haven't you?'

Parker bridled. He sensed the direction in which the conversation was moving.

'No, I have not. He's been in contact with his accountants. I know that for a fact because they served a notice to quit on Julia Hamilton. He wants her out of Harbour Buildings. I knew nothing about it until afterwards.'

'How would he have contacted them?'

'By phone, I presume. He is allowed to make phone calls from prison. But you would know that, wouldn't you? I assume you've been monitoring them. I certainly warned him that you would be.' He paused. 'I suppose he could have written to them as well. That's a possibility, but you would know about that too?'

'We should have done. I'll have to check that out.'

Parker relaxed a little. 'I suspect he's had quite a lot of contact with them. They're helping with his problems with the Revenue.'

Hood looked anything but pleased. Something had obviously gone wrong somewhere.

'Anything else?'

'Yes. The windows had been blacked out but I was just able to see that a mattress and a blanket had been left inside – they had definitely not been there before. I was going to ask Doyle about it this morning, but he hasn't got here yet. There's been some incident at the prison apparently.'

'So I heard. Did you report any of this?'

'No, I didn't. I didn't see the point. Especially as the title is about to be transferred.'

'Could Doyle have known about the mattress and the blanket?'

'I don't think so. He might have known about the padlock – if he asked the accountants to improve the security. But as for the rest? How could he? Ever since he and that Hamilton woman split up he's become obsessed about her claiming some of his assets. And she has certainly threatened to do so. For some reason he thought she might be targeting this farm, though why he should think that I cannot say.'

'If she'd moved in, could it have scuppered the sale?'

'Of course not. The title has effectively passed now that the condition has been satisfied. It's only a matter of dealing with the paperwork. She'd simply be a trespasser. It would be comparatively easy to get her out. But I never understood his concerns. Julia Hamilton wouldn't want to move into a place like that anyway. It's uninhabitable. It'll be demolished once the deal is finalised.'

'Demolished?'

'Oh, yes. The planning permission includes authorisation to demolish the whole lot, house, outbuildings and both barns. The developers want the site completely cleared.'

'When is that scheduled?'

'Not my concern. But it must be pretty soon. We've been waiting on the planners for over nine months. The developers will want to get on with it. Time is money you know. They have it all lined up to start as soon as the transfer is effected.'

'And when will that be?'

'Immediately. The paperwork is already drawn up. A few signatures and registering the transfer and they'll be ready to go.'

Hood had an immediate picture of the demolition proceeding with Mrs Campion and the boy locked in the cellar.

'And he didn't ask you to do anything apart from check the place was secure?'

'Absolutely. I thought it was a complete waste of my time.' Parker paused. 'Has something happened there? Is that why you're asking these questions?'

'Again, I'm not in a position to say, Mr Parker. But I'm grateful for your help. I may be able to give you further information later today. Now, if you'll excuse me?'

Hood conducted Parker to the door. He then telephoned Chief Superintendent Craven.

'Ah, Harry,' said Craven. 'Just the man. The helicopter has been over this farm. Nothing to report but we are on our way there. I have a firearms team on hand but I don't think we'll need them. If they're being held there I suspect they'll be on their own. If these kidnappers are as professional as I think they are, they're probably on their way out of the country as we speak. They'll have been recruited to put the frighteners on the judge and abduct his family. Once they had Mrs Campion and the boy securely locked away, that would be their function completed.'

Hood glanced at his watch. It was ten forty-three.

'Let me know if you find anything. The judge is due to sit in less that twenty-five minutes, although there may be a delay. One of the defendants hasn't arrived yet.'

'Will do. We're approaching the drive now. We're disguised as building contractors, so we shouldn't arouse suspicions if anyone is here. We'll speak later.'

The call was terminated. Hood pondered whether he should ring the judge. He decided to wait. He should have some news – good or bad – within minutes. Hooper approached him.

'Message from Group Eleven, sir. Doyle should be here by eleven thirty. The prison is functioning normally again.'

'Does the judge know?'

'The court clerk gave me the information, so I assume he does.'

'Do we know where Julia Hamilton is?'

'She's on her way from London – with Bill Savage. His car has been picked up on the new ANPR cameras on the M1. He went past the Crick junction about fifteen minutes ago.'

'Keep me informed, Andrew. I may want to speak to Miss Hamilton and Mr Savage, especially if they're on their way here.'

A few minutes later his phone rang again. It was ACC Knowles.

'Harry, I've just discovered that someone left a rather odd message for you. Shirley thought it might be important so she got in touch with me when it eventually got to her. We have no idea who it was who phoned it in.'

'What's the message?'

'*Tell Hood Orley Farm. Urgent. It's a matter of life and death*. That's it. It fits in with what you suspected.'

'It certainly does. What time was the message left?'

'That's the embarrassing bit. It was phoned in at 8.05 this morning. Someone's in for a roasting if it turns out to be significant.'

'What?' replied Hood, looking at his watch. 'That's well over two hours ago! Of course it's significant. It virtually confirms my theory. That's where the judge's wife must be. Have you told Tony Craven?'

'Yes. He should almost be there by now.'

'Thank you, ma'am. I'll be in touch.'

Hood terminated the call. He was furious. If anything had happened to the judge's wife and son the police were going to look not only foolish but grossly incompetent. But who could have phoned in such a message? And why? Did someone want the police to find them before the judge gave his ruling? Or was the tip-off from someone who had discovered what was afoot? This was becoming more mysterious by the minute.

Seven minutes later, his phone rang again.

'Harry? It's Craven. We've found them! They're fine; a bit cold and hungry but otherwise OK. No sign of the kidnappers, just as I thought. Your hunch was right. They were locked in the cellar. I'm arranging for them to be brought to the Crown court in a covert vehicle. Can you make arrangements for it to be admitted into the car park? It'll take about thirty-five minutes to get there. You can tell the judge they're safe.'

Hood breathed a huge sigh of relief.

'Will do.'

'And Harry, I reckon there'll be a commendation for this. Very well done! I've just had the chief constable on. He's absolutely delighted.'

Hood looked at his watch. It was ten fifty-three. A commendation was the last thing on his mind, especially as the "tip-off" had never got through to him when it should have done. The chief was not going to be very pleased about that. He made his way to the court office and was directed from there into the judicial corridor. Campion was in his room. He was plainly a man in torment. He stood up as Hood entered. As he looked at Hood's face his spirits rose.

'We've found them, Judge – and they're perfectly OK. They're on their way here.'

Campion sat down heavily in his chair. He placed his head in his hands for a few seconds before he looked up.

'Thank God, and thank you,' he said, fighting back the tears. He stood up and approached Hood, taking his hand.

'I just don't have the words… I shall never be able to repay you.'

'Just doing my job,' answered Hood, shifting from one foot to the other. He decided not to mention the tip-off.

'May I ask something? Where were they?'

'Locked in a cellar in a disused farm in the Vale of Belvoir – a farm that was owned by Michael Doyle until comparatively recently. Well, I say owned by Doyle – it's really owned by one of his companies.'

'Is that so? Not that professional after all then?'

The relief in Campion's voice was plain.

'We mustn't jump to any conclusions – not yet. They should be here in about thirty minutes.'

The judge looked at the clock on the wall.

'Thirty minutes you say? Excellent! I shan't need to sit until they get here. Your little ruse seems to have worked. Doyle won't be here before half past eleven and it will take a few more minutes to get him up into court.'

Hood smiled. 'You'll be able to deal with the case on a proper basis now, will you, sir?'

The judge shook his head. 'Unfortunately, no. I shall still have to recuse myself. Any ruling of mine could not stand in the circumstances. You see, we can't be certain the defendants are behind this.' The judge reflected for a moment. 'But we might be able to expose whoever the kidnappers intended to place in the court. There won't be a problem checking everyone who comes in?'

'There certainly won't. I have already given instructions that no one – and I mean no one – will be allowed to enter or leave without being scrutinised. I'm including counsel and the CPS.'

'Quite right. They could have been bluffing of course, but there would have to be someone in court to check I did as they required.'

'I've also given instructions that all mobile phones are to be handed over on admittance. We don't want any calls being made from inside the court. I hope you don't mind?'

'You have my full authority, Mr Hood. Anything you deem necessary is fine by me. Tell me, how did you find them and in such a short time?'

Hood smiled and shook his head.

'I can't pretend that it was a great bit of detective work.' (Should he mention the tip-off that never got through? He decided not. After all, he had "cracked" the case before he heard of it.) 'Do you know; it was essentially a bit of a hunch. Sometimes that's all it takes. That or someone has been praying very hard indeed. Mind you, Doyle's solicitor played his part, although he may not quite know how. I think we can exclude him from our list of suspects.'

Hood paused.

'Could I ask how you propose to manage things if you can't deal with the case yourself?'

'That's up to you, Mr Hood. As my family is now safe, I am in your hands. I'm quite prepared to give a short judgement explaining why I am recusing myself. That will mean things will be in the open so we might just out one of the gang, assuming they do have someone in court. But if you want the matter to remain under wraps in order to progress your investigation, I shall simply recuse myself without giving any explanation.'

Hood stroked his chin. He was undecided about what to do. 'It will cause a deal of speculation if nothing is said. Let me speak to the chief superintendent. He's in a better position to judge how we should proceed.'

There was a knock on the door.

'Come in,' called the judge.

It was Andrew Hooper. 'Sorry to interrupt, sir, but I thought you should know at once. Julia Hamilton has arrived at court with Bill Savage. They're both queuing at security.'

The judge looked at Hood. 'Is that Bill Savage who's just taken silk?'

'The very man,' replied Hood. 'He's the one she's been with in Brussels.'

'You don't think he could be involved?'

'No sir. Most unlikely. But the lady is a quite different matter. I shall be wanting to speak to her. I would love to see her face if you were able to explain in court why you can't deal with the case.'

Hood chuckled to himself. The judge made a suggestion.

'You'd better speak to your chief superintendent. If she is involved it might just draw her out into the open.'

'Not that one,' interrupted Hooper. 'She's as cool as they come. I'd bet the expression on her face wouldn't change at all.'

'We'll have to wait and see,' said Hood. 'If she is involved, I expect she's the one who's here to see that you stick to their demands. Quite clever, when you think about it – all this pretence that she and Doyle had broken up. Caused some of us to take our eye of the ball, eh, Andrew?'

Hooper smiled but said nothing.

'We'll leave you now, Judge. I have to make arrangements for the vehicle bringing your wife and son to be admitted to the car park. We don't want anyone knowing they're on their way here, and I don't want them to be seen by anyone other than yourself – not yet.'

'Of course. I've already instructed the court manager to co-operate fully. She has no idea what's going on. Only Malcolm Hemming knows the full picture. I shall be waiting at the judges' entrance, if you've no objection? I suppose you'll bring them in that way?'

'Yes. That shouldn't be a problem.'

Hood checked his watch. It was 11.09 a.m.

CHAPTER FORTY-NINE

At 11.29 a.m., Malcolm Hemming unlocked and opened the doors to Court 2. Three uniformed police officers stood sentinel. No one was allowed in without producing evidence of identification. Any mobile phones were temporarily removed and placed in a cardboard box which remained in the custody of one of the officers.

'Is this really necessary?' demanded Bill Savage as he and Julia Hamilton reached the head of the queue, 'I am a QC, you know.'

'Judge's orders,' replied the officer, glancing at the proffered driving licence. 'No exceptions – not even for you Mr Savage.'

'So, you know who I am?'

'Yes sir. You cross-examined me once. I'll never forget it. OK, you and the lady can pass through.'

'I wonder what this is all about?' whispered Jules. 'I don't remember anything like this happening before. Why have they removed your phone? I'm glad I didn't have mine with me.'

Savage puffed out his chest and put on a serious air.

'I've come across it a couple of times – but only in really serious cases. Perhaps they think your ex might try and do a runner if the case goes against him? There's still no secure dock in this courtroom, you know.'

'I can't see Michael doing that. Look, there's his solicitor, Trevor Parker.'

Parker acknowledged both Jules and Savage, but purposively did not approach them. He took his seat immediately behind where Harriet Lassiter would be sitting. Randell Richards then came in; he looked around at the already crowded courtroom before taking his seat in front of Trevor Parker but there was no sign of leading counsel. Malcolm Hemming, acting on Campion's instructions, placed several law reports on the bench together with the judge's red notebook. He looked at the public gallery before disappearing back into the judicial corridor.

'Won't be long now,' said Savage. 'I must say, I can't wait to hear Campion's ruling. I've never been so excited about a case I didn't have a brief in.'

Jules nodded but said nothing.

Downstairs at the judicial entrance Campion embraced his wife and son. Chief Superintendent Craven looked away then whispered to Hood.

'If the judge feels up to it, I have no objection to his giving a full explanation as to the events of the last two days. I'm pretty convinced that the kidnappers are well gone. You can give Julia Hamilton a pull before she leaves the court. We have precious little else to go on. I'll interview Benson and Doyle later. Let's hope that the judge's remarks rattle a few cages. Of course, he'll have to put a ban on anything being reported, at least for the time being.'

Campion led his wife and son upstairs to his room, Christopher wriggling in his mother's arms. The police entourage followed at a respectful distance. Craven continued his whispered conversation with Hood. 'The chief's been told about the tip-off. He's given instructions that it's not to be mentioned to anyone, least of all to the judge. But it means we're going to have to give some serious thought to what was really going on here.'

Hood nodded.

'It doesn't take anything away from what you and your team achieved, Harry. The chief still thinks it was a great piece of detective work – and so do I.'

Hood nodded again. He still couldn't believe that the message had not been passed to him. He had observed on many occasions that the changes introduced through new technology didn't always lead to improved results. People were more important than gadgetry. He and Craven stopped as they reached the judge's chambers. The judge turned and invited them in. They followed Campion and his family into his room.

'I just want to get home,' said a greatly relieved Celia Campion, as she placed her son on the worn carpet. 'That cellar was filthy. Christopher is in urgent need of a bath too.'

Young Christopher seemed unconcerned as he toddled round the room and tried on his father's wig. He'd regarded the whole thing as one giant adventure.

Celia smiled.

'I never realised being the wife of a judge was so high risk!'

Campion kissed her, tenderly.

'You're sure they didn't harm you?'

'Never laid a finger on me. I was blindfolded just before we arrived at the farm, but no one bothered us once we were locked in. I never heard a thing from them. I suspect they left shortly afterwards. I waited for an hour or so then started shouting – but no one came.'

'Hardly surprising. I'm told it's in the middle of nowhere.'

'You can say that again. The drive is about a quarter of a mile long. It's really remote.'

'Do you need anything?'

'Apart from that bath, no. I must smell something terrible.'

Campion kissed his wife again.

'You've never smelt sweeter to me.'

He held her close for several seconds.

'If you can wait about half an hour or so, I'll come home with you. Not that it'll seem like home anymore. I'm glad we're moving.'

'There'll be a police escort and a guard at your home for the next few weeks, sir,' interrupted Craven. 'Until you move or we catch these people. And we shall need to go through things with Mrs Campion in more detail as well. I hope this afternoon will not be too early. The forensic boys should have finished by then. We shall have to ask you to wait until they're done before you return home.'

'I'll be fine, Chief Superintendent. Just give me a few hours and I'll do all I can to help you.'

The judge smiled at his wife and turned to Malcolm Hemming who was standing by the door.

'You can tell the leaders and Mr Cavan-Henry that I shall not be giving judgement today. No need to say anything further. I shall make the position clear when I come into court.'

The usher nodded and departed. The chief superintendent looked at Mrs Campion. Although she seemed remarkably unaffected by her ordeal, he was concerned that her condition might deteriorate. She could easily suffer from delayed shock.

'I can arrange counselling if you like? This must have been a very traumatic experience.'

'No need for that,' replied Celia with a smile. 'A large gin and tonic after a hot bath will do the trick!'

The judge hugged his wife again.

'We shall want to speak to you, Judge, as well. I'll leave the initial questioning to Chief Inspector Hood – he's in the best position to deal with matters at present. It's down to him that we found you, you know.'

'I'm fully aware of that,' said the judge. 'We are both more grateful than we can say.'

Mrs Campion nodded her appreciation and removed her husband's wig from her son's head. Christopher protested but his mother picked him up.

'Daddy needs it. He's got to go into court and deal with these very naughty men.'

'I want my teddy,' said the child.

'Where's his teddy bear?' asked the judge. 'You didn't leave it in the cellar?'

She turned to her husband and spoke a little wearily.

'No I didn't. The superintendent has it – in an exhibits bag! I'm hoping I might have obtained a sample of DNA from at least one of these animals. I managed to rub it against one of them in the darkness when we were en route. She'd lifted part of her mask just before I was blindfolded. Christopher and I were quite a double act, weren't we Christopher?' She stroked the top of his head. 'They're not as clever as they think they are.'

'She?' echoed Craven.

'Oh, yes,' replied Mrs Campion. 'One of them was definitely a woman. I recognised her perfume – L'Air du Temps. I sometimes use it myself.'

The judge smiled broadly and brushed his face against hers.

'So you have been listening to some of what I've told you about DNA evidence?'

His wife did not react other than to raise her eyebrows. She was obviously very tired.

'Can we get this over with, darling? I could really do with that gin and tonic despite the hour. I've lost all track of time.'

'Of course.'

The judge smiled again as he put a protective arm around his wife and son. Christopher made a final but unsuccessful attempt to grab the judge's wig. His father avoided his little hands and placed it on his own head.

'I've learnt one thing from all this,' he said philosophically.

'What's that?' asked Celia, taking his hand and kissing it.

'Never reserve judgement. If I'd given my decision last Wednesday, none of this would have happened!'

★★★★

The two silks and Cavan-Henry, still in his junior's robes, entered the courtroom after reluctantly proving who they were. Markham-Moore followed them.

'Here they come,' whispered Savage. 'They look very pensive. I wonder if they already know how he's going to rule?'

As leading counsel took their seats, there was a loud knock on the judge's door. Malcolm Hemming appeared and surveyed the crowded court.

'All rise,' he commanded. He then stepped back as Campion strode in, bowed and took his seat. The clerk stood up.

'Put up Benson and Doyle,' she ordered.

The door in the dock opened and two security officers appeared, followed by the defendants. They were identified and told to sit. Hood saw Julia Hamilton glance towards the dock. There was no sign of recognition from Doyle.

Harriet Lassiter was quickly on her feet.

'May I apologise for the late arrival of Mr Doyle?' she said. 'Apparently there was some sort of incident at the prison and his departure was delayed for well over an hour.'

Campion smiled. He seemed remarkably relaxed. Quite different from an hour and a half before.

'No need to apologise, Miss Lassiter. These things happen.'

'Well, I'm grateful your Honour was prepared to wait until he was produced.'

'Again, there is no need to apologise. Mr Doyle is entitled to be present at all stages of the hearing of his case. That is his constitutional right.'

The judge emphasised the last two words. Doyle nodded in the dock. Lassiter sat down. Campion opened his notebook and withdrew a few sheets of paper from the back. He glanced at the dock then at the public gallery. He noticed Bill Savage sitting next to an attractive looking woman. He rightly surmised this was Julia Hamilton. He recalled that he had seen her in his court on previous occasions sitting behind counsel. He cleared his throat and began to speak.

'Last Wednesday, I heard submissions from counsel concerning two applications to dismiss the charges faced by the defendants Charles Benson and Michael Doyle. Both applications are opposed by the Crown. I should say at the outset that I am very grateful to counsel. This is an unusual and difficult issue and I have been greatly assisted both by the written arguments and the oral submissions. I have prepared a written ruling which I had intended to hand down this morning. In it, I come to the conclusion that I am driven to accept the submissions advanced on behalf of the defendants and dismiss the charges.'

There was an almost audible groan from Markham-Moore. Doyle stood up and punched the air in delight. He was immediately told to sit down by the dock officer. Campion looked up. A wry smile crossed his face. A similar expression could be seen on Hood's face. They both knew what was coming next. Neither of the leaders nor Cavan-Henry reacted. They, too, knew that Campion would not be giving a judgement. But they were not expecting what occurred moments later.

'As I was saying,' the judge continued, 'I had prepared a ruling which I *had* intended to hand down this morning. But that is no longer necessary.'

He paused. Counsel looked first at Campion then at each other. The smile on Hood's face broadened. Doyle became agitated.

'Yesterday morning at about 4.45 a.m., an incident took place quite without precedent in this country. My home was unlawfully entered by a gang of armed criminals. My wife and two-and-a-half-year-old son were abducted. I was assaulted and held prisoner in my own home until just before seven thirty this morning.'

A loud murmur passed round the courtroom. Several people gasped in astonishment. Campion looked directly at Julia Hamilton. As Andrew Hooper had predicted, her expression remained quite impassive. Harriet Lassiter seemed shocked. Trevor Parker shook his head in disbelief. His immediate thoughts were that Doyle was behind this and he now understood what had informed the questions Hood had asked him earlier. Bill Savage's jaw fell open. The usher called for silence. The judge continued, touching the bruise on his forehead as he did so.

'I was told in the clearest terms that unless I ruled in favour of the defendants, my wife and son would be murdered.'

The judges voice faltered for a moment. Audible gasps were heard from all round the court.

'A gun, which was undoubtedly loaded, was pointed at me from a distance of no more than three feet as this demand was communicated to me. Under the direction of this gunman, I prepared the ruling to which I have referred.'

He paused and looked up.

'I have no intention of complying with this demand or handing down the ruling that was procured by these threats. Had I not been subject to such intimidation, I cannot say what decision I would have reached. The arguments are finely balanced and I had yet to come to a final conclusion before my home was invaded. Happily, thanks to the brilliant work of the police, in particular Chief Inspector Henry Hood and his team of detectives, my wife and son were located less than an hour ago. They are now safe. In the circumstances, I do not feel able to continue with this case. I am sure that *almost* everyone in this courtroom will understand why. I therefore propose to recuse myself. No doubt the events of the last two days will fall to be investigated by the police. That will, I am sure, be a careful, extensive and drawn-out inquiry. Whether these defendants were in any way involved in these events, I simply do not know. That will be a matter for the police to inquire into. But for the moment, both will continue to be remanded in custody. I shall contact the senior presiding judge and inform him of what has occurred. Another judge will be assigned to this case. That is all I propose to say for the moment. The case will stand adjourned until a date to be fixed. I direct that unless and until the court orders otherwise there must be no reporting of my remarks. I shall make an order under the provisions of the Contempt of Court Act. If the press or other media have any concerns about such an order, they will be free to make submissions later.'

Campion looked towards Malcolm Hemming.

'The court will rise,' shouted the usher, scowling towards the dock. For his part, Malcolm Hemming had no doubts as to who was responsible. The court did as he requested. Campion bowed to counsel and quickly departed. There was an immediate disturbance in the dock as Benson shouted to anyone interested in hearing him that it had nothing to do with him. Doyle was silent and ashen faced. Both men were bundled into the secure holding room immediately adjacent and the door firmly closed.

'Absolutely unbelievable,' whispered Cronshaw to Harriet Lassiter. 'I have never heard of such an outrageous thing in all my life. To kidnap a judge's wife and child; why, it's diabolical!'

'If Doyle is behind this he can kiss goodbye to seeing the outside of a prison for the next thirty years,' replied Lassiter. 'Poor Tom Campion – he must have been through absolute hell! And as for his wife and son, well, it doesn't bear thinking about.'

The increasing noise in the courtroom made further comment pointless. Two members of the press rushed up to Cronshaw.

'Does that mean we can't report any of this? This is the biggest news story we've ever had. Nothing much ever happens in Leicester. Surely it's in the public interest that we should be able to report it?'

'I'll check with the judge when I have the chance. He may allow a report providing these defendants are not mentioned. They still have to be tried you know. But for the moment, you abide by his ruling, clear?'

'I suppose so.'

Julia Hamilton and Bill Savage made their way towards the exit in silence. Savage was quite affected by what he had heard; Jules remained quietly composed. There were a number of people in front of them which delayed their departure because identification had again to be established to the satisfaction of the police officers and mobile telephones retrieved. Hood intervened.

'Could I have a word?' he said quietly.

'This has nothing to do with me,' insisted Julia Hamilton quickly. 'I've only just got back from Brussels.'

'True,' confirmed Savage. 'We went there last Wednesday. Miss Hamilton has hardly been out of my sight.'

'Then we'd like a word with you too, sir. If you've no objection?'

'Of course not,' replied Savage, looking more than a little flustered and embarrassed. 'Only too eager to assist, but I really don't know anything.'

'If you would go with Detective Sergeant Hooper, sir. I would like to speak with Miss Hamilton in private.'

★★★★

'I'm sure he's telling the truth, sir,' said Hooper, as he reported back to Hood following his interview with Bill Savage. 'He's produced their travel documents and the receipt from the hotel. There's no doubt about it, they were in Brussels for six nights – cost him a small fortune. And it looks like he paid for everything.'

'So he's smitten with her too, is he?'

'Looks that way sir, but I think he's more concerned about his career at the moment. He can't afford any scandal in his position.'

'What about his mobile phone?'

'He's no objections to our interrogating it, but he says he's hardly used it while he was abroad. He says he rang his clerk a couple of times but that was about it. He has a fitting arranged at Ede and Ravenscroft in the morning.'

'Did Julia Hamilton use his phone at all?'

'Not that he recalls.'

'She hasn't got a phone with her,' said Hood. 'She says she left it in her flat at Harbour Buildings and didn't take it with her to Belgium. Ian Lunn's gone over there with her to get it. She volunteered the information so you can guarantee there'll be nothing on it.'

'But if she was behind this, sir, she could have used a phone at the hotel.'

'The Belgian police are looking into that – but she's too clever to have left any trace – assuming she was involved. We're also checking the hotel at Heathrow. She might have been in touch with the kidnappers last night. It's all just a bit too convenient, don't you think? The perfect alibi – out of the country and with a new QC as a witness. She's denied everything, of course, and we have nothing concrete to challenge what she says. I hope Tony Craven gets somewhere with Benson. The word is he's really worried about being dragged into the kidnapping plot – so he might just open up.'

'What did she say about Doyle? Are they still an item?'

'Not according to her. It's all over, or so she says. But, frankly, Andrew, I don't believe her. I think she's using Savage to give us the run around. By the way, did you tell him that she's pregnant?'

'No I didn't. I wasn't sure. Has she confirmed it?'

'Not exactly, but that was one thing she didn't deny. And I can tell you, she's pregnant all right. It's got to the point where she can't hide it any longer – if you know what you're looking for.'

Hooper smiled. 'I suppose you would know, sir. What about the accountants? Any joy there?'

Hood sighed.

'You won't believe this. The deputy governor at the prison who was supposed to be overseeing the monitoring of Doyle's calls treated the accountants as if they were lawyers. Because they were advising Doyle about his position with the Revenue, the governor reckons that legal professional privilege applies; so his calls to the accountants were not recorded.'

'Is that right?'

'Well, it's a bit of a grey area and I don't pretend to understand the whys and wherefores, but it means we have no record of about half a dozen calls that Doyle made to them. I'm going to have to interview the partner who was dealing with him – when I have the time.'

'Are you going to arrest her, sir?'

'Not yet. I've asked her to come back next week. I want to wait and see if the chief super gets anywhere with Benson. He will be the easier of the two to crack.'

'What about Doyle?'

'Craven is seeing him tomorrow morning. I'm hoping to go with him. They're transferring Doyle to Wakefield. He's been reclassified as Cat "A". That'll teach him. If he thought Leicester was bad, he's not going to enjoy Wakefield.' Hood smiled. 'We thought we'd let him sweat for a bit. He'll have been told by now that he's going to be on remand for months with no chance of bail. That should undermine his confidence a bit.'

'If he and Hamilton are deceiving us about their relationship it might well shake him up if he discovered we had arrested her?'

'I agree, but we have to have some evidence first. The chief is taking a direct interest in this investigation now. So we can't afford any mistakes. Tony Craven and I have been summoned to the presence the day after tomorrow. There's going to have to be a major rethink in respect of judicial security too. Judge Campion's been contacted by the Lord Chief Justice. He was apparently furious. There's going to be a fundamental review of the whole system by the Met commissioner. We can't have anything like this happening again.'

'So we won't be involved in that?'

'No Andrew. We've got the easy bit. We just have to find and arrest the kidnappers, that's all.'

CHAPTER FIFTY

Thursday, 8 April 1999

'I can assure you, Mr Cavan-Henry; I had nothing to do with it. I knew nothing about it – until the judge raised it yesterday morning. I mean it. Who would kidnap a judge's wife? You'd have to be stark staring mad!'

Cavan-Henry and his instructing solicitor's representative had travelled to Woodhill Prison in Milton Keynes to which establishment Benson had been transferred immediately after his brief appearance before Judge Campion. Woodhill was a category "A" prison and he had been confined in the high-security wing where his activities were under constant surveillance.

'Kidnapping a judge's wife and child in an attempt to force the judge to decide a case in favour of the defence is unheard of in this country, Mr Benson,' said his barrister. 'Both you and Doyle are likely to be treated as suspects, although I'm bound to agree I haven't come across any evidence that suggests you were involved.'

'Of course you haven't – that's because there isn't any. What will happen to me though, if I get done for it?'

'I don't think there's any doubt about that. If you are "done for it" as you put it, they'll want to make an example of you. Oh, yes. There's no doubt about that! The establishment will come down on you like a ton of bricks. It'll be life imprisonment without a doubt. It wouldn't surprise me at all if you ended up before the Lord Chief Justice.'

Benson dropped his head. His eyes filled with tears.

'But I really wasn't involved. How could I have been? I don't have the contacts. The only person whose been to see me apart from you and Miss Riley here is my fiancée – although I don't suppose she'll stick around for much longer when she hears about this.' He looked up and spoke angrily. 'If anyone is responsible for this, it'll be Doyle.'

'Be careful what you say, Charlie,' interjected Miss Riley. 'Remember the police are coming to see you later.'

'Don't worry. I shan't tell them anything – apart from the fact this is definitely not down to me.'

Benson looked at Cavan-Henry; tears were now running down his cheeks.

'Look, Mr Cavan-Henry, I know you think I'm guilty of the robbery and I'm not so stupid that I don't know this DNA thing is just a technicality, so tell me what would I get for the robbery if I pleaded?'

Cavan-Henry pursed his lips. 'If they dropped the attempted murder, which they probably would in your case, and you were not prosecuted for the kidnapping, about fourteen years I would have thought.'

'Fourteen years? As long as that?'

'One of the guards was shot, remember? And there was nearly two million stolen.'

He dropped his head again. 'And how long would I actually have to serve?'

'Two thirds, although you could apply for parole after half.'

'Seven years?'

'Yes. But you shouldn't assume you'd necessarily get parole, certainly not at the first time of asking, but your previous good character would be a help.'

Benson nodded. He was now calm. 'All right. See what you can do, will you? If they'll take the robbery, I'll plead – but I'm not dropping anyone else in it. I want to live.'

'Those are your instructions?'

'Those are my instructions.'

'You don't want us to run the admissibility argument? That's still open to you, you know. The fact that Judge Campion has withdrawn from the case doesn't affect the matter one iota.'

Benson shook his head. 'No. I don't. I admit I was there. I wasn't armed and I didn't know that madman was going to shoot anybody. That wasn't part of the plan.'

The barrister looked hard at Benson but said nothing for several seconds.

'All right, Mr Benson,' sighed Cavan-Henry looking at his instructing solicitor, 'I take that to be an admission. I shall draft something for you to sign. We don't want any ambiguity about this.'

'No. I want to come clean. I would have admitted it before if I hadn't been so scared. But I got myself involved with some pretty dangerous people. I must have been off my head.'

'So it would seem. It would reduce your sentence, you know, if you were to agree to assist the prosecution with the others.'

'No way! I'd be a dead man before I got to court. Anyway, I don't even know who the others were. I don't know their names or anything about them. That's the way Doyle works.'

'So Doyle was involved was he?'

'I didn't say that.'

He turned away for a moment. 'The truth is he wasn't even there. And I'm not saying anything else – so don't ask me. I'll plead guilty but I'm not saying a word about the others and I want that made very clear. I want you to tell Doyle's solicitor that.'

He became distressed, his eyes filling with tears once more. He was plainly worried about his safety.

'They'd have no problem seeing to me in here. I'm going on rule 43 as it is.'

Cavan-Henry started to collect his papers.

'What about your share of the money? If that was recovered that might help.'

Benson shook his head.

'You probably won't believe me, but I haven't had my cut yet. All I was given was seven and a half thousand to tide me over, and most of that has gone.'

Cavan-Henry glanced at Miss Riley.

'All right. I shall ask Miss Riley to take a full proof from you but it's up to you what you say. And I strongly advise that you should have her with you when you speak to the police this afternoon, understand?'

'Yes, sir. I think that would be a good idea.'

CHAPTER FIFTY-ONE

Friday, 9 April 1999

Chief Superintendent Craven and Chief Inspector Hood travelled up to Wakefield Prison where Doyle was now being held. The judge had revisited his order under the Contempt of Court Act and allowed the facts of the abduction to be reported, subject to the proviso that the defendants and the nature of the case he had been trying remained confidential. Inevitably, all the newspapers led with the story the following day. "An attack on the very foundations of British justice" thundered *The Times* in a leading article. The tabloids were less prosaic and, in the absence of any hard facts, allowed their imaginations to run freely in describing the devastating effect on the judge's wife and son. Several journalists and photographers were virtually camped outside The Old Bakehouse; a couple of the more enterprising, from the *News of the World,* had pretended they were bona fide potential purchasers of the judge's home in an attempt to get inside, but the police frustrated them. No one was allowed within 400 metres of the house without passing through a heavy police cordon and the house was temporarily taken off the market.

Michael Doyle had been depressed beyond description, as he had worked his way through two newspapers en route to Wakefield in the early morning of 9 April. He appreciated, of course, that as he would have been the principal beneficiary of the ruling the judge had prepared, but not delivered, he would be in the frame for the kidnapping and blackmail. Perpetual imprisonment seemed to be stretching out before him. Neither was the irony of the situation lost on him. He genuinely knew nothing about it. Absolutely nothing! While he marvelled at the lengths Jules was prepared to go to ensure his release, it had never entered his head that such a dramatic solution would be attempted. His only consolation was that it demonstrated as nothing else could, the strength of her feelings for him and her absolute commitment to him and their child. At least that is what he chose to believe.

But it had all gone wrong. How and why he didn't know. And he didn't want to know. He realised, of course, after Trevor Parker had, in all innocence, delivered the message from Jules "we'll always have Paris" that something was in the wind. But he had been deliberately kept out of the loop, for his own protection, or so he assumed. That was how he and Jules operated – on a need to know basis. Now it had rebounded and there was nothing he could do about it. As far as he could see, he would only be able to clear himself by revealing Jules' part in this latest conspiracy and if he did, he probably wouldn't be believed. It would simply be assumed that he was part of the plan. So, he resolved, that was something he would never do. She had stood by him loyally. The least he could do was to stand by her in return. But he needed to see her. He didn't care how it was done; he simply had to see her. Only by looking her in the face could he be really sure she was still his. Trevor Parker would have to arrange it, somehow.

Harriet Lassiter had seen him briefly before he was removed from Leicester Crown Court after the hearing. He had assured her, quite truthfully, that he had not been involved in the abduction. She, for her part, had told him that there would be no trial for several months on the original charges. The kidnap and blackmail would have priority and the investigation would be anything but rapid.

'I'm afraid you're going to be on remand for a long time,' she had said solemnly.

'What about this legal point of yours,' he had asked. 'Does it still apply?'

'In theory, yes, but a lot will depend on what Benson decides to do. He seems very panicky to me. If he were to abandon the point and plead guilty, the prosecution could rely on his conviction to prove the connection between the two of you. The DNA would no longer be relevant.'

'But he won't do that will he? Not when he still has a chance of going scot-free?'

'I don't know,' Lassiter had replied, coolly. 'He'll be in the frame for the kidnapping too. He might well prefer to do his time for the robbery if it keeps him out of a kidnapping charge. We'll have to wait and see.'

'Will you be able to find out?'

'I can ask his barrister, but he isn't obliged to tell me.'

As Lassiter and Randell Richards had left the cells and made their way to the robing room, Harriet was crestfallen.

'Do you think he was involved in this, Randell? If he were, they'll throw the key away and I'd have no great desire to continue representing him.'

Randell Richards had been giving the matter a great deal of thought. This was, by far, the biggest and most lucrative case he'd had in years. He had no intention of allowing the junior brief to slip from his grasp. Not if he could help it.

'I don't think he was, you know. How could he have organised it? He's had no contact with anyone but his lawyers for weeks. And why would he have sent Trevor Parker round to the very place where the kidnappers were going to hold Mrs Campion? It doesn't make sense.'

'Trevor's told you about that has he?'

'Yes – and he's also told the police. I think Chief Inspector Hood was speculating that our very ethical instructing solicitor might have been acting as Doyle's errand boy. Trevor was anxious to make it clear that he wasn't.'

'That might make his position rather difficult with Doyle?'

'It might, but he's retiring in July and he said the delay in any trial is not going to affect his decision to go.'

'That's all we need. A new instructing solicitor taking over. I can tell you one thing, Randell. I'm glad that my clerk insisted on having the brief fees up front. I have a nasty feeling this case is going to fall apart under us.'

While Randell Richards shared Harriet's sentiments about his brief fee he was determined to ignore anything that might tell against his continuing in the case.

'What, even if there's no real evidence that he was involved in the abduction?'

'Yes, but he might have known it was going to happen all the same? That girlfriend of his or one of the other gang members might have put the whole thing in motion. I noticed that Hood wanted a word with her this morning.'

'That wouldn't make him guilty though, would it? He would have had to have agreed to it and done something in furtherance of the conspiracy. Simply expecting something to be done to help him wouldn't be enough. And everyone has assumed that he's the brains behind this robbery. Suppose he isn't? Suppose someone else is the mastermind and that someone else was simply making sure he got out?'

'Your faith in our client is quite touching, Randell – but the police will have a damn good go at putting him in it up to his neck. And they wouldn't need much in the way of evidence either. A jury will have no sympathy with anyone involved once they hear the full details from Mrs Campion. And who was going to benefit from this had it worked out? Michael James Doyle.' She sighed in exasperation. 'Why on earth couldn't he have left it to us?'

'Well, as long as we can continue to act. I don't see that this causes us any professional embarrassment.'

Harriet half smiled.

'Not at the moment, no, but I don't like it. I don't like it one little bit.'

★★★★

'That didn't go too well, did it?' said Craven as he and Hood made their way out of the prison. Hood was deep in thought. They'd spent forty minutes interviewing Doyle about the kidnapping. He had said nothing, other than to deny he had anything to do with it.

'We are going to have a problem in pursuing this allegation against him,' said Hood.

'You mean the tip-off?'

'Exactly. At some stage of this investigation, we are going to have to disclose it. If it was received at 8.05 a.m. – and it has been logged on the computer at that time – it must undermine the case against Doyle. He'd hardly have arranged for a message like that to be sent to the police. If we'd acted on it at once, we'd have discovered Mrs Campion well before the judge was due to give his ruling – which would have defeated the purpose so far as he is concerned.'

'I can see that, Harry. But there's no need to disclose it yet. It would not be in the public interest. We need more time to find out exactly what was going on.'

'Perhaps. But I can't be party to covering it up if it comes to charging Doyle.'

'No one's saying you should. I agree with you – it will have to be disclosed at some stage. All I'm saying is – not yet. And remember. The chief has given strict instructions. No one else is to be told about it. It's not to go beyond the main members of the team.'

'And just how long does he think that's going to last? He'll throw the book at whoever failed to pass the message on. It'll get round – these things always do.'

The two men did not speak for a few moments. Then Craven revealed what he was thinking.

'You don't think all this could simply have been arranged to drop Doyle in it?'

'That's what's been passing through my mind. He'd be the obvious suspect because the kidnappers made it plain that the whole thing was for his benefit'

'But who would want to do that? It doesn't make sense.'

'I don't know – unless the Hamilton woman really has finished with him. If he went down for the robbery and the kidnapping, we'd both be drawing our pensions before he saw the light of day. Perhaps that's what she wants? Michael Doyle permanently out of her life. And there's no way he could have made that phone call. Not at five past eight in the morning.'

'But whoever made the call – the fact remains that the judge's wife and son were abducted – and an attempt made to blackmail the judge. That's what's important, not someone trying to drop Doyle in it. That's just an added bonus.'

CHAPTER FIFTY-TWO

Monday, 19 April 1999

'You have Miss Hamilton's comprehensive statement, Mr Craven,' said the solicitor. 'While she is prepared to answer further questions there are certain matters of a highly personal nature which she is not prepared to discuss.'

'Does that include her relationship with Michael Doyle?'

Craven looked at Jules and smiled. The solicitor answered for her.

'As she makes clear in her statement, that is all in the past. She has had no contact with him for over five weeks now.'

'And her pregnancy?'

Jules interrupted.

'I have confirmed that I'm pregnant – at the moment. I have no intention of identifying the father. That's entirely private. Besides, it's none of your business.'

She sat back in her chair and folded her arms. Craven glanced towards DCI Hood then looked at Jules.

'It might be – if Doyle is the father? You were still in a relationship with him when the child must have been conceived.'

Jules looked at her solicitor before she answered.

'As I've said, I'm not prepared to discuss it. My private life is my affair.'

Craven was not prepared to leave it there.

'You see, what troubles me, Miss Hamilton, is this. You and Doyle might be trying to pull the wool over our eyes. You and he might still be involved with each other. For all we know you could just be trying to give the impression it's all over between you?'

Craven thought he might have touched a nerve. Jules' reaction was swift and heavy with sarcasm.

'What you think is not evidence. Either charge me or release me. There's nothing else to discuss.'

She glared at the chief superintendent then smiled sweetly at Hood.

'As I said earlier, Miss Hamilton, you're not under arrest. You can leave at any time. But it might be less inconvenient to you if you stayed and heard me out.'

Jules remained motionless for a moment.

'Very well. But I really do not think I can tell you anything about this kidnapping. Whoever carried it out must have been mad or…'

Craven interrupted.

'Or desperate! Desperate to ensure that the father of her child was released from custody? You've been working in the law for some years, haven't you? You'd have known that if the charges were dismissed that would have been the end of it. Even if the prosecution appealed, Doyle could not have his acquittal overturned. That's the law.'

Jules gave as good as she got. Hood smiled to himself. He could not fault her reply but he was troubled that the chief superintendent had not disclosed the tip-off.

'What if I did? I also know that a decision of a judge that is brought about by improper pressure could not stand. It would be set aside. Quite simply, it would be a nullity – so it would be no advantage to anybody. I don't think whoever carried this out knew much about the law.'

Craven was not put off.

'Yes, but if this conspiracy had worked, Doyle and Benson would have been released – and twenty-four hours would have gone by before the judge's wife and son were freed. Plenty of time to get Doyle out of the country – by some illicit means.'

Jules shook her head. She came straight back with her answer.

'And what about all his assets in this country? It would have taken a lot longer than twenty-four hours to deal with those – or perhaps he was just going to abandon the lot. Somehow I don't think so, Superintendent. The Michael Doyle I *used* to know is very attached to his property – and his money.'

Touché, thought Hood, but he said nothing. Craven frowned. He realised he was not going to make any progress with Julia Hamilton this day.

'Tell me,' he said. 'Does Mr Savage know you are pregnant with Michael Doyle's child?'

Craven had no doubt that he had touched a nerve this time.

'That's it,' responded Jules, angrily. 'I'll tell you for the last time, I know nothing about this kidnapping. I was out of the country at the time. It had nothing to do with me.'

She stood up.

'I'm leaving now; I see no purpose in continuing this discussion.'

'We may wish to speak to you again.'

'Well, if you have any grounds to arrest me, no doubt you will. But be very careful, Mr Craven. I shall not hesitate to bring proceedings for false arrest and malicious prosecution. Good morning to you.'

Her solicitor smiled as he scrambled out of the room after her. If only all his clients were so self assured!

Craven sighed and wiped his brow.

'Well, Harry, that certainly didn't go to plan either.'

Craven closed the file he had earlier placed on the table.

'She's a right one, isn't she? A really cool customer! If anyone's capable of organising something like this, she has to be the favourite!'

Hood, who had been sitting quietly in the corner, observing, agreed.

'Yes sir. But the trouble is, we haven't any evidence that she did. And she knows it. She also means what she says. If we put a foot wrong with her, we'll be bombarded with legal proceedings. It's all very well for the chief to suggest arresting her and then finding some evidence to justify charging her, but I prefer to do things the other way round. Evidence first and then the arrest.'

Craven laughed.

'I think the chief thinks that if we arrested her and got her banged up for a few days, there might be some movement on the part of Doyle.'

'But it wouldn't be for a few days; her lawyers would have her out on bail in no time. We have to get something more substantial than mere suspicion. And I still think we'll get nothing from Doyle. He and the Hamilton woman might still be as thick as thieves – as we think – but they'll not give one another away.'

Craven stood up and walked away from the table. He then turned and faced Hood.

'I agree. What we need is a way to prise them apart. To inject a bit of mistrust. If Doyle thought Hamilton had said something to us – or vice versa – things might start to move – in our favour.'

'We'd have to be very careful,' cautioned Hood. 'We are at something of a disadvantage compared to them; we have to stick to the rules. And there's still the question of the tip-off.'

'What do you mean? It doesn't affect any case we might be able to build against her, does it?'

'I'm not so sure. It depends what that case is. If she is behind this, it can't be because she wanted to help Doyle. Quite the opposite in fact – if we assume that she engineered the tip-off too.'

'Perhaps we shouldn't assume that? Supposing the tip-off is nothing to do with her or Doyle? It's always possible that it came from someone else. It's certainly something we need to think about very carefully.'

Hood said nothing. He was a stickler for keeping to the rules. The chief superintendent continued to speculate.

'I wonder how Doyle might react if we told him that someone had tipped us off? He's not stupid. Whether he was behind this or not it might just unsettle him if we told him his chance of walking away scot-free had been scuppered by someone betraying him. He might well think that someone was Hamilton.'

'Yes, sir. He might. But we'd have to have a bit more than we have at the moment before we could plant that suspicion in his mind. If he still has contacts on the outside, something very unpleasant could happen to her. We do owe her a duty of care – in the absence of any real evidence she was involved.'

'I suppose that must be right. Anything's possible. Doyle could have been behind it and in cahoots with Hamilton? There again, he may be entirely innocent. Perhaps we should proceed cautiously but I'm not for excluding Doyle – or her – at this stage of the investigation.'

'Neither am I. But it's up to you, sir. Do we disclose the tip-off or not?'

The chief superintendent stroked his chin but said nothing. He reflected on what Hood had said – and knew he was right. The tip-off would have to be disclosed – eventually.

'Not yet Harry. My instinct is that we hold fire for the present. We need to know a lot more before we decide on our final course of action. Remember, I want these kidnappers caught and put away – whatever their motive may have been. If Julia Hamilton is involved in any way, I want her too. If Doyle is involved – the same goes for him. The gravamen of these offences is the effect it had on the judge and his family – and the course of justice. I'm not over interested in the internecine squabbles of a bunch of gangsters.'

Hood nodded. He remained concerned but was prepared to go along with it – for the time being.

'If we are going to keep the tip-off under wraps for the time being, I suppose our best prospect is Bill Savage, you know, the new QC she's been stepping out with. There was a bit of a reaction when you asked her directly about the child's father. I'd lay even money she hasn't told him she's pregnant with Doyle's child. If I were Savage, I'd be a bit concerned if it got about that I was in a relationship with a woman who might have been involved in kidnapping a judge's wife – a woman who was due to give birth to Doyle's offspring. Wouldn't do his new career as a silk much good, would it?'

Craven agreed.

'Perhaps you should have a word with him, Harry? A very discreet word, of course!'

'Perhaps I will, sir. Sergeant Hooper took a brief statement from him on the seventh, but he was, perhaps, a bit too discreet!'

Craven smiled.

'By the way, did your man Lunn get anywhere investigating the potential purchasers of the judge's home?'

'He's not completed the task yet, but he's been in contact with most of them. So far, they're all genuine. Young Craddock has been assisting. He's been quite a find. I'm very impressed with him, as is Sergeant Lunn.'

'Is he? He used to be on my team when I was a DI, did Lunn. We never really got on. Didn't see eye to eye on things.'

'I have always found him perfectly satisfactory – although he does prefer to work on his own. He's not what I would call a team player.'

'Well, I suppose it takes all sorts. Which potential purchasers have not been accounted for?'

Hood looked at his notebook.

'A couple from Buckinghamshire – they're on holiday at present – and an American woman. She said she was the wife of a visiting American professor. Craddock is checking out local universities, but he's not come up with anything yet.'

'What name did she give?'

'Epstein. Karen Epstein. According to the judge's wife, she said her husband was an associate professor of American literature somewhere in Pennsylvania. She didn't catch where. Craddock's going through all the colleges in and around Philadelphia with PC Munt. There are dozens of them apparently. I never realised the Americans were so keen on further education.'

Craven laughed.

'Did Mrs Campion give a description?'

'Yes. But she's not confident at this stage that she would necessarily identify her. The woman wore dark glasses – never took them off. She said she had trouble with her eyes. Mrs Campion was a bit distracted at the time as young Christopher was playing up and she left the woman to look at some of the house on her own. Another thing. She never took her gloves off. Mrs Craven particularly remembers that. She thought it was odd. It's a pity the agent didn't send someone to show her round.'

'That was probably planned too. Insisting on a viewing at such short notice that no one from the agents could attend. Very astute.'

'Undoubtedly. No fingerprints either if she never took her gloves off. SOCO have been all through the house but nothing of evidential value has been found so far. We should have their final report in a few days.'

Craven sighed.

'When did she view the house?'

'Well over six weeks ago now, on 24 February. The agents never heard anything more from her and they've been unable to contact her. She picked up a copy of the particulars at the house too – the agents left several with the Campions. The phone number she gave is no longer live. It's a pay-as-you-go mobile, so there's no chance of running her down from that.'

'Surely they had an address?'

'Unfortunately she gave the address of a hotel in Market Harborough. She insisted on seeing the house immediately because she said she was flying back to the States the next day. That's why they didn't have anyone available to show her around that afternoon – so it fell to Mrs Campion to do the honours.'

'We've checked the hotel I presume?'

'Of course. Someone of that name did stay there – for one night – but no one can remember much about her – and she paid in cash, so there's no credit card trail.'

'Remind me, Harry. When was the so-called bust-up between Doyle and the Hamilton woman?'

'Around the beginning of the second week of March.'

'Sounds like the American might bear further investigation. Could it have been Julia Hamilton? She's quite the actress, as we've just experienced.'

'We're certainly regarding it as a possibility. We've had one bit of luck. Ian Lunn's rung in – he's looking at the CCTV at the hotel. He's identified Alex Stringer dropping off a woman on the night in question, and he was driving a dark-coloured Range Rover.'

'Was he, indeed? Now what would Alex Stringer be doing in Market Harborough and driving a Range Rover? I think we'd better bring him in.'

★★★★

There was a wry smile on Julia Hamilton's face as she headed for the exit doors of the police station, her solicitor following in her wake.

'I think you put them in their place,' he assured Jules, who of course, needed no such assurance.

'One simply needs to treat them firmly,' she responded. 'After all, they're used to dealing with halfwits, not intelligent people.'

The double entrance doors suddenly swung open and Raymond Craddock rushed through, his head down, quite oblivious to her presence. He almost collided with her.

'Sorry,' he muttered, looking up, briefly. Then he halted sharply.

'Moira?' he said. 'Is it you?'

Jules, as always smartly dressed, her blonde hair carefully arranged, her blue eyes sparkling, curled her lip as she replied. She certainly didn't sound like Moira. Not a hint of an Irish accent.

'Are you referring to me?' she asked, adopting a very superior tone The look she gave Raymond certainly did not remind him of Moira. 'I think you must be mistaken.'

With that she swept through the doors, followed by her solicitor.

Raymond did not move for a few seconds. He thought back to the photograph he had been shown of Julia Hamilton when he had started to review the CCTV. Back then, he had persuaded himself that Moira and Julia Hamilton were not one and the same. The postcard he had received from Cork, seemingly signed by Moira, had removed the last vestiges of doubt. But seeing this woman as he had, those doubts returned with a vengeance. He imagined for a moment how Julia Hamilton might look in a red wig and green shaded contact lenses. He had noticed too, the lingering aroma of the perfume he associated with Moira as Julia Hamilton passed him by. He winced as he recalled what he had told Moira both in the hospital and when they had met in the pub in Hull. Was this woman Moira? Had he simply been used? Had he unwittingly revealed confidential information to Michael Doyle's lover? He couldn't believe he had been so naive.

'Are you all right, Raymond?' inquired the desk sergeant. 'You look as if you've just seen a ghost!'

'It's nothing, Sarge. Just someone who looks like a girl I used to know, that's all.'

The sergeant grinned. 'Aren't you the lucky one.'

CHAPTER FIFTY-THREE

Ian Lunn walked casually into the detention area at Central Police Station. The custody officer looked up from the newspaper he was reading. They knew each other very well and exchanged greetings.

'I see Forest beat the Villa – but I doubt if it will save them from the drop!'

The sergeant, a life-long Nottingham Forest supporter sighed but put his newspaper down. 'What can I do for you, Ian? It's pretty quiet in here tonight.'

'I hear you've got Alex Stringer under lock and key, George. Apparently he wants a word with me.'

'Does he now? He didn't have much to say when DCS Craven interviewed him last night. No comment all the way through – or so I heard.'

Lunn smiled.

'That sounds like Alex. He never would say anything on tape.'

The custody sergeant looked for the custody record, found it and stretched it out on the desk.

'Do you think you'll do any better?'

Lunn shook his head.

'I'm not here to interview him. He wants to see me – I have no idea why.'

'Well, you'll have to sign in. I don't want any comebacks.'

He picked up a pen and offered it to Lunn.

'If he says anything you won't be able to use it, you know.'

Lunn put his initials in the appropriate column and noted the time.

'I'm aware of that George. But he might say something useful. Everything helps in an inquiry like this – and I have the DCS's approval.'

'He must be desperate!'

The sergeant sighed again and called to the constable in the back room.

'Stuart, get the keys and show Sergeant Lunn in to cell 5. Don't forget to lock him in. I don't want Stringer going walkabout.'

He glanced at Lunn.

'You'll be OK with him, will you? Just press the buzzer if you need us.'

'No problem. Alex and I go back a long way.'

Lunn followed the detention officer along the corridor and into the secure area. As the cell door was opened, he recalled his last conversation with Stringer when he had driven him back to Nottingham from Loughborough Magistrates' Court. It seemed that Alex had ignored his advice. He was in serious trouble as the expression on his face confirmed as Lunn entered the cell. The door was quickly locked behind him.

'Good of you to come, Mr Lunn.'

He indicated the bench and invited the detective sergeant to sit down.

'I'll stand if you don't mind, Alex. But you sit down if you want.'

Alex Stringer sighed, but remained standing.

'I need your help Mr Lunn…'

'Now Alex, remember my position. I had to get the DCS's permission to see you as it is.'

'Craven?' Stringer shook his head and turned away. He walked towards the bench that had served as his bed. He sat down and faced Lunn.

'Anything I say is off the record?'

'Of course it is Alex. I haven't cautioned you and I'm not going to. Whatever you say will be used for intelligence only, always supposing you tell me something useful.'

Stringer hesitated.

'You know me, Mr Lunn. I'm no grass…'

Lunn nodded.

'…but they reckon I was involved in kidnapping that judge's wife and kid.' He stood up and almost shouted. 'That's absolute bollocks! I wouldn't get involved in anything like that!'

'But it is you on that CCTV, isn't it?'

Stringer looked away but did not answer immediately. He turned and peered towards Lunn, anxiously, before sitting down again on the bench.

'If it is me, Mr Lunn – and I'm admitting nothing – what had that got to do with kidnapping this woman and her kid?'

'Come on, Alex,' replied Lunn, trying his best to sound sympathetic. 'The DCS explained all that to you last night. The woman you drove to the hotel – she was casing the judge's house. She had to give the agents' an address – or she would never have got inside. We've already established the kidnappers knew the place inside out. *She* gave them the information.'

Stringer looked down.

'But I didn't know that, did I? It was just a driving job – that's all.'

'That might be for a jury to decide, Alex – unless you come completely clean with me.'

Stringer's expression changed. He no longer looked quite so desperate. There was hope in his eyes.

'What do yu mean?'

'You know the drill, Alex. You help us and I'll see what I can do.'

The anxiety returned.

'What guarantee have I got? How can I trust you?'

'There are no guarantees, Alex. It's up to you. But if you go down for this, you don't need me to tell you the likely sentence.'

Stringer placed his head in his hands.

'I know Mr Lunn. I know. They may as well throw away the key. I'll never get out. With my form, they'll think I was one of the kidnappers. But I was at my flat all that night.'

'Got any witnesses?'

'Of course I haven't. I was on my own.'

Lunn put his hands in his pockets and took a couple of steps towards the door.

'Well, it's up to you Alex. I can't hang around here. I've got work to do.'

Stringer stood up and walked towards Lunn.

'All right. I'll tell you what I know – but you have to promise to keep my name out of it. If it gets out I've said anything, I'm a dead man.'

Lunn turned and faced Stringer.

'No holding back now, Alex. You tell me everything, understand?'

Stringer hesitated then nodded. He returned to the bench and sat down.

'It was around the middle of February. I'd not long been in my flat in Beeston. I had a call from someone…'

'Who?'

'I don't know Mr Lunn. He didn't say and I didn't ask…'

'Go on.'

'He asked if I'd like to earn a few hundred. Five to be precise. He said it would be easy and legal.'

'Did he, Alex? And you believed him?'

Stringer looked down.

'Well, he never mentioned anything about a kidnapping.'

'Go on.'

'I was told some keys would be put through my letter box and that the car they were for would be parked in the precinct. A Range Rover. I was given the registration number – but I can't remember what it was – so don't ask me.'

'What? Nothing?'

'It was "S" reg… but that's all I recall.'

'Colour?'

'Black – seemed quite new. Only five thousand on the clock – I remember that. And another thing. There was an insurance certificate in the glove compartment – in case I was stopped.'

'What name was it in?'

'I don't remember. And before you ask, yes, I've still got my driving licence.'

'Which insurers?'

'Can't remember that either. It didn't seem important.'

Lunn tried not to sound too dismissive.

'So you had a good look around it, did you?'

Stringer nodded.

'And?'

'I was to pick up this woman – from Leicester Railway Station at 6 p.m. She would be wearing a dark blue coat and a black scarf and carrying a green zip-up bag.'

'That was Julia Hamilton, wasn't it?'

Stringer half smiled then shook his head.

'I don't know who she was Mr Lunn. I'd never seen her before. But it wasn't Julia Hamilton. I'd have known her. It definitely wasn't her.'

Lunn failed to hide his disappointment.

'Remember what I said, Alex. You tell us everything.'

'But it wasn't her, Mr Lunn. Honest.'

'What happened next?'

'I drove this woman – whoever she was – to the Green Dragon Hotel in Harborough. I parked up in the rear car park and carried her bag into reception. She insisted I did that – but it wasn't heavy. She could have done that herself. I wondered at the time why she was so keen that I should. Now I know why. To get me on the CCTV!'

'Did you spend the night in the hotel too?'

'No. I parked up in that lorry park near Lutterworth. I spent the night in the Range Rover. I wasn't going to waste money on a hotel room.'

'Then what?'

'I picked her up the following afternoon at about 1 p.m. and drove her to that village near the locks – Foxton, I think it's called. I dropped her off there – near the church. She walked towards it. I remember that. I thought she might be going to a funeral or something. I was told to skedaddle until just after two thirty – so I did. I had no idea where she went after that.'

'Did you go to the judge's house?'

'No. I didn't know anything about any judge or what she was up to – and I didn't ask.'

'You must have been suspicious though, Alex. Why would anyone pay you five hundred pounds for a driving job if it was above board? And let you use an expensive motor like a Range Rover? It doesn't make sense. I hope you're not keeping anything back.'

'God's honest truth, Mr Lunn. I've told you everything.'

Lunn scowled.

'I don't think you have, Alex. When did you pick her up again?'

'Sometime after half past two I think it was. I remember I had to wait quite a bit for her. Oh, and there's something else. I was parked up near the church and some Australian-sounding woman asked me what I was doing there. Very forthright she was. She was carrying a lot of flowers into the church. She'd be able to confirm I was there.'

'Would she? We'll have to ask around.'

'You do that Mr Lunn. There can't be too may Aussies living around there.'

Lunn continued.

'The woman in the scarf. Did she have anything with her when you picked her up?'

'Not that I can remember, no. Hang on a minute. She did have something. Yes. She had some sale particulars for somewhere.'

'What happened to them?'

'She didn't leave them in the motor. She still had them when I dropped her off.'

Lunn sighed.

'You know the search team found a copy in your bin, Alex? The sale particulars for the judge's home.'

'Not in my bin, they didn't. Anyway, my bin's been emptied more than once since then. Someone's put them there – to try and incriminate me. Stands to reason, doesn't it?'

Lunn did not reply. He returned to the narrative.

'Where did you take her after you picked her up from the church?'

'Back to the station at Leicester. I got the impression she was going to London. I don't know why – that's just what I thought.'

'Why not Harborough? You can get a train from there to London.'

'I don't know, Mr Lunn. I just did as I was asked.'

'Can you describe her?'

'She looked a bit like Jules – but it wasn't her. About the same height I would say. She had fairish hair – not as blonde as Jules though. She never took the scarf off and she wore dark glasses all the time – and gloves. She didn't say much either. That's why I thought she might have been to a funeral. She certainly didn't seem very happy.'

'Could it have been Jules in disguise?'

'No way, Mr Lunn. I'd have recognised her. I've not had a lot to do with her but I've seen her around. I wouldn't make a mistake like that.'

Stringer thought it better not to reveal the full extent of his dealings with Jules.

'She didn't give you a name?'

'No – and I didn't ask. Not my business.'

'Did you notice anything about her accent?'

'Not really – though she did sound a bit American, when I think about it.'

Lunn paused.

'What did you do while you were waiting for her?'

'I drove down to the locks – there's a car park there. I had a smoke and popped along to that cafe on the side of the canal. They'd remember me. I was their only customer to begin with.'

Lunn said nothing for a few seconds.

'Does Orley Farm mean anything to you?'

'Orley what?' Stringer looked puzzled.

'Orley Farm. It's in the Vale of Belvoir. One of Michael Doyle's properties.'

'Never heard of it, Mr Lunn. Is it important?'

Lunn changed the subject.

'How were you paid the five hundred quid?'

'Came through the letter box the next day. I left the Range Rover in the precinct. I was told to leave the keys in the exhaust.'

'Who was it who phoned you, Alex? How did he know your number?'

Stringer dropped his head and looked away. Lunn persisted.

'Come on, Alex. You must have had some idea who it was.'

Stringer looked up.

'Well, I did have an inkling Mr Lunn. It was a long time ago, but the voice did ring a bell – not that I could swear to it.'

'Who do you think it was?'

Stringer was reluctant to answer but eventually he did.

'A bloke called Duffy. I never knew his first name. He used to work for someone you and me both know. But I haven't seen him for years. He must have asked around to get my number.'

That was a name Ian Lunn hadn't heard in a long time. He recognised it immediately, but he wasn't going to let Stringer know that.

'Who did he work for Alex? I can't help you unless you tell me everything you know.'

Stringer turned his head away. He appeared genuinely afraid. He was plainly reluctant to name names. Then he blurted it out.

'Gus Grayling – the Fish. But don't let him find out I told you. Promise me, Mr Lunn. My life wouldn't be worth a candle if he found out I'd said anything. You know what he's like.'

Lunn frowned.

'I know what he's like all right. I know exactly what he's like.'

CHAPTER FIFTY-FOUR

'Thanks Andrew. That's very good work by you and Malcolm. Not that it helps us.' Hood dismissed the detective sergeant, leaving the chief inspector alone with Ian Lunn.

'Nothing's coming together, it seems, sir.'

Hood shook his head.

'That's right Ian. And to make matters worse, DCS Craven has gone off sick too.'

'Nothing trivial, I trust.'

Hood tried not to smile.

'Quite the reverse. Apparently he's gone down with shingles! I just hope he hasn't given it me. My wife is pregnant and that would create real problems. As it is, he'll be off for at least three to four weeks.'

'Do you think you'll be able to wind up both investigations before you go off to Brum?'

'You can forget Birmingham,' said Hood, failing to conceal his disappointment. 'I didn't get it. The board was postponed twice because of this inquiry. And I've just heard they gave it to one of their own. I don't think they liked the publicity they received about the possibly unlawful retention of Benson's DNA.'

Lunn appeared shocked.

'That was hardly down to you, sir.'

Hood shook his head.

'I know – but that's obviously not how they see it.'

Lunn paused.

'I'm sorry sir. That's really hard on you.'

Hood smiled. 'There'll be other opportunities. Now what happened when you saw Stringer? I take it you've spoken to him?'

'Yes, sir. I didn't want to say anything while anyone else was in the room. What he told me mustn't go any further.'

Hood's interest was aroused but he remained sceptical.

'Whatever he may have revealed, do you think he was telling you the truth? He's not exactly noted for his honesty, is he?'

'On the whole, yes. I think he was. Knowing Alex, though, he'll have kept something back. He always has something in reserve.'

Hood invited Lunn to take a seat. Craven had authorised Lunn to speak to Stringer to try and get a handle on the kidnapping. Hood had questioned the wisdom of allowing the meeting to take place at all but he had been overruled.

'He's as good as admitted it was him on the CCTV from the Green Dragon. Trouble is, he says the woman he dropped off there was definitely *not* Julia Hamilton.'

Hood did not appear in the least surprised. He sighed, stood up and placed his hands in his pockets and walked towards the window that overlooked the car park.

'He's probably right about that – unfortunately.'

'What do you mean, sir?'

Hood turned and faced Lunn.

'Hooper and Munt have been going through Hamilton's work records. On 24 February, she was in Worcestershire – at Hewell Grange Prison to be precise, taking instructions from a client of Trevor Parker. The appointment was from 1.00 p.m. to 1.55 p.m. It's all been checked out. She didn't leave the prison until after half past two so she can't have been anywhere near Foxton when the American-sounding woman viewed the judge's house. So you see, Ian, we're back to square one.'

Lunn took stock before he spoke.

'Not quite sir. From what you've just said it sounds as if Alex Stringer really was telling the truth.'

'Go on.'

Lunn related everything that Alex Stringer had told him.

Hood looked slightly put out.

'This may change the shape of the whole inquiry, Ian. If Gus Grayling is involved…'

He paused.

'The question is why would he have become involved? Was he behind the robbery or was he brought in – by Hamilton perhaps – to kidnap the judge's wife to apply pressure to get the case dismissed?'

'But what about the tip-off, sir? Why would Grayling want to tip us off?'

'That's the difficult bit, Ian. It doesn't really fit, does it – unless Hamilton did it to make sure Doyle stayed inside?'

'But it was a male voice that left the message.'

'According to the dozy individual who failed to pass it on. I don't think we can put much store on that!'

Hood did not try and hide his anger at the failure of the officer to pass on the message as quickly as he should. Lunn made another suggestion.

'Perhaps Doyle has crossed him in some way – and this is the Fish's method of getting his revenge. Very shrewd when you think about it, sir. Getting us to do his dirty work for him...'

Hood did not dismiss the possibility out of hand but he remained sceptical.

'I don't know, Ian – it's all very speculative. And according to some research Debbie did before she went on maternity leave Grayling's been quite ill recently. Hardly leaves his home these days. He has very bad emphysema, apparently, as well as other problems. I did a check with the Sussex police. He's at death's door, according to them.'

Lunn was hardly sympathetic.

'Well, he should knock a bit louder!'

Hood failed to conceal a smile.

'And it's a lot of trouble to go to, don't you think? Just to have a pop at Doyle? It would have taken a great deal of organisation, not to mention the expense. And very risky too. And it could have all gone very wrong. If I hadn't got lucky, Doyle and Benson could have been long gone.'

Lunn put forward an alternative theory.

'Perhaps Grayling did want them out – and someone in his organisation took a different view? Then made the call to the switchboard. It does happen. And if Grayling is as ill as you say, there could be a bit of competition to replace him. Perhaps Doyle has himself down as a contender?'

Hood shook his head. 'But Doyle was planning to move abroad. And when he disposes of all his assets here, he'd have no problem paying off Grayling and the Revenue. It just doesn't add up. There must be something else to it – something we're missing.'

He turned and looked out of the window again.

'Tell me, Ian, do you still go fishing?'

Lunn smiled.

'When I have the time sir, yes. But I haven't had much to spare recently.'

He joined Hood at the window. They looked out into the rain swept car park.

'Ever fished for grayling?'

Lunn grinned.

'Not specifically, sir, no. I believe they're not easy to catch!'

'So I hear. Apparently they prefer fast-running water, with deep currents. The best method of catching one is to use a maggot that rises and falls with the current – you know – to tempt him into biting on the hook. Am I right?'

Lunn agreed.

'Yes, sir. Trouble is, they usually fight like mad. It's all very well getting one to bite – landing him is quite another thing.'

Hood stepped back from the window and moved towards his desk.

'Gus Grayling was well named don't you think? What are our chances of landing him?'

'Not good. We'd need better bait than Alex Stringer – maggot though he may be! Grayling would have no trouble devouring him – hook an' all.'

Hood laughed.

'You're probably right. And if he is about to expire we'd be wasting our time. We'd never get him into court.'

'So, sir, what's our next move? What about Stringer?'

'Do you really think he's holding something back?'

'Yes, sir. He always keeps something in reserve, does our Alex.'

Hood frowned. 'I know I was against your seeing him, but it seems I was wrong. Perhaps I should speak to him, officially? We don't have to make a decision about him until tomorrow morning, do we?'

'No sir, Mr Craven got an extension from the magistrates' court. It runs out at eleven o'clock.'

'Right, fix it up will you, Ian? Early tomorrow morning. And get him a solicitor if he wants one.'

Lunn frowned. 'Not Alex, sir. The last thing he'll want is a solicitor!'

'And let me have your notes too. I don't want to blunder in and make things worse.'

Lunn smiled. 'He also mentioned another name from the past, Derick David Duffy. He was into armed robbery, big time. I haven't heard of him recently. Not since before Stringer was jailed. He might be worth talking to – if we can find him. I checked on the computer. He hasn't surfaced for ages. He had a couple of years knocked off his sentence by the Court of Appeal and he hasn't troubled us since he was released. Another thing, probation has lost touch with him. He's in breach of his parole licence. Apparently, there's been a warrant out for him for well over three years.'

'And he's not been arrested?'

'No sir. He seems to have vanished completely.'

There was a knock on Hood's door and Wendy Knight came in carrying a photograph album.

'Do you have a minute, sir? Raymond and I may have come up with something.'

Hood indicated a chair and Knight sat down in front of his desk.

'I'll let you go, Ian. You'll let me have a copy of your notes – on that other matter?'

'Yes sir.'

Lunn nodded and left the room. Hood turned to Wendy Knight. She placed the photo album on to the desk and turned several pages over before removing a photograph and handing it to Hood.

'Where has this come from, Wendy?' asked Hood, looking at the photograph, then turning it over to see if it was dated. No such luck.

'From Doyle's penthouse flat, sir. Raymond and I took your advice to heart and have been going through all the exhibits systematically. We found a couple of photos that may be of interest. There's another one a few pages on.'

Hood looked at the photograph again. He opened his desk drawer and took out a magnifying glass. With the aid of the glass and the lamp on his desk he was able to make out the several persons appearing in the photograph more clearly.

'This looks like a Doyle family portrait. Is the girl with the red hair a younger version of Julia Hamilton?'

'That's what we thought at first, sir. But if you look at the other photograph – she reached over and turned three pages on – the same red-haired woman appears in a picture *with* Julia Hamilton.'

Knight removed the photograph and handed it to Hood. He placed both of them on his desk – side by side – and studied them with the glass. After a few moments, he looked up.

'Good Lord Wendy, these two could be sisters. Do we know who the red-haired girl is?'

Knight picked up the second photograph.

'Raymond and I have been researching Doyle's family – but more thoroughly this time. His father's whereabouts are unknown – he seems to have left his wife while Doyle was still a youngster. His mother lives in Ireland with his younger sister, who goes by the name of Mary. She was linked to a man called Donnelly from County Waterford, but they separated years ago, and, wait for it, she's a qualified nurse.'

'Is she indeed! Has she ever worked over here?'

'We think she has. Raymond saw a nurse when he was on bed watch. She came in to see Doyle when he was still in a coma. He reckons this could have been her. She was using the name Moira.'

'Did he get a surname?'

'No sir. He only saw her a couple of times.'

'Did he now? Did he find out anything else about her?'

'She said she came from Cork and that her mother was unwell. She was going back to Ireland on account of her mother's illness.'

Hood said nothing more for a time, then picked up his telephone. Knight placed the photograph back on the desk.

'Shirley, get DC Craddock in here will you? I don't care what he's doing, I need to see him urgently.'

He replaced the receiver. Knight stood up.

'He's not far away, sir. He thought you might want him.'

'Why didn't we pick this up before, Wendy?'

'I don't suppose anyone thought this album was of any interest. It's not exactly central to the inquiry, is it?'

'But we did a check on the wider Doyle family, didn't we?'

'Yes, sir. But we didn't know what his younger sister looked like and we had no reason to believe she was relevant to the inquiry. His older sister lives in New Zealand. So we can exclude her as being of any interest.'

'We've heard nothing from Inspector Crawford in Hull, I take it?'

'I've been in touch, but he's still waiting for a response from the hospital. They're very slow. They obviously don't regard this as being high priority.'

Hood scratched his head.

'Well I do. I want you and Raymond to get over there. We can't wait for the hospital to get round to giving us the answers. We need to know *now* if she was working there earlier this year. It could explain a great deal. If she's been helping out Doyle it must have been with Hamilton's connivance. She could even have passed herself off as Julia Hamilton on occasions. All it would have taken is a wig and a bit of nerve – and the Doyle family seem to have that in abundance.'

He picked up the photographs, looked at them again and held them in his outstretched hand.

'These two really could pass for twins. I think we may have to speak to Mary Doyle, or whatever she calls herself. Do we know where she is at the moment?'

'No sir. Raymond received a postcard some time back. It was postmarked Carrigaline – that's in County Cork. Whether she's still living there I don't know. I've put a call through to the Garda in Cork – an Inspector Ryan – he said he would make some enquiries and ring you tomorrow. I have the telephone number in case he needs chivvying. He didn't sound over interested.'

'We'll have to make him interested then, won't we? And what was young Craddock doing receiving a postcard from her?'

'I think he tried to chat her up when he was on bed watch at the hospital.'

'Did he now? Perhaps I should have words with him?'

'He's a bit embarrassed about it, sir. I don't think he knew enough to give anything away.'

'Let's hope so. Look, tell Craddock I'll see him tomorrow. The two of you better get over to Hull and see what you can find out about Doyle's sister.'

Knight handed over her note of the telephone number. As she made to leave the room, Hood's telephone rang. He indicated for her to continue on her way, waving her out of the room as he picked up the receiver. He was somewhat surprised when the caller revealed his identity.

'Hello, Mr Savage. What can I do for you? I hadn't expected to hear from you again.'

Hood listened as the barrister disclosed a piece of potentially helpful information. He had been reviewing his credit card bill which covered the trip he had taken to Brussels with Julia Hamilton. Hood grabbed a pen and started to make notes on a scrap of paper.

'That's very interesting. But are you sure about it?'

'I'm absolutely sure that when we left Waterloo, Julia Hamilton had three pieces of luggage: Two suitcases and a medium-sized handbag. I wondered why she needed to take so much with her at the time. We were only going to Brussels for six days. The two cases matched – they were obviously part of a set. One of them – the larger of the two – was quite heavy. I distinctly remember the porter complaining about it when he placed it in the compartment. It was the same at the other end. The taxi driver, who spoke only French, wondered what on earth she had in it.'

'Did you ask her?' inquired Hood.

'No. I didn't think it important at the time.'

'So you never found out what was in it?'

'No. But that's not the point. What is significant about my credit card bill is not what's on it; it's what isn't on it.'

'I don't follow.'

'That piece of luggage – she didn't bring it back with her. If she'd returned with it, I'd have had to pay excess baggage, and I didn't. She only brought one suitcase and the handbag back with her. She obviously left the other one in Brussels. She must have. I remember it crossing my mind as we got into our suite at the hotel that I'd be lumbered with an excess baggage claim when we flew back. The suitcase seemed so heavy.'

'Did you pick it up yourself and feel the weight?'

'No. I don't think so, but I saw a couple of porters struggling with it.'

'And you didn't see what was inside it?'

'Never.'

'You know what will have been in there, don't you?'

'I don't *know*, but I could take a pretty good guess. Cash from the robbery?'

'Exactly. She was using that trip to smuggle some of the proceeds stolen from the Charnwood into Holland via Belgium – which is what Doyle was trying to do when he had his little accident. Someone must have picked it up from her.'

'Which means', said Savage, 'that she was using me in more ways than one.'

'And it proves something else,' said Hood. 'It confirms what I've always thought; she and Doyle are still an item. That's why she went to Brussels with you – not just to give herself an alibi – but to use you as cover to smuggle the cash into Belgium. It would have been child's play to get it into Holland afterwards.'

Savage let out a lengthy sigh.

'And to think she almost had me eating out of her hand. The sexual chemistry she exudes is unbelievable. I've never felt anything like it. She almost had me falling in love with her.'

Savage laughed as he continued.

'You'd better be careful if you arrest her, Mr Hood. She might have the same effect on you.'

Hood had no such concerns.

'Of course, this is not going to be easy to prove, is it? I don't suppose you want to make a statement about it?'

'I'd rather not,' replied Savage. 'I have to think of my position. Couldn't you get the people at the hotel to assist you? The porter will certainly remember us.'

'I'll see what I can do. I'll have to get in touch with the police in Belgium again. But thank you anyway.'

Hood put the phone down. Now he had something tangible to put to Julia Hamilton.

But she would have to wait until he'd interviewed Alex Stringer. In the meantime, he would ask DC Eccles to make contact with the police in Brussels and obtain statements from staff members at the hotel. He was sure that the delectable Julia Hamilton would be firmly lodged in their memories.

CHAPTER FIFTY-FIVE

'Hello, again, Mr Lunn. Come to release me? 'Cos I'm in no rush, I can tell you.'

'Not quite Alex. Time doesn't run out until later this morning – and my boss wants a word with you.'

'Who, Craven? I'm not speaking to him again. No way, Mr Lunn.'

Ian Lunn sighed.

'Not the DCS, Alex. Mr Hood. He's in charge at the moment. The chief super's gone off sick.'

Stringer became agitated.

'Why does Mr Hood want to see me? I've told you all I know.'

'I don't think you have, Alex. I know you of old. You're holding something back.'

Stringer turned away and placed his forehead directly against the white tiled wall of his cell and started striking his head repeatedly.

'I've nothing further to say.'

'Well, it's up to you Alex. But Mr Hood proposes to interview you – upstairs. Shall we go?'

Stringer turned round.

'Do I have to, Mr Lunn? I thought you were going to help me – after what I told you?'

'I am trying to help you Alex. But it's down to Mr Hood – not me. He needs to see you in order to decide whether to charge you or not. I'll tell you this much – it's in the balance. He's not made a decision yet. You might yet make bail.'

Stringer grunted and half laughed.

'But I don't want bail, Mr Lunn. I want you to keep me in – at least until Thursday.'

Lunn looked at him.

'What do you mean, Alex?'

'I'll tell you upstairs but not on tape. I'm saying nothing on tape.'

★★★★

Stringer was already sitting in the interview room with Ian Lunn when Hood appeared. Lunn introduced him. Hood nodded in acknowledgement of the man he had never met before. He was not impressed with what he saw. He sat opposite Stringer, placing a small file on the table and withdrawing from it a copy of the sale particulars of Judge Campion's home. Stringer winced as he recognised it. Hood then switched on the tape machine, asked Stringer to identify himself and administered the caution. Stringer gave his name, declined the assistance of a solicitor and said he had nothing further to say.

'That's a pity,' rejoined Hood. 'I was thinking of bailing you. I just need your assistance on one matter.'

Stringer looked up. He then stared at the tape machine.

'I have nothing to say,' he insisted.

Hood continued unabashed.

'The people you mentioned to Ian Lunn yesterday…'

Stringer raised his hands and pointed at the tape machine; he was obviously anxious that neither Grayling nor Duffy should be mentioned while the machine was running.

'Don't concern yourself,' added Hood. 'I shan't mention them by name…'

Stringer sat back in his chair, much relieved.

'What do *you* think they were up to?'

Stringer became agitated again.

'I have nothing to say, Mr Hood. Charge me. I won't be asking for bail.'

He looked at the machine again. Hood took the hint.

'Very well, I shall bring this interview to an end. The time is' – he looked at his watch – '8.16 a.m.'

Lunn stretched over the table and switched off the tape recorder. He then looked sympathetically towards Stringer.

'This is your chance, Alex.'

Hood said nothing. Anything Stringer said with the machine switched off could not be used in evidence. He knew that; so did Stringer. Stringer was now breathing heavily. He looked at Hood.

'Off the record?' he pleaded.

'The tape has been switched off, Alex. You know what that means. You've been in this situation before.'

Although Lunn spoke softly, there was a degree of insistence in his voice.

Stringer looked at him then at Hood.

'All right. I'll tell you. But if this goes any further…'

'Intelligence only,' promised Hood.

'Duffy is taking over from Grayling… they reckon the Fish is on his last legs.'

Hood shook his head and smiled.

'I think we already knew that, Alex. Tell us something we don't know.'

Stringer took out a handkerchief and wiped his brow.

'He was planning a job in these parts.'

'Go on,' encouraged Hood.

'Doyle got in there first.'

Hood and Lunn looked at each other.

'What do you mean?' asked Lunn.

'Duffy and Grayling had planned to rob the security van at the Charnwood on the Sunday morning. I was supposed to be part of it – not that I had any intention of turning up.'

Both Hood and Lunn raised their eyebrows, cynically.

'Duffy had information from someone at the bank.'

'Who?' asked Hood.

'I dunno. I would never be told anything like that, would I?'

'What happened?' asked Lunn.

Stringer took a deep breath. 'Well, it's obvious isn't it? Doyle's mob got there first – on the seventeenth – and you lot had the place locked down afterwards so the whole thing was called off. Grayling was furious. He reckoned there'd be two million quid in used notes ripe for the taking on the Sunday morning. Doyle hadn't told them what he was up to – and he owes Grayling big time. I was told to say nothing and to lie low until I was contacted. I heard nothing until Duffy got me to do that driving job. I had no idea what that was about. I just did as I was told.'

'And the kidnapping?'

'I know nothing about that.'

He looked away.

'I think you do, Alex.'

'Leave it out Mr Lunn. I've told you everything. If they find out what I've said so far, I'm a dead man. They don't mess about.'

'Who do you reckon was behind the kidnapping? Was it Grayling and Duffy or Julia Hamilton?'

His head dropped.

'I don't know, Mr Hood. Honest.' He paused. 'All I know is Duffy wanted to get his hands on Doyle. He still does. If the Fish was behind it, it wasn't to help Doyle escape you lot. You can take that as read. He probably wanted to cause him serious damage – or worse.' He paused. 'And he still does. Doyle doesn't know how lucky he was being moved from Leicester. I hope he's safe where he is. Grayling was going to have him shanked in Welford Road. It's easily done you know, if you have the contacts.' He looked at Hood. 'That's all I know.'

'Where's Duffy now?'

'I don't know, Mr Lunn.'

'I think you do, Alex. You must have the means to contact him.'

Stringer dropped his head. His body started to shake.

'Give me a break Mr Lunn. If you go after either of them, they'll know I talked. They'll know I've been in here for the last two days. They have more contacts than you know of!'

He raised his head. There was fear in his eyes. He looked away and sighed.

'Look. They're planning a repeat performance on a security van from the counting house at Retford. The Charnwood job was a dress rehearsal. Had they pulled off the robbery at the Charnwood they thought you would have been concentrating all your resources on that.'

'Were you supposed to be in on the Retford job?'

Stringer shook his head.

'No way. Duffy was bringing over some hard man from Ireland. He didn't want me. That's why he's thrown me to the wolves on the kidnapping. He thinks I don't know about it.'

Hood eyed him cynically. 'How did you find out about it?'

'Because I keep my ears open, Mr Hood. One of the others who was supposed to be in on the Charnwood job let it slip. They've been waiting for a big build up of used notes. Duffy must have someone on the inside.'

'Does he now? When? When is the Retford job?'

Stringer paused. He was reluctant to continue. Hood pressed him.

'Come on, Alex. Spit it out.'

'This Thursday morning – early. It's Duffy's team, but the gunman is the Irishman. He's a contact of Grayling – comes over specially.'

'Name?'

'I've no idea who he is, but he's dangerous. That I do know. He's killed before, according to what I heard.'

Hood stood up and paced the room.

'That's a National Commercial operation near Retford, isn't it?'

'I think so. Does it matter?'

'Who gave the information?'

'I don't know Mr Hood. All I know is it's someone on the inside – it has to be. Stands to reason, don't it?'

Hood sat down again and looked intently at Stringer.

'You're not just making this up, are you, Alex? Trying to impress me?'

Stringer shook his head. 'No I'm not.' He looked at the sales particulars on top of the file and jabbed his finger towards it. 'Some bastard's planted that, you know. I reckon they want me to go down for the kidnapping. They've set me up. I'm just returning the compliment.'

Hood paused and glanced at Lunn then at Stringer.

'If you're making this up Alex…'

'Why would I do that?'

'I don't know. To send us on a wild goose chase, perhaps, while they pull a job somewhere else?'

Stringer looked down and shook his head.

'No way, Mr Hood. I wouldn't do that.'

'Wouldn't you? Tell me this then, Alex, why would someone like Duffy rob a security van when everyone knows that they're using these new cartridges now. It's been given a lot of publicity recently. The cash would be covered in purple ink as soon as they tried to bust them open. There'd be no point to it.'

Stringer looked up and smiled, knowingly.

'Not on this trip, Mr Hood.'

Hood narrowed his eyes.

'What do you mean?'

'This isn't a delivery in the usual sense. This is the one they've been waiting for – an inter-bank transfer – that's what they call it. The Retford unit is closing down – didn't you know that?' He laughed. 'Call yourselves detectives! Duffy's been waiting for this for weeks. It's been delayed at least twice.'

He laughed again then spoke in a barely audible whisper.

'He's been told they're moving over 3 million quid to Bridgeford House. It'll be in one of those cage things – not packed in them cartridges.'

Hood had a vague recollection that Reg King had said something about Bridgeford House expanding its area of operation. But he hadn't mentioned that Retford was closing down. He hadn't mentioned Retford at all.

'Which security firm is being used?'

'Dunno, Mr Hood.'

'And you don't know where Duffy got the information from?'

'No idea. Duffy wouldn't tell anyone that, would he? He'd keep it to himself. But it must be someone at the bank.'

Hood glanced at Lunn.

'This is serious Ian. We're going to look complete idiots if they pull this off.'

'Well, we can stop it by giving them police protection, can't we, sir? Armed units escorting the security van would put them right off. They wouldn't risk a shoot-out in the street.'

Hood nodded and indicated to Lunn to follow him out of the interview room.

'You stay where you are, Alex. I haven't finished with you – yet.'

Ten minutes later, Hood and Lunn returned.

'We need one further piece of information from you, Alex.'

Hood sat on the edge of the table as he spoke. Lunn seated himself in a chair.

'I've told you all I know, Mr Hood. Charge me with something, for God's sake and let it be known that I've said nothing. I'm going to need police protection from now on.'

'On one condition, Alex. Tell me, where is Duffy hiding? Sergeant Lunn has checked him out. He's not registered anywhere. Not with DVLA at Swansea or the benefits office and he's in breach of his parole licence; he's vanished completely. If he's planning a job like this, he must have a safe house or something not far from Retford. You tell us where he is and we'll go along with what you want. We'll put you on witness protection.'

Stringer became agitated.

'Witness protection? I'm not putting my name to a statement. You can forget about that.'

Stringer went through his pockets looking for a cigarette. He found one and Lunn lit it for him. He took a long drag and looked nervously at Hood.

'What about the kidnapping?'

'If you're telling us the truth, you needn't worry about that. We'll charge you with it – for the sake of appearances – but drop it later.'

Stringer sighed.

'How can I trust you? I want something in writing.'

'We haven't time for that, Alex. You've got no choice in the matter. If we let you go, they'll be on to you. They won't want you running about if they're planning a robbery on this scale.'

Stringer put his head in his hands for several seconds.

'All right. But you didn't get this from me, right?'

'Right.'

'It's off the Ollerton Road. An abandoned industrial unit. There's acres of space there and a lot of large warehouse-type buildings. Duffy's holed up in the old manager's bungalow – or at least he was. I've only been there once. It's pretty remote. No one ever goes there now.'

'Is he armed?'

'I should think so. He's supposed to be providing the shooters for the heist. The Irishman won't be bringing them over with him – that would be too risky. And knowing that mad bastard – they'll be loaded.'

Lunn stood up and sighed wearily. 'And you told me you'd given all this up, Alex.'

Stringer shook his head; he did not reply.

'Well, this'll be the best outcome for you Alex; you'll be retiring now – permanently. You have no choice in the matter. We're going to have to move you to another part of the country. Got anywhere in mind?'

CHAPTER FIFTY-SIX

Hood had to move fast. He drove with Lunn to police HQ. An urgent meeting had been arranged with the ACC.

Stringer had been charged and was due before the magistrates' court in Leicester at 11 a.m. The prosecuting solicitor had been briefed to ensure that it was stated in open court that Stringer had refused to answer any questions when interviewed under caution – which was the literal truth. His refusal to co-operate would be put forward as a reason for refusing him bail – not that Stringer intended to make an application. He was too scared that it might be granted. Hood was relying on the fact that as the first person to be charged with the kidnapping conspiracy, Stringer's case would receive maximum publicity. He had also made arrangements to continue holding him at the police station. He wasn't prepared to risk a remand to Welford Road.

'This is very risky,' cautioned Margaret Knowles as she looked at Hood's extensive note of his conversation with Stringer and his detailed plan of the intended operation. 'You're going to use armed officers?'

Hood nodded. 'We have no option – we have to assume the robbers will be armed.'

Knowles placed the documents on her desk.

'And the dog section too?'

'Yes, but just as backup.'

Knowles adopted a business-like manner.

'I've asked Inspector Rowan to join us from the firearms unit. He's on his way here. He'll have to OK the use of his team and go through the details.'

'Danny Rowan? – He used to be with West Yorkshire, didn't he?'

'Yes. Not enough excitement for him up there apparently. Do you know him?'

'We go back a long way.'

'Good. You'll have to make any alterations he deems necessary.'

'Of course, but I think he'll agree with my proposals. I did serve with him in Leeds for twelve months and I am an authorised firearms officer.'

Knowles was only partially reassured.

'But you're not a specialist firearms officer?'

'No ma'am.'

'You're up to date with your training though?'

'Yes. I completed the refresher course only six months ago. I'm fully certified as is Sergeant Hooper.'

'But not me,' interjected Lunn.

'Well, I think the chief will want only SFOs on this operation – apart from you, of course. Then there's the question of the dogs. I haven't contacted the dog section yet. Sergeant Whitely has a training session this morning. He'll ring you at lunchtime.'

'I don't know him, ma'am, but I hear he knows his stuff.'

'Lee Whitely is the best dog man we've ever had. His team have had excellent results of late. But remember, Harry, they're only to be used as backup. The last thing I want is one of the dogs getting hurt. You know how the public reacts if that happens? They don't care about us – but if a dog goes down, we'll never hear the end of it.'

Hood smiled.

'I doubt if we'll need them, ma'am. But they ought to be on standby.'

'Well, we have two and a half days to set it up. The chief wants to see every detail of the operation. I shall show him what you've planned so far, but he won't give the go-ahead unless every eventuality is covered. He'll simply order us to warn the bank and stop the delivery or provide a highly visible armed escort.'

That was the last thing Hood wanted.

'It's crucial, ma'am, that nothing is said to the bank. Someone has tipped these people off, and there may well be a connection with the Charnwood robbery. The Loughborough managers have access to the details of the operation at Retford. They share information about the availability of used notes – something Reg King forgot to mention in his original statement.'

'Do you think he might be involved?'

'I don't know. It's something I shall have to give careful consideration to – after Thursday!'

'And Stringer? We can trust what he says?'

'I think so, yes. He's going to have to go into witness protection – which he will hate. He wouldn't make up something like this.'

'I don't know, Harry. Safety first has always been my motto. Think of the consequences if it all goes wrong.'

Hood tried hard not to show his exasperation.

'There's another reason, ma'am, why we have to arrest this bunch of villains as they're about to pounce.'

'Another reason?'

'I think there's a good chance this may be the team who kidnapped Judge Campion's wife and son.'

Knowles appeared quite taken aback.

'Yes, ma'am.' Hood explained his theory in detail. He was very careful not to exclude Julia Hamilton's possible role in the affair.

The ACC walked around her desk and sat down.

'But do you have any evidence? It's all very circumstantial.'

'There's nothing wrong with circumstantial evidence. It's frequently more reliable. And we do have that as yet unidentified DNA from young Christopher's teddy bear.'

Knowles was silent for half a minute. She perused the conclusion of Hood's report again.

'Did Stringer tell you how they were going to go about it?'

'No, ma'am. He doesn't know. He says he wasn't going to be part of the team.'

'And you believe him?'

'He's probably lying about that. But everything else he's said checks out.'

'So you have no idea what their plan might be?'

'No, ma'am. That's why we have to be flexible. But the direct route from the counting house goes past the entrance to where we think they are. If I were planning such a venture, I'd have some means of stopping the security van as it approached the entrance.'

'You mean some trick to get them on to the site?'

'Perhaps; or they may take a more traditional approach and just ram the security van.'

That was the last thing the ACC wanted to hear. 'How many will be in this gang?'

'I don't know for sure. Five or six at the most. If they hope to get their hands on 3 million, there'll be a limit on their numbers. They're playing for big stakes so they won't want to divide it up between too many. It might be significant that they're not using Stringer now – I reckon they'll be pretty low on numbers.'

The ACC sighed and pursed her lips. 'All right. We go for it – always assuming the chief agrees. But Harry, it's essential that this is stopped before there's a gun battle in the street. You must move in before there's any direct confrontation with the security van. If at all possible.'

'Agreed, but we have to have a backup plan – just in case. Fortunately, Langdales has been contracted to do this delivery. Simon Langdale has promised his full co-operation. He's also confirmed the details of the consignment. It fully supports what Stringer has told us.'

'You're intending to replace the guards, I see?'

'Yes, ma'am. Simply as a safety precaution. His own men won't even know about it. They'll be driven to a different destination – a last-minute change of schedule.'

'And he'll keep it to himself; Langdale, I mean?'

'Well he kept this delivery to himself. You would have thought he'd have asked for a police escort given the size of it.'

'Yes, that's a bit odd, isn't it?'

'Down to Retford, apparently. It's up to them to request our assistance – and they didn't. I wonder why? Especially after what happened at the Charnwood.'

'But will Langdale keep it confidential?'

'I don't doubt it. The last thing he wants is another successful robbery. It would ruin his business. We'll be using armed officers inside the security van. They'll be told to co-operate and let the cash be stolen if we're not able to make an arrest before the van is attacked. But this really is a remote prospect. The whole area will be surrounded. We'll move in as soon as the van is stopped. And we'll have the advantage of surprise and heavily outnumber them.'

'If everything goes to plan!'

The ACC still did not sound over-optimistic.

'Yes, ma'am. There can be no guarantees, of course. But I think we can proceed on the basis that they won't get as far as accessing the security van.'

'You realise there'll be hell to pay if they get away with the money? We'll be criticised for not warning the bank. They could replace the cash with something else if we disclosed this intelligence.'

'I realise that ma'am, but this is our best chance of cracking the whole case. There's a leak at National Commercial – I'm convinced of it. If we warn them, the mole will go to ground and we'll never identify him. And then there's the possible link with the kidnapping. Seriously, ma'am, it's the only way.'

CHAPTER FIFTY-SEVEN

The chief constable eventually approved Hood's carefully planned operation, whilst at the same time distancing himself from responsibility if anything went wrong. 'Try not to kill anyone,' he said, dismissively, as Hood and Rowan left the presence. Hood had already discussed matters over the telephone with DCS Craven, whose recovery seemed to have been quickened by the excitement of recent events.

'I don't know what he's so worried about,' grumbled Rowan as the two officers walked across the car park at police HQ. 'We haven't fired a gun in anger for over eighteen months.'

'Let's hope it stays that way,' replied Hood.

The security van was due to leave the Retford counting house at approximately 4.45 a.m. Sunrise was only fifteen minutes later. Hood was hopeful that there would be sufficient light when his team struck to ensure that visibility was good enough to avoid any unfortunate accidents. He had acquired a scale plan of the entire site from the agents handling the sale of the property which had lingered on the market for over three years. No one, it seemed, was interested in purchasing it. Lee Whitely's dog section had taken up position under cover of darkness in an adjacent farmyard. It was hoped that the occasional barking of the dogs would not alert the robbers. Fortunately, the co-operative farmer had three dogs of his own, lodged in a stable in the yard, which were anything but quiet. Four officers and four dogs were in Whitely's detail, including Police Dog Troy who had been trained specifically to deal with offenders in possession of firearms. Three other dogs, Rebus, Alfie and Ritchie had their own individual talents and responsibilities. Lee Whitely would decide if and when a particular dog and his handler were to be deployed at any stage of the operation after liaising with Hood. Marked and unmarked police cars were in position and several armed police officers had quietly placed themselves around the site some hours before in accordance with Hood's directions. The chief inspector, in direct radio contact with Rowan and Whitely and each firearms officer, was sitting in the front passenger seat of an unmarked police car driven by Hooper which was discreetly parked in the driveway of a gravel pit a few yards from the site entrance. He adjusted his bulletproof vest and prayed that the manufacturer's description of its qualities was accurate. His police baseball cap, to be worn if he left the comparative safety of the car, rested in his lap. He patted the holster containing his police issue Walther P99 and hoped he would not be forced to draw it. Three fast response vehicles with full markings and armed crews were hidden across the main road, one behind the open gates of the same gravel pit where Hood was situated, the others in two tracks on either side of the site entrance. Their task was to ensure that the main road was blocked in the event of a break out.

It had not proved possible to identify the number of individuals inside the premises. The former residence was in darkness until shortly after 3 a.m., at which time lights started to appear in various rooms, only to be switched off after a few minutes. The electricity supply to the dwelling had been cut off when the business closed; plainly, it had been reconnected illegally. Hood was initially concerned that there appeared to be no vehicles in the vicinity of the former manager's bungalow. He had calculated that the robbery could not be attempted without at least two, possibly three, vehicles so he was relieved when a report reached him of a light-coloured Range Rover secreted in one of the barns. His confidence grew after he was told that police markings had been attached to the vehicle and a blue lamp fitted to the roof. He was also told that a Honda motorcycle parked next to it had been disguised to look like an official police motorbike. 'That must be how they're intending to pull the job,' he whispered to Hooper. 'They're going to pretend to be police officers and flag down the security van.'

'That should get them a few more years,' commented the sergeant, acidly.

At 4.46 a.m., Hood received a message from Ian Lunn, who was watching the exit gates of the counting house just outside Retford. The security van was departing. It would be passing the entrance to the old packing station in approximately twelve minutes. The roads were almost deserted and the early morning sun was starting to break through the clouds in the east. The action was about to begin.

At 4.47 a.m., the side door of the bungalow opened. A solitary figure walked towards one of the barns and disappeared from sight. He was dressed as a police motorcyclist, his helmet making identification impossible. Moments later the sound of a motorcycle engine starting up disturbed the almost eerie silence of the morning. The dawn chorus was beginning as a second individual left the bungalow. He, too, was dressed in what the average person would have taken to be a police uniform, the high-visibility jacket standing out in the half-light. He disappeared into the same barn and moments later, the engine of the Range Rover could be heard bursting into life. A genuine police observer, hidden in a small copse on the boundary of the site, noted both the absence of any registration number and the heavily tinted side windows as the vehicle emerged slowly from the barn. He wasn't impressed with the attempt to mock it up as a police vehicle, but at that time of the morning it would have fooled most people he supposed. A few seconds later, a third individual also dressed in what would have passed for a police uniform walked from the bungalow towards the Range Rover. He appeared to be carrying what was described over the radio to Hood as a pump-action shortened shotgun. Little did he know that he was continually in the sights of another officer's Heckler and Koch MP5 as he climbed into the passenger side of the Range Rover.

'I could drop him in less than a second,' whispered the SFO, as he lined up his target.

'I don't think Mr Rowan would be very pleased if you did,' replied the observer to his immediate right. The SFO smiled, but said nothing.

'Neither would the chief inspector in charge,' grunted Hood, who had heard the comment though his earpiece.

Hood became quite excited as this report reached him. Could this be the very vehicle involved in the kidnapping of Celia Campion and her son? It was the wrong colour, but given that it had been got up to resemble a police vehicle, its original shade could easily have been altered. He instinctively checked his gun. Moments later, he was almost taken by surprise as a tipper lorry overloaded with wooden pallets and travelling in the direction of Retford suddenly halted just past the site entrance. A man, dressed in a boiler suit and sporting a dark-coloured balaclava jumped from the passenger side of the vehicle and ran to the rear. He then directed the driver to reverse a few yards and eased him along the road to the south of the entrance. The driver stopped, then drove the lorry awkwardly on to the grass verge, causing it to lean sharply to its left and almost overbalance. The tipping mechanism was put into motion.

The driver descended leaving the door wide open and the headlights on full beam. He stared briefly at the cloud of dust rising from the pallets as they spread noisily across the road blocking it completely. Hood, using powerful binoculars, observed the proceedings and noted one of the men jogging to the north of the entrance with an emergency warning notice which once set up started to display flashing amber lights. He described what he could see over his radio and warned his team to be ready to move. As he did so, he received a message from the most northerly placed armed response unit that the security van was in sight. The two men from the lorry then stripped off their boiler suits and removed their balaclavas, to reveal police uniforms underneath. Hood almost swore as he noted that one of them, a tall man, was dressed as a chief inspector, complete with medal ribbons on the left side of his chest. Both men then retrieved high-visibility jackets from the lorry and placed police caps on their heads. With torches in their hands, they walked slowly past the entrance towards the approaching security van. The one posing as a chief inspector also had a radio in his hand. The Range Rover, preceded by the motorcycle, with blue lights flashing somewhat dimly, emerged from the drive on to the Ollerton Road. The Range Rover blocked the highway to the north of the entrance, straggling the centre white line, while the motorcycle followed the two men on foot. As the security van appeared, the "chief inspector" raised his hand and directed it to stop. The police officer who was driving the security van disguised as a Langdale employee was fully prepared. He had heard Hood's account of what was happening over his radio. He was not going to be fooled by these *faux* police officers. He partially wound down the window on his offside and listened as he was informed there had been a major accident a couple of hundred yards ahead.

'It's going to take a while before the road is opened again,' he was told.

A uniformed hand pointed down the road.

'There's a drive on the right about 75 yards along. You can turn into there and head back towards Retford. You'll have to find an alternative route.'

'That's a bit of a bugger,' replied the driver, playing his role convincingly.

'You'll be perfectly safe,' he was assured. 'There are several police officers on duty. They'll assist you.'

'Anyone hurt?' asked the driver, straining to get a better view of the accident.

'No. The lorry shed its load, that's all.'

The driver resisted smiling and did as he was asked, edging slowly along the road until he reached the entrance. As he began to turn into the drive, two men wearing police uniforms and motorcycle helmets raced from the Range Rover, leaving the engine running. Each was pointing a gun and screaming for him to stop. The motorcyclist jumped from the machine and pointed a shortened pump-action shotgun directly at the rear of the security van. 'Get out of the van!' they all screamed, repeatedly. The security vehicle was now virtually off the road, but partly blocking the entrance. The robbers had moved fractionally too soon. Had they waited a few more seconds it would have been well into the drive and could have been attacked away from the road. The two who had been on foot pulled what appeared to be pistols from their jackets. No one inside the security van reacted. The driver pretended to stall the engine. As he did so, one of the robbers fired his gun into the rear doors of the van. Before a second shot could be fired, Hood ordered his team into action.

'Go, go go!'

Three armed response units emerged from their hiding places, blocking any possible escape along the Ollerton Road. The blue lights from the police vehicles flooded the scene in vivid strobes of colour rendering the lights from the Range Rover and the motorcycle ineffectual. Inspector Rowan's voice could be heard, clearly magnified through the loud haler he held in his left hand. 'Armed police. Get down on the ground. You will not be hurt if you do as I say.' The two from the Range Rover and one of those who had earlier emerged from the lorry obeyed instantly but not the individual dressed as a chief inspector. He threw open the driver's door and leapt into the Range Rover. Ignoring the warning, he reversed it past the site entrance then headed for the narrow gap between the stalled security van and the gatepost. He smashed into the offside of the Langdale vehicle, pushing it to its left and forcing his way through, taking the gatepost out as he did so. Three of the robbers dropped their weapons and lay on the road, their hands stretched out before them. Armed police officers rushed forward, seizing their guns and handcuffing them. Their helmets were pulled off and they were dragged, struggling, to their feet.

'We've been grassed up,' cursed one of them.

'Shut up,' said one of the others. They were taken away and placed in separate police vehicles, the caution ringing in their ears as they were pushed along. The fourth robber ran back towards the motorcycle.

'Stop or you will be shot,' shouted one of the SFOs.

'Drop your weapon, remove your helmet and lie on the ground,' called his partner.

The would-be fugitive followed the instructions, throwing the shotgun on to the grass verge, and turning towards the officers and scowling before removing the helmet and dropping it. A mop of flowing light brown hair was released as the helmet was taken off. The motorcyclist slowly knelt, then lay on the hard road surface. The two SFOs approached warily, their MP5s carefully pointing at the prone figure on the ground.

'Look at this, Steve,' said one of them as he scrutinised his prisoner. 'It's a bloody woman!'

'So what? She'll still have to be cuffed.'

As indeed she was. Back at the now crowded entrance of the unit, Rowan repeated his warning to the driver of the Range Rover; he was over-revving its engine in his desperation to escape. Again the inspector was ignored. Two shots rang out and the front tyres deflated, bringing the vehicle, briefly, to a halt. The police dogs, still secured in their cages inside the dog van in the adjacent farmyard, barked furiously. The driver almost lost control of the now damaged Range Rover, skidding on to the verge. He quickly reversed then straightened up and drove forwards rapidly in the direction of the main warehouse, the engine surging and the wheel rims cutting into the sandy surface of the drive. Two further shots rang out and the rear tyres instantly deflated. Abandoning his vehicle, he then ran, zigzagging, towards the side door of the largest warehouse. For a big man, he moved with great agility as he raced up the small flight of steps that led to the entrance. He slammed the door behind him. Before he vanished into the comparative safety of the building, an armed officer had aimed his gun at him and called for him to stop, but was instructed by Rowan not to shoot. Other officers, some armed, ran to cover the other exits. Whoever this was, he would not be allowed to escape.

Hood, baseball cap on his head with Hooper at his side, trotted past the damaged security van towards the warehouse. He was quickly joined by Rowan, his face beaming.

'We have four of them in custody,' he said, 'and listen to this, one of them is a woman!'

'Which one?'

'The one on the motorbike!'

'Who is she?'

'Refuses to say. Any sign of Duffy?'

'He wasn't one of the four?'

'No. Perhaps he didn't come on the job?'

'We'll know soon enough,' commented the SFO who had refrained from shooting the fifth robber. 'One of them made it into this warehouse. He ran across that bit of grass and up those steps.'

'Is he still armed?' asked Hooper.

'We assume he must be,' replied Rowan. 'The others all were and this fellow is probably the leader. It looked like he had a pistol of some kind in his hand when he was on the Ollerton Road. He's obviously desperate not to be caught.'

'Well, he's going to be bitterly disappointed,' said Hood.

He gave instructions for the main road to be closed and requested a team from SOCO to be despatched. He then made a call to the ACC and told her what had occurred. He could sense the relief in her voice when he informed her four of the five were already in police custody.

'Any shots fired?' she asked.

'Four,' replied Hood, 'not counting the one fired into the rear of the security van by one of the robbers!'

'Good God, Harry. I thought you were going to intervene before anything like that happened. Anyone hurt?'

'No, ma'am. Four tyres on a Range Rover blown out; that's all.'

'Not one of ours, I hope.'

'No ma'am – although they'd mocked it up to look like one of ours.'

'And the fifth man?'

'He's holed up in a warehouse. We could have stopped him – with a bullet – but we bore in mind your instructions. We'll soon have him out of there.'

'I'm glad you did. Be careful, Harry.'

Hood terminated the call. He addressed the group of officers who were gathering around him.

'Right, a full search then. At least it's getting light now. But it'll take some time to search this place. Look at the size of it. We may have to call for reinforcements.'

Rowan shook his head.

'That's what he's relying on. He thinks he can sneak out of there while we assemble a search team. But he's forgotten one thing. The dogs! I've called up the dog section. We'll soon find him.'

He gave Hood a knowing look.

'I want the bungalow searched too,' instructed Hood, slipping his plan of the site from underneath his body armour. 'There may be one or more of them still in there. In fact, we shall have to mount a detailed search of all of these buildings. That'll take time, even with the dogs. And we proceed on the basis that if anyone is still on the loose he's likely to be armed. Any dog handler is to have a firearms officer with him at all times. Understood? Everything's gone smoothly so far; we don't want any casualties – and I include the dogs in that.'

'Yes,' said Rowan. 'I suggest we speak with Sergeant Whitely. He's the expert. He's bringing the van up now.'

The vehicle containing both the police dogs and their handlers eased into view and stopped at the right-hand side of the warehouse, a safe distance from the door through which the fifth robber had retreated. Rowan approached Whitely and informed him what had occurred. The experienced dog handler, who had heard everything through his earpiece anyway, jumped out of the driver's seat and looked about him. He then took a few steps over to the rough grassed area in front of the building and kicked at the overgrown turf. Rowan pointed to the warehouse door.

'There's one of them in there – and he's probably armed. Who are you going to send in?'

Whitely frowned.

'I can only send in one dog at a time – and if chummy is armed as you say, I want an SFO with the handler.'

Rowan nodded.

'No problem. The DCI has already said as much.'

Hood walked over and joined the conversation.

'Who's it to be?' he asked.

'Alfie's the best tracker,' explained Whitely. 'But Troy has been trained to deal with gunmen. So I suggest we use him.' He paused. 'I want to make one thing clear though, before I send him in.'

Hood was intrigued. 'What's that, Sergeant?'

'If there is anyone in there and he raises his gun to the dog, we shoot the bastard!'

Lee Whitely's tone brooked no dissent. Hood now looked perturbed as the second most senior SFO appeared by his side. The ACC's instruction that no one was to be shot was still at the forefront of his mind.

'Let's hope it doesn't come to that. I want him alive.'

'Yes, sir,' said Whitely.

'If it does...' whispered the SFO, patting his gun, as he and the sergeant walked towards the dog van.

'All the other exits are covered,' shouted Rowan. 'He won't get out.'

Whitely called to one of the handlers.

'Right, Mark. Can you get Troy ready?'

The handler released the excited dog from his cage at the back of the van and placed him in a check chain. The other dogs barked and pawed and nudged the wire of their cages, anxious that they, too, should be called on to demonstrate their prowess. Whitely walked to the rear of the van so he could speak out of earshot of Rowan and Hood unless he raised his voice. Initially, he did just that.

'We're going to search the main warehouse first,' he instructed. 'There's no electric light in there, but that shouldn't inconvenience the dog. There should be enough natural light through the glass sections of the roof for us to see, but I'm told the place is full of junk, so he could be hiding anywhere. The sun's coming up, but we'll wait a few more minutes. According to the plan the boss has, it's in three sections. They'll have to be searched separately.'

'Who's the SFO?' whispered Mark as he patted Troy and ruffled his coat.

'John Bradley,' replied the sergeant, quietly. 'He's a crack shot – and he won't hesitate if either you or Troy are in danger. You've no worries on that score – whatever the brass may say.'

'What are we waiting for?' shouted Hood, anxious to proceed.

'A bit more light,' insisted Whitely.

Again, his tone made it plain that he would not risk the handler or the dog until there was sufficient light. Hood, who had little experience of the deployment of police dogs, sensibly did not argue the point. Instead, he spread the plan out on the bonnet of a police car, which had made its way up the drive, checking each exit from the warehouse. Ten minutes later the sergeant gave the order and Mark encouraged Troy forward.

'Right. Let's do it. Come on, boy.'

The dog, straining at the leash, was taken to the point of entry across the grassed area over which the target had run. The door was opened and Whitely and the handler went inside, the SFO following. The door was closed. Rowan and Hood glanced at each other, then Rowan walked to the dog-section van and gave further instructions.

'We'll wait until it's a little bit brighter before we search the other buildings, but we'll need the other three dogs.' The handlers murmured to each other. They'd been sitting around for over an hour and three quarters and were not averse to a bit of action. They were always ready to demonstrate the effectiveness of their dogs. So were their charges, as they pushed at their cages excitedly, shaking the vehicle and barking as they did so. They realised something exciting was afoot.

Hood remained at the entrance to the warehouse. He heard the SFO shout first.

'Armed police. Show yourself and you won't get hurt. You have thirty seconds.'

Half a minute later it was the handler's turn.

'Police with a dog. Show yourself or the dog will be put in.'

There was no response.

'Right. I'm releasing the dog. When he finds you, for your own safety you must remain quiet and still and you will come to no harm.'

Troy barked, sending out his own particular warning as he continued to strain on his leash.

'Very well,' said Whitely. 'Release the dog.'

Troy ran forward, his nose to the floor; he had no difficulty in picking up the scent of his target. Hardly anyone had been in the warehouse for several months. He skirted the inside of the walls in the first section, covering the whole area but gave no indication. Then, at a heap of pallets to the right of the building, Troy stopped and barked twice. Whitely pulled a high-visibility police jacket from the top of the stack and allowed Troy to examine it. The dog then continued his search, the three officers following, the SFO with his gun at the ready. The dog ran across to where the next section began, then looked up towards his handler. Although he had picked up the scent again, he had not found the target. Head down, he pushed against a heavy polythene sheet which led to the second section of the building. This area was full of abandoned machinery and hundreds of boxes and wooden pallets stacked as high as the ceiling. All three officers followed. Hood and Rowan, in radio contact with Whitely, monitored the dog's progress from outside. Troy was enjoying himself, his tail wagging, his nose seemingly glued to the floor. He jumped over some old packing cases and nosed along the back of a stack of wooden pallets. Still no indication. He then came to a darkened section of the warehouse. There were no roof lights and two solid, heavy-looking sliding doors barred entry to that section of the building. Troy started to bark excitedly, pawing at the door.

'He's in there,' whispered Whitely.

The dog came to heel, and the handler placed the check chain around his neck. Troy continued to pull hard but obeyed the instruction not to bark. Whitely pressed himself along the side wall immediately adjacent to the sliding doors and pushed one of them open with his foot. He peered into the darkened room. The SFO repeated his warning.

'We know you're in there. Armed police. Throw down your weapon and show yourself and you will not be harmed. The building is surrounded. You have no chance of escape.'

No response.

'I'll have to put the dog in again,' whispered Whitely. 'There's no knowing where he might be. The place is full of potential hiding places. We need to know where he is before we risk going in ourselves.'

Troy was only too keen to oblige; his handler less so. 'He might shoot Troy.' The SFO put his hand over his microphone to ensure his next comment could not be heard by any senior officer.

'It'll be the last thing he does if he raises a gun to him.'

The three officers looked at each other.

'That's what the dog's for,' insisted Whitely. 'He'll be OK.'

Two other SFOs appeared under the leadership of Rowan, who was now armed with an MP5. They had been despatched by Hood who realised the target was in the final section of the warehouse with no means of escape. All the other exits were secured by armed officers. No doubt the senior investigating officer thought a show of force might induce a surrender. The last thing he wanted was a long, drawn-out siege. Rowan indicated by hand movements and whispered instructions how the four would deploy themselves once inside. Troy was released and his unarmed handler and the four SFOs waited until he barked again. They then quickly disappeared through the opened door. Torchlights from the MP5s were shone on to a heap of debris, broken pallets and cardboard boxes in the far corner where Troy was barking excitedly. The handler called the dog and he immediately came to heel and lay down on the floor, his front paws stretched out in front of him.

This time Troy remained free, ready to attack should it prove necessary. Rowan repeated the warning. There was a slight movement behind the stack. Four red tactical lights built into the MP5s played on the heaped enclosure.

'Throw out your weapon,' instructed Rowan. 'We have you surrounded.'

A pistol was thrown forward and a large male, still dressed to give the impression he was a police officer emerged, pushing the pallets and an old carpet away from himself. He had obviously abandoned the high-visibility jacket in the first section of the warehouse. One of the officers picked up the loaded gun and made it safe.

'Remove your hat,' ordered the inspector.

The man did as he was instructed and brushed his hand through his greying hair. He dropped the hat on to the floor. A small two-way radio was taken from him by Rowan.

'Now, lie down with your hands behind your head.'

Again, the man complied. One of the others moved forward, handcuffed him and pulled him roughly to his feet.

'Some bastard grassed us up.' The voice was distinctively Irish. No attempt was made to disguise it.

'Name?' demanded Rowan, briskly.

There was no reply.

The inspector stepped forward and cautioned him. Again, he made no answer; he shook his head as he was marched away. Troy gave him a final victorious bark as he passed.

'Well done,' said Hood as the party emerged from the warehouse. 'Very well done indeed!'

He made to pat Troy but the dog growled and he withdrew his hand.

'Shows you the value of the dog, sir,' said the handler. 'It would have taken all morning to search that place. Troy here found him in under five minutes.'

Hood nodded then supervised the removal of the Range Rover, watching as it was placed on to a low-loader to be taken away for scientific examination. He ran his finger along the damaged paintwork at the side and noted that it had recently been sprayed. He scratched the surface with his fingernail. Underneath it was black. He could hardly contain his delight. He then put in a second call to the ACC.

CHAPTER FIFTY-EIGHT

Wednesday, 19 May 1999

Charlie Benson looked nervously around him as he entered the dock in Court 1 at Nottingham Crown Court. His case had been moved to the largest centre in the East Midlands for him to enter his plea of guilty to conspiracy to rob. Hood sat with Ian Lunn in the public seats. He wanted to be present when Benson pleaded. He'd reluctantly agreed with the decision not to pursue Benson on the attempted murder charge provided he pleaded as promised. Getting a plea out of Benson was essential if Doyle was to be implicated in the robbery.

Charles Cavan-Henry, now resplendent in his new robes as Queen's Counsel, turned and nodded to him in the dock as the usher called for silence. Everyone stood as Mr Justice Cropwell Butler trudged in and bowed to counsel, his red robes providing a distinct flash of colour in the otherwise drab surroundings. Benson remained standing as everyone else took their seats. The judge arranged his book and pencils and whispered to the clerk before she turned and faced the now shivering Benson.

'Are you Charles Anthony Benson?' she demanded.

Benson had difficulty getting the words out in order to confirm that he was but having conveyed sufficient to the clerk to satisfy her as to his identity, he was told to sit. Cavan-Henry stood and asked for count two only on the indictment to be put.

'What about the count of attempted murder?' growled the judge.

Markham-Moore was on his feet in an instant. Cavan-Henry happily gave way.

'The Crown will not be seeking a verdict on that count in respect of this defendant, my Lord, or in respect of count three.'

'Oh, why not?' asked the judge, casting a look of total indifference towards the dock.

Markham-Moore glanced at his opponent then looked the judge firmly in the eye.

'We accept, my Lord, that Benson was not party to the firing of the gun; we accept he had no idea that a gun was to be used. And in any event, it was loaded with salt, not pellets. I think we would be in difficulties proving an intent to kill.'

The judge took a second or two to consider the matter. Benson swallowed hard, his fingers gripping his screwed-up handkerchief.

'Very well. Count two only.'

Benson then pleaded guilty to conspiracy to rob and Cavan-Henry rose to his feet again and requested the preparation of a pre-sentence report. The judge scowled.

'What on earth for? A substantial sentence of imprisonment is inevitable. A waste of the probation officer's time!'

'Benson has no previous convictions,' submitted Cavan-Henry, meekly. Cropwell Butler had the reputation of being a hard sentencer. Anything to assist counsel to soften his attitude would be more than welcome.

'That won't save him,' replied the judge, eyeing the obviously distressed defendant with scant sympathy. 'This was a very serious offence of its kind. Absent the gun, these security men were terrified and the van set on fire. If there is anything to mitigate the offence – and I'm bound to say I can't see anything – his plea apart – you can tell me about it.'

Markham-Moore stood up, Cavan-Henry graciously giving way again. The prosecutor addressed the judge with some diffidence.

'The Crown does not invite your Lordship to sentence today. There is another defendant who faces trial on all three counts. In our submission sentence should await the determination of the jury in that trial, especially as further charges may be sought against that defendant.'

'You mean Doyle?'

'Yes, my Lord. Michael James Doyle. He is charged with attempted murder and possession of a firearm with intent to endanger life as well as the conspiracy to rob.'

'Has he been charged yet in relation to the kidnapping of Judge Campion's wife and son?'

'No, my Lord. That matter is still under investigation. No decision has been made. It is a difficult and extensive inquiry. Others must have been involved.'

'But not Benson?'

'No, my Lord. Not Benson. We are satisfied he had no involvement.'

The judge nodded, made a note in his book, then turned to Cavan-Henry. 'Very well, Mr Cavan-Henry, you may have your report – for what it is worth – it doesn't look like your client will be sentenced for some months, more's the pity. I shall only be on this circuit for another six weeks.'

Thank God, for that, thought Cavan-Henry, although he half smiled as he responded.

'That is a pity, my Lord. But that seems to be the position. It wouldn't be right to sentence Benson with Doyle's trial outstanding. There is no application for bail. Mr Benson recognises imprisonment is inevitable.'

'Very well. Anything else?'

Both counsel shook their heads, then Markham-Moore jumped up.

'Would your Lordship simply confirm that there must be no reporting of what has occurred today? It might otherwise prejudice Doyle's trial.'

'Prejudice?' queried the judge, who had never been averse to a bit of prejudice in a criminal trial. He looked at Cavan-Henry but then drawled, 'Oh very well,' directing his eye over the press bench.

'You know the score, gentlemen? No reporting – of anything!'

The three reporters sitting in the press bench looked at each other, their disappointment quite evident. The judge rose after remanding Benson back into custody, bowed and left the court. Both counsel let out a sigh of relief. Benson was quickly removed from the dock.

Markham-Moore spoke first, as he bundled up his papers.

'I though he was going to be difficult, but we got there in the end. I suppose it could be months before Doyle is tried. I gather they want to finish the investigation into the kidnapping before any trial takes place on this indictment.'

'Understandable, I suppose,' replied Cavan-Henry, taking off his wig.

'I did hear', whispered his opponent, 'that the Lord Chief Justice is considering trying the kidnapping case – if enough evidence emerges to charge anyone.'

'Surely Doyle will be charged, won't he?'

'I don't know, Charles. You'd have thought he must be in the running, but there are complications, or so I understand. The DPP has instructed Harold Cronshaw to advise on the matter; I'm not really in the loop any more. It's all very hush hush.'

'So the DPP has taken the case over has he?'

'Not the robbery – just the kidnapping. Rumour has it that the Attorney-General may turn up to prosecute in person. Now that doesn't happen very often these days.'

'That seems very foolish. Much better to leave it to Cronshaw – if they want a conviction.'

'My thoughts exactly, Charles – but who are we to argue?'

'Well at least Benson's out of it now. I'd better pop down and see him before they take him back to Woodhill. He won't feel safe until he gets back there. He's a very frightened man.'

'Not frightened enough to finger Doyle, I suppose?'

'No. He wants to live.'

'Well, with this conviction, we won't need to rely on the DNA point anymore. Benson's plea is more than enough to prove the link with Doyle.'

'That's what's worrying Benson. He knows Doyle won't like it. He'd better be very careful in the showers from now on.'

★★★★

Hood was really on a roll. Five arrests and further valuable information about Julia Hamilton! The Belgian police had been wonderfully efficient. They had quickly obtained a very helpful statement from one of the porters at the hotel where Julia Hamilton and Savage had stayed. One of the drawbacks of her obvious good looks was that everyone remembered her, just as Hood had hoped. The underpaid porter was able to describe her – and her luggage – with remarkable accuracy. "The beautiful English lady," he had commented, "with the very expensive luggage." He could even identify the make – *Diane Von Furstenberg* – he'd seen similar suitcases before, usually in the possession of wealthy Americans. He had regarded the tip he was given by the "gentleman" as derisory so he felt no particular loyalty to either of them. It was not surprising in those circumstances that he had remembered her suitcases and was prepared to say so. He'd also had to lug them up to the seventh floor (there was a temporary fault in the service lift) and had noted the disproportionate weight of the larger one.

The English couple was also remembered by one of the chambermaids. She had recalled a suitcase separate from the others under the bed which Julia Hamilton had occupied. As an experienced chambermaid, Marta Lenaerts could always tell who had slept in which bed when more than one was available. She had no trouble confirming that both beds had been slept in throughout the six days Julia Hamilton and Bill Savage had occupied the suite. And she was equally certain which one had been used by the lady. She had even tried to pull the suitcase from under the bed on the first occasion when she had cleaned the room but had been unable to do so. She also remembered that a couple of days later the suitcase had vanished. She had never seen it again, although the gentleman's valise and the lady's other case had remained always on view.

Hood had also received a witness statement made by Mary Doyle, or Moira Donnelly as she preferred to be known. She explained the use of the name Moira by pointing out there were several nurses where she had trained in Cork who were called Mary. To distinguish her from the others, several had started referring to her as Moira and the name had stuck when the matron had adopted the practice too. She explained that she had been nursing at the Royal in Hull and had been chatted up by Craddock. She frankly admitted she had tried to find out why the police were so interested in her brother but denied she had been in contact with Julia Hamilton. They didn't get on. The Garda inspector taking the statement from her had also checked her whereabouts both on 23 and 24 February and during the period when the kidnapping took place. It was clear she had obtained a new position and been working in the hospital in Limerick and could not have had any involvement in the events Hood was investigating. She also confirmed she had no professional dealings with her brother but she had heard his name mentioned by one of the medics in the canteen and had checked up on him during one of her breaks. She cheekily added that she quite fancied Craddock and hoped he would be in touch when his duties permitted. Hood didn't believe her. He had no doubt she had been in contact with Julia Hamilton but appreciated he would never be able to prove it.

So he decided to bite the bullet and sent Andrew Hooper and DC Eccles to arrest Julia Hamilton – but not in respect of the robbery or the kidnapping. He had decided to keep things in proportion and low key. The arrest warrant he had obtained specified a single allegation – handling stolen goods – a quantity of cash stolen from the Charnwood. He thought he had just enough evidence to raise a strong inferential case that she had taken some of the stolen cash to Brussels in order to get it laundered. He fully appreciated that while he could go some considerable way to support the accusation that she had left one of her suitcases in Brussels, he had no evidence at all that it was stuffed with cash from the Charnwood robbery.

Neither could he prove with whom she had left it. But he had to inject a degree of urgency into the investigation. The arrests of the would-be robbers near Retford had expanded the investigation and put Hood under additional pressure but he wasn't going to allow that success or the extra work to cause him to lose sight of Doyle and Hamilton or the Charnwood robbery. Doyle's failure to convey to Holland the four hundred thousand pounds he was caught with could be linked to Hamilton's seemingly successful trip to shift a similar sum in Brussels.

He also remained convinced that Hamilton had a hand in the abduction of Judge Campion's wife and son. He had calculated that she had been the instigator, that she had gone to Grayling or Duffy to obtain the necessary muscle but that Grayling or one of his underlings had reneged and made the call to the police in order to ensure that Doyle became the major suspect. Michael Doyle must have crossed him in some way. If Stringer's information was right – and he had proved remarkably reliable so far – the abandonment by Grayling of the plan to rob the security van on the Sunday following Doyle's successful raid on 17 December would have been sufficient for Grayling to seek revenge. It was in his nature. So Hamilton's quite ruthless and carefully thought-out plan to free her lover simply gave Grayling the opportunity to get his own back underlining to all and sundry that no one would be allowed to play him false and get away with it. Sometimes, the money simply didn't matter; it was merely a question of his maintaining his reputation and illegitimate power base so that he had something worth passing on to his anointed successor. Although Hood had considered that the tip-off might have come from Julia Hamilton, he had discounted that as the least likely explanation but had not rejected it entirely and was perfectly happy to permit Doyle to believe it was an avenue he was still investigating. Feeding Trevor Parker this information, which he was bound to pass on to Doyle, might well cause a rupture in the relationship that Hood was convinced still existed between the two. If Doyle could be persuaded that Hamilton could not be trusted and that he alone was master of his destiny, something might give – to Hood's advantage. So he had mentioned his theory to Trevor Parker. He was slightly surprised that Parker had hardly reacted. Perhaps he had reached a similar conclusion himself? Hood, being scrupulous in his compliance with the rules, had also pointed out to the solicitor the potential risks to Doyle if Duffy were ever arrested.

Julia Hamilton reacted to her detention with fury, threatening all and sundry with dire consequences. When she arrived at Central Police Station, solicitor in tow, she was much calmer. She was insistent that full disclosure be made before any interview. Hood was happy to oblige. The statements from Brussels, now translated into English, were provided. The solicitor looked none too happy as he perused them but Julia Hamilton maintained her cool. But when she was asked if she could produce the suitcase which matched the one Hooper had found in her mother's flat – she had moved there a few days before her arrest – she fell silent. She needed time to think and asked for a private consultation with her solicitor. It was obvious what Hood wanted to know and why. Where was the second suitcase she had taken with her to Brussels? When she returned to the interview room and the tape was switched on, she wisely declined to give any clear explanation. She kept things as vague as possible.

'I can't remember,' she said, looking at her solicitor. 'I think I must have mislaid it – in the rush to get to the airport. We overslept and were running late.'

She had calculated that Hood probably had no evidence there was any money in the suitcase. It was mere speculation. She also anticipated that any CCTV evidence from the hotel would be long gone and the chance of anything being seen on CCTV at Waterloo was very remote. Once she was released – and she had no doubt that she would be – she would contact Max in Holland and retrieve the suitcase, assuming he still had it.

Hood moved on to question her about the kidnapping. She looked at him and shrugged her shoulders. Anxious as she was to hear what Hood had to say, she dismissed her solicitor's concerns that she should not be questioned about matters outside the facts which had led to her arrest. She wanted to know exactly how far Hood's investigation had progressed, but she gave nothing away.

'Not that again. I have told you I was out of the country at the time. It had nothing to do with me. And you know it.'

Hood paused. Should he reveal what he believed had happened? He decided the time was ripe.

'I believe you planned this kidnapping then prepared the perfect alibi by going abroad with Bill Savage. At the same time, you took that larger suitcase which contained part of the proceeds of the robbery. You and Doyle were under pressure from the person who had lent him a substantial amount of money some years ago. You were making up for his failure to transport the money we found in the Mercedes after he smashed it up on the way to the ferry. That was one of the reasons you and he tried to make me believe it was all over between the two of you. Very clever, but I'm afraid I didn't fall for it.'

'And your evidence for this ridiculous suggestion? As I have repeatedly told you, I was in Brussels. I have an impeccable alibi.'

'Of course you do, Miss Hamilton. But you wouldn't need to be here if you had arranged for someone else to do the dirty work. Any more than Doyle would need to be at the Charnwood to mastermind that robbery.'

Hamilton shook her head and smiled.

'Where is your evidence for all this? I am sure Mr Savage will confirm I was with him over the entire Easter break – in Brussels.'

'You got Gus Grayling's men to do the deed.'

The smile vanished from her face, then returned, gradually.

'And who exactly is this Gus Grayling?'

'You know perfectly well who he is. He lent Doyle a very substantial amount of money some years ago – at a very high rate of interest. Money that Doyle has been paying back in cash, gradually, but not quite as fast as Grayling required. The restraint order the Revenue obtained meant that he couldn't use any of the proceeds of sale of any of his properties to repay Grayling – hence the robbery at the Charnwood.'

She shook her head and smiled.

'Again, Mr Hood, where is your evidence for this?'

Her hand clutched her abdomen. There was no hiding anymore the fact that she was pregnant.

'The object of the kidnapping was to blackmail Judge Campion in to dismissing the case against Doyle…'

Julia Hamilton appeared irritated.

'We've been through this before. I have nothing more to say on the subject.'

'The one thing I'm not entirely clear about', continued Hood, 'is why they were taken to a property that could be so easily linked with Doyle? Can you help me about that Miss Hamilton?'

She ignored the question and asked for a glass of water.

'It seems to me there are two possibilities. Either you wanted Mrs Campion to be found before her husband gave his ruling, so that Doyle would come under immediate suspicion and stay in custody – perhaps so you could go off with the delightful Mr Savage – or it all went wrong for some other reason.'

She smiled and leaned forward as she spoke.

'And how did it all go wrong Mr Hood? Not that any of this makes any sense to me…'

'Because we received a tip-off, that's why. Three hours before Judge Campion was due to give his ruling, someone telephoned us and gave us information that we should check out Orley Farm…'

Julia Hamilton ceased smiling.

'Yes, Orley Farm. That's where Mrs Campion and her son were taken – as you well know. Now, help me Miss Hamilton. Who do you think would want to lead us to believe that Michael Doyle was behind the kidnapping? Was it you or Gus Grayling?'

Hood thought he detected just a flicker of concern before she adopted her previous stance and gratefully took possession of a plastic cup of rather tepid water handed to her by the uniformed constable. She took a sip.

'No idea, Mr Hood. You tell me. And I ask you again, who is this person Gus Grayling? I don't believe I have ever met him.'

Her reply was heavy with sarcasm. Hood had to admire her. She had guts, there was no doubting that. She took another sip from the plastic cup and seemed satisfied with her answer. Hood then turned to the question of Doyle's sister. He showed Julia Hamilton two photographs from the file in front of him. She looked at them and smiled.

'Not a very good one of me,' she commented. 'It must have been taken a few years ago.'

'Who's the redhead?' asked Hood.

'I do believe it must be one of Michael's sisters. I haven't seen her in ages.'

'Is that right? So you didn't have any contact with her when she was working at the hospital where Doyle was taken following his accident? Bit of a coincidence that, don't you think?'

Hood looked her directly in the face. She remained completely unruffled.

'Coincidences do happen – and I don't recall her contacting her brother. If she did, he didn't tell me.' She handed the photographs back. 'She and I never got on, you know. But I *am* surprised she never got in touch with Michael if she was working there – but I understand it's a very large hospital. Perhaps she didn't know he'd been admitted? It wasn't exactly planned, was it? The accident, I mean.'

She turned towards the solicitor.

'She and Michael used to be quite close, I believe, but they haven't had much to do with each other since she moved to Ireland – and that was long ago, when she was still a teenager.'

Hood caught her attention.

'You could pass for sisters, couldn't you?'

She laughed.

'I don't think so.'

'So, she's never tried to pass herself off as you?'

'Don't be ridiculous. Why on earth should she do that?'

Hood thought he detected another slight frisson of concern, but he let it pass. He was satisfied that the matters he had raised with her would all be disclosed to Doyle in due course, which is exactly what he intended. How she would go about it he didn't know and, frankly, he didn't care. He had surely provoked her enough. Well, almost enough.

'By the way, Miss Hamilton, are you aware that Charlie Benson has pleaded guilty to conspiracy to rob? His case has been adjourned for sentence – to follow Doyle's trial. It hasn't been reported in the papers. The judge put a contempt of court order on it – so as not to prejudice Doyle's case.'

He could tell from her expression that she had been unaware of Benson's plea. She swallowed hard and her hand went to her abdomen again. Hood pressed on.

'We can now rely on Benson's plea of guilty to prove the link with Doyle. We needn't worry about the DNA point any longer. But, of course, you would know all about that wouldn't you, given your legal experience?'

Julia Hamilton was becoming more and more uncomfortable – just as Hood had hoped. She glanced at her solicitor again then looked at Hood, making a supreme effort to sound entirely indifferent to what he had told her.

'That's of no concern to me. Michael Doyle and I are history. I never thought much of the DNA point as you call it, anyway. Trevor Parker will confirm that.'

Hood could not resist smiling.

'He already has.'

She narrowed her eyes and glared at him. He really had her on the run at last. He closed his file of papers. She looked away. There was nothing more she could say. Hood stood up, bringing the proceedings to a halt.

'Miss Hamilton can go – for now!'

She rose to her feet quite slowly. For the first time in all his dealings with her, she seemed somehow vulnerable. Hood never doubted her toughness but she somehow

seemed to be less robust and her confidence had undoubtedly taken a knock. She lent on her solicitor as she walked towards the door.

CHAPTER FIFTY-NINE

Friday, 21 May 1999

'You don't look well, Michael. Is everything all right.'

Parker was visiting his client at Wakefield Prison for only the second time since his removal from Leicester.

'No it isn't,' snapped Doyle. 'I still haven't seen Jules. What's the hold up?'

'I don't know. I passed on your message and asked her to apply for a visiting order.'

'Well she hasn't.'

Parker hesitated.

'There may be a problem.'

'What do y' mean, a problem?'

Parker paused. He had to decide how much he should tell Doyle.

'I suspect she won't be in a position to see you immediately – even if she wanted to.'

Doyle sat up in his seat.

'Oh, why not?'

'She's been arrested. For all I know she may still be in police custody.'

Doyle's jaw dropped.

'For the kidnapping?'

Parker looked puzzled.

'What makes you think she's been arrested for the kidnapping?'

Doyle hesitated.

'That's what Craven suggested when he saw me after I first arrived here. He suggested we were in it together.'

'Things have changed since then. I don't know about Julia – she's not my concern – but I think they'll be hard pushed to prove anything against you so far as the kidnapping is concerned.'

Doyle narrowed his eyes.

'Well, don't keep it to yourself, Trevor.'

'Hood has made a fresh disclosure. I'm not sure what to make of it yet. But it certainly won't harm your position.' He smiled. 'It looks like the police had some help in discovering where Mrs Campion and the boy were being held. They had a tip-off a good three hours before the judge was due to give his ruling.'

Doyle's face froze. This was obviously news to him.

'Who from?'

'They don't know. The caller didn't identify himself.' Parker took off his spectacles and rubbed his eyes. 'You realise, Michael, that this raises a number of possibilities?'

'What d'yu mean?'

Parker replaced his glasses; he was obviously reluctant to answer.

'One possibility is that the whole thing was intended to make trouble for you. The kidnappers used one of your properties to detain Mrs Campion and you were the person most likely to benefit from blackmailing the judge. You were bound to be the prime suspect – which proved to be the case. The anonymous tip-off simply meant the plot had no chance of succeeding – but it still left you open to prosecution.'

'I thought you said it wouldn't harm my position?'

'That's what I've been suggesting to the chief inspector. He isn't quite there yet, but he's definitely having second thoughts about you.'

'And Jules?'

'She's in a different position. She's been arrested on suspicion of handling stolen goods – money from the Charnwood robbery. Hood reckons she smuggled a sizeable sum into Belgium over Easter – making up for the money he says you failed to get there last December.'

'Rubbish! Where did he get that idea from?'

Doyle stood up, roughly pushing his chair away and walking towards the window. He turned and glared at Parker. 'I'm getting the impression you're not levelling with me, Trevor. Are you keeping something from me? Because if you are…'

Parker pointed to the table.

'Why don't we sit down, Michael?'

Doyle scowled, but he pulled out a chair and sat down again. His solicitor took a seat opposite him.

'Does this involve Jules? You'd better tell me everything, Trevor…'

Parker cleared his throat. 'Yes it does. You remember when I mentioned that Julia might be up to something?'

'Go on.'

Parker looked down.

'Julia went to Brussels over Easter. She never bought into the dismissal application. She never thought it would succeed. It had crossed my mind that she could have organised the kidnapping in order to force the judge to rule in your favour. But the tip-off changes all that.' He looked up. 'You know who she went with?'

'No I don't – you tell me!'

'She was in Brussels – with the new QC, Bill Savage. The one who took her to the Law Society dinner.'

Doyle did not react as Parker had expected.

'What if she was? What does that prove?'

Doyle, of course, had worked this all out for himself. Whoever she went with would simply be to cover her real motive of getting the cash into Europe so that Max could deal with it. But he wasn't going to let his solicitor know that. He suddenly flew into a contrived rage, standing up and pacing the room.

Parker raised his voice.

'You're not listening to me, Michael. Hood is on to her and so am I. He reckons he can prove she left a suitcase in Brussels containing cash from the Charnwood robbery. She killed two birds with one stone. Smuggled cash from the robbery into Europe and gave herself a cast-iron alibi for the kidnapping at the same time. Very clever, when you think about it.'

Doyle almost laughed.

'Has it occurred to you, Trevor, that this is just another of Hood's wild theories? He's not really after Jules, he's after me. If there is anything in this, he'll put the whole thing down to me. He'll try and prove that I engineered the whole thing.'

'He might – but I don't think so.'

Doyle looked puzzled.

'Why not?'

'Because if you were involved, you'd have hardly had the judge's wife locked up in a property so easily identified with you and you definitely wouldn't have tipped off the police. Think about it, Michael. Who do you know who would want you sent down for life?'

'Not Jules…'

'Oh, really? With you out of the way, she'd be free to go off with Bill Savage. He's a very wealthy man, you know. He's just inherited a fortune from his great aunt's estate. And you said yourself that Julia's main concern is money! Well, Bill Savage has both money and status. And they spent six days and nights in Brussels – together!'

Doyle stood up and kicked out at the chair, sending it flying across the room.

'Make your mind up, Trevor. One minute she's trying to help me and now she's trying to put me down for life! And she's pregnant with my child, don't forget. I don't think some stuck-up QC would be very keen on taking my child on, do you?'

He walked across the room and picked up the chair and sat down. Parker could see he was under immense strain.

'But she told you the child is not yours?'

Doyle shook his head. 'Well, she lied.' He leant forward. 'I *know* the child is mine, Trevor. I don't pretend to understand why she lied, but she did.'

Doyle put his head in his hands. He needed time to think. But his solicitor was not letting up.

'Perhaps that's why she hasn't arranged to see you.'

Doyle looked up. He was now calm.

'So, she's been abroad with that barrister? It doesn't mean she's taken up with him.' He sighed. 'That was him, was it? The smooth looking bastard she was sitting with at court?'

'Yes.'

'How long have you known about this?'

'Since the hearing at Leicester.'

'And you didn't think to tell me?'

'I didn't want to upset you. I know how you feel about her. But you have to start thinking of yourself, Michael. You must forget about Julia. Whatever she's been up to, she can look after herself.'

Neither of them spoke for some time. Eventually, Doyle looked up.

'I can't believe she's tried to harm me. And she wouldn't know the first thing about organising a kidnapping. The whole idea is ridiculous.' He paused. 'There must be another explanation.'

He turned away from his solicitor.

'There's something else, Michael. Do you know Alex Stringer? Hood has him in custody.'

Doyle sniggered.

'I haven't seen him in ages. Last thing I heard was he was inside – for armed robbery.'

'Well, he's out now – or he was. He's been charged with kidnapping Judge Campion's wife.'

Doyle laughed.

'Alex Stringer? I don't believe it. He wouldn't have a clue.'

'Perhaps he was just following orders from someone with a bit more nous?'

Parker eyed his client.

'You mean me? No way.'

'No, I don't mean you. Julia, perhaps?'

'I'm not going down that road again, Trevor. Jules wouldn't be able to organise anything like that.'

'She wouldn't have to. If she paid someone else to do the dirty work.'

Doyle looked up.

'And where would she get the money from? Kidnapping a judge's wife wouldn't come cheap, you know.'

'Perhaps the money she smuggled into Belgium was to pay for it.'

Doyle knew that could not be the case. If Jules had succeeded in getting some of the cash from the robbery to Max, it was intended for a quite different purpose.

'Tell me, Michael. What do you know about Gus Grayling? That's another name Hood has mentioned. He's a major villain apparently. Hood reckons you've had dealings with him. And I seem to remember he was mentioned in the mortgage fraud…'

Doyle was quick to answer.

'I was acquitted, remember. It never went to the jury. The prosecution dropped all charges. And Grayling was never even charged.'

'But he did lend you a lot of money, didn't he?'

'What if he did?'

'Have you repaid him?'

'What's that got to do with anything, Trevor? I deliberately kept you out of my arrangement with Grayling. So why are you raising it now? It's got nothing to do with my case.'

'Have you not been keeping up with the news?'

'No, I haven't. It's a bit difficult when I'm not allowed to see anyone except for you. Why do you ask?'

'I should if I were you.'

'Why?'

'A few days ago there was a major robbery attempt in north Nottinghamshire. Cash in transit. Five million pounds.'

'What's that to do with me? Have you forgotten, Trevor? I've been locked up for the last three and a half months.'

'Just listen will you, Michael? The attempt was foiled. Five individuals have been arrested. It bears some similarity to the Charnwood robbery. Same bank, same security firm, same area.'

'Perhaps they did the Charnwood job as well,' suggested Doyle, anxious to grasp at any straw in the wind.

'Perhaps some of them did,' agreed Parker. 'Hood reckons it was organised by this Grayling fellow or by one of his lieutenants – a man called Duffy. Heard of him, have you?'

Doyle did not reply.

'I have to tell you this, too, Michael. It comes directly from Hood. Believe it or not, he's concerned about your safety – and Julia's too.'

Doyle laughed.

'Tell me another one, Trevor. Why would Hood be concerned about me?'

'I'll tell you what he told me. He has reliable information – and I mean really reliable information – that Grayling and Duffy were planning to rob the security van that was due to deliver to the Charnwood on the Sunday following the robbery on the seventeenth· The robbery you're charged with put paid to that. The place was locked down and the Sunday delivery had a police escort. Hood has a theory…'

'Not another one, Trevor? What is it with Hood? He seems to have a theory for everything. I thought the police were supposed to have evidence, not theories.'

He shook his head. Parker continued.

'Rightly or wrongly, Grayling blames you. Whoever carried out the robbery on the seventeenth did so without his knowledge or permission and on a patch he regards as his. He's so angry about it the word is that he was organising someone at Leicester Prison to cause you serious damage. You were lucky you were moved here.'

Doyle started to change colour. He became ashen faced.

'But why would Grayling think I was behind the robbery on the seventeenth?'

'Because you've been charged with it, of course. And... Benson has pleaded guilty.'

'He's what? Why's he done that?'

'I suspect he's pleaded because he doesn't want to be done for the kidnapping. It's understandable, I suppose. But it will damage your case. They won't need to rely on the DNA point anymore. They can rely on his plea to prove the connection between you. I've spoken to Miss Lassiter – there's no chance of keeping it out.'

Doyle sighed deeply.

'So that's it, is it? He's dropped me in it, has he?'

'Not necessarily. He hasn't said a word about anyone else. He's refused to give evidence for the prosecution. And we still have the alibi. That can't be broken; and we don't need to rely on Julia. I have statements from six or seven highly respectable witnesses.' The solicitor paused. 'But it's not only you who is at risk.'

Doyle anticipated what his solicitor was about to say.

'You mean Jules?'

'Hood thinks that if Grayling can't get at you, he'll take it out on Julia. But it's not him you should worry about. He's in a bad way. He's not long for this world, apparently. It's Duffy you need to concern yourself with. Grayling's in hospital. But they have no idea where Duffy is. No one has seen him in years.'

'Does Jules know about any of this?'

'No. The police have been keeping an eye on her – but she hasn't been told anything. Not at the moment anyway. She's safe enough in custody. But when she's bailed...? Not that you should bother yourself with her.'

Doyle started to breathe heavily. He was becoming increasingly agitated.

'You forget, Trevor. She's pregnant with my child!'

'I know, Michael. But you have to think of yourself. We can't be sure what Julia's been up to.'

Doyle stood up and started to pace the room again. He spoke with determination.

'There's only one way to be sure. You have to get her in here to see me. I don't care how you do it, but I have to see her. It's the only way.'

Parker sighed.

'That's more easily said than done. She can't be forced to come and see you. And if she's bailed, they could put a non-contact condition on her.'

Doyle spoke forcefully.

'Just do it, Trevor.'

'I'll do what I can but Julia is not my client – you are.'

'But she has to be warned…'

'That's up to the police. It's not my concern. And neither should it be yours. Not any more.'

Doyle sat at the table and put his head in his hands. After a few moments he looked up.

'What do you advise I should do?'

Parker was quite taken aback. Doyle had never asked for advice since his arrest. He had merely given instructions. The experienced solicitor hardly knew how to answer.

'It's up to you, Michael. If this man Duffy gets to you or Julia, I couldn't answer for the consequences. If you want my professional opinion I'm prepared to give it, but you may not like it.'

'Go on then. Tell me the worst.'

'Very well. I don't believe Hood will charge you with the kidnapping. Whether he goes after Julia I wouldn't like to say and it's no concern of mine, but he knows he won't get anywhere pursuing you. The tip-off can't have come from you; if you were involved that's the last thing you'd have wanted.'

'And…'

'The Charnwood robbery is problematical – now that Benson has pleaded, the money you were caught with assumes a greater significance.'

Doyle slammed his hand on the table.

'But it makes no difference. I'm still going not guilty.'

'If those are your instructions.'

'They are!'

'What about Duffy?'

Doyle dropped his head for several seconds then looked up, half smiling.

'Suppose I was to tell them?'

Parker raised his eyebrows.

'Tell them what?'

'Tell them where Duffy is.'

'Do you know?'

'Not for certain, but I could have a pretty good guess, though. But I'm not telling you, Trevor. You leak like a sieve. You get Hood in here and I'll tell him.'

'Anything you say to me is in the strictest confidence, Michael, and I certainly don't advise you should speak to Hood without me being present.'

Doyle scoffed.

'Don't you? Well, we'll have to differ about that. Hood, that's who I want to see. No one else. Hood on his own. No tape, nothing. Just Hood. As you say, it's time I started looking after myself. It's obvious no one else is going to.'

CHAPTER SIXTY

Hood was still waiting for the scientists' reports in respect of the Range Rover detained near Retford. Despite the urgency of the matter, he was informed the DNA results would not be available for another week. Neither had he traced the owner of the lorry that had spilt the pallets on to the Ollerton Road. The registration plates were false and the chassis number had been filed off the engine block. No similar vehicle had been reported stolen.

He had, however, discovered the identity of the Irishman located by police dog Troy in the warehouse off the Ollerton Road. It turned out that the Garda had been interested in him for some time and, fortunately, a minor brush with the law three years before had ensured that his fingerprints and DNA were on record. He was, it seemed, one Joseph Hanlon, forty-seven years of age and originally from County Mayo but nowadays living in Dublin. Irish intelligence suggested he was a former member of the provisional IRA, although nothing had been proved against him. Suspicions as to his alleged activities had never been turned into definite proof because no one had ever been prepared to risk giving evidence against him, such was his reputation for calculated violence. Hood had no such qualms. He had all the evidence he needed to put him away for at least twenty years and if he could establish he was involved in the kidnapping of Mrs Campion and her son, the sentence would, in all probability, be doubled. So that, at least, was progress of a kind.

The female motorcyclist, however, had proved a more difficult nut to crack. She was still refusing to identify herself and there was nothing on record anywhere to establish who she was. Although a solicitor had been provided for her, she had declined to say anything about her origins. Of the other three, Liam Kinch and Adam Leckie had been quickly identified. Both their fingerprints and DNA were on record. But they remained obdurate too. Both had refused to say anything when interviewed as had the fifth man. There was nothing on record to identify him. Reluctant as he was to bail them for further inquiries to be made in relation to the kidnapping, all five had been charged with conspiracy to commit robbery and possession of firearms with intent to endanger life. All had been remanded in custody. Hood had taken special care to ensure they were not remanded to prisons where Benson and Doyle were housed. In the event of evidence emerging that any of them had participated in the the kidnapping of Mrs Campion, further charges would be laid.

Hood's efforts to trace Duffy had also come to nothing. The record showed that Duffy had complied with the requirements of his parole following his release from prison in 1995. For a period of six months he had attended every meeting with his probation officer and complied with all the conditions of his licence. He had then suddenly disappeared. The flat where he had been living in Worksop had been abandoned. All his meagre possessions had vanished with him. There were suggestions that he had left the country or that he had been killed by members of a rival gang, but nothing definite had been established. Hood knew, of course, that he was still alive. He believed what Stringer had told him and he remained hopeful that the scientists would be able to prove he had been in the bungalow at the abandoned industrial unit. It was also clear that the five who had been captured trying to rob the security van near Retford would provide no assistance in finding him. The mere mention of Duffy had simply increased their resolve to remain silent. It was going to take a truly desperate individual to give a clue as to where he might be found. Hood had spoken again, briefly, with Alex Stringer but he was unable or unwilling to give any further information about the mysterious Mr Duffy. So, Hood was forced to rely on the upcoming meeting between himself and Doyle at Wakefield Prison. Could it be that Doyle would disclose something as to Duffy's whereabouts? Hood could but hope. Trevor Parker had complied with his instructions and passed on Doyle's message but he was concerned that his client insisted that no one else should be present.

The chief inspector drove himself up to Wakefield in his Saab convertible. When he met Doyle in an interview room he quickly set out the basic rules of what would be permitted.

'I don't know why you've asked to see me,' he began. 'I understand from Mr Parker that he has advised you against saying anything in his absence. Anything you choose to say will not be used in evidence against you as this is not an official cautioned interview. Anything you reveal will be used for intelligence purposes only. I am not prepared to speak to you about the Charnwood robbery – I want that clearly understood?'

Doyle nodded. It appeared to Hood that the fight had gone out of him.

'I understand, Mr Hood. I don't want anything for myself. All I want is for you to lay off Jules. If you lay off her, I'll tell you how you can find Duffy.'

Hood's eyes lit up. He was, of course, more interested in capturing Duffy than bringing a case against Julia Hamilton but he was not going to give any undertaking in relation to her if some cogent evidence were to come forward which placed her in the conspiracy to kidnap Mrs Campion or the plan to blackmail her husband. He explained as much to Doyle.

'Fair enough. Jules was not involved in that any more than I was. It's the robbery at the Charnwood I'm worried about.'

'I can't discuss your alleged role in that,' insisted Hood. 'Julia Hamilton is different. She has not been charged with anything in respect of that offence. If you give me some real assistance in finding Duffy, that may well help her.'

'I suppose that's the best I can hope for?'

'It is.'

Hood chose not to reveal that Julia Hamilton's missing suitcase had turned up. It had been delivered by an unknown taxi driver to the hotel in Brussels. When the Belgian police opened it, it was full of clothing, including a heavy winter coat easily identified as belonging to Julia Hamilton. Its reappearance weakened the prospect of a successful prosecution against her in respect of the cash although Hood was convinced it was a carefully prepared contrivance which she had put in place. Doyle stretched his arms and yawned. Then he began his disclosure.

'Duffy's surname was originally Maguire.'

He spoke quietly. Hood interrupted.

'We know that. It's on the PNC.'

Doyle smiled. 'That's as may be. It may be on the Police National Computer, but I bet you don't know who his father was?'

'Enlighten me,' replied Hood.

'His father was the late Don Duffy – an associate of the Krays. Died in Parkhurst in the eighties. Duffy never knew his father but he found out all about him after his mother died. That's when he changed his name to Duffy.'

Hood was beginning to think he may have had a wasted journey. Was Doyle going to tell him anything he didn't already know?

'We know all about the Don. It's all on record and we've seen the birth certificate. Duffy Senior put his name to it, although he abandoned the mother a few months later.'

Doyle smiled again.

'Duffy got himself sent down for armed robbery and serious violence. Came out in '95.'

'All on record,' said Hood showing a modicum of frustration. 'You'll have to do better then that.'

'Patience, Mr Hood. I'm getting there. I had brief dealings with Gus Grayling after that mortgage fraud trial – you know the one the police cocked up.'

Doyle allowed himself to smile broadly as he recollected his triumph.

'He lent me quite a bit of money to get back on my feet – the banks wouldn't touch me, even though I'd been acquitted. Duffy was still inside at the time. But Grayling was already setting up a new identity for him, ready for when he came out.'

Hood was now listening carefully.

'Grayling was?'

'Yes. The word on the street was that Duffy had kept quiet about who organised the three robberies he was done for. Grayling obviously thought he should show his gratitude…'

'Grayling was behind the robberies, was he?'

'You don't need me to tell you that. Grayling will have been behind everything Duffy was ever involved in.'

'Go on.'

'When he came out, Grayling insisted he kept his nose clean for six months – then he vanished. The idea was to make you lot think he'd died – or left the country. He was then resurrected. New name, new business venture, a complete change of life. He was Duffy when it came to crime and Mr Respectable the rest of the time.'

Hood looked at Doyle suspiciously.

'How do you know all this?'

Doyle looked about him and laughed.

'Belief it or not, Grayling told me. We were both drunk at the time. He'd lent me the money I needed and he told me the story about Duffy when he was in his cups. I'd never met Duffy at that point, whatever you may think. When Grayling started to sober up, his attitude changed, and quickly. He obviously regretted what he'd told me. He said if I ever revealed what he'd said or didn't pay the money back – with interest – he would do for me and for anyone I was involved with.'

'Like Julia Hamilton?'

'Precisely. I thought we'd reached an amicable arrangement over the debt. I thought Grayling was prepared to wait until I'd sorted my problems with the Revenue. As you know, they have a restraint order against me. Then all this came along and you nicked me. Grayling's supposed to be on his last legs, he can't wait any longer and he's threatened me with Duffy.'

'How was this threat communicated?'

'Through a bent screw. Don't ask me who it is 'cos I won't say. A bent screw is very handy if you're in my position, Mr Hood. You know, for getting those little extras that make life worth living.'

Hood was silent for a few seconds.

'So what's Duffy's other identity?'

'You realise if I tell you, I'll be putting myself and Jules in considerable danger?'

'That had crossed my mind, yes. But you're no longer bothered about her, are you?'

Doyle looked down.

'We'll both need protection. I don't care what you think. I know she's carrying my child – whatever she may have said to you.'

Hood looked at Doyle carefully. He noticed how his expression changed every time he mentioned her.

'You're in love with her, aren't you?'

Doyle looked away.

'Yes, I am. I'm doing this for her – and my son. I don't want anything for myself.'

Hood nodded. 'I understand.' He paused. 'I shouldn't really tell you this, but she says you and she are finished. It's all over between you.'

Doyle turned and looked at Hood. His eyes were moist with tears. He was becoming quite emotional.

'Does she? I'm sure she has her reasons. But that doesn't matter to me. I want my son to be born alive and, incidentally, not in prison.'

Hood sighed. 'Yes. I'm sure you would. But I can't give any guarantee about that. What makes you think Duffy would suspect you to be the informer?'

'Don't use that word Mr Hood – it goes against the grain that does.'

His expression changed. He hesitated then spoke quickly. 'Because only the three of us know about it. Duffy is using the identity of a cousin of Grayling's who was killed in a speed boat accident in Corfu in 1994. His death was covered up. There's never been an inquest or a death certificate – or a body for that matter. Duffy looks a bit like him, so that helped a lot. And they're almost exactly the same age.'

'And…'

'Grayling set up a legit business – well, it appears legit, but it wouldn't surprise me if he's used it in the past in his criminal activities. It's a road transport operation based in South Wales. Lafferty Transport. It's basically above board with a sideline which only Duffy and Grayling know about. Very handy for exporting stuff abroad I shouldn't wonder. Duffy's the chairman, but there's a manager on site who does all the real work.'

'What's the name he's using? You haven't told me his name.'

'Yes I have. It's Lafferty; like the business. Patrick Lafferty. You'll find the address in Yellow Pages. It's near Swansea. He's very well known locally. Has a box at Swansea City's ground too, I believe. They were promoted this season.' He paused then grinned. 'I'm a Leicester City supporter, myself.'

Hood was not interested in football. 'But he doesn't handle the day-to-day running of this business?'

'Of course not. Too busy with other things. It's just for show, but it turns a nice profit, or so I've heard. Must be a good man, the manager.'

'What's his name?'

'No idea Mr Hood, but it shouldn't be too difficult to find that out.'

Hood paused in order to take all this in. 'So, in South Wales he's a respectable business man but in England a major criminal. That's what you're telling me?'

'That's exactly what I'm saying, yes.'

Hood stood up and took a few steps around the room. He looked at Doyle quizzically, trying to make up his mind whether he was being told the truth.

'What about his personal life – in Wales I mean?'

Doyle shook his head. 'No idea, Mr Hood. I only know what Grayling told me. I did hear he has a grown-up daughter. Grayling mentioned that as well, but I don't know anything about her.'

'Does anyone else know about this?'

'Not as far as I know. It's not the sort of thing you bandy about. That's why I need protection – Jules too. Duffy will know I've told you. He's not going to think Grayling's grassed him up, is he?'

Hood frowned. 'Does Julia Hamilton know about this?'

Doyle shook his head vigorously. 'No, she does not. And I don't want her to know. Not until I have the chance to see her and tell her myself. Trevor Parker is supposed to be arranging for her to visit me. I hope you're not going to stand in her way. As for Grayling…'

'You needn't worry about Grayling. I've heard from the police in Sussex. He's still in hospital. He isn't expected to come out alive.'

Doyle seemed to relax slightly. 'As bad as that is it? I'd heard he was ill. Might save me a few bob if he pops his clogs!'

He smiled then added, more ruefully, 'But if you arrest Duffy, he'll know I was the one who grassed him up. He knows I had that session with Grayling years ago and that I owe him money. And if the Fish dies, Duffy will be in control. He's the anointed successor. But I suppose you already knew that.'

'We had an inkling. As for Miss Hamilton, she's been released. It's up to her whether she comes to see you. But I'm bound to tell you, she will be charged if evidence emerges that she was involved in the kidnapping.'

'And Duffy?'

'Well, we'd better give him a pull – and quickly. Thank you for your assistance Mr Doyle. I won't forget it.'

CHAPTER SIXTY-ONE

Lunn and Hooper set out for South Wales three days later, after Hood had run a few checks on Lafferty Transport. He had been in contact with the chief superintendent in Swansea and despatched Wendy Knight to Morristown where the business was based to make discreet inquiries in the immediate locality.

Lunn had taken the precaution of bringing photographs of all the suspects arrested after the Retford attempted robbery. After a gruelling journey, Hooper parked the unmarked police car in the car park of the St Brieuc golf club. The two of them wandered round for a while before walking into the clubhouse bar which was virtually unoccupied. The steward looked up as they entered and viewed them suspiciously.

'Members only,' he announced in a particularly unfriendly manner. Both officers produced their warrant cards which seemed to have the desired effect.

'We're looking for Chief Superintendent Thomas,' said Lunn. 'We understand he's about the place?'

The steward nodded. 'Still out on the course. He's playing with Mr Lafferty.'

He then lent forward, looked about him and whispered towards the officers who were now standing immediately in front of the bar. 'Very slow player is Mr Thomas – now Mr Lafferty, he's a different kettle of fish. Plays off 6, you know.'

'I don't know how they find the time,' said Hooper wearily. He had attempted to learn to play golf in his youth but had abandoned the idea out of frustration and a lack of essential ability and patience.

'Mr Lafferty's hardly away from the place,' added the steward. 'All it takes is practice, or so they reckon.'

'Retired?' asked Lunn nonchalantly.

'Oh no,' replied the steward. 'He's a successful businessman. Runs a haulage company. But it runs itself from what I can tell – it must, the amount of time he spends here.'

'All right for some,' said Hooper. 'Married is he?'

The steward screwed up his face. 'No – not that one. He's more sense than that.' He lent forward again. 'Mind you, he did bring a very attractive woman with him to the Captain's Dinner just before Christmas. I did hear it was his daughter. She was a lot younger than him. Name of Kelly. Didn't catch her surname, although it wasn't Lafferty. I'm sure of that.'

Hooper and Lunn looked at each other. Lunn pulled a photograph from his inside pocket.

'Could this be her?'

The steward took the photograph and studied it for a few seconds.

'Could be,' he replied, handing it back. 'She looks a bit grim there. Nothing's happened to her I hope.'

Lunn shook his head. 'Nothing to worry about. We're just trying to trace her family, that's all.'

'Accident, eh?' asked the steward, a note of concern in his voice. 'She rides a motorbike, you know. I've seen her. Rides far too fast for my liking.'

'Something like that.'

There was a brief silence.

'Well, I'd offer you gentlemen a drink – if I could, but rules are rules. Have to be bought by a member.'

Lunn smiled. 'That's all right. We are on duty. How long do you think they'll be?'

The steward glanced towards the large window, which overlooked the eighteenth green.

'No sign of them. Could be a while yet if they play all eighteen holes. Mind you, if the superintendent is well behind, they may cut a few. I could get you a coffee if you like? No problems with that.'

The officers accepted and sat down at a table, which gave them a fairly good view of the final green. Lunn looked at his watch. It was nearly one o'clock. An elderly couple walked into the bar and sat down and a number of others started to drift in. The steward greeted them and then went about his business. It was obviously his busiest time of the day.

'That's interesting,' said Hooper as he stretched out his legs. 'It looks like Harry may be right. Do you think the woman we have in custody could be the Kelly Maguire who has shares in the haulage business?'

'It's certainly looking that way – I'll pop out and give Harry a ring.'

A few minutes later, after Lunn returned, the steward called to him from behind the bar.

'There they are now,' he said pointing to the eighteenth green. 'Mr Lafferty's the one nearer the hole.'

Lunn walked to the window and observed the two men in silence. They were some distance away and neither of them looked like the Derick Duffy he remembered. The one pointed out by the steward was the right height but he was far slimmer than Lunn recalled. He immediately started to have second thoughts. The man then turned as he lined up his final putt. There was something about the expression on his face that rekindled Lunn's hopes. That was a face he'd seen before. It was thinner and the glasses didn't help. But that was Duffy all right. He'd swear to it. He turned and nodded to Hooper. They were going to get their man after all.

★★★★

Wendy Knight had come up trumps too. She was reporting back to Hood at about the same time that Duffy arrived in Leicester in the custody of Lunn and Hooper. She had done much of her research online and by telephone having spent only one day in South Wales. She had identified Kelly Maguire as a director of the transport business from the records at Companies House. Hood was convinced she was Duffy's daughter. The telephone call from Lunn earlier in the day from South Wales had removed any doubts. But Knight had found out much more.

'This is the really interesting bit. The manager's name is Philip Jarvis. He's the half brother of the former husband of Carol Jarvis, King's secretary at National Commercial!'

'That can't be a coincidence, surely?' said Hood.

'It gets better,' continued Knight. 'According to local gossip, Lafferty and she are involved with each other. She spent the Christmas break there and three days over Easter. I sent her photograph to South Wales yesterday after I got back. It's her all right. The local police have confirmed it. She also picked up a parking ticket in Swansea on Boxing Day.'

'And we thought she was involved with King,' said Hood, shaking his head. 'It just goes to show you…'

'You don't think she's been deliberately giving the impression she was involved with Reg King to cover her relationship with this Lafferty individual?' asked Raymond Craddock, who had been permitted by Hood to sit in as Knight reported what she had discovered. 'Most of the staff at Bridgeford House thought she and King were an item. They thought it was only a matter of time before he left his wife for her.'

'And she could also be the mole,' said Wendy. 'As King's secretary she'd know as much as he did when it comes to deliveries. Everything passes over her desk. I'm surprised we haven't checked her out in more detail before.'

'Are we going to arrest her? We don't want her disappearing, do we?' asked Craddock.

'Not yet,' replied Hood, firmly. 'Let's see where we are with Duffy first. But I would like you two to check her out. The system we set up at the beginning of this investigation has borne fruit. I've been told that Mrs Jarvis has handed in her notice.'

Knight and Craddock looked at each other and smiled.

'Another coincidence, sir?'

'I don't think so, Wendy. You and Raymond will co-ordinate a surveillance operation which concentrates solely on her. She leaves Bridgeford House in the middle of next month. If she's involved with Duffy, which is undoubtedly the case, she'll find out he's been lifted pretty soon. I don't want her vanishing but I don't want her arresting. Let's see if she does something that incriminates her, then we bring her in.'

'Did she give a reason why she's leaving?'

Hood nodded. 'The bank is looking to reduce staff numbers following the closure of the Retford branch. They're transferring some people from Retford to Loughborough. She volunteered for redundancy, which seems to have upset Reg King, I can tell you. He tried to persuade her to stay but she wouldn't hear of it. I've said nothing to them to raise any suspicions that she may have had an ulterior motive. But she's the only member of staff with the necessary access to information who has sought to leave since this inquiry began.'

'What about King? Does this let him off the hook?' asked Knight. There was a distinct tone of disappointment in her voice.

'It may – but it's too early to say. He certainly did nothing to rebut the impression she created amongst the rest of the staff that the two of them were very close. But that could be down to her – and an old man's unrequited ardour!'

CHAPTER SIXTY-TWO

Kelly Maguire – she had admitted her name – was the first to crack. Hood could not interview her further about the attempted robbery near Retford. She'd already been charged, so the rules did not permit additional interrogation on that subject. But after she made her remand appearance at Retford Magistrates' Court, he had her brought to Leicester Central and arrested her for conspiracy to kidnap and blackmail. She had been identified as one of the kidnappers through her DNA that had been found on young Christopher's teddy bear. Hood also made sure that she caught a glimpse of her father as she was walked down the corridor to an interview room. Duffy's fingerprints had been checked and although Hood was still waiting for an up-to-date DNA match, he was more than happy to proceed on the basis of the fingerprint identification. Her reaction when she saw her father was all that Hood could have wished for. Before she was even cautioned she started to weep and within the hour she had told Hood more than enough. She acknowledged that Duffy was her father from a relationship many years before. Her mother, long since dead, had been a niece of Gus Grayling which provided an additional reason why the master criminal had been so keen to assist Duffy when he came out of prison. Although Hood carefully avoided asking her any questions about the Retford offence, she quickly volunteered that Adam Leckie was her long-standing boyfriend; it was he, not her father, who had prevailed upon her to join the conspiracy to kidnap. When Hood pointed out that he already knew that Mrs Jarvis was involved with her father, she clammed up and said nothing further. After Hood disclosed the DNA match from the teddy bear, she started to weep again but denied any knowledge of the planning or purpose of that conspiracy; she had merely been brought in to ensure that the mother and child remained safe. She eventually admitted that she had been one of those who had entered the Campion's home but claimed she had no idea why the judge's wife and child had been abducted.

Duffy was a more difficult proposition. He refused to acknowledge his true identity for over three hours, despite being told that his daughter had confirmed her antecedents. But Hood had more than enough ammunition to undermine his silence. Not only did he reveal that a DNA profile had been obtained from a pillowcase found in the bungalow at the abandoned industrial unit, the search of his home in South Wales had produced damning evidence of Duffy's criminal activities. Hood brought a large exhibit bag into the interview room and slammed it down on the table.

'We've searched your home,' he said. 'Have a guess what we found?'

'No comment.'

'I should tell you we found your floor safe. Very intelligent that, putting it under the fireplace.'

Duffy knew what was coming; he looked around him and silently cursed. Hood was really enjoying himself. Duffy glared at the exhibit bag in Hood's hand.

'Not only did we find your old passport – in the name of Maguire. We seized this too.'

Hood opened the brown paper bag and placed a sawn-off shotgun, carefully wrapped in a towel, on to the table. Placing latex gloves on his hands, he removed the towel, exposing the gun. He picked it up so that Duffy could get a better view.

'This is a Purdey, isn't it, Derick? Now, who would saw off the barrels of a valuable gun like this?'

'No comment.'

'We also discovered over thirty shotgun cartridges in a cupboard under the stairs. What would a respectable businessman be doing with a prohibited weapon like this – and all that ammunition?'

Hood placed the gun back into the exhibit bag and placed the towel in a separate bag and handed both items to the constable standing by the door.

'Get these off to the lab. I want the results back as soon as possible. And make sure they're looked at separately.'

The officer left the room, taking the bags with him. Duffy said nothing but he realised the game was up. He then conceded who he was and tried to cut a deal. He appreciated that he would be going to prison for a very long time so he promised Hood he would spill the beans on everyone involved in both the kidnapping and the Retford offence if he could turn what he called Queen's evidence. He was even prepared to drop his daughter in it.

'She's not told you the half of it,' he sighed. 'Not that she really knew what it was all about.' He looked up and snapped at Hood. 'And I want something in writing. I don't trust you lot.'

Hood left him and made a few telephone calls. James Frazer, for once, moved quickly. He got on to the DPP and thrashed out the outline of a deal. The Attorney-General was then consulted but he balked at Duffy not serving any time in prison. He was no use as a witness unless he admitted his guilt and imprisonment would have to follow given the gravity of his offending, insisted the law officer. Hood saw Duffy again in the late afternoon and assured him he would serve no more than ten years inside if his co-operation extended as far as giving evidence against the others, whatever the sentence imposed by the judge. The prerogative of mercy would be exercised. Duffy looked disappointed. He was expecting to do better than that.

'It's up to you,' Hood informed him. 'The alternative will be to risk a life sentence with no guarantee when you might be released. We already have enough evidence to prove your involvement in most of this. And don't forget, one of the others may well choose to talk before the day is out.'

Duffy asked for time to think. He had no intention of telling the unvarnished truth anyway. But he knew enough to give them what they wanted and to try and ensure his part was reduced to a small cameo role rather than that of a leading player. The next day he had still not made up his mind. Hood told him he would be charged within the next twelve hours, whether he agreed to the compromise or not. Time was running out. No further extensions could be granted by the magistrates' court.

Then an event occurred that changed everything. Hood discovered that Grayling had died in hospital the previous afternoon, unmourned and alone, save for the discreet presence of a police intelligence officer. Hood insisted that Duffy should not be told but he realised the news was bound to get to him. That was all Duffy needed. He now had the perfect opportunity to cast the man the police had always been unable to convict of anything as the prime mover in the whole enterprise. He couldn't be touched now and, more importantly, he was in no position to contradict anything that Duffy might choose to say. The others who had been involved knew hardly anything of the detailed planning that Grayling and Duffy had engaged in; they merely did as they were told. Duffy could now assign all the intelligence, all the planning and much of the blame to a dead man. He couldn't avoid smiling when Hood and Knight, together with his solicitor returned to the interview room.

'It's now or never,' said Hood, as he handed Duffy the document which bore the illegible signature of the Attorney-General, guaranteeing he would serve no more than ten years. He would still be prosecuted, so he had to be cautioned. He could even refuse to answer any question that got too close to the truth. This was going to be a long interview, but Hood didn't mind. If all went to plan he believed it would bring his whole inquiry to a satisfactory conclusion.

'All right, Mr Hood, you win. I'll tell you what I know.'

Not that he did. Not entirely. Duffy denied all knowledge of the Charnwood robbery. In this regard, he was speaking the complete truth. Neither he nor Grayling knew anything about it until they saw it reported on the television news. He agreed, of course, that he knew of Michael Doyle but claimed to know nothing of any loan made to him by Grayling. Hood didn't believe him. He was satisfied that Doyle had told him the truth about the loan. He, unlike Duffy, had no reason to lie.

'You'll have to ask Gus Grayling about that,' he said, pretending he was unaware of his patron's convenient demise. Hood, of course, could not reveal what Doyle had told him but he refused to believe that Duffy had not heard of Grayling's death.

'Don't come that with me Derick. You know I can't ask Grayling; he died thirty-six hours ago. We're not going to make much progress if you hold out on me you know.'

Duffy grinned. 'All right, Mr Hood. So I heard Gus had died. It doesn't alter anything does it?'

'I hope not. For your sake. Do you know how Doyle got the information to carry out the robbery on the seventeenth?'

'No idea, Mr Hood.'

'So it's simply a coincidence is it that two cash-in-transit robberies were planned within days of each other at the same location and involving the same bank and security firm?'

Duffy was adamant. 'I know nothing of Doyle's activities; at least I didn't until Grayling let me in on a few things.'

He knew what Hood wanted to hear and obliged him.

'Grayling had planned to rob the security van on the Sunday after Doyle's boys had pulled the job on the seventeenth. He was furious. You people had the entire shopping centre locked down – so Grayling told me he had no choice but to abandon his plan, which, by the way, was nothing to do with me. He couldn't even find out who the robbers on the seventeenth were, though he had a damned good try. He had his feelers out but nothing got back to him. When Benson was arrested he had genuinely never heard of him.'

'So the robbery on 17 December stymied his plans completely?'

'You can say that again! I've never seen him so angry. He'd invested a great deal in that enterprise, although the Retford job was always the main chance.'

'So he knew the Retford unit was going to close?'

'We all did – it wasn't exactly a secret. He planned to do the security van removing the cash from Retford to Bridgeford House. But he needed to know which of the vans would be carrying that load of cash.'

'But you chose the right target, it seems,' said Hood. 'The van that was attacked on 13 May had over 5 million pounds on board. And it was all in used notes.'

'All in used notes? That would have been an unexpected bonus.'

'Unexpected? I don't think so.'

Duffy smiled. 'Well, Mr Hood. We did have a sort of tip-off. I hope you're not expecting me to tell you who that was?'

Hood expected that and more. 'If you don't, the deal's off.'

Duffy paused. 'You'll probably find out anyway.'

Hood decided to help him out a little.

'We already know Derick. We arrested her this morning. But it will help you of course if you confirm it for us.'

Duffy looked slightly alarmed. He didn't want to say anything that might contradict what the police already knew.

'What's she said?' he asked. Hood hesitated.

'We know that your general manager is the half brother of Carol Jarvis' ex-husband, the manager's confidential secretary at Bridgeford House. We found that out before we arrested you.'

Duffy frowned. 'So you know about me and her as well I suppose?'

'We do. It's not exactly a secret down in South Wales, you know. You should have been a bit more discreet.'

Duffy sighed. 'All right. So you know she was the source – but she didn't really mean to tell me. I had to squeeze it out of her. She just let it slip after a particularly passionate encounter.' He looked very pleased with himself as he recollected the occasion, then his tone changed. 'Not that I'll be enjoying anything like that again for the foreseeable future!'

Hood was anxious to move on. 'So she wasn't part of the conspiracy?'

'No, of course not. She thought I was a respectable businessman, just like that chief superintendent in Morristown. I met her when she came down to see her brother-in-law. Although she was divorced, she always got on very well with him. It was a genuine coincidence. By the way, you should have seen Thomas's face when your sergeant arrested me!' Duffy laughed. 'I'd been playing up to him for the last three years. He never suspected anything. I even let him win a couple of rounds of golf now and again – just to keep him sweet. Lousy player actually.'

Hood restrained himself from commenting – for the moment.

'But she must have given you some pretty specific information. How would you have known which van to attack? There were dozens leaving the Retford unit before it was closed.'

'I twisted it out of her. She was intending to leave the job anyway. They were offering redundancies at her place because of Retford closing down. I blame the manager. You know he was after her? Always harassing her he was and touching her up. He was the one who told her about this delivery. Trying to impress her and keep her on side. She just passed it on in all innocence. She had no idea I was going to do anything with it.'

'And she told you about the cartridges, did she? The ones that sprayed purple dye on the notes if they were interfered with?'

'Get real, Mr Hood. We already knew all about them. That's why Gus planned the job before Christmas. He knew about the cartridges coming in after the holiday period. There's even been a TV programme about them. He also knew the banks were altering their cash dispensers during the Christmas break. That all came out when I raised the question of security with Carol in the context of my business. She had no idea anyone was planning a robbery.'

'But the delivery on 13 May didn't involve cartridges, did it? The cash was placed in cages inside the van.'

Duffy nodded. 'Well, I suppose she did let that slip. She was annoyed with King. He'd tried to grope her when she was doing a bit of overtime. It really upset her and she told him she was going to take redundancy if it was offered and make a complaint to his superiors. He tried to persuade her to stay but she wouldn't have it. She saw the itinerary for moving the cash to Bridgeford House and I wheedled it out of her. But she hadn't a clue we were planning to steal it.'

Hood was not convinced, but he put the question of Carol Jarvis' possible involvement to one side for the moment and turned to the question of Mrs Campion's abduction.

'What about the kidnapping? That's more serious than any robbery.'

Duffy fell silent. He really did not want to talk about that, but he knew he was going to have to.

'Not my idea that, but I'll tell you what I know.' He leaned forward and adopted a confidential tone. 'I only know what Grayling told me. He was approached by Doyle's girlfriend – Jules I think he calls her. She wanted the judge to rule in his favour on some legal point. Don't ask me what it was because I don't understand such things.'

Duffy half smiled as he spoke but Hood could hardly disguise his delight that someone was at last prepared to finger Julia Hamilton.

'But why did she go to Grayling?'

'No idea. But when you think about it, who else could she go to? Only Grayling could organise something like that. No one else would have the nerve. I certainly wouldn't. I've spent my whole life trying to avoid judges. But I'm going to need an understanding one now.'

He smiled again as Hood continued to question him.

'But Grayling was confined to his bed, wasn't he? He was seriously ill. He was hardly hands-on.'

'True, but his brain was still working 100 per cent. He regarded it as a challenge. He knew he was on the way out, so he never thought he'd do time for it if it all went wrong.'

'What did she offer him?'

Duffy looked directly at Hood. 'Doyle.'

The chief inspector couldn't quite believe what he was hearing. 'What do you mean?'

Duffy looked down then raised his head. 'Although she probably didn't know it. She came down to Sussex to see Grayling, by appointment. Don't ask me how she contacted him because I don't know. I was making one of my regular visits. I drove an artic. down to Dover and called in on the way back with Bobby; Bobby Owen – he's one of my drivers. She was just leaving. I didn't even know who she was until Grayling filled me in afterwards. She told him it was the only way she could guarantee that Doyle would be freed. I remember her saying that she thought the judge wouldn't fall for the crafty legal point that was being put forward. She's a bit of a lawyer herself by all accounts and she explained all the details. I didn't follow a word of it, but Grayling did. He was very bright was old Gus. He wasn't at all well but his mind was as alert as ever. She said she'd pay a quarter of a million if he pulled it off. She even offered him a hundred thousand on account, but he wouldn't take it. He realised she'd be paying with part of the loot from the job that Doyle had pulled. And he wasn't going to touch any of that on principle. That's when he became certain Doyle had carried out the robbery at the Charnwood. He knew, of course, that you'd arrested him, but he simply couldn't believe it could be down to him. Not at first. He didn't think Doyle had the brass balls – or the contacts. And he certainly didn't have Grayling's permission.'

Duffy sat back, looking very pleased with himself.

'Did Grayling tell her about the job he'd planned at the same place?'

'Course he didn't. He kept that to himself. It was after she'd gone that he discussed it with me. I had to do the organising 'cos he couldn't, not the state he was in.'

'So he agreed to it – the kidnapping?'

'You bet he did. He had no intention of letting Doyle get away with what he'd done. He fully intended to teach him a lesson that he wouldn't forget. He agreed to fix the kidnapping – for half a million – but he knew he'd never collect because there was never any intention to put the plan fully into effect. The fee he demanded, well, that was just for show. He wanted Doyle to go down for the duration – abducting a judge's wife? – He'd never see the light of day again! Gus said he'd die a happy man, knowing he'd ruined the rest of Doyle's miserable life.'

'But what about the money Doyle owed him?'

'I've told you, I don't know anything about that. But Gus didn't care about money. Not by then. Where he was going money was no use at all – if you get my meaning.'

'So this whole thing was designed to get Doyle sent down for life? For something he hadn't done?'

'Exactly. Sweet, isn't it? Not that Jules would have realised that. Although for all I know, Doyle could have given her the idea of the kidnapping in the first place!'

'Who carried it out?'

'Not me! I was down in Morristown. You can check that out. I was very careful to ensure I had several witnesses who could vouch for me – including that dopey chief superintendent.'

'We need to know who was involved. And you've already admitted you had to run things because Grayling was too ill. So let's have it – all of it.'

Duffy sighed deeply. What he was about to do went very much against his code. But he realised someone must already have talked or he would never have been arrested. He had to get in quickly, before any of the others said anything even more damaging.

'It's the same team that pulled the Retford job, minus one. Hanlon was the main man. Gus had him brought over specially from Ireland. I put my daughter in simply to make sure the wife and child came to no harm – and I want that noted. She had no idea what it was all about. I think she got carried away with all the excitement. Her boyfriend had worked for us before, but I suspect you already know that.'

Hood was unsympathetic. 'She could always have asked, couldn't she?'

Duffy did not reply.

'And the others?'

'Kinch was a mate of Adam's; they've pulled a few jobs together before.'

'We have five in custody – who's the one in the lorry with Hanlon – he pretended to be a police officer on the Retford job? He won't tell us anything and there's nothing on record about him.'

Duffy screwed his face up and was reluctant to speak.

'It's all or nothing Derick.'

'Do I have to? I feel responsible for getting him involved. He's one of my drivers. He was really pushed for money. He has a daughter who is seriously ill.'

'We'll find out who he is in the end. His photo is doing the rounds. It's going on *Crimewatch* next week.'

Duffy let out a deep sigh. 'All right… it's the driver I mentioned earlier, Bob Owen. Lives in Morristown. He's never been in trouble before. I feel bad about dragging him in to this.'

Hood noted the name. 'And they were all involved both in the Retford job and the kidnapping?'

He nodded. 'With the exception of Bobby. He had nothing to do with the kidnap. It was Alex Stringer who helped us out on that one.'

Hood did not react. 'What did Alex do?'

'He wasn't on the job – we weren't that desperate! He drove my daughter to the judge's house. She was pretending to be interested in buying it. We needed to know the layout. It was on the market you know.'

'So Stringer wasn't part of the team that went in?'

'No. I dropped him a few quid for acting as Kelly's transport. We wouldn't use Alex on a job like this. He didn't know what it was about. But I see you've charged him with it. Poor bastard must be wetting himself.'

Hood turned the conversation back to Grayling.

'So Gus Grayling had nothing to do with the Charnwood job on the seventeenth?'

'That's right. If he did, I'd tell you.'

'Who gave you the tip-off for the Sunday delivery? The one you didn't rob?'

'No one; no one specific anyway. Gus worked it out. Christmas was coming up. They were bound to deliver a lot more cash at that time of the year. And cash-in-transit robberies had gone right out of fashion – or so we thought! Surprise was the key. But it was Doyle who surprised us.'

'But you were interested in used notes, weren't you? That delivery was made up entirely of used notes.'

'Was it? I'd gathered from what Carol let slip that a lot of them would be untraceable, but we had no specific information about that. Gus would have had no trouble in laundering new notes anyway. He had his contacts abroad. They'd have been out of the country in no time. He wouldn't have laundered it here.'

'In one of your lorries, presumably.'

Duffy grinned. 'You could well be right, Mr Hood. But it never happened of course.'

'So explain to me why Grayling was so averse to taking money from Julia Hamilton?'

Duffy sighed. 'Do I have to spell it out, Mr Hood? Grayling realised he would never be paid by Jules – once that phone call was made to your lot.'

'So, you know about that, do you? Who made the call?'

Duffy paused. He smiled. 'I did. We wanted the thing over as quickly as possible. The last thing Gus wanted was for Doyle to be released. And I want that noted too! This was never going to be a real ransom demand. From what I read in the newspaper, it sounds as if someone messed up at your end.'

Hood ignored him. 'Why were they taken to Orley Farm?'

'To ensure that Doyle was implicated. Why do you think? I'd lay even money that you suspected him as soon as you heard about the phone call.'

Hood had no intention of revealing he had solved the case before he was told about the call.

'And you were responsible for the additions to the cellar were you?'

'I arranged it, yes. I didn't go there myself, of course. Gus knew about it because Doyle's sale to the developers was in the papers. But we heard he was struggling to get the planners on board. Ideal when you think about it. It's miles from anywhere.'

'So Grayling knew Doyle had sold it?'

'Subject to planning permission, yes.'

'So he knew he'd be coming into money?'

'Yes, but when? The planners were being very difficult and we'd heard on the grapevine that Doyle was in trouble with the Revenue.'

'So Grayling had two potential sources of money? Doyle and the fee Julia Hamilton offered for the kidnap?'

Duffy shook his head. 'Grayling knew he'd never be paid by Jules for the kidnapping – not when the finger pointed at Doyle. But time was getting on and Gus wasn't going to put his hand in his own pocket. Kidnapping a judge's wife doesn't come cheap, you know. He'd not got as much left as you lot would like to think. That's why he'd planned the Charnwood job – the one that never materialised. His medical bills were very expensive. He wasn't on the National Health.'

'But I don't follow. If he needed money, why not take what was on offer from Julia Hamilton?'

'That was much later, when he knew he was on the way out. He gave up his treatment just after Christmas. He'd had enough. He was in a lot of pain and the treatment was worse than the disease. By the time she arrived on the scene, he knew it was only a matter of time. He was just on pain relief and oxygen.'

'I'm not following this at all. If he needed money and Doyle owed him money, why not press Doyle for it? Doyle has plenty of assets.'

'Perhaps he was pressing him; but if he was, he kept me out of it. I've told you, I knew nothing about any earlier arrangement he may have had with Doyle. I was inside until 1995. And we weren't joined at the hip, you know. I don't know everything about Grayling, and he certainly didn't know everything about me.'

Hood wasn't impressed. 'He set you up in Wales, though, didn't he? He gave you his cousin's identity, didn't he? He treated you like one of the family?'

'What if he did? I knew nothing about any arrangements he'd made with Doyle. And I had to pay a price for all the help he gave me. Always at his beck and call, I didn't have much choice, you know.'

'Don't give me that, Derick. You chose the road you went down. Nobody pushed you into it.'

Duffy looked down. 'I don't suppose they did.'

'What about the guns? We collected three sawn-offs and two pistols from Retford. Where did they come from?'

'No idea, Mr Hood. That was down to Gus and the Irishman. Nothing to do with me.'

He turned away, anxious not to look Hood in the face. He eventually looked up.

'And I want to make it clear the gun from my safe has been there for nearly three years. It's never been fired. Your tests will show that. Look, Gus had his own armourer; someone in the East End. He never told me who. The guns were delivered to me in Morristown. I simply passed them on.'

'And the ammunition? They were all loaded you know.'

Duffy sighed. 'And the ammunition. That came with them. I suppose that's going to increase the sentences all round.'

Hood could not resist smiling. 'No doubt about that.'

Duffy started to look very depressed. Hood had no intention of letting him off the hook.

'That shotgun we found in your floor safe looks just like the one used in the kidnapping. There can't be many Purdeys that have been sawn off and the judge gave us a very good description.'

'Did he? All sawn-offs look the same, don't they?'

'We'll be carrying out full scientific tests on it, you know. It's already on its way to the lab.'

Duffy stared straight ahead. 'You do that. I've told you. It's never been fired.' He paused and looked at Hood. 'How did you find the floor safe, anyway?'

'We didn't. That was down to Chief Superintendent Thomas. He obviously feels you took him for a fool. No senior officer can live with that – not without making amends. He had his boys take your house apart at the seams. We'll be doing the same with Grayling's place in Sussex in due course.'

'You do that, Mr Hood. But you'll find nothing. Gus never had anything there. He was always too smart for the police.'

Duffy fell silent.

'Now, about the Retford job…'

'That was already planned before Jules approached him. It was always going to be the big one. It was just a question of when. But we never expected as much as 5 million. You must understand we only knew about that a couple of days beforehand. We calculated it would be no more than three. Gus wasn't going to touch a penny of it himself. Hanlon was to get a cool million and the rest would be divided up between the others. I was there earlier on in the week – but I was back in Wales when it all went off. My cut would not have been that much.' Duffy paused. 'I'd like to know who grassed us up, though? There can't be many in the frame for that!'

Hood then played his ace of trumps. 'You'd be surprised, Derick. We have more sources than even you could ever imagine.'

Duffy concentrated his gaze on Hood. A look of horror passed over his face.

'You don't mean... Grayling?'

Hood smiled. He was enjoying Duffy's discomfort. He had already worked out for himself that Duffy was busily transferring as much of the blame as he could on to a dead man who could not answer back. Hood was quite capable of doing the same; and it might divert the spotlight from those who would otherwise be put at risk. He shook his head.

'Don't I? You know we never reveal our sources. But I can tell you this. We had an intelligence officer sitting with Grayling when he passed on.'

Duffy became agitated. Hood's smile broadened.

'Gus would never do that. Not to me.'

'Really? Can you be sure? Perhaps he wanted all of you to go down? After all that's where he was going – in a manner of speaking. Perhaps it was his way of making amends. His final confession. They say confession is good for the soul, don't they?'

Duffy stood up and started to pace around the room.

'I don't believe it. Gus help you lot? Don't give me that!'

'Sit down,' ordered Hood. 'We need to get on.'

Duffy returned to his seat. Hood continued to needle him.

'All this trouble and expense – just to teach Doyle a lesson? Come on, Derick. There must have been more to it than that?'

Duffy said nothing for some time, then he looked up. His eyes flashed with anger. He had *almost* dismissed the possibility that Grayling had informed on him; surely this was just a device by the police to try and unsettle him? But once planted, that thought would re-occur from time to time, never to be completely vanquished. He chose his words carefully.

'It wasn't just putting Doyle down. Old Gus knew he was dying. It was his one last chance to prove he could run rings round you people. He'd been doing it all his life, if you remember? You never even laid a glove on him.' His tone became arrogant. 'He really enjoyed it, all the planning and everything. He even wrote the script for Hanlon. You know, to make sure he got it exactly right. Gus wasn't leaving anything to chance. The Irishman would never have carried it off otherwise. Gus was cock-a-hoop when he heard that Doyle had been transferred to Wakefield. He opened a bottle of champagne to celebrate.'

He suddenly became thoughtful. 'Last bottle he ever opened. I'm glad he went before it all fell apart. He'd have died a bitter man if he'd lived to see all this.'

He dropped his head. Hood could not resist a final dig.

'I don't suppose he'd have approved of you turning Queen's evidence, either?'

'No comment.'

★★★★

Five days later, Hood and Wendy Knight attended Grayling's funeral at Hastings Crematorium. It was a bright and sunny morning but when the two officers went inside they were somewhat surprised at the small number who had gathered to pay their final respects.

'I expected more than this,' whispered Hood, as they took their places, well to the rear.

'I suppose we have most of the potential mourners in custody,' quipped Knight, with a broad grin on her face. Hood did not reply.

Neither was there a priest or minister in attendance and only half a dozen individuals followed the cortège into the tiny chapel, swelling the congregation to about a dozen. There was no music and a single wreath of orchids rested on the plain pine coffin. Grayling had always lived in the shadows. His final departure was in keeping. Hood had previously established that Grayling's wife had divorced him many years before. His only son now lived in Australia. He had clearly not bothered to make the journey to attend his father's funeral. The undertaker made a brief statement, mentioning the deceased's dates of birth and death and Grayling's body was consigned to the flames without more ado.

'Not much of a send-off was it?' said Hood as the two officers drove back to Leicester. 'I hope I do better than that!'

Knight nodded. 'By the way, sir, Debbie's had a little boy; they called him Harry.'

Hood smiled. 'Popular name, Harry.'

He went on leave for the rest of the week. When he returned, Detective Chief Superintendent Craven was back in harness and had retaken control of the inquiry. The incident room was quite crowded and as Hood passed through the door, applause broke out. He noticed his colleagues were passing drinks around, hardly discouraged by Craven. A champagne cork popped and several opened bottles of spirits were dotted around on the desks and tables. There was a general atmosphere of celebration. It was quite apparent that too much alcohol had already been consumed by most of those present. Craven lifted his hand as Hood made his way to the centre of the room.

'The man himself,' he said, raising his glass towards Hood.

'What's all this then?' rejoined Hood.

The applause ceased abruptly.

'Present from the chief,' said Craven emptying his glass in a single swig, and pouring a drink for Hood. 'They reckon he's on his way round to congratulate you!'

Hood frowned. 'It's a bit early for this, isn't it? We've still got work to do.'

He was not at all happy with the situation. Wendy Knight intervened.

'They've all coughed, sir,' she said, 'with the exception of Hanlon, of course. He's still saying nothing but he'll have to plead when it comes to it. And we've just got the report from forensics on the sawn-off found in Duffy's floor safe.'

She handed the fax to Hood as Craven looked on.

'They've found the judge's DNA on the stock. It has to be the gun he was hit with in his bedroom.'

Hood's mood immediately lightened.

'Anything else found on it?'

'Not on the gun, no – but Hanlon's DNA has been found on the towel in which it was wrapped! So much for his being forensically aware!'

Hood quickly perused the report and smiled broadly.

'A tiny fleck of blood! It's amazing what they can do nowadays. Someone's been very careless leaving that there.'

'That's not all,' said Knight. 'We've also had the report on the Range Rover. Mrs Campion's DNA has been found on one of the rear seat belts. Someone had attempted to clean the inside but they'd missed the underside of the seat belt. There's no doubt about it – that was the vehicle used to take her and Christopher to the farm. And Hanlon's DNA has been found on the steering wheel, but that was to be expected. They were probably going to destroy it after the robbery. Lucky we caught them when we did.'

'Very careless to use the same vehicle, but I don't suppose they thought they'd be apprehended quite so quickly.'

'And a pity upstairs made that agreement with Duffy,' grunted Hooper, who had ambled over, glass in hand. 'We could have proved Duffy's involvement easily with this. He was right about the gun not being fired, though. No evidence of a recent discharge.'

'So it's not the weapon used at the Charnwood,' said Hood.

Hooper shook his head.

'I suppose the chief is coming down to claim the credit, is he?' interrupted Lunn, rolling his eyes. He had always held a dim view of his most senior officer. 'But we know who really deserves the recognition, don't we?'

He raised his glass to Hood and winked. Craven took up the running.

'I would like to propose a toast,' he said. 'I can't pretend I played much of a role in cracking this one, apart from putting Harry here in charge during my enforced absence.'

He looked directly at Hood and acknowledged the laughter and applause of the others.

'You played a blinder, Harry. No one else could have achieved what you and your team have achieved. Well done. Well done to all of you. The chief is understandably delighted.'

He raised his glass once more and smiled at Hood.

'Here's to you!'

Everyone in the room raised their glasses and murmured their agreement. Hood took it all in good heart, but quietly. He knew who had made the most significant contribution to resolving the outstanding issues and he was modest enough to appreciate that it was not him. Without the information from Michael Doyle the police would in all probability never have identified Patrick Lafferty as Duffy. And without Duffy's disclosures the kidnappers may well have got away with it. All in all, it was a close run thing. Duffy's reward for informing on his accomplices had already been approved – and there was no going back on it, providing he gave evidence, should it prove necessary. The question remained as to what was to be done for Doyle? Hood fully intended to arrest and charge Julia Hamilton with involvement in the kidnapping of Mrs Campion in the hope that Duffy would stand by the agreement and give evidence against her. Hood could not take a witness statement from him until after he'd pleaded guilty – so Duffy would have to be arraigned before the others appeared in court. That would have to be arranged as quickly as possible. He didn't want Duffy having second thoughts.

He had also made it perfectly clear to Doyle that there would be no deal to protect Julia Hamilton from prosecution if evidence emerged of her participation in the abduction. The only promise he had made was not to press the investigation as to her possible role in the Charnwood robbery and its aftermath. He was quite willing to do that, but Doyle was going to be upset and angry once he discovered she had been arrested for the kidnapping. And something was going to have to be done both to placate him and to repay him for his valuable assistance. And it had to be done without attribution. If Derick Duffy were ever to discover who had informed on him, Doyle's life would be very much at risk.

CHAPTER SIXTY-THREE

Tuesday, 8 June 1999

'You're sure about this, are you Mr Doyle?'

Harriet Lassiter removed her spectacles as she addressed her client. 'This is quite a turnaround from your original instructions.'

'I know what I'm doing,' replied Doyle, sullenly. 'But I'm not having the attempted murder. That was nothing to do with me. I wasn't even there – and I'm saying nothing about anyone else's role. I want that to be very clear.'

'Very well. I shall speak to the prosecution and see what they say. You appreciate your sentence would be much reduced if you named the gunman and the others who were involved?'

Doyle scoffed.

'No chance. I wouldn't live another week if I did that.'

Trevor Parker intervened.

'You're not just saying this to protect Julia are you, Michael? From what I've heard she's likely to be charged with involvement in the kidnapping so it's no good you admitting something you haven't done.'

Doyle's reply was heavy with sarcasm.

'But I was in on it, Trevor, just like you always thought. I wasn't there, but I was part of it and I was taking my share of the proceeds out of the country when I crashed the car.'

He yawned. It was obvious he wanted the consultation brought to a conclusion as quickly as possible.

'I'm admitting it 'cos I'm guilty, but I wasn't the organiser. That was down to someone else. Someone who was pressing me for money.'

'You mean Grayling?'

'Do I? I'm saying nothing more. The police know the truth of it. You ask them. As for Jules, she knows how to look after herself.'

Lassiter started to pack her papers into her briefcase.

'We shall be in touch after the prosecution has considered your offer to plead to the conspiracy. I don't know if they'll agree your basis of plea, though.'

'They will,' replied Doyle with confidence. 'They owe me – big time.'

Lassiter looked at him suspiciously.

'What do you mean?'

'Wait and see. They'll agree to drop the attempted murder. Trust me.'

Parker guessed what had happened.

'Have you given them some information on the quiet?'

Doyle did not reply.

'If you have, you should tell us what it is, Michael. We need to know. if we are to represent you properly.'

Doyle shook his head and looked at his solicitor with a bemused expression on his face.

'Wait and see. I'm saying nothing more.'

Parker was concerned. He knew, of course, of Doyle's meeting with Hood but had no idea what had passed between them.

'What did you tell Hood when you saw him last month?'

The solicitor was insistent but it had no effect.

'No comment.'

Lassiter sighed.

'Let's go, Mr Parker. I think Mr Doyle has made his position clear. We have our instructions. We must act on them.'

'That's right,' said Doyle. 'I'll no doubt see you both shortly.'

He smiled, stood up, knocked on the conference room door, then turned to speak to Parker before he departed, handcuffed to the prison officer.

'Don't worry. It may never happen Trevor.'

The door closed behind him. Parker sighed. Doyle had not forgotten about the copy ledgers after all.

'I wonder what he's up to now?' he said, as he pulled on his overcoat. 'And why is he being so mysterious?'

'Whatever it is, he obviously doesn't want us to know.'

Parker frowned. 'He's done a deal with Hood. That's what it is. They've arrested and charged the gang who did the Retford robbery; most of them were also involved in the kidnapping of Judge Campion's wife and son. Someone has given Hood some solid information. I reckon it could have been Doyle.'

Lassiter picked up her briefcase from the table.

'You could well be right, Mr Parker. But I don't think he's going to tell us anything about it. If it were to be revealed in mitigation to reduce his sentence the others would know he'd informed on them. He'd be foolish to go down that road. He'll take his punishment and rely on the Home Secretary to release him early – when all the fuss has died down. On balance, it's probably his best option. With Benson pleading guilty, he'd probably be convicted of the Charnwood robbery, despite our best efforts. I just hope he had nothing to do with the kidnapping of Mrs Campion. I really do.'

'I honestly believe that he didn't. But as for that girlfriend of his, it would not surprise me in the least if she organised the whole thing.'

★★★★

Julia Hamilton could not believe it. Not only had she been arrested again, she had been charged with conspiracy to kidnap Celia Campion and her son and conspiracy to blackmail Judge Campion. True to his word, Hood had not charged her with involvement in the Charnwood robbery. But her swift denial of involvement had brought her no relief.

Hood had interviewed her alongside Chief Superintendent Craven. She had made no admissions. Quite the contrary.

'I never met this man Grayling,' she insisted. 'Duffy is a liar. He's only interested in preserving his own skin.' She then added with a flourish, 'And you were wrong about my missing suitcase, weren't you? It turned up after all – just like I said it would. You're just as wrong about this.'

But Hood could see she was worried. Very worried. Duffy's taped interview had been provided to her solicitor and she had listened to it with care. She was the first to appreciate that Duffy's account hung together quite well and provided the most credible explanation for the available evidence. It was not going to be easy to undermine what he had said. But she would do her level best to do so.

Neither had her now quite advanced pregnancy saved her from being remanded in custody. The magistrates' court had denied her bail and her appeal to a judge at the Crown Court had been rejected. She had to look forward to giving birth to her child at Holloway Prison's mother and baby unit with no prospect of being tried before October at the earliest. Bill Savage had sent his condolences but pointed out that he could not represent her, given their former personal relationship. He was very keen to emphasise it was all over. He had also convinced himself he'd never had any real intention of pursuing it to a conclusion. But he was worried that he might have to give evidence at her trial if she relied on an alibi involving him. Still, there were compensations. The tiny pangs of regret he occasionally felt were more than assuaged when the experts confirmed that the painting his great aunt had left him was most certainly the work of Pieter de Hooch. He was laughing all the way to several banks!

At the end of July, at the Central Criminal Court, heavy sentences were handed down by the Lord Chief Justice on Duffy and his associates. Duffy had pleaded guilty four weeks before, then made a comprehensive witness statement that had been served on all the others. Having expressed himself in the most trenchant terms about the iniquity of kidnapping the wife and child of a serving judge and holding them to ransom in an attempt to force him to dismiss the case against obviously guilty criminals, the Lord Chief Justice had imposed sentences of thirty-two years' imprisonment on Joseph Hanlon, twenty-eight years on Kinch and Leckie and twenty-four years on Kelly Maguire. Derick Duffy, who had received several death threats while on remand, had been sentenced to twenty years, receiving what was described as "appropriate credit" for informing on the others. Bobby Owen had been sentenced to fourteen years for conspiracy to rob and possession of a firearm with intent to cause fear of violence. Consecutive sentences of seven years' imprisonment had been imposed on Hanlon, Kinch and Leckie for the Retford offences, reduced as the Lord Chief Justice had stated, to ensure that their overall sentences did not offend against the principle of totality. As an act of mercy, the seven years he imposed on Kelly Maguire was ordered to run concurrently; a similar concurrent sentence was passed on Duffy, he benefiting again from his co-operation with the authorities. It was only their pleas of guilty that had saved them from life sentences.

'She was lucky,' moaned Lunn, afterwards. 'She was no better than the others. Who says woman are treated as harshly as men?'

Julia Hamilton alone had pleaded not guilty. Her trial would take place at the end of November, giving her sufficient time to recover from the birth of the child due in September.

It hardly needed saying that the reaction of Hood and his team was generally ecstatic. A comprehensive judicial commendation had been issued. No one had been omitted; even Police Dog Troy was included.

'Thirty-nine years for Hanlon, that's more than the train robbers got,' exclaimed a delighted Hooper.

'I should think so too,' rejoined Hood. 'The offences against Judge Campion and his wife were far more serious and struck at the roots of the entire criminal justice system.'

'And we still have the trial of Hamilton to come,' enthused Hooper.

'I wouldn't build your hopes up too much about that,' countered Hood. 'We are relying solely on Duffy, a career criminal. There must be at least a possibility that a jury will not believe him. And she has a rock-solid alibi for the period during which the kidnapping occurred.'

'But the others all pleaded after seeing his statement – even Hanlon. That must count for something, surely?'

'It won't harm us, that's for sure, but she could well go for the sympathy vote with the jury. We have nothing to support what Duffy says about her, nothing at all.'

'What about Doyle?'

'What about him? He'll say nothing to harm her, that's as certain as Christmas.'

The following week, Doyle and Benson appeared for sentence before Mr Justice Cropwell Butler at Nottingham. The judge had changed his itinerary to make himself available. Nothing was advanced on Doyle's behalf to take advantage of the invaluable information he had given Hood. He had resisted anything being put before the judge and had said nothing to assist Harriet Lassiter in mitigating his sentence. He was relying on the Home Secretary to discharge him well before his otherwise earliest release date. Hood and the assistant chief constable had signed a letter setting out his co-operation that was placed in a safe at the Home Office, to be opened and reviewed in due course. He was sentenced to fifteen years and Benson to twelve. Doyle smiled to himself. He was confident he would be released well before Benson. Neither man said anything to the other as they were taken down.

As for Alex Stringer, the case against him was discontinued, largely because of the contents of Duffy's statement. He had, nevertheless, sensibly agreed to change his identity and move to Scotland, where he was assisted by a Home Office witness relocation programme. Carol Jarvis was not prosecuted. The DPP took the perhaps charitable view that she had been used by Duffy and not appreciated she was passing information to a criminal. Reg King was moved from Bridgeford House to a mundane position in the bank's regional headquarters in Leeds. His wife stuck by him despite the rumours that had gained wider circulation after the arrest of Carol Jarvis.

The chief constable remained elated. He had received a personal message from the Prime Minister congratulating him on the performance of his officers. Wendy Knight was promoted to sergeant and, much to his surprise, Ian Lunn was made an inspector, although it meant a period back in uniform. Hood was quietly assured his promotion to superintendent would not be long in coming.

'And I shouldn't wonder if there isn't a mention in the New Year Honours,' the chief had assured him with a wry smile.

Of whom? wondered Hood, silently.

Eccles retired from the police service leaving Hooper quietly fuming that nothing had come his way in recognition of his efforts, save the general commendation from the court. Munt returned to general duties with a chief constable's commendation and Craddock was now a fully-fledged detective constable, still secretly hoping that he and Wendy Knight might make a go of things now that Greg Oldham had departed permanently for the United States. He had lost all interest in Moira.

'We never identified the Charnwood gunman, though, did we?' said Knight as she and Hood celebrated her advancement with a drink at a local hostelry.

'Or the leak,' added Hood, ruefully. 'Just like the great train robbery, we never identified the mole.'

'Maybe there wasn't one,' consoled Knight. 'Or perhaps Mrs Jarvis had let something slip that Doyle or one of the others picked up?'

Hood could not accept that. 'No. The two robberies were not connected. Someone else, someone we've missed, gave Doyle the information he needed. And he's not going to tell us. Not now he's gone down for fifteen years and Julia Hamilton is locked up in Holloway.'

'But it's still a great result,' said Knight. 'Fancy another one?'

★★★★

EPILOGUE

It was the second week of September when Amrit Patel and his two university friends arrived at the border between Pakistan and India. It had taken them nearly three months to get there, journeying through Europe, Turkey and the Middle East. His two friends left him after they had spent two days at Agra, visiting the Taj Mahal on the southern bank of the Yamuna River and spending one night in a particularly luxurious hotel, generously paid for by Amrit Patel. After his two friends flew back to the UK, Amrit made his way in his Land Rover to the south of the country. He was heading for his father's home village near Mysore. Hidden in a specially prepared compartment he had constructed underneath the remodelled and restored vehicle was one hundred and twenty-five thousand pounds in twenty-pound notes. He was the mole Hood had failed to detect. He was the student who had been dismissed from Bridgeford House for stealing three hundred pounds whilst working there during a summer vacation. The bank had declined to prosecute him, fearing adverse publicity, but he had maintained his links through his on-going relationship with one of the girls employed in the machine room and through her had learnt of the plan to replace the satchels with specially prepared cartridges from early 1999. He also knew that deliveries to the Charnwood would grow in volume as Christmas approached, thus increasing the number of used notes making up the consignments.

Amrit had also worked as a temporary employee at Langdale Security after losing his position at Bridgeford House, a job his father obtained for him during the university vacations. His studies at Sheffield had included computer technology and software programming, so he proved useful in tweaking Langdale's computers. It gave him the opportunity, too, to alter temporarily the alarm system just before the Charnwood robbery was due to take place. No one had noticed; he was always adjusting things and usually for the better. What he had failed to foresee was his father volunteering for an extra shift on the very night of the robbery. When he discovered what had occurred, he had spent three days and nights in the hospital in Leicester terrified he may have had a hand in his father's demise. No one was more relieved than he when his father pulled through.

He had met Benson on the July course at Newmarket races when both had had a hefty win after backing the same 33-1 outsider. They ended up in the champagne bar rapidly becoming the worse for drink. They exchanged phone numbers and attended the races together on two or three further occasions. It was when Amrit took his girlfriend with him to the Cesarewitch meeting that the plan started to be hatched. Benson took it to Doyle and by the beginning of December everything was in place.

Now he could make it up to his parents. In India, a hundred and twenty-five thousand pounds was a considerable fortune and there were numerous opportunities to start profitable businesses with such capital in the booming Indian economy. He estimated that in two years' time he would have more than doubled his money so his parents could return and live in luxury for the rest of their days. He had no intention of returning to the UK himself.

In Dublin, the Donnelly brothers were much relieved they had declined Jules' offer to assist her in the kidnapping plot. Both Bernard and Colin had decided to retire and concentrate on their various businesses. The sentences imposed by the Lord Chief Justice had deterred them from further serious criminal activity, at least in England.

At Holloway Prison, Julia Hamilton gave birth to a healthy boy on 29 September. She called him Michael, after his father. She knew nothing of Doyle's arrangement with the police and for the time being she was allowed no contact with him, save to inform him of the birth of his son, and that had to be done in writing. But she was already planning in her own mind how she would undermine the prosecution case against her. By the time her counsel had finished with Duffy his credibility would be destroyed and she knew Doyle would co-operate, if necessary. Although her relationship with Savage was over, he would remain a reluctant but valuable witness in support of her alibi. "We'll always have Paris," she had assured Doyle at the end of her brief message to him, "and we'll be there together sooner than anyone can possibly imagine."

ACKNOWLEDGEMENTS

Although this novel comes entirely from my imagination, eagle-eyed lawyers may notice that the decision of the Judicial Committee of the House of Lords in *Attorney-General's Reference No. 3 of 1999 [2000] UKHL 70* played a role in developing the arguments surrounding the admissibility in law of DNA evidence and sheds light on why the novel is set at the end of the 20th century! This decision of the House of Lords removes any doubts about the question which the imaginary Judge Campion was called upon to resolve. So this issue could not arise today. The law in other significant areas has also been brought up to date so there would be no point in anyone seeking to copy the actions of any one of the characters in the novel! The Crown now has a right of appeal if a judge accedes to an applicaiton to dismiss and the Appeal Court can overturn the trial judge and order the continuation of the trial.

I would like to thank Lady (Christine) Peace who religiously read the original - much longer - draft, and several others, including my wife, Alison, and my daughter, Anna, who did the same. Others who helpfully read earlier drafts and made helpful comments include Beverley Tarquini, Jane Hughes, Amalia Antill and Judge Joan Butler, QC. A big thank you, too, to my copy editor, Hannah Eveleigh, who spotted numerous errors and corrected them.

Thanks must also go to Ann Rowan, who arranged for me to spend a day with the Nottingham Constabulary police dog section, where I was able to witness for myself the dedication and training of both handlers and dogs. I am more than happy to dedicate this novel, in part, to Police Dog Troy, who was the first police dog I commended when sitting as a judge following his and his handler's capture of a burglar. Unfortunately, Troy died shortly afterwards from an unrelated physical condition, much to the sorrow of his handler, PC Mark Lambert. But his successors continue to play a quite amazing role in the detection and arrest of serious criminals in the East Midlands. Long may this continue!

The trial of Julia Hamilton is a central feature of the next Inspector Hood novel, "A Private and Convenient Place", which will be published in 2017.